Revenge of the Downtrodden

The Hanging Chads Omnibus Volume 1

Evan Clouse

DEDICATION

This book is dedicated to my beautiful, strong, and intelligent wife, Pam. Without your support, I would never have been able to create this work. I thank you and I love you. This book literally and figuratively represents a new chapter in our adventure together, and there's no one else on this earth that I would want to be on this ride with.

This book is also dedicated to every person who has suffered a loss at the hands of the sadistic bullies in our world.

It is dedicated to our Asian brothers and sisters who suffer from harassment.

It is dedicated to our Hispanic brothers and sisters who are looked down upon by large segments of our society.

It is dedicated to our Native American brothers and sisters who continue to suffer under the yoke of American colonialism.

It is dedicated to our sisters who are losing their rights of self-determination of their personal health care.

It is dedicated to our veterans who have yet to have a national health care system worthy of their sacrifice.

It is dedicated to every person who lost someone to COVID-19 because the lemmings around them weren't taking this shit seriously.

It is dedicated to every person, especially the children, who must carry the scars of mental, physical, and sexual abuse.

It is dedicated to every person who has lost a loved one due to the senseless proliferation of guns in our society.

It is dedicated to every one of our Black brothers and sisters who has lost a loved one by execution on our streets at the hands of our broken criminal justice system.

It is dedicated to every LGBTQ+ person who continues to be discriminated against and marginalized.

It is dedicated to every woman who has to endure the leering glances and unwelcome advances of their male counterparts.

And finally, it is dedicated to every person whose voting rights and voice in our democracy have been compromised because of bullshit, tinfoil-hat conspiracy theories.

I weep with you. I scream with you. I stand with you. And I love you all.

Contents

LINEAGE

ASCENSION

Acknowledgments

I would like to thank so many people whose aggregated influences and inspiration have culminated in the creation of this work. I thank my parents, Mike and Carla, for instilling in me basic ethics and morality. I miss you, Dad, and it is my prayer that this work puts a smile on your angelic face.

I thank my sister Paige for her creativity and decency.

I thank my sister Cory for her boundless optimism and wisdom.

I thank my niece Hannah for being one of the strongest people I have ever known.

I thank my niece Faye for her originality and humanity.

I thank my nephew Thomas and my niece Brin for being the inspiration behind many of Maddy's childlike qualities and for always making me smile.

I thank my in-laws for their welcoming love, cookies, and beef and noodles.

I thank Todd for his friendship and endless patience with me.

I thank Amy for her steadiness, friendship, and going out of her comfort zone to give me feedback throughout this process.

I thank Kara for her irreverent personality and feedback on my work.

I thank Marcia for her kind and gentle soul.

I thank Wes and all of my friends at Pallister's for making me laugh and being my oasis of sanity.

I thank Michael, Mike, Peter, and Bill for providing a large piece of my life's personal soundtrack. Please come back to us. We need you now more than ever.

I thank Bruce Springsteen for teaching me how emotionally moving art can be.

I thank Lux Interior for his attitude and providing me with the basis of Erick's name. Rest in peace, my friend.

I thank Joe Bob Briggs for introducing me to horrific wonders in his most unique manner.

And finally, and perhaps somewhat surprisingly, I would like to thank all of the pricks who have belittled me, lied to me, lied about me, and stabbed me in the back throughout my life. You are the inspiration behind my "fuck off" attitude. You inspired me to create Maddy.

So thank you for being the assholes that you have always been and will always be. Time's up, bitches! Evan out!

Hanging Chads

PROLOGUE

It was always the first thing that she noticed. The faint scent of iron as the sticky thin molasses gently dribbled down the shaft of the knife and penetrated the space between her clenched thumb and forefinger. The faint exhalation of air passing through his mouth that was now permanently formed into a silent scream. Then, the sound of the blood droplets hitting the floor. Slowly at first, like an annoying leaky faucet. Drop . . . drop . . . drop . . . then faster as the taut skin surrounding his jugular gave way completely to unleash a crimson waterfall that hit the hard wood floor as though someone had poured an entire gallon of milk upon it. She pulled the knife completely from his throat while loosening her grip from his hair. Then the familiar thud as the lifeless body succumbed to gravity, completing the merciless fait accompli.

A mischievous smile forced the upward curling of the right side of her mauve-painted lips. This was successful. This was liberating. This was justified. This was...the first time that was completely unplanned. She looked down upon the mess that he had created as the pool of newly released blood expanded outward like a growing hurricane churning above warm water. She had not brought her customary grab bag to provide for the cleanup, change of clothes, and silent escape into the brisk Brooklyn night. Without preparation, there may be too many clues, and her self-appointed reign over the hapless sadists of the five boroughs may be over, replaced by incarceration, prison fatigues, and forced lesbian sex.

Her mind raced as she went through her mental filing cabinet of possible solutions. And *his* face kept popping into her consciousness. *No, not him, there must be another way,* she rationalized. But with each discarded option, there was his image. *No, I can't get him involved in this. I promised myself that I would stop after I met him...my soul mate...my prince. I can't put him in jeopardy. And he can never know about this. Or about the others... Or could he? Could it be that he knows already?* She recalled seeing the flash of rage in his eyes that night, not so long ago, at the bar. The same rage that was so familiar within herself. She felt that she had witnessed a knowing acknowledgment of her complicity as they watched reports of her most recent triumph on the news. He was her soul mate, her prince, and he *already* knew. And she also knew that he would do anything for her. Yes, this would be successful. This would be liberating. This would be the final consummation of their love. She would call...him.

Chapter 1

Raging Eyes

Madeline Ruth Sommers entered the world on May 13, 1988. Even as a newborn, her smile was infectious. But not as infectious as when she would give an unknowing recipient a flash of her emerald-green eyes. Then, to seal the victory over her adversaries' emotions, the batting of her sandy-red eyelashes, leaving her worthy combatant immobilized by her charms and completely at the mercy of the child's whims.

Maddy (as her beloved aunt Patty, aunt Blair, and uncle Joe and her friends would refer to her) was a child with a free spirit and endless optimism. Always seemingly amazed and absorbed by the latest sensation that was introduced into her world, she also was always keenly aware of what other people, especially adults, were doing and saying around her. Each new discovery was greeted with the exclamation "Oh! This is the greatest [ice cream cone, pizza, dolly, movie, etc.] in the history of the world!" Her spirit seemed unbreakable, and her smile was constant. She loved to entertain and to be entertaining. One little trick that she discovered that would elicit the desired response of uproarious laughter from her "audience" was crossing her eyes while smiling and sticking her tongue out from the right side of her mouth. Her loving family members called this her "silly face."

Her mother called it blasphemous. "Madeline," she would say in her frigid, condescending, and slightly nasally voice, "if Jesus had meant your face to look that way, he would have made it that way. Stop that this instant."

Maddy would look up at the person who had given birth to her in her plain long beige dress with a gaudy floral pattern, buttoned to the top. Everything about her was cold and stiff—from her expressionless gray face, topped off with a tight bun of sandy-red hair, to her clenched, almost opaque fingers. Although only twenty-five when she had given birth to Maddy, she always appeared nearly thirty years older than her actual age, making her appearance almost corpse-like even as a younger woman.

Looking for reinforcement, the young child would look to her father (or, as Maddy would later refer to him, "the guy who somehow managed to jizz into that cold bitch"). And Maddy, beginning when she was a child, would never utter the name of those that she held no respect. At best, they were mere annoyances to be disregarded. They were less than her because she knew that her lack of respect for them came from their basic lack of respect for her and others, and that made them merely biologically *Homo sapiens*, not really human with possession of a "soul." Her father would look at her solemnly, with a long- drawn face as if he were saying that he was powerless to help her, which, in fact, he was. Her father was the youngest of his siblings. Whereas his elder sisters, Blair and Patty, had always been outgoing with a zeal for whatever counted as fun (drinking, screwing, partying, music, and the like) during the various stages of their life, he was always an introvert. And he always held a secret admiration of his elder sisters, especially Patty, who had far more success bedding women than he could dream of. He was a follower and held no internal drive, ambition, or personal conviction. He walked through life being willfully ignorant and merely followed those within his orbit at that particular time. So upon meeting the woman who would become his wife and mother to his daughter, he was helpless as she manipulated him into her web of control and radical religious and political fervor. Despite this, and over his wife's protestations, he always insisted that Maddy be a part of his sisters' life to look after her as they had done for him as a child, as if he knew this precious child needed their outside influence in order to be formed into a functional human being.

Receiving no solace from her emasculated father, Maddy's eyes quickly darted across the room and connected with those of her beloved uncle Joe. Joseph Argento, Blair's husband and ten years her senior, met the love of his life while repairing pipes in an apartment building in Madison, Wisconsin. Always good with his hands and possessing a brilliance for mechanics, Joe had always held gainful employment that satisfied him while being able to stay out of the typical banal office politics. He was, in his heart and mind, a fixer. He loved repairing things, whether they be materialistic or emotional. Joe was popular at his local tavern and was the resident "good listener." Always quick with a bawdy comeback or joke, Joe also possessed a great disdain for bullies and would immediately escort anyone who was harassing of the local barflies out of the tavern, usually with a bruise or two to commemorate their experience. And at age thirty-five, he was a confirmed bachelor. Until one frigid December evening when he received a call of distress to fix a broken water pipe from an apartment building. The young woman answered the door, and Joe's heart melted. This, then, was the beginning of the end of Joe's confirmed bachelor status and the beginning of his great romantic love affair with his Blair.

And ten years later, he would find his other great emotional love in the form of his only niece. Upon seeing the newborn's perfectly round and angelic face (complete with her elegant emerald-green eyes), Joe told his wife that they must always be a part of her life in order to provide a counterbalance to the influence of her parents' fanatical views and lifestyle. It was due to this undying love and commitment to this child that Joe would participate in these family gatherings, quietly simmering and tolerating the ignorant chatter being exchanged by the adults. But he was not there for his own amusement. He was there to act in his role of guardian for the child against her mother's frigid cruelty. He would watch. He would wait. He, his wife, and his sister-in-law Patty would quietly mold this young girl in their own way. And if those two bastards ever went too far against his precious niece, he would act with quick, merciless retribution.

Seeing that she had her uncle's full attention (which she almost always had at these gatherings), Maddy would flash her uncle a slight mischievous grin, as if to say, "Fuck her." And her uncle Joe would mirror her expression and sentiment. It was just the two of them silently communicating with each other until Joe would say, "C'mon, buttacup, let's see if we can't find some ice cream." Maddy would place her delicate hand into that of her uncle and smile upward at this mountain of a man with the knowledge that she would always be safe as long as her uncle Joe was around.

Maddy was always allowed to spend Friday evenings and most of Saturday with her aunt Blair and uncle Joe while her parents were off to conduct "adult" church activities (which Maddy later speculated involved the sacrificing of some godless whore followed by a rapturous feast of the poor girl's entrails washed down with her blood. Maddy had no evidence that this was what had occurred. But she had no evidence to the contrary either. So living in this post fact world of 2015 and beyond, she surmised that if other people could believe in made-up bullshit like stolen elections and hydroxychloroquine, then so could she). Her aunt Patty would also be present at some point, usually with her most recent girlfriend. As Maddy grew and was learning about the various forms that romantic relationships could take, she learned from her aunt Patty that relationships could be casual, time limited, and based upon pure carnal pleasure. She learned nothing from her parents' relationship as that just seemed batshit crazy to her. It was distant and uncaring. Why would two people who seem to barely tolerate each other stay together? What was it that bonded them together? It was a mystery to her that after a while she simply didn't care enough to waste time on. But it was the type of relationship that her aunt Blair and uncle Joe had that formed the foundation of the type of relationship that she would long for. They looked longingly into each other's eyes. They were considerate and would do things for each other without being asked. They were playful with each other. And they laughed together. Constantly. They picked on each other mercilessly (which they called "goofing on" each other). It was never done in malice, but more like two kittens wrestling just for the fun of it. Uncle Joe would make a crude joke that would initiate a harsh glance of disapproval from his wife, followed by her breaking down into tears laughing. They cared for each other. They respected each other. They trusted each other. These components, then, became the foundation of Maddy's definition of love.

At the age of four, Maddy watched *Cinderella* for the first time at her aunt and uncle's house (Friday was always movie and junk food night, and Maddy vigorously consumed every frame and morsel of it). Even at such a young age, Maddy could relate to the story of wanting to get out from under the cruelty of her family and into the arms of someone who truly cared for her. Therefore, *Cinderella* naturally became "the greatest movie in the history of the world!" She became obsessed with the concept of finding her own prince and longed for the day that she would go to Disneyworld to meet him, fall in love, and live happily ever after (as that was where all princes lived in her developing mind).

But that childhood dream of visiting this romantic playground never materialized. Her mother considered almost any type of story or entertainment outside of Bible stories to be, at the very least, blasphemy if not outright satanic. Even if there were a parental desire to accommodate their daughter's most precious wish, the family did not have the resources, as much of their excess money was "donated" to the church to which they belonged.

Maddy and her parents attended a church that was, quite literally, a cult. As is the case in some houses of worship throughout the world and of every religious denomination imaginable, its radical, evangelical congregation was made up primarily of two types of people: those who seek total dominion over others (in every way possible including emotionally, physically, and sexually) and those who choose to be dominated and told what to do and believe so as to never have to possess personal responsibility for their own actions. They seek entitlement to the "right" to believe and act however they desire (or how they are told to by the cult leader) without any of the personal responsibility or consequences that result from their misguided, and often destructive, actions. They are above any societal judgment, as their actions are always explained away by their bullshit cop-out "will of God." Or, as in the case of political cults, an exclamation that their treasonous acts are, in fact, some twisted form of "patriotism."

Maddy's parents were the perfect familial microcosm of this cult dynamic, with the mother being the fearmongering dominatrix and the father being the one who was quite willingly dominated. And the Sommerses' church embraced the most radical religious and political extremes in its effort to subvert its congregation into obedience (and, of course, "donations") through fear and hatred of any person, thought, or "lifestyle" (meaning differences in human biology) that was not sanctioned by the church/cult.

And in the middle of this was Maddy who, from birth, was caught between two very different worlds. The world that she spent most of her time in was that of her parents. It was an upbringing based upon cold, fascist authoritarianism where the slightest deviance from the ordained "norm" was met with swift punishment, usually in the form of three strikes upon her backside by a yardstick wielded by her mother as her father impotently sat in another room. Such grave "infractions" ranged from a harmless burp at the dinner table to being caught watching a Saturday-morning cartoon that was deemed unfit to getting a new dress dirty as she played in the grass. This upbringing was about rigid rules with absolute intolerance for deviation. And the one rule that was to be held in reverence more than all others and which must never be broken is that one must never break the silence and disclose what occurs within the family and, by extension, the church. The desired effect of this abusive rigidity is to break down each cult member's personal image and will until that person is also fully indoctrinated and becomes either the dominator or the dominated in their adult life.

But Maddy never became indoctrinated in her parents' cult of fear and pain-based subservience. While Maddy's father had the personal strength and will of a discarded jellyfish helplessly lying on a beach, Maddy got her spirit and will to thrive and survive from two other sources. Her mother, from whom she learned two basic lessons: first, it is justified to be intolerant and punishing of those that you deem "unworthy" and, second, to live her life with an unbreakable rigidity, for flexibility toward others was akin to weakness. Her other sources of her spiritual foundation were her beloved aunts and uncle, from whom she was able to define "unworthy" as people who used others solely for their own personal benefit, using any means necessary, and also that charity and humanitarianism are lofty goals for all of society to aspire to but that those goals can never be achieved without the counterbalance of justice for those who act in opposition to humanity's and the world's betterment. The end result of these diametrically opposed influences was a human being who would never be deterred from her sense of equity for herself or for those that she cared for.

While an evening in her parents' home was spent consuming a bland, tasteless dinner (usually grilled, seasonless chicken or fish with steamed vegetables) followed by her parents' rabid ingestion of radical right-wing commentators' bloviated propaganda on "America's most trusted news channel" and capped off with an hour of quiet reverential Bible study, her Friday evenings and Saturdays were quite different. Her homelife was, at best, drudgery and, at worst, emotionally and physically painful.

Chapter 2

(Ain't Nothin' but a) House Party

Maddy's Friday evenings and Saturdays were the complete opposite. They were rambunctiously joyous. The weekend's festivities would always begin by Maddy's dour mother delivering her to the doorstep of her aunt and uncle's home right after school, always with the firm warning: "Do *not* let her have any sweets. Do *not* allow her to stay up past nine. And *do not* allow her to watch any of your 'movies' or listen to any of your unholy noise that you call 'music.'"

"Of course not," uncle Joe would respond in a subservient tone. "We'll just have a nice, quiet weekend. No need for you to worry."

"Well . . . we'll see," the lanky corpse would reply in her obnoxiously nasal and condescending voice. "Just remember, my allowing her to visit is a luxury that I can take away at any time." "Of course, understood," uncle Joe would say, fighting back the urge to both laugh at and strike out at this most miserable person.

The door would be carefully closed, so as not to even hint at the spiritual insurrection that was about to be unleashed within the house. Giggling, Maddy and uncle Joe would cautiously peer out the curtains as they watched the Sommerses' plain American "made" (as far as they knew) sedan drive away.

"I think the coast is clear," Maddy would say, in a barely audible whisper as though fearing that her mother possessed the ability to still hear her from a block away.

"I think so, Maddy. What should we do tonight?" Joe would say as he looked down on her and beamed with the joy of being in his niece's presence.

Maddy would look down at her shuffling feet and say in a singsongy voice, "Well . . . I was just thinking' that . . . maybe . . . if you want to . . . we could go to the store and . . . maybe"—her delicate face would then lift, slightly cocked to the left with her luscious eyelashes batting rapidly over her infectious emerald-green eyes—"get some treats and a movie?"

This same act was played out over and over in some variation or another almost every Friday night from the time Maddy could put sentences together until she would leave Madison at the age of seventeen. And uncle Joe always greeted this demure but completely transparent manipulation with his boisterous belly laugh while saying, "Yep, let's see what trouble we can find at the store, buttacup." Maddy would let out a high-pitched squeal of delight as she began bouncing around the home's inviting foyer as she now realized her yoke of oppression had just been removed, if only for a short time.

"Blair, honey, Maddy and I are gonna run to the store and pick up a snack. Y'need anything?"

Aunt Blair, always looking ten years younger than her actual age, even with her hair up in a tight black bun and still dressed in her conservative business pantsuit from her day at the accounting office, understood her role in this little ruse and would always warn in a tone of tacit approval, "Now, Joseph, don't be spoiling that girl. Just get a few things." Her conscience would now be satisfied as she had fulfilled her prescribed duty. She had done what she could to moderate their impulsive behavior. There was nothing more that she could possibly do and was now completely powerless (she would rationalize) to stop her two mischievous loves from unleashing their gluttonous carnage on the unsuspecting local market.

Joe, mentally regressing to whatever age Maddy happened to be at the time, would gleefully skip with his energetic niece to whatever red vehicle he currently drove. (He always owned a red car or truck from the time he had met Maddy's mother, just to piss her off, as red was, of course, the color of Satan and whores.) Maddy was never allowed to go to the store with her father on his weekly procurement trips, so Maddy would stare in wonderment at the cornucopia of all of the potential smells and tastes on display in glorious, vibrant colors. She noticed everything, from the light buzzing of the overhead lights to the clacking sound one wheel would make on the shopping cart. She would drag her uncle down every aisle, even the aisles with paper products or cleaning supplies, so as to ensure that she would not miss out on a single opportunity for sensory pleasure. When she would notice an item of interest, she would politely but excitedly say, "Hey, uncle Joe . . . could we get this?"

To which Joe would exclaim, "Why the hell not? Who's to stop us? Put it in the cart!"

Frequently on these trips they would encounter another shopper behaving in a manner that Joe would find annoying, if not intolerable. From taking up an entire aisle with their overly obese body and shopping cart as they methodically read every nutritional label for every brand of ketchup to senselessly berating a sixteen-year-old clerk because their coupon to save thirty-five cents off of shampoo had expired, these inconsiderate demonstrations grated on Joe. And Maddy would frequently ask, "What's *their* problem?"

To which Joe would reply, "That, my dear, is what is known as a fuckin' douchebag."

Following this two-hour trip to the market, the devious pair would return to their home port with their bags of contraband bounty. They would laugh with glee as they poured the contents of the bags upon the mahogany coffee table in the living room. "Look at what *we* got!" they would exclaim, behaving much like victorious pirates who are drunk on the power of their most recent victory.

Then, aunt Blair would enter the room. Maddy and Joe would immediately be quiet, bow their heads in reverence for the entrance of the home's matriarch, and feign embarrassment while also giving each other darting looks of delight with slight, mischievous grins. Blair, her straight jet-black hair now down, echoing visions of the most luxurious of ebony curtains, had her slight and taut frame encased in tight, faded twenty-year-old blue jeans and a slightly torn tour T-shirt from some one-hit wonder '80s band (frequently, it was a Naked Eyes T-shirt). She would wistfully gaze down upon the overabundance of preservative-filled treats. The table was completely engulfed by multiple types of candy, ice cream, crackers (with canned "cheese" spread, of course), potato chips, tortilla chips, pretzels, dip, frozen pizzas, frozen burritos, and, usually, Twinkies.

"Jesus Christ, Joseph, what are you thinking?" Blair would say, attempting to sound exasperated but unable to hide her amusement.

"But, Blair, honey—" Joe would start to plead before being cut off from his most patient wife.

"I know . . .," she would say in an understanding and approving tone, "but the sour cream and onion Pringles are mine. Got it?" The three unlikely co-conspirators would then begin laughing as they dug into their evening's feast while the movie that Maddy had selected began flickering on the screen. To his credit, uncle Joe would always direct Maddy to movies that were, for the most part, appropriate for her age and usher her gaze away from the violent images found on the adult, R-rated titles. Disney movies were a hit with Maddy as a very young child (especially *Cinderella*, which played nearly every Saturday afternoon before her parents were to pick her up). As she grew, her tastes would evolve, and she would become enraptured by the on-screen battles of the various superheroes with their colorful, muscle-bound costumes and their righteous dialogue. The battle between "good" and "evil" was infectious for her as she longed to witness justice being served to those whose characteristics and personalities reminded her of her parents and their church's parishioners.

At the age of twelve, an event occurred that spurred her interest in politics and triggered her exploration of political dramas and documentaries. At the age of thirteen, another event occurred that inspired her to delve into the cinematic world of civil and human rights. And at the age of fifteen, an event occurred that would cause her to be enveloped by the dark themes and intensely violent imagery of psychological thrillers and horror.

By 9:00 pm, Blair, Joseph, and Maddy would be slumped down in their respective nesting places, bloated and fatigued from their grotesque orgy of sugar and edible chemicals. Reluctantly, they would clean up the mess of haphazardly discarded wrappers, crumbs, and quarter-eaten bags of just about everything, as they needed to be prepared for the impending arrival of the evening's final guest.

And then aunt Patty would arrive around 10:00 pm. And all hell would break loose. Aunt Patty, her slender arms adorned with a variety of tattoos ranging from the "anarchy" symbol to an image of an animated '20s flapper, would typically be wearing over her toned body a Ramones T-shirt that hadn't been washed in a while, a black faux leather mini that barely covered the crotch in her well-worn fishnet stockings, and black Doc Martens. One large hoop earring, bearing a skull, would dangle from her right ear just beneath her crew cut of (pink? purple? blue? black? yellow?) hair. She would bound into this Rockwellian scene and exclaim from her black-painted lips, "Let's get this fuckin' party started!" She would briefly introduce whatever girl-toy she had in tow that evening, gallop into the family room, turn on the stereo, and begin playing music.

When Maddy would ask her aunt Patty what it was that they were listening to, Patty would kneel attentively in front of her inquisitive niece and say in a soft maternal voice, "Maddy, my love, what we are listening to is"— Patty would then purposefully contort her voice into a deep, demonic growl —"the music of the gods." Patty would then throw the unsuspecting child to the floor and blow on her belly, eliciting squeals of laughter from her delighted niece. But this "music of the gods" was entirely different from her parents' "godly music," which was dark, solemn, and, quite frankly, just no fuckin' fun (as Maddy would describe it starting at the age of ten). The parishioners would just sit there, expressionless as they sang these sorrowful melodies. If this was the music that God liked, Maddy surmised, then she definitely did not want to be invited to a party at *that* fucker's house!

No, the music that she was introduced to by her beloved aunts and uncle was celebratory. It was loud. It inspired laughter and shouting and unholy gyrations of the human body that held Maddy's attention in both awe and delight. There were no rules (except that the family Chihuahua, Rascal, definitely did *not* like to dance); and Maddy's spirit, enthusiasm, and will to not just be alive, but to actually live and feel and experience was unbridled. Sweat would pour from her constantly smiling face and soak her T-shirt as she bounced from one dance partner to the next in a frenetic blur of excitement.

There was Bowie. And Lou Reed. And the Damned. And the Cramps. And the Sex Pistols. And the Jesus and Mary Chain, to name but a few of the artists from Patty's sonic buffet. Later in the evening, Joe and Blair would usually be able to wrestle control of the party and play songs from their more "subdued" musical library. Their more "mellow" contributions would include Springsteen, Fleetwood Mac, Sam Cooke, Irma Thomas, and, yes, frequently, "Does Your Mother Know" by ABBA, just for the sheer irony of the title and usually by request from a small, sweaty imp. The evening was a sonic smorgasbord of punk; new wave; '60s R&B and soul; '60s garage; and glam and pop from the '70s, '80s, and '90s. But at some point in the evening, Joe would always put on "A Groovy Kind of Love" by the Mindbenders.

"Oh fuck, not this again!" Patty would exclaim as the two soul mates held each other and swayed to their song with smiles of contentment on their faces. Maddy would look on in romantic wonderment as she bore witness to this demonstration of true love and commitment.

The party would usually last until one or two in the morning, which caused Saturday to be a bleary-eyed wasteland of leisurely snacking on the previous evening's leftovers and watching various cartoons on television. Patty and her friend would usually be crashed out in the spare bedroom until noon, their naked limbs both sprawled out and entangled at the same time. In the early evening, Blair would always make a well-balanced dinner for her family. Maddy would either play in the kitchen under her aunt's feet or sit in the living room with Joe and watch *Cinderella* (again). Patty would also be in the kitchen to "help," which mostly consisted of just being in the way, as Patty possessed just enough culinary skills to accurately order a Big Mac from a drive-through. The family would sit down to consume Blair's delicious home-cooked wares. But first, they would hold hands and bow their heads, and each would say a silent prayer to themselves, or say no prayer at all. The choice was for each of them to make. Maddy's prayer was always to be able to live in this loving home forever. As they were eating, Patty would usually say to Maddy, "Sooooo, Mads, watcha gonna tell Mommy?"

Chapter 3

(What's So Funny 'Bout) Peace, Love, and Understanding

Even as a very young child, Maddy instinctively knew that she could not tell her parents about the actual events that had occurred over the course of the past twenty-four hours. She would rehearse her story without being asked. They had dinner of chicken and vegetables. They watched a Hallmark movie (the synopsis of which Maddy would always memorize in the event of an inquisition). She bathed, read a Bible passage, prayed, then went to bed. This, or some variation thereof, is the story that she would tell her parents week after week as "Personality Crisis" by the New York Dolls or some similar musical delight echoed throughout her brain. And they always bought it. Deception of her parents was as delicious as last night's Twinkies, she would gleefully think to herself.

Maddy was twelve years old during the 2000 presidential election. Her parents were, of course, die-hard Bush supporters although they never really bought into the concept of "compassionate conservatism." Her aunts and uncle supported Gore, having no other viable option. Maddy became intrigued by the differing political and societal opinions that surrounded her and began reading news reports at her school library (as she knew that she could not bring that material home) from various sources and critically thinking about what reports made sense and which did not. Even at that age, it did not take her long to realize through basic thought and common sense that the "news" that she was subjected to every evening with her parents was nothing more than made-up bullshit designed to tap into the frightened "moral majority's" emotions so that they would become addicted to this daily infusion of toxic, self-fulfilling rhetoric. Like a junkie, the mindless and emotionally charged audience would dutifully tune in, eager for their next fix, and the advertising dollars would pour onto the propaganda peddlers like wine from Christ's goblet. To Maddy, it was simply obvious that these vicious and hateful diatribes were as fake as the myths that she was forced to endure at church. It was all just a made-up story, not unlike her beloved Disney movies (except for *Cinderella—that* shit is real!).

Maddy would try to discuss actual facts and scientific information with her parents to counter the fantasy that was being ingested by them. Those conversations did not go well and would typically end by her father saying that he wasn't going to raise a feminazi (because he possessed no original thoughts) and her mother saying that she would be nothing more than a godless whore if she did not subscribe to what it meant to be a Christian and true American. But Maddy would persist over the years, to the point of her mother calling her "demonic" and beating her with a yardstick as she yelled, "Blasphemy!" The pain Maddy felt from these mental and physical beatings was real and had an impact on her body and on her spirit. Maddy's eyes would well up with tears as she would rapidly ascend the staircase, fling open her bedroom door, and crash, front first onto her bed. Tears would stream down her face uncontrollably as her developing mind would desperately search for answers to her plight.

The end result of that election did not sit right with Maddy, and her young mind struggled to reconcile it. She, like many Americans, couldn't quite put her finger on it; but it just didn't seem quite fair. And what the fuck were "hanging chads"? How could something so insignificant be so destructively significant as to influence the outcome of a presidential election?

"Yeah, that shit's just wrong," Maddy would say. "We gotta get rid of these 'hanging chads.' They're fuckin' up our world." Maddy began eighth grade when she was thirteen and was assigned a school project with a classmate named Edward. Maddy innocently invited Edward to her home after school to begin the project. Maddy and Edward entered the home and was greeted by her mother's look of shock, then quiet disapproval. "Um . . .," Maddy began to timidly explain, "this is my friend, Edward, and we have a class project to do . . . Is that okay?" "Very well . . .," her mother tersely said. "Just leave your bedroom door open."

"Uh . . . okay," Maddy agreed, although she didn't understand the purpose behind her mother's demand.

Upon her father's arrival home, Maddy asked if it would be okay if Edward stayed for dinner. Her father looked up briefly from his "news" program, looked at Edward, and in an emotionless tone said, "No, Maddy. It's best he run along home now."

Edward and Maddy made plans for their next project session then said their goodbyes.

"I don't understand. Why couldn't Edward stay for dinner?" Maddy inquired.

Her father looked at Maddy with his long face and sunken gray eyes and stated in a dry, matter-of-fact voice, "It's best he stays with his own kind just as you must stay with your own kind. Maddy, don't you ever invite another n——r into this house again."

Maddy was in shock. She began thinking to herself, *Okay, I get that they have some messed-up beliefs and they're pretty isolated from everyone except the church people . . . but . . .* Maddy started thinking about the church's congregation. They were all *white*. Almost all of the hosts and commentators on their "news" programs were *white*. There was that time that her mother immediately left the family gathering at Aunt Blair's house when she saw that Patty had brought along a black friend. *Hooooly shit!* Maddy realized. *This shit's worse than I thought. I'm being raised by fuckin' douchebag racists!*

At this point in her life, Maddy instinctively rebelled and began seeking out anything and everything that ran counter to her parents' indoctrinated beliefs. She wore nothing but black. She dyed her hair black. She would put on black lipstick and eye shadow as soon as she arrived at school. She pored through Patty's CD and record collection, gravitating toward darker artists like Bauhaus, Sisters of Mercy, and the Cure and aggressive punk bands like the Dead Kennedys and Black Flag, which she would play loudly in her bedroom. What could her parents do about it? Berate her? Beat her? That was nothing more than a continuation of her current life, so who really cared? She was numb to it all. Although she felt empowered enough to "act out," she never mentioned anything about the abuse she was enduring at her mother's cruel hands and her father's impotence out of fear that her weekend passes would be forever taken from her.

Her infectious smile faded, and she stopped flashing her "silly face," for she just didn't care about others' reactions any longer, except for on her weekends with her aunts and uncle. She continued to feel genuine joy each weekend in the warm emotional embrace of those that she considered to be her real family. She enjoyed the typical activities that had become ingrained into their Friday-night ritual, but she relished the added dimension of lively discussion and debate with knowledgeable adults over the most complex issues of the day. This was an environment that actually *encouraged* her to question authority and explore the validity of various rational viewpoints. Her thoughts and opinions were treated with the same regard and respect as any of the other conversationalists, and she was not protected from receiving negative criticisms.

It was all just a part of the give-and-take of a respectful but vigorous adult discussion.

One evening in particular, when Maddy was fifteen, Patty's latest "friend" began regurgitating the same neofascist, anti- immigrant, radically pro-gun propaganda that festered from the right-wing talking-points crowd. Patty stopped sipping her gin and tonic and looked over at Maddy, who had a look of delighted surprise on her face. Blair and Joe stared at the trio silently, waiting in anticipation to see who would make the next move. The only sound that was discernible in this suddenly tense room was the slight cracking of the ice casually melting in Patty's glass until Maddy began laughing and exclaimed, "Jesus Christ, auntie Patty, you gotta unload this one. She's not bright enough to hang with us."

Patty shook her head in disbelief as she turned to her soon- to-be former companion and said, "Shit . . . you're hot and all . . . but I know I can't change your mind, and I really can't hang with a fascist, so y'know . . . get the fuck out."

The room exploded into laughter as the wounded and embarrassed figure slipped out of the house and into the night.

"Blair, honey . . . could you go get the fire extinguisher?" uncle Joe inquired. Perplexed, Blair asked why as tears brought on by excessive laughter rolled down her almost-too-perfect cheeks. "Well," Joe explained, "we might want to be prepared for the cross that's gonna be burned on our lawn tonight." Joe's droll commentary resulted in another round of unstoppable laughter.

"This isn't funny!" Patty exclaimed. "Who the hell am I gonna fuck tonight?"

In the meantime, her parents, concerned about the erosion of their power over their teenage daughter's "soul," was conspiring with their cult leader/pastor. Even as a young child, Maddy never was engaged in the sermons or activities of the church. She would simply gaze out the window and look at the beauty of the world that existed outside of the dank gray wooden walls. That is until her mother would give her a sharp nudge in her side, which inspired nothing more than polite staring at the pastor as his meaningless words fell harmlessly away from her consciousness. This polite indifference had now grown into visible hostility toward these rituals, as Maddy would sit in her "Sunday dress," her arms folded with a look of resentment upon her fifteen-going-on-ten-year-old-looking face.

The pastor was a man in his mid to late forties. Slicked- back black hair to match his neatly trimmed goatee topped his ruggedly charismatic face. A tallish man with a reasonably toned body for a man of his age, he was married with two grown daughters of his own, both of whom were attending Bible college. He knew what was needed to guide a teenage girl through the confusion of hormones, peer pressure, and sinful "urges." He knew, he would tell Maddy's parents, how to guide her back onto the Lord's path.

It was then decided that Maddy would go to the pastor's home on Wednesdays after school for private Bible study. It was this private tutoring, he convinced, that would prove pivotal to the salvation of Maddy's soul. But should this fail, they had no recourse but to accept that Maddy's soul had already been consumed by the dark spiritual forces that proliferated throughout their version of the world, and he would advise them to allow their daughter to go onto her sinfully perilous path, so as to disallow her possession from being a corrupting influence upon the family and church.

Following the sermon the next Sunday, Maddy's mother looked down upon her petite daughter, expressionless with the exception of the slightest of wry smirks exposing the cracks from around her serpentine lips. Her father sat alone and motionless, his legs hanging out from the end of a well-worn pew. Looking down with a blank expression as if in a state of forlorn ambivalence, he said nothing.

"Madeline," her mother began with frigid condescension, "a decision has been made. Go to the pastor's office this instant. He will explain. This is your only chance for redemption. Come straight home afterwards. You shall walk home today with your cross to bear."

Maddy walked slowly and with trepidation to the pastor's office and walked in through the open mahogany door. She found herself alone in a room that did not resemble the rest of the church in the slightest. Instead of dark lighting and drearily faded paint that hid much of the disrepair that many of the floors, walls, and pews were in, his office was bright, colorful, and downright opulent. The furnishings in the sitting area were in the best of condition and made from the finest materials. His desk and office chair were enormous and took up a third of the generously spaced room. There were many pictures of the pastor with supposed dignitaries. Maddy recognized many of the faces as right-wing commentators and politicians or from press conferences from outside of a courtroom to protest their latest charges as being a "political witch hunt" or "patriotic prosecution." Maddy felt ill looking at these smiling white men that she knew would never serve the time they deserved for their crimes against humanity and our country. She was alone in the belly of the beast.

Her stomach sank further and began to tighten as she could sense him creeping up behind her. She emotionally recoiled as she felt his meaty and sweaty hands fall upon her delicate shoulders. And she could feel him grow as he subtly pressed his body against her backside. The trauma of this experience was complete for Maddy even before the pastor began speaking in a soft, predatory tone, "Madeline, thank you for coming to see me."

Maddy didn't like the way the word *coming* oozed out of the pastor's mouth. He continued in a soft tone with a methodical pacing, ensuring to drag out almost every word, "Your parents are fine, God-fearing people and true patriots in our congregation. And although it may not seem like it to you now, they have your best intentions in their heart. They want so badly to be proud of you, and I know that you *want* them to be proud of you. Every little girl longs for the respect and love of their parents, isn't that right, dear?"

Maddy knew what was happening and feared for what was about to happen. At the tender age of fifteen, it was a sad commentary on our society that one as young as her must be well versed in the manipulative tactics of molesters and rapists. She knew that she was in danger and was mentally and physically frozen by the situation that she found herself in. Fighting back the tears that had begun welling under her now-dejected green eyes, she was able to say in a subdued and trembling voice, "Y-y- yes, s-sir."

"Gooood . . . that's so very gooood," the pastor continued as he began suggestively pawing Maddy's tightened shoulders. "I know you want to be a gooood girl for your parents, your church . . . and for *meee*, don't you?"

"Y-y-yes," Maddy stammered, her mind racing to find an escape route. Her mind was screaming, "Just run!" but her body would not cooperate.

"Goood. Sooo . . . your parents and I have decided that it would be best for you and I to begin having private Bible study together. Just you and me. Won't that be fun? Every Wednesday after school from three thirty to five. During our sessions, you will learn how to resist the temptations of this sinful world and get you on the Lord's path once again . . . and," he stated in a light snicker, "I know it's a bit naughty, but . . . perhaps . . . if you don't tell your mother . . . perhaps you and I might share some ice cream together. Wouldn't that be nice? I know how you love having ice cream with those you care for."

Fear immediately turned to anger. *That . . . fucking . . . tears it!* Maddy thought in an internal scream. *It's one thing for this fucking perv to want to rape me. It's quite another to use my love of eating ice cream with my beloved uncle Joe to do it!* A wave of fortitude swept over Maddy as she quickly pulled away from the pastor's intrusive touch and turned to face him while wiping the last remnants of tears from her enraged emerald eyes. "Yep, got it. Every Wednesday after school. Lookin' forward to it. See ya then!"

Maddy hastily left the room, walking as quickly as her size 6 feet would go. She left the church and thought, *Oh, I'll bear this cross all right. I'm gonna bear this cross the entire walk home. And when I get home, I'm gonna bury this fucking cross up that bitch's fucking ass!*

Maddy entered her parents' house in a torrent of rage, flinging the front door open and closing it so violently so as to shake all of the rummage sale–purchased religious paintings and decor.

Her mother, seeing the intensity on her daughter's contorted face, hastily stood up and began saying, "Madeline! What is the meaning of—"

At which point, this petite girl who now resembled a cuddly rag doll crossed with Linda Blair at her *Exorcist* "finest," said to her mother in a low, sinister voice, "No, no, no. It's *my* turn, bitch. I understand you people are fucking nuts, I get that. But what I didn't get is that you were so fucking brainwashed that you would serve your own daughter up to a fucking pedophile. So . . . here's how it's gonna be. I'm never going to that douchebag's house, and I'm never going back to that cult that you call a church ever again . . . you got that, bitch?"

Maddy's father sat motionless in his twelve-year-old tan recliner. Looking down and ensuring not to make eye contact with either combatant, he could not help but to display the slightest of congratulatory grins.

Incensed, the woman who gave birth to her picked up the conveniently located yardstick, raised it, and swung with the intent to strike her young daughter as she had done so many times before for the slightest of "infractions." But this time, the result was different. Instead of landing on her daughter's backside with a loud slapping sound, the sound came earlier as a result of landing in Maddy's delicate-looking but forceful hand. Maddy clenched the end of the yardstick that she had snatched from midair, ripped it from the woman's grip, tossed it across the room, and said in a low but intense voice, "Never . . . fucking . . . again. Do you understand me, you fucking bitch? Never . . . fucking . . . again."

For the first time in Maddy's life, Maddy witnessed this woman express emotion on her callous face. And that emotion was fear. This woman that Maddy had always needed to coward from due to the mental and physical abuse that she had endured by her hand was now afraid of *her*. Maddy experienced a wave of an emotion that she had never felt before. It was an odd combination of joy, strength, and assertion. She had never felt so substantial in her life. And she liked it.

"Ju . . . ust go . . . to your . . . room right now . . . young lady . . . and you . . . pray that Jesus can rid you . . . of that . . . d-d-demon inside of you," the woman guardedly and meekly stammered.

Maddy's eyes welled up with tears as she rapidly ascended the staircase, flung open her bedroom door, and crashed, front first, onto her bed. The tears were streaming down her face uncontrollably as she let out the most maniacal laughter that she had ever experienced.

The laughter ended as the realization of what she had just done to the one person who had total legal control of her settled in. *Oh fuck . . .*, she thought, *she could send me away. She could have me committed, or worse. I gotta get the fuck outta here.* Hastily, she haphazardly threw clothing into her backpack, grabbed her purse, and prepared to exit through her second-floor bedroom window. Just before her departure, she caught a glimpse of her bookshelf. *Nope, can't leave that behind.* Maddy scurried down the truss on the side of the porch and began walking toward aunt Blair and uncle Joe's house, her DVD copy of *Cinderella* firmly in tow.

Maddy appeared at her beloved family's doorstep shaken by fear and rage. Uncle Joe answered the door and saw the purse, backpack, and pleading demeanor in his precious niece's green eyes and knew instantly that some bad shit had just gone down. Joe immediately stated in an understanding tone, "Get your fuckin' ass in here, buttacup. Anyone followin' ya?"

"I . . . I . . . I dunno," Maddy stammered.

"Blair, honey . . . why dontcha call Patty. I think we're gonna need her. And tell her not to bring along a friend. This is family business."

The next hour was the most painful and tormenting hour that Blair, Joe, and Patty would ever experience. They listened with guilt-ridden horror as Maddy recounted everything that she had experienced in her life. The constant suppression. The degradation. The beatings. Everything came out, culminating with the latest episode of beginning to be groomed for molestation and her epic confrontation with her mother. Silently, they all stood up, went over to their beyond-her-years-mature niece, and embraced her in a mournful recognition of what this majestic creature had endured right under their noses. Each of them, Blair, Joe, and Patty, tears streaming down their hardened, enraged faces, embraced her so tightly that it was as if they were trying to absorb Maddy's suffering and take it upon themselves. They would never forgive themselves for having allowed this and apologized to Maddy profusely for being so blind to her plight. Maddy pleaded with them to not feel guilty. She had not told them because of her intense love for them and of her fear that her unhinged mother would find a way to keep them away from her if she ever told. The mixed emotions of pride in the strength of their niece entangled with their gnawing guilt was broken by the ring of the harvest gold rotary phone in the foyer. Blair solemnly left the emotional huddle and answered the phone. "Yes, she's here . . . yes, please . . . come on over. I'm sure it will be fine."

Guilt appropriately turned to all-consuming anger for each member of the family as Blair reentered the room, giving her sister and her love of her life knowing glances before she spoke in a controlled voice so as not to unleash the torrent of fury she and the others were experiencing. "Maddy, your parents are coming over. I think you should go up to your room now. We have some . . . things . . . to discuss with them. And do not worry. You are safe, my dearest."

"Fuck yeah, she is . . .," Joe began to express, his voice becoming louder before Blair raised her hand and calmly said, "Joseph, please sit down. There will be a time, but that time is not now." Heeding his wife's guidance (and somewhat of a warning), Joe went to his chair, sat down, and smoldered, just waiting for the moment his wife would give him the clearance to erupt.

Maddy trudged up the staircase as was requested of her and thought to herself, *Oh fuck, this is gonna be good!*

There was a knock at the door. Blair answered and greeted Maddy's parents politely. Maddy's mother entered the room guardedly but with assertion, her slug of a husband just barely behind her as if he were using her as a shield for what he knew was about to be brought down upon him.

It was a warm September evening, but not so warm that air- conditioning was needed. The windows were open to let a fresh breeze of air in. The Argentos' home felt subzero.

Maddy's mother sensed that the mood of the room was as cold as her own heart and politely stated with what appeared to be a slight smile of conciliation, "Good evening. We're sorry to have bothered you. If you would be so kind as to call for Madeline, we'll just be on our way."

Blair raised her hands outwardly and at hip level, her delicate forefingers pointed out in order to preempt any reaction from Joe or Patty as if conducting an orchestra. "Before you go, won't you have a seat? I think we have some things to discuss with you," Blair stated in a constrained voice and with a smile reserved only for a female praying mantis prior to eating its mate's head.

Understanding the situation that she was confronted with, Maddy's mother went on the offensive. She began speaking softly but with a great crescendo with each uttered statement, ending with the manufactured uplifting clamor of the most charismatic of televangelists. "Now . . . look here. She is *our* daughter, and we shall raise her as we see fit. My only regret is that I've allowed her to fall under the influence of such . . . people . . . throughout her life. We *will* see to it that her soul is saved. We *will* see to it that her faith in God and country is restored. We *will* see to it that she attends our church and receives personal guidance from *our* most glorious pastor. And we *will* see to it that she never is in the presence of heathens such as you for as long as I walk this earth!"

There was the sound of slow, mocking applause coming from the corner of the room. Joe lifted his head as he clapped. Blair and Patty, who had been standing in front of Joe as a human safeguard against the carnage that they knew Joe could unleash, silently and knowingly parted, allowing a direct line of sight between Joe and this most vile of women. He stood, silently walked to the slightly trembling mother, and stopped five inches from her face. In a low, barely discernible growl, he stated, "You will now listen to me. And you would be wise to listen to me and believe everything that I am about to say. If anyone ever harms that child in any way, I will tear them apart. With my bare hands . . . and . . . as *my* god is *my* witness, listen to me now and believe me . . . I will tear them apart. I will gladly spend an eternity in hell for sending you there with me. Believe me. And I'll send that worm of a husband there too, just for the fuckin' kick of it. Now . . . watcha gonna do . . . bitch?"

Maddy's mother was frozen by the fearful realization that what this enraged man was uttering was true. But she would not back down. *She* was in control and would not relinquish it to this blue-collar infidel. She parted her lips to begin speaking, when a soft but forceful voice broke the tense silence, "Stop this. Stop this now. We all have Maddy's best interest at heart, so perhaps we can reach a . . ."

"Compromise?" Patty said while looking at her little brother's haggard face.

Patty and Blair looked upon their little brother, a small and defeated man whom they once looked after as a child, five and six years their junior. The boy who was always a bit less than smart but always had the best of intentions. The boy who constantly got his lunch money stolen. The boy who would be laughed at as he entered a classroom with ill-fitted clothing. They had protected him from the bullies who would aspire to take his lunch money or humiliate him just for the adolescent fun of it. They were his guardians and role models. Upon his return from the service, with congratulatory brain trauma, they assisted him in finding employment and a new apartment. But once he met the woman who was to be his wife and he became indoctrinated into the world of cult propogandists, they had no choice but to write him off. Despite multiple attempts at reason, they determined that he was simply no longer salvageable. And they did not speak to their brother except for infrequent occasions. Until Madeline entered the world. They all witnessed this miracle of strength, beauty, and spirit in this small infant and were determined to resolve their differences with their brother and his wife on her behalf.

"Yes, a compromise," the lanky man stated as he climbed from out of his chair and stood next to his rigid wife. "This has gone on far enough. Maddy needs all of us in order to be the God-fearing person we all want her to be."

"Well . . . kinda—" Patty stated until Blair abruptly cut her off, "Yes . . . a compromise. Let's just all sit down and come up with a solution that will be in the best interest of everyone involved."

Maddy's mother sat in the corner, her lips clenched so tightly that they were nearly invisible. She did not speak a word as the principals of this newly formed alliance began negotiating the terms of Maddy's adolescent life. There was give-and-take between the parties, with Maddy's parents insisting that they continue to play a role in their daughter's spiritual development. An agreement was reached, and hands were cautiously and frigidly shaken to seal the deal, except for Joe. "Nope, I ain't gonna shake nobody's hand. This deal ain't done yet. Maddy has to agree, or the deal is off. This is her life, and she gets final say. Anybody got a problem with that?" Maddy's parents silently nodded their tacit approval as Joe yelled up at the ceiling, "C'mon down, buttacup! We got some shit to talk about!"

Maddy descended the staircase and entered the room. Having changed out of her conservative Sunday dress, she was now wearing ripped black jeans and a black Damned T-shirt (both of which were hand-me-downs from Patty who left cool clothes at her sister's house for Maddy to wear). She looked up reservedly at her uncle Joe, her protector and guardian. She exhaled a sigh of relief as he gave her a knowing wink and slight smile.

"Madeline—" her mother began to sternly say before being abruptly cut off by Joe, "Nope, I'll tell her. Maddy, my dear, I think we've come up with a solution. But this is your life, and if you don't like these terms, we'll go back to the drawing board. You are free to express yourself here, and we want your input, understand, buttacup?"

"Yes, uncle Joe," Maddy stated with a newfound sense of ease.

Everyone took a seat and monitored Maddy's reaction as Joe outlined the details of the plan. "Here's the deal. Numero uno: You never will have to go to your parents' 'church'"—he sarcastically emphasized—"or see their douchebag 'pastor' ever again unless you want to for some fucked-up reason.

"Numero two-o"—Maddy loved that her uncle was using their mutual love of their favorite *Monster Vision* host during this presentation, as it placed an emphasis on their bond and was a clandestine "fuck you" to her parents— "you will stay the full weekend with us, from Friday night through Sunday night, unless you got shit going on with your friends. And we're all going to basically do whatever the fuck we want to do . . . *except* . . . your parents insist that you attend Blair's church with her each Sunday morning. And, well . . . maybe I'll pull my old ass out of bed and go once in a while too."

Blair looked at her conciliatory husband with bemusement as she had tried to get Joe to go to church with her for their entire relationship. Despite the church that Blair (and Patty when younger) went to was very "liberal" (as churches go), Joe never placed any trust in organized religion. He always said, "Nope, I got no reason to talk through a fuckin' middleman. If I got somethin' to say, I'll say it directly to the man himself." "Numero three-o, Monday through Thursday, you will stay with your parents, and you will have private Bible study with your mother for one hour each evening. That, we decided, would give everyone the opportunity to give you information that you can then use to decide who *you are* as a person." Maddy scrunched her slight round nose at this suggestion but said nothing.

"Numero four-o, no one . . . and I mean *no one*," Joe stated in a raised voice while staring glaringly at Maddy's mother with her corpse-like rigidity on full display, "will *ever* lay a hand on you again. And, as God is my witness, there *will be* hell to pay. We *will* see to it that you will be able to legally stay with us until you are grown, because these motherfuckers won't be in any condition to look after you anyway.

"So that's the deal. Watchathink?"

Maddy scanned the room and looked at the faces of everyone there. Blair, with her intensely calm face offering her solace. Patty, wearing a wry grin as if to say, "You fuckin' *got 'em*, Mads." Her father, solemn, but with a hint of hopefulness being displayed by his widened eyes and raised eyebrows. Her mother, looking defiant but unable to keep her eyes from expressing the stinging defeat that she had just endured. And finally, back to uncle Joe, his face strong and caring, as if to say, "It's up to you now, and I got your fuckin' back." He had signed off on this deal. So, she surmised, if he trusted the deal, then so could she. "Yeah, okay . . . seems fair. We'll give it a shot," Maddy stated, projecting confidence. "But one last thing. Numero five-o: I'm not gonna be subjected to any more radical, right- wing brainwashing propaganda bullshit on TV or the radio or anywhere for that matter, *and* the fucked-up Bible shit. It's one or the other, got it? You wanna listen to all of that shit, go for it. It's your life. But this is *my* life, and I'm now gonna decide what to listen to and who to believe! You can try to indoctrinate me with one or the other, but not both. If you don't like it, then the deal's off!"

"Madeline," her mother stated through her clenched teeth while impersonating a pacifying tone, " just the Bible study will be fine. And we shall pray that you will become a God-fearing, patriotic American as we spend our time together. Now, please gather your belongings. It's time we take our leave."

"Ummm . . . nope," Maddy stated with an upturned, shaking head, resembling an infant refusing to eat her string beans, "It's Sunday. I'm stayin' here tonight. I'll see ya after school tomorrow. Reaaally lookin' forward to it too." Her daughter's sarcasm and newfound haughtiness was not lost on her parents as they crept out of the house like a defeated army.

Joe beamed with pride for his family as he witnessed Maddy go over to his adoring wife and his sister-in-law and embrace them in a tension-releasing hug. Tears flowed as she said, "T-thank y-y-you all. I-I love you a-all so m-much."

"Fuck this. Where are we orderin' pizza from tonight anyway?" Joe dryly inquired to the response of laughter from his loving family, immediately replacing the almost visible stress of the evening with relief and pure, unconditional love.

CHAPTER 4

TEENAGE RAMPAGE

Approximately three weeks later, the pastor was found beaten in a dark parking lot behind an adult video store, the apparent "victim" of a carjacking. Lying in a pool of his own blood, both arms had been broken. His jaw was shattered as were his teeth, the chipped fragments glistening in the moonlight. Both eyes were a macabre dark purple and swollen shut from the intense beating that they had endured. And every finger on both hands had been meticulously snapped, one by one. His brand-new 2003 Porsche (which he could somehow afford on his "modest" pastor's salary) was found in an abandoned lot a few days later. Its decimated appearance was much like that of its owner, who was lying in a hospital bed recovering. The pastor would never be able to have full use of his hands again. The perpetrator was never found.

A day later, news reports flashed throughout the homes of Madison with details of the gruesome discovery. It was a Friday evening, and Maddy was in her customary position on the dark- green couch next to her Aunt Blair watching the news with her and her uncle before the evening's more raucous proceedings would begin. Blair was knitting a sweater for their Chihuahua, Rascal, who was sleeping on Maddy's lap enraptured by the gentle caress of his belly. The news report of the beating came across the screen. Blair never looked up from her task. Upon hearing this news, Maddy's eyes darted and connected with those of her uncle. Seeing that she had her uncle's full attention, Maddy flashed her uncle a slight mischievous grin, as if to say, "Fuck him." And her uncle Joe mirrored her expression and sentiment. It was just the two of them silently communicating with each other until Joe said, "C'mon, buttacup, let's see if we can't find some ice cream."

Maddy enthusiastically bounced to her size 6 feet and giggled as she followed her uncle's powerful frame through the home's foyer and down the short hallway between the living room wall and mahogany staircase. The hallway walls were adorned with family pictures, most of which would contain Maddy's beaming smile. From birth to her current age, there were images of Maddy in front of or, more frequently, mischievously peering from behind her aunts and uncle, as if she had been a pixie photo bomber throughout her entire life. As they passed through the hallway, Joe can't help but glance at the pictures of his loving family and cherished niece that chronicle her development over these past fifteen years.

Now physically fully grown as she ventured to the edge of adulthood, Maddy stood at a less than imposing five feet, four inches (or as Maddy would say, "Four *and a half* fucking inches, thank you very much!"). Her petitely feminine, slender body remaining constantly toned despite the carb and sugar onslaught that it was forced to endure through Maddy's voracious appetite. Her round modestly freckled face presented a small slightly turned-up nose above her naturally mauve delicate lips and was framed by her flowing blunt bang auburn hair, cut straight at the eyebrows and slightly curled inward at the ends just above the shoulder, giving the appearance of a molten copper waterfall. Showcased within this kaleidoscope of perfect facial features were her fierce emerald-green eyes that flickered through the constant batting of her lush sandy eyelashes.

Sitting back on the couch next to her aunt with Rascal joyously lapping at her spoon following each silky bite of butter ripple, Maddy reflected on how fortunate she was to have such a caring and loving family, fully realizing that there were other children, especially girls and young women, who were left at the mercy of domineering parents and sadistic lovers, their pride and sometimes bones left shattered in their destructive wake. Her heart sank at the thought of what her life might be like without her affectionate support system, and an ember began burning that would later lead her to resolve to do everything in her power to defend others from society's most insidious inhabitants, just as her real family had done for her.

Maddy had a singular thought throughout high school: get the fuck out. Although her homelife was much more stable and much less abusive, she was still confronted daily (well, Monday through Thursday) with snide barbs from her parents as they continued to attempt to indoctrinate their daughter into their twisted world vision. There were constant targeted references to "godless whores" and "infidels" throughout each day's Bible study sessions with her ever-condescending mother, and her father frequently referred to her as "my little feminazi" or "my little commie," in order to belittle her "liberal" but quite mainstream political ideology.

What was so wrong, she thought, on treating our country's citizenry with regard and care? To help them have health care? A social security net to combat economic downturns? To be the beacon for the world's down-trodden as promised by our Statue of Liberty? To have the wealthy shoulder their fair share of the country's responsibilities to one another? To not have weapons of war in the hands of untrained and, often, radically unhinged individuals who use them to commit genocide against those whom they deem unworthy due to their nationality, gender, skin color, sexual orientation, or politics? What, she thought, was so wrong about each of us realizing that we are all a part of this society and that we have the moral obligation to fulfill our responsibilities toward one another in order to collectively protect our inherent rights of "life, liberty, and the pursuit of happiness"? Is the "mortal sin" of so-called "liberalism" as simple as not wanting to pay taxes so that the wealthy can buy another vacation home and the middle-class can upgrade to a fifty-two-inch flat screen in their bedroom to match the ones in their living room and basement family room? Is that what was most important to her parents and those of their ilk?

Maddy found it ironic that her father would rant about "socialism" while eagerly accepting his unemployment check when he lost his latest job, receiving his free health care at the VA clinic, and frantically filling out the forms necessary to receive government energy assistance. It seemed to Maddy that her parents' definition of "socialism" consisted solely of government programs that they themselves didn't receive at that particular moment. If it was a program that *they* did not receive but was beneficial to *someone else* in our society, it was "socialism," and that was evil. If it was a benefit that *they themselves* benefited from, it was something that *they* were *entitled* to.

Maddy also found irony in her parents' protestations of being under the "yoke of government oppression" while supporting a political party that was attempting to exterminate actual democracy through voter suppression tactics and gerrymandering representational districts, among many other things. But, she surmised, this was okay with them, because it was *the other* whose rights were being eliminated and not *theirs*. At least, not yet, Maddy thought as she would say to herself silently in her singsongy voice, "Better be careful whatcha wish for, fuckers . . ."

Shortly after the family's " joint custody" deal was struck, Maddy sat down with her aunts and uncle to reveal her plan for her sought-after independence. Although the plan was sophomoric (as she was, after all, a sophomore in high school), its simplicity had a beauty and determination to it. Maddy stood in the middle of the Argento living room with her adoring family sitting around her. The moment's importance led her to feel as though she were about to deliver something as historic and impactful as the "Emancipation Proclamation" or the awe- inspiring "I Have a Dream" speech. Standing proudly with her shoulders back and wearing a sly smile, she began to speak in a formal tone, her green eyes darting to each audience member from underneath her tapestry of copper hair.

"Good evening. I would like to thank you all for attending my presentation," she stated, looking like an animated fairy addressing the United Nations. "As you all know, I am wanting to leave Madison right after high school. I have chosen a destination. I will be moving to New York City. Why? Because I love the history and the imagery and the dynamic energy there. I need to be in a place with a variety of people and exciting adventures. Plus . . . my parents call it the bastion of sinners, so it kinda sounds like . . . well"—she slightly snickers as she finishes the sentence—"my kinda town." Looking up haughtily, she looked at her family, anticipating knee-slapping laughter for having delivered what she believed was the most clever joke in the history of the world.

Instead, she was greeted with an unenthusiastically delivered "Buddabump . . . ching" from her uncle Joe as he shook his head derisively. Blair just stared at her niece with widened eyes and a bewildered, open-mouthed smile.

"Jesus Christ, Mads," Patty stated, "don't quit your fuckin' day job. Leave the jokes to the professionals."

"Okay, shut the fuck up. I'm not done yet," an embarrassed and slightly annoyed Maddy exclaimed. Regaining her composure, she began again. "I have developed a plan that is both simple and foolproof, and I would appreciate . . .," her voice trailed off slightly before beginning again in a more assertive tone, "a little support, unlike your *lack* of support for my incredible humor," before finishing more softly, "in helping me to execute it."

This last line brought the previously desired effect of knee- slapping laughter from her bemused family as they had just witnessed their diminutive niece fight back and immediately regain her composure in a most adorable fashion.

Fighting through her laughter, Patty exclaimed, "That's right, Mads! Don't let anybody fuck with you . . . not even us!" "Okay then, that's better," Maddy continued with her chin held high and wearing a confident grin as Rascal looked up at her from his nest at her feet. "Okay . . . here's the plan:

Step 1: Work my ass off and save money up for the move.

Step 2: Graduate early with good grades. I figure if I take summer school courses over the next two summers, I'll have enough credits to graduate in January 2006, instead of in May. I can then move, maybe in time for the spring semester at college. Step 3: Get a scholarship to a university in New York. Easy- peasy. I'm smart, fun, and adorable. They'll be falling all over

themselves to bring me in.

Step 4: Move my shit to New York and live happily ever after. Whatcha think?"

Maddy was greeted at first with silence and wide eyes as the impact of her address began to sink into the family members. Tears of pride began subtly welling up in each of their eye ducts as they dramatically stood and enveloped their niece in, first, applause, then their warm physical embrace as six loving arms wrapped around her petite frame.

———

Throughout high school, Maddy attacked her plan with the zealous enthusiasm of an invading army on D-Day. She took a job as a cashier/waitress at a local diner and ice cream parlor, making sure to milk as much tip money as she could from her (usually) male customers through a subtle shake of her adolescent behind while flashing a not-so-subtle wink of her evocative left green eye. *Decent wage, great tips, free food and ice cream to take home and share with Uncle Joe. Who could ask for anything more?* she would frequently ponder as she would eagerly fill a container with soft-serve chocolate to take back to the Argentos' home on a Friday night, her contribution to the enthralling edible and musical extravaganza that she would once again experience.

Maddy was very popular with the owner of the restaurant, as well as her coworkers, all of them female, their ages spanning generations from the sixty-one-year-old owner to the middle- aged and teenage waitstaff. She could be a Lolita-esque seductress in her pursuit of generous tips but then immediately turn into an effective, punishing enforcer of common decency should someone go too far in response to her flirtations. A pat on her behind or an overly suggestive or crude comment directed at her, or any of her coworkers, would be met by her elfin figure gliding back across the restaurant to the offender's booth. She would look down at this man-child and his "posse," guffawing like the jackasses that they were, and say in a soft, almost enticing tone, "Hey . . . so . . . I know you think you're cute and all that, but I just want to tell you that . . . you are insignificant to me, to this business, and to everyone in this business, soooo . . . if you ever do anything like that again in this place, well, let's just say that my saliva in your food will be the least of your problems. You got that, chad?"

The transgressor would visibly gulp and almost whisper through his now-pale lips, "I-I'm sorry . . . I-I didn't mean anything by it."

"Yeah . . . okay, that's what I thought," Maddy would conclude as she glared at this emasculated puddle of a man with her nonblinking, raging green eyes. With each subsequent victory over an unsuspecting and hapless bully, Maddy's ember would burn brighter.

Her increasingly glowing ember would continue to be strengthened during each Bible study session, which frequently needed to be rescheduled to the morning before school to accommodate Maddy's work schedule. Maddy's employment and socking money away of course did not sit well with her parents, who were completely unaware of what their daughter was planning to do with the money and who saw this as yet another threat to their control over their increasingly rebellious daughter. They tried to force her not to work, at first through arbitrary orders to which Maddy would reply, "Ummm . . . nope, gonna work. We'll have to reschedule your indoc sesh. Just how it is." Then, by trying to cripple her financially by demanding she pay rent. Maddy would react with feigned histrionics, "Oh, please, don't make me pay rent! I can't afford to pay! What are you gonna do, evict me? Ohhh . . . pleeeaase don't evict me . . . Where on earth will this poor girl go?" With a slight sinister grin, Maddy would then stare through her ever-weakening mother and say in a sinister tone, "Yeah, evict me, bitch. C'mon. Do me another favor." Regardless of the time that the Bible study (or "indoc sesh") would be, immediately upon the clock striking the top of the hour, Maddy would jump up from her splintering wooden dining room chair and exclaim with fervor, "Times up, bitches! Maddy out!"

Maddy's parents, in reality, had no real reason to be disappointed in their daughter. Her fatal flaw in the eyes of her delusional, disapproving parents was that she was her own person and held on to her own beliefs and sense of self with the same determination and rigidity of her mother. Any set of rational parents in the world would beam with pride if they were raising a child such as Maddy. She held down a job of some responsibility at which she excelled. She never got into the typical teenage trouble of experimenting with drugs and alcohol, partially because she had little time for such exploits, but mostly because she was nearly impervious from the pressures imposed by her peers as she viewed such activities as juvenile. Aside from a bit of awkward adolescent fumbling and groping, she was not sexually active. She was a nearly straight-A student, just missing out on magna cum laude of her graduation class to a female rival. "Yeah, I know how she got that. She supplied the magna and the laude, and some perv teacher at the school probably supplied the cum," she would jealously pontificate upon hearing the news.

Aside from a few petty feuds, she was well liked at school and had a wide array of friends from every walk of life that the city of Madison offered. She was kind to others and especially supportive of her classmates who were frequently on the receiving end of public ridicule. As early as the spring semester of her sophomore year, it had become well known throughout the high school that if someone was "cool with Maddy," it would be wise to leave that classmate alone or risk being subjected to public mockery, if not worse. It was not unusual for a pubescent classmate (regardless of gender) to open their locker and find unwelcome presents such as rotting food, jockstraps that had been purposely soaked in urinals, or used tampons. For especially egregious classmates who simply refused to learn their lesson, a tip-off would be made to school security who, upon opening a locker, would find half-drank bottles of booze along with bizarre manifestos proclaiming violent intentions.

"Morning, chad," Maddy would say with haughty derision as she strode past the "crime scene," mockingly smiling at the security guard and the enfeebled classmate. Although everyone knew who was responsible, there was never any evidence, and the perpetrator would never be found. And the ember would burn just a bit more brightly.

For every action, there is an equal and opposite reaction. Maddy was not a science buff and therefore was not that familiar with Newton's third law of motion that basically says that any force can be undone. This was a lesson that Maddy, who was beginning to develop a slight immature arrogance in the wake of her various "victories" over her parents and deserving classmates, would learn in her junior year at the hands of upper-middle- class deviants (and probable future Supreme Court nominees). Maddy, taking a rare Friday night off from the eatery and her family, walked into the pre-track meet and premature "victory" party with what she felt was deserved regal grandeur. She was greeted enthusiastically by her closest friends and other classmates as they yelled invitations to join them over the intense volume of the drivel of over-produced and completely unoriginal pop hits from 2005. *Fuck, man*, Maddy thought to herself, *I need to call Aunt Patty, 'cause this shit's fuckin' lame. Seriously, people actually listen to this shit? Whatevs . . .*

Throughout the evening, Maddy was frequently offered drinks from the jubilant teens. Maddy always said, "No, thank you . . . not into that shit." But there was one boy, who happened to be the host of the party, who succeeded where others had failed. Not wanting to look "uncool" to her schoolgirl crush, she accepted the innocent-looking red solo cup from this boy who was the best athlete at the school. He had a reputation as a ladies' "man," especially with the cheerleaders (whom Maddy referred to as "the brain-dead fake-tit squad"). Maddy had been infatuated with this boy all through junior high and high school. He was, in her mind, the physical embodiment of a prince. She, on the other hand, held absolutely no interest for him. But he knew of her infatuation as she would always awkwardly avert her gaze away from him and blush when he looked over at her. And his friends knew of the infatuation as well. The same friends who had been subjected to her vigilante locker terror over the years. Tonight was the night that this stuck-up little bitch would get what was coming to her.

After several sips from the cup, Maddy's world began to spin in a wide array of colors and images and sensations. She felt her body go limp, then be dragged until a heavy "thump" upon a soft surface. There was nothing but dark haze surrounding the fondling of her clothes and muffled laughter. "W-what's going on?" Maddy heard herself state, but the actual sound that came from her mouth was a barely discernible whimper. She opened her mouth to say no but was stopped by something with the texture of a hard sponge being inserted into it. She bit down. Hard. Then, the muted screaming of anguish as she felt a blow against her left cheek.

Several party attendees, who also happened to be some of Maddy's close friends, heard the screaming and general chaos and ran to the basement bedroom. Opening the door, they found Maddy, half undressed, her skirt and top pulled up with her panties partially pulled down and her bra torn off. She lay, slumped over on the bed from the impact of the blow in a state of semi-consciousness, looking like an abused rag doll.

"L-listen, she asked for it . . . okay?" the host of the party stammered as two other boys feverishly and awkwardly were zipping up their pants, one pair of which had a significant amount of blood on them. "No one will believe her anyway. And . . . and . . . even if they did . . . my, my dad's got connections. So just g-get the fuck out of h-here and take this little whore w-with you!"

Even in their still-developing adolescent minds, the three teenage friends, two girls and a boy, were sophisticated enough to realize that he was probably right. Rape victims were rarely believed, and even if they were believed, the social pressure that would result from legal action would be a fate worse than death to a teenage psyche. Plus, they had all been drinking and did not want to face the wrath of their parents or be forced to take the social risk of ratting out the party's other attendees. The best thing that they could do was get Maddy out of there. The three friends hastily stumbled with Maddy draped in between them to the 1996 silver Nissan that they had driven there, poured Maddy into the front seat, and took off to deliver Maddy to the Argentos'.

The door knock sounded like an ominous thud. Joseph Argento answered, in lounge shorts and a well-worn Bob Dylan T-shirt. He seemed like a giant, even to this rather tall, lanky girl who awkwardly looked up at him and stuttered, "M-Mr. Argento? W-well, see . . . ummm . . . Maddy . . . ummm . . ." Joe rushed past the girl to the silver car in the driveway. In one swift motion, he opened the car door, lifted his enfeebled niece into his arms, and strode back to the house. He took two steps at a time as he ascended the staircase leading toward Maddy's bedroom.

Patty, having just arrived at the home for the normal Friday festivities, ran up the stairs after Joe. Blair came to the door and in a quiet yet stern voice said, "You and whoever's in the car . . . in the house . . . now."

Joe laid Maddy down on the queen-size bed with the care of a mother with her newborn kitten. Patty, who worked as a registered nurse at an assisted living home, rushed to Maddy's side and began an initial evaluation of her beloved niece's condition. Joe looked on with dreaded anticipation until Patty said, "Well . . . this isn't drunk. I think she's been drugged. She has some swelling on her cheek. Looks like she's been hit. I don't think those fuckers were able to finish what they started. I don't think *that* happened. Can't tell why she has blood on her mouth, but knowing her and what was going on, I can kinda guess. We need to keep watch over her, but I think she just needs to sleep it off. I'll stay up here for a while. Why dontcha let Blair know."

Mixed with rage and relief, Joe descended the staircase and entered the living room where he found his wife sitting with the three humbled yet heroic teens. He gave Blair a subtle "okay" sign before rigidly taking a seat.

Blair, sensing her husband's anger, said in a partially pleading, partially demanding voice, "Dearest, let me do this, okay?" Joe slowly nodded his approval as his wife began the interrogation.

Following the intense questioning, there was not a dry eye in the room. They knew pretty much what had happened and definitely knew who was involved. "Okay . . . first off . . . thank you," Blair stated sincerely. "You have done this family a great service that we will never forget. I can't tell you how proud I am of you all and how thankful we all are that Maddy has such devoted and brave friends. Now, you three have been drinking, haven't you?" The three unlikely heroes solemnly nodded. "Very well. We are going to call each of your parents. We are going to tell them that the four of you went to a party, and when it got out of hand, you had brains enough to decide to hang out here. We will tell them that you are welcome to spend the night for a sleepover with Maddy if that's okay with them, and we'll send you on your way home in the morning. Sound okay?" Visible relief swept over each of the young faces as they realized that their short lives were not going to end that night.

The next morning, Maddy awoke to the sight of her attentive uncle watching over her from the foot of her bed. He was holding her light-blue baby blanket that he used to wrap around her as an infant as he cradled her into an innocent slumber. But this morning, the blanket was more for his comfort than hers. Her eyes immediately locked onto his, and tears began to form as she said, "Oh fuck, uncle Joe . . . I fucked up . . . I'm so sorry." "You got nothing to be sorry about," Joe stated with a compassionate seriousness. "I just got one question for you. Am I handling this, or are you?"

Maddy managed her mischievous grin through her embarrassment and tears and said, "Naw, I can handle these fuckers. They won't get the jump on me again."

"Very well then . . .," Joe stated with a reassured tone, as he now knew that his resilient niece's spirit was firmly intact. "Why don't you get cleaned up and come down for breakfast? If there was ever a time for ice cream, this would be it."

The next day, what seemed to be the entire school and surrounding community arrived at the Sunday-afternoon track meet to witness their track team, and local athletic hero, bring home the medal. Making the event even more important, a number of college scouts were on hand to assess this boy's potential of filling their respective college's coffers from the sale of T-shirts bearing his image. (Suspiciously absent from the event were two of the boys from the party. Rumor and innuendo later turned to fact as it was eventually revealed that one boy had to receive emergency surgery to repair his . . . dangling participle. He would transfer to another school upon his "recovery." Because of excessive nerve damage, his member would never be able to be used for anything more adventurous than common urination. The other boy, as it turned out, suffered from crippling depression and anxiety, exacerbated by his part in the violent rape attempt. During the track meet, he was in a psychiatric hospital. He would later transfer to a private school out of state. The following winter break, he returned home and took his own life by a single gunshot wound. The shot was fired from his father's revolver that had been arrogantly and carelessly left on his nightstand. The boy's blood and brain fragments were splashed across the NRA banner on the bedroom wall.)

The first event started off, literally, with a bang; and the upright colts dashed off on their first step of their brief one- hundred-meter journey. At this most inopportune time, the liquid laxative that had been placed into the boy's water bottle began its desired effect. While in full stride, and leading the pack by a full length, torrents of foul feces exploded out of the boy's shorts and onto the track. Suddenly off-balance, he slipped in the refuge and landed face-first upon the scorching asphalt. Red and brown pools began forming around their respective extremities. Emergency personnel rapidly responded and provided initial treatment to the boy's shattered chin, jaw, and nose and placed him in a neck brace that they feared he required. (Upon further examination at the hospital, the EMT's initial prognosis turned out to be correct. Upon landing, the boy's chin was thrust up with such force that an upper vertebra had been snapped, which would require major surgery to repair. The boy would not experience a painless day throughout the remainder of his life. Needless to say, he never participated in athletics again, which was his only ticket to a higher education as he wasn't terribly bright. He went on to live a loveless and insignificant existence before mercifully succumbing to colon cancer at the age of fifty-two.)

The perpetrator of this most vengeful prank was never found. And the ember that had been momentarily beaten down began to subtly glow and rise once again, like the proverbial phoenix. The stretcher passed right in front of Maddy, who held a premium viewing position just inside the three-foot-high chain- link fence. As the humiliated and seriously injured boy passed with all of the fanfare of a funeral procession, Maddy gleefully exclaimed, "Jesus Christ, chad, when I said run, I didn't mean *that*! You need to watch what you drink!"

Maddy flashed her uncle, who was sitting with Blair and Patty a few rows up, a slight mischievous grin, as if to say, "Fuck him." And her uncle Joe mirrored her expression and sentiment. It was just the two of them silently communicating with each other until Joe came down to the fence, put his arm around his prideful niece, and said, "C'mon, buttacup, let's see if we can't find some ice cream."

CHAPTER 5

GROWIN' UP

The slight seventeen-year-old silently sat on the edge of her bed. The only discernible sound was from her red-stained fingers meticulously tearing out pages from a book that were then being taped together, end to end, forming a serpentine, crimson-fingerprinted train of paper.

She was filled with mixed emotions this frigid January morning. She was so proud of herself for having earned a full-ride scholarship to a college in Brooklyn, as had been preordained in her "master plan." She reviewed her plan one final time as if she were double-checking a grocery list on her way to the checkout counter:

Step 1: Work my ass off and save money up for the move. *CHECK.*

Step 2: Graduate in January 2006 with good grades in time for the spring semester at college. *CHECK.*

Step 3: Get a scholarship to a university in New York. *CHECK.*

Step 4: Move my shit to New York and live happily ever after.

It was this final step that provided a mixture of raw, overwhelming feelings, nearly bringing her to tears. The feeling of loss of her closest high school friends and of her self- made "power" and influence that she wielded with unmerciful abandon. She smirked as she thought back to all of her vengeful "pranks" that went unpunished for her but provided punishment for those that she felt rightfully deserved it. *Yeah . . . I better knock that shit off now.*

Time to grow up. Deal with shit like an adult, she said almost convincingly to herself.

Uncle Joe will be here in an hour. Gotta move this shit along. This is no time to get fuckin' sentimental, she thought as her emotions moved away from loss to the exhilaration of her potential future adventures that she knew she would have. *What new friends will I make? What new restaurants will I love? What new concepts will I discover and explore? What new hangouts will I find? What new bands will I hear? Is this where I will meet my prince? I wonder what kind of ice cream . . .*

Tears suddenly flowed as exhilaration turned once again to loss. But this was a much deeper and painful feeling of loss, which made her feel as though she had sharp daggers stabbing into her side. She was leaving her support system that was made up of her family members who had always cared for her, inspired her, and loved her. She cherished them as much as they had always cherished her. There would be no more Friday-night frenzied orgies of music and snacks. There would be no more of aunt Patty sneaking her into clubs for 21+ shows at the local bars. There would be no more of aunt Blair's carefully chosen words of support to calm her fraying nerves. There would be no more of uncle Joe's powerfully warm embraces. Then, upon reflecting upon her uncle and what he meant to her, she suddenly experienced a new feeling: that of great resolve. She straightened her spine, held her petite head up, and thought to herself, *No, there won't be as many of those experiences now. But they will still happen, just not all of the time. And those experiences just need to be replaced by the experiences that I will have on my own and which will make my family proud. Especially uncle Joe. I will die before I ever let him down. I* will *make something of myself. I* will *find happiness. And I will make him, and everyone else, proud of me. Or else, my name ain't Maddy Sommers. And that's my name, so that's just the way it fuckin' is.*

They had raised her for this moment. They had raised her to stand on her own two dainty feet and to always be her own person. They had raised her to not count on anyone else in this world for her happiness. They had raised her to not just live, but to be alive. And they had raised her to fight back against anyone and anything that ever tried to physically or emotionally oppress or harm her.

Her resolve increasing, she now felt elation at the prospect of never having to see her sadistic mother and pathetic father again. Her mind raced back to a few hours earlier in which she came careening downstairs to proudly inform her parents of the afternoon's upcoming events.

In as powerfully condescending of a voice that she could manage, Maddy began her proclamation, "Sooo . . . listen up, 'cause I've got some news for you. I'll try to put it into little bite-sized chunks so you will both understand. Here's what's happening." Maddy stood, her five feet and four (and a half fucking) inches seemingly towering over her hapless parents, who stared at their daughter pensively. Standing with rigid poise, with her green eyes sparkling as brilliantly as a polished gemstone and her copper strands perfectly framing her youthful but determined face, she began.

"Numero uno: As you know, I've graduated high school, and I've got my diploma in my hand. I know that I told you that I was planning on working this spring, saving money, then going to community college in the fall, but . . . well . . . that was a fuckin' lie. Sue me.

"Numero two-o: I have a full-ride scholarship to a college in New York, 'cause, well . . . I'm like smart and shit, which you may have noticed if you had pulled your heads out of your cult's ass long enough to pay attention to who I actually am . . . but . . . whatevs.

"Numero three-o: I've saved up a shitload of money, so that's not an issue. Oh, by the way, Aunt Blair helped me set up my private account through her accounting firm, so you wouldn't be able to get your hands on it or know how much I had. And you never asked, so no one lied to you about it. Seriously, you two are so out of touch with the world. Did you really think I only made like a hundred bucks a week? Wow, naive much?

"Numero four-o: This past week, I've shipped all of my stuff to my dorm room in New York, so my room's pretty much cleared out except for one suitcase and a few things at aunt Blair's and uncle Joe's house. Oh yeah, speaking of which, in case you haven't figured it out yet," then mockingly adding out of the side of her mouth, "which is kinda fuckin' likely . . .

"Numero five-o: uncle Joe is coming in a couple of hours to get me, drive me to New York, and drop me off at college . . . oh . . . yeah . . . where I fully plan on getting all kinds of nekkid and fucked up!" she stated as she giggled with delight.

"Over . . . my . . . dead . . . body," her mother frigidly stated as she stiffly rose from the tattered, flowered fabric of her living room chair, looking much like a zombie rising in a Romero movie. Her father, averting his eyes, slumped even lower and sadly looked down, acknowledging his defeat.

"You are only seventeen," the icy woman continued with all of the charm of a Nazi interrogator, "and if that heathen of a man comes for you, we *will* call the authorities and have him arrested for kidnapping. We *will* press charges, and we *will* have him locked up for as long as the law will allow."

The woman who had given birth to this sprightful behemoth stood in front of her daughter, hands firmly on her hips while exuding haughtiness.

Maddy looked at her mother with resolve, sighed deeply, and in a calm, almost dismissive voice stated, "So . . . let me take this point by point. Over your dead body? Be careful whatcha wish for, bitch, 'cause that shit can be arranged. Second point. You're gonna call the cops on me and uncle Joe? Go for it. Do you really want *me* talking to the cops? About *you*? About your douchebag cult leader? About a lot of other abusive shit that I know goes on with some of the assholes there? I think not. Third point," she continued, changing her presentation to a saccharinely sweet, singsongy voice, "oh, Daddy dearest, please sign this waiver allowing me to attend college prior to the age of eighteen. 'Cause if you don't, I promise you, the next five months of your life will be a living hell, if you fuckin' make it that long."

Maddy's emasculated father submissively takes the paper and pen that his daughter had dramatically thrust in front of him and signed it, without word. Handing it back to his daughter, he quietly said, "I'll pray for you."

"Don't fuckin' bother," Maddy retorted snidely. "All of your prayers haven't done shit for you. What the fuck do you think they'll do for me?" Maddy then jumped up as if she had just been transformed into the perkiest of cheerleaders (a comparison that no one would dare make to her face) and exclaimed, "Okay! Thanks so much, Mommy and Daddy. I'll stay in touch. Or not. Whatevs!"

The smirk that was generated by this recent memory quickly turned to a painful scowl, as another memory crept into her consciousness. The memory of herself when she was six years old and being struck harshly on her backside three times by that fucking yardstick for the unforgivable sin of putting the toilet paper on the holder the wrong way. "Madeline," her sinister mother said at the time, "there are no small infractions against God. There are only infractions, all of which must be strictly punished. The toilet paper roll is always to be placed so you are pulling from the top of the roll, not the bottom!" Chills ran down Maddy's spine as she could almost feel her nerves painfully reacting to each memorable strike.

Two inviting honks of a horn were heard, eliciting the joyous memories of the final bell at the end of a school year. Both sounds represented the same thing: youthful freedom. Maddy bounded down the staircase, clutching the small suitcase that she had personally packed for most of her seventeen and a half years before going to her aunt and uncle's. Present as always in its contents was an overly played DVD of *Cinderella*. Maddy looked at her demoralized parents, wearing their crippled demeanor on their pasty faces. "Madeline . . .," the mother started to say in a low, defeated voice.

Maddy cut her off by stating, "Save it, bitch. And for the final time . . . time's up, bitches! Maddy out!"

Maddy flung open the door, leaving it wide open. All of the various religious decor that were hanging from the walls of the modest home shook in the wake of its force. One picture fell completely from the wall, shattering the glass and frame as it violently landed upon the faded wooden floor. She bounded to uncle Joe's new 2006 red PT Cruiser (because, at sixty-two, he thought that it made him look "cool").

"How we doin', buttacup?" Joe excitedly stated as Maddy entered the car.

Maddy gave her uncle a full hug around his mammoth neck, looked endearingly at him, and said, "I've never been fuckin' better."

"Well, then let's go!" Joe shouted to the accompaniment of his niece's gleeful squeals as the Cars' primary anthem thundered through the speakers, the sound bouncing off the dim external paint of the Sommerses' home.

Maddy's mother looked on as this most wicked vehicle departed their driveway and disappeared around the corner. She quietly picked up the fallen family portrait. The broken glass had gouged the image of the faces of the mother and the father. But the image of a six-year-old Maddy's face remained unblemished, clearly projecting her hopefulness through a beaming smile.

Maddy's mother tossed the picture and broken frame into the dustbin sitting on the edge of the staircase. Reservedly, she and her husband climbed the stairs for what seemed to them to be an eternity. They cautiously opened the door. The room was completely cleaned out with the exception of the disheveled bedding lying on top of the mattress and a giant red "Anarchy" symbol, which had been haphazardly spray-painted on the wall. In her bathroom, they found the pages of the Bible, meticulously torn out and taped together from the top of a page to the bottom. All of the taped pages had been wound tightly around a toilet paper tube and placed on the toilet paper holder. For added effect, the end of the roll was placed so that you had to pull from the bottom instead of the top.

The drive to New York was long (936 miles to be exact), devoid of scenery outside of lengthy stretches of frozen fields, and three of the best days of Maddy's life. It was just her and uncle Joe, listening to music, joking, and doing spot-on impersonations of her parents in little made-up, only slightly exaggerated, skits.

"Now, Madeline . . .," uncle Joe would begin in a dry, nasally mocking tone, "you know that Jeeesus would never consent to you watching *Sesame Streeet* . . . Those muppets are deeemons sent straight from hell," followed by Maddy rigidly stating in the same nasal impersonation while trying to one-up her uncle by increasing the absurdity, "Now, Madeline . . . Jeeesus only loves those who wear pink dresses on Thursdaaays. Blue dresses on Thursdaaays is the work of the devil . . ."

"Okay, okay . . . how 'bout this?" Uncle Joe would excitedly exclaim. "Now, Madeline . . . I saw a brown-skinned man eat ice cream one time, which means that all ice cream is demonic. Put that cone down this instant or you shall become possessed!"

"Oh my fucking god, maybe they're right," Maddy stated. Through his laughter, Joe inquired, "Right about what?"

Maddy, still snickering, said, "Maybe we are going to straight to hell!"

Joe looked at his niece with feigned concern and said humorlessly, "Yeah, maybe we are. Hand me my CD case, wouldja?" Maddy handed her uncle the case of CDs that Joe had brought for their road trip and looked at him inquisitively. He popped a CD in, cranked the volume, and said, "Well, if we're going to hell, we may as well do it in style!" They both let out another round of explosive laughter as AC/DC pounded at their eardrums.

Cleveland was almost perfectly the halfway point on their journey, so they planned to stop there for the night. They had left on Saturday afternoon and checked into their off-interstate hotel just around midnight. Weary from the drive and constant laughter, they quickly changed into their pajamas and fell into a deep slumber on their respective single beds. Tomorrow was going to be a big day. It didn't hurt that Cleveland was also the home to the Rock and Roll Hall of Fame.

Everything was going according to plan. Cleveland by midnight Saturday, then all of Sunday at the Hall of Fame. Leave early Monday morning for arrival at her Brooklyn dorm by late afternoon. They arrived at the Hall of Fame like two small children getting their first glimpse of an amusement park. They were amazed at all of the heroic artifacts that were upon display there.

Handwritten lyrics, concert-worn costumes, and legendary instruments fully adorned the walls and display shelves. They would eagerly bounce from room to room and display to display. Then, they would stop and look in awe at the priceless artifacts of the greatest musical artists to have ever lived.

"Wow, aunt Patty would love this," Maddy expressed. "Yep, I'm sure she would. But that bitch never invited me to go see Foo Fighters with her the last time they were in town . . . so . . . fuck her too! In fact, let's take a picture of us in front of this Cramps drumhead! That'll piss her off!" Joe snickered with the same glee as a child who had just figured out how to open the cookie jar as they posed in front of the iconic symbol of punk rock wearing wide smiles and uplifted middle fingers.

Patty's response was swift, concise, and brutal. It simply read, "Fuck you both."

Maddy and Joe were still giggling like children at their little prank as they drifted off into a deep and satisfied slumber, visions of rock dignitaries dancing in their heads. The next morning, the two travelers begrudgingly loaded up their belongings and took their respective seats, with Maddy behind the wheel for the first leg of their final stretch. Maddy took a CD out of her purse and said, "Aunt Blair wanted me to play this on the last day of our trip. Wanna play it?"

Joe looked with fondness at the cover of the CD and was delighted by how clever and sentimental his lovely wife was. "Yes. It's perfect. Pop it in, buttacup," Joe stated as he casually wiped a tear from his eye and looked out of his passenger window so as not to risk making eye contact with his niece at this emotional moment. Track 1 of 18 began to play as the red Cruiser pulled out of the hotel parking lot and onto the interstate while Springsteen's "Growin' Up" roared out of the speakers.

Monday's drive was the exact opposite of that on Saturday. Raucous laughter and mocking revelry were largely replaced by quiet introspection with occasional solemn advice from uncle Joe, which his dutiful niece absorbed like a dry sponge. She clung to his every word of sage guidance. Although she had been told all of this before, she listened intently for one new piece of wisdom or one new vocal inflection or emphasis that might entirely change the impact of the words. To each piece of fatherly advice, Maddy would respond with "I will, uncle Joe," "No, I won't forget, uncle Joe," or "Okay, uncle Joe." Except she had a slightly different response to his last pearl of wisdom.

As the pair drove into Brooklyn, they gawked at the red stone architecture and the bustling of humanity while hearing the constant buzzing overtone of the city's traffic and voices. They pulled into the gates of the college and parked in front of Maddy's dormitory. They checked in at the office, retrieved a key, and began loading her previously shipped belongings onto a cart. They silently made their way to Maddy's room. They carefully opened the door to the sight of two sets of metal framed bunk beds, one on each side of the sanitized pale-green room. There were four desks, two in between the sets of bunk beds and one at the foot of each bed. Maddy was the first to arrive and, being preemptively diplomatic, thought it wise to not claim a space for herself before her roommates had the opportunity to voice their opinions.

Fighting back her tears and wearing a forced smile, Maddy said, "Well, this is it . . . I guess."

"Yup, I guess so," Joe stuttered as gruffly as he could muster while avoiding eye contact so as not to reveal the anguish that was gripping his heart. "Aw, fuck, buttacup . . ." Joe struggled to continue. "This won't be so bad . . . You'll visit . . . We'll visit . . . We're just so fuckin' proud of you." Despite his best efforts, this mammoth of a man could not stop the tears that were beginning to well out of the corners of his eyes as he handed Maddy an envelope and said, "Here, this is for you. Blair, Patty, and I . . . well, we've all been putting a little away each year since you were born into this account see . . . and . . . well, we thought you could use it for your college tuition, but you had to grow up to be such a fuckin' smart-ass that I guess you won't need it for that . . . so . . . use this wisely, okay?"

"I-I-I will, Uncle Joe," Maddy stammered as she took the envelope, and her hero took her into his massive arms. Their tight and loving embrace lasted for what seemed an eternity and for just a split second simultaneously.

Before relinquishing his hold upon his adored niece, Joe said with a loving sternness, "Don't let anyone fuck with you. And if they ever do, I'm just a phone call away. You got that?"

Maddy's spine stiffened. She confidently pulled away from her uncle, standing before him with her head held high as tears streamed from her sparkling green eyes and said assertively, "You don't have to worry about me, uncle Joe. No one's gonna fuck with me. If anything, it's the douchebags of this world that should be worried, 'cause I can fuck some shit up." She then flashed her "silly face" at her uncle, her tongue sticking upward out of the right side of her smiling lips while crossing her emerald-green eyes.

Joe exploded into laughter before saying, "All right, I'm gettin' out of here if you're gonna be an asshole like that. You call me, you got that?"

"I-I will, I promise," Maddy said as she watched the only man who had ever cared for her walk out of her immediate life. She opened the envelope. There was a note that simply said, "For our most precious niece and light of our life. Love, Aunt Patty, Aunt Blair, and Uncle Joe." Inside the note there was a check for $170,000. She stared at the check in amazement and loudly said, "Whaaaat the fuuuuck!" She was all alone, standing in the middle of this unexplored world, packed full of her experiences of love and caring as well as pain and grief. But mostly, she was packed with the burning resolve to live up to the expectations of her loving family at any cost.

CHAPTER 6

WE ARE FAMILY

She would not be alone with her thoughts for long. About ten minutes after Joe's departure, a tall young woman entered the room. She was dressed in a sharp gray-and-white business suit complete with blazer, pencil skirt, black stockings, and high heels, which made her already towering frame appear Amazonian. She had long jet-black hair that hung five inches past her shoulders and encased her extended, pretty face with perfect caramel skin, reminiscent of Iman. She looked at Maddy, extended her hand, and in a professional voice said, "Hi, I'm Samantha, but you can call me Sam."

Maddy met Sam's hand and shook it, trying to replicate the firmness of Sam's handshake, and said with her bright smile, "Hiya! I'm Maddy, but you can call me . . . Maddy!" She was met with a stoic stare with no emotional reaction whatsoever. *This bitch is pretty high strung*, Maddy thought. *She should be fun to fuck with.*

"Okay, let's get the business out of the way, then we will get to know each other," Sam bluntly stated as though she were facilitating a business meeting. "First off, sleeping arrangements. We all roomed together last semester. The only reason why our belongings aren't here is because they did deep cleaning over winter break, and we had to move everything out and put it into storage. We lost one of our roommates over winter break. There's no need to discuss that now, but that is why there was room for you here. I'm in the upper left bunk and have the desk at the foot of the bed. Jules has the upper right bunk and has the opposite desk. You will have the lower left bunk with the desk immediately to your left. ____has the lower right bunk with the opposite desk. Clothing, shoes, and other personal belongings are stored in the closet. You will see that there is an even amount of hanger, floor, and shelf space which has been marked by bunk number. Please trust me that it is even. I measured it out and marked it personally. You are bunk number 3 and have the space accordingly allocated. Personal decorations are allowed on the walls of your desk area. Nothing profane, please. There are no visitors in this room past 9:00 pm. This is strictly enforced.

"Questions? Good. Hearing none, let's move on to—"

Sam was then abruptly cut off by Maddy who said to the slightly annoyed Sam, "Yeah, I do have a question. See, profane is kind of a vague and subjective term. What might be profane to one person might be art to another, and I've got these two posters of hot guys who are hung like a horse, which I find to be very . . . artistic, so that'll be okay . . . right?" Maddy flashed her mischievous grin at the expressionless young woman who dryly replied, "Oh good. A comedian. Well, that will take some getting used to. And to answer your question, yes, those images are considered profane and are strictly prohibited."

"Gotcha," Maddy stated while thinking, *Pictures of guys' cocks are out, but sticks up asses are definitely in.*

Sam was about to resume speaking when the door opened again. A medium-built young woman with curly dark-brown hair cascading around her attractive face entered. She was wearing a baggy gray sweatshirt, black sweatpants, and well- worn black skate shoes. She haphazardly tossed her suitcases in front her desk and launched her bookbag onto her top bunk, which made an impressive thud upon landing. "Hey, all," the young woman said in an uninterested voice.

Sam made the introduction. "Jules, this is our new roommate, Maddy. Maddy, this is Jules."

"Hiya," Maddy enthusiastically stated.

Jules looked at her new roomie, gave her the once-over, and said, "Yeah, I guess you'll do. Just stay out of my shit and we'll get along fine."

"Jules," Sam interrupted, "must you use that type of language?"

Jules bitingly retorted, "Oh, fuck off, Sam. I'll talk however I want. Here's a helpful hint, Maddy. When Sam tries to reinstitute the swear jar, the best way to get rid of it is to put used condoms in it. Worked three times last semester. But Sam is a tenacious bitch, so it'll probably make a comeback. Or

. . . a 'cum' back, if you know what I mean." Jules briefly exposed a rare smirk before beginning to unpack her belongings and shove them into the closet.

"Very nice, Jules . . . very nice," Sam stated in a lecturing tone while bristling at the lack of organization of bunk 2's closet space. "Way to make a good impression on our new roommate." "Here's the thing, Maddy," Jules began explaining, "Sam is the resident gestapo, I just don't give a fuck, and _____ is—" The door opened once again, leaving this last thought hanging for a moment. A very petite young Laotian American woman entered. Her pretty, modest face lowered so that it was almost entirely covered by her straight black blunt bang hair.

"Hello everybody," she stated in a quiet voice. Wearing blue jeans, tennis shoes, and a humble flowered blouse, she cautiously walked across the room and gingerly placed her belongings upon the bottom bunk. She carried herself as though she wished to be permanently invisible, rarely making eye contact with the others.

"And this is our resident mouse, _____," Jules continued. "Another piece of advice, Maggy, don't make any sudden movements around her. You'll freak her the fuck out."

"Ummm . . . okay, but it's Maddy," Maddy replied.

Jules looked at Maddy with disdain and said, "Who gives a fuck?"

Maddy, discarding her polite subservience, let out a pronounced laugh and said, "Wow . . . you three are a motley fucking crew now, arentcha? But not to worry. I'll get this troop shaped up in no time, and we're going to be the best of friends or else my name isn't Maddy Sommers. And, well, that's my name, so that's just the way it fuckin' is. Lookin' forward to years of fun and frivolity with you, bitches. Now, where's the closet place to get snacks? I'm fuckin' starving!"

Although the four roommates were entirely different in almost every way, they all shared one similar trait. They were all kindhearted, which, in a short time, grew to tenaciously defending one another. It was perfectly permissible for them to call each other every name in the book while engaged in trivial disagreements over someone borrowing a piece of jewelry without permission or leaving discarded clothing on someone else's bunk. But this was not a courtesy that was extended to anyone outside of this ever-increasingly-tight group, and violators would be immediately and harshly dealt with.

This trait was especially true with Maddy. She very quickly became both disappointed and morbidly enthralled to discover that most of the young men at the college were only slightly hairier and more frequently drunk versions of those from her high school. Instead of being sixteen going on twelve, they were twenty-something going on twelve. And just as in high school, by the beginning of the following fall semester, it was widely known around campus that you simply didn't mess with anyone who was "cool with Maddy."

Throughout her college career, including both her undergraduate liberal arts work and her graduate work in business administration, Maddy took up a new hobby. She became very well versed in the art of stalking. She found it easy to envelop her petite frame in black jeans, hoodies, T-shirts, boots, sunglasses, and ball caps so as to appear completely asexual. Because of her slight size, she could hide away from the sight lines of others behind trees, shrubbery, or pillars in dark entryways. She began what would become a standard practice of having two sets of electronics. She had her personal cell phone and computer that she would use for all of her purposes except for one. She always kept a burner cellphone to send anonymous texts, a cheap digital camera with which to take clandestine pictures, and a cheap laptop whose sole use was the printing of pictures off from the camera. All of these items were relatively inexpensive, small enough to be stored in a small locking briefcase and could be easily discarded into the Hudson once any identifying numbers were removed should the need arise. She had graduated, literally and figuratively, to a new level of sophistication to conceal her involvement in vengeful pranks.

Anyone within her social circle, whether it be her roommate "sisters" or more casual acquaintances who were threatened, belittled, or, in the most extreme cases, assaulted in some way would be avenged in some manner by this sprightful vigilante. She might stand on a table at the student union and gleefully reveal a schoolmate's lack of stamina in bed or his unfortunate "length impairment." "Hear ye, hear ye, everybody . . .," would be the standard bellowing introduction that would invoke painstaking fear in some members of the audience and salacious curiosity from all of the other audience members who were "cool with Maddy."

"Hot off the presses, it's time for another installment of 'As the Douchebags Turn.'" Sam, Jules, and _____ would look up at their friend in giggling delight before scanning the room and mockingly staring at the intended target, who, on this occasion, happened to be a young man who had the poor judgment to call Jules "an uptight bitch," for declining to perform a certain sexual act on him. "Now, you all know me and you know that I do not like to spread rumors, so all I'm doing here is providing a public service . . . but . . . a little bird has told me that a certain captain of the rowing team, who shall remain nameless because it's just too fucking insignificant to waste my breath on, can last in the sack for up to—now, wait for it, ladies—an astonishing three and a half minutes! That's right, ladies, bring your sexual frustration to a whole new level. Act now and you not only get the three minutes, but you also get another *thirty fucking seconds* for free!"

Another young man was targeted after slapping Sam for laughing at him. Upon the removal of his shorts, Sam was dismayed that this incredibly cocky young man wasn't very cocky at all when naked and erect, and it turned out that he was overly sensitive about his condition. So he slapped her. Violently. Through steely-eyed tears, Sam informed Maddy and the others of the incident, and a most appropriate announcement was made shortly thereafter.

"Hear ye, hear ye, everybody . . . I have an important announcement for all of you ladies. There has been an incredible breakthrough in blow job technology!" Maddy would make eye contact and work the entire room, her face beaming with pride as she was dismantling another "chad" through the projection of her verbal missiles in her best infomercial voice. "I can now confirm that *you too* can have all of the satisfaction of giving a blow job without having to worry about that annoying gag reflex. A little bird has told me that scientists from all around the world have perfected the 'suckbutnotgagphallus 3000.' The first prototype is being worn by none other than our distinguished vice president of the Greek council. Sign up now, ladies, before the little bird who told me about this finds it and eats his pathetic little worm!"

Many in the audience would express visible relief when they learned that they were not the latest target and that their tawdry little secrets currently remained just that. The vast majority of the audience would explode into laughter and a standing ovation of applause as the emasculated quarry would slink out of the room.

Another weapon in Maddy's arsenal were pictures of male classmates that she felt were exceptionally demeaning in their sexism or racism or any other "ism" that they might be. The photos would be of the societal bigot in a romantic embrace with someone other than who they should be with. These pictures usually involved another young woman but involved another male on more than one occasion. Maddy would carefully edit the picture to conceal the identity of the other person, as they were not the target of her wrath.

Just as in high school, it was well known who was behind the social carnage. And just as in high school, there was a collective shrug as there was never any evidence found to point the finger at anyone in particular thanks partly to gloves and hairnets being added to Maddy's bag of tricks. It also helped that the selected prey of this hijinks was not well thought of by the general population of the school, including faculty, and they were felt to be deserving of this public comeuppance.

As the years went by and Maddy's wave of humiliation continued, her circle of friends and acquaintances expanded. Retaliation against her by the offended was nearly impossible, as any plan to gain retribution was always reported back. This would initiate a text from a burner phone to the conspirators that always said, "We know what you're planning. Better not fuck with her. This is your only warning." The phone would then be harmlessly discarded without an ability to trace the text back to the author.

From January 2006 until May 2012 when Maddy received her master's degree (once again just missing out on magna cum laude, which was all right with her as that honor went to __), the student body was left with three choices. Option 1: Be "cool with Maddy" and be within her social circle. Option 2: Stay out of her social circle, but make sure you knew who were in it and do not fuck with anyone who was. Option 3: Or fuck with them and wait for the inevitable consequence. Over time, the student body mostly fell into the first two camps.

Maddy's roommates always knew when something was being plotted. There would be a red "anarchy" bandana on the dorm room's handle. This signaled that Maddy was currently in "consultation," and her privacy was respected by all. The classmate (male or female) would leave the dorm room, usually with a look of combined relief and satisfaction. Maddy would be sitting at her desk, wearing her sly grin and doing the best Brando impersonation that her slight female form could muster. It would not be too many days later before Maddy would prepare to go out for the evening while banging her head and playing air guitar to Judas Priest's "You Got Another Thing Coming." With a sly wink of one emblazoned green eye, she would be off into the night seeking " justice" once again for the bullied and downtrodden. Her friends never asked where she was going, and Maddy never offered. Everyone would find out the next day anyway.

Over the years, the four roommates became inseparable. Despite their different personalities and frequent differences, they had mutual love and respect for one another and would be seen out together at the various New York bars and hot spots whether it be seeing a band or performing off-key drunken karaoke to "We Are Family." Dinner together always began with an argument of who would sit next to Maddy, as she had difficulty making up her mind on what to order, and whatever was sitting next to her always looked better, so she would begin eating off her exasperated friend's plate. One evening, Jules stabbed Maddy in the hand with her fork while she was attempting to abduct a french fry.

"What the fuck, bitch?" Maddy exclaimed.

"Keep your fuckin' hands off my fries," Jules retorted coldly. "Jesus, it's a fuckin' fry . . . overreact much?" But from that moment on, the mere motioning of one's hand toward their fork resulted in Maddy's hasty retreat back to her own plate. Maddy's influence had its limits, and those limits stopped at french fries. During their junior year, the four friends rented a four- bedroom flat together eight blocks from their campus. Although small, it was much more space than their dorm and offered considerably more privacy should more intimate activities be pursued. Following their graduation in May 2009, Sam became the first of the friends to take the plunge and get married to a coworker at an accounting firm that Sam initially had interned at, then obtained a prominent position overseeing an entire department at the ripe old age of twenty-two. This left one bedroom open, which was immediately filled by Sam's coworker and official referral, Kristy. Kristy was a small-statured, blonde, perky, outgoing dynamo who enjoyed talking— a lot. She provided the perfect counterbalance to the introverted nature of Jules and _____, while providing Maddy with a verbal sparring partner. Although married, Sam's presence always hung over the group, and the house "rules" that she had implemented remained intact as a sort of homage to their departed self- appointed "leader." The only exception to this was that the dark presence of a swear jar was never seen again, forcing Jules to find an alternative way to discard used condoms.

The young women made a pact on the day of Sam's nuptials. Sam, looking absolutely elegant in her tightly fit pure white wedding dress (which Maddy would call out during her drunken and slurred toast at the reception, "Saaammm . . . I'm sooo happy for youuu . . . buut how the fuuck can you wear white? We know whaat you've dooone." Maddy was taken home by

Jules shortly thereafter) and her best friends looking . . . slightly less than attractive in their (pink?) matching puffy-shouldered bridesmaid's dresses, put their hands in a circle, and swore that no matter where life took them, Wednesday nights would always be theirs and that they would always see or speak with each other on those evenings. This was a tradition that lived on throughout their lives, with the exception of one of the members of this tight circle.

Of all of her friends, which now included the cheerleader- esque Kristy, the Nameless One became Maddy's closest and most trusted confidant. A bitter betrayal twelve years after their initial meeting would lead to Maddy's never uttering, or allowing anyone else to mention, her name again. But up until that point, the two besties were emotionally and usually physically inseparable (unless Maddy had some "business" to take care of). The Nameless One was kindhearted and incredibly intelligent with great attention to detail and a natural proclivity toward math and science, especially electronics and chemistry. But what she possessed in intelligence, she lacked in social skills. She was very poor at picking up on social cues and was incredibly gullible to practical jokes and sarcasm. She always would go along with the crowd and would never express her opinion on matters in order to avoid any possible conflict.

That is, unless she was drinking. Following two drinks of a cocktail, the more cute than beautiful Nameless One would become a shamelessly flirtatious extrovert and became easy prey for the male sharks who would ceaselessly circle the nightclub. Maddy would doggedly watch over her vulnerable friend, frequently turning down offers for drinks or dancing from her own male suitors as she guarded over her friend's escapades. There were many occasions where a young man's hands would immediately move from under the Nameless One's shirt to grasp their suddenly inflamed testicles following a swift and brutal kick from a size 6 shoe. The Nameless One would then be escorted from the club, poured into a cab, and taken home to sleep off the night's events.

The event that solidified the bond between the two happened in the fall semester of 2006. The Nameless One came to Maddy distraught and confused on a crisp late October afternoon. While looking out of their dorm window at the brilliant orange and red leaves fluttering in the light breeze, the Nameless One told Maddy about a conversation that had just taken place with one of her male professors. With tears welling in her forlorn hazelnut eyes, she meekly reported that this professor had told her that in order to pass her class, she would need to do some "extra credit." She began trembling as she described how this late fifties pudgy man asked her to come to his office later that night, and if she didn't, he just wasn't sure that she had the stuff to pass his class. "And wouldn't that be disappointing to your parents? We wouldn't want that to happen now, would we? So just be a good girl and come by at eight tonight, and I'm sure we can find a way for you to earn enough points and make your parents proud." She then said he suggestively patted her on her thigh just above the knee, smiled wickedly, leered into her eyes, and said lasciviously, "Looking forward to tonight."

Maddy stared at her traumatized friend, seething with anger. "Don't worry about it," Maddy stated in a low, intense voice. "I'll take care of it." Her friend looked at her appreciatively, giving her a simple nod of gratitude as her tears began drying on her moist cheeks, with full understanding of the force that she had just unleashed.

The professor turned the corner that led to his drab office and saw a petite young lady, wearing black jeans and a black hoodie facing his office door. He went up from behind the young lady and, upon placing his hands gently upon her shoulders, began lewdly massaging while softly saying, "I'm glad you came. Why don't we go in and take care of your grades?"

The young lady turned around as a familiar chill went down her spine. He was met by the enraged green eyes of someone other than whom he was expecting. "Yeah, Prof . . . let's do that," Maddy said coldly. She flashed a smile that indicated that this would not be a polite social visit.

"Uh . . . uh . . . I'm sorry, young lady, I . . . I . . . thought you were someone . . . uh . . . else," the professor weakly stammered. "That's okay," Maddy began confidently. "We can have our own kind of fun. Why don't you open the door? Believe me, you *do not* want me to leave without hearing what I have to say. Got that, Prof?"

Once inside, the professor cautiously sat behind his desk while Maddy propped her size 6 black Vans up on the other side, a small container of pepper spray clutched in her hand within the hoodie's deep front pocket. "Sooo, Professor," Maddy began in a mocking tone, "let me tell you a little story. And by the way, you would be wise not to interrupt me. So . . . when I first moved into my dorm, I was told that another freshman girl had moved out unexpectedly. And no one would talk about it, which made me a bit curious. So I found out her name and did a bit of research. And do you know what I found out? Well, a little birdie told me that she left school right after taking her final exam with you. I mean . . . she just packed up her shit and left . . . right after her final exam with *you*, which made me wonder, why would she do that? Especially since she had two more finals to go! Makes no sense, does it, Prof?"

Maddy stared at the professor with devilish glee, her auburn hair resembling the flames of hell as the red neon light from the next-door pizza parlor reflected off it. "So it just seemed to little ol' me that maybe there was a connection. I couldn't prove it, and I never reached out to the girl because I didn't want to harm or embarrass her in any way. But I thought maybe I'd follow you around a bit, 'cause I had a suspicion of what had probably happened. And I thought, if I were right, you'd keep doing something bad, and that might impact me or one of my friends. So I was prepared when my friend—y'know, the person that you thought I was—came to me with her little story." Maddy then stood up while taking a brown legal envelope out of her bag, threw it on the professor's disheveled desk, and said with an intense joy, "Prof, you done fucked up. And you might want to get blinds for your window, 'cause that fire escape is really sturdy and comfortable. Now, why don't you take a look at the present I brought for you. Oh, and you can keep those. Trust me, there are *plenty* of others."

Maddy sat back down, propped her feet back upon the desk, and watched with satisfaction as the professor's face became ashen as he thumbed through the graphic images of himself and numerous coeds engaged in various sexual activities. He sullenly looked up as Maddy delightedly exclaimed, "But . . . credit where credit is due. You've got yourself some fuckin' stamina! And you're a helluva lot more limber than your . . . uh . . . body would lead one to believe! Maybe you should hit the gym and go into porn or somethin', 'cause I think you've missed your calling!"

Jokes aside, Maddy began again, earnestly. "Okay, Prof, let's get down to brass tacks . . ." Maddy insisted as if she were negotiating the surrender of a defeated army. "Here's what's gonna happen. Numero uno: You're going to apologize to my friend for the mind-fuck shit you just put her through. Numero two-o: I don't give a fuck how well she's doing in your class— she's gettin' a fuckin' A! Numero three-o: If I ever hear of you doing this to another girl, I will fuckin' expose you! I don't know about those chicks in the pictures. I don't know if they're fucking you willingly or for the grades or what. None of my business. But if this shit ever happens again, I will fucking .

. . bury . . . you. The only reason why I'm being kind to you right now is because I know you have a young child, and I don't want him to learn about how fucked up his daddy is from me. But if you fuck with anybody again, the gloves are fuckin' off, and you will think that tonight was a fuckin' picnic compared to what I will put you through." Maddy paused to take in the expression of pure terror on the professor's face. It was the same look of terror that she had forced upon her mother several years ago. And once again, she liked it. "Now, *thank* me for my kindness, you prick."

"Th-Thank you for your . . . uh . . . kindness . . . The terms are . . . uh . . . acceptable. It will all be taken care of. I promise to never do this again," the emotionally neutered professor humbly said.

"Cool," Maddy stated with satisfied dismissiveness. Maddy's slight frame turned around and walked toward the door. Upon opening it, Maddy turned back once more and flatly stated, "Oh, and one more thing. I think I'll take your class next semester, just to keep an eye on you. I expect that my grade will be reflective of my generosity."

The next afternoon following class, the professor asked to speak to the Nameless One. Avoiding eye contact with his young student, he matter-of-factly stated, "Well . . . it seems as though I owe you an apology. I seem to have made an error in reviewing your performance, and you have already earned enough points to receive an A in this class. Congratulations. Your attendance will no longer be necessary."

"Wow," the Nameless One said with an unexpected confidence, "she really scared the shit out of you, didn't she?" She then smiled, turned, and pranced her way up the stairs and out of the theater-seated lecture hall.

"What did you do?" the Nameless One said to Maddy as she entered her dorm room.

"Some things are best left unsaid," Maddy stated haughtily as the two friends embraced each other and joyfully cried as "Why Not Smile" by REM played out of Maddy's well-worn CD player. At the end of the semester, it was discovered that the professor had taken another position at a community college in Wyoming. About a month later, the human resources director for the school received a tightly sealed legal-size brown envelope. The school decided to rescind its offer of employment.

Maddy was now fully encircled by her support system. She had her best friends in New York, and she had her loving family in Wisconsin. And those worlds would frequently come into contact with one another. Maddy visited

Wisconsin every fall, winter, and spring break as well as a few weeks in the summer. Regardless of her current age, she always felt like a teenager again as she dripped sweat bouncing around the house to the earsplitting music and gorged on snacks and ice cream with uncle Joe. They were so proud of her, and the entire visit overflowed with intense joy. During each visit, on his way back home from picking Maddy up at the airport, Joe would ask, "So anyone fuckin' with ya?"

"Nobody that I can't handle," Maddy would arrogantly reply as uncle Joe would let out his guttural laugh and say, "That's my buttacup, never taking any shit from the douchebags of the world!"

She would even visit her parents and spend an awkward half hour listening to her father rant about the "deep state" or whatever the conspiracy du jour was on that particular day. Her mother would frigidly lecture her on her sins and rigidly plead for their daughter to return home to once again live a "godly" existence. Maddy would say the same thing to herself during each visit over the years. *Is it me, or are these fuckers getting even crazier?* Little did she know that her question would be answered on January 6, 2021. Maddy would always end the visit with "Welp, it's been . . . something. I hope that you guys are happy doing whatever it is that you do. I just wanted to say hi and let you know that things are going well with me. If you ever want to call, you've got my number. Maybe one of these days we'll be able to find a way to be proud of each other. Take care, and I'll see ya next time I'm in town." Maddy would leave her parents' increasingly shabby home with a combined sense of sadness, disappointment, and gratitude. She would return to the humble but immaculate home of her aunt and uncle, wait for Patty (and guest) to arrive, and prepare for the cork to be popped off the evening.

Not a month went by without Maddy seeing her aunts and uncle. They would frequently fly or drive to New York for extended weekends to visit their exuberant niece on the months that she was unable to visit them in Madison. Sam, Jules, the Nameless One, and, later, Kristy became a cherished part of their extended family; and they would revel in the sight of these unlikely sisters partying, laughing, and squabbling among one another. Saturday nights were usually spent with the young pride taking their second set of parents to the local karaoke bar, where on-key and very enthusiastic renditions of the day's greatest hits sung by Maddy were met with not-so-subtle ridicule by Patty. "Jesus, Mads, why the fuck did you sing that? I thought I raised you better. Your next song better be by the Ramones or I'm walkin' the fuck out."

"Quit bein' such an old fuckin' prude!" Maddy would exclaim to the laughter of the entire table. Recipes, stories of exploits, pictures, and advice were frequently shared among all of them through email, phone calls, and "social" media (which Joe and Maddy loathed as they would frequently lecture their friends and family of the insipidness and dangers of these engines of mindless gossip, narcissistic self-indulgence, and political conspiracy).

In April of Maddy's final semester of graduate school, Patty called her niece up and said, "Hey, watcha doin' Saturday night?" "Um . . . supposed to go to a party, but nothin' I can't get out of . . . why?" Maddy inquired.

"I saw that SCOTS are in town that night, and I thought I'd fly out to see them. Wanna go?"

"Fuck yeah, I do. Do you need a ride from the airport?" "Nah," Patty responded. "I'm just gonna fly in, see you at the show, and fly back out the next morning. Just felt spontaneous and wanted to see you."

"This is fuckin' awesome!" Maddy exclaimed as she felt the excitement of seeing one of her favorite bands with her rockin' aunt. That Saturday, as Maddy was leaving to meet her aunt at the show, she turned to the Nameless One and sternly lectured, "No more than three drinks tonight, and no more than one every hour and a half. Got that? I'm not gonna be around to bail your ass out at this party!"

"No worries, I'll be fine. I've got a couple nice guy friends who will be there. They can watch over me," she responded in order to reassure her close friend.

"Well . . . be sure that they do, or I'll fuck them up too!" Maddy exclaimed as she shook the house by the slamming of the heavy oak door.

The cab dropped Patty in front of her hotel, and the aunt and her cherished niece exchanged a sweaty and exhausted embrace goodbye. Maddy got back into the cab and gave the driver his next destination as she thought, *aunt Patty's so fuckin' cool. She even caught a chicken leg.* Her ears still ringing, and gin- infused head still buzzing, Maddy walked into the living room of her shared home to the sight of the Nameless One sobbing, while curled up in the fetal position on the brown leather couch. She was surrounded by the anguished faces of Sam, Jules, and Kristy who were trying to comfort their fallen friend.

"What the fuck happened?" Maddy exclaimed.

Sam, attempting to remain calm, said flatly, "We tried to call, but your phone was off." Then, failing in her attempt to control her emotions, she blurted out, "Oh, Jesus Christ, Maddy, she's been raped." Tears began flowing freely from ten horror-stricken eyes as Maddy joined the somber huddle.

Maddy was nauseous the next morning. Her nerve endings were tingling with rage while simultaneously feeling numb. Her heart felt like it weighed 200 pounds as she mentally kicked herself over and over for trusting her now emotionally battered and sexually assaulted friend to the whims of her "nice guy friends." *I should have been there, I should have been there, I should have been there*, she kept repeating over and over to herself in a macabre mantra. The Nameless One recounted how they had kept bringing her drinks at the party. She was her typical drunken flirty self, and one of the "friends" took advantage of it. She could remember being carried up the stairs as the other friend said, "I don't think you should do this."

"Shut the fuck up," the other retorted. "She wouldn't be hanging with us if she didn't want it. C'mon, she's been all over us all night!"

She vaguely remembered saying "No," or at least she thought that she had, as her underwear was removed, and she felt the pressure of his invasion. She remembered seeing the other friend out of the corner of her eye, just looking down motionless despite her pleas for help. Then, she was submerged into blackness until she saw the face of her friend who had been called to pick her up. Jules, with a rush of adrenaline, picked up her discarded friend into her arms, carried her down the stairs, and placed her carefully into the back of the cab. Upon returning to their home, Sam and Kristy were informed. Attempts to reach Maddy went unanswered.

The police were called. The consultation was pointless. The Nameless One was interrogated about how much she had to drink, what she wore, what did she say, are you sure it was them, did you kiss them first? Tears streamed from the eyes of the victim who was being victimized once again by the callous and almost accusatory nature of the questions and the impolite disregard of the questioner.

Finally, Maddy said angrily, "Okay, that's it. You've been of no fucking help whatsoever. Get the fuck out. We'll deal with this ourselves."

"Now, listen here, miss, these allegations are quite—" the officer began saying until Maddy cut him off, "Did I stutter, motherfucker? Get the fuck out . . . Barney."

The officer shook his head dismissively and said, "Yeah, maybe you ladies just need to watch how much you drink next time. Boys will be boys, y'know." Maddy had to be restrained by Sam and Kristy as the officer strode out of the apartment.

That same officer visited Maddy two weeks later. She knew what it was about and nearly cried as she tried to keep from smirking at the thought of the previous evening's escapades. Over the past two weeks, the stealthy sprite had done her research. She knew where the rapist lived. She had become adept at gaining entrance into areas that she was supposed to be restricted from. She knew approximately what time he would be home and in what condition he would be in. And she was armed with the strongest epoxy on the market. All she had to do was patiently wait and seethe as her internal ember became engorged by vengeful flames.

The rapist stumbled in shortly after 2:00 am. Tripping on a floor rug, he violently crashed onto his mattress. In his nearly blacked-out state, he failed to notice two green eyes that glowed from his corner chair as the faint hallway light hit them. He began snoring; and the clandestine figure slowly rose, walked over to the bed, pulled down his pants, rolled him over to his stomach, and generously applied the epoxy between the cheeks of his buttocks. She then rolled him back over and provided the same treatment to his flaccid genitalia. She placed both of his hands over the blob of glue that he was now encased in and pressed down firmly, so that his hands and genitals were now one mass of oozing and treacherously sticky flesh. For her finale, she applied the epoxy over his mouth. *No one's gonna hear you scream, you motherfuckin' chad*, she thought as she effortlessly floated out the window, down the gutter, and across the lawn on her way home.

The officer was intense in his interrogation, but she had an ironclad alibi. She was out with her friends the night before, singing karaoke. "You can ask anyone, Officer. There were about thirty people there," Maddy innocently claimed. Everyone who was at the bar that night attested to her presence, some with her complete song list as they would chuckle about how off key she had been on some of them. Being "cool with Maddy" was reciprocal, and her friends were as loyal to her as she was to them. All Sam had to do was go around the bar that night and say, "If anyone asks about Maddy, she was here tonight, and here's the three songs that she fucked up." The request was unanimously agreed upon by the bar's regular patrons through slight, knowing nods.

The rapist survived the attack but was forced to endure months of excruciation from the removal of the epoxy and subsequent skin grafts and surgeries. The male penis is homely at best. The rapist's penis ended up being downright grotesque. As the officer suspiciously eyed Maddy as he made his way to the exit, Maddy stated in her most demure voice, "Have a nice day, Officer. I sure hope you get your man." As those words were coming from her mouth, she was internally vowing, *One down, one to go. You better hope I never find you, you pussy motherfucker.*

Chapter 7

This Is Not a Love Song

Romantic involvements for the five friends were as varied as their respective personalities throughout their college years. Jules was a confirmed bachelorette who didn't want to be tied down or have to make the required, usually modest, compromises to build and sustain a relationship. She adopted the same attitude toward men that many men in the world have toward women. It was a utilitarian posture of most men being good for just one thing: raw, emotionless sexual gratification, and maybe hook up a stereo, but that was pretty much it. To Jules, most men were disposable "sticks with dicks" who, over the years, provided her ample condoms for the despised swear jar. Jules held the same outlook toward sex that she did about eating. It was a natural, biological need that could be fun. Her frequent saying was "When I'm hungry, I'll go to a restaurant. When I'm horny, I'll find a cock." It was as simple as that to her with no moral qualms about either activity. If a man ever began to get too emotionally close to her, Jules would let them down as easily as her empathetically challenged persona could by saying abrasively, "Yeah . . . how 'bout we don't fuck this up with feelings and shit? I'll tell you what. If I need to get laid and I don't have any other options, I'll give you a call. You're not bad and will do in a pinch."

The heartbroken young man would leave the dorm, apartment, or cheap hotel room thinking *But isn't that what chicks want? Romance and feelings and shit?* Jules always felt that she was doing these young men a needed service by leaving them questioning their single-minded and grossly simplistic beliefs about the "fairer" sex.

The Nameless One's romantic interests were as roller-coaster in nature as her two extremely different social personalities. The Sober One was far too shy and meek to even make eye contact with a man, let alone flirt with him. The Sober One was gullible and believed anything an interested suitor might say to her in a sweet or flirtatious voice. She would immediately "fall in love" with any man, young or older, who gave her the slightest bit of attention, leading her to multiple heartbreaks upon discovering her latest liaison was married. The Drunk One was overly amorous, which was advantageous for predators who wanted to seduce her into making bad decisions. This is where her friends, usually Maddy, would be forced to come to her rescue and figuratively spray her down like a dog in heat. Following her rape in the spring of 2011, the Drunk One never came out again unless in the safest of surroundings, and the Sober One's gullibility transformed into a deep distrust, fear, and resentment of men in general.

Sam's marriage lasted five years. Neither party was really to blame; they simply grew apart and realized that they weren't a good fit any longer. Upon announcing her impending divorce to her friends, Sam noticed the vengeful expression beginning to manifest itself on Maddy's face. Sam looked at Maddy and sternly said, "Maddy, do not do anything to him. He's a decent guy. He didn't do anything to hurt me, so just let it go, okay?" Maddy nodded in agreement. Once a pact was made within the circle, it was never to be broken. Sam's divorce was as organized and efficient as all of the other aspects of her life, and she remained friendly with her ex her entire life, on occasion with benefits should the need arise for the two of them. Sam was career oriented, which left little time, or interest, for serious relationships; so she engaged in numerous short-term liaisons. Her attitude toward love resembled that of her attitude toward business. If the right deal came along, then sign up for the merger. Otherwise, use the other party to its maximum benefit, then discard it once there was no longer an upside to its continuation.

Kristy's romantic life resembled that of her outgoing positive attitude. She fooled around a bit during college as most young people do; but at twenty-five, she met the man of her dreams, was married at twenty-six, and went on to have three children in their lifelong relationship. The initial meeting between Kristy and her future husband, Jason, was less than romantic, however. While Kristy and Maddy were onstage at the karaoke bar about to begin singing a duet, a table of three slightly drunk and more than slightly obnoxious businessmen yelled up to the pair, "Show us your tits!"

As two of the three men brazenly tittered at their crude gesture, Maddy could be heard saying, "Okay, pause the fuckin' song!" The entire bar went quiet as the anxious, anticipatory eyes of the crowd followed Maddy's lithe frame down the stage stairs and over to the bar. In a voice drenched in faux innocence, she politely asked the bartender for two large beers. She then turned with purpose and approached the offending table, ensuring to accentuate the swaying of her hips as she did so, while wearing her maniacal grin. Upon reaching the table, she stood between the two giggling hecklers while holding the heavy glass mugs precariously over their heads. Demurely, she stated with a Monroe-esque sigh, "I owe you two an apology, and I need to make it up to you. I didn't mean to make you two all hot and bothered, so how about I treat you both to a little head?" The frothy amber suds of ale cascaded down upon the previously perfectly manicured faces of the men. As the drenched and humiliated men left the bar to the roars of the satisfied bar patrons, Kristy and Maddy began the first lines of "Brass in Pocket" by the Pretenders.

Laughing hysterically upon their return to their table, they received victorious high fives from their friends as Maddy exclaimed, "That's what I'm fuckin' *talkin'* about!" The pair then looked up into the remorseful eyes of the third man from the offending table. He was short, somewhat stocky with his twenty-seven-year-old head presenting prematurely thinning brown hair. He had difficulty making eye contact with the ladies as he stuttered, "I, I just want to . . . um . . . apologize for my friends' . . . um . . . behavior."

"Yeah, you wanna make it up to me?" Kristy inquired. "Get up there and sing me a song."

"I, I don't really know how to . . . um . . . sing," he shyly responded.

"Then keep your apology to yourself," Kristy stated as she turned back to converse with her tablemates.

Twenty minutes and four singers later, the bar was "treated" to the soft, out-of-tune mumblings of a humbled man attempting to sing. Maddy looked up at the singer, then back to Kristy, and said, "Jesus Christ, he's horrible!" It was arguably the worst rendition of "Johnny B. Goode" ever performed. Kristy thought it was the cutest thing that she had ever seen. The two would wed almost exactly one year later in a ceremony that was flooded with perfectly white imagery, from the bridal gown to the flower arrangements and everything in between. Maddy, loving weddings with an open bar, was continuously steered away from the microphone throughout the entire evening so as not to risk a repeat of her debacle at Sam's ceremony. The next day, Maddy asked how her toast went. She received the same reply from everyone she asked. It was perfect.

Following Kristy's wedding, the remaining four women in the rented flat moved into their own respective homes. Their Wednesday evenings remained sacred, and they would rotate their weekly gatherings between their homes on a schedule that was developed by Sam. Kristy only missed two Wednesday evenings with her friends. Once, in order to give birth to twin boys approximately two years later. Undeterred, wine and cheese were snuck into the hospital waiting room by Maddy, Sam, Jules, and ____; and they were quite lit when an excited Jason came to tell them and the rest of their family the joyous news. They were fairly lit again on another Wednesday evening two years later when Kristy's daughter entered the world. But this time, one member of the group was no longer there, and another member sat in the corner more consumed with her seething thoughts than the revelry of the occasion.

And then there was Maddy's love life, whose eternal search for her prince led her to boyfriend after boyfriend, always turning out to be disappointments. They were all just typical self-absorbed "guys" who cared for her only to the extent that she was willing to be their personal maid and/or on-call sex toy. As soon as Maddy would make this revelation, the undesired suitor would be unceremoniously discarded, and the search would begin again. One boyfriend in particular got the door slammed in his face and told to "fuck off and don't call me again!" when he unexpectedly appeared at Maddy's doorway with his laundry bag. The young man left her apartment building frustrated and confused. *"Isn't that what girls are supposed to do?"* he thought as he trudged down the cracked sidewalk.

It didn't help that Maddy's opportunities for male suitors during her college years were significantly limited on campus by her avenging reputation. Despite her self-described, and generally agreed upon, "adorableness," most campus hetero males were frightened of the retribution that they might experience should a date or, god forbid, a sexual experience not be up to Maddy's standards. They had seen other young men's reputations be destroyed and did not aspire to join that statistical demographic.

Maddy became inspired by Kristy's good romantic fortune (although she didn't initially understand why Kristy was attracted to that "fuckin' dork") and became determined that it was surely her turn at the altar of happily ever after. Those desires came to seeming fruition at her and her friends' graduation party shortly after Kristy met Jason.

Aunt Patty, determined to not slow down at the age of sixty-one, spent the party engaged in drinking games with her younger counterparts, expressing glee as they acquiesced to her alcohol-fueled dominance one by one. She would frequently yell at Maddy to "change the fuckin' song! This shit sucks!" Aunt Blair played hostess and was a blur of activity as she threw away discarded plates and cups, cleaned up spills, and refreshed the appetizers, all the while marveling at the incredible person her beloved niece had become. Uncle Joe sat in a corner of the room watching his niece with admiration while sipping his never- ending beer. He had held Maddy in his arms shortly after she entered the world and had helped in shepherding her through all of her life's burdens and triumphs. Now, looking at his recently turned twenty-four-year-old niece flutter through the crowd while engaged in endless laughter-filled conversations, he couldn't help but experience feelings of pride swelling in his heart, which emerged through his tear ducts. At one point in the party, Joe interrupted his socialite niece who was speaking to a handsome tall man. Joe couldn't help but think that this man seemed out of place at this gathering somehow.

Joe went up to Maddy and said, "Hey, buttacup . . . can I see ya for a sec? I just have something that I want to give you for your birthday."

"Of course, uncle Joe!" she said as she politely excused herself while provocatively indicating that she would be right back.

The emotionally inseparable pair went into Maddy's bedroom, and Joe presented her with a haphazardly wrapped box, as this was the one gift that Blair had not been asked to work her magic on. She was surprised by the additional gift, as her family had already given her multiple presents of housewarming gifts that they felt she would need when she moved away from her friends. She tore open the wrapping paper and flung open the box with the same glee that she had as a child on Christmas morning. Inside was a large photo album. Through water-blurred vision, she began leafing through the pages and looking at the images of her entire life with her loving family.

Joe then said, "This book is to help you remember where you came from and who you are," before handing her a smaller box from the bottom of the package. "And this is to help you get where you need to go."

Maddy opened the box with anticipation. Inside was a set of well-worn and brownish stained brass knuckles. Maddy and Joe gave each other their knowing smiles, their glistening eyes mirroring each other, before she said with sincere gratitude, "Thank you, uncle Joe. I will cherish these . . . and put them to good use . . . y'know . . . if I need to." She delicately placed the book on top of her dresser and the other box deep under the multiple colors of fabric in her underwear drawer before the two rejoined the party.

Many people were invited to the soiree, including friends and acquaintances from both on and off campus, so it was not unusual that Maddy did not know the man standing in the corner looking at her from the corner of his eye. He was tall, probably about six foot two. He had a rich, smooth complexion with a perfectly groomed goatee and was dressed immaculately. He did not have one slicked-back black hair out of place. His shoe size seemed impressive as well. He looked as though he had just stepped off a fashion magazine cover. Maddy thought that he was the most beautiful man that she had ever seen and immediately began to swoon.

She casually sauntered over to the man and struck up a conversation. Upon learning from an interrupting old man that not only was this a party for her graduation, but it was also to celebrate her recent twenty-fourth birthday, the man snuck out of the party, only to return a short while later with a dozen red roses and a bottle of expensive red wine. The amorous gesture was rewarded by an invitation to stay the night.

The whirlwind romance began; and Maddy felt like a princess as she was showered with f lowers, candy, and sentimental cards from her elegant suitor. He was a thirty-four-year-old associate professor of psychology at another university and was quite adept at reading other people's personalities . . . and their vulnerabilities. He instinctively knew what to say with the perfect tone and air of sincerity to endear him to any person or group of people from any walk of life. Maddy was impressed by his ability to be the perfect conversationalist and to be accepted by all of her friends . . . with the exception of Jules, who found him to be "smarmy." However, there was a rule within the circle. Unless one had actual evidence of potential harm from a romantic interest, you were to keep your personal opinions of another's love interest to yourself. They were all grown women who were fully capable of making their own choices without the interference of others, and those choices would be respected by the group. So Jules kept her thoughts to herself.

Maddy had never wanted to be the "other woman," but she wasn't bothered that he was currently married. He had convinced her that his second marriage was coming to an end, which it did two months later. He was quite complimentary of his previous wives, explaining that both marriages had ended amicably and that the memorable experiences had inspired him to be an even more thoughtful and giving partner when he marries for the third and final time. On their third month of dating, the man looked into Maddy's welcoming emerald eyes and said, "I love you." He pulled out an impressive engagement ring, the perfectly cut center diamond showering the room with its prismatic beams. He gently asked, "Will you marry me?"

Maddy dreamily responded "Yes." The ring fit onto her finger as perfectly as a slipper, and shortly thereafter, the couple began making plans for marriage to be held eight months later. Her fiancé's family wasn't necessarily *unfriendly* to her. They just treated her with disregard as if she were nothing more than a piece of furniture in their ornate upper-middle- class home that they had to now navigate around. Whereas her family and friends' reaction to the joyous news was cheerfully congratulatory, his family's reaction held the same bored reaction that one experiences flipping through the TV channels.

Maddy didn't care. She was conciliatory and polite with his family. She was determined to be eventually accepted and would put her best foot forward toward that effort. She sent handwritten birthday wishes to his parents and elder brother. She began speaking "properly," abandoning her well-versed profanity. She dressed in conservative, "ladylike" dresses rather than her flirtatious tops, minidresses, and skirts or torn jeans and rock T-shirts. She politely disengaged whenever political issues were brought up, leaving the sometimes-heated dialogue exclusively to the men.

She learned how to cook (somewhat) and would make desserts from scratch to take to family gatherings. She would become the perfect wife and daughter-in-law, because he was her destiny.

The change in her personality was not lost on her family and friends. The person who was once a vivacious extrovert was now a reserved, overly polite young "lady." She would immediately shut down after receiving a glance of disapproval from her future husband, and her boisterous laughter became a reserved titter. She quit her job at the bookstore that she had worked at since she was an undergraduate on her fiancé's insistence. She was in line to become manager with a substantial salary for the sprawling new and used bookstore that also sold various novelties and records. But he felt that holding a full-time job would compete with her household obligations. Unknown to her, he also was attempting to chip away at her personal and professional support system so that, over time, she would be completely dependent upon him for all of her needs if not for her very survival. He refused to travel to Wisconsin, so her opportunities to see her family became less and less over time. She was "allowed" to see her friends on Wednesdays, but only because those were the evenings that he typically worked late grading papers and preparing lesson plans.

On the day of the wedding, just before he was to walk her down the aisle, uncle Joe said, "Are ya happy?"

"Y-yes, I think so, uncle Joe," came Maddy's weak reply. "Well, just remember," Joe continued while staring straight ahead, "selling your soul isn't worth trying to prove something to your parents. Be who you are, not what you are expected to be. And if you can't be who you are, get the fuck out."

Maddy walked down the aisle silently but with the full understanding of what her uncle had just said to her. She was trying to be something other than who she was. And she was doing it to prove to her abusive parents that she was a good person who deserved happiness. In that moment of realization, the wedding ceremony became stripped of emotional significance for her and became nothing more than a contrived pageant. She would go through with this, and she would build a successful marriage, but it would be on her own terms, just as everything had been throughout her life. What she failed to realize was that she was about to go up against the most emotionally destructive force of her life.

CHAPTER 8

Bad Moon Rising

Maddy stared emotionless at the photo album smoldering in the fireplace, one final glowing image of her and uncle Joe succumbing to the flames licking around its edges. She wondered how she had allowed this to happen. She wondered if she would ever be able to regain control over her life or make sense of the world again.

It was May 13 of 2017. It was her twenty-ninth birthday, and the present she received from her husband of four years was the malicious destruction of her most prized possession. She remembered a conversation with his mother a month before their wedding. Maddy had asked her why she didn't like her. His mother had replied, "I do like you, dear. That is why I'm trying to get rid of you. You're too special to be with my son." That was only one of many warnings. There was the tense silence of Jules every time he was present or mentioned. There was aunt Patty mockingly referring to her as "Stepford." There was uncle Joe's advice during the wedding procession, followed by constant reassurances and veiled warnings from him about "certain types of men." There was the time that aunt Blair emailed her the criteria for narcissistic personality disorder and would make psychological references to a certain political candidate while wondering aloud how anyone could trust a man such as that. It had all been lost on Maddy who was in her own psychological battle for her soul. But she had mistakenly began to define her soul as the soul of her marriage. In her mind, if her marriage failed, then she had failed, and "they" would win. And besides, _____, her best friend, really liked him. She felt like such a fool in retrospect to have placed so much emphasis on the judgment of her sweet but socially impaired confidant. The election of 2016 was another blow to Maddy's psyche.

Her parents, and their radically energized ilk, had won. And she feared her country would never be the same as fringe conspiracy theories, lies, and propaganda were increasingly becoming mainstreamed and were swelling the ranks of antidemocracy forces. And the other side was feckless at best. They would drone on about the virtues of "bipartisanship" while the fascists were taking a flamethrower to the political and societal norms that held our republic together. She felt helpless and hopeless on that election night, finally giving up any hope of a sane outcome once she saw Pennsylvania turn red. She turned off the TV, crawled into bed, curled into the fetal position, and quietly wept.

Her husband, who initially had been the epitome of charm, class, and respect, turned out to be a self-serving chameleon who used his conversational prowess and charisma solely for his personal advantage. He craved attention and praise so much that he would frequently belittle those around him in order to feel more powerful, including Maddy. At first, she thought his jabs were his way of joking, and she had begun to become indoctrinated to them. But methodically over time, they became increasingly biting and purposefully hurtful. Nothing was ever good enough. That wasn't what he wanted for supper. He'll just go out and get some real food. The house was never clean enough. Her clothes made her look like a little girl or a slut or whatever shameful name he could conjure up as she emerged from the bedroom ready to go to that evening's engagement. She had had so many boyfriends in college because she was a whore; and he, and he alone, could make her appear virtuous. Her friends were bitches or whores or idiots. She came from a family of toothless Midwestern simpletons. She was uncultured. She was crude. She was losing her looks. One day she would be a harlot, the next day she would be a prude. It was the same pounding sledgehammer to her brain, day in and day out, that she had endured from her parents. Why had she not recognized this? How had she allowed her spirit to once again be beaten down by a sadistic fuck? Where the fuck was her fight? It was then that she realized that she hadn't said "fuck" in well over three years. *Well, that's gonna fuckin' change,* she thought to herself as she valiantly attempted to piece together her shredded dignity and regain her lost self-image.

Her scrambled brain tried to figure out why she had stayed with him for so long. She didn't need his money. He had no idea that she had $170,000 invested from twelve years ago, which was now worth considerably more. For some subconscious, perhaps protective reason, she had never mentioned it to him. What she truly yearned for was the unconditional romantic love of someone, and that was something that she thought she had found. She surmised that, unlike her parents, he was a con man whose behavior served his interests solely. Her parents, she thought, at least were genuine about their fucked-up ideas and lifestyle. He wasn't. He purposefully manipulated her, drawing her in, then, over time, began and accelerated a continuous campaign of psychological abuse designed to make her subservient to his emotionally sadistic whims. And unlike her relationship with her parents, Maddy had *wanted* this to work, so she made every attempt to satisfy him so that she may find her own happiness through his. But her actions and intent didn't matter to him. The more she acquiesced, the crueler his attacks became, culminating in this evening's murder of her cherished photo album. He knew what her family meant to her, and this was his way of telling her that he was willing to burn down her entire life, just for his own twisted amusement. She wasn't stupid. She was a victim of a sadistic, narcissistic con man. What *would* make her stupid would be to not admit her error in judgment in the face of clear evidence to the contrary. And what would make her a perpetual victim would be to do nothing about it.

Stiffening her spine for the first time in four years, she took one last mournful look at the ashes that had previously been a tribute to her most adored memories. She went to the kitchen and, having to stand on her tiptoes, pulled the canister of his designer coffee from the top cabinet shelf. She returned to the fireplace and scooped the ashes into the coffee container, shook it vigorously, and returned it to the exact resting place from where it was found as Lesley Gore's "You Don't Own Me" played on her phone.

She went to the basement and searched through the neatly stacked cardboard boxes until she found the one that she needed. She took out the required belongings, stripped nearly naked, and replaced her conservative dress with black jeans, socks, boots, T-shirt, hoodie, and ball cap. She found the pepper spray and shoved it into her left hoodie pocket. She found another small box, took out its contents, and lodged the item into her other pocket. Before leaving her now-foreign-feeling home, she took a long look at herself in the hallway mirror. She saw a wicked smile cross the face of the young woman in the reflection, her green eyes resembling an emerald burning ember. For the first time in over three years, she recognized herself again. "You're Maddy *fuckin'* Sommers," she said audibly to her own reflection in a low, determined voice. "You weren't raised to put up with this shit. Time to fuck some shit up!"

On her walk toward her husband's office on campus, she reflected on the evening's events that initiated the conclusion of her marriage and this ultimate showdown. It was a Saturday, and she was planning on going to karaoke with her friends for the first time in a long time to celebrate her birthday. She had pleaded with him to allow her to go and to join her, but he didn't want to, preferring a quiet celebration in their home away from her "whore" friends. In his overly pompous tone, he lectured her on the company that she kept and insisted that she remain home rather than pursuing her "childish" hobbies. She was determined to stand her ground and told him, albeit meekly, that she was going and that she hoped that he understood. His tone then changed. Speaking in a calm, sweet voice, he said, "I do understand, darling. I'm sorry. I know how much they and your family mean to you. I really don't want to go, but you may if you would like. All that I ask is that we spend a few quiet moments by a beautiful fire, before you depart. Would you mind getting some firewood?"

"N-No," a pleasantly surprised Maddy stuttered. "Thank you. Thank you for understanding. I'll be right back."

Upon her return, she found him sitting in front of an already built fire, his maniacally twisted face glowing from the violently crackling flames. She said enthusiastically, "Here's the wood!" He stood up from the fire, grinning, and said in a low, disingenuously endearing voice, "Oh, that is all right, darling. I found something to burn that we won't have any use for any longer." It was then that she saw the photo album, engorged in flames. The adored images of her childhood being consumed by the violent inferno of his creation. She felt as though she had just been kicked in her stomach.

Tears began streaming as she stuttered, "W-W-Why?" Still wearing his terrorizing grin, he said matter-of-factly,

"Because I can. Because I own you. I own your every thought and your every emotion. You will do what I want to you to do, and you will feel how I want you to feel. And right now, I want you to feel the same sense of hurt and abandonment that I do. And now you do. And it pleases me. And that is what you were brought here to do. To please me. And now, it pleases me to go to my office and finish up some work. If you are not home when I return, those pathetic pictures will be the least that I destroy. Happy birthday, darling."

Without a shred of hesitation, Maddy flung open his heavy oak office door and found her sweating husband panting behind a half-naked young woman bent over the side of his desk. He looked at her and smiled. "Hello, darling. I thought you might come. Would you like to join?"

Maddy removed the hood from atop her head and sternly said, "Out, bitch." The confused and embarrassed girl dislodged herself from her paramour, swiftly reorganized her disheveled clothing, and departed the room.

Zipping up his pants, the husband said, condescendingly, "Now, that isn't necessary, is it? You really don't learn, do you? I guess you will be a bit more of a project than I thought, but breaking you will be amusing. Just as it was with the first two." His Cheshire grin was suddenly wiped away by the blur of brass landing upon his jaw, flinging him onto the floor as blood spewed from his mouth. Like a lynx, Maddy pounced upon her surprised and befallen prey holding the bloodstained brass knuckles in her right hand and the pepper spray in the other, just an inch from his quivering eyeball.

The petrified look on his face was familiar and intoxicating to her as she said in a deep growl, "Now look here, motherfucker. I don't want shit from you. All I want is a divorce and all of my personal shit. That's it. And you are going to grant me that divorce, or, as God is my witness, I will fucking destroy you. I will destroy you physically. I will destroy your career. I will destroy you emotionally. I will fucking destroy you. You have no idea what you have unleashed. I know that you're nothing more than a bully who pisses himself at the first sign of strength, so don't fuck with me, because you have never come up against a strength like mine. Give me my divorce and my shit and leave me alone, and I'll do the same. But if you don't"—her brass knuckle–adorned fist then punched him in his now-pale face three times with the quickness and ferocity of a prize fighter before continuing—"this is the least that I will do to you."

"F-fine," he stammered. "J-just get out of here. I'll have my attorney take care of it." As he watched this five-foot-four-(and a fucking half)-inch terror approach his door, he had the initial impulse to attack her from behind and physically beat her into submission. He then felt the intense pain from the swelling, cuts, and flowing blood from his beaten face and decided to let her go. She was a waste of his time, and there would be others, he thought. But he would play one final psychologically devastating card before the evening was through.

Maddy contacted her four friends who all met at Sam's single-story, two-bedroom brick home. Maddy recounted the events of the evening in a calm, almost self-congratulatory manner. Wine, gin, and vodka began flowing as the five friends laughed, hugged, and cried together. It was an emotional reunion of sorts, as the Maddy they had all come to love had returned completely to the fold. Arrangements were made for Maddy to stay temporarily with Sam until she was able to find her own place. It was negotiated that there would be no swear jar. The owner of the bookstore that she had resigned from three years prior had recently reached out to her, once again inquiring about her availability for the manager position as she had been unable to find anyone trustworthy and bright enough for the position. With her intelligence, pleasant demeanor (toward customers and staff), keen eye for business, and understanding of the vast shop, Maddy would accept the offer and return to the professional embrace of its delightful owner, Monica. The dark cloud that had hovered over Maddy, and, by extension, the group, had come to an end. The five friends would march together toward the future, with a new pact that anytime a romantic involvement started to become serious, the suitor would be screened by the group. Opinions on harmless personality quirks, appearance, and choice of (legal) profession were off limits. But they would have the responsibility to give their unvarnished truth about any red flag that they considered to be an actual threat. They had just joyously toasted to Sam's newly written agreement, when _____'s phone went off.

_____looked at her phone and immediately turned from the group. There was a simple text that read, "Only twice. Too bad. Deal's off."

"Everything okay?" Jules inquired.

"Um . . . um . . . um . . .," was all ___ was able to get out as Maddy's phone went off. There was an email from her soon- to-be ex with the subject line saying, "Divorce Arrangements." "Well, well, well . . .," Maddy began gleefully. "Let's see if the douchebag is gonna cave or if he's gonna be a glutton for punishment." Sam, Jules, and Kristy began laughing along with Maddy as she read the message aloud. "Okay, check *this* out, girls. It says, 'Contacted my attorney. It will be simple. All we must do is sign. Our attorneys will work on a mutually beneficial time for you to pick up your belongings. I will not touch anything before you do so. I wish you nothing but happiness in the future.'"

"Aaawww," the four mockingly vocalized through their cackles, before Maddy concluded reading, "So in the spirit of full disclosure, I believe you might want to know who else I've been fucking." Maddy scrolled down to find ten pictures of her husband, smiling at the camera as he was engaged in a variety of sexual positions and techniques with another woman. The woman's identity was shielded due to the angle of the camera or the type of activity until picture number 6.

Pictures 6 through 10 clearly identified _____ as the other woman. It was then that the rest of the group looked up to notice that _ had yet to turn back around. She was standing there with her head down and her back to the group, quietly sobbing. "You . . . fucking . . . bitch," Maddy stated in a hurt and horrified voice. "It's one thing to be betrayed by that douchebag . . . but . . . my best friend? After all we've been through together? After all of the times I've protected you? After all of the times you listened to me about my suspicions? Why . . . how could . . ." Maddy's bewildered voice trailed off as _____ said with her back still turned, "M-M-Maddy . . . I'm . . . s-so s-s-sorry. I . . . I . . . I—"

Maddy then cut her off and said while wiping away newly formed tears, "Y'know what? It doesn't fucking matter. Why should I be surprised by anything that happens in this fucked-up world anymore? Just get the fuck out. I never want to see or hear from you again. Just fucking disappear, or I swear to god, I'll . . . I'll . . ." Maddy didn't have the opportunity or desire to finish her threat as the Nameless One hastily left the home and ran down the street.

The four remaining friends sat on their respective cushions staring straight ahead and expressionless in complete silence. They were completely shell-shocked by this diabolical revelation. They had been sisters, in the best sense of the word, for so long. They had never betrayed or lied to one another. It shook their faith in humanity to its very core. The deafening silence was broken as Maddy said in a flat voice that was completely devoid of emotion, "I don't want to ever hear that bitch's name again. Understand?" The other three solemnly nodded in unison as Maddy got up and began walking toward her new bedroom with the energy of a funeral procession.

Jules was elected by Sam and Kristy to try to reach out to the Nameless One (as she would now be known, even outside of Maddy's presence) quietly and obtain some form of an explanation. She let three days pass before making her first attempts. Her phone number had been disconnected. She was no longer in her apartment. She no longer worked at the financial institution where she had been employed. All of her social media accounts had been deactivated. No one could or perhaps would give any information on her whereabouts. Jules even began scanning hospital admissions and obituaries in the event that something unspeakable had occurred, but to no avail. Maddy's dictate had been fulfilled. She just fucking disappeared.

The divorce was handled between the attorneys and was indeed simple and efficient. Maddy retrieved her belongings without incident with the assistance of her three remaining friends, family, and several rather large male acquaintances from around the neighborhood. Two weeks had passed since the confrontation, and Maddy did not personally see her ex that day, who was keeping to himself in another part of the house. But Patty and Blair took it upon themselves to seek him out. They found him in his small study off the kitchen in the back of the house.

While gazing out the window at the now-weed-infested flower garden that had previously been attended to by Maddy, he stood silently as Blair said, "I asked Joseph to not help with this part of the move. It is not a courtesy that I will ever extend again, do you understand?"

The beleaguered man turned to stare at the sisters, wanting desperately to say something to regain his control over the situation. But seeing the resolve on the ladies' faces, he wilted and merely nodded. As he had turned around, Patty presented a satisfied grin and said mockingly, "By the looks of your face, I don't know that Joe is going to be needed. You picked the wrong girl to fuck with, and she has plenty more to dish if she needs to . . . you fuckin' pussy." With that, the sisters departed the room, leaving the man to his impotent attempts to console his shattered ego.

Maddy fell into her role at the bookstore seamlessly. As she entered the building, the longtime employees applauded, and she was greeted with an enveloping bear hug from the shop's owner, Monica. Monica was a jovial Haitian refugee who had gained her citizenship and built her business up through a small business loan program. She had been a librarian in Haiti and loved the ability to spread art, knowledge, and competing ideas through books and other forms of media. Over the thirty years of being in business, her shop became known not only for new and used books but also for rare limited and first editions. Maddy was especially adept at playing the sleuth and tracking down editions that were desired by her customers. She was talented at brokering deals for these rare treasures and could change her persona to meet the needs of the negotiation. Frequently, a brief flash of her smile and the batting of her emerald eyes was all it took to seal a fiercely negotiated in-person deal.

After what seemed like an eternity, Monica whispered into Maddy's ear, "Welcome home, child," and released her from her vise-grip embrace.

Maddy, wiping a tear from her eye, looked up and said, "Hiya, everybody! It's great to be back! Now, let's sell some freakin' books!" Maddy, having placed herself on hiatus from any entanglements with men, threw herself into her work, relearning the shop's vast inventory of books, periodicals, records, DVDs, and novelty items. She quickly brought herself up to speed on the various systems for the operation of the business and personally met with each of the employees. Following their initial meeting, Maddy would make a mental note as to which employees she wanted to retain and which she would like to . . . upgrade. She also began making contacts with publishing houses and literary agents in order to establish her shop as a desired destination for book tours. Maddy also began reading more, as she now had free access to the greatest books ever written, including *Auto Mechanics 101*, which she thought might come in handy just in case she felt like fucking up a certain ex's precious BMW. An astonished Monica would stand back and watch her pint-sized dynamo take the reins of her business. She was convinced that Maddy would be the one to carry out her legacy once she decided to retire.

About four weeks into her new career, Maddy received a brief text from Patty. It simply read, "Call me now."

This can't be happening, Maddy's racing mind thought as a cab was taking her to the hospital from Dane County Regional Airport. She thought back on her phone conversation with Patty.

"Hey, Mads," Patty's weary voice had answered.

"What the fuck's so urgent? I'm at work," Maddy impatiently replied.

Patty responded with "Yeah, you gotta drop that shit and get here." Patty's voice began to crack under the weight of her sorrow as she struggled to continue. "I-I-It's Joe, Mads. It's n-not good. H-here, I'm s-sorry. Talk to B-Blair."

Tears were already beginning to form in Maddy's eyes as she heard the haggard but soothing voice of her Aunt Blair. "Maddy, I'm so sorry to tell you this. Joe is in trouble. He got into an . . . altercation last night trying to break up a fight between a couple. The man pulled out a gun and shot Joe. At first, we thought he would be all right, so we didn't bother you with it right away, but things have taken a turn for the worse. You need to get here if you want to say goodbye."

"Oh, Jesus fucking Christ, I'm on my way!" Maddy exclaimed as she hung up the phone. She hurriedly ran to Monica's office and apologetically explained the situation, hailed a cab, and went directly to the airport. She would land in Madison approximately five hours later. During her flight, she furiously searched for news articles about the incident. Authentic media outlets simply distributed the factual information of the case.

At approximately 11:30 last night, a Madison, Wisconsin, man was shot outside of Wayne's Pub. Initial reports indicate that Joseph Argento, 74, was attempting to break up a domestic dispute between a man and a woman when the man, identified as 27-year-old __ __ pulled a gun and shot Mr. Argento in the abdomen. Mr.

_______ is currently in custody awaiting release on $100,000 bond. Mr. Argento is currently listed in critical condition.

The propaganda outlets had a decidedly different take as they screamed headlines such as "Wisconsin Man Stands His Ground against Vicious Attack," "Gun Advocates Rejoice As Madison Man Protects Girlfriend," and "2nd Amendment Protects Our Freedom Again!"

Seething from both the tragedy of her uncle's condition and at how he was being portrayed by the self-serving right-wing blowhards, Maddy pulled out her second phone, which had yet to be used, which was not connected to her identity, and which would be quickly disposed of upon her arrival in Madison. *I've got your name, motherfucker*, Maddy began thinking to herself. *Now . . . who the fuck are you . . . chad?*

He was an insignificant nobody who had caused significant damage. He had a string of domestic abuse and assault charges but had never been convicted, usually due to the women involved dropping the charges or failing to appear. He had a license to purchase and to conceal carry firearms, which Maddy thought was yet another example of her country's misguided outlook on what "personal freedom" and "public safety" meant. He was a job hopper with vast gaps between employers, leaving one to wonder what his primary source of income truly was and what potential grudges might exist against him. His mug shots identified a number of tattoos including the Confederate flag, the swastika, the number 14, and a weird frog-like image. He lived in a run-down trailer park, complete with a broken toilet lawn "ornament" (*Naturally*, Maddy thought), and drove an Orangutan Orange 1969 Dodge Challenger. There were three taverns in his area that he frequented.

Once he's released, he' ll end up at one of those, Maddy speculatively plotted.

The cab arrived at the hospital, which resembled a tall gray tombstone in the evening's eerie June moonlight. There were several muted clangs as the pieces of a cell phone, which had been disassembled in the airport ladies' room, hit the bottom of the sewer grate, a petite woman ignoring the sounds as she strode into the hospital with as much composure as she could manage. She entered the hospital room and found Blair and Patty standing over a bed. Without saying a word, the three women embraced as Maddy looked down upon her still-larger- than-life uncle who was nearing submission and took his firm hand.

Joe's sunken eyes scanned the room at his loving family. His sister-in-law and close friend and confidant, Patty, consoling him with a calm expression as if to say, "It's okay to let go now, Joe. We'll see you again soon." Then to his adoring wife, Blair, her eternal love and caring for him etched across her sixty-four-year-old face. *She still doesn't look a day over twenty- five and is the most beautiful woman I have ever seen. She remains exactly as I found her. What a lucky fucker I've been*, he thought through his intoxicated haze before his sullen gaze fell upon the emerald-green eyes of his beloved niece. For a brief moment, his dull brown eyes regained their sparkle. He managed one final mischievous grin and a sly wink as if to say, "It's all okay, Buttacup. You will be okay. I will always be with you. Fuck those douchebags."

Maddy, fighting through her anguish and tears, flashed her uncle the same slight mischievous grin, as if to say, "Yeah, fuck them, Uncle Joe." It was just the two of them silently communicating with each other as his eyes peacefully closed on his niece for the final time.

The annoyingly persistent, one-note ring of the electrocardiogram was joined in a morbid harmony by the excruciated wail of a young woman who had just realized that she had lost the only man who had ever cared for her. Maddy's tear-soaked eyes perfectly matched the electric green displayed by the flatline.

CHAPTER 9

DON'T LET ME BE MISUNDERSTOOD

Once upon a time, there lived a lovely young lady named Maddy. From the time Maddy could speak, all that she longed for was the unconditional love, caring, and recognition of her prince.

They would play games, hold hands, and, mostly, laugh together for their entire lives. But there were evil people in the world who would try to keep this determined damsel from achieving her dream. Her parents would mock her, ridicule her, beat her, and try to indoctrinate her into a fantastical world driven by fear, power, and greed. Young men would trick her into drinking a spiked elixir in order to take away the magic of her self-confident sexuality. Another man would, in fact, succeed in this heinous quest with her best friend whom she would then be forced to avenge. That best friend would reward her gallantry through an unimaginable betrayal.

A man posing as her valiant prince would turn out to be a vile goblin who attempted to consume her soul and place it into his servitude. And now, the evil ones of the world had taken away the only man that she had ever felt safe with in his strong embrace. He was her role model for what a prince should be. And now he was needlessly gone, through a cowardly act performed by an insignificant gnome who wielded the calamitous weapons of the weak minded and hearted. The woman was now filled with resolve that had been instilled within her by the years of built-up emotional scar tissue. She now realized that there were truly evil people in this world and that some of those people were, for one reason or another, beyond the reach of the laws of her civilized society. She would still seek out her prince, for she knew he was out there, somewhere. But she would now be driven by the higher purpose of carrying out the sentence of the ultimate justice on those who violently preyed upon the vulnerable and crushed them emotionally, physically, and spiritually. This was now her calling, she thought as she painfully clutched the well-worn handle of uncle Joe's homemade night-stick. The final switch had been flipped, and the ember that had been smol-dering for the past twenty-nine years now roared to life, becoming a blazing inferno.

Over the next three days, as funeral preparations were being made, the Argento home was enveloped by a cloud of anguish. Everyone went about their assigned duties silently and without question. Blair, who was internally wrecked, presented herself with the same steely resilience that she had through any crisis. She was the family's matriarch who kept everything in check, and she would not fail her husband or family now by wilting under the weight of her devastating heartache.

Two days before the visitation, Sam, Jules, and Kristy arrived. Sam hugged Maddy and her aunts, took one look at Blair's beleaguered face, and asked her for the to-do list. "Good, now go upstairs and get some rest," Sam suggested to Blair before turning to Jules and Kristy and began barking orders. "Okay, ladies, we've got work to do. Once each assigned task is complete, you will report its completion back to me. And Jules . . . you can say 'fuck' as much as you want. Let's go, girls." Looking fondly back down the stairs at her trio of soldier ants, Blair thought how much she loved these members of her extended family. Blair collapsed into bed and began to lightly snore the moment her head hit the pillow. All of the assignments had been completed, and arrangements had been made by the time she awoke seven hours later according to Sam's official report.

Patty and Maddy were tasked with suggesting the photo for the funeral program and three songs for the service. Although their hearts were shattered, they were able to find some solace through trying to think of what songs they could play that would most piss Joe's spirit off.

"Hey, Mads," Patty would say as her eyes fought to regain their sparkle, "wanna get struck by lightning? How 'bout we open with something off of this?"

Maddy let out a cathartic laugh as she looked at the CD cover of *Pat*

Boone's Greatest Hits. "We wanna piss him off, not be damned to hell for all eternity! Why the fuck do they even have this?"

Patty chuckled and said, "I think it was a gift from your parents." The next sound that was heard was from the impact of the CD jewel case smashing up against the wall. Shards of plastic gleamed in the afternoon sunshine that was beaming through the window. This scene was played out seven more times as they rummaged through the collection of albums and CDs.

Maddy would ask, "Where the fuck did they get *this*?" followed by Patty's dry response of "Your parents." *Smash! Smash! Smash! Smash! Smash! Smash! Smash!*

Patty, looking at the plastic shrapnel strewn about the room, said, "Hey! Clean this shit up. I shouldn't have to suffer for your parents' shitty taste in music."

Three songs were finally chosen the night before the visitation and presented to Blair for her approval. Blair looked at the song titles, wiped a tear from her eye, and said, "Yes. He would love this." Blair then stood and called for Sam, Jules, and Kristy to join them. Standing tall while straightening her velvet black hair, she addressed her sisterhood. "Ladies, we are going to be okay. We may not have Joseph any longer, but we have each other. The most important thing that I learned from Joseph is that everything will be all right if we are able to put away our pride and allow those who love us to lift us up in times of need. And this is not the first nor will it be the last time of need for us all. But we have each other and Joseph's spirit to lean on. This is not an ending for us. It is only the beginning." The last sentence was delivered directly toward her niece who understood its implication. "Now, let us all lift each other up and march together towards our futures. And may God have mercy on anyone's soul who dares to stand in our way." The group tearfully laughed as twelve arms became entangled in an inspirational embrace celebrating their love, strength, and empowerment.

There were three harsh knocks at the door. Kristy answered the door and was greeted by the sight of a small man standing behind a lanky pale woman who looked to be in her late seventies. "Yes, may I help you?" Kristy inquired.

Through her thin, pursed lips, the woman said, "Is Madeline here?"

"Uh . . . yes . . . may I ask who is calling?" Kristy inquired. "Why, dear child, we are her parents."

Oh my god! Kristy thought to herself. *Maddy wasn't exaggerating. These two are creepy as fuck!* "Um . . . yes . . . so nice to meet you both . . . Won't you both come in?" Kristy said as cheerfully as she could muster.

Kristy stood to the side as the pair slunk into the foyer of the home. Maddy's father sincerely said, "Blair, Patty, Madeline . . . I'm so sorry for your loss . . . If there's anything that I can—" before being cut off by his domineering wife. "Yes, it is indeed a tragedy . . . of sorts. We wanted to pay our respects and offer you all the opportunity to seek salvation within our congregation now that you see what such a . . . lifestyle . . . can lead to." Maddy understood this contemptuous act for what it was. It was an attempt by her soulless mother to once again gain the upper hand and to exact revenge upon uncle Joe and the entire family for their earlier acts that had wrestled control away from her. And she was making this power play at a time when she thought the family, and most importantly, her daughter, would be at their most vulnerable. A sly, cracked sneer crossed the mother's face as Maddy silently approached the pair. She looked up at her mother, noticing the same flaming auburn hair that she saw in her own reflection each day. Blair, along with the entire sisterhood, watched in hushed anticipation as the two stared each other down. The tension was palpable. A size 6 foot fiercely struck her mother in the crotch, causing the emaciated- looking woman to fall to her knees. Maddy grabbed the tight copper bun that clung to the top of her mother's head and pulled it up so that her mother was forced to see the raging glow in Maddy's virescent eyes. Maddy struck her mother in the face repeatedly, causing blood to fly from the newly formed gashes upon her pallid face. Maddy tossed the limp body onto the floor as if discarding a used tissue. She licked a trail of blood from the engorged knuckles of her right hand before going over to her speechless father, pulled his shirttail from his pants, and wiped the rest of the blood onto it.

"Take her home, Dad," Maddy ordered. "Oh, and if you want to call the cops, just know this . . .

"Numero uno: The cops probably won't do anything because they loved uncle Joe as much as we do. Plus, then I'm gonna spill about everything that I know about you and your fucking cult. Numero two-o: Even if I do get into trouble, it won't be that much, and I'll be out reaaal soon. And numero three-o: The moment I get out, I'm coming directly to your house, and you both are gonna think this was a sunny day at the beach compared to what I'll do to you . . . if you know what I mean, and I think that you do."

Maddy's visibly shaken father assisted his beaten, bloodied, and bewildered wife to her feet. Both parents' clothes were covered in scarlet as they stumbled out of the house and toward their car. Patty, Sam, Jules, and Kristy observed the entire scene with looks of fearful astonishment plastered upon their faces. Sitting motionless, they resembled mannequins watching the most grotesque of horror films. They all knew that Maddy was capable of destruction. But until this moment, none of them knew the level of ferocity that Maddy could call upon to fulfill her vengeance. None of them except for one member of the group.

Blair sat in her chair wearing an expression of satisfaction as she secretly spoke to her husband. "I told you, Joseph, that there would be a time and a place. And this is it. She will struggle for a bit, but she will be all right. We will all be all right. The torch has been passed. You can rest easy now."

"Sorry for the mess, Aunt Blair, I'll clean it up." "Nope, I got it," Patty said in reverence.

"Okay . . . listen . . . I got some shit to do and to think about. I'll be back in a bit. Anyone need anything while I'm out?" Maddy inquired.

Blair looked at her triumphantly calm niece and simply said, "Yes, if you don't mind, why don't you get me some Sour Cream and Onion Pringles? And some butter ripple ice cream." With a nod of acknowledgment, Maddy left the house and started the red Cruiser. "No More Mr. Nice Guy" by Alice Cooper was playing on the radio. The car's tires squealed out of the driveway; their sound drowned out by Maddy's piercing voice singing at the top of her lungs.

———

Maddy didn't need much for this adventure, but she did need to conceal her identity as best she could on a warm June evening. She went to a secondhand store furthest from the Argento home and found everything that she needed. She purchased a small black wool cap to put her hair under, a generic black ball cap to wear over it, sunglasses, a humungous black T-shirt, baggy black jeans and black shoes, two sizes too big, and a small duffel bag. She paid in cash. She then drove to the supermarket nearest her home and purchased Blair's requested snacks before returning.

She placed the items in the kitchen and began back down the hallway beside the staircase. It was then that she noticed trace blood spatters remaining on the base board and lower portion of the staircase. *Fuckin' amateurs*, Maddy thought as she completed the cleanup from the earlier brutal beating. Everyone in the household was emotionally and physically exhausted and in their respective bed when she had arrived, so she was very quiet as she went to the basement and retrieved the necessary tools from Joe's toolbox. She placed the tools, small flashlight, and nightstick into the duffel followed by a large garbage bag that now contained the purchased clothing and proceeded to her bedroom.

As Maddy and Patty had been searching for songs for the service earlier that day, Maddy had opened a small record box. On the very top of the pile was a 45 record, which immediately transported Maddy back to her childhood. As a very young child, Uncle Joe would tuck her into her bed, with her blue baby blanket right next to her. He would then play this record on her child's record player while beaming down at his precious niece. She would drift off to sleep enveloped in the warm cocoon of her bedding and her uncle's adoration while listening to that song.

Tears began to well once again as Maddy lowered the needle onto the well-worn record, the blue and gray "Fontana" label spinning at 45 rotations per minute. She lay upon the bed, clutched her blue baby blanket, and curled into the fetal position as she listened to the soft and reassuring melody of the Mindbenders' "Uncle Joe the Ice Cream Man."

The visitation was not scheduled until five in the evening and would go until ten. Sam and Jules went to the supermarket to get groceries, which contained waaaay too much "healthy shit" for Maddy and Patty's liking. "Healthy body, healthy mind," Sam would cheerily lecture as she was putting the groceries away.

"Oh, fuck it. I'll just go get a burger somewhere. You comin', Mads?" Patty inquired.

"Naw, they went to all of this trouble. I'll just deal with it," Maddy responded.

Patty, now realizing how rude she was being to her generous adopted "nieces," sat her taut sixty-five-year-old body down at the table and with a resigned sigh said, "All right, I guess I had to try fruits and vegetables sometime. Thanks, girls, for doing this. It was supersweet." It was then that Jules displayed a rare grin, took a box of frozen burritos out of the bag, and handed it to the nutritionally challenged pair.

"That's what I'm fuckin' *talkin'* about!" Maddy exclaimed as she ripped open the box and placed four burritos into the microwave.

Sam just shook her head in bewilderment and thought to herself, *My lord, they look like vultures devouring roadkill,* as Patty and Maddy covered their burritos in heated canned chili, salsa, and shredded cheese and dug into their feast.

Kristy spent most of the day on the phone with her understanding but completely overwhelmed husband who took time off from work to care for their one-year-old twin sons while Kristy was away. There were multiple, oftentimes frantic, conversations about nap times, where certain items were located and what they were allowed to eat. At one point, Jason sent a text with a picture. The image was of the two angelic faces, as well as the kitchen floor, covered in ketchup, canned pasta, and what might have been flour. "So . . . that just happened," was all that the text read. Kristy proudly showed the picture to the sisterhood, which provided yet another well-needed release of tension.

"You're gonna have to blow him hard when you get home, you realize that, dontcha?" Jules matter-of-factly said to Kristy as another round of laughter poured out of the six bereaved yet spirited women.

The impossibly long line of visitors parted with reverence as six black-clad women made their way into the funeral home. There was a beautiful slideshow of pictures of Joe posing seemingly with everyone from his neighborhood that Kristy and Jules had arranged. The beaming face of a photo-bombing Maddy was frequently featured. Images of Maddy's parents were absent from the presentation, with the exception of one picture of a smiling Joseph holding a six-year-old Maddy on his lap, her fearful green eyes focused to her left as a lanky dark shadow towered over the image of the pair.

Tears flowed as freely as outrageously funny stories throughout the evening. There were multiple attempts at impersonations of Joe telling a joke, but none of them had the same comedic timing as the original. In addition to various cousins and extended family, everyone from the neighborhood and beyond made an appearance—from his friends from the local pub, to neighbors, to employees at local businesses, to local police officers. Hugs and gracious offers of assistance were plentiful as Blair, Patty, and Maddy fully realized the impact that their beloved Joe had had on so many lives. It filled their hearts with solace, pride, and resolve.

At around 8:30 pm, Maddy looked at her uncle's casket and went up to all five of the ladies in the receiving line and said, "I'm exhausted. I need to go lay down for a bit in that little side room, okay?"

Blair looked at her niece with a tender and understanding expression and said, "Of course, dear. We'll make sure nobody bothers you while you rest. But you need to be back out here by nine thirty, understand?"

"Yep, no prob," Maddy replied. "I think an hour should do it."

Maddy went into the side room and placed her purse, which contained her cell phone, on the couch. A few minutes later, a red car without headlights crept out of the funeral home parking lot, turned left, and headed west toward a neighborhood of trailer parks and taverns.

The obscenely orange Challenger was not located at the first bar on the tour. But it was found parked way behind the second bar under the darkness of large tree limbs. *Oh, he's making this too fucking easy,* Maddy thought as she silently drove around the corner to a dark adjacent lot, parking behind a large dumpster. She took the garbage bag out of the duffel, leaving the empty bag wedged under the rear tire for later use, and put on the jeans, shirt, wool cap, ball cap, sunglasses, and shoes over her thin dress, as she had rehearsed earlier that day. She found a hole in the chain-link fence that separated the two areas and, being careful to not make contact with the jagged barbs of metal, crawled into the other lot and underneath the targeted vehicle. *Now, what did that book say about brake lines?* Maddy thought as a faint snipping sound could be heard.

A seemingly well-rested Maddy emerged from the funeral home side room and returned to the reception line at 9:38 pm, just in time to hear Patty whisper to Sam, "When can we get a fuckin' drink?"

Maddy took her place next to Blair who said, while continuing to shake hands and receive the hugs of the last remnants of well- wishers, "Did you have a nice rest, dear?"

"Yup," Maddy replied, "I feel much better now."

The funeral was at ten the next morning, and the ethnically diverse crowd was standing room only. The preacher from Blair's (and occasionally, Joe's) Methodist church presided over the solemn event. The morning began with the heart- wrenching version of "In My Life" performed by a near-end-of- life Johnny Cash, his haggard vocals accentuating the finality of the proceedings. The preacher then began her introduction, purposefully avoiding specific biblical passages in reverence to Joe's generally suspicious nature of organized religion. Instead, her soothingly righteous voice focused on the primary themes of biblical scripture and general Christian beliefs that epitomized Joe's character such as community, the sacred bond of family, the embracing of others' differences, and the concept of selfless charity. She concluded by presenting a brief overview of Joseph's life, including an emotional nod to those in his immediate family that he had left behind. Maddy gained strength from her stoic Aunt Blair and remained composed as the preacher concluded, "Joseph Argento was much like our biblical Joseph. He never failed to find shelter for those in need. And we can find solace in the belief that his smiling face is looking down upon us at this very moment and guiding us toward the shelter that we are currently seeking. And now, his cherished niece, Maddy, would like to say a few words."

Don't fuckin' lose it, don't fuckin' lose it, don't fuckin' lose it, Maddy silently repeated to herself as she approached the podium, flanked by her three outwardly emotional "sisters," their carefully applied mascara running down their faces like the future 2020 images of the running hair dye of an inept, vain, and bafoonish attorney. Maddy began, "Jesus . . . I haven't seen some of you for so long . . . Oh, fu—I mean . . . um . . . I shouldn't have said Jesus . . . I mean . . . you can *say* Jesus . . . but . . . um . . . shit, let me start over."

Maddy looked at her carefully prepared notes and thought to herself, *What is it that these people need to know about uncle Joe?* She set her notes to the side and just began speaking from her heart to the highly attentive crowd in the same entertaining manner that she had made her vengeful declarations in college. "My uncle Joe was the greatest man to ever walk this earth as far as I'm concerned. No, wait. That's a fact! There was a scientific survey conducted to find who the greatest men in the history of the world were; and it turned out that uncle Joe was number one, followed by Gandhi, I think, then maybe Desmond Tutu. I'm not sure. I didn't read the whole thing. But my point is, that's science! And you can't argue with science!" There was a slight, uniform chuckle throughout the amused crowd as they watched this adorable and much beloved niece pay tribute to her uncle as only she could.

"Listen," Maddy continued, "uncle Joe never looked for fame or fortune or praise. He just wanted to do what he could to help other people. The appreciative smiles on their faces were enough for him. He didn't want his name in big gold letters. He just wanted people to respect one another. It didn't matter who you were, where you came from, who you slept with, or what your skin color was because he knew that that shit was stupid. He knew that it was just stupid to judge other people on that type of bullshit. He helped *everyone*, and he did it *equally* no matter who they were. During the height of a blizzard, he was out there in trapped people's homes fixing their pipes or whatever or delivering meals that my aunt Blair had prepared. You got a flat tire? Uncle Joe was there. Stuck in the mud? Uncle Joe was there. Need someone to take care of your dog when you have to go out of town? Uncle Joe was there. Need help carrying your groceries? Uncle Joe was there. Need to get out from under the thumb of a fuckin' bully?" Maddy paused and looked down again, unable to hold back the torrent of built-up tears any longer. "Well . . . he sure as hell was there for me," Maddy quietly stated before raising her head, her tear-soaked emerald eyes piercing through the congregation. "And he was there for a lot of you too. Maybe we all need to just take a page out of uncle Joe's book and stand together against the fuckin' bullies of this world. I know I'm gonna. He was my guardian. He was my savior. And he was my hero. And I will pay tribute to him the rest of my life." With that, she nodded at the funeral director, who shook off his shocked expression and began playing the Bill Withers classic "Lean on Me."

Upon the song's completion, there wasn't a dry eye in the house. Blair sat silently between Patty and Maddy, her hands clenching theirs tightly as if they were her personal lifesavers saving her from going under frigid waves of despair. The preacher got back up, thanked everyone for being there, and made the announcement as to the location of the gravesite service and subsequent reception.

The final song was then played. It was the song that Joe would sing as he repaired someone's home. It was the song that he sang to comfort his cherished wife following a tough day at work. It was the song that he would sing to a child who had fallen off their bike. It was the song that he would always sing to try to bring comfort to those in need. Indeed, it was the song that he quietly sang at Maddy's bedside while clinging to her blue baby blanket while watching over his viciously assaulted niece.

The opening chords began, and everyone gave each other knowing smiles before joyously singing along to the opening lines of Bob Marley's "Three Little Birds." The entire flock sang full throated while holding hands, swaying and smiling as Joseph Argento's anthem was played in his honor for a final time.

Fuck! Maddy thought. *This is where I got the whole "a little bird told me" thing.* Maddy chuckled to herself as she looked up with her mind transporting her beyond the ceiling and into the universe. *Thanks again, uncle Joe. I will always love you.*

CHAPTER 10

CHERRY BOMB

As Blair, Patty, and Maddy were walking to their red Cruiser following the gravesite service, another funeral attendee approached the trio of mourning women. Maddy immediately felt a chill run down her spine and a shot of fearful adrenaline as she thought, *Oh fuck! The duffel bag is still in the trunk! Just be cool. Just be cool. Just be cool.*

Detective Simmons spoke to the ladies in his most sincere voice, "Ladies, once again, I am so sorry for your loss. It's a loss for all of us in this town. Joe did more for us all than a lot of people realize."

Blair gave the detective a knowing nod before saying, "Thank you, Officer, for your kind words and for attending today and last night. Your presence was . . . reassuring."

Maddy thought to herself that this conversation was kind of creepy, as though these two seemed to be speaking in code. *What the fuck is up with these two?* she pondered.

"Well, I know nothing can bring Joe back, but at least you won't have to go through the stress of a trial for the dirtbag that did this," the nearly retired fifty-three-year veteran of the force continued.

"W-what do you mean, Detective?" Maddy inquired demurely.

Donning his official voice, Detective Simmons began explaining, "Well, it hasn't hit the news yet. We wanted to keep this under wraps until after the funeral, y'know, just out of respect for all of you. But that guy was in a car accident last night. He drove his car right into a light pole. The entire front end was smashed all the way into the cabin, and his head was planted into the pole. I've never seen anything like it. A light pole with the back of a head of hair sticking out of it. He died on impact. Strangest thing though. The impact must have caused his brake lines to be cut somehow. And his accelerator was stuck." He then looked right at Maddy. He knew her reputation in high school for hijinks and that she was always suspected of what had happened to the local track star. But there was never any proof, and she was Joe's niece, so the investigation as to the identity of the perpetrator was perfunctory at best.

Maddy looked directly into the eyes of the detective as he spoke to her with her eyebrows raised and bottom lip slightly puckered out so as to appear as innocent as possible.

"Well, this guy had a long list of enemies. You folks were just the most recent, and I know where you all were last night. I saw you all at the visitation myself, so my guess is that this one's gonna go cold pretty quickly. Besides, there's not much appetite for finding the killer of the man who murdered a local hero. So you all rest as easy as you can, all right?"

As the detective walked away from the three relieved women, Patty said to Blair, "Goddammit, Blair, this shit's gotta end."

Blair looked at her niece, the nervous sweat beginning to dry on her brow, and smiled. "I have no idea what you're talking about Patty."

"Oh, fuck it!" an exasperated Patty exclaimed. "Let's blow off the reception and go to the Diner. You know that's where Joe would have gone after a shit day like this."

"Fuuuck yeah!" Maddy excitedly exclaimed. "I'll call Sam and the girls and have them meet us there! Oh shit . . . what will I order?"

Jules drew the proverbial short straw and was seated next to Maddy at the diner. She thought that her meal might be shielded due to Maddy being distracted by her former coworkers coming up to her with joyful greetings and mournful hugs while discussing an upcoming sandwich that the diner would begin to feature. The "Joe Argento" would be a grilled roast beef and provolone on pumpernickel topped with fresh tomato slices and homemade creamy Italian dressing. Everyone at the table ordered one except for Jules. She foolishly ordered herself a patty melt. As she didn't care for roast beef, she thought that the grilled hamburger on pumpernickel would suffice as a tribute and be close enough to the "Joe Argento," so as to ward off Maddy's provocative advances toward her lunch. She was mistaken. Thinking it too harsh to stab Maddy with a fork at this time, she simply slapped Maddy's invading hand and said, "Keep your fuckin' hands off of my food!"

Grins and chuckles were evident around the table as Maddy retorted in a childlike voice while looking down at her "injured" hand, "Geez, it's just a bite of a sandwich and . . . I'm in mourning, y'know? Some friend you are."

Jules let out an exasperated sigh, looked up at the ceiling, and said, "Fine, but just one bite and just this one time. Any other time and I'll fuck you up!" Maddy gleefully took the half sandwich off Jules's plate, tore off the top, squirted a healthy glob of mustard, replaced the top, and took a huge bite. Jules, who also despised mustard, just shook her head as she said, "You are such a fucking bitch."

A muffled retort of "Takes one to know one!" came from Maddy's bulging face that displayed an ornery smile and puffed- out cheeks that resembled a chipmunk collecting nuts.

Everyone in the household was exhausted physically, emotionally, and spiritually that evening and collapsed into their respective beds by 9:00 pm, except for one dark silhouette sitting alone beside the firepit eating butter ripple ice cream while watching the contents of a discarded garbage bag burn to ashes. Looking out at the lone figure from her bedroom window, her niece's emerald eyes mirroring the dancing flames, Blair thought, *Well, it's not the first time the pit has been used for that . . . and it won't be the last.*

———

As the plane glided closer to New York and away from her familial support system, a deep depression was beginning to take hold of Maddy. By the time the plane landed, she was filled with internal despair. She felt as though she had no control over her life following the takeover of her nation's decency, the betrayal by her best friend, and the tragic loss of her spiritual anchor. She was a rudderless ship in the eye of a storm and felt powerless to find a direction to steer herself, choosing instead to emotionally list helplessly as hurtful waves of torment battered her soul.

Maddy outwardly was able to put on the act of holding everything together. She had had years of experience of keeping personal tragedy hidden behind her charming smile, off-beat sense of humor, and boisterous laugh. But internally she was a tortured soul whose outlook seemed hopeless. And, as with most people who suffer from clinical depression, Maddy began to self-medicate. By day, she was an efficient manager of a thriving bookstore, helpful neighbor, and loyal friend. By night, she transformed into a party girl, wearing slinky short dresses, drinking excessively, dabbling with drugs, and frequently bedding a disposable distraction.

A new young lady started employment at the shop about two weeks after Maddy's return. She presented multiple bruises on her arms and legs when her long sleeves or hem of her dress would be forced to rise up while performing her job's responsibilities of stocking or retrieving merchandise from higher shelves. When asked, Amanda would always say that she's " just such a klutz" and laugh the inquiry away. Maddy saw no evidence of her being a "klutz" as she would effortlessly move from one responsibility or customer to another, never coming close to running into anything or falling.

On July 3, Amanda's husband came into the shop to visit. Accompanying him was their seven-year-old daughter. Maddy could not help but notice that the daughter displayed the same klutz-like injuries as her mother, so when the family went behind a secluded book rack in the back of the store, Maddy nestled herself behind an adjacent rack, listening intensely to the conversation that had already begun.

"Listen, don't make this a fuckin' thing, all right? It's just a party. We're gonna go to Hampton Beach, watch some fireworks, and blow some shit up . . . Do you *really* wanna make this a big deal?" the husband exclaimed in a threatening tone. "N-no," Amanda began, "b-but you said we were spending the evening together tonight. You promised us . . . you—"

It was then that Maddy heard a firm slapping sound followed by "Listen, bitch, I know you thought you could tie me down by having this fucking kid, but it didn't work, okay? I'm going to that party, and you two had better be home when I get back tonight. You know I'll fucking find you wherever you might try to hide, so don't even try it!" Maddy then heard the husband's heavy footsteps growing fainter as the pair of desperate sobs from behind the other rack grew louder.

Amanda composed herself and said to her traumatized daughter, "Okay . . . smiles, okay? Listen, I've got to work, but maybe I can have you look at books in the children's section until I get off, okay?"

"Y-yes, Momma," came the daughter's defeated reply. The pair left and returned to the front of the store. Maddy slipped through the locked file room that was in the back middle of the store and was at the front counter seconds before the pair arrived. Upon seeing her boss, Amanda apologetically said, "Maddy, um . . . something came up with my husband and, um . . . I don't have anywhere for her to go until the end of my shift . . . so . . . um . . ."

"That's okay," Maddy enthusiastically exclaimed. "I'll tell ya what, sweety. I have a TV and DVD player in my office. Why dontcha go pick out a movie and you can watch it in there until your mom can take you home, all right?"

"Thank you!" the little girl said with a forced smile upon her face that was all too familiar for Maddy.

As Maddy was leaving for the evening, a coworker said, "Hey, Maddy, big plans tonight?"

Maddy, not breaking stride, replied in a deep, determined voice, "I gotta party to go to. Really lookin' forward to it."

Hampton Beach was a place where Maddy and her friends frequented often, especially during college. They had found a little alcove that was surrounded by rocks that they could drink and cavort at without the prying eyes of the cops or unwanted advances of muscle-ripped Romeos. The one drawback to the area is that the tide would come into this alcove earlier than the rest of the beach, which would cut the evening a bit short. That final feature went from being a liability to an asset on this particular evening. Maddy placed her prepared duffel bag in the alcove along with a beach blanket and a six-pack. In the bag, she had assembled everything that she needed for her evening's festivities. The contents of the bag would become a staple for Maddy that she would have available from that evening on— just in case a "chad" reared its ugly head. Change of baggy dark clothes, shoes (two sizes too large), garbage bags, smelling salt, nightstick, pepper spray, zip locks, burner phone, wig, ball cap, sunglasses, scalpel, hunting knives, sleeping pills, body wash, binoculars, multiple types of gloves, hairnets, and the ever-popular duct tape. There were three more items in the bag this evening just for this special occasion.

Bands of revelers with their explosive entertainment and coolers of libations in tow began arriving at various points on the beach. Maddy crouched in the shadows of the rocks and through her binoculars scanned the various groups for her unsuspecting prey. She found him about fifty yards down the beach with a group of about twelve other people. He began drinking as soon as the cooler was placed in the sand. She made her way to an area about twenty yards away from the party and stooped behind a tall stretch of beach grass. The sun began to set, and the celebratory explosions began to light up the darkening sky. Maddy just waited.

She did not have to wait long. After about twenty minutes, the husband went to the grassy area only about ten yards from where Maddy was lurking. He let out an audible "Whooo!" as he relieved himself. He zipped his pants and turned back toward the direction of his party only to be met with a petite young lady walking toward him. She was barefoot, wearing Daisy Duke denim shorts and a tight red tank top.

"So is pissin' the only thing that cock is good for?" she inquired, wearing a lascivious smile.

"Fuck no," the man replied.

"Yeah? I'm feelin' a little frisky tonight. You wanna show me some real fireworks?" Maddy brazenly asked. "I found a quiet little spot just a little way down the beach. I've got beer, a blanket . . . and me! Wanna play?"

The slightly intoxicated husband arrogantly didn't think twice about the offer and assertively said, "Fuck yeah, baby. Let's go." The dark pair sauntered thirty yards down the sandy trail and disappeared behind a large grouping of rocks as an exploding kaleidoscope of color showered down upon the gathered crowd.

Upon reaching their destination, the man grabbed Maddy and began to aggressively kiss and grope her. "Whoa, whoa, whoa . . . slow down, tiger!" Maddy said as she nudged the man away from her, still smiling. "I'm up for it and everything, but I'm *not* into sand in my ass, so be a dear and spread the blanket out first, okay?" The man begrudgingly took the blanket, unfolded it, and bent over to lay it upon the ground.

The next image he saw was a smiling Maddy, her maniacal green eyes being illuminated by a detonating red Roman candle. She had smelling salts under his nose in her left hand and a wooden nightstick in the other. And he couldn't move. Not a muscle. His hands were bound behind his back, and his feet were bound together. He felt several objects in his mouth which he attempted to push out with his tongue, but his mouth had been secured shut in a viselike grip by multiple layers of duct tape being applied from over his head to under his chin.

He began struggling against the zip locks that bound him while expressing muffled cries of desperation.

"Hey, hey, hey . . .," Maddy began in a gently reassuring voice, "it's going to be okay. I just want to talk to you a bit about statistics, then this will all be over, so just chillax, okay?" He quit struggling and stared at Maddy with confused and fear- filled eyes.

Before beginning, Maddy surveyed the scene to make sure she was prepared to make her hasty exit. The garbage bag was at the ready as were her change of baggy black clothes and a hunting knife. Everything that was not needed at this point had been packed back into the duffel bag and secured under a rock overhang on the other side of the alcove so as to avoid becoming contaminated. "Yep, let's get started," Maddy stated as she turned back toward the quivering disoriented man.

"Did you know," Maddy began as though she were beginning an academic lecture while waving the nightstick like a baton, "that about ten million people are victims of domestic violence every year and that 25 percent of women are victims of this abuse at some point in their lives? Did you know that, chad? Did you know that over four million children are identified as victims of abuse each year? *Four fucking million!* And that's just the one's that we know about! That's a lot of people who are put through physical and emotional trauma, chad. A lot of fuckin' people who are now so damaged that they're gonna have to really struggle to be able to lead normal lives or find healthy relationships. It really makes them all sorts of being fucked up in the head!"

Maddy then crouched right in front of the man with macabre illuminations and shadows fluttering about her face as the booming explosions continued. "I've always wondered what would drive a man to beat on a woman or child . . . or pet for that matter. I've really thought about that, and do you know what I came up with, chad? I came to the realization that"—her face immediately transformed from bemusement to stone-cold determination before continuing—"I don't give a fuck. There *are* no reasons to beat on another person, especially someone who's much smaller or physically weaker. I don't give a fuck what your reasons are or why you get off beating your sweet wife or that adorable little girl. Daddy didn't love you enough? Waaaaa! See a fuckin' therapist. Bad day at work? Waaaaa! Get another fuckin' job. Self-image problems? Waaaa! Put down the potato chips and hit the fuckin' gym. Low self- esteem? Waaaa! Put down the fuckin' video games and go do something with your life. There are no reasons and there are no excuses for your adding to these horrible statistics. I've looked into the eyes of your wife and child. And do you know what I saw? Hopelessness and fear. No one should have to live with that. Fuckin' no one. So . . . since you're really into adding to statistics, I thought I'd do you a favor and volunteer your name to a statistic. I'm just not sure which statistic it will be. Will it be missing persons? Will it be people lost from the undertow? Will it be murder victims? Or will it be . . ."

Struggling to fit her slight hand into the constricted denim, Maddy pulled out a lighter and showed it to the cowering man, the sweat pouring down his face the only motion his bound body could perform. "Fireworks casualty?" Maddy concluded. Her maniacal grin returned as she lit the fuses of two saran- wrapped M80s and one cherry bomb (mainly as a tribute to ice cream sundaes) that were lodged in the man's mouth.

Maddy got up and quickly ran to the edge of the surf, giggling in anticipation. She turned around to see the man desperately flailing his head as the glimmer of sparks drew precariously closer to their finality. Then . . . *boom!* An explosion was added to the chorus of explosions from the nearby parties. Brain, flesh, blood, and bone particles rained down upon the alcove like gooey confetti in a demented ticker tape parade.

"Whoaaa!" Maddy excitedly exclaimed through her continued laughter as she jumped with joy and clapped her hands. "That . . . was . . . fucking . . . *awesome!* Best fuckin' Fourth *ever!*" Maddy went over to the fresh corpse. The jaw and top of the head had been completely blown off and decimated. She removed the zip ties and the traces of remaining duct tape with the knife and tossed them into the garbage bag. She jumped into the surf to wash away the chad's remnants, removed the wet clothes, put them into the garbage bag, and changed into the baggy black clothing. She put on the black ball cap, looked down, and became royally pissed. "Goddamn that motherfucker!" Maddy exclaimed.

"He got his brains and shit all over the beer! Gaaawwwd! Now I'm getting wet again!" she lamented as she rinsed the six- pack off in the rising surf.

As she approached the bookstore on July 5, the Brooklyn sanitation department was removing the refuse on the block as normally scheduled. A large dumpster was lifted and dumped into the back of the impressive truck, its contents becoming smashed. Maddy stood and watched for a moment as a familiar- looking garbage bag was deposited. She turned and began to head toward her work. Upon her entry into the store, her coworker inquired, "How was your party the other night?"

Maddy dryly responded, "Didn't go. Thought all the loud noise would give me a headache, so I just stayed home and did some . . . research. Hung with my friend Kristy and her kids last night though. Did sparklers and shit. Ate some of Jason's grilled burgers and hot dogs. Kristy's potato salad didn't have enough mustard but was edible with enough salt. Y'know, typical Fourth shit."

Amanda filed a missing person report on the same day. A look of worry covered her face as she expressed her concern about her husband's where-abouts. Maddy listened graciously while holding her trembling hand. The following Monday, Amanda came into the shop wearing a bit more makeup than usual and a considerably shorter dress. Her daughter was holding her hand. The adorably freckled face could not hide her ease as she heard her mother explain to Maddy, "Hey . . . I'm gonna have to be a bit late this morn-ing. I'm really sorry, but I have to fill out some papers at her new day care. You see . . ." She began explaining what Maddy had already learned. "Well . . . they found him. Or . . . parts of him. He apparently got drunk and got swept up in the tide and got eaten by the . . . fish . . . or whatever."

"I'm so sorry," Maddy replied as sincerely as she could muster. Amanda looked at Maddy with piercing eyes and said, "Yeah, well . . . I told him not to go to that party. When will men ever learn?' She then turned to leave before abruptly rotating back, handed Maddy a CD, and said, "Do you think we could play this over the system today? I especially like track 5."

"Sure, why not?" Maddy agreed as she looked at the Chicks album *Fly*. She turned the disc over and read that track 5 was "Goodbye Earl."

CHAPTER 11

ASHES TO ASHES

It was December 5, 2018, and Jules and Sam were tittering in the corner of the hospital waiting room, slightly buzzed from the wine that they had snuck in to consume while they awaited the birth of Kristy's latest addition to her and Jason's brood.

"C'mon, Maddy, quit your pouting, get your ass over here, and have a drink with us," Sam ordered to the black-clad figure sitting on the opposite side of the room. Her black hood was up over her sunken head. She was more consumed with feelings of shame and rage at this moment than celebratory for Kristy and her family.

It had been exactly two weeks since she was last in this hospital, but for a drastically different reason. She once again reflected on her mistakes from the past year and a half that had threatened her relationship with her best friends, her family, and her very life. Her depression had caused her to bottom out in her social life, and she began engaging in risky behavior that increased as time went on as she searched for a more impactful high to drown in. Almost every evening, except for Mondays, which became widely known as her night to stay in to read or to do research, she was out at the clubs. Even her sacred Wednesday evenings became an obligatory appearance with her friends before jetting off to the next party. Her drinking had become excessive, and she had begun dabbling in drugs. Maddy had shunned anything stronger than the occasional hit of pot out of fear of becoming addicted. She understood how obsessive her personality could be and that even the slight dabbling with hard drugs may send her down the rabbit hole of lifelong addiction. That hole was beginning to be dug.

And then there were the men. Almost every evening there was a new, disposable male distraction to play with. Sam and Jules enjoyed playing around, but Maddy was taking it to a whole new level. She was usually intoxicated at the time of these hookups, so was vulnerable to any type of sexual or physical abuse. She had always had a strict rule about becoming involved in any way with married men, but adherence to this rule evaporated as the white lines in the ladies' room became more prevalent. She was searching for anything or anyone that could momentarily shield her from the intense feelings of loss that were consuming her, and what those distractions were became less and less important.

Maddy met a young man in a run-down, seedy bar on the extreme south side of her neighborhood in early November. He was twenty-two, eight years her junior, which was a change of pace for her. He was dark and sullen. He had endless grievances against the people and societal systems in our world, and Maddy felt an instant kinship with him. He reflected her own darkened outlook on life and society. Around him, she thought, she could drop whatever prescribed act that was required by any particular social scene and just be her own morose self. He was also a junkie. He was renting a room in a shoddy flophouse that he paid for through same-sex favors to the landlord and his associates. He was a self-described artist but had no real talent to speak of, so he had no legitimate prospects when he moved to the heart of the city away from his upper-middle-class and quite privileged suburban upbringing. He thought of himself as a rebel and as one of the few people in the world who could see the "truth" behind corporate and political greed. Through her painstaked eyes, Maddy initially saw him as a modern-day prophet.

The rest of the world, or at least those that noticed him, saw him for what he was. He was an insignificant spoiled brat rich kid who thought he was something important but gave no effort to try to accomplish anything. He was a user, not only of smack, but of people; and instead of applying himself, he quickly retreated into the constant cycle of hustling people in order to obtain his next high. And one of the best ways to use people is to get them hooked on him and his injected venom. In him, Maddy saw a visionary. In her, he saw a meal ticket, not unlike other meal tickets, both male and female that he had charmed into a heroin-fueled haze, only to then hand them off to depraved others to sexually exploit through prostitution or worse. He was, in essence, the neighborhood groomer for the local sex traffickers; and in Maddy, he had found the perfect emotionally vulnerable victim. Her looks didn't hurt either. *Damn, I'm gonna live for a year off of this little piece*, he conspired to himself.

Maddy's friends became increasingly concerned as they watched their friend's self-medication increase to dangerous levels. All lights began flashing red when they learned where she was hanging out. They knew that area of town and knew the trajectory that their friend was on. They also knew that the bottom that Maddy was about to hit was one that many aren't able to return from. So on Wednesday, November 21, Sam prepared Maddy's favorite appetizers for a pre-Thanksgiving feast, gathered Jules and a very pregnant Kristy, and awaited their friend's arrival.

It did not go well. Upon her arrival, Maddy exclaimed through her now rapidly paced cadence. "Hey, all! Can't stay long. Gotta see my new guy. Just gonna stay for one drink, then gotta split!"

Sam countered with "C'mon, Maddy. Look, I made those fried pizza things you love. Just hang with us for a bit, okay?"

"Nope, not hungry, but thanks for the effort. Where's the gin?" Maddy retorted.

Sam, never one to be known for her patience, quickly became irritated and ordered, "Maddy, sit down!" It went downhill from there.

"What the fuck, bitch, I'm not your fuckin' kid, all right?" Maddy incredulously stated.

"Listen, Maddy," Jules chimed in, trying to salvage this rescue mission, "we're just worried about you. We know where you've been hanging out and what you've been up to. We just think that maybe you should get some . . . professional help . . . y'know . . . before this shit gets really bad. I mean, what would your uncle Joe say?" Jules knew that this last line was a mistake before it exited her lips.

"Don't . . . you . . . fucking . . . *ever* . . . !" Maddy began, her voice rising into a rapid-fire cadence. "What would Uncle Joe say? I think he'd say that I'm doing fine . . . yeah . . . that I'm finally hitting my groove and am finally happy. That he's glad that I've met someone who sees the world as it actually is, not how you bitches see it from inside your own asses! What the fuck am I doing that's so different, huh? You all party. You two fuck anything that moves, and you, Kristy, with your perfect little family. Yeah, I bet Jason has all kinds of fucked-up secrets that you don't know about. I bet he's banging his secretary even as we speak! But you wouldn't see that in your perfect little world, raising your perfect little kids!" Maddy's jealousy of her friend was laid bare.

Kristy looked up at Maddy with tears beginning to form and said, "Why would you say that to me? What have I done to make you say such a hurtful thing?"

Kristy's emotional plea momentarily broke through Maddy's cocaine-fueled fog. She felt a brief instant of remorse, before realizing that she didn't want to feel that or anything ever again. "Y'know what? Fuck this!" Maddy said in conclusion. "Do me a favor and just disappear like that other bitch did. I don't need you dragging me down!" There was the harsh slam of the heavy wooden door, and the scene was over. Or was it?

"This isn't over," Sam bluntly stated as she regained her self- assurance and began barking orders.

Maddy went to the cheap hotel that her man was at with the requested amount of heroin and required paraphernalia. "Yeah, babe, that's my girl," he said while lying on the stained mattress as Maddy entered the room. The wall-paper was shredded as cockroaches emerged from cracks in the wall. There was the stale scent of urine and sex. And Maddy didn't mind. She described the earlier confrontation with her friends as she unpacked her wares and undressed.

This is perfect, the opportunistic grifter thought to himself. "Yeah, babe. People like that just don't get it, you know? C'mon . . . let me turn you on. Let me show you the world as it really is."

Maddy awoke the next day to the vision of aunt Blair's solemnly stern expression. "W-where am I? What's going on? W-why am I restrained?" Maddy awkwardly blurted out.

"Well, dear, you nearly died," Blair began. "I'm going to get a nurse to get you checked out and give you some time to orient yourself. Then . . . you and I are going to have a little chat." Maddy didn't care for the tone of that last remark.

The doctor came in, checked Maddy out, and said flatly, "You're damn lucky to have the friends that you have. If they had found you ten minutes later, you would be dead right now. We need this bed, so we're discharging you in an hour. You'll be all right, I guess. I hope to never see you in here again, but I probably will. It's usually just a matter of time for you people."

Under ordinary circumstances, Blair would have recoiled at anyone speaking to her beloved niece in such a manner and leapt to her defense. But today, all that was heard from the figure in the dark corner of the room was "Thank you, Doctor."

"Oh fuck, aunt Blair, I'm so—" Maddy began before being abruptly cut off by the direct voice of a visibly disappointed Blair.

"No . . . it isn't going to be that easy. You are going to lay there, and you are going to listen to me. I want you to know what you have put us all through. I know that you don't want to feel anything anymore. I know that you've been through a lot these past two years. But so have I. And you don't see me lying in a hospital bed, causing my loved ones to hurt the way you are doing to all of us right now. Today, my dearest, you are going to feel again. You are going to feel what we are all feeling. You will then be allowed to apologize. And then"— Blair purposefully paused dramatically, leaned over, and stared into her niece's soul—"you, young lady, are going to get your fucking shit together."

Blair then described the events of the earlier evening. How Kristy, fast approaching her due date, was dispatched to her home to call Blair and Patty and to be the main point of communication. She would relay updates to the aunts and closely monitor police emergency dispatches. Jules and Sam split up and began scouring the seedy neighborhood that they knew Maddy had retreated to. Both women had to use pepper spray to ward of respective would-be assailants. About a half hour into the search, Sam was nearly run over by a fleeing skinny man while she entered a dilapidated hotel. She threatened the hotel manager with calling the police if he didn't tell her which room the girl in the picture was. "Yeah, fine . . . she's in room 18. What the fuck do I care anyway?" came the manager's response. Sam opened the door to the sight of her convulsing naked friend, gagging on her own vomit. She quickly turned her over with one hand and dialed 911 with the other. She began manually scooping the vomit out of Maddy's mouth to clear the air passage while calling Jules. "I've got her! It isn't good!

I've called 911! Call Kristy and get over here!" Sam frantically stated.

The police and paramedics arrived and immediately administered naloxone to the obviously overdosed woman. They put her on a stretcher and rushed her to the hospital as the dazed faces of Sam and Jules looked on. They hailed a cab and arrived at the hospital twenty minutes after the ambulance. They pleaded for information but were told that they were not entitled to any. They would have to wait until next of kin arrived. It was the most heart-wrenching four hours of their lives.

Blair arrived, immediately identified herself, and insisted that she see her niece. It was only when Blair gave the pair of heroines a thank-filled hug that Sam and Jules knew that their friend had made it. The information was relayed to Kristy, and the three friends broke down in a release of tense emotion.

Blair concluded with "I left Patty at home. I didn't want her to see you . . . like this. Now, your friends are in the waiting room and would like to see you. I suggest you let them in. And I suggest you make it good." Maddy just slowly nodded, tears streaming down her face as she watched her aunt depart.

A very similar scene was played out as Blair made Sam, Jules, and Kristy repeat the exact same story, but from their perspective and through their own emotional trauma. This was the intervention that the ladies had hoped for the previous night. They were filled with regret that its success had to come at such a traumatic price. Kristy was the final woman to speak. Her final line to Maddy was "I forgive you for what you said to me because I love you. But if you ever say something like that about my husband or family again, our friendship is over. Do you understand?"

Maddy looked up at the four sober faces standing around her. She had always taken great pride in her personal strength and her ability to use that strength to protect others. But when the chips were down, she folded. She realized that it was the strength and support of these women that had sustained *her* and not the other way around. She timidly bowed her head in reverence to these models of feminine power and said, "I don't know how, but I'm going to make this up to each one of you. I don't have the words to express how ashamed I feel right now or how grateful I am to have you all in my life. My life that I nearly ended by my stupidity and immaturity. And I'm so sorry that I've ruined everybody's holiday. But this year, I truly understand the meaning of Thanksgiving, because I am so thankful to you all for saving my life. I can never fully repay you, but I'll do everything that I can to be the best friend and niece that I can be. That's my promise to you."

"We're gonna hold you to that, bitch," Jules callously responded. "Now, put on these clean clothes and let's get you out of here. Oh, by the way, I called your work and gave your boss some bullshit excuse as to why you're not there today. You're welcome . . . again."

Two weeks later, Maddy found herself in the same hospital with the same friends and remembered her promise to them. She took her hood off her head and looked at her two giggling companions. "Yeah, okay, enough of the pity-party shit. Let me have a swig of that wine."

Jason came into the waiting room a short while later with the same proud expression that he had carried two years prior. "It's a girl!" he exclaimed as the three friends enveloped him in a congratulatory embrace.

Jesus, Kristy's one lucky bitch. He really is a nice guy, Maddy thought as she collected her things, including a black duffel bag. "Hey, where are ya going?" Sam inquired with a concerned expression.

"Listen . . . I'm okay. I just have something that I need to take care of, okay? I'll talk to you all tomorrow."

As Maddy walked along the downtrodden side streets of the neighborhood that had nearly terminated her, she thought about people who carried the horrendous affliction of substance abuse, especially opioids. There were millions of people who had gotten hooked on that shit, many of whom were innocent surgery patients who had been duped by "Dr. Feelgoods" who traded their Hippocratic oath in for kickbacks from some pharmaceutical companies who put profit above the common welfare of society. It was as disgusting as it was predictable. Not every addict is to blame for their plight, she thought. But every "chad" is responsible for the havoc that they unleash upon others. This motherfucker wasn't a victim. He was a gutless "chad." She called him on her burner phone.

"Hey, babe, where are ya at? I've got some candy," she innocently inquired.

"You . . . you're all right . . . but I thought . . . I mean . . .," the stuttering grifter stated surprisingly.

"Naw, I'm fine. Just first-time jitters, I guess. C'mon, where are ya? I wanna see my guy!"

Maddy went to the cheap hotel that her former man was at with the required amount of heroin and paraphernalia. "Yeah, babe, *there's* my guy," she said while observing him lying on the stained mattress. The wallpaper was shredded as cockroaches emerged from cracks in the wall. There was the stale scent of urine and sex. And Maddy didn't mind. She described a brief reaction to her hit from two weeks ago, and the clueless con man ate it up through the haze of his last fix.

This is perfect, the opportunistic executioner thought to herself. "Yeah, babe. I think I'm really starting to get it, you know? C'mon . . . now let me turn *you* on. Let me show you *my* world as it really is."

Maddy just sat there silently and watched. She watched through her emblazoned emerald eyes with a sly smile on her face. She watched as he mumbled something incoherently. She watched as his pupils dilated into nothingness. She watched as he began shivering, then convulsing. She watched as vomit began spewing from his mouth, encasing his entire face. She watched as he violently gasped for breath, shooting geysers of vomit into the air as he did so. She watched as his body twitched one final time, the entire contents of his stomach oozing down his face and resting on the stained carpet in chunky tan pools. *Well,* that *was kinda gross,* Maddy thought as she grabbed the man's wallet from the nightstand. *Fuck, he musta scored sucking cock or dealing or somethin',* Maddy speculated as she removed $180 from his wallet. Her petite gloved hand tossed the wallet back onto the nightstand as she turned toward the door, never looking back.

CHAPTER 12

SPRING HEALED JACK

The bustling Christmas season finally concluded, and Maddy decided to spend New Year's back in Madison. She would arrive New Year's Eve, spend the next day at home to recover from her anticipated hangover, and fly back on January 2 in order to attend her weekly Wednesday ritual with her friends, which would be held at Kristy's house to celebrate her new daughter. She had not been back since her uncle's funeral, and she wanted to start the new year by visiting his gravesite. She also had bridges to rebuild with her two aunts.

She rented a car at the airport and drove directly to her uncle's gravesite. His tombstone was three feet taller than most in the cemetery as many people in the community had chipped in to purchase a most elegant tribute to their local luminary. There was a light dusting of snow, which Maddy carefully brushed away from the black marble. The surface of the stone glistened in the afternoon sun, and the engraving appeared to jump off the surface. There was no wind whatsoever, and her copper strands just lay motionless upon her solemn head as she stood in the frigid temperatures, reading this most beautiful and simple tribute.

Joseph Angelo Argento October 1, 1942 to June 5, 2017
Beloved Husband, Brother-in-Law, Uncle, and Friend
Shelter to Many, Justice for All

"Well . . . I suppose you heard about the stupid shit I've been up to," Maddy began embarrassingly, looking down and shuffling her small feet as she spoke as though she were a five- year-old trying to explain where the cookies had gone. "Well, I don't have any real good excuses. I allowed my head to get fucked up. And I put a lot of people through needless worry. That's on me. I alone did that shit, and I alone have to fix it. I promise you, starting this year, I'll do better. I'm not one for New Year's resolutions, but I'm gonna make you my New Year's promise, so here it goes . . ." Maddy straightened herself, looked directly at the black marble, and began in an assertive voice:

"Numero uno: No more fucking drugs . . . ever! That shit nearly killed me, and I liked it too much, so that shit's done!

"Numero two-o: Drinking back to normal levels. Y'know, just fucked up enough to have a good time, but not so fucked up that I'm gonna put myself in danger.

"Numero three-o: No more sleeping around . . . very much. I mean . . . y'know . . . if it's kinda a boyfriend, then I guess it's okay . . . but . . . well . . . no more one-night stands I guess is what I'm trying to say . . . unless they're supercute . . . but probably not even then. And definitely no married guys."

Her voice dropped to a whisper as she leaned into the ebony gravestone and concluded with

"Numero four-o: Don't kill anybody this year. Even if they have it coming. I've gotten lucky so far, so I'd better hang that shit up while I'm ahead."

She stood upright once more before concluding, "Okay . . . that's it. I love you, and I miss you every fucking day, and I hope you're giving angels a bunch of shit about what's going on down here, 'cause they seem to be just sittin' on their asses. Okay, I'm going now." She finished by wiping frozen tears from her lightly freckled beet-red cheeks. As she walked toward her car, a light breeze ruffled her copper strands as a lone bird chirped in the distance.

Maddy arrived at the Argento home and was immediately embraced by aunt Blair. "Welcome home, dear. We're so excited to see you!"

Aunt Patty walked into the foyer and gazed upon her niece with a worried expression. "Aunt Patty . . . I'm so sorry. I-I swear, I-I'll never . . . oh please don't hate me!" Maddy broke down in tears as the elder aunt embraced her tightly and said soothingly, "I could never hate you . . . You are the light of my life. Just don't pull this shit again, okay?" Maddy nodded to her aunt as she relinquished her grip, both women wiping the tears from their eyes and smiling at each other. "So . . . let's get ready for this fucking party! I'm ready to get fucked up!" Patty exclaimed as the three women initiated their hasty preparations. There were about thirty people at the Argentos' home that evening, most of whom were close family friends. Patty, at sixty-six, still had a knack for attracting companions ten to fifteen years her junior; and tonight was no different. Her still- toned legs were encased in black fishnets that were, in turn, frequently wrapped around a fifty-something bleach blonde who was adorned with tattoos and a Black Flag long-sleeved T. Maddy kind of liked this one. She had "TUFF" tattooed on the knuckles of one hand and "LUV!" on the other. When not enveloped with her latest conquest, Patty was changing CDs or records on the stereo. Especially when somebody dared to put on something that she found to be too "mellow."

"Who is fucking with the stereo?" she would bellow as an embarrassed guest would hastily try to put away something in the vein of Andrew Gold's greatest hits. "Okay, bitch, I love you, but you're banned from the stereo for tonight. This is a fuckin' party, not a family vacation," Patty would scold as she scoured the music collection for something more appropriate.

Aunt Blair circulated around the party as she had always done, refreshing drinks, cleaning up, and engaging in idle chitchat. There was one man at the party that Blair seemed to spend more time with than others. His name was Edgar and had been a family friend for many years. He was seventy-two and had lost his wife a few years earlier to cancer.

As the evening wore on, Maddy finally summoned up her courage and found her aunt in the kitchen filling the potato chip bowl. "Um . . . aunt Blair . . .," Maddy awkwardly began. "Um . . . so . . . y'know . . . what's up with you and Edgar?"

"Well, dear, there are some things that I do not feel I need to explain. But since you asked, we have known Edgar for a very long time, and he has always been a nice man, so we have been seeing each other from time to time to . . . comfort each other." A rare blush encased Blair's perfect cheeks before she haphazardly picked up the bowl, spilling half of its contents upon the floor. "Well, now, isn't that nice?" Blair said with exasperation.

Through a half chuckle, Maddy said, "It's okay, aunt Blair. That's your business, and I'm sorry I asked. But . . . you're kinda acting like a schoolgirl, and I'm not the only one who noticed so—"

Blair cut her off immediately and sternly said, "Oh, a schoolgirl, am I?

Well, listen here, little missy . . . I . . .” Blair and Maddy broke down into laughter and embraced as Blair stated, “Okay, but even at this age, I still have needs, and I really don’t want to discuss this any further . . . okay?”

“Yup . . . got it,” Maddy replied as she began to sweep up the tragically wasted salted snack treats.

Blair straightened herself and began leaving the kitchen before turning and saying, “Thank you for cleaning that up. And thank you for your understanding. You need to know that nobody can ever replace my Joseph.”

“I get it,” Maddy stated in conclusion. “You’re just a horny old bitch. Good for you is what I say! Just keep a lot of blue pills on hand!”

Patty concluded 2018 by playing a raucous rendition of “Auld Lang Syne” by Me First and the Gimme Gimmes. She welcomed 2019 by playing the uplifting “Let the Day Begin” by the Call. The last of the guests left the party around three thirty in the morning, and the fatigued and inebriated hostesses (and their companions) poured themselves into their respective beds. Maddy was drifting off to sleep when she heard the telltale sound of creaking bedsprings coming from Blair’s bedroom. “Ohhhh, fucking gross!” she loudly exclaimed as she wrapped her pillow around her head, attempting to purge the sound from her consciousness.

The following evening, Maddy and Blair were alone in the house. A college bowl game was on the TV. “Why is this on? You don’t like football,” Maddy inquired.

“No, but my Joseph did,” Blair sentimentally responded. “It wouldn’t be New Year’s if it wasn’t on, and I find it comforting. Please, dear, sit with me. I need to have a discussion with you.”

Uh-uh, Maddy thought. *What did I fuck up now?*

Blair began in a serious yet thoughtful tone. “I need to speak with you about responsibility. When one starts down the trail of . . . justice, shall we say . . . there are certain rules that must be abided.”

“Ummm . . . Aunt Blair . . . I’m not gonna—” Maddy attempted to retort before being interrupted by Blair.

“Please, dear. Just listen to me. When one engages in these . . . practices . . . it must be for the right reasons. It must be someone who has done something terrible or is a significant threat to someone else and who is out of the reach of conventional . . . punishment. It must never be done for petty infractions or differences and must *never* be done solely for our own gratification. Do you understand so far?”

"Uh . . . yeah . . . I know, but—" Maddy replied before once again being cut off.

"Yes or no is all that I need from you at this moment. Now, let's continue. And there are many bad women out there as well, but I have never believed that any one of *us* should *ever* do anything to permanently harm one of our sisters. For them, I believe that their punishment, *if* deserving, shall come in its own natural due course.

"Now, if someone is to do something to another person, then that someone needs to be careful about it and take others' safety into consideration. Let's take, for example, the fiend who gunned down your uncle. He got what was coming to him, but whoever did it was sloppy. Someone innocent could have been injured or killed that way. Do you understand?" Maddy just nodded her head. She had been driven by pure emotion on that evening and had not stopped to consider that someone else could have been harmed through the actions that he had forced her to take. "On the other hand, if your employee's husband's . . . accident . . . had not actually been an accident, well, that was quite clever. As was the misfortune of your former . . . boyfriend."

"How . . . how did you know about those . . . um . . . accidents?" Maddy sheepishly inquired.

"Oh, I make it my business to know about a lot of things that happen in this world, especially in my neighborhoods. And through you, your neighborhood is my neighborhood. So consider me to be . . . well informed. I want to leave you with this. If someone is going down the path of creating . . . accidents . . . then it would be wise for that person to never keep any souvenirs of their exploits, and they need to create these . . . accidents . . . in a variety of ways. And finally"—Blair looked at her niece with the same seriousness that she had just a few weeks before in the hospital bed—"this conversation never happened and will never happen again. Now, let's see what we can scrounge up for dinner, shall we?"

As Blair got up and cheerfully pranced toward the kitchen, Maddy thought, *Holy shit. She is the most loving person in the world and the coldest bitch all in one. I'm never gonna get on her bad side.*

The year 2019 was a year of mostly good times. Everyone's careers were going well, and their love lives continued on their predictable trajectory. Kristy relished being a housewife and raising her three lovely children alongside her dutiful and sweet Jason. Jules's importing business was thriving, and she continued discarding used condoms as the need arose. Sam entered her second romantic "merger," which turned out to be an efficient six-month escape from the dating scene before the deal fell through. At the annulment meeting, the pair shook hands, wished each other well, and went back to their respective lives. Maddy was once again ordered to stand down.

Blair and Edgar continued their very casual relationship. They never were to fall in love, but the companionship and biological benefits helped to soothe their personal angst. And Patty just continued to be Patty. Blair and Patty visited New York six times that year to visit their actual niece and their adopted ones. They loved Kristy's children, although Patty refused to hold them if they were "smelly," so she didn't hold them very often. And the karaoke Saturdays continued with the friends' singing starting out pretty well before deteriorating into drunken slurs of off-key shout singing by the final song. Edgar accompanied the pair on one occasion. Maddy returned home from work to find Patty sitting alone on the couch.

"Hey, wuzzup, where's aunt Blair and Edgar?" Maddy inquired as she entered her small, two-bedroom apartment.

"Where do you think?" Patty responded with a growl. "They're in the bedroom fucking . . . again . . . I'm tellin' ya, Mads, it's fuckin' gross."

Maddy burst into laughter as she said, "Oh, that's fuckin' funny coming from the broad who's had a virtual pussy buffet since she was a teenager! Leave 'em alone and let them have their fun, for Chrissakes!"

Maddy's career continued to thrive at the bookstore while her love life was a bit more of a . . . struggle. She had three "boyfriends" that year, with the definition of a "boyfriend" being that if they stuck around past three dates, then she would sleep with them. At that point, she would see where things lead. All three times they led to the same place. Being asked to leave the man's apartment following sex (usually because the guys were coming over to watch "the game," which led Maddy to wonder, *How many fuckin' games could there possibly be?*), being called up by the man for no other reason except to come over and have sex and having the privilege to do the man's housekeeping and laundry because they had . . . sex. It was all too predictable and disappointing, but Maddy never sought any revenge upon them. She would just break up with them as only she could by stating, "Okay, this shit isn't working for me. If you just want a cum bucket, go inflate one. If you want a personal maid, then hire one. I'm looking for a man who cares about me and supports who I am, not just a lay. So good luck or whatevs, and don't call me again." They weren't bad people, Maddy thought. They just haven't caught up yet in our society's evolution. They're just man-child knuckle draggers. They're not a threat—they're just going to be some poor bitch's less-than-attentive husband.

These men were not in any way evil, unlike Jack the Ripper, who had most definitely been a threat and was most definitely evil. Maddy, perhaps trying to find more appropriate outlets for her darker impulses, became infatuated by the enigmatic historical serial killer. She was both repulsed by him, because of his choice of victims, and intrigued by his ability to have never been identified, even though all of his victims were from the same London neighborhood, worked in the same profession of solicitation, and completed his murders in basically the same way. She read about additional serial killers as well and realized that the Rippers, Gacys, and Bundys of the world appeared to carry the same personality traits. They were narcissistic sociopaths who acted out to fulfill their emotional personal need for power. And they were indiscriminate in their victims. It did not matter to them who the person was, necessarily (although they all had a victim "type" whether it be children, young women, young male homosexuals, etc.). What mattered was that the victims, in the killer's mind, were weaker than them and could be easily dominated. Their victims acted as a magnifying glass for their tiny ego and probable tiny penis. They were demented individuals who took bullying to a whole new level not unlike . . . "Holy shit!" Maddy exclaimed to herself upon reaching her epiphany. "They're just like every fascist world leader who has killed hundreds of thousands if not millions of people all for their own self-satisfaction. These motherfuckers are small-time Hitlers!"

New Year's 2020 arrived and was joyously celebrated by the four friends as well as Blair and Patty who flew to New York for the occasion. The clock struck midnight, and Maddy went to a dark corner of the club by herself and spoke to her beloved uncle. "Okay, uncle Joe. I'm just gonna keep going on my promises from last year. No heavy drugs, don't get too fucked up on booze, and avoid one-night stands as much as humanly possible. Okay? I love you, uncle Joe. Happy New Year." There was one promise from the previous year that she had omitted. Although her black duffel bag may have been lying on her closet floor collecting dust, she had begun carrying a scalpel with her in her purse for personal . . . protection. Or so she had told herself.

The ominous dark cloud was rapidly spreading from China, throughout Asia, Europe, and now had arrived in the United States. Everyone knew that this was going to be bad as they watched in horror the rapidly escalating hospital and death rates from overseas. A confused and terror-stricken public searched for answers, and toilet paper, as the nation's public health experts were kept on a short leash by a power-hungry, small-handed troll of a man who trumpeted conspiracy over scientific fact, further dividing an already contentious population on something that was absurd to be divided about.

It was announced that all nonessential businesses in New York City would be shut down March 20, 2020, due to the very real and very deadly threat of COVID-19. So Maddy and her friends decided to do what many people in the city decided to do. They decided that they would go to an all-night dance club on March 18 with the full realization that this might be their last Wednesday night together for some time. They had dinner at 8:00 pm and attended a live music club at 10:00 pm before arriving at the dance club just after one in the morning. They (meaning Sam) decided that they would rotate who would hold the table while the others danced and flirted around the club, except for Kristy who was more than happy to dance and flirt with her bashful husband who was allowed to attend on this occasion.

As the clock approached three in the morning at a far too rapid pace, a somewhat tall fit young man approached Maddy at her round purple plexiglass table that she was standing at and saving while her friends drunkenly gyrated on the dance floor to the insipid, overly amplified sound that the patrons called "music."

He leaned over to meet her eyes and said in his most suave voice, "Hey, beautiful, can I buy you a drink?"

Never one to look a gift horse in the mouth and thinking that this might be her last chance for a good lay in a while, Maddy provocatively looked at the man, flashing him her most wicked smile, and said, "Sure, but only if you join me."

"What would you like?" the man said, fighting back the anticipation of his certainty of bagging his latest conquest.

"Whatever you're having," Maddy replied.

"Gin and tonic?" came the response followed by Maddy purring, "Perfect." Maddy intensely watched the man as he approached the bar and ordered the required libations that he was sure would end up in eight (thirty in his mind) minutes of sexual bliss.

Yeah, I could fuck him, Maddy thought until she witnessed him putting something into one of the drinks. The man returned to the table with the drinks, and Maddy couldn't hide her slight grin as she thought to herself, *Yep, rule numero uno when accepting a drink from a stranger: always order the same drink that they do so that they don't notice when you . . .* Her thought trailed off as she excitedly exclaimed while pointing to a scantily clad young woman standing behind the man, "Get a load out of *that* chick's dress, wouldja!" As he turned to look, Maddy stealthily reversed the two glasses.

The man turned back around to see Maddy eagerly sipping on her drink. "Yeah, that's really something. Some girls have no shame, huh?" the man said with an anticipatory grin.

"Yeah, some guys don't either. Why dontcha drink up and maybe we can find some other place to have some fun?" Maddy replied, mirroring the man's anticipatory grin while thinking, *Well, I guess it's time to come out of retirement.*

The man guzzled his drink and said, "Okay, wanna get out of here?"

"Sure do," Maddy confidently stated as she firmly grabbed the man's hand and began leading him to the exit of the dance club. They were just two faceless dark silhouettes in a sea of faceless dark silhouettes that were frequently highlighted by the flashing colorful strobes, pulsing to the monotonous thumping of the electric "drum" beats. The pulse of the computer- generated drivel matched the pounding of Maddy's anticipatory heart as her adrenaline began to rush.

As they reached the exit, the man suddenly felt woozy and slightly stumbled. "Hey, you okay?" Don't worry, I've gotcha," Maddy protectively stated. Once outside, they were greeted with a torrent of crisp rainfall. "Hey, let's go over here, and I'll call a cab," stated Maddy as she led the man to an overhang in the dark alley next to the club. Pushing him down upon the ground between two conveniently placed rusted dumpsters, Maddy gleefully said while removing her coat, "Have a seat. I'll fix you right up . . . chad."

The man looked up with a perplexed expression, followed by one of horror as he felt the blade of the scalpel entering his neck and the sticky warmth of his blood running down to his collarbone. "Now, chad . . . why didja go and do that?" Maddy's maniacal smile peered down upon him like a demented rag doll. "If ya wanted to get into my pants, all you had to do was ask. I was up for it."

Her steel-toned monologue continued as she forcefully inserted the scalpel into his neck, over and over, splattering blood onto her hands, forearm, and dress before turning her attention to wild slashes upon his face.

Streams of crimson covered his dying expression as she concluded, "How many chicks have you raped, anyway? How many women's lives have you ruined? How many, chad? How many? Well, no more for you. You will never send another woman into a physical and emotional hell ever again." Pleased by her latest work, she stared at him with a slightly cocked head, her rage-filled green eyes meeting his that were now near lifeless. She provided one more blow by fiercely plunging the scarlet-covered scalpel into his heart while saying, "This one's for ruining my dress, prick." Maddy confidently stood and stepped out from under the overhang and into the foggy cascade of chilled rainfall. Diluted pools of blood appeared at her feet as her body and clothing were being washed clean from the evening's violent escapade. She looked down the alleyway. Noticing that the bustling city's inhabitants were completely unaware of anything outside of their own personal interests, she put her coat back on over her drenched party dress, turned, and strode down the alley in the opposite direction, hailing a cab at the next street. She quickly texted Sam and said, "Just not feelin it anymore tonight. Grabbed a cab. Goin home. Call tomorrow. Music sucked." She had not bothered to take a final look at the brutally slashed corpse, passively lying there with the rest of the city's refuge. He was too insignificant to waste a final gaze upon.

CHAPTER 13

No More Hot Dogs

New York City, like most of the world, was a dystopian existence with people forced into isolation from one another due to the steady march of the COVID pandemic. Making matters worse, family members and neighbors were pitted against one other by tinfoil-hat conspiracy theories at a time when we most needed to be working together as a community.

In Wisconsin, Blair and Edgar decided to pool their resources, both economic and emotional and move in together for the duration of the virus. Due to their age, they both were of higher risk of hospitalization and death should they contract the virus. They both watched in horror as friends around their own age began succumbing to the cruel pandemic. They spent many nights holding each other on the couch watching the news and weeping. Blair also spent time each day monitoring death reports in the Brooklyn area. Out of concern for her niece, she closely watched the progression of the virus as well as reviewed the cause of other deaths in that area.

Patty, at the age of sixty-eight, was planning on retiring in mid-2020 from the fifty-six-bed assisted living complex that she was employed at but decided to continue working there out of her great sense of responsibility to her clients and employer. It was not uncommon for her to work sixteen-hour shifts or more as the virus deteriorated the nation's nursing and medical workforce. Patty threw herself into her work and remained mostly on emotional autopilot as she watched many of her cherished clients pass away, usually because a staff member had brought the virus onto the premises. Of the fifty-six people living there, nineteen had died by the end of 2020. Patty herself contracted COVID in the fall of 2020 but did not require hospitalization. She was down for the better part of a week and back at work within two weeks of her initial positive test. When Blair, who was unable to see her sister throughout this period, asked Patty over the phone why she thought she did not have a worse case, Patty simply said, "Clean fuckin' living" as she took a shot of tequila while smoking a cigarette on one of her few off days.

Maddy's parents, like the rest of their congregation, refused to abide by shutdown orders for large gatherings and continued to attend their church/cult services. Their rhetoric matched that of the rest of the unhinged right in the nation and preached about their "personal freedom" to do what they wished. This, to Maddy, seemed contradictory to the preaching of Christ, who held that we should work toward the common good of everyone, not just ourselves. There were also vile disparagements placed upon esteemed scientists and medical professionals whose only crime was trying to help the world out of an international pandemic with the least amount of lost life possible. As is always the case with these types of people, the foundation for their propaganda was their own perceived benefit over the common good of others in our communities.

Uncle Joe would take a flamethrower to this fuckin' place, Maddy thought as she heard reports of these large congregations flaunting their nose at everyone else's safety and well-being. In their minds, they were the "chosen ones" whom God Almighty would shepherd through this hardship. Personal responsibility based upon facts once again lost out to the willfully ignorant cop-out of "God's will."

Predictably, their church, like many throughout the nation, experienced a harsh outbreak. Maddy's parents were afflicted, with her father being hospitalized for five days on a ventilator before being released. Her mother carried long-term symptoms permanently. Eight members of the congregation perished. And her parents never conceded that they or anyone in the congregation had it. They held on to their lies willingly in the face of actual personal experience. They held on to those lies as fiercely as they would hold on to the laughably transparent lies of a stolen election at the end of that year and would march to the capitol (despite being quite short of breath) to illegally overthrow the United States government during the domestic coup attempt of January 6, 2021.

When Blair told Maddy about the church outbreak including the condition of her parents and the deaths of the others, Maddy's only response was "God's will, I guess. Shoulda worn a mask, motherfuckers." When Blair told Maddy about her parents' peripheral involvement on January 6, Maddy's response was "Fuck. I really need to change my last name," followed by laughter and a mocking chant of "Lock them up! Lock them up! Lock them up!"

During the shutdown period of the pandemic, Maddy was as isolated as everyone else, for the most part. However, the bookstore was booming as mail orders from bored homebound people used the pandemic as an opportunity to catch up on their reading, learn new skills, or as a simple escape from the daily stress. Maddy's staff were all laid off but taken care of for the most part through the Paycheck Protection Program. She increased her work hours and was alone in the store processing deliveries and shipping orders for ten to twelve hours per day, seven days per week in order to keep up with the demand. It was also a needed distraction from the emotional, mental, physical, and political tragedy that was unfolding daily. Watching the deterioration of communities through sickness, death, and societal disharmony was like watching a slow-moving train wreck that you had no control over. Monica frequently offered to come in and assist Maddy but was always told, "Nope, I got this. Just enjoy your time off as best you can. I'll call you if I need you." The bookstore also offered a large private space to hold a safe, socially distanced gathering each week with Sam, Jules, and Kristy. Each lady would bring their own snacks and drinks, sit in a large circle in the back of the store, and reengage each other with their weekly tradition. Upon its completion, Maddy would sanitize the entire area.

When not working, Maddy was also expanding her reading list as well as going back and watching some of her favorite movies such as those directed by Quentin Tarantino. During this time, she subscribed to a horror streaming channel and would lie in bed under the covers eating junk food and shudder in delight at the images from classic slasher and giallo films. One of her and Uncle Joe's heroes had also revived his career around this time, and Maddy both wept during and laughed at the offbeat commentary during breaks in the presented movie while talking to the spirit of her uncle.

"What's Joe Bob got for us tonight?" she would inquire of Joe's spirit as she settled into the four-to-five-hour splatter- and joke-filled marathon, butter ripple (when she could find it), dripping down her chin and onto her top cover.

Due to employee shortages and disrupted supply chain issues, basic goods were often in short supply. These problems were exacerbated by hoarders and, especially, black market operators who never failed to seek personal gain from human suffering. This was true at the onset of the pandemic in 2020 and experienced a resurgence as the omicron variant once again severely stressed the nation's health care system. The intensity and destruction of the variant was unnecessary. Following a brief reprieve and ray of hope of the pandemic's conclusion in the summer of 2021, tens of thousands of willfully unvaccinated people perished that fall and winter. And those ill-informed or simply apathetic people risked the lives of the civilized, vaccinated people who were at higher risk due to their age or underlying health conditions. It was in this environment that shortages again became pronounced, especially baby formula.

Maddy climbed the stairs toward her second-floor apartment when she heard sobbing on the floor above. Sitting on the top step was a despondent Abana and her three-month-old son. Abana and her military husband had moved into the building a few months before her son's delivery. She was soft-spoken and mostly kept to herself, although she would always present a pleasant greeting when encountered.

"Hey, wazzup?" Maddy cautiously inquired.

Abana blurted out through her anguish, "Oh, Maddy . . . I don't know what to do. I stood in line for three hours to get formula today, and they were out by the time I could get in there. It was the only place that got a shipment today, and there's no place that's getting any for the next two days. I don't know what to do. How will I feed my baby? What will I do? The churches are out too! I just don't know what to—"

"Hey, hey . . . calm down just a sec, okay?" Maddy interrupted in a soothing voice, reminiscent of her aunt Blair's. "Just go into your apartment and let me see if I can figure something out, okay? I'll be up in a little bit."

Maddy's stomach sunk as she descended the staircase and entered her apartment. She thought that she knew where she could get some formula. A little bird had told her that the same guy who had sold her the heroin that nearly killed her had branched out during the pandemic and was dealing in essential black-market goods. She had never wanted to see his face again but could think of no other options. She pulled the black duffel bag from her closet floor and took out the latest burner cell phone. As the phone rang, she was changing her clothes. Gone was the cute olive autumn dress over the tan leggings; and on were the black jeans, baggy black hoodie, and size 8 boots. With the addition of the sunglasses and black COVID mask, she looked like the world's least ferocious ninja.

Maddy's side of the conversation went like this: "Hey, I heard you have baby formula, that true? . . . How much? . . . A better price if I do *what*? . . . Well, maybe. Where are you and we can negotiate once I get there."

She knocked on Abana's door who graciously invited her in. "Okay, I got a lead on some, but no promises. Two questions. Can you get someone to watch the kid, and do you have access to a car, preferably a van?"

"Yes, my neighbor can watch him, and I think that I could borrow our church van for a while," Abana replied.

"Good. I'm gonna go see if I can strike a deal. If I do, I'll call you. Be ready to pick me up with the van. And Abana, this shit's illegal as fuck, so no questions, and we have never had this conversation. Got it?"

"Y-yes," Abana replied, now wondering what she may have gotten herself into.

Maddy arrived at the small storage building in a mostly abandoned industrial park. She gave the signal with four rapid knocks, immediately returning her right hand to her hoodie pocket in order to clench her stun gun. This matched her left hand that was already clenching her pepper spray. The heavy steel door opened with an ominous squeak. Inside the doorway was an unshaven, long-haired, and overweight middle-aged man wearing a dirty sweatshirt and sweatpants. He was eating a hot dog as ketchup slovenly rolled down his chin.

"I see you haven't changed your look up much," the man dismissively said.

"Yeah, you're lookin' great too. Let's not fuck around. How much stuff ya got?" Maddy inquired hastily.

"I've got ten cases, six big cans per case. For you . . . $500 a case," the man replied.

"You're fuckin' nuts!" Maddy exclaimed. "That shit goes for less than $200, retail. And since I know you didn't pay a fuckin' dime for it, that's what I'll pay. Two thousand dollars cash for all ten cases. Take it or leave it."

The man presented a devilish grin before saying, "What about my little offer on the phone? Five thousand cash or . . . two thousand and you suck my cock . . . naked. Take it or leave it." Maddy shook her head in disgust. A familiar feeling that was part anger, part vindictiveness, and part exhilaration was beginning to sweep over her. It was bad enough that these vultures were exploiting the lower- and working-class families during this time of crisis, but to require blowing his sweaty cock too? "Dude, you reaaally shouldn't push me on this, 'cause I'm *not* in the best of moods. I'm gonna shoot you one last offer, and I suggest you take it. For starters, I'm not putting your COVID cock in my mouth, so how 'bout this? You sit in that chair, I'll do a little tease for you down to my bra and panties, and then give you a hand job. But my gloves stay on! Deal?"

"Yeah . . . all right, baby . . . I've always wanted to see what you've been hiding under all of that black."

"Oh . . . you're gonna find out all about me today, big boy," Maddy innocently replied as she began removing her boots and socks. She then began swaying her hips while sliding out of the baggy jeans, kicking them far away from the chair. She sauntered closer to the chair while lifting the black hoodie over her head, discarding it at his feet with the right pocket easily accessible. She got on her knees in front of him. With her left hand, she pulled down on the waistband of his sweatpants. With her right hand, she pulled out the stun gun.

"Ya ready to have some fun?" she breathily whispered, attempting to channel Marilyn as she lifted his hairy and sweaty roll of fat to reveal his fully erect four-inch penis.

"Oh, fuck yeah, baby, let's have some fun!" the man excitedly screamed. His scream increased in volume, pitch, and shrillness as fifty thousand volts flowed into his body through his testicles. Zip ties were immediately removed from the black duffel and placed around his ankles and wrists, tying him to the chair. Duct tape was placed over his mouth, before the smelling salts were applied. The disoriented man alarmingly reentered consciousness and looked into the steely emerald eyes of a barely dressed mini assassin. She was holding a knife and wearing the grin of a demented clown.

"Now . . . we're gonna figure out if *my* definition of fun and *your* definition of fun are the same thing. I'll tell ya what . . . I'll start." Maddy then jumped and squealed with delight as she said, "Oh my fucking god! Do you know what this reminds me of? It's just like that scene in that Tarantino movie . . . y'know, where the guy dances around the tied-up guy and cuts off his ear and shit? And . . . you did say you wanted to see me dance, so this feels like a win-win. But I don't want to totally rip off the master . . . plus I'm a red, not a blonde, so . . . what shall we dance to?"

"Oh . . . I know . . .," Maddy deviously stated before getting in the man's face, bouncing her head back and forth while beginning the introductory laughs of Hasil Adkins's "No More Hot Dogs."

She then began singing the verses of the most demented song that she had ever heard. It was a song about a person being decapitated and their head being mounted on the wall. It was graphic and twisted. Needless to say, it was one of Maddy's favorites.

Maddy pranced around the room, occasionally sticking him in nonlethal areas of the body with the knife. As she glided around her quarry, she was certain that she was perfectly emulating the coolness of Michael Madsen in *Reservoir Dogs*. In reality, she looked more like a recovering hip surgery patient having a seizure. Her jerky contortions only contributed to the man's confusion and horror as Maddy sang verse after verse, adding the required demented laughter and smiling with her copper hair bouncing in a frenzy.

At the song's conclusion, Maddy got back down on her knees in front of the man. She looked up and stared at the crimson pools at various places on his clothing. "Okay . . . I say that was fun. Now, it's your turn. Let's see here . . . I don't really wanna give you a hand job at this point, so how about I do something else for you and let you have one more hot dog?"

With a maniacal look of glee, Maddy began sawing through the now-flaccid penis with her serrated knife. "Jesus Christ! This is harder than cutting through raw chicken!" Maddy grunted before the penis completely separated from the body, a torrent of sticky blood hitting Maddy right in the face. "Oh fuck, fuck fuck . . . *fuck*! I didn't expect you to jizz that much blood! And during COVID too, you prick!"

She got to her feet, looking much like the title character from the finale of *Carrie*, her auburn hair, face, and body saturated with the crimson molasses. "Okay, motherfucker, here's your last hot dog!" she stated as she pulled back the duct tape, shoved the dismembered penis into the man's mouth, and placed the duct tape back. She then put duct tape over the man's nose. As she watched the man gasping for air and grasping for his life with him bleeding profusely out of his groin, aspirating from the lack of oxygen and gagging on his own phallus, Maddy thought, *I'd hate to be the coroner who has to figure out* this *cause of death. Maybe they'll just check off everything on column A and be done with it.* There was a final exhale as the man's frozen face projected the very definition of fear.

Maddy cut off the zip ties and duct tape and placed them in the garbage bag. The mutilated penis hanging out of the man's mouth looked like a piece of half-chewed, uncooked pork. She was about to wash herself off in the sink when a glistening metal object caught her eye from the corner of the room. "Oh, fuck it, I'm already covered in blood and shit. May as well go all the way," she said aloud to herself as she picked up the newly discovered axe.

She stood with her hands on her barely clad hips and looked with pride at the head that she had just mounted on the wall. "Fuck, man," she said aloud, "I've outdone Hasil. I've put *two* heads on the wall, and, as they say, two heads are better than one." Upon saying this, Maddy immediately became despondent as she realized that she had no audience to hear what she was sure was the greatest joke in the history of the world.

Maddy finally went to the industrial sink and completely washed herself before placing her bra, panties, and gloves in the ever-present garbage bag. She then put her black clothes on including new gloves and called Abana. "Get your ass over here with the van . . . now!" Maddy ordered. Thirty minutes later, Maddy and Abana were loading the borrowed van with ten cases of formula plus several packages of diapers and a box of various medications that Maddy had already placed outside of the locked building. Before leaving the site, Maddy unlocked the door to the building and cracked the door open. *Looters will be here soon. They'll take as much shit as they can and leave tons of evidence. The cops'll never figure this one out . . . even if they want to.*

Maddy was soaking in a well-deserved hot bath that evening, steam rising around her sweat-covered, lightly freckled face that carried a look of relaxed self-satisfaction. She thought back to the conversation that she had with Abana on the way back home. Upon Abana's inquiry as to what she owed her, Maddy simply said, "You don't owe me shit, except to never talk about this, okay? Oh, and if I ever need you to say that I was with you at some point, you'll do that for me . . . okay?"

Abana smiled and said, "Of course . . . that's the least I can do. Thank you for helping me and my baby."

The conversation ended with Maddy's dismissive and rather arrogant comment, "No prob . . . it's what I do or else my name isn't Maddy fuckin' Sommers. And that's my name, so that's what I do."

At the moment that Maddy was soaking in her bath, nearly 1,100 miles away a man was going berserk. He was taking an aluminum baseball bat to every electronic device in his home. Shards of plastic were flying like shrapnel as the man thrashed every television, phone, and computer in his path, his enraged red face engorged with blood. The man's wife was screaming at him to stop, which he eventually did, but not until his destruction of the devices was complete and the home resembled a disaster area. He was filled with both rage and remorse as he watched her leave the home with her hastily packed suitcase. He then said aloud, "Fuck this, I'm going to New York."

CHAPTER 14

BRIDGE OVER TROUBLED WATER

Once the COVID vaccines became widely available in the spring of 2021, Maddy resumed her search for a romantic life partner. But this time, at the wise old age of thirty-four, she was armed with two new weapons. The first was what she referred to as her "prince checklist." It was a list of ten characteristics that any potential suitor would have to possess, with no compromises offered. The "applicant" would get up to three dates with her to make it through the checklist. If he was able to accomplish this feat, then, and only then, would she consider becoming intimate with him. If, in the process of dating, the applicant failed on any one of the checkpoints, he was eliminated from the competition. She now viewed dating as an interview process and felt great empowerment as she turned the power dynamic tables.

She wanted a man who truly liked who she was as a person, so she presented her full personality complete with vulgar language, bad jokes (which they would be wise to laugh at), and ordering something considerably more substantial than a salad at dinner, placing her voracious appetite on full display. She would pepper her date with questions, each designed to investigate another aspect of the checklist, and she made it clear that she doesn't do *that* until at least after the third date. This approach led to many free dinners, ten occasions of walking out (after taking her last bite of dinner) on a man discovered to be married, six second dates, zero third dates, and one occasion on New Year's 2022 that made her take a sabbatical from dating for a while.

"Fuck, I'm gonna have to substantially increase my battery budget," she would lament after each failed attempt.

Her second weapon was the COVID vaccine. Her attitude was that, unless the man was unable to receive the vaccine due to some form of health condition, anyone who willingly did not receive the vaccine was placing her and all of society at risk due to contributing to the spread of the constantly mutating variations of the virus. Before agreeing to a date, she would request to see the man's vaccination card. Several men sneered at the request, which elicited an immediate response from Maddy of "Then fuck off, slackjaw!" These people, she thought, had no right to hide behind their "personal freedom" to put her and others' safety at risk. She did not care if their refusal to get vaccinated was for religious reasons, political reasons, or out of willful ignorance. To her, it was " just fuckin' stupid," and she resented these people being allowed to mingle in public, knowingly undermining the efforts that members of civilized society were making in controlling and ending the pandemic. Her new rallying cry was "No Vax, No Vag!" which became the standard for many of her single friends as well.

When the bookstore reopened for walk-in business, all of Maddy's employees returned and were greeted with a hearty elbow bump by a smiling, masked store manager, which only served to accentuate her glistening emerald eyes and copper lashes. Monica returned to her business as well but never entered the sales floor as she was unable to receive the vaccine due to her health conditions. Maddy had moved Monica's office to a large conference room on the second floor of the building so that Monica was able to preside over socially distanced meetings with her employees. Patrons were required to show a vaccination card and be masked prior to entry, a rule that Maddy enforced rigidly. Maddy's justification for this rule was "If you're too fuckin' stupid to not get vaccinated, then you're probably too fuckin' stupid to read, so what are you gonna buy in here anyway?"

In early February 2022, a new patron began coming into the store. He would walk around and browse at various items before proceeding to the children's section. Once he arrived there, he would lurk around for about thirty minutes constantly looking at his phone.

What the fuck is this guy up to? Maddy wondered. She asked her assistant manager, Sean, to get the guy's name and contact information so that he could receive publicity emails and be entered into a monthly cash prize giveaway.

"Um . . . what cash prize giveaway?" Sean inquired.

"Just fuckin' do it, please," Maddy impatiently responded. Maddy looked up the man on the internet and discovered that he had just moved to Brooklyn from Greenville, Florida. *What the hell are you doing almost 1,100 miles away from home? This is going to require a bit more investigation,* Maddy thought.

It was New Year's Eve 2021, and Maddy had a hot one on the hook. Not married, great job, and devastatingly handsome. *Three off of the checklist right out of the gate,* Maddy enthusiastically thought as she wrapped herself in a large black overcoat, covering her gold sequined party dress that looked to contain less material than an average bathing suit. He took her to Peak at Hudson Yards, and she looked over New York City in amazement from nearly 1,300 feet in the air. Specialty cocktails flowed, as did the spirited conversation over the exquisite dinner. Maddy was mentally checking off the prescribed requirements from her list and waiting in anticipation for an offer of a second date when the man suavely said, "So how about you and I go back to my place and ring in the New Year with our own fireworks?"

"Um . . . well, I would love to, but . . . um . . . I really don't go back to a guy's apartment until I get to know them a little bit better. You understand . . . right?" Maddy replied with the last line being more of a plead than a question.

"Oh, sure, I understand," the man said as Maddy breathed a sigh of relief. "I understand that you're nothing more than a little cock tease. C'mon, baby, you know the score. I take you out for a nice dinner, I pretend to be interested in whatever you've been rambling on about, you come back to my place and take care of me, then I send you on your way. What about that do you not understand, you little tart?"

Maddy's face became as red as her cranberry-based libation. Feeling part shock and part disappointment but expressing full rage, Maddy said loudly, "You fucking sexist piece of shit! What is it with you guys? Is that all you care about? Do you not realize that we are human beings and not just a fuckin' hole to stick your dick in? Just fuck off! I don't even want a slimeball douchebag like you to pay for my dinner. I've got the check, because I also have money because I also have a brain and talent and shit. I hope you get fuckin' herpes tonight, you fuckin' prick!"

Every woman in the restaurant applauded as the publicly neutered man slinked out of the exit, while every male patron sat silently, desperately rethinking their strategy for the evening. Maddy fuckin' Sommers had just provided the biggest single- handed cock block in the history of the world. And that was a scientific fact. The elevator's swift plunge from the 101st floor matched that of Maddy's plunging broken heart. *That's it . . . I'm fuckin' done with guys for a while. This shit's like torture!* Maddy said to herself as she embarked on yet another lonely ride home.

———

I fuckin' hate *Valentine's Day!* Maddy thought to herself as she assisted clueless male patrons pick out the "perfect" gift for their wife, fiancée, girlfriend, or potential conquest. It had been six weeks since her last date, and she vowed to keep that streak alive as she was appalled by married man after married man brazenly hitting on her while purchasing a gift for someone that they had vowed to love. *If one more fuckin' guy hits on me today, I swear I'm gonna*—her thought was interrupted by a soft male voice from behind her.

"Excuse me, miss?" the voice stated.

Maddy thought, *Here we fuckin' go again*, as she put on her fake smile, turned around, and stared into the hazel eyes of the unfamiliar male patron. "Yes, may I help you?" Maddy professionally inquired.

"Yes . . . um . . . I was told that you have used records here, and I was wondering if you could tell me where they're at?" the man inquired.

Maddy gave him a quick once-over. About mid-forties, average build, average brown hair, average top half of his face, average . . . *What the fuck does his sweatshirt say?* Maddy almost burst out laughing as she read the man's sweatshirt that said, "Real Men Love Cats." *Okay,* this *motherfucker's not trying to hit on anyone! Not wearing that!* Maddy thought. She then said while still attempting to contain her laughter, "Sure, what type of music are you into so I can point you to the right section?"

"Well, I have pretty eclectic taste in music, so that might be a lengthy discussion," the man answered.

"Well . . . let's start with this. What do you think of the song that's playing in the store right now?" Maddy asked, not realizing that her subconscious was leading her to an early test of this man.

"I think that this is a very sweet version of a very good song," the man replied. Maddy felt a tinge of disappointment before the man said, "But the Mindbenders' version is much better in my opinion."

"Huh," Maddy said while giving the man another once-over. "Okay . . . good response. You, sir, have just won yourself a personal tour back to the record room. C'mon, follow me." The pair began their journey through the vast labyrinth of books and novelties toward the new adventures awaiting them in the record room as the Phil Collins version of "A Groovy Kind of Love" swept into their ears from above.

"Well, here we are!" Maddy excitedly exclaimed as she spread her arms out and twirled.

"Holy fucking Christ!" the man loudly stated as his bulging eyes quickly surveyed the vast racks of colorful aged cardboard and vinyl that covered the full length of the building adjacent to the bookstore. "This place is incredible! And that smell . . . there's nothing like the musty smell of musical history."

"Yeah, we have a few records . . . like . . . kinda everything . . . so what are you into?" Maddy again inquired. The man began listing some of the artists that he enjoyed off the top of his head. There was Bowie. And Lou Reed. And the Damned. And the Cramps. And the Sex Pistols. And the Jesus and Mary Chain, to name but a few of the artists from his more aggressive tastes. But he also enjoyed more "mellow" artists that would include Springsteen, Fleetwood Mac, Sam Cooke, Irma Thomas, and yes . . . when the mood was right, ABBA. His musical tastes encompassed a sonic smorgasbord of punk, new wave, '60s R&B and soul, '60s garage, and glam and pop from the '70s, '80s, and '90s.

"Wow, dude, is that it?" Maddy playfully inquired.

"No, I could go on if you would like," he responded before Maddy said, "Nope, I think I've got the picture. Hey, by the way, since it's not crowded back here, we can take our masks off if you're comfortable with it. You are truly vaccinated, right? You didn't show a fake card at the door?"

The man removed his mask and revealed a clean-shaven, slightly wrin-kling face that was carrying a wide smile as he said, "Am I vaccinated. Yeah, I've got more than two brain cells to rub together, so . . . yeah . . . I'm vaccinated."

Maddy loved the response so much that she couldn't help but feel that she could maybe play with this new customer a bit. "Okay, mister . . . I gotta ask . . . what's up with the sweatshirt?" The man paused for a moment before his serious reply. "Well, there are a couple of things about this sweatshirt. Numero uno:

It happens to be true."

Whaaat the fuck did he just say? Maddy thought before responding, "Okay, mister, I'll bite. How is it true?"

"Well," the man continued, "if you ever meet a guy that *doesn't* like cats, unless it's because of an allergy or something, that guy is always a self-centered narcissistic douchebag who doesn't like cats because they are *so* self-centered that they can't handle the indifference of cats and how cats offer their love on their own terms. And numero two-o: Sometimes people make fun of me when I wear this shirt, and y'know, I'm forty-six years old, and I really don't have anything to prove to anybody. I think I'm a decent guy, and if people like me, then that's great. And those that don't can just fuck off, if you know what I mean, and I think that you do." A mischievous grin replaced the serious expression on his face as he delivered the last line.

Maddy just stood there in her maskless shock for a moment while thinking about what he had just said to her. *Well, I guess the language gloves are off with this guy. And did he just reference . . .* "Okay, one more question. Did you just quote Joe Bob to me?" The man, his smile changing from mischief to delight, replied haughtily, "Did I not say that I have more than two brain cells to rub together? Of course, I just quoted Joe Bob. It's nice to meet another fan."

The pair burst into laughter for the first of what would be many times. "So . . . I haven't seen you around before. Are you new here?" Maddy innocently inquired.

The man paused, his face once again becoming serious before he said, "Yeah . . . I'm from Jefferson City, Missouri. I used to be an eighth-grade schoolteacher, and I've been saving and investing my money since I was sixteen, and I just decided I needed a . . . change of pace, shall we say. I've always been intrigued by New York, and I found a decent deal on a small one bedroom a few blocks away, so I decided to try it. If I don't like it, there's always Boise or some shit like that."

"Or Des Moines," Maddy added.

"Why the fuck would I move to Des Moines?" the man incredulously asked.

"Uh . . . I don't know . . . it's another city," Maddy replied before the man said, "Yeah . . . kind of, I guess . . . I'm Erick, by the way."

Erick presented his hand as Maddy excitedly exclaimed, "Hiya! I'm Maddy! Nice tameetcha!"

"Yeah, I know," Erick arrogantly replied.

A chill went down Maddy's spine. *How does he know my name?* she thought as a couple of previous stalkers ran through her mind. She cautiously stopped shaking his hand and pulled it back as she asked, "Um . . . how do you know my name?"

Erick flashed his mischievous smile once more before replying, "Because it's on your fuckin' nametag."

The two burst into laughter once again before Maddy excused herself to return to the sales floor. "Are ya gonna come back?" Maddy asked.

"Yeah, I think I might come in on Tuesdays to start looking at the LPs and Wednesdays to start on the 45s. That way, I might be done by the time I die."

"You should come in on Fridays too!" Maddy blurted out. "Um . . . okay . . . why?" Erick inquired.

"Well," Maddy began explaining, "you see, Fridays are the day we put out all of the stuff we've accumulated throughout the week, and since I now know what you're interested in, if I see something that you might like, I'll hold it back so you can check it out. There's no obligation to buy it or anything, but"—she paused for a moment wondering why she was giving so much attention to this new customer—"if you don't come in on Friday, then that shit'll just go out onto the floor, and you'll miss out, mister! Besides, you're kinda fun to talk to, so come on in and we can visit some more."

"Okay," Erick confirmed, "Tuesday, Wednesdays, and Fridays around one. So . . . I'll see you tomorrow."

The following day, Erick entered the mammoth storefront at 1:03 pm and was immediately greeted with an enthusiastic "Hey, you!" Looking to where the voice had come from, Erick saw Maddy, grinning ear to ear, bounding toward him.

"Wassupbuttacup?" Erick responded, then, just as quickly, attempted to retreat from his exclamation with an embarrassed "Oh my god, I'm so sorry Maddy! I don't know why I said that. It just came out! I hope I didn't offend you."

Perplexed, Maddy said, "Uh . . . nope . . . why would that offend me?"

"Well," Erick attempted to explain, "we've only just met, and that greeting seems a bit informal."

"Nah, it's cool," Maddy replied. "I kinda like it. My uncle used to call me that, sooo . . . it's cool."

"Well, in that case," Erick continued in a sarcastic sneer, "why dontcha answer the fuckin' question? *Wassupbuttacup*?"

Maddy carried a momentary shocked look on her face, which quickly transformed into a knowing grin. "Oh, first off, fuck you, and secondly, nothin' is up, except I'm having to deal with a smart-ass customer right now who really should learn to watch his language 'cause I don't care for such talk as that," she said with a lilted, arrogant head and noticeable sarcasm.

"Well!" Erick retorted with fake exasperation while making sure to place an emphasis at the beginning of every word he is about to utter. "*May*be I *will* watch my *fuck*ing *lang*uage!"

"Well," Maddy countered using the same verbal cadence, "*may*be you *sho*uld *wat*ch your *fuck*ing *lang*uage!"

"Okay, *then* I *fuck*ing will!" he said before her retort of "Good, I'm *glad you*'re *fuck*ing *doing that*!" They looked at each other with full recognition and appreciation of the other's playful grins before descending into uncontrollable laughter.

This is going to be fun, they both silently thought before Maddy said, "Wanna continue our discussion from yesterday? I'm on lunch break."

"I would love nothing better. Lead the way," Erick stated eagerly.

Upon reaching a long brown leather couch in a reading area of the store, Erick asked, "So did you have a nice Valentine's Day?" *Ohhhh . . . here we go*, Maddy thought. *He's tryin' to figure out if I'm involved with someone. Well, kinda nice change of pace from guys who don't care. Should I lie to him and tell him I have a boyfriend or . . .* "Why, yes, I did, thank you so much for asking," Maddy replied. "I had a hot date with a pizza and a Rob Zombie double feature."

"Cool," Erick responded excitedly. "What did you watch? The Halloween remakes . . . or two from the *Firefly* trilogy . . . or something a bit more obscure like *Lords of Salem* and *31*?"

Impressed once again, Maddy replied, "I went with *House of a Thousand Corpses* and *Devil's Rejects*. You're into Rob Zombie movies too?"

Once again Erick put his arrogant sarcasm on display as he said, "Okay, Maddy . . . once again . . . I have more than two brain cells, so yes, I'm into Rob Zombie films. In fact, *The Devil's Rejects* is my second all-time favorite movie."

"Second favorite?" Maddy retorted with an attitude. "What the fuck is better than that?"

"Well, I shall tell you," Erick countered. "*Return of the Living Dead.*"

Feeling slightly out of her league, Maddy sheepishly replied, "Um . . . okay . . . I've heard of that movie, but I've never seen it." Erick, now sensing Maddy's vulnerability in the situation, rolled his eyes and let out an exaggerated sigh. Faking incredulousness, Maddy stated loudly, "What the fuck is the matter with you, mister?"

In an overly judgmental tone while looking down at her with his hazel eyes, Erick stated, "Geez, Maddy. How can you call yourself a horror fan and never have seen that? I'm just so deeply . . . disappointed in you right now."

"Oh . . . fuck . . . you!" Maddy immediately responded. "It's not *my* fault that I wasn't born before the stone ages, so you can just get off of my ass, mister!"

"Nope," Erick immediately responded with the same intensity of a returned volley in a tennis match, "I'm not gonna let you off of the hook that easily. Some of *my* favorite horror movies are the ones from Hammer Studios that were made before *I* was born, so your age is no excuse. You wanna hang with the cool kids? Then I suggest you watch that movie." The last line was delivered as he leaned toward her wearing a huge smirk on his face as his hazel eyes danced with playful delight. "Okay . . . fine . . . I will," Maddy conceded. "But then you have to watch a movie that I pick out, and we're gonna discuss it . . . in detail . . . so no fast-forwarding through it!"

An agreement was reached that afternoon that became the springboard for many pointless but entertaining discussions.

The pair immediately fell into a deep friendship. Every Tuesday, Wednesday, and Friday at around 1:00 pm, they would sit on either end of the long brown leather couch in the reading area of the store and discuss music, movies (especially of the horror variety that Maddy had selected), and other general interests. Neither were into sports or the outdoors. Both were into drinking, animal rights, human rights, and New York's nightlife. In March, their discussions became deeper as they mutually wrestled with the images of the genocide that was unfolding in Ukraine. They would attempt to quell their empathetic pain with frequent jokes. They laughed together constantly. "That's what she said," was uttered by one, if not both simultaneously upon any mention of size, width, length, stamina, liquidity, or sensation. Combined, they shared the sense of humor and maturity of an average twelve-year-old.

At one point upon telling Erick about her close friends, Maddy stated,

"Yeah, my friends and I have a tradition. We've been meeting at one of our places every Wednesday night pretty much the entire time we've been friends. We just hang out, drink some wine, and—"

Maddy was abruptly cut off by Erick who said in his overly condescending tone, "Maddy, I'm a man of the world, and at this point in my life, I think I have a pretty good understanding of women. So you don't need tell me what you do, because I know what's going on there."

"Oh, do you now, mister?" Maddy responded snidely. "Okay, enlighten me, fucker."

Erick's lips deviously curled upward as he said, "Pillow fights in panties and tank tops. I'm right, aren't I?"

Maddy had a shocked look of enthrallment on her face. Determined not to let him best her, she responded, "Oh . . . my . . . fucking . . . god! You are such an old perv! Panties and tank tops? You know *nothing* about women! We do that shit completely nekkid, and it usually ends with some lezzy 69ing. So what do ya think about that?"

"I don't think much of that at all," Erick responded dismissively. "It's just as I would have expected." The pair looked at each other for an instant before breaking out into uncontrollable laughter once again.

"We are sooo not good for one another," Maddy stated through her chortles.

"Nope, we're the worst. You're the type of person that my mother warned me about. But she's kind of a right-wing lunatic at this point, so what the fuck does she know?"

That last line opened the door to deeper revelations as Maddy confided in her newfound friend about many (but certainly not all) of the aspects of her past. She talked about her upbringing with her mentally and physically abusive parents and her love of her aunts, uncle, and best friends. She confided in him about bottoming out emotionally following the loss of her marriage, best friend, and uncle Joe, although the embarrassing details of that period were omitted.

Erick would sit quietly on his end of the couch and nod empathetically as this delightful but pained woman began trusting him with what he thought were her darkest secrets. He listened intently and merely voiced his understanding instead of offering unsolicited advice. There were times during these discussions that he would have a fleeting thought of holding her in a comforting embrace, but such thoughts seemed ridiculous to him and were quickly discarded.

Maddy had never had a male friend such as this. He never made passes at her or hit on her. He listened to her without judgment. He laughed at her jokes, even when she knew that they weren't very funny (which was extremely rare in her mind). They could call each other out when one of them would make a ridiculous statement without the fear of offending the other person. They could laugh with or at each other. She was free to speak her mind, and he was free to speak his. And they did, frequently disagreeing on such important topics of the day such as "Which Cramps song was the best" or "If you were stranded on an island, who would you rather be with? Christopher Lee or Peter Cushing?" That last discussion resulted in them folding their arms in disgust and not speaking to each other for . . . about eight seconds before the laughter began. They then compromised and decided that it didn't matter who they were stranded with because whoever it was would put their head on a spike anyway, so what difference did it make?

He respected her. She felt comforted during their time together. She felt that he was on her side. And she could trust him with most of her inner secrets, just as he could trust her . . . *Wait a minute,* she thought to herself in early April. *He has hardly told me anything about* his *past. What's that about?* As those thoughts went through Maddy's head, Erick approached the counter with a smile and a copy of *Simon & Garfunkel's Greatest Hits.*

He paid for his record and began to leave before turning back around and saying, "Hey, Maddy . . . can I tell you something?"

"Of course," Maddy replied.

"Well," Erick began, "I just want to thank you for your friendship. I walk around the city every day just feeling . . . angry . . . about a lot of stuff in this world. But I never feel angry when I'm here, looking at records or goofing around with you. This place is like my . . . oasis of happiness. I feel comforted here. So I wanted to thank you for that and tell you how much I appreciate you and your friendship. And . . . just one more thing. I think you're a really cool chick, but I get the feeling that maybe you don't think that you are, so . . . let me give you a piece of unsolicited advice: don't let any motherfucking douchebag ever try to change you, because you're perfect just the way you are . . . okay?"

"Uh . . . yeah . . . okay," Maddy responded while thinking, *Where the fuck did* that *come from?*

CHAPTER 15

I'M GONNA FOLLOW YOU

As Maddy's friendship with Erick was flourishing, she was also becoming involved in the life of another man. From the middle of February when she had first noticed him lurking around the children's section of the bookstore until mid-April, Maddy had found out where the man lived and stalked him in order to learn more about him and his patterns. In her ever- present baggy black clothes, hoodie, sunglasses, and COVID mask, she would virtually disappear into the bustling mass of humanity of the Brooklyn streets.

The man had only come into the bookstore on three occasions. Each time, he browsed his way casually over to the children's section. Upon reaching his destination, he would take his phone from his pocket and look at it while pointed in the direction of one of the children who were innocently flipping through the pages of one of the colorfully illustrated stories. He was always sweaty, regardless of the temperature inside of the store, and his eyes would frequently dart quickly around his immediate surroundings before returning to the image on his phone. On the second occasion, a store employee introduced himself and asked him to fill out his contact information in order to receive email notifications from the store and to be enrolled in their, "um . . . monthly cash prize giveaway. It's . . . um . . . a really cool promotion . . . All of our regular customers have signed up, so . . . if you could . . . ." The man hesitantly agreed to the request, took the clipboard, and completed the information in order to not arouse suspicions.

On the third occasion, Maddy approached a shopping mother of a three-year-old child who was a few feet away in the children's play area. Maddy casually asked the mother, "Hey, is that your husband or something?" as she pointed out the man loitering with his phone pointed at the woman's toddler son.

"No . . . he's . . . um . . . excuse me please," the woman replied before instinctively going over to her son. She leaned down, took the boy's delicate hand, looked up at the man with a stone face, and said coldly, "C'mon, sweety. Let's go to the next store." The man never returned to the store again.

Through her investigation, Maddy learned that the man was an overnight delivery person for a local food distributor. He was always home in the evening. His silhouette could be seen behind the newspaper-covered windows before the lights went out, usually around six in the evening. Maddy would return around midnight to observe the man leaving to go to the food distribution warehouse. He would return home around eight thirty the next morning, leaving Maddy just enough time to get to work herself. She was unable to observe him during the daytime hours, except on the weekends.

She purchased a new burner phone and began delving into the man's past. He was a thirty-two-year-old man who had recently moved to New York from Greenville, Florida, where he had lived for about two years and worked in a similar position. He was also recently divorced from his wife of eighteen months. He had no children. He had no criminal record with the exception of one arrest for solicitation of a prostitute. The prostitute had also been arrested, and Maddy learned that she was known for dressing up as a child in order to fulfill her john's twisted "daddy" fantasies. The arrest had occurred one week prior to the divorce filing in October of the previous year.

While scouring the web for clues to help her assess the threat that this man presented, a news article from December of 2021 caught Maddy's eye. Her eyes quickly welled with tears as she read the headline that screamed off of the page, "Body of 2nd child found. Search continues for 3rd." Maddy's heart sank as she read about the three children. Two of the bodies, a four-year-old boy and a five-year-old girl, had been found by search dogs buried in shallow graves in a wooded area about twenty miles north of Greensville in southern Georgia. A nine-year-old freckly faced little girl was still missing. Maddy stopped reading when the article began to describe the state that the bodies were found in. She did not need the sensationalized imagery in order to understand what had happened. The ember began to glow anew as she began to delve further into the man's past.

Prior to living in Florida, the man had been raised in Salem, Arkansas. He had been a high school dropout in the tenth grade and was employed in a number of menial jobs until he obtained his commercial driver's license and began work at an area distribution center. He left the area and moved to Florida in September 2019. Maddy began searching news articles from around that area from 2019. *Oh fuck, please don't let me find anything. Please let me be wrong about this*, Maddy pleaded with the universe. Her pleas were not heard, nor did they last long. Beginning in 2011, there had been seven reports of missing children ranging from the ages of four to twelve in and around the Blue Hill area. Only one child was located. A six-year-old boy's body had been found by hunters in a shallow grave in a densely wooded area about twenty miles north of Blue Hill in . . . "Oh, goddamn it," Maddy said aloud in a defeated voice. The boy's body was found in southern Missouri. That was the pattern. Abduct the children that he probably saw in the morning going to school or playing outside as he completed his deliveries for the day in whatever town he might have been assigned to. Do his fucked-up, twisted, and evil shit. Bury them not only in another jurisdiction, but in another state in order to take advantage of law enforcement's frequent lack of cross communication. And New Jersey was right across the Hudson River.

Maddy began removing the numbers from the phone and disassembling it. She went to her black duffel bag and took inventory. She put on her baggy black clothes and went to the Hudson River. The river's waves pounded violently as the strong winds continuously blew Maddy's hood from off her auburn strands. As she tossed the parts of the phone into the surging waves, Maddy thought, *Not on* my *watch, fucker.*

Maddy was at a distinct disadvantage when it came to monitoring the man's movements. He was on the move while she was at work, and he was dormant at her peak stalking times. But there was no time limitation on the weekends. And he had a very distinct pattern. He would go to a local park around 8:30 am. He would watch (or probably record) the playing children there. He would stay for about two hours; at which time he would go to a large discount store. He would loiter around in the toy department and pull out his phone whenever a child entered his aisle. He would quickly turn and leave as soon as an adult approached. He would do this until around noon, at which time he would go into the men's room for about fifteen minutes.

Fuck, I'd hate to be the janitor in this place, Maddy thought as she could imagine what activity the man was engaged in. He then would leave the store and go back to his apartment for the remainder of the day.

On one such Saturday morning in the park, Maddy looked up from behind the tree she was encompassed by. About thirty yards away was the beaming smile of Erick as he said, "Hey! Wassupbutta . . ." Maddy quickly turned and walked away.

He heard Erick shout after her, "Sorry! I thought you were someone I knew!"

Nope. You don't know who I am right now, and you never will, Maddy thought as she felt the comfort of sweeping relief. *You can't know. It's not safe for you.*

Well, fuck! Maddy thought to herself as she pondered the plight that this degenerate had forced her into. She needed to do something, and fast. He may have already identified his first victim in Brooklyn. She began thinking about her options. *Break into his apartment and wait for him there? Nope, I can't see what's in there through the newspaper-covered windows. He may have booby traps and shit. At the park? Nope. It's broad daylight and too far from the subway. Plus, I'm not gonna have kids see that shit. Wait for him at the distribution center? Nope. Too many other people milling around there including security. At the discount store? Nope, too many cameras and too public and . . . wait a minute. Maybe a public display is just what this fucker deserves. I need to get some flesh-colored gloves and go shopping.*

It was the first Saturday in April. Flowers were blooming in the park, and leaves were budding on the trees. Birds were heard chirping from all directions in the still chilly morning air. Maddy's alarm went off. She extended her entire body with a satisfied exhalation as she completed her morning stretch. *No point really of showering,* she thought as she put on her hairnet, black "boy" wig, baggy black jeans, black hoodie, sunglasses, COVID mask, and flesh-colored gloves. She looked at herself in the mirror. *Oh fuck . . . I look ridiculous. I look like one of those weird space elves from* Star Wars.

She entered the subway station three stops from her regular stop and took it north into Jackson Heights. She then took the train back south to the required Brooklyn stop. She went into the discount store with her head down in order to avoid any part of her face being caught by the cameras. She retrieved a shopping cart and made her way through the store, placing miscellaneous items in the cart as she went. It was eleven, and he was here. She went in the opposite direction from where she had spotted him and proceeded to select the two items that she truly needed for her macabre endeavor.

At 11:45 am, the discount store cameras captured a small black-clad figure push their shopping cart into the corridor where the bathrooms were located. What the cameras could not capture is the same black-clad figure removing two items from the cart and entering the men's room. Nor could they capture them going into one of the stalls, locking the door, and squatting above the toilet. The cameras also failed to register the rapid heartbeat of this person as the anticipation of completing their self-justified horrific deed swelled.

She heard someone enter. She listened intently to the sound of shuffled footsteps, followed by the creak of the stall door farthest from the entrance. There was the click of the door lock, then an almost silent thud as something was laid on top of the porcelain tank. The unzipping of the pants. Then, the expected primal panting.

Within seconds of each other, Maddy kicked open the stall door. With her left hand, she plunged an arrow through the man's rectum, exiting halfway through his erect penis. With her right hand, she fiercely slammed his head with a hammer. The unconscious man collapsed to the floor with a heavy thud. Maddy looked at the image on the phone that he had been watching. It was the image of a three- or perhaps four-year-old little girl gazing in wonderment at a multicolored toy unicorn. She looked down upon the man with a combination of disgust and self-approval. Blood from the entrance and exit wounds was beginning to flow and well up around his shriveled testicles. She took a piece of paper and slid if halfway down the shaft of the arrow. She then rapidly left the store, returning home using the same out-of-the-way route. Soiled clothing was removed, bagged, and discarded. *Now I can finally take a fuckin' shower!* Maddy thought as she pondered where she and her friends would go for dinner before karaoke tonight. She settled on a place with good shish kebabs.

The police were notified of the murder as soon as a large pool of blood was seen seeping out of the bathroom stall by another customer. They took pictures of the crime scene, including the frozen face of shock and brutal pain on the face of the "victim." They looked at the paper that was left on the shaft of the arrow. The typed letters simply read, "Greenville, FL Blue Hill, AR." The following Tuesday, news of the gruesome discovery was still buzzing in the community. People were appalled at the amount of child pornography and images of some of *their* children playing in the park or at local shops that were found on multiple electronic devices in the pedophile's apartment. A wide variety of people were questioned, including Maddy and Sean. They both replied that he had been in there a couple of times and that they had obtained his contact information. Maddy reported that she had made a child's mother aware of the man's suspicious activity, and no, she didn't know her name.

"Well," the detective confided, "a million cameras in this 'burg and not one usable image of the guy that did this. But . . . maybe that's for the best. If you folks think of anything, give me a call, all right?"

"Will do, Detective!" Maddy offered disingenuously.

As the officer turned to leave, the concerned face of Erick was seen by Maddy. "Uh . . . wassupbuttacup?" he tentatively inquired.

"Hey, you!" Maddy excitedly exclaimed. "Nothin'. Just asking everybody about that murdered perv. Wanna go to our spot and talk?"

Once they arrived and had planted themselves in the well- worn grooves of the leather sofa, Erick said, "Y'know, it's just too sad to talk about, but . . . well . . . I'm not one for the death penalty, but some people . . . well . . . I just think that whoever did that to that motherfucker . . ." Maddy began sweating, and her heart began pounding, afraid to hear how Erick would finish the sentence. "Well . . . I think they deserve a fuckin' medal, key to the city, and ticker tape parade. But that's just me." Maddy's heart swelled as she felt something that she had thought she had felt before. But not like this. It was almost as though she was developing . . . feelings greater than friendship for him. *What the fuck is going on?* Maddy thought as she returned to her office. She then took a deep breath, reached into her purse, and pulled out the prince checklist. *Okay, this is fuckin' stupid. He's just my friend . . . but . . . let's just get this over with.*

MADDY SOMMERS PRINCE CHECKLIST
BY MADDY SOMMERS
NUMERO UNO: Can't be married. Not even "separated."

Ummm. Okay, undetermined. I don't think that he is, but he's never really talked about it, so . . . undetermined.

NUMERO TWO-O: Treats me with respect.

Yup, he totally treats me and my opinions with respect. I'm sayin' check.

NUMERO THREE-O: Listens to me.

Yup—that's all we do is talk and listen to one another. That's another check.

NUMERO FOUR-O: Won't try to change me.

Well, he just said the other day to not let any motherfucker change me, so . . . check.

NUMERO FIVE-O: Handsome.

Uh, yeah . . . he is handsome. I mean, I just haven't thought of him that way before, but yeah, I'll give him another check.

NUMERO SIX-O: Financially independent.

Well, it sounds like he's not rich, but he has enough to live here without working. He has his own place, so he won't be sleeping on my couch because he can't afford the rent, so . . . check.

NUMERO SEVEN-O: Intelligent.

Oh fuck. He's rifling right through these. Check.

NUMERO EIGHT-O: Common interests.

Not into sports or the outdoors, so won't be going off with "the guys" to do their stupid "man" shit. Loves music, horror movies, drinking, and going out. What more could a girl ask for? Check.

NUMERO NINE-O: Makes me laugh.

Are you kidding me? That's all we do together. We laugh at stupid jokes or asshole people or freakish-looking kids. I sometimes laugh so hard that I gag. That's what she said. Shit, I wish he had been here for that one. Check.

NUMERO TEN-O: Has to have the same political ideology. No patriotism, no pussy! No shit.

Ummm . . . I really don't know. I mean, he's certainly not a fan of dictators, but I still don't know, so . . . undetermined.

Maddy ran out of her office onto the sales floor just in time to see Erick about to leave. "Stop that man!" Maddy yelled out without thinking. Four patrons and an employee quickly surrounded a completely confused Erick who said, "What the fuck, Maddy?"

"Oh shit . . . sorry!" Maddy embarrassingly stated. "I just . . . uh . . . needed to talk to him for a minute. Sorry I was so dramatic about it. Uh . . . you can like . . . stand down or whatever."

The people separated themselves, revealing a rather annoyed Erick. "Okay, so . . . what's so important that you nearly had me lynched?"

Maddy's mind was racing. What can she say? Then it hit her. "Hey . . . sorry about that," she began sheepishly as she slowly approached him, cocking her head slightly and batting her eyes.

What the fuck is up with her? Erick thought.

"It's just . . . well, I just got this box of 45s in today, and I haven't looked at them yet, except for one, and . . . I thought you might want to check them out before you left."

"Oh . . . cool. Yeah, that's worth getting nearly lynched for. Go get them," Erick replied sincerely without a hint of sarcasm. They returned to their respective positions on the couch. Maddy had a box of records. Erick was literally and figuratively salivating.

"Okay . . . I just looked at one, and that's why I ran out to stop you," Maddy felt a tinge of guilt about her deception.

"And what record was so special to cause such a threat to my physical safety and outstanding reputation?" Erick inquired. "Okay, so . . . it's an original pressing of 'Love Me' by the Phantom and—"

"How much for the box?" Erick immediately inquired. "Okay, so there's fifty records in the box, and I have no idea what's in here, and we only gave $30 for them, so . . . how about $2 a record, a hundred bucks for the box."

"Oh god no, Maddy," Erick countered.

"What the fuck is wrong with that? That's a great deal!" Maddy incredulously replied.

"Yeah, I know. It's too good of a deal. I feel like I'd be taking advantage of you at that price. How about $4 a record, two hundred for the box?"

"Okay, let's be reasonable about this," Maddy stated as she adopted her "negotiator" demeanor complete with cocked head and batting copper eyelashes. "How about we just compromise at $3 a record, $150 for the box?"

At that moment, Amanda walked by the sofa. "Hey, Amanda, could you come here for a minute?" Erick requested.

"Sure, how can I help you?"

Erick began explaining, "Amanda, I am going to write you a check for that box of records that Maddy is holding. This check is going to be for more than the $100 that she wants me to pay, but less than the $200 that I feel is reasonable. You shall take this check, put it in the cash register, and accept it as payment for this box of records, okay?"

"Sure, whatever," Amanda stated as she accepted the check and began to leave.

"Amanda, hold it!" Maddy ordered. "Just tell me. Is that check for less than $200?"

"Yes, it is," Amanda replied.

"Fine. You sir have just purchased a box of vintage 45s. It is my sincere hope that they will bring you countless hours of enjoyment."

This exchange led to another hour of enjoyment for the friends as they joked around and discussed Maddy's flawless negotiating tactics. Maddy then looked at Erick and said, "So . . . tell me . . . how come a nice guy like you isn't all settled down and married and shit?"

Erick's demeanor immediately went from jovial hijinks to depressingly somber as he said with a tear forming in each hazel eye, "Well, I was married, and I lost my wife last fall to COVID because . . . because . . . because . . . those fucking right-wing douchebags murdered her through their hate-filled indoctrination of their insane motherfuckin' propaganda and . . . and . . . I'm so sorry, Maddy . . . I just can't talk about this with you."

Erick grabbed his box of records and dashed out of the store, leaving a bewildered Maddy in his wake. She sat there with the mixed emotions of sorrow for her friend's loss and exhilaration at what was just revealed and what could potentially come out of it.

NUMERO UNO: Can't be married. Not even "separated."

Check.

NUMERO TEN-O: Has to have the same political ideology. No patriotism, no pussy! No shit.

Big fuckin' check. *I think that I've just met the one person who hates those fascist motherfuckers more than I do.*

She pulled out her prince checklist. A teardrop fell upon theunfolded paper as she read the last line of the page:

If you have met a guy that has successfully navigated himself through this most treacherous quest, then congratulations! You, Maddy Sommers, have just met your prince. Now go get him and go get busy!

Maddy went to the cash register and opened the drawer. She took the check out and smirked as she looked at it. *Well, he'd better come in tomorrow,* she thought, *'cause now I've gotta get him to fall in love with me, and . . .* She looked at the check that he had written for $199.99. It said, "Gotcha!" in the memo line, complete with a smiley face for the "O." *And I'm sorry to say that I'm gonna have to cut that smart-ass's balls off!*

CHAPTER 16

THE MORE YOU IGNORE ME, THE CLOSER I GET

Oh fuck . . . I'm in love, Maddy thought as she strode to Kristy and Jason's town house after work on Wednesday and reflected on the day's events. Erick had returned to the shop at his usual time earlier that day and apologized for his emotional reaction from the day before. Maddy was apologetic as well, but Erick insisted that she had no reason to apologize. She had no idea why he had really moved to New York because he had not told her, and for that, he was extremely sorry.

"So why *did* you move to New York then?" Maddy had inquired.

Erick responded with "Do you remember a few weeks ago when I told you that I walked around angry all of the time and this place was my oasis of happiness? Well, I'm going to tell you everything that I walk around angry about all of the time. I haven't told you before this because I just didn't want to spoil the one place that I can let all of this go, and I didn't want to burden you, my good friend, with my issues."

"You can tell me anything," Maddy offered sincerely.

"Okay, but this isn't going to be fun," Erick began as his head bowed with a despondent look upon his face, a single tear rolling down his cheek. He explained that he and his wife had met as teenagers in Jefferson City, Missouri, and had become high school sweethearts. Both attended Mizzou, and they were married shortly after their college graduation. He became a junior high public-school teacher. She worked in health insurance and steadily climbed her respective corporate ladder. And she was beautiful, always was in fact. She was intelligent and had a carefree spirit that made him eager to return home each evening. They laughed together during happy times and cried together during times of loss and sorrow. They vented to each other about their daily professional stressors. They were each other's support system, always having each other's back. From the time they had met at the age of sixteen until the year 2020, it had been a wonderful twenty-eight-year relationship.

He had always been an independent politically, leaning slightly right of center if he had to categorize his position. He had voted for Obama in 2008 but switched to Romney in 2012 out of his belief that the Affordable Care Act was an unfair burden to businesses. She was politically apathetic for the most part but always voted for the candidate that she felt "had the best heart," regardless of party affiliation, policy issues, or ideology. They rarely discussed politics, let alone argue about it. Maddy recalled that as Erick spoke, his face became increasingly redder, and his voice became louder and more pronounced.

Then came COVID. Their families had both succumbed to the radical right-wing propaganda that was spewed by narcissistic, greedy blowhards on the internet and cable television, and these family members were increasingly whispering in their ears. To Erick, their attacks upon lifelong medical professionals while watching the circus of self-gratifying daily press conferences was pure insanity. Then came the transparently stupid attacks upon the 2020 election with a who's who of right-wing freaks leading the charge against our constitutional democracy. The right-wing party had become one that was advocating dictatorship over democracy, marginalization of minorities over equal rights for all, and fantastical worldviews over fact-based reason. Basic human rights and public health measures were not just being ignored but actively attacked by the people who were electronically injecting this vile Kool-Aid into their system on an hourly basis, and Erick could not wrap his mind around what was happening. There seemed to be no ability for these people to be reasonable. Any fact-based arguments were greeted with the immediate response of "fake news!" He tried to put on a smile and enter into polite conversation with these people, including members of their families. He would end up sitting in the corner shaking his head in disbelief at the utter madness that he was forced to listen to from people who were otherwise reasonably intelligent. Oftentimes, he would just leave early as he felt his blood pressure rise, with a full understanding now of how Nazi Germany had come into existence through the indoctrinating messages of hate into a willfully ignorant and self-serving public.

And in their isolation, his wife became one of them. It was not as though she woke up one day and was a completely different person. It happened slowly, over time, as she was increasingly bored at home and spent more and more time listening to broadcasts that had been recommended to her by her family and friends. Erick tried to offer counterprogramming, but his offers were ignored, if not outright mocked. She began calling him "sheeple." He received the vaccine as soon as it was available to him. She did not because of government microchips or some such nonsense. Therefore, they basically lived in separate areas of the home as Erick did not want to risk contracting the virus and spreading it to his students and their families. They were increasingly isolated from each other, but she had her large "tribe" of like-minded "thinkers" to support her. Erick did not. He felt as though he were a tiny speck of rational blue in a sea of increasingly red hysteria.

Then in the fall of 2021 came the attacks upon school boards and teachers, including Erick personally, for teaching the actual history of our country, warts and all, instead of some whitewashed "America first" propaganda designed to alleviate "bad feelings" that white students might harbor for the atrocities of their distant and not-so-distant ancestors. There were death threats via the telephone, email, and notes left on the front door. All for trying to explain to the children of our country how the depravity of slavery continued to impact all of our society to this very day. It was a fact that Erick failed to understand opposition against. Finally, at a school board meeting in October, Erick was personally attacked outside of his car. With their unmasked, unvaccinated spittle flying into his face, he was called a traitor. He was called a commie. He was called a libtard. And those were the kind words. Erick had opened his car door, looked each of his attackers in the eye, and simply said, "I can't stand watching you people fuck up your children anymore! You're just too fucking stupid to waste my time on! If any of you motherfuckers try to take a swing at me, I'll fucking kill you! Now, fuck off!" And with that, Erick's twenty-two-year career had come to an end.

He returned home and explained the reprehensible scene to his wife, hoping that this level of insanity might shake her from her self-imposed pod of ignorance. Instead, she looked at him with a blank expression and said, "They have a point. Why do you hate our country?" And Erick lost his shit.

He casually walked over to the kitchen door, picked up the aluminum baseball bat that he had placed there for protection, and, in a frenzied blur, proceeded to destroy every phone, computer, radio, and television in the house. Fragments of the devastated electronic devices were flying throughout the home as Erick was completely absorbed by his blind rage. She screamed at him to stop. He did not hear her, nor did he stop. She left him that very night. He never saw or spoke to her again. Two weeks later, she contracted COVID. Three weeks later, she was dead. He was devastated by the loss of his lifelong love and his impotence at not being able to do something about it. He had been saving and investing his money since he had begun working at the age of sixteen. He wasn't wealthy, but he had enough to live on for a while anywhere he chose. And he chose New York. He put his house on the market, most of his belongings in storage, and moved there on January 1, 2022, with a simple New Year's resolution: "Don't kill anybody this year."

Erick looked up at Maddy and saw his tear-filled reflection in her understanding tear-filled emerald eyes. She had wanted to reach out to him in a comforting embrace but felt that she could not. Here was a man who understood the deterioration of our basic societal norms, just as she did. Her emotions swelled from romantic interest to adoration. She still would not admit to herself that she had fallen in love however, until Erick looked up, wiped his tears from his cheeks, flashed his ornery grin, and said, "But the real reason I moved to New York is because . . . well . . . it's my kinda town."

"Oh . . . my . . . fucking . . . god!" Maddy exclaimed. "That is the best fucking joke I've ever heard!" The pair burst into hearty laughter while looking admiringly upon each other. And with that, Maddy Sommers was the first to realize that they had fallen in love.

The only trick now was to get a Mr. Erick Parker to fall in love with her. This required a great deal of thought, organization, and a foolproof three-step plan that Maddy unveiled to her friends that Wednesday evening. As appetizers, wine, and gin were being consumed, Maddy proudly stood before her trio of sisters and presented her strategy. "Okay, gang, thanks for listening to this. Okay . . . I've finally met my prince. I know it sounds weird, but it's almost like the universe or something has, like, brought us together or something. So I think we're meant to be together, but Erick's like still going through survivor's guilt and stuff, so I need to be cool about this. Here's my plan:

Numero uno: Get him to ask me out on a date. Numero two-o: We fall in love.

Numero three-o: We live happily ever after.

"What do you think?" The three just stared at Maddy in disbelief. Each knew that any form of contradiction would be unwelcome at this point. Sam and Kristy looked at Jules in order to nominate her as the spokesperson.

Jules let out a heavy sigh and said flatly, "Yep . . . we like it. Not too many details. What could possibly go wrong?" "Awesome! Thanks for your support. I'm getting another drink. Anybody want anything?"

The trio shook their heads, and Maddy triumphantly left the room. They continued shaking their heads in amazement as Kristy said, "Well . . . this is going to be either really good or really bad."

"Yup," Sam agreed, "we'd better check this guy out. She won't survive another relationship like the last two. And . . . we'd better give Blair a heads-up." The pact was made. Erick was about to endure the most comprehensive investigation that could be performed short of an anal probe. And even that was not necessarily off the table.

As Maddy was making her drink in the kitchen, she saw six brilliant blue eyes peering at her from around the corner of the staircase that led to the family room. She stared at them, and they stared back. She suddenly felt the gruesome weight of the tragedy that had befallen the missing children and broke down into tears. The six-year-old twin boys and four-year-old girl made their way into the kitchen. "Aunt Maddy," the towheaded girl said while looking up at Maddy with a worried expression, "why are you crying?"

Maddy forced a chuckle, wiped her tears, and got down on one knee. "I'm crying," Maddy began, "because I'm the luckiest girl in the world to have such great huggers in my life." With that, the three children enthusiastically charged Maddy, knocking her over and pinning her to the floor in their ornery but loving embraces.

They rolled around on the floor, tickling each other and laughing when Jason came upstairs and said, "Um, Maddy . . . everything okay?"

Maddy playfully shoved her three cackling attackers onto the floor, stood up, and said, "Yes, everything is okay, because these lovely children have a wonderful man who will always protect them. I know how much Kristy appreciates you. And until the events of this week, I didn't realize how much I appreciate you too. Why don't you take a break? I'll watch these guys for a while."

When Kristy came downstairs to check on things, she found Maddy asleep and encased by her three beautiful blonde children. The children were all lying on her in a variety of near-impossible angles mesmerized by their first viewing of *Cinderella*.

On Friday morning, Maddy was once again arming herself for battle. She looked at her black duffel bag, kicked it to the side, and dug into her closet for the cutest pair of pumps that she had. She got dressed and looked at her reflection in the mirror. She was wearing her formfitting purple dress, stopping just above the knees, and black strapped pumps. *Yup . . . fucking irresistible. Okay, Mr. Parker, prepare yourself to get royally fucked . . . well . . . hopefully.*

"Wow, you look great," Erick said as he greeted Maddy at the store that afternoon.

"Oh . . . this old thing?" Maddy demurely replied while batting her eyes. They took their spot on the long couch and began their conversation with the typical bad jokes and discussions of current events. Maddy searched for the perfect opportunity to begin her romantic assault, but there were no natural openings. That is until later when Erick came up to the counter with a record to purchase. As Maddy looked at the cover of "One on One" by Cheap Trick, she said, "I've heard this record is really good, but I haven't heard it."

"Well, you can borrow it if you would like," Erick replied. "Well . . .," Maddy began innocently while looking down, "I actually don't have a turntable. I'd have to go to someone *else's* house to listen to it." This resulted in a deep sigh of exasperation and rolling of the eyes by Erick. "What the fuck is wrong with you, mister?" Maddy exclaimed.

"Okay," Erick began, "do you remember a while ago when I told you not to let anybody change you."

"Yeah," Maddy responded with her full attitude on display. "What does *that* have to do with anything?"

"Well," Erick continued, "I'm only human, and there's only so much that I can take, so . . . why does a cool chick like you not have a turntable? Get a fuckin' turntable so that you can borrow this record, okay?" This resulted in another round of "arguing" as the pair went back and forth with "*Fine,* maybe I *will* buy a turntable!"

"*Good,* I think you *should*!"

"*Great,* then I *will*!"

"*Awesome,* I'm *sooo* glad that you're *doing* that!"

Spontaneous laughter ensued as Erick said, "This has been fun. See ya next week! But seriously, get a fuckin' turntable."

As Erick left the store, Maddy thought, *Well, we kinda missed the fuckin' point there now, didn't we?*

"Strike 1!" Sean said as he walked past Maddy with a slight grin.

"Shut the fuck up, Sean," came Maddy's bitter response. The following Tuesday, with Maddy adorned in a cute low-cut sleeveless flowered top and midthigh-length pink skirt, Maddy said, "So . . . what are ya doin' for supper tonight?"

"Oh, I'm going to eat a Bercelli's," came Erick's reply.

"Yeah . . . I've always wanted to try that place, so . . . are ya goin' with friends or . . ."

"No, just dinner by myself. But . . . do you like spicy food?" Erick answered.

"You know I do. Why?" Maddy replied demurely while batting her eyes as her heart began racing, and she thought, *Oh fuck! It's happening!*

"Well," Erick began, "if you ever go, try the marina with spicy sausage and red peppers. You'll love it!"

"Yup . . . I'll be sure to do that," Maddy replied as a lonely trombone was heard in the distance going "Mwaaa, mwaaa, mwaaa."

"Strike 2!" Sean gleefully said as he paraded by his frustrated boss.

"Shut . . . the . . . fuck . . . *up* . . . Sean!"

Sean came back over to the counter and said with a hint of sarcasm, "Hey . . . do you want some pointers on how to pick up guys, because I've really been hitting the mother lode recently." His beaming smile faded as Maddy raised her head, and he saw her deeply annoyed and perhaps violent expression. "Okay . . . guess I'll get back to work now," he said as he left the counter, silently chuckling.

The following Wednesday, with Maddy wearing a black T-shirt with silver sequins that spelled out "The Ramones" and tight blue jeans, Maddy said, "Hey, if you ever hear of a band coming to the club that I would like, let me know, okay . . . 'cause . . . I'd really like to go!"

Her eyes were batting as fast as they could go as Erick replied, "Yeah, I'll do that! Maybe I'll see ya there! See ya Friday!"

Maddy frustratingly thought, *Okay, mister. You know what would be a surefire fuckin' way of seeing me there? If you'd realize that we're meant to be together, and you ask me out and we go together. That would be a surefire fuckin' way of seeing me there now, wouldn't it?*

Sean began approaching the counter. Maddy looked up

and said, "Don't *even* fuckin' say it, Sean!" Sean stopped, gave Maddy a sly grin, and held up three fingers. The ink pen narrowly missed the back of his head as he made a hasty retreat back to the storeroom.

That night at Jules's apartment, a frustrated Maddy was expressing her bewilderment to her friends and aunts who were in town that week. "What the fuck is this guy's deal? I mean, we get along great! We have the same interests! We both have great senses of humor!" That last line caused everyone in the room to look down so that Maddy could not see their eye rolls. "And," Maddy continued, "I'm fuckin' adorable! So . . . what the fuck?"

"You sure he's straight?" Jules inquired flatly.

"Yeah, he's fuckin' straight," Maddy answered annoyingly.

Kristy chimed in and said, "Well . . . maybe you're just not his type." Maddy just stared at her coldly and slowly shook her head.

"Ummm . . . well . . . I'm sorry. I've got nothing," was Sam's brilliant contribution.

Blair then added her voice to the chorus. "Dear, he's just had a traumatic loss. He may not be ready to date yet. If it's meant to be, then it will be in due time. And always remember. I know it sounds old fashioned, but I've always felt that a lady should wait to be asked out by the gentleman."

"Fuck that!" Patty exclaimed. "If I lived by that rule, then I'd never get laid, because my dates are always chicks! But if that's how ya wanna play it, Mads, remember that this dude hasn't asked a girl out in like, what . . . thirty years or something? This motherfucker has no idea what he's doing! If you want him to ask you out, you're going to have to hit him over the head with it!" Blair looked at Patty in order to make her understand who it was that she was talking to. Patty hastily retreated. "I mean . . . figuratively, not literally. Don't *really* hit him over the head. Guys don't like that . . . I've heard."

Okay . . . new plan, Maddy thought.

It's brilliant! Maddy thought. *I'll go out with another guy a couple times. I'll tell Erick about it. He'll get jealous and ask me out. Fuckin' brilliant!* The full range of Maddy's junior high maturity was on display as she regaled Erick about the new guy that she had started seeing. It didn't work.

"That's really nice. You deserve to find someone cool. Hey, have you seen the new Netflix series?" was Erick's uninterested response.

The following Tuesday, Erick was at the counter purchasing his latest treasure. Maddy was also at the counter desperately contemplating her next offensive when the man that Maddy had dated a couple of times came strutting into the store. His shirt was unbuttoned halfway down his slender chest with three gold chains prominently displayed. "Hey, babe," the man stated as he seductively leaned across the counter at his assumed paramour. *What the fuck is this guy doing here?* Maddy thought. *Oh shit.*

I was supposed to go out with him tonight. And . . . when the fuck did we get to "babe"? "Uh . . . hey . . . what are ya doin'?"

"Well," the man replied alluringly, "I just wanted to come in and tell you how excited I am about our . . . you know . . . third date."

Maddy immediately thought, *Fuck! Why did I even tell him about that! He thinks he's getting laid! Think fast, think fast, think fast . . .* "Uh . . . yeah . . . about that. Listen, someone called in sick for tonight, so I'm going to have to work, and I'm pretty booked up the rest of the week, so . . . maybe I'll give you a call next week or something."

The man immediately became despondent and said in a childlike whine, "But, babe, it's . . . y'know . . . our third date. What am *I* supposed to do?"

Maddy callously replied, "I don't know what to tell you. Build a model airplane. Stream a movie. Adopt a shelter animal. I don't know, but I have to work."

"Fine, just forget it then!" the man angrily exclaimed before turning and leaving the store.

Cool, that was easy. Now . . . about Erick, Maddy thought as Erick then came up to her laughing.

"Wow, that guy *really* wanted to go on a third date with you," Erick playfully stated through his chuckles.

Okay, this is it, Maddy schemed. *I'm gonna wipe that smug smile right off of your face and we're going out tonight or else my name's not Maddy fuckin' Sommers. And that's my name, so that's what's happening whether you like it or not!*

Maddy was looking down at a paper, pretending to be filling out a form as she began in her most alluring voice, "Yeah . . . that's not going to work out. Besides, I just went out with *that* guy a couple times to try to make this *other* guy that I *really* like jealous. So . . ." She then looked up and gave Erick the Full Maddy. Head slightly tilted to the left. Her radiant copper hair framing her beautiful freckled face. And those emerald eyes glistening as flashes of auburn batted over them. "Why can't a nice guy like you ask me out sometime?"

Erick's eyes widened as his smug smile disappeared. He just stood there looking at her with a shocked and dumbfounded expression. He finally was able to stutter, "Uh . . . uh . . . ummmm . . . there's another record that I was going to buy. I'll be right back." And in that moment, although he would not yet admit it to himself, Erick Parker realized that he had fallen in love with her.

"Well, I think he finally got it," Sean dryly stated.

"Yup, the ball's in his court," a hopeful Maddy replied. "And if he doesn't hit this ball back, then he's not gonna have any balls left to play with!"

What the fuck was that? Erick thought in a state of confusion. His mind was swimming. *What did she mean by that? Should I ask her out? Should I feel guilty about asking her out? Jesus, I haven't been on a date in thirty years! I don't even* want *to date anyone. But . . . it's Maddy, so . . . yeah, it's just Maddy. She probably meant for us to just go out as friends. And certainly, there's nothing wrong with asking a friend out. Yeah, I'll just ask her if she wants to go to the show tonight, and she has to work anyway, so she'll turn me down, and I'll come back in tomorrow, and everything will be normal. Yep, this will be fine.* Erick had difficulty in repressing the knowledge that his rationalization was ridiculous.

Erick summoned as much courage as he had available to him and attempted to be cool as he strutted over to the long counter, as though he were grooving to a T. rex song. Maddy looked up at him expectantly and batted her lush eyelashes once more as he said, "Y'know, it's . . . uh . . . it's too bad you gotta work tonight, 'cause . . . uh . . . I'm seeing a really cool band at the Club, and I think you'd really like them . . . y'know . . . if you were inter-ested . . . but I know you gotta work, sooo—"

Maddy immediately cut him off, not allowing her prey to wriggle his way out of the romantic trap that she had sprung. "That sounds really cool, um . . . who's playin'?"

These two friends had never had a moment of awkwardness or trepidation between them from the moment that they had met. They knew each other so well, and their bond of friendship was so strong by now that their trust in each other was absolute, and they were both surprised at the tension that surrounded them in this moment. It was as though they were two combatants feeling the tight anticipation of an upcoming battle. The pressure was immediately relieved when Erick confidently said, "Um . . . they're called Southern Culture on the Skids. They've been around for, like, thirty years or something, but they play really cool, what I would call, Swampabilly, and I think you might dig them."

"Seriously?" Maddy stated excitedly. "They're in town? How the fuck did I not know that?"

Erick flashed his mischievous smile as if he knew a game between them was now afoot and said in as condescending manner as possible, "Now, Maddy . . . you really don't have to try to look cool around me . . . I know you have cool taste in music, but you really don't have to pretend you know who this bands is." His face beamed with arrogance as he was sure he had caught his friend in an embarrassing predicament and was mentally preparing his victory speech.

"Well . . . listen here, mister," Maddy began in an overly emphasized annoyed tone while mirroring the arrogance plastered on his face, "I'll tell you what. If I can name ten SCOTS songs off the top of my head, then you're buying dinner and drinks tonight . . . and let me tell you, I'm gonna be one expensive fuckin' date. And if I can't . . . well then, I will, of course, pay, which, I can guarantee you, will *not* be a problem. Deal?" Each word dripped with satisfaction as she knew she had just kicked his ass—brutally and quite publicly.

The arrogance faded from Erick's face once he heard her refer to the band as "SCOTS." He knew he was fucked, but the points had yet to be officially scored, so he retorted with false confidence, "Yeah, okay . . . you got a bet. And oh, by the way, I like really expensive cocktails, and I'm in a three-appetizer mood, so you might wanna check what you have in your bank account, 'cause this might get ugly." He felt that the only way to throw her off her game would be to project such overconfidence that it might affect her ability to concentrate. Maybe she would only be able to come up with eight or nine song titles, and a hard-fought and well-deserved victory would be secured over his worthy, and now surprisingly alluring, opponent.

Maddy locked her fired-up eyes upon Erick's, took a deep breath, and began rapidly firing out song titles. "'Friedchickenandgasoline,' 'Doublewide,' 'Firefly,' '8PieceBox,' '69ElCamino,' 'CamelWalk,' 'VivaDelSanto,' 'BananaPuddin',' 'DirtTrackDate,' and . . . um . . . oh shit, I need one more!" There was a glimmer of hope in Erick's eyes as he began to lift himself off the virtual ropes that this musical juggernaut had mercilessly knocked him into until Maddy said in her most pompous voice, her head held high with her lips open and spread upward in the most conceited smile in her arsenal, "Just fuckin' with ya. 'Soul City,' muthaaafuckaaa! Maddy out!"

Erick burst into congratulatory laughter as he enthusiastically joined the celebration of his friend's decisive victory over him. It was never about winning with them. It was all just for the sport of it all, and he reveled in the moment as he gazed upon the prideful expression on her precious face. She had bested him, and he loved it as he sensed that their "battles" had just been taken to a new level. She may have won this round, but there would be many more to come. This kittenish war was far from over.

CHAPTER 17

EIGHT-PIECE BOX

Maddy, taking her aunt Patty's advice to heart, took control of the arrangements for their first date. But first, they had to agree that it was, in fact, a "date" as Erick had taken their previous exchange completely as a joke.

"So," Maddy began, attempting to control her excitement by playing it "cool," "that sounds superfun. So what did you have in mind?"

"What do you mean?" Erick inquired, now realizing that she was really serious about going out together.

"Well . . . would we grab a bite to eat first, or . . ."

"Oh . . . uh . . . sure. I mean, you won the bet and all so . . .," Erick replied as he desperately attempted to find his footing in this unfamiliar discussion. "Um . . . I was just going to go the burrito joint, but we could go anywhere you like, and since I'm stuck with the bill, you should probably pick some-place better."

"No, I love the burrito joint, but they're just so huge!" "That's what she said!" was Erick's response followed by laughter by the pair and pathetic eye rolls by a listening Sean. "Well, okay," Erick continued, now feeling surer of himself after his perfectly timed joke, "how about we meet at the burrito joint at six, split a burrito, go to the show, and maybe we could grab a drink after-wards . . . y'know, if it wasn't too late."

"So . . .," Maddy countered demurely with her head slightly cocked to one side, "this would be like a *date* . . . right?"

"Ummm . . . well . . . ummm . . . I don't know that we have to put any pressure on it by labeling it. How about if we just go out and see if we have a good time and then decide what it is?" Erick knew this response was ridiculous as the words haphazardly fell from his mouth. He also knew that he had just set himself up for yet another round of humiliation at the hands of his pint-sized adversary.

And Maddy didn't disappoint him. As she listened to his ridiculous comment, she immediately thought, *Oh . . . I am soooo gonna fuck him up right now.* And she did. "Okay . . . let me get this straight. You're taking me to dinner . . ."

"Well . . . it's just the burrito joint," came Erick's embarrassed reply. He lacked the courage to even look at Maddy's piercing green eyes as she gleefully tore apart his argument.

"Yes, but it's still dinner," she calmly said to which Erick replied deflatingly, "Yeah . . . I guess so."

"And you're taking me to a show," Maddy's voice continued to lilt into a singsong cadence as she spoke.

"Yeah," came the timid reply.

"And you're taking me out for drinks afterward." "Well . . . if it's not too late."

"And it *might* be a date!" Maddy concluded.

Erick, rediscovering his fight and realizing the absurdity of the situation, looked right into Maddy's eyes, smiled, and exclaimed, "Exactly!"

Fuck it, close enough, Maddy thought to herself as she said, "Okay, this sounds like fun. Let me see what I can do."

Maddy departed back to her office, and Sean approached the counter, shaking his head in disbelief at the awkward encounter he had just witnessed. Erick immediately began performing emotional damage control as he spoke to Sean about the most likely scenario. "Well, I'm sure she's back there just trying to find a way to let me down easy. I know she can't go because she has to work, so . . ."

Sean burst out laughing. "She doesn't have to work! She just said that to blow that other guy off. *You're* the one she wants to go out with. She's been hitting on you for like two months . . . did you not know that?" Erick just shook his head with a confused expression as Maddy reentered the area, fresh off calming her emotions, putting on her "cool' demeanor, and establishing her plan for her novice paramour.

"Okay," Maddy began confidently, "I would love to go out on this *date* with you, but I have a couple of conditions first. Numero uno: You can't buy these records today," she said as she took his records and placed them under the counter. "Nor can you buy them tomorrow. You're going to come in on Thursday and buy these records *from me*, and we're going to have an open and honest discussion about whether we should go out on another *date* or just be friends." This first condition was based upon Maddy knowing that Erick was going to have to take a day and process his feelings of survivor's guilt, probably by talking with Pastor Tim. "Numero two-o: I get to ask you any question that I want, and you promise to not get offended and to answer completely honestly . . . deal?"

"Counterproposal," came Erick's surprisingly confident reply.

Counterproposal? What the fuck? Maddy thought.

"I will take tomorrow and think about our time together, and I will come in on Thursday and have an open discussion about where we should go from here. And you can ask me anything that you want, but any question that you ask me you must be also willing to answer. Deal?" The ensuing formal handshake was the final nonintimate moment that the pair would experience for the remainder of their time together.

Erick was sitting at a sidewalk table in the warm but completely cloudy and gray late-May New York evening. He was watching the throng of pedestrians pass by, nervously awaiting his friend . . . or date . . . no, friend. And he was talking to the universe. *Okay, this is ridiculous. Why would a cool chick like her have any interest in me? This is just stupid. Listen, if there's anybody up there that's been pulling some strings or whatever, please just give me a sign that I'm making a fool out of myself. Have a bird shit on my head, or . . .*

At that moment, he looked down the street and saw Maddy standing at the corner wearing a beautiful canary-yellow sundress with a white geometrical pattern. He looked at her. She looked at him. Their eyes met. And at that moment, the slightest parting of the clouds occurred, and Maddy was backlit by a single ray of sunshine. She was a bright, glowing vision in the ashen gray city. And Erick audibly said, "You gotta be fuckin' kidding me."

The "date" went off without a hitch. Once their mutual nerves had calmed, they threw themselves into a deep "philosophical" discussion about which SCOTS album they should take should they be stranded on a desert island. It was not lost on Maddy that Erick had placed them both on the island together in this scenario. Maddy vehemently argued for *Mojo Box* while

Erick lobbied in vain for *The Electric Pinecones*. In the spirit of their first "date" or whatever it was, they compromised on the obvious. If they ever were to be stranded together on a desert island, they would take *Dirt Track Date*.

Erick and Maddy were sitting at Erick's preferred table about ten yards from the main bar and thirty yards from the stage as the opening act performed. "Ummm . . . aren't we going down front?" a confused Maddy inquired.

"Yep, just wait for it."

"Wait for what?" Maddy asked.

"For *it*. For the last song of their set. Don't worry, I'll let you know when it's time to move." Maddy sat there impatiently while wondering how she was going to catch a piece of chicken from *here* as Erick went to the bar and got two drinks for each of them. There was a final power chord struck as Erick handed Maddy her two drinks and said, "Now!" The entire floor audience turned to face the pair that was moving in the opposite direction. They were like salmon going against the current until they reached their destination. Erick smiled at Maddy triumphantly and said, "See? Front of the stage!" Maddy squealed with delight and wrapped her delicate arms around Erick for the first time. The brief embrace was simultaneously awkward and comforting.

The performance was exhilarating. They danced. They laughed. They sang along. They were covered in sweat as they would wrap an arm around the other's waist in order to shout something into the other's ear. And Maddy caught her piece of fried chicken that was tossed from the stage by a provocatively dancing go-go girl as the band tore through "Eight-Piece Box." Maddy snatched it from the air and began immediately devouring it.

"Ummm . . .," Erick awkwardly said, "that's really supposed to be used as a prop. It's not really to be eaten."

"What? It's fuckin' chicken, isn't it? I'm vaccinated, so I don't care where that bitch's hands have been. Fuck it, I'm starvin'!"

Erick just smiled and shook his head in approving wonderment.

Following the show, the pair went to a small tavern, and Maddy began peppering Erick with rather intimate questions. She found his responses to be predictably rather boring. *Well, at least he's not a freak who's gonna tie me up and spank me and shit,* she thought. She then made an error. She asked him how many women he had slept with, to which he immediately answered, "One."

"How the fuck is that even possible?" Maddy exclaimed in disbelief.

"Well, I told you how long I was with my deceased wife, and I've never even thought about having a one-night stand or anything like that. I mean, I need to have an emotional connection before I'm comfortable with that. And of course, I would never dream of cheating on someone that I was involved with, even as she changed into another person that I didn't recognize. I just wouldn't be able to live with myself, Maddy." "Okay . . . well, I guess that's commendable or something."

It then dawned on her. She had to answer the same question.

Erick immediately sensed her discomfort and said, "You can take a pass on this one. That aspect of your life is yours and is really none of my concern." A wave of relief swept over her as they finished their drinks, and he offered to walk her home.

On the three-block trek, Maddy reached out and grabbed Erick's hand. Erick gave her hand the slightest squeeze as if to say, "Yeah, that's okay."

"Well, this is me," Maddy awkwardly stated upon their arrival to her apartment building.

"Well, I really had a nice time tonight, Maddy, and . . . um . . . I've got a lot to think about. I will definitely be in on Thursday so we can . . . y'know . . . talk."

"Ummm . . . well . . . it's not really *that* late," Maddy stated alluringly as she wrapped her arms around his waist. "And . . . I'd really like to listen to those records you bought, so . . . how about we go back to your place and we . . . y'know . . . listen to records."

Erick was not adept at picking up on social cues, especially provocative passes, but this was so blatant that even he understood its intentions. He thought, *Yeah, she wants a needle in a groove, but it has nothing to do with music,* before saying, "Okay, Maddy . . . I really did have a wonderful time tonight, but . . . I just don't want one of us to wake up in the morning and think, 'What the fuck have I done?' I just don't want to rush into anything because the most important thing to me is your friendship, and I would just hate myself if I did anything to damage that."

"Okay . . . but I want a good-night kiss then." Their lips met for the first time. It was the most tender kiss that she had ever experienced, sending electricity through her entire body. He said good night. As she floated up her stairs, she thought, *Fuck, I'm really gonna have to buy some more batteries.*

The following day, Erick was filled with anxiety, exhilaration, and guilt.

He needed to talk to Pastor Tim. The first week that Erick was in New York, he wandered down a mostly residential neighborhood and found a small nondenominational Christian church. More spiritual than religious, Erick kept walking until he noticed the various banners waving outside of the church. Pride, peace, and BLM flags were prominently displayed and flapping in the frigid January breeze. He didn't so much willfully enter the building as he was drawn into it. He took a seat in a modest back pew and looked at the eclectic medium-sized congregation that was made up of various genders, ages, and races. He listened to the pastor whose sermon was about mutual respect and caring for others in our communities, regardless of our differences. The pastor asked for the congregation to rise and sing a hymn, then left the stage. Erick got up and turned to leave when he was greeted by the pleasant smile of one Pastor Tim. "Hello, I don't believe I've seen you here before. It's nice to meet you. I'm Pastor Tim."

"Yeah, hello, I just thought I'd come in from the cold and see what this is all about. It was, uh, nice. So I guess I'll be going now."

"Won't you stay for a bit? I make a mean gin and tonic, if you're into such things." Erick thought that he had never been in a more peaceful and comforting presence in his life.

Pastor Tim and his husband, Jeremy, became foundational influences for Erick. He could be completely open with them and unearth his various feelings, including the hatred he harbored at his wife's "murderers." They would listen and always have a piece of advice that would soothe Erick, at least in the moment. It was, in fact, Pastor Tim who had suggested that Erick build a new record collection and mentioned the bookstore with all of their used records. That conversation was held on February 13. Erick began attending the small church regularly, usually the Wednesday-evening services. Following the service, he would hang out in Pastor Tim and Jeremy's home, have a few drinks, and discuss various topics, sometimes very emotional, other times not. The evening almost always ended in disgusted laughter at one of Erick's more vulgar jokes. Although a devout man of God, Pastor Tim was not devoid of a strong and somewhat twisted sense of humor. As March extended into April and then into May, the conversation would often become about "my friend Maddy." The references to her became more frequent as Erick would say things like "Oh, you should have heard what my friend Maddy said today," "Maddy had the greatest laugh when I said this," "Oh, I really got Maddy good today. Let me tell you what I did . . .," "You know what I really like about Maddy? She just has the most perfect smile." Pastor Tim would sit and listen while frequently giving his husband knowing glances who would, in turn, lightly tap his heart with a swooning expression.

Therefore, it was no surprise to Pastor Tim and Jeremy when Erick showed up on their doorstep on that Wednesday afternoon in late May. "Oh fuck, guys, I think I have a problem," Erick rapidly stated as he entered their home and flopped into one of their oversized couch cushions. Pastor Tim and Jeremy sat on the adjacent love seat, held hands, and patiently listened with bemused expressions on their faces as Erick unloaded his torrent of information including everything that had happened on the previous evening's "date."

"And it was a date! It was! What do I do? Do I ask her out again? Should I feel guilty about asking her out again? I'm not even looking for this! I have a very nice emotional ecosystem here, and getting involved with someone is just gonna fuck it up! What if I ask her out again? If I do, I'm tellin' ya both, I'm gonna fall in love with her. And then what? What if I get emotionally destroyed again? Why aren't you guys saying anything, and why are you smiling at me like that?"

Pastor Tim looked at his beloved husband, let out a slight sigh, looked at Erick, and said, "We all know what you are going to do. You're going to ask her out again. And you are going to do it because you already know that you have nothing to feel guilty about. We do not find love—love finds us. And finally, you know just as we do that you have already fallen in love with this girl. We've known it for some time."

Erick incredulously responded, "Uh . . . no, you don't. You don't know that. And . . . uh . . . neither do I, but . . . well . . . if I do, I'm holding both of you personally responsible for what happens!" Erick stormed out of the home.

Jeremy looked at his husband and said, "I'm okay with taking responsibility for this. How about you?"

"Definitely," Pastor Tim replied as they both began howling with laughter.

That Wednesday evening, Maddy recounted the same scene to her friends. "What do you mean he turned you down?" Sam exclaimed.

"I know, right? How the fuck does that happen? How does he resist *this* shit?" an exasperated Maddy retorted.

"Toldja he was gay," came Jules's dry response.

"He's not fuckin' gay. He's just . . . he's not like any other guy I've been with. He, like, respects me or something. I mean, he told me he wasn't into one-night stands, and that must be the case 'cause I offered this shit up on a silver platter, and he sent it back to the kitchen! I mean, what's he doing? Conning me so he can get into my pants some *other* time? Doesn't make sense. Plus, he said the most important thing to him was our friendship. And if that's true, that means he cares about who I am as a person. I'm not just a piece of ass to him. I'm a human being that he enjoys being around, y'know?"

Then Kristy asked the million-dollar question, "What if he doesn't ask you out again? What if he says he just wants to be friends?"

Maddy annoying replied, "Okay, Kristy, I love you; but if you don't have something intelligent to contribute, then please just don't say anything. Of course, he's going to ask me out again. He has to 'cause we're on step 2 of the master plan, so that's happening. Plus, a guy doesn't kiss a girl like *that* and not be into her. Nope, tomorrow night, we'll be going on our second date. And then the fuckin' world better watch out because we're gonna be unstoppable!" As Maddy was relaying her argument to her friends, she was silently thinking, *Oh fuck. I'm gonna die before one tomorrow. C'mon, Erick, let me in.*

A new retail development was beginning to be built in a run- down Brooklyn neighborhood. Construction workers were being brought in from around the country for the massive undertaking. As Maddy and Erick were processing their feelings and plotting their next romantic moves, a large rusty black pickup truck arrived at the local motel that was housing the construction workers. The back end displayed an out-of-state license plate, a Confederate flag sticker, and a red political sticker carrying an insipidly simple message. Beneath the license plate dangled a pair of "truck nuts," just to accentuate the intent behind driving the laughably large vehicle. Two men emerged from the truck carrying duffel bags and a cooler. After checking in at the front desk, one of the men said, "So ya know any good bars around here? We're lookin' for some big-city pussy."

CHAPTER 18

GIRLFRIEND IS BETTER

Erick was pacing outside of the bookstore. His heart was racing, and his palms were sweaty. "This is stupid, this is stupid, this is stupid," he kept repeating to himself until he heard the "click" of the front door of the shop being unlocked. He reactively turned in the opposite direction, then hesitantly turned back to face the door. *Oh, fuck it, what's the worst that could happen?* he thought as he opened the door. Ten feet away was a petite sprite walking away from the door. She heard the front door buzzer and immediately spun around. Her face beamed with excitement as she exclaimed, "Hey, you!"

"Wazzupbuttacup? How are you?" Erick immediately replied, attempting to retain some sense of normalcy.

"Nothin, 'cept I'm excited to see you. What's up with you?" Maddy replied.

"Ummm . . . well . . . I have a couple questions to ask you," he stated to Maddy before she said tentatively, "Yeah? What would *those* be?"

"May I *pleeeease* buy my records now?" Erick questioned in a childlike pleading voice as though he were begging for another cookie.

"Yes, you may," Maddy stated as she lilted her head, "right after you ask your second question."

"Well . . . ummm . . .," Erick began. They were staring into each other's hopeful eyes, fully understanding what this moment meant. "I just wanted to ask you if . . . y'know . . . if . . ."

Just fuckin' say it! Maddy was screaming at him from her inner thoughts.

"Well . . . if you're not busy or anything, if you'd like to have dinner with me tonight?"

Maddy felt that her response to this moment had to be perfect. It couldn't be too anxious but not be dismissive either. She completely fucked it up. "Oh . . .," she began sarcastically, "well, *tonight* I'm going out on a second date with this guy that I'm *crazy* about!"

A defeated Erick simply said, "Oh . . . okay . . . maybe some other time then," before turning toward the door.

Oh fuck, he's literal, Maddy thought before grabbing Erick's arm, spinning him around, and saying, "You big nudge! *You're* the guy I'm going out with that I'm crazy about!"

She was looking up at him into his eyes as he said, "Wow . . . I'm really bad at this, aren't I?"

"Yeah, you're the worst," Maddy purred in response. "You're lucky I found you. You'd be lost in this world without me."

"You might be right about that," Erick replied in a whisper. The front door buzzer sounded as another customer entered, breaking their spell. They nervously laughed and made the arrangements for Erick to pick Maddy up at her apartment at six then go to a Chinese restaurant. Erick floated out the door.

Maddy floated back to the counter where Sean said, "Hey. He forgot his records."

"That's okay. He'll be back," Maddy dreamily replied.

Erick arrived at Maddy's apartment at 5:53 pm and rang her buzzer at exactly 6:00 pm. She buzzed him up and told him that she would be ready in a moment. She was dressed to kill, figuratively speaking. Slinky red dress resting midthigh, red strapped pumps, and black stockings. She looked at her reflection and thought to herself, *This fucker's going* down *tonight . . . I hope.*

Her entrance garnered the desired reaction as Erick's eyes nearly popped out of his head at this sultry vision. "Wow, you look great!" Erick stammered.

"Oh . . . this old thing?" Maddy demurely replied before Erick burst out laughing and said, "You're the worst fucking liar in the world!"

"Um . . . actually I'm not, but, well, I just wanted to look nice tonight."

"Mission accomplished. Should we go?" Erick excitedly offered.

"Yeah, but before we go, I thought it might be nice to start our second date with a kiss."

Erick took her into his arms. The kiss was tender at first, much like two nights before. But then it became much more passionate. It was a moment that neither wanted to end, but they knew that it must. Otherwise, they would definitely miss dinner. "Okay, let's get this over with . . . I mean . . . um . . . let's go to dinner, okay?" Maddy stated while trying to conceal her flushed complexion.

The food arrived, and Erick ignorantly had ordered something different from Maddy. He watched her with bewilderment as she immediately said, "Wow, yours looks great!" before proceeding to shovel his sweet and sour chicken into her mouth. Three healthy bites in, Maddy suddenly realized what she was doing, looked up into Erick's shocked but amused expression, and said with her mouth full, "Ummm . . . do you want to try some of mine?"

"Sure," Erick exclaimed through his laughter. *It's like I'm out with a full-grown six-year-old*, Erick thought as he shook his head in wonderment.

Several bites into dinner, Maddy said flirtatiously while gazing at Erick with her sparkling green eyes, "Y'know . . . I'd *still* really like to listen to those records."

Erick softly replied, "I'd love to listen to records with you," before hastily saying, "Now, Maddy, when we say 'listen to records,' we're not *really* talking about listening to records . . . are we?"

Maddy's expression was one of shock and delight before she burst out laughing, leaving an anxious Erick's question hovering in the air. Maddy composed herself, looked Erick square in the eyes, and said, "Okay, Erick. I'm going to be as blunt as I can be with you. Fucking, Erick. I'm talking about you and I fucking." "Okay, good," a relieved Erick replied. "That's what I thought, but I didn't want to be too presumptuous."

They arrived at Erick's apartment. The Chinese food was thrown into the refrigerator. They stared at each other for the briefest of moments before exploding into passionate kisses. In the height of her passion, Maddy failed to notice if there were chains hanging from the walls, a creepy doll in the corner, or a mentally unhealthy shrine to his mother. Fortunately for her, all that the sparse apartment held were two chairs, a small sofa, a television, and the framed autographed SCOTS album from the previous show.

After Maddy's earlier hopeful wish was granted, Erick went to . . . insert Tab A into Slot B before he exclaimed, "Oh god, Maddy, I'm so sorry!"

Well, Maddy thought, *he hasn't been laid for a while and I'm pretty fuckin' hot, so hopefully I can get him going for a round 2 . . . but I didn't* feel *anything.* "What's wrong?" Maddy breathily asked.

"I'm so sorry. I didn't think to buy any condoms!"

"It's okay, I'm on birth control," came Maddy's impatient response.

"No, really, I'm so sorry. I—" Erick continued before Maddy cut him off and said in a demanding voice, "It's okay! Just fuck me!" So he did.

Lying in the aftermath, Maddy asked if she could use his shower as she felt a bit "sticky." "Of course," Erick replied, "but, um, before you do . . . well . . . I know you have to work early tomorrow, but . . ."

Maddy's mind began racing. *No! He's going to kick me out! Not him! I never thought he'd do that! How fucking disappointing!* Erick continued awkwardly, "Well, I just thought, y'know, if you'd like to . . . well . . . you're welcome to spend the night . . ." Then he rapidly said, "'Cause I've got shorts and shirts and stuff you could wear, and I bought an extra toothbrush . . . y'know . . . just in case."

A visibly relieved Maddy coyly countered, "Do you *want* me to spend the night?"

Erick looked Maddy in her glowing emerald eyes and said, "I would absolutely love it if the first thing that I saw when I wake up in the morning is your beautiful face." About thirty minutes later, they both *really* needed a shower.

As Maddy was preparing to leave the room to take her shower, she turned back around and said, "Okay, I can't let this go. You thought that this might happen tonight, right?"

"Well, I thought it was a possibility," Erick replied.

"And you bought a *toothbrush* but not *condoms*? What are you *thinking*?" They both exploded into laughter as the silliness of the situation swept over them.

Erick did understand women profoundly. This was a sleepover, and he knew that no sleepover with a woman was complete without a pillow fight, typically in bra and panties. So he instigated one. While watching a topless scene in *Return of the Living Dead*, Maddy not so innocently inquired, "So who has better tits, me or Linnea Quigley?"

"Okay, Maddy," Erick began with a hint of being annoyed. "I'm going to answer your question, but it's an unfair question, and I'm going to explain why it is unfair. First off, you have the best tits there have ever been, are currently, or will ever be, so that should take care of that question for all time. Now, when women ask their partner a question like 'Do you think that other woman is pretty?' it's an unfair question. They already know the other woman is pretty. Otherwise, they wouldn't be asking. And it leaves the guy in an impossible position. He either has to say, 'No, that other woman isn't pretty,' which is an obvious lie, so now he's untrustworthy. Or he has to admit that yes, in fact, the other woman is pretty. So now he's in trouble for noticing another woman. So it's an unfair question, and for that, you must be punished."

With that, Erick (barely) hit his inquiring adversary in the face with a pillow and began laughing. "Oh . . . you just started World War III, mister!" Maddy exclaimed.

"What the fuck are you going to do about it?" came Erick's arrogant reply. Maddy answered his question by picking up a pillow and viciously wailing on his ass. Erick was defenseless, as he would not hit her very hard, nor would he strike her with his pillow above her waist. All he could do to defend himself was lightly tackle her and delicately pin her to the bed.

"Hey! No fair! You're cheating!" Maddy exclaimed with the maturity of a ten-year-old.

"Well, all's fair in love and war," Erick softly stated before giving her a passionate kiss. As they kissed, Maddy thought that this had indeed been the best slumber party she had ever been to.

Maddy woke up the next morning and was greeted by two sets of inquisitive eyes staring at her from the foot of the bed. Maddy wiped the sleep from her own eyes, smiled, and said, "Hey . . . who are you guys?" The two nine-month-old black cats took this greeting as an invitation to pounce upon their newfound friend, and they began purring and rolling around on her chest.

"Oh, I'm sorry," Erick stated as he entered the room. "I didn't mean to let them in."

"It's okay," Maddy replied through her laughter at the frolicking kittens. "What are their names?"

"Well, Maddy, I would like to introduce you to Hunky, because he's a bit of a chunk. And this little princess is Dory because . . . well . . . she's a-dory-able."

"Oh, wow . . . I've gotta teach you joke lessons. That was really bad," Maddy replied with fake disgust.

"I got up early and picked up your coffee and favorite scone from your coffee shop . . . I hope you don't mind."

"Of course not! Yummy! I'll be right in!" Maddy excitedly exclaimed.

Erick was nervously pacing in his small kitchenette as he watched his houseguest wolf down her scone and coffee. Finally, he summoned up his courage and asked, "So . . . ummm . . . can I call on you again?"

Maddy's immediate laughter was not the response that he had hoped for. "Can you *call on me* again?" Maddy astonishedly gasped. "I mean, I've just had the best two dates of my life, and I've just had the best mind-blowing sex of my life! Uh, yeah . . . It's a pretty safe bet that we'll be doing *this* shit again," she concluded as she took another bite of scone with crumbs tumbling all around her. "Plus, who the fuck talks like that? Can you *call on me* again? What are we, second cousins from Appalachia? *Uh . . . Durrrr . . . Does ya wanna go-a-courtin'?*"

They both exploded into laughter as they made arrangements to meet up at the club later that night following Maddy having dinner with her friends.

Sam, Jules, and Kristy had done their homework on this guy, minus the anal probe. They could find nothing that he had lied about, nor any major red flags of warning. Following Maddy's overly animated (and slightly exaggerated) recap of the previous night's events, Sam bluntly said, "Okay, Maddy. I'm officially calling it. This is getting serious, and you know what that means, don't you?"

Maddy let out a sigh of resignation, looked down, and said, "Yeah . . . I'll get him to meet you guys tomorrow night. Just don't be too hard on him . . . okay?"

Following dinner, Maddy saw Erick standing at "his" table, and she was not pleased by what she saw. A young brunette was obviously flirting with him complete with shoulder pats, overly exaggerated laughter, and hair flips.

Who the fuck is this *little skank?* Maddy thought as she approached the table. "Hey, you!" Maddy excitedly stated before planting a big kiss on Erick's surprised face.

"Wazzupbuttacup? Hey, I'd like you to meet my friend, Julie. And, Julie, this is—"

Before he could finish his introduction, Maddy jutted her hand out in front of her new nemesis and enthusiastically exclaimed, "Hiya! I'm Erick's *girlfriend*, Maddy!" The two shook hands and smiled while telepathically saying to each other, "Fuck *you*, bitch." "Oh yeah, well, fuck *you*, whore."

Erick, unable to pick up the frequency of the female telepathy, just stood there and thought, *Girlfriend?*

As the evening progressed at the Club, Maddy was surprised at how many people Erick knew. She had known him only from the bookstore, which was almost exclusively one-on-one interactions. But here, especially during a local talent showcase where only the currently performing artist's parents were paying any attention, he was greeted by seemingly everybody there. He made multiple introductions of his, "ummm . . . friend Maddy" following a handshake, brief hug, fist pump, or, on one occasion, being lifted from the floor and twirled around by a biker-looking dude.

"Goddammit, Jerry, put me down!" Erick exclaimed. "Maddy, this is the owner of this dump, Jerry. He's such a fuckin' Jerry . . . and, Jerry, this is—"

"Hiya, I'm Erick's *girlfriend*, Maddy!" Maddy was determined to get the term *girlfriend* into Erick's introductory vocabulary. That victory was complete the following morning as Erick asked if she had meant that during their introductions. "Well . . . how did that make you feel?" Maddy hesitantly inquired. "Oh, I really liked it. And . . . well . . . I have no interest in seeing anyone else or anything like that. I just need to make sure, y'know? I'm not sure if you noticed, but I'm not that great at picking up on signals."

"Noooo shit, huh? Like that chick Julie?" Maddy said in an interrogating tone.

"Julie, what about her? You don't think . . . Oh, Maddy, don't be silly. That girl has no interest in me like that."

"All right, I'm just gonna let that go," Maddy strategically replied. "So since you seem to do all right with blunt talk, let me be as blunt as I can be. You are my boyfriend, and I am your girlfriend, and we are now in an officially exclusive relationship. Got that?" Before Erick had a chance to reply, Maddy broke out into tears.

"I can't . . . I can't do this to you," Maddy began with anguish in her voice.

"W-what's wrong?" a confused Erick asked.

Maddy, incapable of looking at him and with tears streaming down her face, said, "I can't let you get too deep with me until I tell you about my past. It's just not fair to you. You need to know what you're getting involved with, before things go . . . too far." Erick sincerely replied, "Maddy, you don't have to do this.

There isn't one thing that you could *ever* say to me that would make me change how I feel about you. This isn't necessary."

"Yes, it is . . . and I hope what you just said is true, but I have to tell you this." Maddy then spoke of her mentally abusive upbringing and marriage, the betrayal by her best friend, and her disillusionment in her country's current state before giving a vivid description of her bottoming-out period from a few years prior complete with a graphic description of her dalliances while calling herself such names as "slut" and "whore." She also confided in him about her near-death experience and how her family and friends had saved her from herself. There was no mention, however, of cut brake lines, exploding heads, scalpels, intentional overdosing, or decapitation. A girl's gotta keep her secrets after all.

She had never been so afraid in her life and could not bring herself to look at whatever expression that Erick was wearing on his face. She was sure that the look would be one of judgment and disappointment in her. She concluded by stuttering, "S-so, I j-just hope that y-you can s-see that I-I-I'm not that person anymore and h-how much I-I care for y-y-you."

"May I say something now?" Erick inquired in a soothing voice.

"Y-yes," Maddy hesitantly responded.

"Okay, first of all, our actions are not necessarily who we are as a person. For example, I could be cornered in an alley and have to murder someone to survive, but that doesn't make me a murderer. That was just what I had to do in order to survive in that moment. So I would submit that your actions from that time in your life are not a true representation of who *you* are as a person."

Why the hell did he use that *as an example?* Maddy wondered. "Secondly," Erick continued, "I don't know if anyone has told you this before, but I would suggest that you are suffering from post-traumatic stress disorder from all of the mental abuse that you have had to endure. And one of the hallmark symptoms of that disorder is clinical depression. So I think you may have been clinically depressed at that point of your life, and you were trying to accomplish three things through your . . . ummm . . . behavior. Firstly, it was a big 'fuck you' to your parents and probably ex-husband. Secondly, you felt that your life was out of control, and that was the one thing that you could use to try to grasp on to some sense of control within your life. And third, I think that that was your way of self-medicating, because that . . . um . . . activity releases endorphins in the pleasure centers of our brains and you were looking for at least some temporary relief from your pain."

What the fuck is going on? Maddy thought. *He isn't judging me. He's just explaining my behavior.*

"Okay, the next thing that I would like to point out," Erick continued, "is that we have no control over what we have done in the past, so you might want to consider dropping any guilt that you may feel about things that you have no control over and focus that energy on your future. And finally, we are all made up of our past experiences. We are who we are today because of what we have experienced in the past. And if you could go back and change just one little thing about your past, you may not be the exact person that you are today. And, Maddy . . ." At this point, Erick put his index finger under her saturated chin and gently lifted it up so that his eyes met hers. "I really lo-*like* the person you are today. In fact, I have a greater respect for you and care about you even *more* now that I have a better understanding of what you have had to endure to become this incredible person sitting before me now."

A pleasantly bewildered Maddy then exclaimed, "You mean, you really don't care that I've had way more, y'know . . . partners than you?"

Erick calmly replied, "Well, it isn't so much that I don't care as it is that it simply has no impact on how I feel about you. And besides, as far as I'm concerned, we're even in that department."

"How the fuck does *that* math work?" an even more astonished Maddy blurted out.

Erick, with a slight chuckle, said, "Well, it may be true that you have me beat in quantity of partners, but I believe that I have you beat in quality of experiences, because all of my intimate experiences meant something to me. So as I said, as far as I'm concerned, from the time of our first date, we're perfectly even."

Maddy's mind was racing. *What had he just done? He didn't judge. He didn't scold. He didn't lecture. He just explained the situation and then said that we were even! He's totally letting me off the hook! But I have to make sure.* "S-so . . . you're not gonna break up with me?"

Erick delicately lifted her head once more so that she could see the tears forming in his eyes. "Maddy, at this point, I can't imagine my life without you in it. But I'm telling you right now, Maddy. No one, including you, *no one* will ever say a disparaging word about you or threaten you in any way as long as I'm around. I simply won't hear it, Maddy, because, to me, you are perfect in every way. Now, if you don't mind, I could really use a hug."

Maddy fell into his soothing embrace, sobbing. They held each other until he softly whispered into her ear, "Now, I need a favor from you."

"Y-yes, anything. W-what is it?" Maddy submissively inquired.

Erick, sensing her vulnerability, took full advantage of the situation as he said, "Would you please pick out a place for lunch, 'cause I'm fuckin' starving." The pair burst into tension- releasing laughter as Dory chased Hunky under the chair.

———

"Well, I hope you're fuckin' happy!" Erick exclaimed as he flopped down on the oversized couch cushion that Saturday afternoon.

"What are we supposed to be happy about?" a smiling Pastor Tim inquired.

"Oh, wipe that fuckin' smirk off of your face, both of you," Erick exclaimed, attempting to project being annoyed. "I told you . . . I told you *both* that if I went out with her again that I'd fall in love! And that's exactly what has happened! In fact, she confided in me about some things from her past today. And she put *so much* trust in me that now I know that I can put all of *my* trust in her. And that made me fall even *more* in love with her! So . . . *that's* just fuckin' great!"

"Well," Jeremy chimed in, "have you told her?"

"Told her?" Erick replied incredulously. "Fuck no! I'm gonna totally pussy out, and if she feels the same way, maybe she'll say it first. Then, I'm off the hook, and all I have to do is reciprocate. Okay, that's enough of this shit. I've gotta go home and get ready. I've gotta meet her friends tonight. Pray for me."

CHAPTER 19

REAL MEN

Maddy ushered Erick into the packed karaoke bar. While winding her way through the celebratory crowd to her customary "throne" at the table in front of the stage, Maddy introduced Erick to her friends and acquaintances. Maddy introduced Erick as "my boyfriend," which he was still getting acclimated to. He would smile, say, "Nice to meetcha!" and shake hands. More than one patron issued a stern warning to Erick that night that it would be best for him to treat Maddy well. Erick, impressed at the loyalty that Maddy commanded from this eclectic group of people, would just smile and say, "I will. I just think she's wonderful." This was her tribe, her people, and it would take quite the effort to win them over. He began wondering if it was worth the effort. This was exactly what he had wanted to avoid, putting on a mask and playing a part in order to be accepted so as to be involved in a relationship. He wasn't happy having to do that in his previous life, and he didn't want to do it now. Additionally, he thought, there were the emotional trials and tribulations and all of the life compromises that come along with an intimate relationship with another person. At forty-six, it just wasn't important enough to him. *Maybe we should just be bookstore buddies,* he thought, *and leave it at that.*

Just before they arrived at the front table, Maddy turned around and flashed him a reassuring smile as if to say, "Don't worry. I've got your back." And he believed her. He knew this was going to get rough, but his "girlfriend" was there for him. And *Goddamn it!* he thought, he was both begrudgingly and enthusiastically there for her too. He would play the part tonight, because she was worth it. He was driven to see where this would lead, whether it be a storybook ending or smashed upon jagged stones. There was a special connection between the two of them, whether he wanted to admit it or not. And there were those fucking beautiful green eyes, lush copper eyelashes, and winsome smile that intoxicated him into blissful submission. But he would play his part on his own terms and allow the chips to fall where they may.

They approached the front table; and he was immediately introduced to Sam, Jules, and Kristy. He politely shook their hands and offered his obligatory greetings. He then sat down, spread his arms out, and bellowed, "Let the inquisition begin!" Maddy burst out laughing as she realized that this motherfucker wasn't going to play with these bitches.

"Here's the deal, ladies," Erick began. "I understand what this is, and I respect it. You're checking me out in order to protect your friend, and I have nothing but respect for that. And you can ask me any question that you want. I'm an open book, and I'll answer them as completely and honestly as I can. There isn't a topic that's off of the table. But . . . here's the thing. I'm not going to try to impress you. I'm forty-six years old, I am who I am, and hopefully you like me. But if you don't, well . . . I don't really give a fuck. Now, who has the first question?"

Maddy sat there overseeing the conversation as intently as a mother cat watching over her playing kittens. The questioning began innocently enough. Where are you from, what did you do, how were you able to retire so early, why did you move to New York, blah, blah, blah. They were the same questions that Maddy had already asked with the answers having been reported back. But they were being asked again by these three in order to detect any variation of the story or defensiveness while answering any particular topic. Predators were very clever and were everywhere. Their job was to ensure that their friend wasn't falling for another one of them. Erick answered their questions, sometimes matter-of-factly, sometimes with a sense of self-deprecating humor.

Jules asked at one point why he had moved to New York. She knew the answer that he had given Maddy but wanted to hear it for herself in order to gauge the truthfulness of the story. Upon hearing the question, Erick's face immediately became somber, and he averted his gaze downward toward the table. "Okay, there's the story I gave Maddy and then . . . well . . . there's the *real* story." He looked up at Maddy apologetically as she looked back at him with a reserved inquisitiveness. "I'm sorry I didn't tell you the whole story, Maddy. It's just so hard . . . to talk about." He looked up at the ceiling, trying to hold back his tears. "You see, I really came to New York to have . . . penis reduction surgery, and, well, something went wrong, and now I'm referred to as . . . Buttonmushroom Fungi!"

He immediately turned to Maddy and flashed her a wicked grin and wink as she exclaimed, "Oh . . . my . . . fucking . . . god! You are such a *dick*!"

Erick couldn't hold back his tears of laughter any longer and said through his snickering, "Well, I *used* to be!"

"Great," Sam flatly said. "Another comedian. Yeah, you two are perfect for each other. I have just one more question. Maddy said you've only slept with one other woman, which makes you either the worst lay in the world or a fucking liar. Which one is it?" Sam then began a pompous titter that was quickly joined by Kristy.

"Well, it's definitely not the first one," Maddy quietly said as Erick slowly righted himself in his chair, then leaned over the table while staring directly at Sam.

"Okay," Erick began rigidly. "I think I've been a pretty good sport up to this point, and again, I respect what you are all doing, but it's my turn now." Erick looked at his three interrogators with a stern seriousness before continuing. "Now, I have a couple of questions for you. What number could I have given you that doesn't make me a man-whore but also doesn't make me an object of your ridicule? Five, ten, twenty, thirty? I don't know, you tell me. And what character profile would you prefer your friend to be involved with? Someone who had a lifelong relationship with one woman and never cheated or had a string of one-night stands or someone who *did* cheat on his wife and began banging every skirt he could find as soon as he put her in the fucking ground?" It was this last line that made Sam and Kristy realize that they had fucked up. Maddy watched with the same passive intensity that one would have while witnessing a horrendous accident.

Sam opened her mouth to say something, which Erick immediately countered, "Nope, not done yet. Listen, I know there are a lot of assholes in this world. Please believe me when I say that. And I am truly sorry if you've had bad experiences with men. But it isn't fair for you to project *your* bad experiences onto me. I'm not an asshole *just because* I have a dick. I have an obligation to try to earn your trust and respect. But *you* have an obligation to at least give me that opportunity and to not prejudge me just because of my gender." The area around the table was energized with tension as Erick lowered his voice once again while staring right at Sam and said, "And finally, I may not have much in this world, but I do have my integrity, and I am basically an honest person. And I'm telling you right now, if you ever call me a liar, then you had better know what the fuck you are talking about. If you find something out about me from my past that should be a red flag for Maddy, by all means, tell her. I really don't have to worry about that because there's nothing there, but if you *were* to find something, tell her. You have an obligation to tell her. If you see me out romantically involved with another woman while I'm involved with Maddy, by all means, you have an obligation to tell her. But if you ever call me a liar, you had better have evidence, and you had better know what the fuck you're talking about, because *I will* defend myself." Erick leaned back and surveyed the faces from across the table, which were desperately searching for an appropriate response. He decided to let them off of the hook. "And with that, ladies, I'm going to step outside for a moment. I'll be right back!"

Before departing, Erick leaned over to Maddy and quietly said into her ear, "Is it okay to kiss you?"

"Yeah, why wouldn't it be?" Maddy inquired in the same hushed tone.

"I dunno. I just don't know what the fuck I'm doing," Erick replied.

"Fuck, you are going to be a project, aren't you? Just shut up and kiss me," Maddy stated through a chuckle. They kissed, he departed, and then Maddy went to work.

"What the *fuck*, you guys!"

"Okay, okay," Sam began in an attempt to perform a hasty retreat. "We messed up. We'll apologize when he gets back . . . okay?"

"What's this *we* shit?" Jules snidely countered. "I didn't say shit. Besides, I kinda like him. He's no bullshit. I mean, I'm sure he wants to make a good impression on us, but that doesn't mean he's going to put up with our shit. And what guy lies about how many women they've slept with *like that*? Oh sure, they'll lie about it, but they always exaggerate the number because they think we get turned on by a guy with lots of sexual conquests when, in fact, we just want a guy who will be true to us, like Kristy's dude. And now, it would appear Maddy has found a guy like that, and what do you do? You laugh at him. Not cool, bitches. Not . . . cool."

Erick returned to the table, gave Maddy a soft kiss and slight smile, and sat down to survey the damage. He knew what he had done, and he had done it purposefully. He was drawing a line in the sand at the beginning of this relationship so everybody would be aware of just who they were getting involved with. His intent was not to harm, but to send a message that he would be his own person, just as Maddy would be hers. "Sooo . . . hey, listen . . . I think I went a bit too far and owe you an apology," Sam said regretfully.

"Thank you. I appreciate that," Erick said with a comforting tone. "You know what? As you get to know me, you'll find that I have a tendency to take things too far as well. I can pretty much promise you that there will come a time where I will unintentionally offend you. In fact, it'll probably end up being tonight. So don't sweat it. And now, as a form of peace offering, may I buy you ladies another round?"

Tense discussion turned to spirited conversation as the five of them began discussing various topics and making off-color jokes. "That's what she said" was thrown out anytime a size reference to anything was made, followed by immature, tipsy laughter. Every singer received enthusiastic applause following their respective performance, especially "Dynamite and the Firecrackers," who performed almost exclusively together. During their rousing rendition of "Love Will Keep Us Together," Erick couldn't help but think that they . . . weren't half bad. Erick had been to many live shows and considered himself to be a bit of an expert on the subject. Sure, Kristy was a bit "screechy," and Sam tried to steal the show by singing overly loud, but Jules could actually carry a tune, and Maddy's voice was . . . perfect. She had an imposing stage presence despite her petite frame, and she used her darting emerald eyes as weapons against anyone who dared to not pay attention. Watching her as she periodically would sing a line from the song directly to him with a voice reminiscent of a cross between Natalie Merchant and Rickie Lee Jones, he asked himself, *How the hell did I end up with her?* He was simultaneously filled with gratitude for his good fortune and dread that he might do something to cause its demise.

That dread came to fruition upon the quartet's return to the table with Kristy inquiring, "Okay, when are *you* gonna get up there?"

"Excuse me?" Erick stated in a timid tone as his eyes pleaded with Maddy for support.

"Yeah, this is a singers' table. If you want to sit here the rest of the night, you have to do at least one song," Sam, the architect of this arbitrary rule, haughtily chimed.

Maddy almost apologetically said, "Yeah . . . that *is* the rule . . . I've made people do it myself, so . . ."

Erick confidently reached out his hand and said, "Give me the book."

Erick's name was called. He drew one of the shortest straws in the house as he had to follow Robbie, born Roberta, who identified as male and had arguably the greatest vocal and song selection range in the bar. As a victorious Robbie once again left the stage to thunderous applause, Erick assuredly made his way up the three short stairs on the side of the stage to face three females, giggling in anticipation of his impending embarrassment, and one wearing the expression of pleading hopefulness. Maddy knew that he had a vast music collection. What she didn't know is how much he enjoyed singing along to his collected recordings, and although he had never done so publicly, he was sure that this was his opportunity to win over the hearts of Maddy's friends and acquaintances. And the song that he had chosen was perfect for this moment. A delightfully light pop song depicting the very beginning of the exploration of a new love that was sure to make Maddy's heart swoon. It also didn't hurt that it was penned by one of the greatest song writers in history, Carole King. He had chosen the most perfect weapon, and victory would be his.

As he began singing Herman's Hermits' version of "I'm into Something Good," the various faces throughout the bar changed into one of uniform astonishment. They sat there, including Maddy, hanging on his every perfect note, with their mouths agape at his riveting performance. Upon the song's conclusion, Erick said a polite "Thank you," and took a slight bow to dead silence, immediately followed by voluminous applause.

Erick strode down the stairs and back to the table with an arrogant strut. He sat down, awaiting his much-deserved praise. "Well, you had the balls to do it at least," Jules stated matter-of-factly.

"Yeah . . . it was . . . something," Kristy added without knowing what exactly to say. Sam had turned away from the group to hide her laughter. She was unable to hide the convulsive rising of her shoulders as she attempted to muffle her exhortations. Confused, Erick looked to Maddy, who held an expression of someone who had just lost their beloved pet.

"Okay . . . well . . . the *good* news is that you don't have to do *that* anymore to sit with us . . . and . . . well . . . the song selection was great!" Maddy flashed her smile, trying to reassure her fallen beau.

"Y'mean, it wasn't any good?" Erick pleaded. "I mean, everyone applauded, didn't they?"

Jules responded, "Yeah, they do that. They applaud especially loud for people who sing that bad but have the balls to get up there and make asses of themselves. Dude, you're fuckin' tone-deaf."

Mustering what remained of his shattered dignity, Erick righted himself in his chair and stated in a resolute voice, "Well . . . can't sing and a small dick . . . Fuck it . . . Who wants a drink?" He smiled at the group as if to give them all the green light to release their pent-up howls, got up from the table, and made his way to the bar all the while receiving "congratulatory" backslaps. Rosetta, a medium-built woman in her late fifties who was best known in the bar for her spot-on renditions of Etta James, and her tall, lanky husband, Charlie, who absolutely killed on everything from the Temptations to James Brown, approached Erick at the bar.

"Child," Rosetta began, "that was not pleasant." "Sure wasn't, baby," Charlie echoed.

"Yeah . . . I know . . . I'm sorry," Erick responded sorrowfully. "Don't be sorry—be better," Rosetta lectured. "I've seen Maddy with a lot of different guys, but I've never seen her look at any one of them the way she looks at you. She looks at you the same damn way that you look at her. Yep, unless you fuck this up somehow, this is a done deal. And the best way to surprise her when you propose is to kick the shit out of a song, and that's just what we're going to get you to do!"

Erick began stuttering, "Wait . . . what . . . propose? What do you mean? We've just started going out and—"

"Shut the fuck up, man," Charlie interjected. "We may not know much, but we know two things. We know how to make someone a singer, and we know two people in love when we see it. Now, seems to us we might be able to help you out a bit in both those areas, dig? Here's my number. Give me a call. We'll getcha ready."

"Uh . . . Okay . . . thanks?" Erick stuttered as the pair retreated back to their table.

"What did Rosetta and Charlie want?" Maddy inquired as Erick returned with the drinks.

"Ummm . . . they said that they could teach me to sing," Erick answered.

"Uhhh . . . yeah . . . maybe . . . that would be cool, I guess," Maddy replied unconvincingly. There was a new game afoot between them, and Erick decided that this was one that he was going to win. Decisively. He smiled and kissed her forehead before returning to his drink and the general revelry of the table. The following morning, as the pair were frying bacon and eggs in Erick's kitchenette, they discussed the parameters of their new relationship, frequently with one arm wrapped around the other's waist. Due to Maddy enjoying her quiet Mondays alone and Wednesdays with her friends, it was decided that Tuesdays and Thursdays would be their "date" nights, with Fridays being a "maybe" depending on what they were both doing and Saturdays together at karaoke. Maddy would stay over on all three and maybe four of those evenings. That left Sunday, which was today. Maddy decided to put it into play. "So what are your plans for today?"

"Oh, nothing much. I need to go to the gym and the grocery store, but other than that, I have no plans," Erick replied as he tossed small pieces of bacon onto the floor for the "starving" kittens.

"Really? 'Cause I was just thinkin' that maybe, y'know, if you'd like to . . . maybe I could hang out *here* again tonight," Maddy replied in a childlike voice as she innocently avoided direct eye contact. It was a manipulation tactic that she had perfected with her uncle Joe, and it proved to be once again effective.

"That would be great!" Erick excitedly exclaimed before assuming a more seriously bashful tone. "But . . . ummm . . . Maddy, if you're going to be staying here four or five nights a week . . . then . . . well, it just doesn't seem fair!"

"What doesn't seem fair?" Maddy defensively retorted, now preparing mentally for "the talk" about what their roles would be. She was sure that this was Erick's prelude to introduce her to the joys of being his personal domestic servant, which was an expectation that she was going to immediately stop.

"Well," Erick explained, "I get the pleasure of your company, and you have the burden of having to schlep stuff back and forth between apartments . . . so . . . if you would like . . . and we're *definitely not* moving in together! It's *far too early* to talk about *that*! But . . . if you would like to bring over some of your stuff, I'd be happy to clear out some space for you. And if you would like, on Mondays when I do my laundry, I could just throw yours in with mine; and that would be one less thing that you would have to worry about."

This did not go at all the way Maddy had anticipated, and her off-balanced response came off as being more pissed than astonished. "Say *what* again? Did you just offer to do my *laundry*?"

"Uh . . . yeah . . . I didn't think it was a big deal . . . I'm sorry . . . Have I said something wrong?"

"No, no, you haven't," a pleasantly bewildered Maddy replied. "Please, just sit next to me for a moment. I need to explain something to you."

Erick sat next to her gingerly, as though he were awaiting to see the principal. "Maddy, I'm sorry if I said something wrong. I—"

Maddy put her index finger up to his lips to silence him and said, "Please, just listen to me for a moment. Usually at this stage of a relationship, the guy expects the girl to start doing all of his housekeeping and shit, y'know, just because she's a girl . . .," to which Erick exclaimed, "Well, that's just a bunch of sexist bullshit!"

"And I agree with you," Maddy continued in a calm voice, "but ever since I met you, you have treated me with nothing but respect, and this is just another example of this. So I'm going to jump in the shower before I go home and do some things. While I'm in there, I want you to *really* think about whether you *want* me to bring some of my stuff over and whether you *want* to do my laundry. And *it's ok*ay to change your mind. You *don't* have to do that for me."

"Well," Erick replied, "I don't have to think about it. I've already thought about it. But Maddy, I do laundry on Monday afternoons. If an item is in the laundry hamper on Monday afternoon, then I will consider it to be laundry. If it is . . . somewhere else"—Erick briefly paused and looked around the room at the various clothes that had been left haphazardly around his apartment—"well . . . you're on your own with that." Maddy chuckled and said, "Got it. Put my shit in the hamper. Not a problem." Erick smiled, kissed her forehead, and began walking back to the kitchenette. "Hey . . . wait a minute You're not offering to do my laundry just so you can sniff my panties, *are you*?" Maddy playfully inquired. Erick adopted a serious expression, turned back around, and sat next to her once again. *Oh fuck! That's a new kink! Oh well, as long as I'm getting my laundry done*, Maddy thought to herself.

"A couple of things about that," Erick began seriously. "First, if I *wanted* to sniff your panties, I could already do that because they're *kinda laying* all over the place." Maddy looked around the room. There was a pair on the arm of a chair. Another pair was being carried around the house by Dory, and a third pair was on the kitchenette floor for some unexplained reason.

Valid point, Maddy thought.

"Secondly," Erick continued, "it kind of defeats the purpose to *wash* the panties. There's no point in sniffing clean panties. So no, I'm not into sniffing panties." He got up and began the six-foot journey back to the kitchenette. He then abruptly said, "But I'm not ruling out wearing them around for a while before I put them in the wash!"

"Fine! Just don't get a hard-on and stretch them all out!" came Maddy's immediate playful reply.

"Not much danger of that happening! They don't call me Buttonmushroom Fungi for nothin'!"

A wadded-up skirt barely missed his head and landed on top of the bacon. "Ummm . . . I'll put that one in the hamper," Maddy offered.

The pair spent Sunday evening eating homemade nachos and putting Maddy's belongings away. She had brought three large suitcases, one of which was just for shoes and a smaller suitcase for her "makeup and shit."

I thought I said we weren't *moving in together*, an amused Erick thought as he hung yet another blouse in his increasingly shrinking closet.

Chapter 20

A Groovy Kind of Love

The following Tuesday morning, Sean paged Maddy to the front counter. "Delivery for you," Sean said with a hint of jealousy. Maddy looked at the counter where there rested a vase with twelve roses, six yellow and six white. "Oh!" Maddy excitedly exclaimed. "Are *those* for *me?*"

She opened the card, which simply read,

Maddy, one week ago I went out with this incredible woman who looked so beautiful in her yellow and white dress and these flowers remind me of that magical evening. See you soon.
Erick
PS. That incredible woman was you in case I wasn't clear enough.

Tears welled up; and Maddy picked up the sparkling vase, turned, and abruptly went to her office. After slamming her heavy oak door, she sat down and broke down crying. There was no denying it at this point. She had fallen in love, and she thought that he felt the same way. *But I'm not gonna tell him first,* she thought as she wiped joyful tears from her cheeks. *He's gonna have to step up to the plate first before I allow myself to be that vulnerable. And why the fuck am I using a basketball term? I hate sports!* She then reread the card and began chuckling at the last line. *Oh, Christ! He's so fucking clueless! What a big nudge!*

Erick sheepishly came into the shop at his customary time and was greeted with the equally customary "Hey, you!"

Okay, Erick thought, *I think the flowers went over all right.*

Maddy thanked him for the flowers and commented on how beautiful they were and how thoughtful he was to send them to commemorate their first date. "And it *was* a date now, wasn't it?" Maddy arrogantly inquired with her head lifted conceitedly. "Yeah, yeah, yeah . . . it was a fuckin' date," Erick conceded before saying sincerely, "I'm really glad that you like them, because I really lo-*like* you a lot."

That's the second *fucking time he's done that!* Maddy thought as she tried to slow the rapid pace of her heart.

———

Saturday night. Showtime. Time to make up for my embarrassment from last week. I'm going to blow her fucking mind, Erick confidently thought as he strode into the karaoke bar.

"Oh . . . you came back," Robbie jokingly stated. "Leave my fuckin' man alone!" Charlie bellowed.

"Erick, get your ass over here!" Maddy looked over to see that Erick had arrived and said to her friends, "What the fuck is he all huddled up with Rosetta and Charlie for?"

"I dunno," Jules dryly responded. "Weird threesome? Creamy center of an Oreo cookie?"

"Would you shut the fuck up?" Maddy screamed as she threw ice down Jules's shirt.

The five friends, who now (mostly) included Erick, engaged in their typical revelry. There was much laughter at immature jokes and loud singing along with the featured performers as well as from the stage. Maddy (or Dynamite as was her "stage name"), who did not sing without at least one of her "Firecrackers" very often, sang "My Guy" by Mary Wells to her . . . guy. Jules led her friends at the surrounding tables in eye rolls and pretending to vomit as Maddy performed, drawing a scornful stare and scolding from Erick.

"Hey! Knock it the fuck off! Maddy's singing!" Everyone immediately stopped their immature antics.

Fuck, this guy's serious, Jules thought.

Maddy was on top of the world. She had just once again "killed" on stage. She had found her prince and was in love. And she was sure that he was in love with her as well. Her friends liked him; and her aunts, who would meet him in late July, were supportive as well. And she was saving money on batteries and now, laundry. Plus, he knew about her sordid past (at least the part that she had revealed), and it did not affect their relationship. There was nothing that could bring her down on this first Saturday in June. *Nothing.*

Then suddenly, a dark cloud hovered over the table as an ominous hush fell over the crowd. The karaoke jockey had just announced Erick's name to come to the stage, and his name seemed to echo chillingly throughout the bar. "What the fuck are you doing? Ummm . . . I mean . . . are you going to sing again?" Maddy asked with trepidation. Erick said nothing. He gave her a kiss on the forehead and a reassuring smile as if trying to comfort a family member after being diagnosed with a terminal illness. He took the seemingly long walk from the front table to the stairs and up to the stage. He stood before the crowd who held the same uniform expression as race car fans anxiously awaiting the next fiery crash. He heard Kristy say, "I can't watch this . . . It's just too disturbing." Sam had her head buried in her hands while Jules stared at him with an amused smile, munching on pretzels. He looked at the woman who was his playful adversary and that he now loved. He gave a playful air-kiss and a knowing wink at her beautiful but concerned face.

He then looked at Rosetta and Charlie who were standing at their table with their arms wrapped around each other. They were beaming at him with the same pride as a parent at a school recital. He mouthed "thank you" to them as he thought about his efforts from the previous week. Every day during the past week while Maddy was at work, Erick was at the home of Rosetta and Charlie. On Monday, Rosetta played a single note on her piano and asked Erick to match it. He did. "Okay, dumplin', you're not tone-deaf. You just lack the experience and natural ability to find the right key on your own. We can help you with that. Let's get started." He selected the song that he wanted to sing, and they practiced for hours every day until the correct key was etched into his vocal cords the moment that he heard the introductory accompaniment.

"Do you think I'm ready?" Erick asked the couple on Friday before going to the bookstore.

"Yeah . . . you're ready," Charlie proudly stated as he smiled and wrapped his lengthy arms around Erick's torso.

The opening chords began of a different version of the song that was playing in the bookstore the day that he had met her. He began singing the opening line of the Mindbenders' version of "A Groovy Kind of Love," and the audience let out a collective sigh of relief. Sam began peering at the confident crooner from between her fingers, then slowly lowered her hands. Jules just kept eating her pretzels but did so with nods of knowing approval. Kristy had a look of amazement. And Maddy's face immediately went from dread to her excited smile as she witnessed her guy kick everybody's ass with his serviceable rendition. She felt a single tear run down her cheek as she envisioned her uncle Joe swaying with her aunt Blair from a long-ago Friday evening.

The song ended. Erick took a respectful bow. Maddy stood up on the table and shouted, "That's what I'm fuckin' *talkin'* about! Give it up for my guy, you muthaaafukaaaas!" The bar erupted in genuine applause, and Erick felt pride and vindication but mostly relief as he sat back down at his table. Maddy threw her legs over his lap, her arms around his neck, and exclaimed, "I love you!" before planting a big kiss on his lips.

While still kissing him, Maddy realized what she had just done with her now-widened eyes looking sideways at the shocked expressions on her friends' faces. They were communicating telepathically as Maddy said, *"Oh fuck! What did I just do?" "What the fuck did you just do, Maddy?"* came their psychic response. *"Oh shit, what the fuck is he going to say?" "What's he going to say, Maddy?"*

Erick began chuckling and gently pulled his lips from hers as he thought, *Sweet! I'm off the fuckin' hook!*

"Well . . . I love you too . . . sooo *that's* out there now . . . and now for five minutes of awkward silence," Erick calmly said before giving Maddy a huge smile.

"Oh, fuck it! I looove you!" Maddy exclaimed as she once again threw her arms around his neck and kissed him.

"Well, I guess *this* shit's happening then," Jules stated. "Yup," came the simultaneous response from the other two stunned friends.

Erick asked Maddy if she would like to join him outside. On their way out, Maddy noticed Julie watching them. *What the fuck is* that *little bitch doing here?* she wondered. Once outside, Erick leaned up against the brick exterior of the bar and said, "Y'know, Maddy, there are only two times when saying those three little words is a bad thing. One is when someone says it and they don't mean it. The other is when someone says it and they mean it, and the other person doesn't say it back. So you said it and meant it . . . right?"

"Absolutely," Maddy immediately replied.

"Okay, and I said it and I definitely meant it. So I think this is a really good thing. We've simply expressed how we feel about each other, and we both know that we're in the same place in our relationship. And besides, I owe you one."

"What do you mean?" Maddy inquired.

"Well, you've now said it twice, and I've only said it once, so I want to make myself perfectly clear to you." With that, Erick turned to Maddy, gently placed his hands on her shoulders, and looked into her emerald-green eyes. "Maddy Sommers, I am completely, totally, *hopelessly* in love with you." He kissed her. And she broke down . . . again.

Erick and Maddy approached their table. Maddy's eyes were red and puffy from her tears of joy. Erick excused himself to go to the restroom, and Sam said, "Are you okay?"

"Y-yes, he just told me he was h-hopelessly in love with m-me, and I've never been so h-h-appy!" she stammered through another torrent of tears. Julie's face could be seen peering over the crowd, surveying the events at the front table.

Upon Erick's arrival, Maddy excused herself and said, "Okay, my turn. Be back in a sec." Following her into the restroom was a curious Julie.

"Heeey, sweetie," Julie began in a fake voice of concern, "are you all right?"

"Yeah. Fine. Thanks for asking," came Maddy's curt reply. "Ohhh, good. I just saw that you were crying, and I wanted to make sure that everything was, y'know, all right."

Bullshit! Maddy thought. *This little skank is just trying to find out if there's trouble in paradise, and if there is, she's gonna be a vulture and try to swoop in on my guy! I'm gonna put a dagger in this bitch's heart once and for all!* Maddy gingerly reached into purse and pulled out her . . . lipstick.

"Hey . . . yeah, thanks for asking," Maddy began innocently. "No, I'm fine. It's just that we said 'I love you' to each other for the first time, and I've never been happier, so I guess I just got a little emotional." Maddy watched Julie's hopeful expression turn to disappointment. *Heh, heh, heh, fuck you, skank*, Maddy thought.

"Oh, hey, that's great. I'm . . . really happy for you," came Julie's reply, which increased in sincerity as she came to terms with what she had just heard. "Listen, I know you've picked up on my vibe that I'm kinda into him, but now that I know how you two feel about each other . . . well . . . you don't have anything to worry about with me, okay? From this point on, he's just a friend, and I truly am happy for you both."

"Thanks, that's really sweet of you to say," Maddy replied. "But I was wondering if you could do me a favor?" Julie inquired.

"Uhhh . . . maybe . . . what is it?"

"Well, his friendship is truly important to me, and I don't think that he's picked up on my flirting with him—"

Maddy cut her off, "Yeah, probably not."

"Yeah, what's up with that?" Julie exclaimed. "It's not like I was being subtle about it!"

"Yeah, I noticed," came Maddy's annoyed response followed by "I don't know. He's like autistic or something when it comes to that shit. So what's the favor?"

"Well," Julie said with hesitation, "I know you'll probably tell him about this at some point, but I was wondering if you could just hold off for a little while. I just don't want him to feel weird around me."

"Yeah, I can do that," Maddy agreed as the two gave each other a friendly embrace.

Maddy returned to the table, threw her legs over Erick's lap, and gave him a kiss. Kristy said, "So what did that Julie chick want?"

"Oh, Julie's here? Where is she?" Erick stated as Maddy gave him an irritated look from the corner of her eye.

"Oh, nothin' much," Maddy began. "She just happened to see that I was crying and came in to check on me. When I told her what had happened, she just said that she was happy for us. That's all."

Erick was now presented with a choice. He could choose what was behind Door Number 1 and say nothing. Or he could choose what was behind Door Number 2 and say something completely stupid. He made the wrong choice by saying in a condescending tone, "See, Maddy, I told you that it was just silly to think that Julie was interested in me, you silly, silly girl. See, we're just friends."

Maddy, biting her lip, said, "Yup, I understand that now. You're just friends." Internally however, Maddy was thinking, *Oh, Mr. Parker. You just dug your own fucking grave. Another victory shall be mine! Heh, heh, heh.*

———

Several weeks later, Erick came into the karaoke bar, took a seat at the counter, and began chatting with the bartender, Lee. He heard a couple of hicks who were sitting in the corner of the counter make a reference about "kung-flu" and laugh as they glanced over at Lee. She just stared at Erick as she let out an exasperated sigh. Noticing another white male and mistaking him for a member of their "tribe," one of them said to Erick, "Hey, buddy, this a good place to pick up some big-city pussy?" Erick took one look at them and immediately didn't like them. They both presented scruffy beards, mullets, and shirts with an absurd, flaming "Q." The Confederate flag tattoos didn't help matters either.

"Nah, this is just a friendly neighborhood bar. We're like family around here and look out for one another, so you're not going to find anyone who's interested," Erick coldly replied.

"Well, we have sumthin' that we kin put in their drink to make them all friendly like," one said as they laughed and nudged one another.

As Erick's blood pressure began to rise, one of the hicks exclaimed, "Well, hello there, little red!"

Erick looked in the direction of their leering gazes. Maddy and her friends had just entered the bar.

"Yup, that's the one," the other hick replied. "Let's separate her from the pack, and we'll drug her and plug her."

The sound of a heavy glass being slammed upon the bar echoed throughout the room. Everyone looked over as Erick stared at the hicks and said in a deep voice with a slow, methodical cadence, "I've tried to be polite to you two, but when you talk about drugging and raping women, well . . . that's where I draw the line." Erick's voice continued to deepen. Lee would later describe it as a demonic rattle. His face became redder and became contorted into the embodiment of pure rage. And he stared directly at them without blinking as he continued, "And when you talk about raping my girlfriend, the woman that I love . . . well . . . now you've just made it personal. So here's what you're going to do. You're going to get your asses off of those stools and you're going to leave. Or . . . I'm going to kill both of you motherfuckers."

Maddy watched with a perverse intensity. She saw the look of blind rage in his eyes. She *recognized* the look of blind rage in his eyes. And she knew that she would have to step in and save him from himself. There was suddenly a blur of activity as one of the hicks laughed. Erick came off his barstool and began rounding the corner of the bar. Tony, the bouncer, grabbed the two hicks by their arms and ordered them to leave. Erick was right behind them walking with the intensity of a popular slasher while staring straight ahead with outraged intensity. Then, as quickly as he had started, he stopped. Standing before him with her hands on his shoulders was a five-foot-four- (and a fuckin' half)-inch woman.

"Hey, hey, it's okay . . . They're leaving . . . It's okay," Maddy anxiously said to her love. Erick did not respond to her words or light shakes of his shoulders, instead just staring ahead with his twisted crimson face. And he did not blink until she said, "Hey, you!"

Erick then blinked and looked down. His face softened slightly as he exclaimed, "Maddy!" and enveloped her in his arms, clinging to her as if she were his life preserver preventing him from being swallowed up by his violent waves of anger.

"Hey, hey, hey, it's okay," Maddy quietly whispered into his ear.

Erick whispered back, "I will kill any motherfucker who ever tries to hurt you, Maddy. I am not exaggerating, and this isn't hyperbole. If I ever see those two motherfuckers again, I will tear them apart with my bare hands, and there's not a fucking thing anyone will be able to do to stop me." Maddy believed him as she felt a twisted sense of comfort.

CHAPTER 21

BOYS WHO RAPE (SHOULD ALL BE DESTROYED)

It was early July, and Maddy had sworn off her more violent extracurricular activities. *Nope, I'm done with that shit. I'm not gonna risk my relationship for other people's problems. Aunt Blair knew about uncle Joe. Erick doesn't know about my shit. Different situation. I love him. He loves me. And I'm not gonna let someone else's problems jeopardize that.* Then, she experienced a sinking feeling as she realized that the episode at the bar between Erick and the hicks wasn't someone else's problem. It was hers.

Ever since that night, every time they went out, Erick had been on high alert. He would constantly scan the throngs of people mingling on the street or in the various establishments. He was tense. He was ready. He was looking for them. And Maddy did not know if she would be able to stop him a second time. *It's one thing to coldly plan for your . . . er . . . justice,* she thought. *It's quite another to pop off publicly. The first approach insulates you from legal problems, if you do it right. The second approach leaves you as a sitting duck for a prison sentence.* And it wasn't like she could give him tutorials on the art of murder (*At least not yet,* Maddy chuckled to herself, *but the big nudge has got potential*). So she prepared, just in case the hick chads did something to provoke her or Erick. *But dammit, this is definitely the last one!* she screamed to herself.

She thought that their construction site might be the best location, *If I need to do something, which I probably won't.* There were two bars in particular that they would frequent most evenings. Interestingly enough, Maddy thought, was that there had been an uptick in rapes in that area over the past month. *Probably a coincidence*, Maddy rationalized. The bars were too public. There were too many cameras at their hotel. There were plenty of dark areas between their hotel and the bars, but there was too much unpredictable foot traffic. *Yep, the construction site would be perfect*, Maddy determined. She checked it out on a Wednesday night after spending her evening with her friends. It was dark. The foreman's trailer was easy to break in to for cleanup. *For fuck sakes, this is New York! Why the fuck are you using this cheap-ass lock?* Maddy internally scolded them. There was a toolshed that was equally easy to get in to. *Yup, the gang's all here!* she thought as she surveyed the glistening buffet of potential weapons. But most importantly, there was a cement mixer and plenty of holes that needed to be filled. *I could Hoffa these motherfuckers!* Maddy excitedly thought, before collecting herself and thinking, *But I probably won't have to. Just leave us alone motherfuckers, and you can go on to lead whatever you call a life.*

They did not listen. Maddy received the call late that Friday evening. Robbie was in the hospital. Maddy and Erick rushed over to find many of the bar patrons wearing deeply concerned expressions. No one was allowed in to see him. He was in serious condition. He had been brutally beaten, raped, and sodomized. The police had been there and interviewed Robbie. Maddy, looking for a way into Robbie's room, encountered a pair of officers around a corner. From there, she overheard an officer say, "Yeah, but *she's* or *he's* . . . I don't know what to call these fuckin' freaks anymore. Anyway, *he's* drunk and doesn't know the names of the attackers. All *he* could say was 'hicks.' We're never gonna figure this one out."

I've gotta get Erick out of here before he hears this shit, Maddy thought as she returned to the packed waiting room. Maddy took Erick by the arm and said, "C'mon, we're not going to be able to see him. It sounds like he's in really bad shape but will be all right. There's really nothing else we can do." The somber pair returned to Erick's apartment where they held each other and wept.

The following evening, Rosetta stood proudly atop the stage at the karaoke bar and said, "I don't know how it is that God would allow such evil to exist in this world, but it exists. Whether it be on a large scale like the geno-cide that has occurred to our Ukrainian brothers and sisters or on a small scale like what has happened to our loving friend, Robbie. It exists. And maybe it is our test to do everything that we can to *stand up* to evil whenever and wherever we encounter it. And I don't know *how*, and I don't know *when*, but justice *shall* ultimately prevail. So won't you all please"—Rosetta paused, looked down, and wiped a tear from her eye before standing upright once again with a compassionate smile—"stand and join me in singing Robbie's favorite anthem." The entire Saturday night congregation stood and joined Rosetta as she sang Pete Seeger's "We Shall Overcome." Erick had his arm around Maddy as they sang. Maddy wore a blank expression as her mind meticulously plotted.

It was the following Monday afternoon, and Maddy decided to take a brisk walk on her lunch break. Her constitutional took her to the area of the construction site. Wearing a short black skirt, heeled sandals, and a flowered tank top, the blonde- haired, blue-eyed beauty was the recipient of many calls and whistles as she strutted by. *Fuck, I hate wearing these contacts, and this fucking wig's too tight*, she lamented as she strode over to two construction workers eating their sandwiches alone.

"Hey, boys," she flirtatiously said while leaning over a barrel and exposing a healthy amount of cleavage. "Do you *really* know how to use all of this *big, strong* equipment?"

"Shore do," one of the hicks responded as mustard slovenly dribbled down his chin.

"Want us to show you how we use our *big, strong* equipment?" the other chimed in.

"Well . . . I can't right now, silly, not with everybody lookin' and everythin'," Maddy replied with a giggle. "But maybe later tonight we could meet up and have some fun . . . whatdayasay?" "Yeah, baby, we could show you a few things," one of them said as they began circling her while leering at her through their discount mirrored sunglasses.

"Well, how about one tonight? I'm kinda into . . . different locations . . . might be fun. But just you two. Also, no names and don't tell anyone, all right? A girl's got a reputation to uphold, y'know?"

"Yeah, no problem, baby. We won't tell a soul. And you kin call us whatsever you like. I'll tell you what. We'll bring the drinks and the . . . equipment. All you gotta bring is your smile and that hot lil' body a-yourn."

"Okay . . . bye now, chad . . . and chad," Maddy said as she provocatively waved and giggled.

Fuck, men are stupid, Maddy amusingly thought to herself as she shook her head in disbelief and left the site. "There would probably be more of them alive if they'd just jerk off more often, although that probably won't help much. I don't think the big head is any smarter than the small one for most of these douchebags."

Her heart was racing as she was on the phone with Erick that night. She was excited because she was in love, and her dependable beau had once again called her at exactly nine on the dot. As soon as the clock on her phone changed from 8:59 to 9:00, she would count, "One . . . two . . . three," and her phone would ring followed by her customary greeting of "Hey, you!" and his customary response of "Wazzupbuttacup?"

"What did ya rehearse today at Charlie's?" she inquired.

"Ummm . . . well . . . I'd kinda like to make sure I can pull it off before I tell you that," came his secretive response.

"Yeah . . . okay . . . whatevs," she replied as she struggled to focus on the conversation at hand due to her mind being on a continuous loop of the required preparations for later that evening. The conversation ended by Erick's now-standard "Luvya madly, Maddy!" She hung up the phone, let out a deep dreamy sigh, and went to her closet. She was smiling ear to ear as she pulled out a black duffel bag and began undressing.

She heard them coming. *Fuck, they're loud! I'm gonna have to do this quick. No time for speeches,* Maddy thought as waves of anticipation rushed through her body. They approached the agreed-upon meeting area while drunkenly laughing.

"Where the fuck is that little bitch? I'm gonna plug every hole she's got!" one exclaimed before the other let out a high-pitched squeal. A tiny black figure had jumped out from between two concrete barriers and planted a pickaxe into the abdomen of the now-screaming chad. Intestines collapsed onto the ground in a slushy pile as she struck the other chad in the temple with the pick, sending shards of skull and hair flying through the sultry summer breeze. A geyser of blood spewed from the side of his head as Maddy dislodged her weapon and his lifeless body collapsed to the ground.

"Well, *that* was fuckin' anticlimactic!" Maddy exclaimed. "I didn't *think* you boys would last too long with me," she said to the lifeless bodies, wearing a knowing grin. She then noticed a shallow gasping from one of the chads. He was lying on his side clutching his slimy entrails with a look of desperation. "Oh, still with us, huh? Cool. I thought my fun was over. But since you're wanting to hang around for an encore, I guess I won't disappoint. See, this is my final performance, guys, so I decided I needed to make a statement. You know, always leave 'em wanting more. And you guys are a bit too heavy right now to do what I want to do, so I'm gonna have to lighten the load. But first, about those pesky dental records . . ."

A sledgehammer collapsed the side of the head of the gasping chad. A second blow caused the top of his skull to pop off like a cork as his brains erupted out of the newly formed opening. A third blow left his face looking like melted gelatin with weird fruit in it. The second chad's head and face experienced the same procedure; and chucky pools of blood, bone, and cartilage formed around a pair of size 8 boots.

"But that doesn't take care of your weight problem, so let's shed a few pounds," Maddy enthusiastically exclaimed as she began singing Olivia Newton John's "Physical" while severing their arms and legs away from their torsos with a sharpened axe. Leaving their limbs lying as haphazardly as her worn panties in Erick's apartment, she dragged their torsos that were topped off by "heads" that resembled oozing pink, kneaded dough, over to a steel cable. She placed the bodies back-to-back before wrapping the steel cable, which was attached to a pulley, around their gooey necks. She hit the button on the pulley and lifted the bodies ten feet into the air. Placing her hands on her hips, she looked in admiration at her final piece of work. *This*, she proudly thought to herself, *was the greatest final performance in the history of the world!*

Following bagging her clothes and cleaning up in the foreman's trailer, she tossed the bag of saturated evidence into a hole and filled it with cement. The torsos were left hanging above the ground, and the various weapons and removed limbs were lying wherever Maddy had left them. The scene looked like a wicked child's room that had left her demented toys strewn about. Before departing the scene, she could not resist one final quip. "Well, boys . . . *now* you're hung enough for me. Heh, heh, heh," a grinning Maddy said to the decimated corpses. "Shit, man . . . I gotta find a partner in crime to tell my jokes to. This shit's gold!"

The following evening was a "date" night, and Maddy and Erick were lying in their bed watching the news following their earlier more rambunctious activities, including a one-sided pillow fight. The report of the impossibly gruesome discovery came across the screen. Pictures of the identified "victims" were then shown. Erick immediately looked at Maddy with a shocked expression. Maddy, seeing the expression on his face, mirrored it. They then simultaneously looked down and averted each other's gaze.

"Hey!" Erick excitedly exclaimed. "You know what sounds good? Ice cream! I'll tell ya what, I'll just run out and get some, okay? I'll be right back!" Erick was out the door before Maddy had a chance to reply.

Maddy was frantically pacing around the living room wearing Hunky and Dory like a feline shield. *Oh fuck, oh fuck, oh fuck . . . He knows, he knows, he knows . . . He's telling the cops right now! He's ratting me out. I can't blame him. I mean, for all he knows it's pillows one day and fuckin' chain saws the next! But still, it's really uncool of him to rat me out. It doesn't take a fuckin' hour to get ice cream! I'd better get out of here. I'd better—*

"Hey! Sorry it took me so long. I had to go to three fuckin' places to find your butter ripple. But the upshot is . . ." Erick removed a gigantic container of ice cream from the bag. "Look at the *size* of this fuckin' thing! Wanna share?"

"That's what she said," came Maddy's response as all of the tension in her face was replaced with relief. *Okay . . . maybe he doesn't know. I'm serious. No more of this shit. That was a close call.*

As they lay in bed watching a giallo film with melting ice cream being lapped off the side of the container by two enraptured kittens, Erick said, "Hey . . . um . . . there's something that I would like to talk to you about."

"Ummm . . . okay," came Maddy's fearful response.

"Well, it's not really a big deal . . . I was just thinking that . . . ummm . . . well, I'm not planning on leaving New York because, well . . . you know. And I was just thinking that if things keep going well, which I'm sure they will, that there might be a time that we . . . y'know . . . maybe move in together." Maddy's heart began pounding from joyful anticipation instead of terrified anxiety.

"So . . . I have a line on a three-story brownstone that's a bit farther from your work, but not too far, and it's a really great price because it's in a kinda dilapidated neighborhood. But the house itself has recently been remodeled and is beautiful, and the real estate agent said that there were developers looking at revitalizing that area, so it might double in value in the next few years if we can handle all of the noise from the construction. And so I'm supposed to look at it on Thursday, and I was wondering if maybe you would like to look at it with me because . . . well . . . if we *do* ever move in together, I don't want it to be you moving into *my* place. I want it to be you moving into *our* place. So what do you think?"

Maddy was speechless and only able to rapidly nod her head. "Okay . . . cool . . . so just one more thing. I was thinking that y'know, if things keep going well that . . . now, Maddy, I'm not proposing this right now—I want to be perfectly clear about that! But . . . maybe if things keep going well that maybe at some point, we might want to *think* about *talking* about marriage. What do you think about that?"

Maddy stared at him while trying to regain her composure. She now realized that she had the upper hand in this situation and decided to play it "cool." "Well, mister," she began with a coy assertiveness, "I'm not going to tell you what I think about that. Nope, if you want to know what I think about that, then you're gonna have to pop the question. And I might say yes, or I might say no, but if you want to know, then you're gonna have to pop the question. But . . . *if* you propose to me and *if* I say yes, then . . ." Unable to hold her excitement any longer, Maddy began rifling through the wedding plans that she had been obsessing over. "I think that we should get married next April because we will have known each other for, like, fourteen months and been together as a couple for, like, almost a year, so nobody can accuse us of rushing into anything. And I think we should get married at Pastor Tim's because it's really the only church I've ever felt comfortable in, and he and Jeremy are supercool, and we can invite all of our friends, and my aunts can fly in, and I know several places that could cater it and—" Erick interrupted her by asking, "So do you have the wedding dress picked out?" to which Maddy excitedly replied, "No, but I have a friend of a friend who's a designer, and I'm sure she could design something for us!"

"Us? I'm not wearing a dress," Erick surprisingly stated.

"No, of course not," Maddy replied while giggling like a teenager after her first glass of champagne. "She would design you a suit!"

"Ummm . . . Maddy . . . I was kinda hoping that maybe it would be a bit casual so that I could just wear jeans with a nice shirt and shoes. That would be okay, wouldn't it?"

Maddy looked at Erick with feigned disgust and said sternly. "You're not wearing fucking jeans to our wedding."

"But, Maddy . . .," Erick pleaded.

"You're *not* wearing fucking jeans to our wedding," she commanded.

"But, Maddy, please listen . . .," Erick attempted to say in a final appeal.

"Gaaaawd! You're impossible! For the last time . . . you are *not* wearing *fucking* jeans to our wedding! And now that that's settled, if you would please excuse me for a moment, I'm going to use the restroom."

Erick heard the bathroom latch click followed by a muffled scream of exuberance. *Okay, well, that went well. Now it's time to start on my master plan.*

Step 1: Keep Maddy out of prison.

Step 2: Propose.

Step 3: Get married.

Step 4: Surprise her with a honeymoon to . . . where should we go?

CHAPTER 22

RAVE ON

It was the last Thursday in July, and Erick was on the way to the airport to pick up Blair and Patty. His mind was whirling as he processed all of the events that had led him to this pivotal moment. The radical right-wing indoctrination of his beloved wife leading to her deteriorating mental health and untimely and tragic death. His abrupt decision to move to New York. His meeting Pastor Tim and Jeremy. The meeting and development of a deep friendship with Maddy. Their first date followed by an almost immediate emotional and intimate romantic relationship. His discovery that Maddy had murdered two people and quite possibly a third, as he thought that the pedophile's grisly demise may have been at her hands as well.

He wondered if her aunts knew about what he thought he knew. He didn't really *know* if Maddy had murdered the hicks. It was only the shocked look of a child who had been caught with her hand in the cookie jar that night watching the news report that led him to that assumption. So he didn't really *know*. But deep inside, he knew.

He thought about that night and how he didn't know how to respond to this realization. He needed to get out of the apartment and process his thoughts and feelings, so he went out for ice cream. He did, in fact, go to three places to find the right flavor; but he had taken his time as he slowly trudged from store to store in his search. He was tormented by the discovery and wasn't sure about how that realization may alter their relationship. He was bothered by not being bothered about it, and he was bothered by the fact that his lovely girlfriend had the balls and intelligence to do what he had secretly thought about doing himself.

Rosetta was right the other evening at Robbie's tribute. There *is* evil in the world. And there are times that that evil is left unchecked or unpunished by the proper authorities for one reason or another. And that in his estimation was unfair. And now someone, most likely the woman he shared a bed with five nights a week, was taking out those who were able to cause great physical and emotional destruction to others in our society without suffering the consequences of their grave indiscretions. He wasn't bothered at all by what he thought she had done. In fact, he admired her for it and found his love for her to be even stronger and unwavering than before. He was bothered by his own spineless timidity.

The world was upside down. Self-appointed internet "celebrities" standing in front of a blue screen depicting Paris and holding up a bottle of perfume was now considered to be real. The actual attempt to overthrow our constitutional democracy, the beneficial effects of the COVID vaccine, the actual statistics of deaths because of the proliferation of guns were all somehow unreal. People could create and live in their own reality simply by saying, "Fake news!" They could create and live in their own reality through their self-obsessed posting of "selfies" in order to get "likes" for their fragile egos and apathetic and vapid personalities. Erick found it to be all too depressing and disgusting.

So, he surmised, if people can create and live within their own sense of reality, then why could Maddy not create and live within her own sense of justice? Why could she not provide the justified consequences to the sadists who live on our streets that the decaying societal infrastructure was unable to provide? His appreciation and love for her grew with each step he took back toward his apartment. If he was right, then that was Maddy's business to share. He would keep his suspicions to himself and respect her right to share with him what she desired to share. He was in love, and he was ready to put all of his trust in his adored and probably quite violent soul mate. As he entered his building and began up the stairs to his second-floor apartment, he chuckled to himself as he vividly pictured her diminutive figure chopping limbs off torsos with an axe. *Fuck, this could be more fun than I thought*, he pondered as he entered the apartment with a beaming smile, large tub of butter ripple, and prepared apology for his tardiness. *I'd better make this good. I* really *don't want to piss her off,* he thought amusingly.

Hugs and enthusiastic introductions were exchanged at the airport baggage claim between Erick and the sixty-nine- year-old Blair (she could easily pass for, like, fifty-five, Erick thought) and seventy-year-old Patty. He loved Patty's yellow skeleton emblazoned "Cramps" shirt that had obviously been purchased well before the turn of the century, which provided a springboard for an ice-breaking discussion of music.

Their open and lively discussion continued for two hours back at Erick's apartment as many bawdy jokes were exchanged between Patty and Erick. Blair sat and would calmly yet strategically bring the pair back to more relevant topics, all of which were designed to detect whether this man was healthy for their beloved niece. As Erick discussed his feelings for Maddy, politics, or his views on social issues, the pair of sisters would give each other a knowing glance and nod approvingly. Erick knew that this was his final audition for his role as Maddy's life partner, and he was hamming it up as though he were a freshman theater major in a bad production of Shakespeare.

Toward the end of the discussion, Patty said, "So . . . I like fuckin' chicks! What do you think about that?"

"Hmmm . . .," Erick began as he weighed his response. "Well, for starters, I guess that means that I don't have to worry about you hitting on me, so that's a good thing. I mean, most hetero women find me a bit . . . irresistible. I can barely walk down the street without them tearing the clothes off of my pudgy ass."

Erick's self-deprecating sarcasm was on full display as Blair and Patty erupted in shocked laughter before Blair said, "Well, *we've* certainly hit another gear now, haven't we?"

"But seriously," Erick continued through a slight self-imposed chuckle, "I have two responses. On the one hand, I don't think about that at all. On the other, I think quite seriously about it." Blair and Patty leaned forward a bit in their seats, wondering what this man was going to say. Up to this point, the audition had gone quite well. Would he now crash and burn? "You see, I personally don't give much thought about someone's biology, whether that be race, height, hair color, or sexuality. It is beyond me why so many people obsess about another person's natural biology. And not only do they obsess about it, but they turn that obsession into hatred, which leads to societal persecution of an entire group of people. And it is that last point that I think quite seriously about. But generally speaking, I just don't give a fuck about what genitals another person enjoys licking."

"Okay . . . good fuckin' response," Patty stated in a satisfied tone. "This motherfucker's all right by me."

"I have just one more question," Blair said calmly but seriously as she looked intensely into Erick's hazel eyes. "Our niece is . . . special. She has some . . . natural abilities that you may not be aware of and may never be aware of. These are abilities that she has displayed in the past, and she may never speak of them. Having said that, what are your long-term intentions with our niece?"

Their eyes continued to be locked, and Erick knew exactly what Blair was speaking of. "Well, Blair," Erick began with the same calm seriousness and intensity while holding Dory and lightly kneading the back of her neck, "I would prefer to answer that question fully in Maddy's presence. But . . . I can pledge this to you. *No matter what* she does, I will *always* be with her." The intensity of the moment was broken up by loud "Clomp, clomp, clomping" up the apartment building's stairs followed by the abrupt opening, then slamming of Erick's heavy oak wooden door. Shoes were kicked off and went flying, causing Hunky to begrudgingly jump off Blair's lap and retreat to the safety of the bedroom.

"Hey, you!" an exuberant Maddy exclaimed as she bounced on her tiptoes over to Erick, giving him a firm kiss.

"Wazzupbuttacup?" came Erick's obligatory but equally exuberant greeting. "How was your day?"

"It was fine," she replied before turning to her aunts and embracing them both simultaneously as she said, "It's so great to see you!"

A brief recap of the earlier discussion was held followed by Blair saying, "But there was one question that he *did not* answer for us."

"Really? That's not like you," Maddy said in a confused tone with her left hand concealed behind Erick's back. "What was the question?"

"Well, we asked what his intentions were with you, and he said that he wanted to wait until you were here before he answered. And you are here now," Blair answered pointedly.

"Heeeyy . . . yeah . . . that is a good question," Maddy mischievously said to Erick. "I'd kinda like to know the answer to that one myself. What *are* your intentions with me, mister?" Erick whispered something into Maddy's ear. She adopted her ornery grin and coyly said while removing her left hand from behind his back, "Well . . . last Saturday he gave me this."

On her hand was an engagement ring.

Blair and Patty simultaneously said, "Oh my god . . . is that . . ."

"Yup! We're getting' fuckin' married!" Maddy screamed with the delight of a child opening presents on Christmas morning. "My lord, child. That ring is . . . beautiful," Blair stated in amazement.

"Yeah . . . it's all right, if you like that sorta thing," Maddy playfully replied before turning to Erick and smiling while sticking her tongue out of the right side of her mouth and crossing her eyes. Erick exploded with laughter. Blair and Patty exploded into tears.

"Oh . . . my . . . god," Patty stated. "We haven't seen you make that face in well over twenty years." The two sisters enveloped Maddy in a huge hug before beckoning Erick to join them. "Get in here, motherfucker," Patty ordered. "You may as well get used to being a part of a huggy family."

Sam, Jules, and Kristy arrived at the apartment and embraced their "aunts" in an emotional reunion.

"Hey! Have a seat! I'm about to tell them the engagement story!" Maddy ordered excitedly.

"Oh fuck, not this again," came Jules's curt but resigned response.

"Just sit the fuck down and listen. I have to listen to all of *your* wild nights fucking strangers, so you can listen to this. Maybe you'll learn something," Maddy demanded.

"Not fuckin' likely," came Jules's response followed by an exasperated eye roll.

Following an intense stare of warning directed at all three of her giggling friends, Maddy put on her innocent smile and began in her lilted, singsongy voice.

"Once upon a time, there was a man and a woman who were soul mates that the universe brought together . . ."

"Oh, Jesus, Maddy!" Kristy exclaimed.

"Shut . . . the . . . fuck . . . *up*!" Maddy angrily demanded before returning to her previous demeanor. "Fine. I'll just tell the story. But it's not the same without my God-given dramatic flair! So . . . we were all to meet at karaoke last Saturday night. Erick was already there, which wasn't out of the ordinary because he liked to go over what song he was planning on singing that night with Charlie and Rosetta. Everything was completely normal. They called

Erick up to sing. He gave me a kiss on the forehead and whispered, 'Wish me luck.' I said, 'You don't need it,' to which he replied, 'Yeah . . . I kinda do. This is the most important song that I've ever had to sing,' which I didn't think anything of because I didn't know *what* the fuck he was talking about.

"He got up there, and he kicked the shit out of 'Rave On' by Buddy Holly. And he mostly sang it to me, but sometimes he would play to the rest of the crowd too. After he was done singing, everybody was applauding of course, and he said, 'If I could just have everybody's attention for a moment, I promise I won't hold karaoke up for too long.' Now, I had no idea what he was doing, so I'm rolling my eyes at him and making faces and saying, 'Don't hold shit up! Get off the fuckin' stage!' and laughing. He ignored me of course because he's mean to me like that. So then he says it again, 'So if I could just have everybody's attention, there's just something that I need to say.' And everybody got quiet and looked at him, except me because I'm just fuckin' laughing at him because I think he's just being a big dork. But then he said, 'But I'm getting kinda old, and my legs are a bit sore, so I think that I need to get down here to do this.' And he got down on o-one kn-knee . . ."

"Oh god, here we go . . .," Sam said as Maddy's voice began cracking under the weight of her heartfelt joy.

"And he l-looked at me and s-said, 'Maddy S-Sommers, these last f-few months with y-you have been s-some of the h-h- happiest of my l-life. And it is m-my prayer that w-we will have many m-m-more months and years of h-happiness together. A-A-and I want to a-ask you if you would m-m-make me the h-happiest man in the w-world and m-m-marry me!'"

Maddy wiped her tears from her eyes and gave a slight embarrassed chuckle before speaking rapidly. "So I just screamed and ran up to the stage and threw my arms around him and kissed him, right. Then, the karaoke guy decided to be an ass, and he said, 'Well, I didn't hear an answer!' So I stopped kissing him, and I yelled out, 'Yes, I will marry you!' But he was holding the microphone really close to our faces, so I screamed it into the mic, and it was really fuckin' loud. So everybody started laughing and cheering and stuff. And then the karaoke guy asked Charlie and Rosetta to come up and sing a song for us to dance to because Erick had arranged for them to do that. So he got off of the stage, put this fuckin' ring on my finger, and I just fuckin' lost it. And I turned to these guys and said, 'Guys, I'm gettin' married! Look at the size of this fuckin' thing!' to which they of course said, 'That's what she said.' So Rosetta and Charlie are singing 'How Deep Is Your Love' by the Bee

Gees, and we're dancing, and I'm just a fuckin' mess, and he was too, but he won't fuckin' admit it because he's like a *man* or something. But whatever, then of course everybody was hugging me and stuff, and then I felt a little light-headed, so Erick asked if we should go home, and I said yes.

"So we're all walking back to his place, and we were standing at a corner, and I made the mistake of looking down at the ring, and I just fuckin' lost it again. So I'm sobbing, they're all sobbing, and Erick's holding me when a cop pulled up the corner. Now, he doesn't know what the fuck's going on. All he knows is that there's four chicks crying and a guy trying to comfort one of them. So he comes up and says, 'Is everything all right here?' to which Kristy said, 'Yes, Officer. They just got engaged, and she's just a little overwhelmed.' So I can't even fuckin' talk, so I just put my left hand out and nodded into Erick's chest, and the cop goes, 'Well, if someone had given me a ring like that, then I guess I'd cry too. Congratulations and have a good night!'

"So then, Erick lifts my head up to look at him, and he says, 'If you don't calm down, you're gonna get me ass raped in prison,' to which I said, 'Oh, you'd probably like it, you old perv,' to which he said, 'Well, it's not a matter of if I would enjoy it or not, but if I'm going to get ass raped in prison, I'd prefer it be on my own terms,' and then we all laughed.

"Okay, so we get back to his place, and he says, 'Why don't you all just sit and relax, and I'll make us some drinks because it's been kind of an eventful evening.' And I just fuckin' lost it and said, 'Kind of an eventful evening? Jesus Christ, man, do you think that's the understatement of the century? It was just a little over a week ago that you even *mentioned* marriage, and now I'm your *fuckin' fiancée*!' And then he just looks up at me with that fuckin' smart-ass grin that he gets and goes, 'Yeah, like I said, kind of eventful, durrrr.'

"So we're sitting there, and he says, 'Would you like to see the wedding band and hear the meaning behind the ring?' And I said, 'Yes,' and 'What the fuck are you talking about?' And he said that he had actually designed the ring and that there was a special meaning behind each part of the ring. So I'm like, 'Yeah, may as well get all my fuckin' tears out,' because I know that this is going to be supersweet. So first, he says that this is white gold, not silver, and there's a reason for that that he'll explain in a moment, and I go, 'All righty then.' 'So you see this outer band on the ring with the diamond in the center with the two emeralds on either side?' So he says that 'these are emeralds, which is *your* birth stone and your favorite stone, and this band represents you as an individual who will always have her independence.' Then, he gets out the wedding band, which is exactly like the emerald band except the stones are on the opposite side and are opals instead of emeralds. So he says that this is *his* birthstone, and 'this band represents me as an individual who will always have *his* independence. And when we get married, we will be two coequal independent individuals coming together out of pure love, trust, and respect for one another; and that's why I chose white gold to represent the purity of our love. And the diamonds represent our love, and the other two stones represent trust and respect. And I wanted a large diamond in the middle, because, although we are beautiful and strong independently, once we come together, we will be unstoppable. And these smaller diamonds splashing out from the center diamond represent my hope that our love will be *so* strong that it might serve as an inspiration for other people to find love in this fucked-up world. And that's the meaning behind the ring. What do you think?'

"Now at this point, I'm fuckin' cried out. I have nothing left after hearing the sweetest fuckin' thing I've ever heard in my life. So I just stared at him and said, 'Jesus Christ, man. What the fuck are you gonna do for an encore?' And he just smiled at me and put on a record that he found in the box of 45s that he fuckin' overpaid for. In fact, let me play it!" Maddy jumped up and found the record she was looking for on top of the pile. She placed it on the turntable and gently lowered the needle onto the spinning vinyl. She looked at her fiancé, smiled, and held out her hand. Erick got up and took her in his tender embrace. Blair, Patty, Sam, Jules, and Kristy looked on with reverence as the tearful lovers swayed to "No Matter What" by Badfinger.

CHAPTER 23

CURTAINS

It was February 3, 2023, and Maddy enthusiastically greeted her houseguests. Blair and Patty had already arrived; and they were joined by Sam, Jules, and Kristy. Erick was in the expansive kitchen of the three-story brownstone that they had moved into in October the previous year. The intoxicating aroma of freshly baked lasagna wafted through the open floor plan of the bottom floor with one continuous room containing the living room, dining room, and kitchen. Behind the kitchen wall were a storage pantry on one side and a small bathroom with laundry on the other. Outside the back door was a small back porch and a fenced-in concrete slab, just large enough for Erick's vehicle. The scent of Italian herbs, garlic, and tomatoes ascended the metal staircase to reveal a large master bedroom on the right of the white-tiled hallway and two medium-sized bedrooms to the left. The one nearest the staircase was large enough to house three full-sized beds and two dressers, one of which stored extra clothing for Maddy's friends should they pass out or feel the need to spend the night after a raucous night of partying. The other served as Maddy's reading room and walk-in closet. Erick vowed to never step foot into that room. This was not due to respect for Maddy's personal space but rather to avoid the anxiety he would feel at witnessing the explosion of clothing and books lying haphazardly throughout the space. At the end of the hallway was the master bath complete with a whirlpool bathtub and shower combo.

The sounds of the outside construction permeated throughout the home until you entered the space on the third floor and shut the door. Then, it was deafeningly silent. The entire space had been soundproofed. Black and white tiles checkered the floor with deep red walls accenting the DJ stand in one corner and the bar in the other. The walls were adorned by various posters and pictures of their favorite bands, movies, and celebrities including a large poster of Christopher Lee and Peter Cushing locked in a ferocious battle. The poster hung behind the bar with a sign that Maddy had hand stenciled that read, "What do you mean you're out of ice?" This was the party room, and Maddy used it primarily to recreate her jubilant Friday nights of her youth. It also worked out that Erick had an expansive music collection that he had brought from his storage shed in Jefferson City and organized meticulously on the shelves behind the DJ stand. Patty and Blair were there two Friday nights a month as they had sublet Maddy's apartment and were now splitting time between Madison and New York. Patty would nod, drink, or stagger approvingly at the choice of the piercing chords and driving rhythms that shook throughout the room on a weekly (at least) basis, as Maddy and Erick were careful not to play any of their "pussy shit" when she was in attendance.

Jubilant discussion ensued over dinner as Erick would frequently get up and put on another 45 record. He would retrieve it from the same box that he had purchased nearly a year prior for $199.99. He never took those records out and organized them with his others, preferring to keep this eclectic collection of '50s, '60s. and '70s 45s as they were the day he had purchased them. Or so he thought.

Upon yet another telling of the story, Maddy suddenly thought to herself, *Fuck! I've never told him! Oh . . . this is gonna be fuckin' great!* before saying to Erick, "Hey, I'm getting the story right, aren't I? There were *fifty* records in that box, right?" Erick immediately corrected her, "Actually, Maddy, someone must have miscounted, because there were actually fifty-four records in that box. See? So I got an even *better* deal for my . . . heh, heh, heh . . . *$199.99.*"

Maddy answered demurely, "Huh, I wonder how *that* could have happened? I'm always so precise when I take inventory of stuff . . . Oh, wait . . . I remember what happened now. See . . . you were such a smart-ass about the check with that 'Gotcha!' bullshit that I went through our inventory, and I found four records that I thought that you would like that we were selling for around twenty-five bucks a piece. So I took those records and on the first night I stayed over at your place, I put *those* records in *that* box while you were in the shower. So you see, you paid $99.99 for those four records, and you paid $100 for the box of fifty records . . . just as it was supposed to be!" Everyone around the table held amused expressions as they anxiously awaited the response.

"You didn't . . .," Erick incredulously stated.

"Oh, I most certainly fucking *did*!" Maddy retorted arrogantly. Erick attempted to present an angry expression; but it immediately deteriorated as Maddy smiled, stuck out her tongue from the right side of her mouth, and crossed her eyes. He was once again defenseless as he, along with everyone around the table, burst into laughter.

"Okay, that will be quite enough of that, missy," Blair interjected.

"What's the fuck wrong with you?" Maddy aggressively inquired.

"I think you've picked on him enough for one evening. Now, it's your turn. Patty, do you remember that time when Maddy was around five years old and wanted ice cream?" Patty simply nodded as her mouth was full of garlic bread. "All right, everyone, I would like to tell you all a little story about Little Miss Thing over there," Blair began as Maddy lifted and turned her head away from the table while saying confidently, "Go ahead. You don't have *any* embarrassing stories about me."

Erick was on pins and needles and held an expression of delight before Maddy said, "Wipe that fuckin' smirk off your face. She hasn't got shit on me."

"Well, let's see about that," Blair interjected before beginning her story. "Oh, I swear to you all, I could have wrung that little bitch's neck that day."

"Hey! That's not nice to say!" and overly dramatic Maddy exclaimed.

"Well, it's the truth, dear. Maddy was around five years old, and I was preparing dinner with Patty . . . well . . . being in the way when this sweet, delightful, innocent little face looked up at me and said, 'Auntie Blair, you know what would be a good idea?' And I said, 'No, dear, what?' And she said, 'I think it would be a good idea if we went and got some ice cream.' Then, I said, 'No, Maddy, we're going to have dinner in just a little while, and you ate enough junk last night, so there will be no ice cream tonight.' She then said, 'Okay,' and left the room.

"Well, that just felt too easy. So Patty and I hid around a corner behind Joseph's chair, and sure enough, there she was saying, 'Uncle Joe, you work awfully hard, don't you?' And Joseph said, 'Why yes, buttacup, I suppose I do.' Now this sweet little girl was about to spring just about the most manipulative trap that I've ever seen, and she said, 'Well, you work so hard that I think you deserve a treat.' And Joe said, 'Well, what kind of treat should I have?' And Maddy said while looking down and shuffling her little feet, 'Well . . . I think you should treat yourself to some ice cream . . .,' and then she lifted her little head and batted her eyes at him and said, 'And since you're going anyway, maybe I can come along too?'

"Well, certainly Joseph wouldn't fall for such an obvious manipulation, I thought, until I heard him explode with laughter and yell out, 'I think you're right! I think we both deserve a treat. Blair honey, Maddy and I are going to step out for a moment. We'll be right back!' Well, I was just fuming until Patty calmed me down by saying that Joseph would probably just get her a baby cone, just to keep her happy. And of course, I thought she was right. So imagine my surprise when I went into the living room with Joseph slurping on the largest chocolate shake they had and this little girl sitting in my *good chair*, her little feet just wagging back and forth, her face covered in the chocolate and vanilla swirl ice cream with it running down her arms and *onto my good chair*. This damn thing was so big she needed both of her hands to hold it. And she looked up at me and just smiled as if to say, 'See what *I* have, bitch?' I didn't know whether to burst out laughing, because it *was* so damn cute, or slap that cone right out of that little bitch's hands!"

"Hey! That's not nice! Stop saying that about me!" an "injured" Maddy demanded.

Blair simply ignored her and continued, "So, I calmly asked Joseph to come into the kitchen and informed him that that little girl was going to eat every bite of her dinner, which she did. But the kicker is, about an hour after dinner, she came up to me and said, 'Auntie Blair, my tummy hurts.' And I said, 'Well, it's no wonder after all of that ice cream you ate!' And she said, 'Oh no, Auntie Blair. It wasn't the ice cream. You just made too much for dinner.' I looked over at Joseph who couldn't even make eye contact with me as he tried to keep from laughing. I went upstairs, screamed into a pillow, and that man slept on the sofa that night, let me assure you."

Everyone burst out laughing, except for Erick. He saw the slight tear in Maddy's eye as her uncle Joe's name had been mentioned. He leaned into her and said softly in her ear, "I think that's the most adorable story in the history of the world." Immediately after dinner, Maddy excused herself. It was only eleven days until the wedding, as they had decided to wed on the one year anniversary of their first meeting, and she needed to go for a fitting of her wedding dress. Erick, still attempting in his futile attempt to lobby for jeans, boycotted the fitting by saying he needed to stay home, clean up, and say good night to their guests. "Uh-huh," an obviously annoyed Maddy said as she left their home and entered the world of pounding jackhammers and whistling construction workers.

Following the fitting, Maddy thought, *If he shows up to our wedding in fucking jeans, I swear I'm gonna . . .* Her thoughts were interrupted as she spotted a familiar face across the street. *What the fuck is he doing here? And why is he going into that S&M shop? Not my problem. Gotta get home.*

But you've found him.

Don't care. Not doing that shit anymore.

But he's right in there.

I don't fucking care. I'm done with that shit!

It would be so easy.

Hey, little voice in my fucking head. Let's get this straight. I'm not hanging myself out anymore for someone else, especially not for her. Fuck her and fuck him. So just shut the fuck up!

But you've looked for so long. You've finally found him. He's right in there. It would be so easy. He's right there. Finish what you started. You've found him. You've . . .

Oh, goddammit! Fine! But this is definitely the last fucking time!

The man exited the S&M shop and began walking down the street back to his home when a slight auburn-haired woman with intoxicating green eyes stepped out of the darkness of an entryway and said, "Hey, sexy. Got anything fun in the bag?" "I . . . uh . . . I . . .," the man began to stutter.

"Let me guess," Maddy purred. "You're kinda into being dominated, aren't you?"

"Well . . . uh . . . yeah . . . uh . . .," the man breathily tried to reply.

"Well, sailor, you're in luck because I kinda get off on . . . *dominating* . . . if you know what I mean, and I think that you do." The man began breathing heavily in anticipation as this slight temptress continued, "So, *worm*, here's what you're gonna fuckin' do. You're going to go back into the store and buy me the following items—"

The man attempted to interject by saying, "Um . . . I have some things . . . at my place . . . already . . ."

"I don't want your crusty cum-covered shit! You're going to buy me *new* shit, and don't you *ever* interrupt me again! Got it, worm?" The man nodded feverishly. "Now, get your fucking worm ass in there and get yourself a cute little pair of tight, and I mean *tight*, vinyl, shorts. Get me a full black vinyl bodysuit . . . and nothing crotchless, you fucking perv! Black vinyl boots, black vinyl gloves, cuffs for both your wrists and ankles, a ball gag, and a riding crop. You've got ten fucking minutes to meet me back here. If you're not back by then, I'll be whipping some other pathetic worm's ass, got it? Now go!"

The man rushed back into the store, his engorged penis straining against his tan khakis. He returned in eight minutes with a large bag while breathing heavily. "Okay, worm. Where do you live?" The man immediately gave his address as sweat was beginning to pour from his forehead on this ten-degree evening. "Okay, leave the window by the fire escape open. I'll be up fifteen minutes after you go in, and you'd better have those fucking shorts on, and all of my toys laid out nice for me! And no names. You can call me . . . Josie. And I'm gonna call you . . . Chad. Now fucking *go*!"

The man rushed down the block and turned left as Maddy casually followed, attempting to stay in the shadows with her head down. She climbed the fire escape and entered into the living room window to find the most pathetic site she had ever seen.

"Oh, Mistress Josie . . . I've been so bad . . . I need to be punished!" the man exclaimed from his knees and wearing the very tight black vinyl shorts.

"Fucking stay right there, Chad. I'll be right back. Or maybe I'll take my time and let you sit there on your knees and think about what you've done, you fucking worm. Now, thank me!"

"Th-thank you Mistress Josie," the man feverishly exhaled as Maddy fastened the ankle and wrist cuffs . . . tightly.

Wow, this is some fucked-up shit, Maddy thought as she wriggled her way into the skintight vinyl. As she pulled up the final zipper on her black boots, she thought, *Fuck, I really need to shed a couple pounds before the wedding.* She entered the room to find the emasculated puddle of a man quivering in anticipation for his punishment. She placed the ball gag over his mouth and said, "Now we're gonna have some fun. I think you'll find this to be an experience to *die* for. Laugh, worm! That was a great fucking joke!"

He laughed nervously through the saliva-covered ball gag as she pulled his head back by the top of his hair so that he was forced to look straight up at her. He witnessed his enraptured reflection in her pair of intensely green eyes. "Yeah, I bet you're not just into *this*, are you?" Maddy softly inquired with a firm grip on his thinning hair. "Yeah, I bet you like to watch too, don't you?" her voice became louder with each uttered syllable. "I bet you like to watch while some helpless girl is getting viciously raped by your best friend, don't you!" His expression immediately changed to shock and horror as he felt the blade of the knife sever the artery in his neck as Maddy screamed, "This is for *Lucy*, you pussy motherfucker!"

It was always the first thing that she noticed. The faint scent of iron as the sticky thin molasses gently dribbled down the shaft of the knife and penetrated the space between her clenched thumb and forefinger. The faint exhalation of air passing through his mouth, which was now permanently formed into a silent scream. Then, the sound of the blood droplets hitting the floor. Slowly at first, like an annoying leaky faucet. Drop . . . drop . . . drop . . . then faster as the taut skin surrounding his jugular gave way completely to unleash a crimson waterfall, which hit the hard wood floor as though someone had poured an entire gallon of milk upon it. She pulled the knife completely from his throat while loosening her grip from his hair. Then the familiar thud as the lifeless body succumbed to gravity, completing the merciless fait accompli.

A mischievous smile forced the upward curling of the right side of her mauve-painted lips. This was successful. This was liberating. This was justified. This was . . . the first time that was completely unplanned. She looked down upon the mess that he had created as the pool of newly released blood expanded outward like a growing hurricane churning above warm water. She had not brought her customary grab bag to provide for the cleanup, change of clothes, and silent escape into the brisk Brooklyn night. Without preparation, there may be too many clues, and her self-appointed reign over the hapless sadists of the five boroughs may be over, replaced by incarceration, prison fatigues, and forced lesbian sex.

Her mind raced as she went through her mental filing cabinet of possible solutions. And *his* face kept popping into her consciousness. *No, not* him, *there must be another way,* she rationalized. But with each discarded option, there was his image. *No, I can't get him involved in this. I promised myself that I would stop after I met him . . . my soul mate . . . my prince. I can't put him in jeopardy. And he can never know about this. Or about the others . . . Or could he? Could it be that he knows already?* She recalled seeing the flash of rage in his eyes that night, not so long ago, at the bar. The same rage that was so familiar within herself. She felt that she had witnessed a knowing acknowledgment of her complicity as they watched reports of her most recent triumph on the news. He was her soul mate, her prince, and he *already* knew. And she also knew that he would do anything for her. Yes, this would be successful. This would be liberating. This would be their final consummation of their love. She would call . . . him.

"H-h-hey, you . . .," Maddy fearfully said upon Erick's familiar answer.

Sensing her trepidation, Erick urgently said, "Where are you, and what do you need?" Upon receiving his instructions, he exclaimed, "I'll be there in thirty. Don't move!

"Okay, okay, okay . . . just be cool. Okay, black change of clothes, garbage bag, and two sets of rubber gloves for me." He threw the items into another garbage bag and hastily went into Maddy's "closet" where he retrieved a black duffel, which was covered in fallen blouses, dresses, and skirts. He parked five blocks away from his final destination on a shadowy residential street. He pulled the hood over his head and hastily walked with his head down toward the given address.

He approached the door of the apartment. Taking a deep breath, he attempted to gain his composure for what he was about to witness. He gently knocked and said, "Wassupbuttacup, you in there?"

"Hey, you, yeah . . . come on in," she replied with continued trepidation. He entered the room cautiously and looked at his beloved fiancée. The woman who had healed his scarred heart and had given him renewed life. The woman who had given him a reason to live again. She was standing in the middle of the room, blood spatters haphazardly scattered upon her beautiful face and body that was painted in a shiny black vinyl as crimson casually dripped off of it. Beneath her bloodstained shoes on the floor lay the lifeless body of her latest "chad," his limbs contorted in impossible angles and drenched in his own blood. She was still holding the stained knife, tonight's chosen instrument of her brand of justice. She had been frozen in the same position since she first called him. They said nothing to each other as he slowly walked toward her, making a sploshing sound as his newly soiled shoes slipped through her victim's not yet congealed blood on his journey to console his love. She looked up at him with a bat of her sandy-red eyelashes, creating a kaleidoscopic vision of her beautiful emerald-green eyes. The right side of her lips curled up in a mischievous smile. He wrapped his arms around her in a firm and supportive embrace and closed his eyes. He felt her heart's pace quicken. Upon opening his eyes, he saw the shadow as she raised the knife behind his back. He then heard a muted thud on the hardwood floor as the knife harmlessly landed upon the saturated surface. He whispered into her ear, "Teach me . . ."

Song Reference List

The author would like to thank the countless musical artists that have enhanced his entire life. In particular, the author would like to give a heartfelt thank you to the following artists for enhancing the experience of both writing and reading this book.

Nick Lowe – "Raging Eyes"
J. Geils Band – "(Ain't Nothin' but a) House Party" ABBA – "Does Your Mother Know"
The Mindbenders – "A Groovy Kind of Love"
Elvis Costello – "(What's So Funny 'Bout) Peace, Love, and Understanding"
New York Dolls – "Personality Crisis"
Sweet – "Teenage Rampage"
Bruce Springsteen – "Growin' Up"
The Cars – "Let's Go"
AC/DC – "Highway To Hell"
Sister Sledge – "We Are Family"
Judas Priest – "You Got Another Thing Coming"
REM – "Why Not Smile"
PIL – "This Is Not a Love Song"
The Pretenders – "Brass in Pocket"
Chuck Berry – "Johnny B. Goode"

CCR – "Bad Moon Rising"
Lesley Gore – "You Don't Own Me"
The Animals – "Don't Let Me Be Misunderstood"
Alice Cooper – "No More Mr. Nice Guy"
The Mindbenders – "Uncle Joe the Ice Cream Man"
Johnny Cash – "In My Life"
Bill Withers – "Lean on Me"
Bob Marley – "Three Little Birds"
The Runaways – "Cherry Bomb"
The Chicks – "Goodbye Earl"
David Bowie – "Ashes to Ashes"
Zombina and the Skeletones – "Spring Healed Jack"
Me First and the Gimme Gimmes – "Auld Lang Syne"
The Call – "Let the Day Begin"
Hasil Adkins – "No More Hot Dogs"
Simon & Garfunkel – "Bridge Over Troubled Water"
Phil Collins – "A Groovy Kind of Love"
Pat Benatar – "I'm Gonna Follow You"
The Phantom – "Love Me"
Morrissey – "The More You Ignore Me, the Closer I Get"
Southern Culture on the Skids – "Eight-Piece Box"
Talking Heads – "Girlfriend Is Better"
Joe Jackson – "Real Men"
Captain & Tennille – "Love Will Keep Us Together"
Herman's Hermits – "I'm into Something Good"
Mary Wells – "My Guy"
The Raveonettes – "Boys Who Rape (Should All Be Destroyed)"
Pete Seeger – "We Shall Overcome"
Olivia Newton John – "Physical"
Buddy Holly – "Rave On"
The Bee Gees – "How Deep Is Your Love"
Badfinger – "No Matter What"
Elton John – "Curtains"

LINEAGE

Hanging Chads Book II

PROLOGUE

Maddy's piercing screams echoed off of the sickly green hospital walls as she was rolled down the sanitized hospital hallways on a rickety gurney. She didn't know what hurt worse: the sting of the bullet hole in her shoulder or the constant knifelike jabs from her broken ribs or perhaps it was the emotional scars that once again were being recalled as she feared she may be taking the final ride of her brief thirty-six-year existence.

A kaleidoscope of images and memories was flashing in her pounding brain: the beatings at the hands of her mother as her impotent father looked on; the love of her beloved aunts and uncle; the Friday night dance parties, the smorgasbords of junk food; the cross-country trip to college with her beloved uncle Joe; and the laughing and singing with her friends and babysitting Kristy's delightful children. This last image put a slight smile on her tortured face.

The smile quickly faded as her thoughts turned to her mentally sadistic ex-husband and the execution of her uncle. Intense outrage replaced hopelessness as she relived her brand of justice that she had applied to the insignificant deplorables that found their way into her world. The white trash that had murdered her uncle leading her to cut his brakes and plant his head into a pole. The wife and child beater that discovered that fireworks in the right hands could be quite deadly. The deadly overdose that she injected into the arm of the man who was grooming her to be a sex slave and who had nearly killed *her* with the same intravenous venom. The would-be date rape druggist who she ripped to shreds in a dark alley. The black- market pandemic profiteer of essential goods who has eaten his last hot dog. The serial rapist and murderer of children who received a righteous arrow through his rectum. The pair of redneck rapists who she publicly left dismembered and hanging. The voyeur of her best friend's rape that she eliminated in a most sado-masochistic manner. Her work couldn't be over yet. She and Erick had so much more to do.

Then her prince's face flashed before her eyes. She looked up at her aunt Blair who was gripping her sweaty hand as the gurney rumbled along. "Erick! Where is Erick? I need him now more than ever! Where is he?" Maddy screamed. "He'll be along dear," Blair replied in as soothing of a voice as she could muster. "You're in good hands. I'm here. Patty's here. The doctors will take care of you. Erick will be here as well. Please don't worry. Just try to relax. We are all here to take care of you and—"

At that moment, the gurney turned a sharp corner and entered an operating room. Maddy could hear voices say, "We have to take her now!" "But, Doctor, she's in too much pain!" "I know, but dammit, it has to be now if she's going to make it through!" She was transferred onto a bed and the bright lights shone down upon her, immediately dilating the pupils of her fading emerald, green eyes. Something was being injected. Her aunt's grip was steadfast. And the only thought in her mind was "Erick, where are you?"

Chapter 24

(Your Love Keeps Lifting Me) Higher And Higher

Erick looked lovingly into Maddy's emerald, green eyes that were framed by freckles and blood droplets. He smiled and kissed her gently. It was the same tender kiss as their first date. She let out a slight sigh of relief and comfort as their lips met. He then gently pulled his lips from hers, smiled, and looked down at the violent carnage that lay beneath their feet.

"Maaaddddyyy, you got some 'splainin' to dooo!" Erick bellowed in a poorly imitated Cuban accent while smiling. "What the fuck was that?" Maddy tersely inquired. "It was a joke, y'know. . . what Desi used to say to Lucy on *I Love Lucy*. Pretty funny, huh?" Maddy let out an exasperated sigh and said in a lecturing tone as the pool of blood was beginning to congeal around their boots, "Okay, you're new at this so let me explain a couple of things. Numero uno: you're fuckin' old and nobody under sixty would get that reference so no, it wasn't funny. And numero two-O: I make the jokes around here. You simply lack the experience to try to be humorous in these situations, so just leave the jokes to me. Got it?"

"Okay, well make one then," Erick requested. "Yeah, see, it doesn't work like that," Maddy began explaining. "See, there needs to be a setup and context in order to make the joke work." "Right," Erick agreed, "like when I walked in, took a look around at the mess, and said, 'Maaaddddyyy . . . you got some splain—'" Erick was immediately cut off by Maddy's blood- covered latex fingers over his mouth. "Okay, it wasn't funny the first time so why the fuck do you think it would be funny the second. Please, you're embarrassing yourself. Just leave the humor to me." "Okay, you're the expert. You just point me in a direction and tell me what to do," Erick conceded.

"Okay, here's the plan. Pull the garbage bag out of the duffle. I'll remove my clothes and then—" "Awwww, really?" Erick whined, "you look fuckin' hot right now!" "Yes, I suppose I do, but we need to consider this outfit ruined. If you'd like, we can run by the dirty store on our way home and see what they've got. I need a new French Maid outfit anyway. You tore the fuck out of that last one! Now, may I continue? This is kinda serious seeing as how we're standing in the middle of a murder scene, okay?" "Yup, I'm sorry. I'm all ears," Erick replied. "Okay, we go into the bathroom and into the shower, remove our clothes, and put them into the garbage bag. We then immediately put on new rubber gloves and take a shower. We pour bleach down the drain. We put on our fresh clothes and carefully walk back into the living room, making sure not to rub our fabric on anything or step in any blood. We then will throw some water on any area that has any type of footprints so that the prints are washed away. We then quietly, and I mean *quietly*, leave, get back to the car and get the fuck back home. Got it? Any questions?"

"Yes, I have two questions." Erick seriously stated. "First question: We're going back home *after* the dirty store, *right*?" "Yeah, yeah, yeah . . . after the dirty store, you old perv. What's your second question?" a resigned Maddy replied. "My second question is, are we going to steal his money out of his wallet? I mean, with the way he's dressed and the ball gag and everything, we might be able to make it look like a robbery, y'know, like a call girl did it or something." Erick then presented an excited smile as he enthusiastically exclaimed, "Call girls gone wild! Get it? It's a play on the *Girls Gone Wild* videos . . . get it?" "Yeah, I get it," an increasingly annoyed Maddy countered. "I get that *someone* doesn't know how to follow the *fuckin' rules*! For the last time, *I* make the jokes! In this situation, you're just my, I don't know, my murder scene man slave or something. Okay? Got it?"

"Yeah, I got it. It just seems as though you're really not coming up with any so I'm trying to fill the void. If you'd step up your game, you wouldn't have to worry about it," Erick arrogantly countered as an irritated Maddy stared at him with her blood-covered latex arms folded while slowly shaking her head. They executed the plan to perfection in the shower, and Erick put on the final rubber glove onto his right hand with a "snap." "Okay, if you would please now bend over, heh, heh, heh," he mockingly said. "Okay, I'm fuckin' serious. One more fuckin' attempt at a joke, and you'll be *begging* to look like that motherfucker in the living room. Got it?" Maddy said to Erick who was trying in vain from bursting out laughing. "I'm sorry, Maddy, but this shit just pops into my head, and I can't keep it in. This shit's gold!"

"No, it's not fuckin' gold because *my* shit's gold so please just knock it off. Okay, well since we're in here, and all nekkid and shit . . . are you gonna fuck me or what?" Maddy sternly inquired. "Yeah, sure . . . but Maddy—" "Yeah, what is it *now*?" an exasperated Maddy replied. "Well, I really am gonna need you to bend over then." "GAAAWWWD! Fine! There! Now fuck me!" Maddy ordered. So he did.

As they approached their car that was parked in a darkened area five blocks away, Maddy thought, *Well, I guess I don't have to worry about him canceling the wedding or anything. In fact, he's downright enthusiastic about this shit. I'd better be careful, though. I think that I've created a monster!* And with that, she finally found her solution to the problem that had been bothering her all evening as she bellowed, "It's aliiive! heh, heh, heh." "Uh, what's alive?" Erick asked as he unlocked the driver's side door on his 2017 red Accord. "Uh . . . y'know . . . you're so enthusiastic that I think I may have created a monster, so . . . y'know . . . it's aliiive!" Maddy sheepishly explained. "Yeah, but you didn't set it up, so it didn't make any sense," Erick critiqued. "Yeah . . . I know . . . but I set it up in my head," Maddy argued. "What the fuck good does that do me?" Erick countered. "I can't read your fuckin' mind. Are you sure you're the one that should be making the jokes because you're really bad at this." "Just get in the fuckin' car and let's go," an annoyed Maddy retorted tersely. "Yeah, okay," Erick said through mocking chuckles as he thought, *Oh, I sooo kicked her ass tonight!* Then Erick asked, "Hey, can we get some ice cream after we're done at the dirty store?" "Of course, we can get some fuckin' ice cream. That's another stupid fuckin' question tonight. I'm tellin' you, mister, you're totally getting on my last nerve tonight." "Yeah, I know," Erick replied through his giggles.

They went into the dark backside of the dirty store, where Maddy tossed the garbage bag into the dumpster. "Are you sure it's all right to put that in there?" a concerned Erick inquired. "Yeah, it's fine. Who the fuck is going to dig around in a dumpster behind a porn shop?" Maddy confidently replied.

"Well," Erick began timidly, "Actually, I've found some pretty interesting things in there . . . I mean . . . where do you think I get the cream for your coffee?" You . . . are . . . so . . . fucking . . . GROSS!" Maddy exclaimed before laughing and saying, "I thought that cream tasted familiar."

Following the passionate destruction of yet another French maid outfit, the loving couple was lying in bed when Erick cautiously said, "Sooo . . . I'm kinda guessing that that guy wasn't your . . . y'know . . . first time . . . right?" "Uh . . . well, no," Maddy replied. "Sooo," Erick continued with continued cautiousness, "ummm . . . not that it's necessarily any of my business, but . . . umm . . . well, since I know about this one, I guess I'm kinda curious about the others and . . . well . . . what made you so mad to . . . y'know . . . do that."

Maddy, sensing her mate's trepidation began explaining. "Okay, first off, there's *nothing* anybody can do to piss me off so much that I would do that shit to them. The pricks that I . . . take care of . . . all have it coming for one reason or another. Yes, some of them have touched my personal life, but it's very dispassionate. I don't really *feel* anything but generic rage at the moment when I do that shit. And once it's over, the rage just melts away and it's like they never existed. They are so insignificant to me, that it's like I just don't acknowledge them anymore. I just walk away and go back to work or go back to see you or whatever I'm doing. I don't think about them any more than I think about discarded trash. Because that's what they are to me. They're society's trash that I'm taking care of because the rest of society doesn't have the balls to do it. They're fucking *rapists* and *murderers* and *wife beaters* and *child molesters* and shit like that. I don't off somebody just because they were rude to me or upset me in some way. I off them because they're an insignificant fucking worm that is a threat physically and emotionally to all of us. *They* are responsible for what I do to them. *They* have made me who I am. Is this making sense?" "Yes, it does," a relieved Erick replied. He didn't think that his soon-to-be wife was a threat to him. But on the other hand, it wasn't like he had been involved with a serial killer before, so he thought that it might be prudent to get confirmation of that. "So . . . would you mind giving me the details?"

Maddy laid out each of her kills in excruciating detail including the reasons behind the murders, the specific way she had planned them, the specific techniques that she used, and of course, her final quips. "So . . . then *I* said, Two heads are better than one!" Get it?" Maddy burst out laughing as

Erick meekly stated, "Ummm . . . yeah . . . that's pretty funny." "Okay, okay, you probably had to be there to get the full comedic value." Maddy rationalized, "So . . . how about this next one?" She excitedly dove into the details of the two rednecks that she had dismembered and hung at the construction site and finished by saying, "So *now* you're hung enough for me! Get it?" Upon finishing her last sentence, she literally slapped her knee and laughed hysterically. "Yeah . . . I get it . . . I probably just needed to be there too. It's just probably not as good outside of the moment," Erick meekly stated as he tried to protect his fiancée's ego. "Yeah . . . whatever . . . some people just don't have a natural sense of humor," Maddy tried to explain away.

"Wow," Erick then realized, "you're kinda like if *Dexter* had a baby with *Jessica Jones*." "What the fuck are you talking about?" Maddy incredulously retorted. "I've *never* heard of those motherfuckers. Nope, I'm a fuckin' original!" "Yeah, okay, you're *completely* original. Whatever you say," Erick replied through mocking chuckles. "Fuckin' whatever," Maddy retorted with an attitude, "Listen, we've got to have a serious talk now. You need to understand something. This shit isn't planned. It's not like I'm going around looking for this shit. It's just shit that comes up in life that I find myself having to take care of. I don't know why that is. It's like I have a little murder cloud hanging over my head or something. And the rednecks were supposed to be my last one, until . . . well . . . they weren't. But this *last* one tonight is *definitely* my last one, okay? I've gotten *really lucky* so far in not getting caught or injured and I just want to live a normal life with my soulmate . . . and my cats!" she exclaimed as she lifted Dory into the air and rubbed her nose against hers. Hunky would have received the same treatment, but his weight impairment made it impossible for him to jump into bed.

"Okay, I suppose that's for the best. But I need you to make me a promise." Erick stated resolutely. "You need to promise me that if something *like this* comes up in your life again, you will inform me and you will include me. I know that I don't know what I'm doing and that you're the expert on these matters, but we're a family. And I'm going to be involved in any of the family business regardless of what that may be or what I might have to do. Promise?"

"Yeah, I promise," Maddy agreed. "It's kinda funny that you should phrase it as a 'family business.' Sooo . . . I guess I'd better call Aunt Blair and let her know what has happened tonight." "Blair?!?" Erick surprisingly exclaimed as Maddy dialed the phone and said, "Hey, Aunt Blair. Could you come over for a bit? I think we need to have a conversation that never happened and will never happen again . . . again." A remorseful- sounding Blair said, "Yes, of course, dear. I'll be right over. There's something that I need to tell you as well."

As Maddy recounted the evening's earlier events and the conversation that she and Erick had just concluded, Blair's eyes would scan over to meet Erick's in order to gauge his reaction. Was he frightened? Was he overly intrigued? Was he nervous? Does he now pose a threat to her family's most vulnerable secrets? Would he become a murderous loose cannon? What she saw in Erick's eyes was . . . Erick. Sitting upright by Maddy's side. Resolutely dutiful and proud of his love. What she saw was someone who had been and would continue to be Maddy's greatest support in her life. Following that analysis, Blair felt comfortable contributing to the conversation that never happened.

The seventy-one-year-old family matriarch sat upright in her chair. Her timeless raven black hair cascaded down upon the shoulders of her Oingo Boingo "Weird Science" sweatshirt. She looked intensely first at Maddy and then at Erick before she began as if she were reciting off of a prepared script. "Erick, Maddy has heard this before, but I think that it is necessary for you both to hear this together."

"Aunt Blair," Maddy interjected, "I really don't think that this is necessary. We really aren't going to do any of this anymore. We promise." Blair, completely disregarding her beloved niece's empty promise then began. "When one starts down the trail of . . . justice, shall we say . . . there are certain rules that must be abided. When one engages in these . . . practices . . . it must be for the right reasons. It must be someone who has done something terrible or is a significant threat to someone else and who is out of the reach of conventional . . . punishment. It must *never* be done for petty infractions or differences and must *never* be done solely for our own gratification. There are many bad women out there as well, but I have never believed that any one of *us* should *ever* do anything to permanently harm one of our sisters. For them, I believe that their punishment, *if* deserving, shall come in its own natural due course. And yes Erick, I am including *you* when I refer to *us*."

"Now, if someone is to do something to another person, then that someone needs to be careful about it and take others' safety into consideration. There is to be *no harm* to anyone other than the target. I want to leave you with this. If someone is going down this path, then it would be wise for that person to never keep any souvenirs of their exploits and these exploits need to be conducted in a variety of ways. And finally," Blair looked at her niece and Erick with grave seriousness as she sternly said, "this conversation never happened and will never happen again. Do you both understand?" Maddy quickly responded yes as Erick nodded his head. Upon seeing Blair's serious expression, Maddy nudged Erick in the ribs and whispered, "She has to hear you say it." "Oh, okay . . . sorry," Erick stammered before looking Blair in the eyes with the same serious expression and saying, "yes, I understand."

"Good," Blair began once again. "Now, to some serious news. As you know, Edgar's health began rapidly declining last year shortly after he turned seventy-five to the point where he needed to be placed in a nursing facility. And I am very sad to say that he passed away last night."

"Oh, Aunt Blair. I'm so sorry." Maddy stated in a comforting tone. "It's all right, dear," Blair replied. "It was his time. He was such a good friend and kind companion to me after I lost my Joseph. But he was never my Joseph. So I need to tell you that I will be unavailable to assist with the wedding preparations this week as I need to return to Madison and oversee the funeral arrangements. And I was going to do this a bit later, but I suppose I should do this now."

Blair then reached into her large floral embroidered carry- all and pulled out two large photo albums. "Maddy, this photo album is an exact replica of the one that Joseph made for you for your graduation that was destroyed by that . . . man. We had all of the negatives still. But I wanted to wait to give it to you until I was sure that you were with someone who would appreciate its meaning as much as you do. And I am pleased to say, Erick, that I believe that you are that man. Thank you for being who you are so that my niece can be the dynamic force that she truly is. I am forever indebted to you."

Erick began stammering, "Blair, I just don't know . . . what to say . . . I feel so . . . honored." "There is nothing you need to say. Just continue to be who you are for my niece. Here you are, dear." Blair handed the photo album over to Maddy. She silently began thumbing through the photos that she thought had been destroyed forever. Tears began to flow over her lightly freckled cheeks as Erick placed his arms around her shoulder and lightly kissed her on the side of her forehead. He did, indeed, understand the meaning of this moment.

"This second photo album is from my personal collection. And although

I have made duplicates, I want you both to have the originals. Besides you, my dear, this album is my most prized possession. This album chronicles our lives. Mine along with your aunt Patty and Joseph. This book is our story. You knew who Joseph was as a person. Now, I'm going to tell you what he encountered and what he did to become that person. I am going to tell you the story of my Joseph Angelo Argento."

CHAPTER 25

FEED THE TREE

Joseph Angelo Argento entered the world on October 1, 1942. His parents had immigrated to New York City from Palermo on the island of Sicily in 1938. Although the young lovers' life there was ideal for them, they were increasingly frightened of and disgusted by the fascist government of Mussolini and of the unspeakable atrocities that were raging across Europe, especially to their Jewish friends. So they decided to move to the shining beacon of democracy, believing that the United States of America was a just and fair society for all who lived there. What they found upon their arrival, however, was a very similar fascist state that was disguised as a democracy. They found a society whose promise of true freedom and prosperity was divided between classes. Rich and poor. Male and female. White and black. Christian and Jew. And most impactful for them, natural-born citizens and immigrants.

This was tragically evident as Joseph's mother, Giuseppina, attempted to find health care when she experienced a problem with her first pregnancy in 1939. She miscarried as she and her husband, Angelo, went from hospital to hospital seeking care. A second child who was to be a son was still born in 1940, primarily due to incompetent care.

By the time of her third pregnancy, Angelo had affiliated himself with some of the more influential Italian immigrants in their neighborhood and his wife received the best of care, resulting in the birth of their son Joseph.

Wanting their child to have the best of opportunities in their new home, they named him Joseph as the more American-sounding version of his mother's name. His middle name Angelo was taken from his father, and because his mother exclaimed upon his birth, "Il mio bambino è un angelo [my baby is an angel]."

Shortly after his birth, the family moved to Madison, Wisconsin upon the suggestion of Angelo's associates. Angelo opened an Italian bakery while Giuseppina labored as a free- lance seamstress as well as assisting her husband in the bakery. This was especially true when Angelo was needed back in New York upon his associates' request. Giuseppina never inquired about her husband's activities while he was away, and Angelo never offered.

From a young child until his early teens, Joseph was a slight and sickly child. He missed many days of school from a variety of ailments and spent his sick days looking out his window at the squirrels, birds, and other wildlife that frolicked in the trees outside. He developed a love for animals and would frequently be caught sneaking a portion of his dinner outside to give to the stray cats that seemed to multiply by the day as word got around in the feline community that there was a sucker at the Argento's house. Upon being caught, his loving mother would give a slight shake of her delicate head while wearing a knowing smile and go back into their cozy home.

Joseph loved his parents and they, in turn, adored their son. They provided him with a comfortable middle-class upbringing in a comfortable middle-class neighborhood. They ensured that he was able to receive the polio vaccine in 1955 as soon as possible. They taught him to stand up for himself. They taught him to question authority but also to respect authority when warranted. They taught him about the evils that he would have to face in life from the greedy, backstabbing businessmen to the perils of indoctrination into any one particular ideology or dogma. Although raised Roman Catholic, Joseph never fully subscribed to what was preached to him at the services. He especially didn't understand all of the various sacraments that he was told were necessary for his ascension into heaven. He would frequently say things like, "Really? God gives a fuck if I eat meat on Fridays? With all the shit that's going on in the world, I think I'll be all right. God's got bigger fish to fry. Get it? Fish? Oh, never mind." He would then explode into a deep, boisterous laugh before taking another huge bite of his cheeseburger at his favorite local diner. But the greatest lesson that was instilled in Joseph from his birth was the difference between commitment and respect *for* your family and subservience *to* your family. The Argentos wanted a strong-willed son who was reverent to them when appropriate but independently minded and able to make his own decisions without their constant approval.

Joseph hated school, and it became believed by his parents that perhaps Joseph was exaggerating his illnesses a bit in order to miss another day or two. He hated the rigid authority that the school represented. He hated having to line up in order to do anything, from eating lunch to using the restroom. He especially hated his second-grade teacher who was swift with a yardstick upon your behind upon the slightest infraction. This was especially true for Joseph who took every opportunity to buck her authority, frequently by blatantly smacking his gum in class. It may also have been that Joseph was the only boy in the class with his particular complexion.

One day, the second-grade teacher turned around from the antiseptic green chalkboard to address whoever was giggling behind her. She looked directly at Joseph and coldly said, "Was it you, Mr. Argento?" "No, it was me" came a firm reply from a white boy in the corner of the room. A young Edmund Simmons rose from his seat and said, "I'm sorry, but your fat ass just makes me giggle." The teacher's face turned bright red as the entire class burst into laughter. Except for Joseph who had in fact been the one giggling. He sat there in amazement as he watched this popular boy from an affluent family get marched out of the room toward the principal's office. As he was exiting the room with the teacher's hand firmly gripping his thin bicep, Edmund looked at Joseph and mouthed, "Fuck her."

From that moment on, Joseph and Edmund became the closest of friends. And no one ever bullied Joseph ever again, as he was now officially "cool with Edmund." Their bond grew stronger every year that passed. Another thing that grew stronger with each passing year was Joseph who, by his sophomore year of high school had developed into a physically formidable six- foot, three-inch young man. Edmund would plead with Joseph to join him on the various sports teams at the school to which Joseph would reply, "Fuck that. I don't need some douchebag yelling at me just to put a fuckin' ball in a hole. It's all so fucking meaningless."

One extracurricular activity that the duo would enthusiastically share however was hunting. The pair would develop lists of classmates who were bullies and terrorizing the smaller kids in school. Edmund would do the research and reconnaissance and Joseph would provide the beatings, which grew increasingly brutal. The "victims" of the assaults knew better than to name their assailant, fearing an even more extreme form of retribution. Therefore, there was an unusual number of boys who were seriously injured by tripping and falling down the stairs between the years 1958 and 1961. Joseph's parents always found it curious that on certain evenings before going out their son would play *quell'orribile racchetta* (that horrible racket) called "Rumble" by Link Wray.

Upon their graduation in May 1961, the friend's lives diverged. Edmund joined the police academy. Joseph, impacted by his parents' history with fascist, authoritarian regimes, enlisted in the United States Army in order to do his part against the perceived scourge of communism. Despite his anti-authoritarian streak, Joseph became a model soldier throughout his multiple deployments due to his belief that he was serving a higher calling that would make the world a fairer and safer place for everyone.

That was up until 1966, however. Joseph was deployed in Viet Nam that year and was immediately repulsed at the events that unfolded in front of his bewildered eyes by soldiers who were supposed to stand for the goodness and kindness of democracy. Under the authority of his sergeant, he witnessed villages being burned, executions of civilians, and the raping of village women. As these atrocities were being conducted by his men, the sergeant would stand there with his hands on his hips while chewing a cigar with a maniacal grin on his face. Joseph would always find a way out of participating in the monstrous actions, usually by volunteering to patrol the dense and dangerous surrounding jungle. That came to an end one evening when the sergeant forced him to watch as he raped a young Vietnamese girl in front of her family. When he had finished this lascivious act, he lined the helpless and distraught family up and shot each one in the back of the head. The final shot was for the young rape victim, whose brains and blood were splattered upon Joseph's American uniform before her limp body fell to the floor. Joseph looked down at the innocent girl's blood dripping from his uniform's name-plate and began weeping.

Three weeks later, Joseph found himself alone with the sergeant while the pair were on patrol. They weren't on patrol for enemy combatants, however. They were on patrol for what the sergeant called "g**k pussy." And they found what they were looking for. Nestled in a small clearing was a small hut with a young Vietnamese woman cooking over an open fire. The sergeant looked behind him at Joseph with his devilish grin. "Looks like it's supper time, and you're gonna get a taste this time too," the sergeant sneered just before feeling intense pressure on his trachea from a pair of massive hands. He was forced face-first into a pool of mud and viciously strangled and drowned simultaneously to the point of unconsciousness. Joseph dragged the body of his motionless sergeant to a nearby pond and threw it in. The emerald, green moss exploded out of the water as the near-lifeless body made an impact. The sergeant came to just in time to see Joseph sitting on the bough of a tree while chewing a cigar with a maniacal grin on his face. At the next moment, a crocodile bit through the sergeant's face. A pool of red immediately replaced the soft blue of the water and the emerald green of the moss as the crocodile took its dinner to the bottom of the now tranquil pond.

An investigation into the sergeant's death was conducted, and Joseph was completely truthful when interrogated. He told them honestly that the sergeant had been grabbed and eaten by a crocodile. He did omit, however, the events that led up to the sergeant being near the pond in the first place. Although suspicious, the army closed the investigation and granted Joseph's request for an immediate honorable discharge from service. As he boarded the plane to begin his long journey home, Joseph vowed to himself that he would never take orders from anyone ever again in his life. It was a vow that he would break only twice as he would later find himself helplessly under the spell of his future wife and future niece.

Joseph settled into life with his family back in Madison. He began working for his father at the bakery and looked after things when his father was away on business trips to New York. And he dated . . . a lot. He became known as a ladies' man and frequented local taverns in his search for consensual companionship, which became increasingly easy to find as the hippie, free-love culture was blooming. It didn't hurt that he had become a staunch anti-war activist as well. He was a confirmed bachelor, and no one would ever change that . . . or so he believed.

In August 1968, Joseph was staggering home after an unusually unsuccessful evening of cavorting with Edmund. The pair of friends were swaying down the street with their arms around each other as they loudly and badly slurred a song that had played on the jukebox earlier that evening. As they butchered the words and notes of "In My Life" by The Beatles, an explosion rocked the neighborhood from two blocks away. The two friends immediately found their sobriety and rushed to the sounds of a violent inferno and falling debris clanking upon the street's pavement. Edmund stood there in shocked disbelief as his life-long friend fell to his knees and painfully screamed at the universe. The only home that Joseph had ever known had been blown up. And his beloved parents were in there.

There was nothing left of his parents to bury. They had been unceremoniously and prematurely cremated. Following a brief police investigation, Edmund told Joseph that the act was purposeful. Joseph sat silently at the front pew staring at the two opulent urns. He was seething with rage as the traditional Roman Catholic eulogy fell away from his deaf ears. He was gently nudged by Edmund, who gingerly said, "Hey man, you're up." Joseph Angelo Argento climbed the adorned stairs and took his place behind the podium. He looked out at the throngs of neighborhood friends and well-wishers. "I'm not much of a talker, so I don't have much to say," he began earnestly. "My parents were loving. My parents were loyal. And my parents did not deserve to die like this. If anyone in this room has any information, let me know. I'll owe you one. And believe me, I *always* pay off my debts." His voice then descended into a dark growl as he concluded, "Because I'm gonna kill the motherfucker that did this."

Following the service, while completing his obligation of shaking the hands of the ceremony's attendees, he saw Edmund speaking with three unknown men who were dressed in black. The men left and Edmund approached Joseph. "Hey man, see me when you're done here. You know where I'll be."

Joseph entered his neighborhood pub. His large haggard frame lurched forward as he made his way through the establishment until he got to the last booth. There, he saw Edmund who gave his best friend a meek smile of condolence. Edmund pulled out two pieces of paper from his black suit pocket. He handed the first piece of paper to Joseph and said, "This is the address of who you are looking for." Joseph glared at the words and numbers written on the paper. The final letters spelled out "Brooklyn." Edmund then handed the second paper over. "And, if you go to the first address, then this second address is an invitation." The two men gave each other the same knowing nod that they had given since beginning their hunting expeditions in high school. It was a nod that communicated understanding. It was a nod that ensured that this conversation had never happened.

Joseph lurked in the shadows inside a Brooklyn home. His eyes emanated a fiery glare as the meek-looking man of Laotian descent entered. He threw down his keys and entered his modest kitchen. He opened the refrigerator door. Standing behind him, the face of an enraged Joseph was illuminated as the refrigerator light flipped on. The man felt the pain of a jagged knife going into his back, severing his spinal cord. His legs went numb, and his body collapsed upon the white and black checkered tile.

Joseph turned the man over. His face was frozen in fear. "So you probably know who I am," Joseph began with a chilled calm. "And you probably know why I'm here. So there's no need to waste time with that. Let's just get on with the revenge, shall we . . . you motherfuckin' douchebag." With that, Joseph put a gag in the man's mouth. "Can you still feel *this*?" Joseph gleefully inquired as the man let out a shrill, muffled scream as his right index finger was meticulously sawed off by the serrated edge of the knife. "Good," a pleased Joseph responded to the man's tortured vocalizations. "We're going to take this *very* slow. One by one. And when I'm done with each of your fingers, I'm going to move up to your elbows. I'm going to slowly saw through your flesh, your muscle, your bone. Then, I'm gonna cut your fuckin' head off. Any questions?"

Following his shower and change of clothes, Joseph peered one last time into the kitchen. The blood had completely covered the black and white checkered tile and was beginning to seep out onto the tan dining room carpet. The man's arms were circulating above the room, having been tied to the blades of the overhead ceiling fan. Blood continued to fly, creating Pollock-esque streaks on the walls, curtains, and appliances. The fingers had all been placed between two pieces of bread and left on a plate on the tangerine kitchen table. "Heh, heh, heh, finger sandwiches," Joseph chuckled to himself. He had placed the head in a pot of water that was now boiling, slowly tenderizing the flesh and peeling the skin away from the skull. "Hey, nice of you to invite me for dinner, but I'm in the mood for Italian tonight. Burn in hell, motherfucker."

Joseph cautiously knocked on the unassuming door of the second residential address he had been given. The door opened to reveal one of the three men that he had seen at his parent's funeral the day before. "Please, come in, Mr. Argento," the man said invitingly. Joseph was taken to the basement where he was greeted by the other two men and three others. A large man was sitting behind a grand mahogany desk puffing on his cigar. "Please, Joseph, it is all right to call you Joseph, isn't it?" the man said politely. Joseph nodded and the man continued. "Good, please Joseph, have a seat, won't you?"

Joseph took a seat and looked around the dark room. Six stern faces were staring at him, their hands firmly placed inside their coat jackets. The walls were papered in red velour, with gold accents. Multiple priceless paintings from some of the world's artistic masters adorned the walls. The furniture was all deep brown heavy oak with cushions that matched the walls. The man behind the desk said, "Gentlemen . . . we're all friends here. Please remove your hands from your coats and join us." The men looked at one another, then at Joseph. They nodded to the large man and took their seats on the adjacent sofas on either side of the desk.

"Now, Joseph," the large man began, "I'm going to tell you some things, but it is on the condition that you never utter a word of this to anyone . . . that would not be good for your health . . . do you understand?" "Yes" came Joseph's firm reply. "Fine. Let us begin then. I want to speak to you about who we are, what we can do for you, and what you can do for us.

What you see in this room are six of the most lethal hit men in the country. Your father was the seventh and regretfully, we now have an opening. A number of years ago, we were all affiliated with different . . . shall we say . . . organizations. We all grew tired of being under someone else's thumb and of the . . . randomness of the orders that we received. We just didn't want to kill people because of someone else's petty beefs anymore. It just wasn't a very fulfilling work environment. So we quit, and we formed this organization, the name of which is only known by our members. But in the right circles, we are known as *Murder, Incorporated*."

Joseph gave a nod of understanding before the man began again. "Yes, we are contract hitmen, and some may frown upon such a trade. But we have a code of ethics that we live by. First, we don't do this just for the money. The hit has to be on someone who is truly deserving of it. Someone who causes pain and suffering to people who don't deserve it. We don't off someone just because he's stooping someone's old lady. And if anyone ever hires us under false pretenses, then . . . well . . . how does that saying go boys? What comes around goes around."

The room filled with laughter before the man began again, "Our former employers have been trying to get us back. Your parents were a message. It never should have happened. Another part of our code is that we all look out for one another. We missed this one and we're deeply regretful. We all loved your father. He was, in many ways, the best of us. But I can assure you . . . we *won't* miss again. We just didn't anticipate them going outside of their . . . family . . . to do a job. Now, we have already sent our reply and taken care of the men behind the hit. It was our duty to do that. We thought you might want to take care of the trigger man yourself and . . . well . . . it was a bit of an audition. And I must say—" the man began chuckling before continuing, "I really don't get the whole boiling head thing but who's to question the tactics of a mourning son, eh? And I've gotta give it to you. That was one creative fuckin' murder scene!" "So . . . we want to offer you your father's seat at the table.

You have military training, some God-given ability, and one massive fuckin' chip on your shoulder. You'd fit in perfectly. Whadoyasay?" Joseph sat and thought in silence for nearly five minutes. His brow was pensive when he finally replied, "Gentlemen. I truly appreciate your offer, but I'm not a killer. At least I don't want to be. I truly honor the respect that you had for my father, but that was him, not me. So I'm going to have to respectfully decline your generous offer." Joseph looked at the man's stone expression. He was anticipating a move and was preparing himself for battle.

The move came in the form of the man saying, "All right then boys! We have our answer. But know this, Joseph Argento, this is a standing offer. If you have a change of heart, you know where to find us. And also know this. Your father was family, which means *you* are family, which means if you get yourself a pretty little wife with cute little kids, they *too* will be family. And we will be at your service should you ever need us. As long as you keep that clam of yours shut. Understand?"

Joseph returned to Madison and placed flowers upon his parents' grave as he silently wept. He returned to Edmund's one- bedroom apartment and crashed on the couch. He immediately fell into a deep slumber as he dreamed of himself as a young boy being lifted into the air by his father's powerful arms as his mother danced and giggled around them with glee. When he woke the next morning, the couch cushion was saturated by his tears.

Joseph started his own handyman business and quickly became known in his neighborhood as the fixer. He could fix anything. Lawnmowers, appliances, roofs, flooring, plumbing. Or, if you had a more personal problem, he could also fix an annoying stalker, an abusive husband, or a random neighborhood bully. The only tools that he needed to fix *those* problems were his deep voice and two fists. And sometimes a little off-the- record information from Edmund. The message was always sent, and the problem was always fixed, usually with minimal bloodshed but always with plentiful bruises and broken bones.

He was also known as the fixer for the lonely single women of Madison who, with a wink of an eye and shake of a rump, were easily able to employ his services. Many of these young women attempted in vain to lasso him into something more serious than casual canoodling. But to their disappointment, all of those hopeful attempts were rebuffed by the confirmed and carefree bachelor. That is until a broken water pipe on a frigid December 1977 night sent Joseph Argento's life onto a completely different and unexpected trajectory.

———

Erick's arm was around Maddy's shoulders when she exclaimed, "Holy fuck! I knew Uncle Joe was a badass, but I had no idea! And at how *funny* he was! Finger sandwiches! That's fuckin' *classic!*" A solemn Blair, ignoring her niece's exultations, turned the page of the photo album and said, "Now, this is me as a newborn with your aunt Patty who was about one at the time."

CHAPTER 26

___

ONE WAY OR ANOTHER

Patricia Mercy Sommers entered the world on January 23, 1951. Only eighteen months later a second blessed cry from a Sommers newborn was heard as Blair Aubrey Sommers entered the world on July 16, 1952. From the moment Patty, as she would be known, set eyes on her younger sister, the two were inseparable.

The Sommers family were your stereotypical, white suburban family complete with the shag-carpeted split foyer home and white picket fence. Hank Sommers, their father, made a stable, middle-class living as an insurance salesman in Madison who enjoyed golf, fishing, watching sports, and a dry martini accompanied by a puff off of his pipe upon his return home from work. Betty Sommers, the girls' mother, was a content stay-at- home house-wife who, alongside her domestic responsibilities, hosted Tupperware parties, bake sales, and book clubs with her other housewife friends. They attended a mainstream Methodist church, and the girls attended a mainstream public school. Every summer, there was a mainstream weeklong family vacation. They would pack up their bright silver airstream with coolers filled with pop and lovingly prepared ham sandwiches, climb into their newest Buick, and head out to such glorious wonders as the Grand Canyon, Yosemite, or Niagara Falls looking much like a picture from a JC Penney catalog.

The girls loved rock and roll and would plead with their father to find the next rock radio station in the area as the previous one was fading out as a result of the Buick cruising down the highway. "All right, girls, all right," Hank would say in order to keep the peace as he twisted the silver radio dial until static turned to the latest wonderous hit from Elvis, Buddy, Ricky, or whoever was on the cover of *Teen Magazine* at that particular moment. Laughing and singing would emerge from the backseat as the parents would smile, shake their heads and roll their eyes at one another.

Their childhood was near idyllic, from a mainstream white American point of view. The sisters were best of friends and shared everything. One of their favorite past times as children was to play with their vast collection of paper dolls, especially those of the most popular actresses of the time. As Blair delighted in finding pretty dresses to put on their likeness of Marilyn Monroe, Patty was equally delighted in undressing her. She would become mesmerized by the shapely curves of the two-dimensional cardboard cutout that was adorned only by her undergarments.

The pair never argued but would engage in petty bickering constantly. "Where is my sweater?" "What did you do with my hairbrush?" "Stop hogging the bathroom!" and "Don't look at me like that!" were common refrains every evening at the Sommerses' home. "Girls," Betty would say in her soft, loving voice, "Please stop your bickering this instant." "Sorry, Mom!" would come the response from the girls in unison which was quickly followed by, "Oh my *Gaaawwwd*! Get off the phone!"

Even the arrival of a brother on April 1, 1957, could not shake the foundation of the bond between the two sisters. Upon his birth, the doctor commented that this was the only child that he had delivered that did not make a sound upon his emergence into the world. This was a trait that would hold true for most of his life. He would sit quietly in the corner and play with his diecast cars and trucks or play by himself in his sandbox with toy soldiers. He was largely ignored by his two older sisters, who due to his misfortune of having been born on April Fool's Day, was dubbed "______the Fool." They would pick on him mercilessly by holding him down and tickling him or other torturous acts such as noogies, wet willies, or "Indian" burns on his arms. He burst into tears at the age of four when the pair *proved* to him that Santa did not exist. That little trick resulted in the girls' Christmas presents being donated to a local charity for underprivileged children and having to complete the clean-up for their brother's wrapping paper on Christmas morning. They sat on the couch with their arms folded glaring at their brother while he enthusiastically tore open each brightly wrapped package, screaming in delight as he looked upon his new toy gun, cowboy outfit, or football. Without saying a word or looking at anybody, Blair would pick up a piece of discarded paper and drop it into a garbage bag that was being held open by an equally stoic and unresponsive Patty. The girls learned an important lesson that day. They learned that they had to terrorize their brother to such an extent that he would never *dare* to tell their parents about anything that involved them ever again.

Although rather cruel, the girls' antics toward their brother were more out of mischief than malice. They secretly loved their younger brother and could be frequently seen placing first aid cream and a bandage on a scraped knee or repairing one of his frequently broken toys. One of them would read a story to him every night before kissing him lightly on the forehead and turning out the light. Patty, however, frequently could not resist the urge to torment him one final time that day by saying as she closed his bedroom door, "And don't worry about that *monster* under your bed. MMWWAAA-HAHAHAAA!"

Outside of the home, the Sommers sisters were highly protective of their brother. It was all right for *them* to bully their younger sibling. It was not all right for *anyone else* to do so. Should any of his classmates call him names or pick on him in any way, Patty would thrust the child's face into the ground, preferably in a mud hole, and say gruffly, "Leave my fuckin' brother alone! He's mine!"

Blair's approach was much more indirect and much more effective. Never one to get her own hands dirty, literally or figuratively, Blair would enlist one of the many boys that she had manipulated into servitude to take care of the problem at hand. By junior high, Blair had mastered the art of being flirtatious, complete with the provocative flipping of her raven black hair, the perfectly timed giggle, a playful pat on a shoulder, or the batting of her jet-black eyelashes over her rich mahogany eyes. The ill-prepared boys in her class were powerless against such seductive assaults and would fall over each other to do anything that she asked in order to win her favor, which usually resulted in a couple's skate at the roller rink or an accompaniment to a school dance. The more generous token of gratitude of a make-out session behind the bleachers, complete with awkward groping was reserved for the most appreciated services of a male suitor.

Patty was feared for her gruff exterior and swift retribution upon anybody who messed with her friends or family. Blair was feared due to the number of people that she had control over, her patient and calculating nature, and the sheer ruthlessness of her orders. By high school, it was widely known that one should not mess with anyone who was "cool with Blair." While a sophomore in high school, a junior high bully had punched her ten-year-old brother in the stomach and called him a "f****t." Blair approached one of the tougher boys in her school who was standing behind the gym, smoking a cigarette, and lying about the number of sexual conquests that he had had. With an accentuated motion of her hips, Blair glided over to the denim- clad high school junior as "Groovin'" was heard coming out of a nearby transistor radio.

"Hey, man . . . who does this song? It's really cool," Blair began innocently. "The Young Rascals" came the boy's eager response. This was only the third time that Blair had ever spoken to him, and he began to immediately wonder what task he might have to perform in order to get her to go out that night. "Rascals," Blair said with bemusement. "That would make a cute name for a dog. Anyway, soooo, listen, my little brother has a bit of a problem, and I was wondering if maybe you could take care of that problem for me." "Uh . . . uh . . . sure. Just let me know who it is, and I'll take care of it," the boy awkwardly stammered. Blair put her delicate hand upon the boy's shoulder, looked into his eyes, and said coyly, "That's soooo sweet of you. I'll tell you what. As a thank-you, how about if I meet you at the park tonight at midnight? And I'll *really* be grateful if you bring me his teeth."

That evening, a dilapidated red 1962 Plymouth Valiant pulled up into the park. The boy stepped out of his car and saw Blair casually swinging with the breeze causing her short skirt to rise provocatively high. She jumped off of the swing and sauntered over to the boy. "So if you have something to show *me*, well . . . I'd probably have something to show *you*." The boy pulled out a bloody handkerchief. Inside were eight teeth from the boy that he had just brutally beaten. Blair squealed with delight and said, "Maybe we should go to your back seat. What I have to show *you* is a bit more private." For the first time in his life, the boy did not have to lie about a sexual conquest. And for the first time in *her* life, Blair had a complete understanding of the power a woman's sexuality had over the immature and emotionally fragile men of the world. It was a power that she would enthusiastically use from that point on and that she would never relinquish. To Blair, the human body became an amusement park. And she was going to ride as many rollercoasters as she saw fit.

Blair and Patty both enjoyed their sexual experiences in the free love culture that was late '60s America. But while Blair was able to present herself publicly as she truly was, Patty had to *suppress* her true sexuality from the scornful eyes of neo-puritan Midwest America. Patty went on a few uninspired dates with boys which almost always ended up with her listening to Blair aggressively make out with her date, as Patty would say, "You want any more popcorn" to the boy that *she* had the misfortune of sitting beside. Blair was known to be warm and inviting to the boys that she was interested in. Patty was known to be cold and unapproachable. To boys, that is. For girls, Patty was not only warm but downright hot-blooded and could be obsessively affectionate. Patty secretly had engaged in a number of clandestine sexual experiences starting as a freshman in high school with girls that she thought might be as interested in her as she was in them. Patty *really* enjoyed slumber parties and she began to hone her ability to sense when another girl was looking at her in a way that was beyond friendship. This would be the girl that she would choose to share a sleeping bag with as Patty always conveniently forgot to bring one. Gym class also became one of Patty's favorite activities as Patty would frequently find herself entangled in the limbs of a girl that she had noticed while showering.

Patty excelled in school through her natural intelligence and abilities. She was especially adept at math and science and was intrigued by the workings of the human body. But in the fall semester of her junior year, her favorite subject became geometry. The class was now being taught by a newly hired female teacher. She was a twenty-eight-year-old petite blonde with a perfect figure. She also had tragically lost her husband of three years in the atrocity that was the Viet Nam war. Patty, smitten with her new teacher and sensing that this older woman might need some comfort began an exploratory mission of mild flirtations. Her suspicions were confirmed one afternoon as Patty, who was sitting at a front row desk, was casually crossing and uncrossing her legs that were barely covered by the psychedelic mini dress that she was wearing. She saw the teacher's eyes dart down under her desktop, then immediately dart back up as her pretty face became flushed. This was the beginning of a two-year relationship that the two engaged in through private meetings at cheap hotels or in the back of a car in a secluded area. The affair ended when her now-former teacher told her that she was getting married. Patty was heartbroken and vowed to never fall in love again.

"Wow, that really sucks," Blair sincerely said to her sister through their bedroom walls upon hearing the news. They were each playing their respective stereos loudly as they were getting ready to go out that night and were yelling their conversation over the incompatible combination of notes and rhythms. Patty was cranking "Kick Out the Jams" by the MC5 as she curled her shoulder-length light brown hair while Blair was swaying to "Sugar, Sugar" by The Archies as she applied blue eyeshadow. "Oh my god, Blair! How can you *listen* to that shit? It's a fuckin' *cartoon* for chrissakes!" Patty would bellow at her sister disapprovingly. "Fine!" Blair would angrily reply before placing "Hair" by The Cowsills on her turntable. Patty, known for her musical snobbery, found *that* selection to be only a minor improvement. "Girls! For the love of Pete, would you *please* turn that racket down and stop your bickering?" their father yelled up at them. "Sorry, Dad!" came the response in unison. Neither of them adjusted the volume on their stereos.

"So who is she marrying?" Blair yelled into her sister. "Oh, that fuckin' gym teacher, football coach dick!" came Patty's response. Blair erupted in laughter and exclaimed, "Don't worry, Patty! I think she's gonna get bored with him *real* fast!" Patty rushed into Blair's room and excitedly inquired, "How do you know that? What do you know? Blair . . . did you . . . fuck that guy?" While continuing to look into her mirror as she applied her makeup, Blair stated in an uninterested tone, "Yeah . . . just once. I thought it might be useful to have somebody on the faculty on my team, y'know? But let's just say that I was extremely disappointed in his . . . performance. I mean, the guy's just not packin'." The pair exploded into laughter before Patty exclaimed, "Fuck! We *have* to go to that fuckin' wedding!"

The happy newlyweds were beaming with joy as they graciously shook the hands of their family, friends, and well-wishers in the receiving line. Their smiles immediately disappeared and were replaced by blushing faces and awkward expressions as they looked into the eyes of the Sommers sisters, who said in a rehearsed sing-song unison as they shook the sweaty hands of their respective ex-lovers, "We're *soooo* happy for you both. We're *sure* that this is just going to be *great*. If there's *anything* that you need, just let us know." They then gave the teachers a not-so-subtle wink before flying down the sidewalk arm in arm, giggling. Mutual suspicion about the odd encounter on their wedding day led to drunken confessions by the newlyweds which lead to an annulment of their marriage exactly seven days later, which led Patty to one final passionate evening at a cheap hotel with her former teacher before Patty dumped her. "Sorry, teach," Patty stated flatly but with a hint of revenge as she took long puffs off of her cigarette while zipping up her white vinyl boots, "but this just doesn't work for me any longer. You've taught me all that you can about love, and now I'm done with it. Thanks for ruining any chance that I may have had at romance." Her former teacher had her head buried in her hands and sobbed as Patty slammed the red door of room 17. Both teachers resigned from their positions and left Madison shortly thereafter.

Following their respective graduations from high school, Patty enrolled in nursing school and Blair enrolled at the University of Wisconsin, majoring in accounting. Blair excelled in her studies and graduated near the top of her class. It didn't hurt that most of her professors were male. Patty excelled in her studies and graduated near the top of her class. It didn't hurt that most of her instructors were female. Patty went on to her career as a nurse in a local hospital followed by a lengthy stint at an assisted living home from which she would eventually retire. Blair took a job at an accounting firm and became the manager in three short years. She remained there until her eventual retirement following a tragic loss in 2017.

Although they now lived apart, they saw each other frequently, often-times at locally held concerts or in various nightclubs. Patty would sweat profusely as she bounced to the rapid rhythms of The Ramones, The Damned, Blondie, or Iggy Pop. Blair would lightly sway during performances of Fleetwood Mac, Carly Simon, or James Taylor. But they would always be completely in sync when it came to one performer. This performer could make them shout, make them sing, make them cry, make them swoon, and most importantly, make them physically and emotionally exhausted. His name was Bruce Springsteen.

Patty continued with her informal and non-committal dalliances. Blair, on the other hand, grew more romantically inclined as she aged into her mid-twenties. She didn't want to simply use men anymore for sexual gratification or feelings of power. She began longing for someone that she could laugh with. Someone that she could smile with. Someone that she could dance with. Someone that she could share her life with. Someone that she could look upon as her equal. Someone that she could protect and who would protect her. And most importantly, someone that she could have a child with.

Shortly after moving to a new apartment in another neighborhood in Madison, Blair was walking up her street with a bag of groceries, fumbling to find her keys in her jacket pocket, when she ran into the back of a man.

Apples, milk, bread, and lunch meat fell upon the grey, cracked pavement. "I'm so sorry, miss," the man said politely. "No, it was my fault," an embarrassed Blair stammered. The pair began picking the items from the ground and placing them back into the partially torn paper sack. "Well, no harm done, I suppose, have a nice day, miss," the man said as he smiled, and proceeded to cross the street and enter a small neighborhood tavern. He was as sweet as he was big, brawny, and beautiful, Blair thought as she swooned. Blair had a long history of manipulating men into doing her bidding. What she wondered now was if she had the power to manipulate a man into falling in love with her.

"Okay, I have met my future husband and I have a plan!" Blair excitedly exclaimed to her sister as Patty was cuddling with her latest nineteen-year-old toy that she had met at a club a week earlier.

"Step one, I need to find out if this guy is married or not. I'm not into messing around with married guys . . . anymore.

"Step two, if he's available, I'll start hanging out at the places he goes and make myself, y'know, conspicuous.

"Step three, he'll notice me and ask me out. That will be easy.

"Step four, we fall in love. Also, easy. "Step five, we get married.

"Step six, we have a kid or two. What do you think?"

"Uh . . . sure . . . what could possibly go wrong?" Patty replied uninterestedly as she resumed cavorting with the giggling bundle sitting next to her. "All right, cool. I'll keep you posted. Do you want to go to the disco with me Friday night?" Blair was greeted by an expressionless Patty as a reply to her obviously stupid question.

Blair's hunting ground became the bar that her unsuspecting prey frequented. He became open season when she discovered that he was not married. In fact, he did not have anything that closely resembled a committed relationship. She became increasingly frustrated, however, as she found it impossible to compete for his attention against the group of like-minded young ladies who constantly surrounded and blocked her quarry. Regardless of the provocative nature of her appearance and multiple flirty glances in his direction, she failed night after night to have her rich mahogany eyes make contact with his. She would watch with frustration as her target would exit the smoke-filled bar with his powerful arm wrapped around the shoulder of yet another tittering ingenue.

Frustration reached a fever pitch on the night that Blair fell in love with him from afar. On her fifth mission to the bar, a male patron was getting rough with his girlfriend in the corner.

"Just shut the fuck up, bitch! I'll stop drinking when I want!" the man yelled before slapping her harshly across the face. Blair watched her mountain of a man get up from his red, cracked vinyl stool at the bar. His mostly female congregation parted as he purposefully strode toward the abusive man, grabbed him firmly by the arm, and dragged him outside of the front door. The rest of the patrons at the bar turned back to their drinks, conversations, or flirtations. It was just another Tuesday night. One bar patron, however, flew to the picture window to observe the events occurring outside. As her eyes adjusted from the glare of the neon beer sign that she was peering through, Blair adoringly watched as her future beat the man over and over again with his concrete fists. Blood and teeth flew as the man begged for mercy. None was given until the man's eyes were completely swollen shut and his face resembled bloody silly putty. Blair's heart was racing rapidly, and her face was filled with both admiration and anticipation as her future then lifted the man from the ground with one hand and warned in an ominous voice, "If I *ever* see you hit a woman again, I'll fuckin' kill 'ya, 'ya fuckin' douchebag."

Night after night, Blair tried to garner his attention. And night after night, she was hopelessly disappointed as she watched him leave in the arms of another. Over a Rockwellian Thanksgiving dinner at their parents' house, Blair lamented her failures over the previous month and a half. As Patty observed their mother hand their father yet another dry martini while stealthily taking the carving knife away from him, she said, "Just fuckin' *trap him*, Blair!" "Patty," her mother scolded as she began carving the turkey as her bleary-eyed husband looked on, "*Must* you use that language at the dinner table?" "Sorry, Mom" came Patty's insincere reply as she turned back to her sister and said, "It's almost winter. He's a handyman, right? Who loves to play the hero, right? Wait for a really fuckin' snowy night. Do something to a water pipe and call him to come over. Sound *really* fuckin' desperate. Answer the door in the shortest bath towel you've got. Once he's fixed your pipe, comment on how bad the snow is outside and invite him to stay over to . . . y'know . . . fix your pipes." "Oh, for the love of Pete girls. *Please* don't talk this way in front of me" came the father's slurred admonition that was barely heard over the blaring Panasonic as the Bears were thrashing the Lions . . . again.

Later that evening, Blair and Patty were in Blair's bedroom going through her old '45s and pondering what their oaf of a brother might be doing for Thanksgiving at his deployment in Korea. She found a record to her liking and squealed. As she placed it upon her well-worn turntable, she said, "Remember this one?" As The Monkees' version of "Pleasant Valley Sunday" came out of the overly trebled speakers, Blair said, "Wow. It sounds like Goffin and King were flies on our wall when they wrote this. I think we may have had the most hum-drum middle America upbringing ever." Patty went into her room and could be heard rummaging around in a chest before she returned, handed Blair a record, and said, "Yeah, but sometimes when Dad got *really* drunk, it was a lot like this." The next record that the sisters played was "Only Women Bleed" by Alice Cooper.

The pipe under Blair's bathroom sink was more stubborn than she had expected. She grunted as she pulled the wrench or plyers or maybe it was a vice or something toward her one final time and the pipe came loose unleashing a torrent of water upon her bathroom floor. Her prayers from the previous two weeks had been answered. There was a blizzard in Madison. And not just any blizzard. It was thundersnow with the sheets of frozen precipitation falling at three inches per hour as they were frequently illuminated by a bright flash of lightning creating a brilliant kaleidoscope of colors outside of her frosted apartment windows.

"Yes, hello, I'm so sorry to call you on such a night as this" came Blair's panicked voice over the phone. "It's just that I heard you could fix things, and my bathroom pipe has broken and I just don't know what to do!" "It'll be all right miss. I'll be over in a jiffy" came the pleasant voice of the handyman. After getting stuck twice and finally skidding to a stop in front of the three-story apartment building, the brawny handyman trudged up the stairs. His arm, chest, and back muscles were evidently bulging, even under his heavy coat, from the weight of the tools he was carrying as the apartment door slowly opened.

There was a flash of lightning quickly followed by a boom of thunder. The electricity in the air was palpable as Joseph Angelo Argento stood there and looked upon the demure feminine figure standing before him. She had a bright pink towel wrapped around her body that covered her only from mid-breast to the top of her thigh. Her beautiful face was encased in a mop of damp, raven-black hair. Blair took one look at his shocked expression and began making wedding plans in her mind. Her ruse had worked. She decided that she would seal the deal by saying, "I'm so sorry. I'm still a bit . . . wet. Won't you please come in?"

Attempting to be as professional as possible, Joseph said, "Well, miss, where is this broken pipe of yours?" Blair fought the urge to use yet another entendre, thinking it too forward, so she simply said, "In here, in the bathroom. Under the sink." Joseph took one look at the obviously sabotaged pipe, with the wrench lying right next to it, and immediately knew that he had been duped. And he didn't care. As he was working for the three minutes that it took him to re-attach the pipe, Blair said, "Y'know . . . it's just so *awful* out and I *do* so appreciate you coming to help me on such a night. If you would like, I would be *more* than happy to make you a hot meal. And since it's just *so* awful out, you are most welcome to stay the night. I would *hate* to see anything bad happen to you over silly ol' me."

As the pair ate a hastily cooked, but previously prepped dinner of grilled pork chops with a steamed garlic vegetable medley, loaded baked potatoes, dinner salad with homemade ranch dressing, and freshly baked cherry pie topped with butter ripple ice cream they talked and laughed together. They spoke about their upbringing, although the more sordid details of their past were omitted. They spoke about their love of movies. Joseph loved science fiction and horror and excitedly discussed the spectacles that were *Star Wars, Jaws,* and *The Hills Have Eyes.* Blair, falsely claiming not to like the sight of blood, preferred such recent releases as *Saturday Night Fever, Slap Shot,* and the latest Mel Brooks romp, *Silent Movie.* Joseph would make a bawdy joke and Blair would genuinely burst into uncontrollable laughter. *This is a person that I can be myself with,* they both thought simultaneously before taking a final bite of the sweet- tart pie. As the pair were cleaning up after dinner, the radio began playing "A Groovy Kind of Love" by The Mindbenders. Joseph put his wash rag down, dried his hands, and took Blair into his massive arms. They swayed to the delicately played and sung notes and stared into one another's inviting mahogany eyes. Joseph Angelo Argento stayed the night with Blair Aubrey Sommers. And he never left.

———

Erick, unsure of which part of the story to comment on chose what he felt was the least controversial and said, "Wow, I guess the apple doesn't fall very far from the tree, now does it?" "What the *fuck* is that supposed to mean?"

Maddy replied as she feigned being annoyed. "Well, it just seems to *me* that *Blair* pursued *Joe* and then *you* pursued *me* and so—" Erick was immediately cut off by his soon-to-be wife as she said, "Oh, get over yourself. I didn't pursue you! I was just kinda interested and . . . well . . . okay, fuck . . . I got nothing. I did pursue you. And you're better off because of it, mister!" "I never said that I wasn't," Erick softly replied as he gave a light kiss to his love's forehead. "Now, this is the first picture of Joseph and me right after we got together," Blair continued as she turned the page of the photo album.

CHAPTER 27

MY BOYFRIEND'S BACK

I should have been there. I should have been there to protect her, was what kept being repeated, over and over, in Joseph's anguished mind. He was standing in a dark corner of the room, his entire six-foot-three-inch frame shrouded by dark shadows as the full moon hid behind the ominous clouds of an impending storm. He was seething in anger and wondered how he would be able to control himself once he saw them. Fuck that, he thought. There will be no control tonight. There will be no mercy. These motherfuckin' douchebags are gonna feel my full wrath. He felt in his back jeans' pockets for the only two tools he would need tonight. A hammer and a pair of plyers.

As he impatiently waited for his prey with his heart pounding blood through his tense body, he thought back to six months ago when this had all started. Not unlike a mighty, proud tree that falls hard when it is confronted with a force of nature greater than itself, Joseph had fallen hard when he went up against the incredible force that was Blair Sommers. Her intoxicating gales of beauty, charm, intelligence, sense of humor, and innocent sultriness swirled around him and blew him over on that fateful December night. He had become a willing victim as she unleashed the full force of her seductive power upon him. He just stood there and allowed this tempest's provocative winds to penetrate through his muscular frame into his very soul.

The couple spent their first evening together. It was both wonderfully exhilarating and peacefully comfortable at the same time. They fell into each other's worlds as though they had been pre-destined. They fit together perfectly, both figuratively and literally. They laughed, talked, and made love until the early hours of the next morning. Upon awakening, Joseph looked out of the frost-covered windows at the spectacle of colors as the bright sunshine reflected off of the pure white snowfall. Blair woke up and burst out laughing when she saw the hulking figure standing at her window. She had loaned him a pair of her pajama bottoms and a large blue baggy Donna Summer T-shirt, and his appearance was hysterically absurd. The T-shirt was stretched to its limit on his muscular torso and her equally strained pink pajama bottoms clung to his waist while hanging down to the middle of his calf. "This is *not* one of my finer moments," he said while chuckling and climbing back into the bed that the two would share for the next forty years.

After a full day of helping people shovel out their driveways, sidewalks, and vehicles, Joseph met Blair at the local bar. He was sitting on his customary stool, laughing boisterously with the group that was gathered around him when Blair entered. She took off her full-length faux fur coat to reveal a tight, silver sequined halter top. Her bell-bottomed, purple-glittered slacks clung to her hips, backside, and shapely legs. Her lithe frame was being held up by a pair of silver platform boots.

She had not dressed for the weather. She had dressed to make a statement. *That's right bitches*, Blair thought to herself as she sauntered ever closer to her new mate while wearing a diabolical smile. *You missed your chance. He's* mine *now.* She planted a long and passionate kiss on Joseph's rugged lips and said, "Hey, lover, buy me a drink?" Every woman in the bar bombarded this interloping ingenue with visual daggers, wishing that their glares could actually penetrate her pale skin.

Throughout the evening, women would approach Joseph. And throughout the evening, each woman was greeted by a friendly smile and casual conversation until Blair would whisper something into his ear and his attention was immediately returned to her. As the jilted woman's expression changed from seductive flirtation to angry disappointment, she would glower directly into Blair's eyes. Blair would make direct eye contact as her mahogany iris appeared to turn as jet black as her hair and give her adversary a confident grin. Every defeated woman understood the meaning of the look and would retreat back to their seat. The meaning of the look was "Don't fuck with me."

Joseph committed to Blair as strongly as he had previously committed to confirmed bachelorhood. Gone were the evenings of carefree carousing. They had been replaced by evenings of carefree cuddling. He spent Christmas at the Sommers' home and was delighted to be welcomed by Blair's loving family. They had even bought him a sweater. Two sizes too small and a putrid green color, but the thought behind the gift was deeply appreciated.

As the sisters were in the kitchen refreshing the drinks later that evening, Patty said in a hushed voice, "Jesus, Blair. *I'm* even tempted to fuck him. And I'm *totally* not into cock." Blair just smiled and winked at her sister as they entered the living room with a tray of fresh drinks. A few hours and more than a few martinis later, Hank slurred, "Well, it's so nice to know that at least *one* of my daughters will be happily married. You see, Patty? Maybe there's someone out there for you too once you get over your confusion. Joe, old chum, maybe you got someone that you could fix our Patty up with."

Joe looked at Patty's smoldering and embarrassed face. He then looked at the pleading expression of his Blair and flashed her a mischievous smile as if to say, "Fuck him." It was just the two of them communicating silently before Joseph said, "Well, Mr. Sommers, Hank, well, I think it might be a bit too early for us to be talking about marriage, but I appreciate your blessing. And yeah, I could *totally* set Patty up. Just leave it to me. I know *all kinds* of young ladies who I'm *sure* would love to get to know Patty better. But I'm afraid I can't help you with the marriage part. This country's too fucking backward to allow everyone who loves one another to get married. I mean, who the fuck *cares*, right, Hank, Betty? Who the fuck *cares* if someone is attracted to a man or a woman? Who the fuck *cares* who someone falls in love with? I'll tell you who. Self-righteous puritan motherfuckers who want to have control over everything we do. Everything we feel. Everything we think about. They don't believe in individual rights. They only believe in *their* perceived right to discriminate against others and to force others to live according to their fucked-up worldview. They want us all to live under the thumb of *their* fucked-up mythology. So I'm very sad to say that I can't help Patty find a wife right now. And I probably won't be able to help her find one in my lifetime. But Hank? I'll tell ya what I *can* do. I sure as hell can help Patty find a piece of ass that she might grow to love."

Hank, recovering from his initial shock, said, "You know what, Joseph? You may have a point there. I really hadn't thought of it that way, old boy." Betty, releasing her pent-up tension for the first time since Patty began playing with her paper dolls, grasped her husband's hand and smiled. In the span of five minutes, Joseph Argento had fixed Patty's parents. At least partially. And he had earned Patty's unwavering lifelong respect.

Two weeks later, Joseph moved out of his shabby two-room apartment and took up residence with his new love. Joseph enlisted the aid of Edmund, who he uncharacteristically had not seen in nearly a month as he had been nesting with his new girlfriend. As the best friends pulled up in a haphazardly packed U-Haul to his new home, Edmund said, "Okay, man. You know I love you, so I just got to ask you this. Are you *sure* you know what you're doing? I'll support you in whatever you do, but if I smell a rat, I'm going to let you know." "I would expect nothing less from you, my friend" came Joseph's wistful reply. "But you don't have to worry. She looks at me the way my mother looked at my father. I guess I didn't know it, but maybe I've been looking for her all along. I feel like I'm a better person when I'm with her, and *nobody* has ever made me feel that way before."

The two brawny men entered the apartment to find Blair with disheveled black hair and wearing a pair of cutoff jeans and an old, sweat-covered T-shirt as she was feverishly reorganizing the living room. "Oh . . . hello . . . you must be Edmund," Blair said in a breathless voice. "I've heard so much about you. I'm so sorry that I look such a . . . mess. But . . . moving day, y'know?" Edmund took one look at this vision of beauty and immediately understood his friend's abrupt turnaround. The pair shook hands, and the men went back out to the truck to retrieve another load. "Yeah, okay," Edmund said. "Yeah, you know what you're doing. That chick's a keeper. Just, take it slow, and be sure, okay?" Edmund's request fell upon deaf ears as Joseph looked up to the third-floor window and gazed at his future's smiling face shining down upon him.

Several evenings later, Joseph was pacing around the apartment, anxiously taking short drags off of yet another Pall Mall when Blair entered the living room following her shower. "Hey, babe, what's wrong?" a concerned Blair inquired through the smokey haze. "Blair, honey, listen. Before this gets too deep, I really need to tell you some things about me. They are things that I'm not ashamed of, but I'm not necessarily proud of either." "All right, dear," a calm Blair stated as she folded her feet behind her on their couch. "You can tell me anything. And I, in turn, will tell *you* everything."

"Well," Joseph began sheepishly, "you know I have a bit of an . . . angry streak." "Yes, I do," Blair purred as blood rushed to her face. "Well," Joseph continued, "there have been a couple of times that my anger took me *beyond* just beating someone up." He then spoke about the "accident" of his sergeant, how his parents had been murdered due to his father's involvement in a hit man syndicate, and how he had taken care of the hit man of his parents. This last part of the story was *very* detailed as he wanted to gauge Blair's reaction.

"Soooo," Blair began inquisitively, "you cut off the arms and tied them to the ceiling fan, *because*—" "Well," Joseph tried to explain, "I just thought the blood would leave cool patterns on the wall. And well . . . they kinda did." Blair then said, "And the purpose of the boiled head was *what* exactly?" "Uh . . . I'm not really sure," Joseph replied. "Inspiration just struck, and so that's what I did. There really isn't a reason behind it. I guess maybe I wanted the cops to think it was some deranged lunatic that did it or something."

"I see, I see," Blair responded, attempting to keep her composure. Her body was beginning to slightly quiver from the tension of the moment. "So are you now in this . . . syndicate?" "No," Joseph firmly replied. "I turned 'em down flat. I told them that I really didn't want to be a killer. That it was just something that I had to do this one time. They said that I had a standing offer to join them and to call them if I ever need anything. But, my darling, I never will. I promise you that. And you have to know that I would *never, ever* harm you or anyone that doesn't have it coming for that matter. I'm really not a violent man . . . usually. *Please* don't be frightened of me. I *promise* you that I'll never kill again."

Blair looked perplexed and said, "Why not?" Joseph, now mirroring Blair's confused expression said, "Uh . . . uh . . . well . . . I didn't really think that you'd want to be with someone who was a killer, so I'm not going to do that anymore." "Well," Blair began, "I *certainly* wouldn't want to be with someone who just ran around killing people at random. That would be . . . wrong. But it seems to me that the two men that you *have* killed, and all of the ones that you have beaten, were men who deserved a certain amount of . . . justice. I see you more as a *justified executioner* than as a *killer*. So should you find yourself in a situation like that," she then stared at Joseph knowingly and said, "or if *Edmund* tips you off about a situation like that, then we will have a discussion that never happened and determine what the right amount of . . . justice . . . should be applied. Agreed?"

Joseph just nodded his head while wearing an amazed expression. He didn't think that it was possible to fall in love any further with Blair. He had been wrong. "Now, Joseph, let me share a little about myself." Blair was completely open and honest as she confided in her new love about the tasks that she used to assign to the boys and men that she would seductively manipulate. When she recounted the story about fucking the boy after he showed her the teeth of the boy that he had just beaten, Joseph looked at her in amazement. He then burst into laughter. "My lord, Blair. And I thought *I* was fucked up. We make quite the pair, don't we?" "We're a perfect match, Joseph. And I love you more *now* than I ever have," a sentimental Blair replied. "And I, you," Joseph softly stated as he looked deep into her eyes, lifted her from the couch into his brawny arms, and laid her gently upon their bed. Their pact was sealed that evening. Joseph would do what he felt he needed to do in order to right neighborhood wrongs. But Blair would have the final say over the ultimate sentence. And Patty, who had a tendency toward loose lips and oversentimentality, was never to know.

Tuesday, February 14. Valentine's Day. Blair was in the bathroom applying her makeup and getting ready for work when Joseph asked for her to come into the living room. "Just a sec!" Blair yelled out as she buttoned her conservative blouse and put on her dark blue blazer. She entered the living room and found Joseph wearing a suit, on one knee and in the middle of rose petals on the hardwood floor. Blair gasped, put her hands over her mouth, and stood motionless in anticipation. "Blair, honey. I know we haven't been together for too long, but it just seems like this was meant to be. I never thought I would ever feel this way about anyone in my life. But then I met *you* and you are all that I think about. I love you. I want to be with you. And I want to ask you if you would do me the honor of being my wife?"

For the second time, Blair Sommers bowled Joseph over. Only this time, it was literal as she squealed and ran into his arms knocking him backward to the floor. The pair were laughing hysterically when Joe said, "So I can take that as a yes?" Blair stopped laughing, looked into her lover's eyes, and said with seductive satisfaction, "Yes. It would be my honor to be your wife."

That evening, Joseph had prepared Valentine's Day dinner that was to be ready upon Blair's arrival home from work. It consisted of burnt steak, burnt baked potatoes, burnt mixed vegetables, and a salad that was not burnt. They ended up eating the salad to accompany a delivered pizza as they discussed possible wedding plans and dates.

"Well, Blair," Joseph began, "I don't know that we need to have *too* big of an affair. Just the usual. We can get married in your church if you would like because I hardly ever go to mine, and it really doesn't matter to me. I mean, does God really give a fuck where two people in love get married? I don't think so. So let's just keep it simple. Bridesmaids, groomsmen, a flower girl. Oh, we'll need a ring bearer. And a photographer! We can't forget that! And a caterer for the reception. And a DJ! Gotta have a DJ! Oh . . . and a cake . . .a really big one! And flowers of course! Lots and lots of flowers! And rice! That's still a thing, right?"

An amused Blair peered at her fiancée in a comforting silence as he excitedly listed all of the arrangements that he felt they needed for the wedding. His arms were flailing, and his cadence became increasingly fast as his voice became louder with each passing thought until Blair interrupted and said, "Or . . . we *could* just fly to Vegas Friday night."

"But . . . but," a confused Joseph began stammering, "don't you want a church wedding . . . and what about your family? And friends? Don't you want—" Blair placed a single slender index finger up to his lips. She looked into his eyes and said, "Joseph, all I want is to be your wife. And to be with you. And to have *children* with you. This is all that I want. Call Edmund. I'll call Patty. We'll fly in on Friday night. Patty, although she will hate it, will take *me* to a male strip club. Edmund will take *you* to a female strip club. That will be our bachelorette and bachelor parties. We will meet the next day at a chapel, preferably *without* an Elvis, and we will pledge our love to one another. We can have a reception for everyone else later. All I want right now is for you to commit to me as much as I am going to commit to you."

"Okay, okay, okay," a nearly hyperventilating Joseph began. "But . . . but . . . what about *my* ring? I need a ring too!" Blair casually chuckled and said, "Oh, my dear Joseph. I bought *your* ring the day after I met you. The day after an oaf of a girl ran into your muscular back and spilled her groceries all over the sidewalk. The day after that man was so sweet and so kind to me. I bought *his* ring the day after that." "That . . . was you?" a shocked Joseph inquired. No words were exchanged for the rest of the evening. The only exchanges were passionate kisses as they made love.

"What the *fuck* are you doing?" Patty screamed at her sister in the ladies' room at the airport. "I'm getting married. I've found my present and my future. And I'll thank you for not questioning me any further" came Blair's terse response before saying in a playfully determined voice, "Now, let's go to Vegas and have some fun."

A bleary-eyed Edmund stood next to his equally bleary-eyed friend. The memories of tastefully placed pasties and engorged speedos were vague at best by all involved. The wedding march began over the tin-sounding in-ceiling speakers. And a vision of beauty came walking down the aisle. Blair, with her raven black hair lightly cascading down to the delicate shoulders of a white with red-accent dress, sauntered down the aisle. Patty, struggling to avert her gaze from the thighs of the Casio keyboardist, stood alongside with her beloved sister. Simple vows pledging their love and loyalty to one another were exchanged. The Wayne Newton impersonating official declared them married. The tin speakers then filled the tiny chapel with the pop chords of "A Groovy Kind of Love." Blair and Joseph kissed, then danced, then laughed. It was the same ritual that they would perform over the next forty years.

In April 1978, Blair announced to her husband of two months and to her family and friends that she was with a child. Hugs and tears were shed as Joseph sat in the corner, sipping his Olympia, and beamed with joyous anticipation. Joseph and Blair Argento were going to have their first baby, and the child would be nothing short of miraculous.

"My *lord*, Joseph. It's a *plate*. I can pick up a *plate*," a scolding Blair told her husband and father of their unborn child as he was hastily clearing the dinner table. "I know, I know, dear. But it's just better to be safe than to be sorry. Oh, let me get that for you, dear," he said as he picked up her cutlery. The phone rang. Joseph answered and said, "Yes . . . I can be there in ten minutes, Edmund."

Joseph returned in less than an hour, his breath emitting a slight scent of gin. "Blair, honey, I have something to tell you." Blair turned off the re-run of *Happy Days* and turned her full attention to her solemn husband. "This is the first time that I have turned Edmund down," Joseph said earnestly. "I need you to listen to me and tell me if I'm doing the right thing. Edmund told me about a cop who beat the fuck out of a Black kid in a holding cell. This kid is pretty fucked up I guess, and Edmund's really pissed about it. He's fuckin' tired of working for people who are abusing the people that they're supposed to protect. He doesn't think that he can talk to anybody internally. So he asked me to . . . y'know . . . take care of it. I looked at the name on the card. And I thought *really hard* about it. I *wanted* to do it. I *wanted* to fuck this guy up. But then I thought . . . a cop who beat the shit out of a Black kid. The cop turns up dead. Who are they gonna blame? Blair, honey, the cops in this town are gonna have a fuckin' *field day* on innocent people. Just because they happen to be black. There will be retribution for what *I* did . . . against people who did *nothing* and who have *no protection* against the local government. So I said no. It's not the right play. Figure out another way. My killing him would only lead to more unnecessary bloodshed of innocent people. Blair, did I do the right thing?"

Blair Argento looked at her husband with admiration. He possessed the rage that she coveted. But it was tempered with reason. If it had been *her* in this situation, she would have ripped out the throat of the abusive cop, without regard to the possible future consequences upon innocent people. But Joseph was able to see beyond immediate gratification. It was a quality that she yearned to possess. "Yes, Joseph. You made the right decision."

Several weeks later, the phone rang. Joseph answered. "Blair, honey! I gotta go fix a broken pipe on the other side of town. I'll be back as soon as I can." "Okay, baby, we'll be waiting for you," Blair responded as she caressed her belly. Ten minutes later, two men broke into the Argento's apartment door. "No, please . . . I'm pregnant!"

Joseph rushed into the hospital, his face a combination of grief and rage. He had returned home, and a neighbor had told him that an ambulance and a police car had arrived. He flew to the hospital, ran down the hallway, and was greeted by Edmund. "Hey, okay, listen to me, buddy. It's not good, but she'll be okay. We'll take care of it. Just be with your wife. Joseph, we *will* take care of this."

Joseph went into the hospital room and peered down upon his beaten wife. Her jaw was purple, matching the color of her swollen right eye. She looked up at him with her left eye and said, "Joseph, call them." "Call who, baby?" a panicked Joseph replied. "You know who. Call them. Call them and avenge me. Call them and avenge *our child that they murdered*. Avenge *us*, Joseph."

Joseph went to a pay phone and dialed a number that he never thought that he would need. "Yeah, this is Joe, Joseph Argento. I need to speak to the boss." "Joseph, it has been so long" came the voice on the other end of the phone. "To what do we owe this pleasure?" Joseph told the man about his wife being brutally beaten about the face and stomach before the assailants left with a few of their possessions. He then said in a dark voice "So help me find them. Don't do anything to them. They're mine. But if you help me find them, then, I'm in."

Twelve hours later, Joseph had returned to his wife's bedside. "Blair, honey. I have their names. They are—" Joseph was interrupted by Blair's weary voice saying, "No, Joseph. *Never* utter their names. Do not give them the *dignity* that comes from having a name. They are worthless. And the worthless have no names. Just . . . take care of this . . . filth."

Two men entered the tin shack that was on the outskirts of the local industrial park. They were drunk and laughing as they stumbled into their makeshift home. Neither of them noticed the hulking silhouette lurching toward them, then striking them upon the head.

"Hey, hey, man, what the fuck *is* this?" a bound man said with confused desperation after having cold water dumped onto his face. His partner in crime was gagging as he tried to spit out the water that he had swallowed. "This . . . is your final hour," a dark voice replied from the hulk standing over him. The pair of confused and anxious men struggled to get up but realized that their legs and arms were fully extended and had been chained to cinder blocks at the elbows and mid-calf.

"Yeah, you fucked up, boys. You killed my unborn child. You nearly killed my wife. And now—" Joseph's voice deepened into a frigid growl. "I'm going to kill *you*. But not before we have some fun first. Are you boys familiar with 'The Hokey Pokey'? It was one of my favorites as a kid, and I thought it might be a fun thing to play tonight . . . with a little twist. First, let's take your left leg out!" A singular loud CRACK! Then a second came followed by screams of anguish as Joseph stomped on their ankles which were hanging over the cinder blocks with all of his weight, snapping their shin bones which then jutted out through the skin, hurtling streams of blood into the air.

"You're doing fine, boys," Joseph continued with a dastardly calm as the men began desperately pleading for mercy. "No, no mercy for the wicked tonight. I must admit, it was pretty clever of you boys to get me to go out on a bogus house call. But for what? Just to steal a few of our things. And why did you have to beat my wife? If you had just ripped me off, then sure, I would have beat the fuck out of you, but we wouldn't have to go through the rest of this trouble. But you didn't, so . . . now, how about those right legs?" *CRACK*! SCREAM! *CRACK*! SCREAM! It was followed by maniacal laughter. "Oh, fuck boys, I've got to thank you. I haven't had this much fun since . . . well . . . since I boiled a man's severed head. Are you starting to get the picture boys? Are you beginning to realize what I have in store for you tonight? Yes? No? Well. How about those left arms to make it clear for you?"

CRACK! SCREAM! *CRACK!* SCREAM! followed Joseph's full-weight assault upon the men's lower radius and Ulna bones causing them to snap and violently protrude through the skin on their arms. "Hard to tell who the winner is. You're both suffering equally. Let's try to break the tie, shall we?" Joseph continued in his deadly calm cadence. *CRACK!* SCREAM! *CRACK!* SCREAM! echoed through the tin makeshift home as the right arms were snapped. Blood was pouring out of the gaping wounds of the men's extremities as Joseph said with amusement, "Okay, boys, that was a tie, and I'm tired of playing that one. So what else did I enjoy playing as a child? Oh, I know, how about operation? He then straddled the chest of one of the men while holding a pair of rusty plyers. Except, in *my* version of the game, we're going to focus on the mouth." With that, he forced open the mouth of the first man, grabbed his tongue with the plyers, and ripped it from the opening. Gurgled screaming was heard as Joseph got up and went over to the second man, performing the same demented deed.

"Let's just lay these tongues over here for a moment, shall we?" Joseph said with unnerving tranquility. "We may need these for our last game. But we're not done playing operation yet." He returned to straddle the first man, once again forcing his mouth open, and began to meticulously remove the man's teeth, one by one with the plyers. The teeth were dropped into the underside of a dented hubcap, resulting in an ominous "clanging" sound following the violent extraction of each tooth. The sound created bounced off of the tin walls and rang like morbid church bells.

After all of the man's teeth were in their rightful place in the hubcap, he turned to the second man, straddled him, and said, "Open up and say AWWW . . . FUCK!" and Joseph began the same demented ritual over again.

The clanging sound mercifully stopped. All teeth were present and accounted for in the hubcap. "Whew, that was work, boys!" Joseph stated as he looked down at the two sobbing men laying in pools of their own blood as he wiped the sweat from his brow. "And I'm starting to get tired. But we still have two more games to play. Do you boys remember that child's toy where you would hammer these colored wooden dowels into a little workbench? I spent *hours* and *hours* with that thing as a toddler. Just loved it. I discovered then that I just really *loved* to hammer things, and I'm in a hammerin' mood!"

He then mounted the chest of the first man and began diligently hammering the teeth into his forehead while whistling the tune of "My Boyfriend's Back" by The Angels. When he had finished, he looked at his work. On the forehead of the first man, he had hammered the teeth to spell

"FUCK" and in the second it spelled "YOU." "Now, I hate to tell you boys this, but playtime's just about over. I need to go see my wife . . . y'know . . . in the fuckin' *hospital*," Joseph stated coldly. "But one more game to play. Do you boys remember that game with hippos and marbles?" With that, he balled up the two tongues in each of his clenched fists and rammed them down the throats of each man. He then pinched the nose of each of the hysterical men and watched them gasp for air before they succumbed to the violent suffocation.

Blair woke up in the hospital and found her beloved husband gazing down at her. His face was riddled with concern. "I'm okay, Joseph. I will be all right" came Blair's weak attempt at reassurance. "But, Joseph. They have said that I will never be able to have children. I'm so sorry." Uncharacteristic tears welled in her mahogany eyes as Joseph laid a bloody handkerchief on his wife's bosom. Blair opened it. Inside were the bloody leftover teeth from the evening's earlier events. Blair smiled with satisfaction at her husband. He smiled back. And although weakened and sore, three nights later, she was slow dancing with her hero in their living room. The song that they danced to was "Never Going Back Again," by Fleetwood Mac.

———

"Holy fuck, Aunt Blair, I never knew, I'm so sorry," Maddy mournfully stated as a solemn Erick was clasping her hand. "It's all right, dear," Blair softly replied. "As they say, God works in mysterious ways. Our child was taken from us. But we were *all* rewarded with you. But not, I must say, without some further trials over the next ten years." Blair turned the page of the photo album and began once again. "This photo of Joseph, Patty, and myself was taken following your grandparents' funeral in 1979."

Chapter 28

Long Time Running

Although not of Irish descent, Hank and Betty Sommers, like most red-blooded Americans were never ones to miss a good St. Patrick's Day celebration. It was one of the few days of the year that Hank would trade in his signature martinis for a good ol' fashion green beer. And this was true once again on March 17, 1979, as the Sommerses were in attendance at a business associate's lake view house in Shorewood Hills, about twelve short miles from the Sommerses' home.

Traditional Irish folk songs were being slurred with very poor imitations of Irish accents by drunken men as their tittering wives looked on with expected reverence. With their shirt tails out, the men's spittle would fly as they attempted to out-volume one another in their swaying haze of revelry. As the lapping waves of Lake Mendota began reflecting the brilliant oranges, pinks, and reds of the setting spring sun, the remaining revelers sat in the spacious living room on the all-white plush furniture in their respective pairs preparing to play a game. There were eight couples remaining, all in their mid-forties to mid-fifties. The Sommerses had planned on spending the night at their hosts' home. This was why Betty had few concerns over her husband's alcohol consumption on this particular evening. It was not until the sloven, giggling men began putting their keys into a large crystal bowl that Betty realized the *real* reason why they were spending the night. She looked at the other guests in horror, then looked at her smirking husband pleadingly. "Awww, c'mon honey, it's just a bit of fun" was the reply she received as Hank pulled his keys out of his pocket and dropped them.

Just before they reached the bowl, the keys were caught by Betty's gentile, outstretched hand. "Hank, I think that it's time for us to say our goodnight's now," Betty said sternly to her husband. "You're embarrassing me . . . in front of my colleagues" came Hank's response that he thought he was whispering but was in fact stating quite loudly.

"Thank you all for a lovely evening, but I think that I need to get this one home," Betty stated cordially before making eye contact with each of the women in the room and saying coldly, "he wouldn't be any good to any of you tonight anyway. Come along, Hank dear. We're going home."

The ingredients for the perfect accident are as follows: You take one part of a lost argument about who would drive home + one part of a *renewed* argument about a husband's infidelity + one part deer running into the highway + one part very large tree + twenty parts too many of alcohol. Mix well, and there you have it. A high-speed crash into a tall oak that decimated their brand-new Buick Regal.

The entire front end had been compressed to the very back of the front seat. The Sommerses' bodies were crushed and impaled by the steering column, dashboard, and engine block. The pictures from the investigative report revealed snapped limbs, oozing entrails, and internal organs, and completely unrecognizable faces. The crash had been so intensely violent that one of Betty's eyes had popped out upon impact and was lodged in the tree. It provided the perfect snack for an opportunistic hawk that had just happened to survey the entire event as it had gracefully glided above the highway.

––––

A phone rang in a rather nondescript home in Brooklyn. "Hey, boss, it's Picasso's wife, she says it's urgent." "Yes, Blair honey, what can we do for you" came the boss's reply as he answered the phone. Blair, attempting to remain reserved said, "I'm very sorry to be bothering you. I know that I'm not supposed to call unless it's an emergency. But will you please tell my Joseph that my parents have been killed in a car accident and that I need him home as soon as possible?"

"Awww, hell honey, I'm so sorry to hear that. Yeah, we'll get him back to you right away. He's probably just about finished with his latest work anyway. If there's anything that we need to do just—" the boss was cut off by Blair's curt voice who said, "No, your assistance in this matter won't be necessary. I just need my husband home. Thank you."

———

"See? Now, *this* is what happens when you try to force helpless old ladies out of their apartments and put them out onto the streets. And for what? So you can put up yet another hideous condo? I mean, just ruining the beauty of the natural architecture of this neighborhood is bad enough. But to threaten the lives of the *elderly*? And their *children*? And . . . oh for fucks sakes . . . even their *pets*? C'mon man, you gotta find a better way to make a living." Joseph then began chuckling as he sliced open yet another three-inch wound in the panicked man's chest and placed a yellow game card into it.

The man was howling in pain as Joseph continued his diatribe. "Do you know what the boys in *Murder, Inc.* call me? Well, now, first off, that's not *really* their name. Only members get to know their *real* name. Hell, my wife doesn't even know. To know their *real* name is to either belong to the club or be dead. But I digress. Anyway, they call me Picasso. Wanna know why? Sure, you do. They call me Picasso because they think the way I complete these tasks is very artistic. And kinda like a Picasso painting, I tend to leave the bodies a bit . . . disorganized. So anytime a more creative message needs to be sent, they give me a call. Now, I don't *have* to take every call. I just gotta accept at least one job a year to stay in good standing. And you're my third. And I *really* wanted to take this one. I *really* wanted to make art out of you. I find you *inspirational*."

With that, another three-inch wound was slashed into the screaming man's inner thigh with another game card placed into it, this one depicting a train. "Heh, heh, heh," Joseph chuckled to himself as he watched the blood ooze out of the fresh wound, saturating the card, "Yeah, I wanted this one. I wanted to end the douchebag who has been threatening and terrorizing an entire neighborhood of fine working-class folks just so he could monopolize the housing in the area. So I thought that if that was your goal, to own every little piece of property so that you could become rich, well . . . I just thought I'd grant you that wish and give you *every piece* of property that you deserve."

With that, another slice of flesh as another game card was shoved into the skin under the wound.

"Well, you now have the complete set of purples and reds and yellows and those really expensive fuckin' blues. You've even got control of the utilities and railroads! Fuck, man, you're a fuckin' tycoon! Now all you need to do is start puttin' up some high-priced houses and hotels and you're golden!" Joseph then took a corkscrew and twisted it in various places over the man's body, creating half-inch holes before jamming small red and green plastic game pieces into the wounds.

The gagged man choked out cries for mercy. They went unheeded. Until there was a voice heard behind Joseph. "Hey, Picasso." "What the fuck, man? I told you fellas not to bother me while I'm workin'!" Joseph bellowed. "Yeah, sorry about that, but your wife called. She needs you home. Her parents have been killed in an accident."

"Awww fuck, all right," Joseph responded with contrition. "Oh, my poor, lovely Blair. And Patty. Jesus, what they must be going through. It's not unlike what the parents of that little boy went through a week ago." Joseph's attention returned to the bound naked man who was pouring blood out of gaping lacerations that had game cards and plastic pieces sticking out of them.

"That little boy that died in that elevator that you had rigged to crash. I saw the pictures of that sweet little boy's body. I saw the anguish on his parents' faces a few days later." Joseph wiped a tear from his eye before concluding, "And it was all because of *you* and your *fucking greed*. There's a sweet little boy who died an agonizing death because of you. So you wanna get rich, motherfucker? Well, here ya go!"

With that, Joseph forced a metal car and a metal thimble up the man's nostrils. He took a large wad of paper money and forced it into the man's pleading mouth and just held it there until the mouth stopped making any sound and the body ceased moving.

"Wow, Picasso," the lackey stated reverentially, "it really is a pleasure to watch you work. That was really somethin'." "Yeah, whatfuckinever," Joseph snarled, " just get me cleaned up and back to my Blair. And tell the boss that I'm on vacation for a bit, all right?"

———

"Goddammit, I knew his fuckin' drinking would lead to this someday," Patty lamented through her tears as the Sommers family left the gravesite where their parents' ashes had just been interned. Blair was holding Patty's hand as they made their way to their car with their younger brother following several feet behind in silence.

The Sommers family licked the wounds of their tragic, but not unpredictable loss and went back to their lives. Patty returned to work at her assisted living home where she found value in bringing joy to those who did not have many joyous days remaining while spending her evenings in the arms of some new pierced plaything.

Blair buttoned up her business suits each day and continued managing the accounting firm where she was employed. Despite her tightly bunned hair and conservative pantsuits, she would frequently be catcalled, whistled at or propositioned by her male subordinates. Blair would give them a cold smile and nod. About a week later, she would give them a pink slip, making sure that the picture of her brawny husband was seen by the emasculated man as he crept out of her office with his box of belongings, frequently containing a photo of his wife and children. New female arrivals at the accounting firm were made aware that any unwelcome advances by their male co-workers would be met with swift retribution by their manager. Every female in the firm was "cool with Blair" and the men who worked there soon found out that it was wise for them to be so as well.

Joseph continued with his thriving handyman business fixing things and helping others throughout the community. At times, a certain Det. Edmund Simmons would meet Joseph at their regular booth in the back of their regular bar and would slide a name over to Joseph that needed to be fixed. More often than not, the fix didn't need to be permanent. Just a little adjustment that needed to be made. And Joseph never turned Edmund down. Never once. And that included a certain police officer that had severely beaten a Black man while he was in custody several months earlier. It was found out that certain police officer had a juvenile penchant for illegally fishing with dynamite in a nearby pond. Because he was a "sportsman." And one week before Joseph's latest "trade show" in New York, there had been an unfortunate accident with the dynamite. To the naked eye, it was impossible to determine what pieces of shrapnel were from the wooden boat and which were human bones. And no Black residents of Madison were questioned following the mishap.

The sisters' younger brother returned to active duty in the army, this time stationed in Germany. Throughout his entire life, the army was the only place where he had been able to truly function. Having no real sense of self or convictions to speak of, he found it comforting to simply follow the orders of his superiors without having to give any thought as to why he was doing what he was doing. He was the perfect subservient soldier who never aspired for promotion and never caused any waves. He was dutiful. He was diligent. He also wasn't especially bright.

Following his rounds on guard duty at a munitions site, he had left open a large door of one of the buildings . . . again. This, plus other minor infractions led to his being asked to accept an honorable discharge. And the accidental dropping of a live grenade near a fueling station which caused him to sustain a traumatic brain injury didn't help matters either. He was discharged and returned home to Madison in 1983.

He lived with Blair and Joseph for about three months before he was able to find employment at Patty's assisted living home in the kitchen and move into his own small apartment. While living with his sister and brother-in-law, he had a certain amount of structure to guide him, although he found Patty's Friday night antics to be too out of control, so he usually retreated to his room shortly after her arrival. "All right, nice to see you *too*, freak!" Patty would yell up at him as he trudged up the Argento's staircase.

In search of any type of structure, he began listening to fringe right-wing radio programs and joined a radical evangelical church, both of which preached hatred over humanity, all in the name of their god or their assumed white male privilege . . . and also in the name of greenback sacraments to their religious and political overlords.

Patty, Blair, and Joseph attempted in vain to convey to him that his best interests were not being served by such mind- controlling propaganda, but those attempts were permanently extinguished in the summer of 1984. Blair was hosting a Sunday afternoon dinner with ham, scalloped potatoes, fresh green beans, homemade rolls, and cherry pie. Patty also contributed to the banquet. She brought a bag of potato chips and a small, half-eaten container of onion dip. And the obligatory twenty- something toy complete with brightly colored new wave hair and florescent leggings.

It was exceptionally warm, even for July. Joseph was pondering whether he had finally met his match with an appliance as the air conditioning unit refused to cooperate with the twisting of his tools through a constant barrage of obscenities. But with one final bang on the side of the unit and just as the younger brother was entering the home with a lanky, corpse-like woman, the cold air immediately began to circulate, dropping the temperature in the room twenty degrees seemingly instantaneously.

"Hello, it's so nice to meet you all," the copper-bunned woman expressed in an annoying, nasally, and condescending tone. Patty leaned into her sister's ear and said, "What the fuck . . . is *that*?" *That*, was, in fact, a female human being. Although only twenty-one at the time, she did not look a day under fifty. And it appeared to have been a really hard fifty. She was buttoned up from head to mid-calf in a dower flowered dress and wore no makeup or jewelry. A silver crucifix hung sadly from her neck as if it were asking to be put out of its misery of servitude.

Joseph came in from fixing the central air unit and accidentally brushed up against the woman that he may have mistaken for a bean pole. "Oh, hey, sorry there . . . what are . . . I mean . . . who are *you*?" This initial interaction would represent the high-water mark in the relationship between this woman and the Argentos.

Following a frigidly silent dinner, Patty was once again in the way in the kitchen as Blair was doing dishes and Joseph was performing a mock exorcism in the dining room. "Okay," Patty began, "I get that the little fucker needs to get laid. But how do you fuck *that*? I mean, that bitch is wound so tight that you'd need the fuckin' *jaws of life* to part those spindly legs! She's so fuckin' tight, I bet she's got a fuckin' *pearl* in that snatch!" Suddenly inspired, she bellowed, "Fuck! That would make a great song title! 'Hot Pearl Snatch!'" Little did Patty know how prophetic her exclamation would be as a song by that title would appear on an album by The Cramps just two years later.

Patty and Blair made every attempt they could to de-program their younger brother over the next year. Their efforts to wrestle him away from the toxic manipulation of his glacially bitter girlfriend, then fiancée, and finally wife in 1985 proved fruitless. "He's fuckin' gone!" Joseph announced in September 1987. "Let him go. He's made his lot with that one. And quite frankly, I'm telling you both that I will never step foot in the same room again with that fuckin' icy bitch! I am *done* with the holier-than-thou condescension and the freakish, insane conspiracy theories. Plus, her face could melt fuckin' paint off of a wall! I'm done, ladies. If you want to continue to try to save him from his self-made hell hole of domination, go for it. I'm out!"

His proclamation lasted all of one month. In October, an announcement was made that their younger brother had apparently obtained the jaws of life and that he had managed to pry open his frigid wife's legs. Equally surprising, especially to Patty, was that he was somehow able to achieve orgasm under the harshest of conditions. "It would be like trying to cum into a glacier in Siberia!" was Patty's exact expression. But most surprising to everyone was that a lifeform was actually able to be sustained under the tortuous conditions within this morally barren womb. It would be many years before anyone would realize the irony that the proclamation of this blessed event was made on October 31.

On the car ride home following the announcement which was made with all of the fanfare of a funeral dirge, Blair stated to her beloved husband, "This is simply not fair, Joseph. How is it that they can be so blessed while we . . . we . . ." Blair broke down into uncharacteristic tears as her loving husband's brawny arm reached around her slender shoulders and said softly, "It's going to be all right, dear. These fuckers don't know it yet, but this child is going to be ours. We're not going to let them destroy an innocent little baby and indoctrinate her into their fucked up and twisted land of hate. They have done us a favor, dear. They have given us a child. And it will be so or my name's not Joseph Angelo Argento. And that's my fuckin' name, so *that's* how it's going to be."

———

Where there is a will, there is a way. And there is *nothing* that can stop us once our most primitive instincts are engaged. And *his* had *most certainly* been engaged. By *her*. He saw his quarry, but she had not yet seen *him*. She was just innocently sitting there, completely unaware of what was about to be unleashed. He knew that he was too heavy to be able to get up to where she was sitting without assistance. He scanned the area and found exactly what was needed. There was a slight creak as his full weight was placed upon the wooden frame that would carry him to what it was that he had to have at this moment. He stopped. She had not noticed. She was so unaware, so innocent, so tantalizing. He crept up behind her with his head lowered so as not to cast any type of shadow which might tip her off as to his impending attack. Unbridled desire caused every muscle in his body to tense until he suddenly sprang upon her. She let out a blood-curdling shriek.

"Jeeezus, Hunky! You scared the shit out of me!" a shocked Maddy exclaimed. Erick and Blair let out hearty laughs as they witnessed this rotund ball of purring fur rolling around in complete rapture on his quarry's lap. "How the hell did you get up here?" Erick inquired as he scanned the room. "Oh, I left the bottom drawer of the nightstand open. He must have climbed up that." Through her laughter, Blair turned the page of the photo album. "Now, this is Joseph holding our Maddy on the day of her birth."

Chapter 29

The Baby Screams

Madeline Ruth Sommers entered the world on May 13, 1988. Even as a newborn, her smile was infectious. But not as infectious as when she would give an unknowing recipient a flash of her emerald green eyes. Then to seal the victory over her adversaries' emotions, the batting of her sandy-red eyelashes leaving her worthy combatant immobilized by her charms and completely at the mercy of the child's whims.

As he held this delicate bundle in his massive arms, Joseph Argento had fallen in love for the second and final time in his life. And it was through the eyes of yet another Sommers girl that would penetrate his loving heart, leaving him helpless to her every whim. He began softly singing the song that had been playing on the radio as he and his wife had screeched into the hospital parking lot. As his soothing voice was recreating the words of The Foundation's "Build Me Up Buttercup," his loving wife Blair looked on with uncharacteristic tears welling in her eyes. Also looking on with a defeated expression was the child's father.

Maddy lay there in his arms staring up at him, contently cooing. She was wrapped in a blue baby blanket that her uncle had brought for her. The blanket provided warmth. It provided comfort. And it provided unconditional love. The child continued staring, frequently batting her tiny copper eyelashes over her electric green eyes and this mountain of a man stared back at her, beaming with joy. It seemed to him that at one point, Maddy had flashed her uncle a slightly mischievous grin as if to say, "Fuck her." In response, her uncle mirrored her expression and sentiment. It was just the two of them silently communicating with one another. At this moment, he was no longer Joseph Argento, the neighborhood fixer nor was he the brutal hit man known in the right circles as "Picasso." At this moment, he had been transformed into the greatest and most important role of his life. He became Uncle Joe.

Uncle Joe walked over to his loving wife and lay the content child into her awaiting arms. As the couple looked down upon this precious gift, they gave each other a knowing glance. All of the arrangements had been made. Their new home somewhere on the East Coast had been secured. The U-Haul was packed. And their papers for their new identities, complete with a birth certificate were secured. All that was left to do was a minor payoff for hospital security and the Argentos would whisk their new child away into the night and away from her parents' destructive forces in Madison. And no one would see the Argentos again. Not even Patty.

The child's father was slumped in the pale green vinyl hospital chair as he watched this loving scene between the Argentos and his daughter. He had a myriad of thoughts going through his addled mind. He knew instinctively that this was the critical moment if he were to be able to raise his daughter. He had seen the U-Haul parked behind the Argentos' home. He saw the look on his sister's and brother-in-law's faces as they cuddled with his daughter. He knew the impossibility of changing his sister's mind once she had come to a decision, and he knew that Joseph was just as strong-willed as she. He also knew, deep down inside that, he did not have the strength to confront this unified force once they had started the wheels of their plot into motion. He did not know exactly what their plot was. But somewhere in his soul, he *knew*.

He then pondered how this episode with his daughter was so much different than the scene between Maddy and her own mother a few minutes earlier. Upon her vulnerable daughter being placed into her chilled and bony arms, the mother looked down at the grimacing newborn and said in her cold, nasally voice, "Yes, I suppose she will do. Come child and eat now."

Upon placing her engorged breast in the baby's mouth, Maddy let out a horrific and chilling scream. It was as though the child instinctively knew that the creature that was holding her was incapable of providing her with any form of sustenance whether it be nutritional or emotional. The child continued screaming until the impatient mother said flatly, "Fine, then. Take it away and give it formula. It must learn to respect me before it feeds upon my God-given milk."

The child's screams continued as her father picked her up, took her into another room with her awaiting family, and tried to comfort her in his own awkward way. He caressed her. He sang to her. And she would not respond. Finally, from a darkened corner of the room, a hulking figure stood up and said, "Give me that fuckin' kid." The infant was immediately enveloped in the warmth of her blue blanket and the warmth of a face wearing a smile and kind eyes. And the infant's emerald eyes stopped crying.

The father now knew three things. That his sisters and brother-in-law would give his daughter the unconditional love and warmth that she required as a counterbalance to her frigid mother, that the Argentos would take his child away unless they were guaranteed that opportunity, and that he lacked the strength to stand up to his wife or the Argentos once their clash of wills came to fruition. So he felt it best to act now when he had the chance and some semblance of leverage over the soon- to-be warring parties.

"I would like to suggest something," the father began meekly. "Yes?" came Blair's inviting response. "Yes," the father continued, "I understand that you don't agree with the beliefs that my wife and I hold. I can also see in your eyes the love that you have for our child. And Madeline *is* our child. And we shall raise her as we see fit. But I believe that Madeline would also benefit from the love of her extended family. So I would like to propose that Madeline stay with you on the weekends, so that she may have a balance in her life between your unconditional love and her mother's . . . efforts."

It was at this moment that Blair knew that her younger brother understood the environment that he and his frigid wife would provide to this child. She also knew that he was at least suspicious of what she and her husband were plotting, greatly intensifying the risk. And not truly wanting to leave Madison to begin a whole new life while constantly looking over her shoulder, she looked at her beloved Joseph and gave him a nod. "That bitch wife of yours has to agree" came Joe's surly reply. "Of course," the encouraged father replied, "I will go and explain the . . . situation to her. I'm sure it will be fine. She may even welcome the break for a day or two each week. I'll go to her now."

What was said between the father and the mother on that fateful afternoon was never discussed. It was surmised by the Argentos that the father had impressed upon the mother the benefits of having some free time on the weekend so that they could be fully enveloped in their church's activities without the burden of having to tend to their child. It was also surmised that her weekends with the Argentos could be used as a teaching tool about the folly of the world's sinners, thereby further indoctrinating their Madeline into their worldview. And it was definitely surmised that the father impressed upon his wife just how dangerous his sister and brother-in-law could be and that they would need to relinquish some control over Madeline in order to retain their *ultimate* control over her.

The father re-entered the room ten minutes later. "Yes, we have an agreement, with some . . . conditions." Hands were shaken as the terms were agreed upon. Maddy would stay with Blair and Joseph from Friday evening to Saturday evening. The parents, meaning the mother, would have full control over what her daughter consumed including her diet, television, movies, music, and books. As the father left the room, he looked sheepishly at Joseph and said, "You can unpack your U-Haul now."

"Holy fuck, Mads!" Patty exclaimed to her newborn niece that she was holding, "We're gonna fuckin' *party*!" She then began dancing around the room with the smiling infant as she sang "Stay Up Late" by The Talking Heads. "What's this about a U-Haul anyway," Patty asked her sister. "Oh, it's nothing," Blair replied. "I think perhaps he is a bit confused about something. You know how he can be. We're just . . . cleaning some things out of the house." "Okay, whatever," an uninterested Patty replied as she stared into Maddy's gleeful eyes and began singing once again, her skull earring dangling just inches from the innocent face.

And party, they did. Friday nights were filled with junk food, loud rock music, dancing, sweating, and laughter. Saturdays were made up of hangovers. Alcohol hangovers for Patty and her latest guest. Sugar hangovers for Maddy. It was also made up of another obligatory viewing of *Cinderella*. Almost every weekend was chronicled through photographs. Where there was a camera lens, there was the beaming face of an auburn- haired Maddy, whether she was the intended subject of the picture or not. It made it nearly impossible for Patty to capture images of her latest giggling conquest. "Mads, would you get the fuck out of the way?" Patty would bellow at her tittering niece. "I'm trying to take a picture of this hot chick!" Starting around the age of five, Maddy's standard response was, "What for? *I'm* the one that's fuckin' adorable!" immediately followed by Maddy crossing her eyes and smiling while sticking her tongue out from the right side of her mouth. This would initiate loud guffawing by Uncle Joe and a stern reprimand from Aunt Blair. Followed by uncontrollable guffawing by . . . Aunt Blair. On Saturday evenings, darkness would encase the Argento home. The temperature would drop inside their home as they once again watched their beloved niece look back at them pleadingly as she was forced to hold the bony hand of her mother and was escorted out of her nurturing womb and back into the cavernous darkness that was her life with her parents. Every Saturday night, Patty would exclaim, "Fuck this. I can't fuckin' take this every week. I'm goin' out." And every Saturday night, Joseph and Blair would hold each other on the couch weeping and silently begin counting down the hours until the next Friday evening would arrive, and their world would be made whole once again.

As Maddy entered her teenage years and wild-eyed stories about a vengeful sprite terrorizing the bullies in her school would abound, Uncle Joe would often intercept the reports, with the help of his best friend Edmund, from the school officials so that her parents would remain unaware of the "obviously bullshit allegations against my niece! Look at this face!" Uncle Joe would yell at the vice principle with his bright red face contorted in anger. Maddy would sit there and coyly look up with her head slightly cocked while batting her copper lashes over her glimmering green eyes and slightly puckering her lips. "Would this face be capable of such things? It's preposterous!

Besides, I heard that the little bastard who got shit thrown into his locker deserved it. *He's* the real problem here! Why aren't you going after the fuckin' prick little bullies in this school? Why are you harassing innocent girls? And if you think you've got something on her, call the cops! If they find some *real* proof, then I'll listen to you. But until then, this is all a bunch of bullshit! C'mon, Buttacup, let's get the fuck out of here and get some ice cream!"

The pair would silently march out of the school's administration office and march down the sanitized hallways with their indignant heads held high. Upon reaching the car, they would begin giggling. "Okay," Uncle Joe would inquire, "what the fuck did you do *this* time?"

"Well," Maddy would chime in response, "see, this fuckin' douchebag has been stealing the smaller kids' lunch money, so I figured he must be really hungry. So I took a bunch of rotten leftover food from the dumpster behind the diner and stuffed it into his locker. Then, I left a note that said, *here's your all-you- can-eat buffet, motherfucker*! Pretty good, huh?"

Uncle Joe burst out laughing and exclaimed through his joyful tears, "Oh . . . my . . . fucking . . . God! All-you-can-eat buffet! Oh, that's fuckin' gold, Buttacup! Fuckin' gold!"

And when a certain track star's water was tampered with causing him to slip in his uncontrolled diarrhea, the police investigation, headed up by Det. Edmund Simmons, was perfunctory at best. "Well, Joseph, Blair, Maddy, there were no witnesses. No fingerprints. And I *personally* saw *you* Maddy standing at the fence line around the track. So I think these accusations are baseless. We'll probably never figure it out. Have a nice evening all."

A visibly shaken Maddy let out a deep sigh of relief as she watched Blair walk Detective Simmons out of the room and say something to one another. "Thank you once again, Edmund. We'll try to keep her out of trouble."

"Why?" came the surprising response. "This kid's a rapist prick. If I could *I'd* fuck them up or have Joseph do it. But they're minors, so I guess it's for the best that we have another minor on our team. Just make sure she's careful. There's only so much interference that I can run and if there's ever any *real* evidence against her, well . . . my hands are gonna be tied."

"All right, Edmund," Blair responded. "But never on *that* team, do you understand? *Never* on the *Brooklyn* team. Promise me that." "Of course, Blair dear. I promise. Never on the Brooklyn team" came Edmund's sincere reply.

———

As the saying goes, it's always darkest before dawn. This was true when a fifteen-year-old Maddy had been served up by her mother and impotent father to their pedophile cult leader, in order to cure her of her "sinful ways." She knew that if she succumbed to the will of her parents that the serpent posing as a prophet would sexually assault her . . . repeatedly. The episode led her to run away to her aunt and uncle's house and fully disclose all of the abuse, both physical and mental, that she had endured at the hands of her mother and the cowardice of her father which, in turn, led to the ultimate showdown between Maddy's parents and the Argentos.

A truce, once again initiated by Maddy's father, had been struck and the foundation of the remainder of Maddy's formative years was complete. She would live with the Argentos Friday evening through Monday morning. She would live at her parents' home on the other days. She would not have to ever go to her parents' church again but would have to endure one-hour indoctrination sessions with her mother each evening. It was a deal that would save true bloodshed. It was a deal that would save Maddy's spirit.

On the following Monday morning, Blair and Joseph watched as their Maddy triumphantly strode out of their home on her way to school, her copper locks bouncing to the cadence of her invigorated steps. They took their seats at their kitchen table, sipped their coffee, and read their respective sections of the newspaper.

"You understand, Joseph," Blair stated calmly, "that so- called preacher needs to have a visitor." Without looking up from his paper, Joseph stated flatly, "Understood, dear. Is there anything that you would like me to bring home for dinner tonight?" "Perhaps not for tonight, dear. But when the time is right, I want to see a few of that bastard's teeth" came Blair's steely answer. "Consider it done, dear," Joseph replied. "Oh, for fuck's sake! Just look at this score! When are the Brewers gonna get *rid* of that bum?"

———

It is so fucking typical, Joseph thought to himself as he lay underneath a brand new 2003 Porsche in the parking lot behind a local adult shop. *Almost all of these fuckers are hypocrites. They're so fucking holier than thou and sitting in judgment on the rest of us while they're bilking their followers out of their life savings and trying to rape their children. They are the absolute lowest form of douchebag there is. To twist people's faith and trust for your own greed and sexual pleasure. If there is a hell, then all of these cult motherfuckers will surely be there. And if there's not . . . well . . . maybe that's what God put* me *here for. It would be too easy to kill this motherfucker. He needs to suffer more than that.*

A pair of patent leather shoes appeared on the pavement at the driver's side door. Joseph heard the door unlock, then open. Before the cult leader could close the door, Joseph had rolled from underneath the vehicle, grabbed the open door with his left hand, and smashed the skull of the preacher with his homemade nightstick with his right. He pulled the pedophile cultist out of the car and shoved him behind the rusted dumpsters. His enraged face was covered with a stocking cap, except for his mouth. The cult rapist watched in horror through his mental shock as a maniacal smile crossed his assailant's face while putting on a brown-stained set of brass knuckles. His screams were muffled by the pounding of a hardened, brass-covered fist on his face and mouth over and over again.

Joseph had learned over the years just how badly you could beat someone without causing them to go unconscious while still inflicting as much pain as possible. Blood and teeth were flying through the air as the merciless attack continued. Deep facial lacerations were gashed onto the cult rapist's face over and over until his face was completely covered in streaming blood and was completely tenderized as if it were ready to be put on the grill.

Then, one by one, his fingers were meticulously snapped in not one, not two, but three separate areas. Each of these fingers that had lasciviously kneaded his niece's shoulders looked like the letter "Z" before the assault was complete. Then, using his own knee and pulling with all of his massive strength, Joseph cracked the pseudo-messiah's arms in half causing the bones to protrude through the skin. And finally, the man's eyes were beaten over and over until they were completely swelled up in a macabre dark purple. One last kick was delivered, shattering his jaw, and finally rendering him unconscious. "*Now*, you've got something to pray about, motherfucker," Joseph growled at the contorted body laying beneath his feet.

The glowing ember of a lit cigarette emerged from the dark bushes across the parking lot. "You about done here?" the observing Edmund inquired. "Yeah, I'm done with this douchebag. For now, at least" came Joseph's reply. "All right," Edmund answered. "I'll follow you down to the abandoned lot and you can work off the rest of your anger on his car. But I have to say, my old friend, that it's just a shame that it had to come to this. That is one fine automobile." "Yeah, it's a shame I have to fuck *it* up too," Joseph countered as he picked up four of the bloody teeth from the cracked pavement. In his entire time with his beloved Blair, Joseph Argento never once forgot to bring home *anything* that she had requested for dinner.

———

Monday, January 9, 2006, was one of the saddest days of Joseph Argento's life. Although he was exceedingly proud of his beloved niece for having graduated early and enrolled in a college in Brooklyn, he couldn't help but lament the fact that his weekends would never be the same without her bright face, boundless spirit, and lame attempts at jokes. *My kinda town*, Joseph thought to himself, *Jesus, Buttacup, you are so bad at jokes, heh, heh, heh. That's one of the things that makes you so precious to me. God, how am I gonna get through the week without your smile?* He then shook his head vigorously and said aloud, "What the fuck are you doing? *Guys* don't get empty nest syndrome! Quit bein' a pussy and let's get to work."

He wiped one final tear from his eye as he approached his red Cruiser in the college dorm parking lot. He opened the trunk, unzipped a black duffle bag, and quickly scanned its contents. *Yep, I got everything. I may as well get this over with. I need to get back home to my Blair.*

———

"Pleeeease! Pleeeease! Stop! I—I—I'll t—tell you anything!" screamed the man who had a hook in his spine in the middle of a freezing meat locker. "I don't need you to tell me anything," Joseph's voice emerged in a dark snarl. "We already know everything. Did you really think that you could double-cross *Murder, Inc.*? Did you not understand the pact you made when you joined? Did you not understand what we would do to someone who broke his oath of office? What we would do to someone who we placed our trust in only to have you betray that trust, you traitorous *fuck*?"

Following that statement, Picasso picked up a rusty chainsaw and pulled the cord to initiate its menacing roar. "I know this isn't very original, but I need to make this quick. I need to get back home to my wife." The chainsaw effortlessly ripped its way through the skin, tendon, muscle, and bone of the man's knee. The moment the tattered appendage hit the floor, Picasso picked up a small shovel that had been waiting in a metal tub of white-hot embers. He placed the shovel onto the wound, immediately cauterizing it to stop the blood flow.

The man's anguished screams echoed off the metal walls as Joseph said coldly, "But not *too* fast. See, you really fucked up when you made this personal. To double-cross us is one thing. But to bring my niece into it is quite another. Did you motherfuckers not learn your lesson when you murdered my parents? You really thought that you could try to send another message? Against *us*? Against *me*? Against *her*?" The chainsaw roared back to life, this time severing the man's left arm three- quarters through. Picasso just left it dangling there as the infernal heat of the shovel immediately sealed the wound.

The screams continued. "Fuck, man, you sound great! This sounds like the opening melody of . . . what is that song again? Oh, yeah." Joseph then began harmonizing with the man's morbid howls with the words to "All I

Have To Do Is Dream," by The Everly Brothers. "Yeah, your father is probably rolling over in his grave right now. One of the originals and you took his place as a legacy after his passing. I guess that organization thought his being gone would be a good time to try to get to us once again. They thought wrong!"

The chainsaw's rusted teeth chewed through the man's other knee causing it to fall to the floor. As Picasso was applying the shovel, he continued in his sinister monotone. "So you fuckers thought you could get to us by threatening my beloved niece? You found out she was coming here, and you told them. And they were going to send you to rough her up, right? You were going to beat and torture my beloved niece. I saw the plans. You were planning on leaving permanent scars upon her sweet little face, weren't you? And for what? Greed on your part? Power for them? Well, let's just show everybody once and for all where the real power lies. *We* are the real power! All of the motherfuckers behind this plot have been taken care of! And for you, *I* am the real power! And right now, *I* am going to use it all on your *doomed ass!*"

The chainsaw ripped through the man's tender abdomen. He let out a heinous roar as he felt his entrails plummet out of his body cavity and land on the cold cement with a sloshy thud. As the man was taking his last breaths, Picasso nailed a note to the man's forehead. It simply read, *LEAVE HER ALONE.* The message had been sent and received. And an unsuspecting Maddy Sommers was now free to enjoy her life in New York without fear from the organized criminal element in her newly adopted home.

As Blair and Joseph were sitting on the couch, trying in vain to become absorbed in a situation comedy, Joseph bellowed, "Oh, fuck, Blair! I miss her so fucking much!" "I know dear," Blair's attempt at a soothing voice said. "But she will be all right. You have seen to that. And we will see her every month. If she isn't able to come here, then we will go there, as will Patty. It is time for her to fly, Joseph. She is our little bird who is all grown up now. She must make her *own* choices and make her *own* mistakes. And if she makes *too* big of a mistake, well . . . that's why we belong to *them.* Now, I would like to suggest that we make this a glass-is-half-full situation." She looked seductively at her husband, her hazel eyes glistening within the frame of her jet-black hair that cascaded down her delicate shoulders, resting just above her breasts. "Hey, Mr. Argento. The kids are all gone. We have the house to ourselves. Let's get drunk and nekkid."

They fell into each other's arms with combined tears and laughter as Joseph thought to himself, *I am the luckiest fucker to have ever lived.*

———

"Holy fuck!" Maddy exclaimed as Erick was thinking *What have I gotten myself into.* "Are you telling me that this hit man syndicate thing has been, like, watching over me and shit?" "Well, not exactly" came Blair's soft reply. "Let's just say that they are the reason that I have been able to keep track of all of your . . . exploits over the years. But that life is not for you, Maddy. You must promise me. I am not afraid of *them*, but I *am* afraid of what they will bring into your world. You must prom—"

Blair was interrupted by the ring of Maddy's phone. "Hey, what's up, Kristy? Say what again? Are you fuckin' *serious*? Fuck, man, okay thanks for letting me know, I'll see you tomorrow." "What's going on?" Erick inquired. "Our doctor at the women's health center," Maddy began, her face becoming more enflamed with each passing word, "has been murdered. Some freak right- wing fuck hid in her car and killed her with piano wire. He left a note that said "Pro Life." We'll see how fuckin' pro-life he is when he's begging me to kill him. I am going to fuck him up, Erick! Wanna play?" She looked long-ingly into his shining brown eyes. As the intensity of his eyes grew, she had her answer. Erick did indeed want to play.

As Blair was walking home from her niece's brownstone, she placed a call. "Yes, hello, this is Blair. I need you to find some information for my niece. No, not that. Just a name and an address will suffice. She will take it from there."

CHAPTER 30

DIG A HOLE

Maddy was reluctantly pushed upon the multicolored lighted stage by her cackling friends on this frigid night of February 13. "Goddamn, you bitches!" Maddy was yelling as her slight frame was tugged by Kristy and pushed from behind by Sam and Jules. "I *knew* you would pull some shit like this! Fine! Let's just get this shit over with. Bring out Schlongzilla or whatever the fuck he's called!" It was her bachelorette's party the night before her wedding and her best friends, along with Blair, Patty, Amanda, Abana, Sean, Monica, and Rosetta were in attendance as a visibly annoyed Maddy was placed on a chair in the center of the stage at the male exotic dance club. She sat there with her gaudy yellow sash draped over her white party dress and with her arms defiantly folded as the MC bellowed, "All right, little lady, let's see if you still want to get married after *this*!"

And then it began. The perfect male physical specimen entered the stage, dressed in a tear-away black glittered tuxedo and gyrating to Billy Idol's "White Wedding" (of course). He stripped away each layer of fabric until all that was visible were his oiled-down glistening muscles and a rather large protrusion from his black tuxedo speedo which was being flung back and forth just inches from Maddy's irritated face. Everyone sitting at Maddy's table held the same look of astonished desire as they drooled down the straws of their respective drinks except for Patty who was too busy trying to look up the skirt of a fifty- something brunette sitting across from her.

Following the performance, Maddy exclaimed angrily, "Great! Nice job! You're very uh . . . talented. Can I get the fuck out of here now?" "C'mon Mads, get a little strange!" a slightly intoxicated Patty yelled out to the roar of laughter from the entire crowd, drawing a suggestive glance from the fifty-something brunette. The MC playfully put his arm around Maddy's tense shoulders and said, "Okay, now. After seeing what you're gonna be missing for the rest of your life, are you *sure* you wanna get married tomorrow?"

Maddy plucked the microphone from the man's hand while brushing his arm off of her shoulder and said sternly, "Why yes, Mr. MC, I am because I have found my prince. I have found someone who cares about *me* and who *I am*. I have found someone that not only doesn't *judge* me but who *supports* me and would do *anything* in his power to *protect* me. And *I* would do the same for *him*. Do you know what that sweet man is doing tonight? While I'm out with these *stupid bitches* looking at fuckin' *man meat*, he's helping my friend's husband babysit their kids. He's watching fucking Nickelodeon and making macaroni and cheese and chicken nuggets for seven-year-old twin boys and a four-year-old little girl. Just so that I can go out and have a good time, which I'm *not* fuckin' having right now. So I don't care how many inches Mr. '70s porn mustache has over there. There is *no* size dick that can take the place of a man who truly *cares* for you and *respects* you. Plus, he's *pretty fuckin' good* with his tongue, so there's that!"

Maddy stormed off of the stage to uproarious applause and laughter. As her size six strapped pumps hit the landing, a tall man handed her a piece of paper and turned and left before Maddy could finish saying, "Hey, dude . . . not interested in a porn shoot!"

She read the typed letters on the blue piece of notebook paper. It had the name of the murdered health clinic doctor and the date of her murder. And it had a man's name and an address. Her face immediately became as engorged with blood as the previous dancer's penis had been. She rushed back to her seat and grabbed her burner cell phone from her purse and dashed off. As she was making a hasty retreat, she turned back to her guffawing friends and said, "Yeah, real fuckin', funny bitches, gotta make a call. I'll be right back."

Erick answered his burner phone which he referred to as the "Chad line." "Hey, wassupbuttacup?" "Hey, you, listen, I was just coming off of the stage where a male stripper was dancing for me and—" Erick cut her off by saying, "Was he well hung?" "Yeah, he was hung like a fuckin' horse, but that isn't the point," an impatient Maddy replied. "As I was coming off of the stage, this guy handed me a piece of paper, and—" She was interrupted again by Erick as he said, "Does he want you for a porn shoot or something else?" "No, would you just fuckin' listen?" An increasingly annoyed Maddy yelled-whispered, "The paper has the name and address of the guy. You know . . . *the guy.* And I want to take care of it tonight. You in?"

"Yeah, I suppose, but Maddy," a hesitant Erick replied, "this means that there is at least one person out there who knows we're looking for this guy. So if we take care of it and leave the body, then this person is going to know it's us. But, if there *isn't* a body, it may or may not be murder. So if we do this, we need to make sure the body is gone, and the scene is clear. And then, we need to figure out who this guy is that gave you the note. I'm assuming he's a friend, but we need to find out."

"Yeah, you got a good point," Maddy conceded as her wheels began spinning, "but fuck, man, we don't have *time* to find a place for him." "Don't worry about it," Erick said reassuringly. "I already *have* a place we can put him." "What the fuck are you talking about?" Maddy exclaimed while wondering what her future husband had been up to. "Don't worry about it," Erick countered. "Trust me. I'll explain later. I'll tell you what. The kids are asleep over here, so I'm gonna say my goodbyes to Jason and head over to the address and scope it out then head home. You tell Blair that you aren't feeling well and need to go back to her apartment, since y'know, we're not supposed to see each other after midnight or some shit like that. But come here instead. I'll be back by then, and we'll make our strategy. Cool?" "Yeah, all right," Maddy agreed. "Fuck man, you're getting kinda good at this." "You don't know how many of these I've planned in my mind before I met you" came Erick's alarmingly cool reply.

———

As the pair were in their respective rooms taking inventory of the contents of their black duffels and dressing for the occasion while listening to their individual choices of preparation music, Maddy exclaimed, "Hey! So we can just use the dude's car and dump it then?" She had to yell over the volume of her latest song to get her jazzed up for the evening's events. As she had graduated from harmful pranks in college to actual murders, she had changed her preparation song from Judas Priest to The Cramps' version of "The Crusher."

"Yeah!" came Erick's reply. "Fuck! I can't hear you! I'll come in!" Maddy yelled as she entered their bedroom and saw Erick putting on his hair net and black ball cap. "And just *what the fuck* are you listening to?" an exasperated Maddy exclaimed. "Sailing" by Christopher Cross, came Erick's blunt reply. "Why the *fuck* are you listening to that *now*?" came Maddy's retort. "It calms my nerves," Erick replied flatly. "Okay, see," Maddy began in a lecturing motherly tone, "you're supposed to listen to something to get you amped the *fuck up*! We're about to *off* a guy! You don't *want* to be relaxed!"

"Listen," Erick countered, "you prep for a murder your way, and I'll prep in my way. And I certainly do not need a lecture from you about music. I think I've got the bases covered. Or have you *not* seen our party room?" "Fine, fuck it. Listen to whatever you want. But you just need to know mister that you're *doing it wrong*!" Maddy stated as she stormed out of the room to complete her transformation from a pre-wedding party girl to a vicious killer.

It was almost too easy. A side living room window of the run-down cottage-style home had a small piece of glass out of it, creating the perfect entry point. He lived alone. His heavy snoring could be heard from the bedroom. They looked around the living room and saw radical paraphernalia and literature strewn about detailing everything from anti-abortion rhetoric, to how to stage a coup to bomb-making. There were guns and ammunition lying around everywhere, their metal frames glistening as the chilled moonlight came in from the opened window. And there was a large map of the New York metropolitan area with crosshairs over pictures of medical personnel who worked at women's healthcare clinics.

"This motherfucker was just getting started," Maddy whispered through her black mask to a nodding Erick. A quick "thunk!" of Uncle Joe's wooden nightstick and the man was completely out. He was duct taped by the wrists and ankles and gagged. They strained to carry the nearly 250-pound man to the open trunk of his car, tossing him haphazardly into the rusting mid-90s sedan like a discarded garbage bag from a cat box.

They got in the car and Erick started it. "Where the fuck are we going?" Maddy inquired. "Well, I hope this doesn't upset you, but last August, I got to thinking about your ex. I got to thinking about how he is a textbook sadistic narcissist, not unlike many of our glorious nation's so-called conservative politicians and pundits, mind you," Erick concluded with a sarcastic and disgusted sneer.

"And I got to thinking about the qualities that all of these assholes have. How they *never* admit defeat and *never* let go of grudges. And I just thought that once our engagement was announced that that douchebag might rear his ugly head again and try to hurt you. And if he did, then he just invited *me* to the fuckin' dance, and that I was going to be prepared for him. I didn't want to tell you about this because you might be a natural suspect, and I wanted you to be able to honestly answer questions should they come up."

"So starting last August, every Wednesday night, after I left Pastor Tim's house and for about two months, I took back streets and roads that didn't have cameras about eighteen miles outside of the city. I found a densely wooded area and I dug a hole. It's six feet deep and about four feet in diameter. I then hammered stones around the wall to keep it from collapsing. I covered the hole with several really large rocks and covered the dirt pile with shrubbery. Not unlike the shrubbery from *Monty Python's Holy Grail*, heh, heh, heh." This last line caused Maddy's look of shock to transform into one of reserved bemusement. *Yeah, that was kinda funny*, she thought to herself without giving her love the satisfaction he so craved.

"I then hid the shovel and a pickaxe in the dense woods. And I've been waiting to use it ever since. Just in case." "Okay," Maddy began reservedly. "First, I appreciate your enthusiasm and how you're trying to look out for me. I truly do. But a couple of points here. Numero uno, I don't think we have to worry about the douchebag. I haven't personally heard from him since the night I kicked the shit out of him. And numero- two-o, we're a team, all right. I promised you that I wouldn't do anything to anyone without your knowledge and I expect the same amount of professional courtesy from you. So long story short, you don't make a move against *him* or *anyone else* without my green lighting it, okay?"

"Yeah, you're right. I'm sorry. I won't hide anything from you again," Erick sincerely replied. Little did he know that only a few short months later, he would break this promise and hide something else from his wife. Right under her nose. In their basement.

They pulled into the wooded area. While conducting a very poor John Cleese imitation, Erick removed the shrubbery from the piles of dirt and the rocks revealing a perfectly preserved hole as Maddy opened the trunk of the car and began cutting off the clothes of the still unconscious domestic terrorist. She then threw the clothes into the bottom of the hole. They audibly grunted as they lifted the naked man from the trunk and rolled him into his dank and frigid fate. With a faint "thud," the man's crumpled body lay feet first at the bottom of the hole with the top of his head about three feet from the ground.

As the limp body plopped into the hole, Maddy said sternly as she poured water onto the frigid man at the bottom of the dark pit, "Don't even *think* about quoting Bill Murray from *Caddyshack* right now." Erick took the warning seriously and immediately closed his mouth.

The man awoke with a start and immediately began violently shivering. "Cold night, huh?" Maddy inquired flatly. "Not as cold as your heart, motherfucker. You like to kill innocent doctors, do you? You like to kill them because you're so fucking *pro-life*, right? Because you want to impose *your* made-up beliefs upon someone else. Because *you* think that women are so worthless that the government should have control over their fucking bodies, *right*? *You* are the king of morality. *You* know all that there is. *You* don't give a *fuck* about whether the woman will be re-traumatized because she was raped by a stranger or by daddy. *You* don't give a *fuck* if the woman might die during childbirth. *You* don't give a *fuck* if the woman doesn't have the resources to take care of a child. In fact, *you* want to *prevent* that woman from having any resources once the child is born! Shame her into having the kid then shame her again when she can't feed it! Double holier than thou points for you, right, motherfucker? It's all *her* fault for being a fucking whore, right? And the guy who jizzed in her gets off literally and figuratively, right? He bears *no* responsibility because he's *a man,* and he should be able to fuck anything that moves and then call her a *slut* as he's wiping his cum covered dick on her curtains."

"And if someone doesn't agree with you then you get to act as judge, jury, *and* executioner. All based upon your made-up bullshit interpretations from your made-up bullshit old man in the sky. Well, buddy. I've got good news for you. We're kindred spirits. See, I *also* believe in executing people that don't agree with *me*. And I just don't agree with murdering innocent people who are simply trying to provide needed health care. So what I'm saying is, you're fucked. And not in the enjoyable way, either. So enjoy your womb without a view, motherfucker."

With a nod of her head, a chuckling Erick began shoveling dirt onto the hysterical and freezing man. His screams became muted as the dirt reached his mouth. There was very little movement once the dirt was at the top of his head. And there was no movement at all as the large rocks were once again placed over the newly minted grave. As Erick was completing his work, with a proud Maddy observing and her hands placed on her hips, he said, "Nice speech and a pretty good joke." "Thanks, baby," Maddy replied with a grin, "we'd better hurry. We're getting married in like twelve hours!"

They thoroughly cleaned off all of the dirt from the shovel and pickaxe and placed them in the still-running and warm car. They removed their soiled clothes and placed them in the garbage bags from outside of the vehicle, all the while exclaiming in unison, "Fuck, it's cold! Fuck, it's cold! Fuck, it's cold!" They put on fresh gloves and hair nets before entering the car and putting on fresh shoes and clothing. The duffle bags, which now also contained heavy stones, were placed into two large, clean, garbage bags and placed in the back seat. And all the while, Erick patiently waited.

He patiently waited on the drive back to the city. He patiently waited as they abandoned the car in a secluded area along the Hudson and threw their bags and tools into the violently churning water, watching as their maniacal deed sunk out of view and out of consciousness. He patiently waited as they began the long trek to their respective subway stations, one which would lead Maddy back to her former apartment now being sublet by Blair and Patty, and the other to take Erick to the home that he would share with his wife for the remainder of his days.

Finally, he simply couldn't wait anymore. "Maddy, I've waited for like *two hours* to make a joke and I think I've been quite patient, and I have one. So can I *pleeeaaase* make my joke?" "Yes, you may," Maddy allowed haughtily. "Okay, this is an original. How does the wife of the radical preacher get him to fuck her?" "Uh, I dunno" came Maddy's intrigued reply. "She dresses up like the Bible because that's the only thing he'll bang!"

Maddy let out a roar of laughter as she collapsed into Erick's inviting arms and said, "Fuck man, I fuckin' love you. I can't wait to become your wife." "Well," Erick stated softly as he gazed into his lover's inviting green eyes, "You won't have to wait much longer." As he watched her short baggy frame fade into the distance, he yelled out to her, "Hey! Are you gonna dream about that stripper's massive dick tonight?" Maddy turned around and flashed him a beaming smile. "Fuck yeah, I am! That muthafucka could stretch this little bitch *out*!"

CHAPTER 31

THE KILLING MOON

On the morning of her wedding day, Maddy watched *Cinderella* again . . . for the final time. She ejected the well- worn DVD and placed it gently into its protective case. As she looked at the cover graphics, a single tear of joy fell. The tear rolled down the plastic cover as it was thoughtfully placed on her bedroom shelf between her two prized photo albums and her photo with Erick with Southern Culture on the Skids that had been taken on their first date. All of these items would be taken back to her new home after the wedding, but she wanted them here with her on the most important day of her life. A smile of combined joy and relief swept over her face as she heard the boisterous arrival of her friends in the living room while gazing at the dirt under her fingernails from the previous night's escapades.

"Mads!" came Patty's demanding voice. "Get your fuckin' ass up and out here! We got shit to do!" "Hey, everybody," Maddy stated as she entered the living room and beamed at the faces of Sam, Jules, Kristy, Kristy's daughter, Alexa, and her twin sons Adam and Aaron. "So . . . anyone wanna help me get hitched?"

There was a flurry of activity over the course of the next two hours. Aunt Blair oversaw each detail as she ensured that pretty yellow sleeveless dresses were put on by the bridesmaids and the adorable flower girl. The two equally adorable pint-sized ring bearers were put into smart blue slacks with white shirts and yellow bow ties. Between assisting everyone in the party getting dressed, she would fly into the kitchen for another round of snack crackers and strawberry juice with the stern warning, "Do *not* get this on your clothes." "We won't, Aunt Blair!" came the response from the three children in unison. It was not lost on Blair later that there were multiple pink stains on the children's clothing as they marched down the aisle.

Blair's ears perked up when she heard Jules ask, "What the fuck happened to *you* last night? You missed some Grade-A beef, bitch!" "Yeah, well, I don't need to see Grade-A beef" came Maddy's arrogant reply, "'cause I've got Erick!" Everyone was huddled around a large bedroom mirror putting on their makeup as they burst out laughing. Immediately realizing her misstep, Maddy attempted to perform damage control and defensively said, "I mean, like, Erick's like Grade A too. I didn't mean it like . . . that . . . I mean . . . Oh just shut the fuck up!" Then, in giggling unison, Kristy, Sam, and Jules bellowed, "Well, they don't call him *buttonmushroomfungi* for nothing!" "Hey, bitches!" Patty ordered, " just listen here! Don't be making fun of her! I mean, hell, I've been able to have a successful sex life without a dick too!" The entire wedding party nearly wet themselves from laughter as Maddy stormed out of the room and slammed the door of the adjacent bedroom.

Blair entered the bedroom, sat next to Maddy on the bed, and began delicately brushing her lush copper locks as she said, "Are you excited, dear?" "Yeah, I'm so fuckin' excited I might hurl" came Maddy's indelicate response. "And are you happy?" Blair gently asked. "I'm so fuckin' happy right now, I might pass out in my own vomit!" came Maddy's response as she stuck with her theme of regurgitation. "One final question, dear," Blair softly inquired as the teeth of the brush gently massaged down Maddy's scalp, "Did you and Erick find what you were looking for last night?" "Yep" came Maddy's confident reply, "but no one *else* will, heh, heh, heh." Blair turned Maddy's head and stared at her beloved niece with a smile of contentment. "My lord, dear. Look at how beautiful you are. Your Uncle Joe would be so proud. Today, you truly are a princess. Oh, and don't worry about the man who gave you the tip. He is no one you need to worry about and no one we need to speak about again."

———

Erick had a problem. A very *large* problem as he stood in his bedroom in his jockey shorts. He, Charlie, Jeremy, and Jason were staring at the bed. "So what are you going to do?" Jason asked. "I dunno . . . I mean . . . she *really* wants me to wear these slacks that she had made for me, but they're so fucking uncomfortable. I told her that I just wanted to wear jeans. Why can't I do that?" The pair of jeans and the pair of shiny blue slacks were laying on the bed as if they were taunting him.

"Okay, let me make this easy for you, m'man," Charlie interjected. "Now, if you *don't* wear the nice slacks, what do you think she's gonna do to your balls?" "Well," Erick thoughtfully replied, "she will probably cut them off." "And," Charlie continued, "do you *like* your balls where they're at?" "Yes, I do," Erick flatly responded. "So it seems to me that you'd better wear the slacks or else you're gonna get really good at singing Roy Orbison songs," Charlie concluded.

Erick thought for a moment about the impossibly high vocal range that Charlie had just referred to. Five minutes later, Erick was adorned in sleek blue slacks, a sharp white shirt, bright- yellow tie, and a slick blue blazer that matched the slacks. "Okay, how do I look?" Erick sincerely inquired as he emerged from the bedroom. "Well, if I wasn't already married, I'd fuck you" came Jeremy's mischievous reply that was followed by the loud guffawing of the group of male friends.

———

Once upon a time, there was a young princess named Maddy whose dream of marrying her prince had come true. The slow cadence of the wedding march echoed in her ears as she strode down the aisle behind her three bridesmaids, her two small ringbearers, and an adorable flower girl who had used up all of the yellow and white petals within the first three feet of the procession.

She was wearing a backless, strapless, and sleeveless white gown with subtle yellow streaks throughout. Below the waistline was a full-bodied skirt with the hemline cut diagonally from the middle of her left calf to the middle of her right thigh, giving observers a flirtatious glimpse of her yellow garter as she completed each step. The intensity of her emerald, green eyes was only slightly obscured by a yellow mesh veil that was cut diagonally from right to left over her joyful face.

She held a bouquet of six yellow and six white roses which matched the floral arrangements at the ends of each pew of Pastor Tim's freshly adorned church. On her feet, were a pair of yellow plexiglass high-heeled slippers that Erick had purchased for this occasion. They fit perfectly.

Marching alongside her to her right was Aunt Patty, in her yellow pantsuit with Pride flag earrings dangling from her earlobes. She was already fighting back the tears as she looked straight ahead and avoided eye contact with the large congregation of friends and well-wishers. She didn't even look at the fifty-something woman that she had picked up at the strip club the night before. To her left was her Aunt Blair, adorned in her tasteful yellow dress and carrying a picture of a joyous Uncle Joe holding his beloved niece on the day of her birth.

The music continued in its measured procession as Maddy looked at the smiling faces of Erick's groomsmen, Jeremy, Charlie, and Jason. And then, her green eyes rested upon the man that she was about to commit herself to. Her heart swelled as she realized that her journey had finally concluded in a happily ever after. She had found what she had been looking for. She had found true love, caring, respect, and support. And she would love, care for, respect, and support *him* as much as he did *her*. *And* she had found a man whose balls would remain intact as she noticed his sharp blue slacks covering his "Grade A" beef.

She took his hands and whispered, "Hey, you." "Wassupbuttacup?" came Erick's immediate reply. "Uh . . . nothin', except I'm kinda in the middle of getting married" came Maddy's playful reply. "Yeah? Me too!" Erick countered. "Since we're both doing that, maybe we should do that together." They looked into each other's eyes as Charlie and Rosetta began singing a perfect rendition of "It Takes Two," by Marvin Gaye and Kim Weston. As they gazed into one another's hopeful eyes, they each shed a single tear, then exhibited a look of shock. It was then that they both realized that they had each completely forgotten their wedding vows. As the final wonderous notes of the song echoed throughout the cavernous church, Erick leaned into his love's ear and said, "It's okay. We'll wing it."

"Erick, Maddy," Pastor Tim began, "I cannot tell you what an honor it is to be proceeding over your wedding today. And it is such a pleasure that two of the finest people that I know have found each other." *Okay, whatever you wanna think*, Maddy thought as she internally grinned. "We are here to join you two in an equal partnership of loving matrimony. Maddy, if you would like to recite your vows now."

Oh fuck! Maddy thought, *just speak from the heart. This is your big moment! Don't fuck this up*!

She fucked it up. "Uh . . . so, Erick . . . um . . . well, like I totally promise not to fuck with you and shit, so . . . will you like . . . be my husband or something?" Erick burst out laughing as he said, "I do." A slightly embarrassed Maddy placed his wedding ring onto his finger. The ring was white gold with an emerald and an opal on either side of a center diamond. The entire congregation shook their heads in amused disbelief.

"Maddy Sommers," Erick began. "I need to thank you. Thank you for healing this heart that no other person in this world could heal. Thank you for giving me a world of sanity in the middle of an insane world. Thank you for being exactly the perfect person that you are. And I promise you that I will never intentionally hurt you and I trust that when I do something stupid to hurt you that you will find it in your heart to forgive me. Just as I will with you." He then looked intensely into her eyes and said softly, "There isn't *anything* that you could do to shake my love, respect, and trust in you. *Nothing*. And with that, will you be my wife?"

Maddy's veil was covered in the joyful tears that her copper eyelashes were batting onto it as she said, "Well, yeah, of course, I will! But fuck, man! Yours was like way better than mine! When you said we were gonna wing it, I didn't realize yours would be so good!" A chuckling Erick placed the diamond and opal wedding band on her delicate finger as Maddy completed her exclamation with "*GAAAAAWD*! Oh well, fuck it. It's too late now. Let's just get this over with, Pastor Tim."

Pastor Tim just stood there for a moment in disbelief. Jeremy had to not so subtly clear his throat to prompt Pastor Tim into continuing. "Okay . . . well . . . I guess I shouldn't be surprised that these have been the most . . . *interesting* vows that I've been a part of. So does anyone here have a reason why these two shouldn't wed?" Erick and Maddy glowered at the congregation as if daring someone to protest. "Okay, good," Pastor Tim concluded, "then I declare you both husband and wife. You may kiss the bride!" "Where?" a giggling Erick inquired as Maddy grabbed her husband's face and said, "just shut the fuck up and kiss me!"

Following an uncomfortably long and passionate kiss, Maddy looked at her audience and yelled, "Hey, everybody! We're fuckin' married!" as the opening drumbeat of "Bohemian Love Pad" by David Johansen roared out of the church's speakers. The entire congregation got up and began feverishly dancing as Maddy whispered into the ear of her husband, "This is the perfect ending to our fairy tale." Erick placed his index finger upon her delicate lips. He stared lovingly into her eyes as he said, "No, Maddy. This isn't the *end* of the fairy tale. It's only the *beginning*."

The revelry continued back in the party room of Mr. Parker and Mrs. Sommers. Patty was the DJ, which explained the large amount of seventies punk and sixties garage songs being played with the more commercial suggestions being conveniently ignored. "Uh, yeah, I'll try to get to that," Patty would growl as she wadded up the suggestion and threw it on the floor behind the DJ stand.

Then the cake made its grand entrance onto the dance floor. It was a two feet long by two feet wide monstrosity in the shape of a six-inch-high heart. The bright pink raspberry frosting was adorned with pink roses, each containing about ten thousand calories. Maddy drooled. Erick and Maddy took their place next to the cake, each grasping the handle of the large butcher knife in their steady hands. They gave each other a maniacal grin as they thrust the knife violently through the middle of the heart twice, creating two uneven pieces. The bright crimson of the red velvet cake was gashed open as the liquid raspberry center oozed out of it.

As Erick picked up a piece of the cake, he glared at Maddy with a twisted face. The shape of the heart. The knife. The bright red. The oozing scarlet center. It had all combined to flip his maniacal switch. *This* would be his revenge. *Revenge* for all of the jokes he was unable to tell. *Revenge* for losing arguments on what to have for supper. *Revenge* for having to pick up her panties on a daily basis. And finally, *revenge* for having to wear those uncomfortable slacks. It would be literally sweet revenge. And no one could stop him. "Don't you *even* think about it mist—" Maddy's warning was cut off by a gleefully grinning Erick shoving the cake into her mouth.

"Oh, you're fuckin' dead," Maddy said in a dark voice as she took her piece of the cake and smeared it all over Erick's delighted face. By the time the uncontrollably laughing pair embraced in a kiss, the cake had been completely decimated. This once beautiful piece of culinary art had been reduced to looking like the leftovers of a pack of starving hounds. "Well, *that* was a waste of money," Sam was heard saying. Maddy and Erick were completely covered in cake, frosting, and red gelatin as they kissed. "Y'know," Erick whispered into Maddy's ear, "it seems as though I've seen you like this before." He then gave his wife a knowing smile as he said arrogantly, "Oh, and thank you for engaging in this food fight with me. Now I get to put on my jeans." "You motherfucker!" Maddy screamed as she chased a giggling Erick out of the room and down the stairs toward the shower.

———

"Here ye! Here ye, all you single muthafuckas!" Maddy yelled into the microphone. "Get your asses onto the dance floor! A little bird's gonna tell us who's gonna get hitched next! Men on that side, women on that side! We'll do the guys first to give them a chance to sneak out while we do the ladies! Now let's go!"

A mostly reluctant grouping of humanity stumbled onto the dance floor and gathered with the tribe of their respective gender. There was nervous banter among them with little eye contact with the members of the other group as they heard Maddy yell once again on the microphone, "Hey, Jules! Jerry! Get your asses out here! Coming to the wedding together doesn't count, so get out here! Don't worry, neither of you will fuckin' catch it anyway, but it's a fuckin' tradition so let's go!"

Jules and Jerry looked awkwardly at each other before Jerry said, "Yeah, uh, we're not exactly . . . um . . . *eligible* . . . I think." "Yeah," Jules chimed in, " just let us sit this one out, okay?"

"Uhhh . . . *noooo*," Maddy said defiantly. "If you're not married, then you gotta play. It's fuckin' science. So unless you're *married*," Maddy's voice trailed off as she and the entire crowd burst out into laughter at the very thought of the confirmed bachelor club owner Jerry and the confirmed anti-marriage and mostly anti-man Jules becoming married. "Why the fuck aren't you two laughing?" Maddy asked them. "Just the thought of it is hysterical!"

More laughing ensued until Jules said, "Yeah, so . . . we were gonna wait for a couple of weeks before we told anybody . . . y'know . . . to see how every-thing worked out." "Yeah, and—" Jerry interrupted, "plus, we didn't want to overshadow your big day so . . . um," Jules and Jerry stared at each other. They couldn't help but smile when Jules said, "So a couple of Saturdays ago, we flew to Vegas and got hitched."

Every mouth in the room, without exception, was agape. "So . . . is anyone gonna say anything?" Jules quietly inquired. The response that she got was that every mouth in the room, without exception, was agape. There was dead silence until Blair walked across the floor, shook Jerry's hand, and embraced her adopted niece warmly. "Well, this truly is a blessed day. Congratulations to both of you. We all wish you nothing but happiness. Oh, and I guess this proves that hell is capable of freezing over."

The entire room laughed once again as Jules and Jerry were embraced in heartfelt congratulations by the entire group. Except for a pair of single male guests who were standing in the middle of the dance floor. "Dammit," one was heard lamenting, "I was gonna try to fuck her tonight. I heard she was really easy at weddings." The other just sadly nodded.

The garter was shot like a rubber band into the mass of testosterone. A delighted squeal was heard. "Yes!" I've always *dreamed* of getting married!" an excited Sean exclaimed. "Just not to someone who would wear *this*."

The bouquet was tossed haphazardly into the air and bounced off of one of the disco lights that draped from the ceiling. It ricocheted directly at Patty who defiantly hit it away like a volleyball. "Aw fuck," Patty exclaimed as the bouquet landed in the arms of the fifty-something plaything from the nightclub.

Erick played one more song before the evening ended. As the blue jean-adorned loving couple swayed to "I Try" by Macy Gray, Erick said, "We should get to bed soon, we need to get packed." "What the fuck are you talking about?" a slightly intoxicated Maddy yelled, causing the entire room to look at the couple.

"Oh, right, you don't know about this. We have a plane to catch tomorrow afternoon." Erick explained. "A plane? What are you talking about? Where are we going?" an annoyed Maddy demanded. "Okay, well to answer that question, I need to put something on your head, so if you would please turn around," Erick urged. "Uh, no, why don't you just tell me what the fuck is going on," an increasingly agitated Maddy exclaimed. "Okay," Erick stated, "Listen. The more quickly you turn around, the more quickly I can put something on your head, and the more quickly you will know where we're going." "Oh, fuck it, fine!" Maddy stated incredulously.

She turned around with her arms crossed defiantly. She heard the soft rustling of a bag behind her and then felt something being placed on her head as a rubber band was lightly snapped under her chin. She saw tears welling up in the eyes of her aunts as she reached up to feel what had been placed upon her head.

What she felt was a black beanie with two large circles on either side. "These are-these are-" She stuttered excitedly before turning to face her beaming husband. "Are we going to the theme park? Are we? *Please* tell me! *Please!*"

Erick took his beloved wife into his arms, looked her lovingly in her emerald, green eyes, and softly said, "You didn't need to go to a theme park to find your prince. You just needed to find your prince so that he could take you to a theme park."

As the pair gazed into each other's eyes and swayed to Dion and the Belmont's version of "When You Wish Upon a Star," Jules said, "Well, that fuckin' beats *us*." "Yup" came her husband's reserved reply. "Fuck it. Let's go to my club and fuck on the stage." "Yeah, all right," Jules agreed.

CHAPTER 32

HOLIDAY ROAD

First Evening of the Honeymoon

Following a long day of travel, Erick and Maddy basking in the February warmth on the small patio of cottage at the Florida theme park. They were drinking customary gin and tonics. Erick had just taken the last sip of his first. Maddy had just poured her fourth when another young couple came around the corner and said, "Hey there! We thought we heard some other night owls and we thought we'd just come over and say hi!"

Maddy, noticing the couple's "Born Again. Born Pro-Life" T-shirts said, "Oh hey, yeah, have a seat. Do you wanna drink?" "Oh, no, thank you. We don't drink" came the scruffy bearded male's almost condescending reply. "So what are you guys doing?" the female enthusiastically inquired.

"Oh, we're just playing a game," Erick answered. "A game? We simply adooore games, don't we, hunny bunny?" "Yes, we do, darling," the male replied.

"Okay, we'll show you a couple of rounds," a delighted Maddy exclaimed. "Okay, here we go. Now concentrate Erick. *The Hills Have Eyes.*" Erick immediately replied, "*The Hills Have Thighs.* New round. *Romancing the Stone.*" Maddy squealed, jumped up, and began clapping as she said, *Romancing the Bone!*"

"Um . . . um . . . umm," the young female stammered. "What . . . exactly are you two playing?" "We're taking *actual* movie titles and turning them into *porn* movie titles. Wanna jump in this round?" Erick answered nonchalantly. "Ummm, noooo. I think it is getting a bit late, but sooo nice to meet ya'll." "Okay, whatevs . . . see ya!" Maddy shouted to the hastily retreating couple. The couple then heard Maddy's voice say, "*The Hunt for Red October.*" They quickly covered their ears before they could hear Erick's reply.

Honeymoon Day 1

Following a far too early and far too greasy breakfast, Maddy and Erick were standing in line to get on their very first ride. Maddy, in full animated regalia complete with her novelty cap, said, "Oh, I don't feel so well." "Well, maybe we should wait on the rides for a bit then," Erick offered.

"Noooo! I don't want to miss a moment of this! I'll be fine, don't worry," Maddy pleaded. The pair were strapped into the ride. "Uh, oh. I think I might get sick," Maddy exclaimed. "Please don't" came Erick's stern response.

The pair disembarked the ride and were walking through the exit. Both of their newly purchased souvenir outfits were covered in Maddy's vomit. "I think that maybe I should lay down for a while," a pale green Maddy slurred. "Yup, probably a good idea," Erick tersely replied. "And ummm," Maddy began again, "maybe we should go to a different park tomorrow." "Yup. I'm never showing my fucking face here again," Erick agreed.

Maddy spent the rest of the day and evening sound asleep. Her loyal Erick spent the rest of the day and evening watching re-runs of *Forensic Files*.

Honeymoon Day 2

"What the fuck?" Erick exclaimed as he awoke with a startle from his deep slumber to find Maddy sitting on her knees on the bed staring down at him. "Oh good!" she exclaimed. "Are you up?" "W—what time is it?" Erick inquired drowsily. "It's like five-thirty! So are you up?" Maddy excitedly replied. "Five thirty?" came Erick's exasperated reply. "Leave me alone! What the fuck?" Erick rolled over to face his backside toward his wife. The technique didn't work. Ten seconds later, Maddy began tapping him on his head and said, "So when do you think you'll be up?" "I don't know, not for a couple of hours! Please Maddy," Erick pleaded, "*I* didn't sleep all of yesterday away. Just let me sleep for a bit!"

Every five minutes came a tap on his head as Maddy would whisper, "Are you up yet?" Erick turned on the shower at 5:55 AM.

As the pair were sauntering arm in arm down the walkway from their cottage, Erick spotted a black-clad blur dart around a corner. "Oh my God! There she is again! She followed me to Florida!" "Who?" Maddy asked. "That fucking nun! I've been telling you, Maddy, ever since we got engaged last summer, I've been seeing this blonde-haired nun following me around! And now she's here! It's an undercover cop! I just know it!"

"Okay, just calm down," Maddy replied in a reassuring voice. "For starters, you're being fucking paranoid. So stop smoking dope. Second, why would a cop be trailing you from last summer? You weren't involved in anything until February. Third, it's probably just a coincidence. There are a lot of blonde nuns . . . probably. And fourth, I have never seen her, and we're together almost all of the time. So just chillax the fuck out. We've got a full day of magic to enjoy."

"Okay," Erick hesitantly replied as his darting hazel eyes continued to survey his surroundings.

They arrived at the lobby and found their overly bubbly neighbors. "Oh, *hey,* you two! Are you having the best time here?" the woman exclaimed. Erick looked at the matching shirts the pair were wearing. There was the image of an AR-15 semi-automatic assault rifle with the phrase *And Jesus said if you don't have an AR-15 sell your coat and buy one, Luke 22:36.*

Oh fuuuuck, Maddy thought as she also saw the shirts right before Erick said, "Oh *hey,* you two. So *glad* we ran into you. There's something that I wanted to say. And that is that those are the *most idiotic fucking shirts I have ever seen in my life, you stupid fucking cunts*! Are you fucking *serious*? For starters, there weren't guns in Jesus's time, so it's pretty fucking stupid right off the bat now, isn't it? And the passage says 'cloak, not coat.' Oh, but the stupid fucking manufacturer didn't want to be sued now, did he? Oh, and he's talking about a sword. A fucking sword! Not an assault rifle. Kinda big difference, don't cha think? Do you think you can mow down twenty little school kids in seconds with a sword? Nope, didn't think so. And from all that *I've* heard, Jesus is kinda into peace and love and shit, not mass murder, you ignorant pieces of shit! It's people like *you* and *your fucking corrupt politicians* who are responsible for every shooting in this country. *You* are *personally responsible* for creating a paranoid fucking country and placing those guns in those murderous hands. And every time, *every fucking time,* that a child gets cut in half by the bullets from a military weapon, their blood is on *your* fucking hands! *You* are personally responsible! How can you motherfuckers say you're pro-life when you support the rampant murder of innocent children?"

The man began to puff out his chest and took a step toward Erick as Maddy looked on with gleeful anticipation. "Oh . . . really motherfucker?" Erick stated as his voice dropped into a demonic growl, and his face became contorted into a blind rage. "You wanna take a swing at me? Go for it. Fucking go for it. Don't you feel kinda naked without your big, long, hard gun, you little pussy? Huh? I know why all you motherfuckers are into guns. I know why you go *deep* into the *dark* woods with your little *boy toys*, all dressed *matchy-matchy* carrying your little *gun* purses and your adorable little *ammo* purses. Oh, I bet you look so *cuyute* when you pull out your *big, long, hard guns* and blow your *loads* all over the woods. I know why you do that. It's because you can't handle the fact that secretly you want to suck a cock and you think that there's something wrong with that. I'm right, aren't I? Your face isn't red from *anger*. It's from *blushing*. Because you *really* want to suck *my* cock right now, don't you? Well, sorry champ, I don't swing that way. But have fun jerking off to your dreams of me tonight. I'll be the one in the yellow speedo and I'll be waiting for you . . . cowboy. Now, you'd better take a step back motherfucker because if you don't, I'm going to make your dream come true. Only it's going to be *your* cock that I'm shoving down your fucking throat."

As is true with *all* blowhard bullies, they always back down when confronted alone. They only find "bravery" when they feel protected in their like-minded tribes. Because they have no personal convictions, fortitude, or resolve. They are merely weak creatures made up of small egos and self-preservation who only care about their immediate safety and fragile emotional needs. So the man puffed one more time and said to his wife, "C'mon, he's not worth it," as the pair hastily slunk out of the lobby listening to Maddy and Erick break out into laughter.

"Wow," Maddy stated. "y'know, between those two and my vomiting yesterday, we're *really* making a lot of friends here." "I know!" Erick squealed in delight. "Isn't it *great*? Best fucking honeymoon *ever*!" "How the fuck did you know that Bible passage?" Maddy inquired. "I dunno, I think I'm learning some shit from Pastor Tim," Erick answered.

Maddy turned around and began walking back toward their cottage.

"Hey, where are you going?" Erick yelled after her. "We need to go back to the room," Maddy responded. "I'm totally fucking wet right now. Come on!"

It was the only ride the two would take that day.

Honeymoon Day 3

"Finally! We get to go on some fuckin' rides!" Maddy shouted as she entered the shuttle to take them to their chosen park. Her exclamation was greeted by a scornful look from a twenty- something couple with a toddler. "Oh, fuck off," Maddy countered. "Your fuckin' kid has heard worse. Just fuckin' chillax!"

Upon entry to the park, Maddy immediately began bouncing from sign to sign, shop to shop, character to character, and attraction to attraction. "Oh, fuck man, take my picture in front of this!" She would yell at Erick who, without exception would say to his beloved wife, "What do mice eat?" "Cheeeeeeeeese!" would come Maddy's bubbly reply as her dimples were stretched to their limit. The pair would embrace while laughing as on- lookers shook their heads in disbelief or, more often, disgust.

At lunch, Erick exclaimed, "These hot dogs are huge!" "That's what she said!" came Maddy's immediate reply followed by the pair laughing so hard that mustard and relish would fly onto their newly purchased character-clad apparel. By the end of their day, their shirts looked like a demented Monet painting as they had been covered in an unholy swirl of multiple condiments, cotton candy, ice cream, and it was hoped, sour cream. On-lookers would shake their heads in disbelief or, more often, disgust. More than one on-looker consulted with a friendly security guard who would ask the couple to please watch their language. "Yeah, fu . . . I mean, yeah, okay," Erick would reply as his wife grinned up at him.

At 1:00, the happy couple was finally in line for their first vomit-free ride. "I'm so fuckin' excited!" Maddy screamed. She then looked up into the judgmental eyes of yet another security guard. "Ma'am, Sir, I'm going to have to ask you to come with me."

"Fuck, we're in theme park jail!" Maddy lamented as they were waiting to meet with the park's head of security. They entered the man's office and gingerly sat down on the hard yellow plastic chairs. "Madam, Gentleman," the man began, "You have been warned several times about your antics. There was even a report of some unusual activity inside a men's room stall."

"Okay, I've gotta stop you there, commandant," Maddy retorted defensively. "What the fuck is so unusual about giving my husband a blow job on our honeymoon, *hmmmm*?" The answer as to whether it was sour cream on her shirt had been answered.

"I'm sorry," the man said in a measured tone as he slowly shook his head, "but I'm afraid that you will both be asked to leave the park, and there will be no refund. We can assist you in finding alternate lodging until your return to . . . wherever you may be from."

"Nooooo!" Maddy pleaded as she cocked her head and batted her copper eyelashes furiously. "Pleeeease! I'm sorry! *We're* sorry! I promise, we'll be on our *best* behavior from now on. We only have one day left of magic. *Pleeeeease?*"

"Very well," the man stated, "but we are going to ask you to return to your cabana for the rest of the day. And you need to choose a different park to go to tomorrow. And I assure you . . . you are both going to be watched *very closely*. One foul word. One moment of . . . marital bliss . . . and you will be escorted back to your cabana to collect your things and taken to alternate lodging. Do you both understand?"

The pair looked at each other silently with slight grins, as if to say, "Fuck him." It was just the two of them silently communicating with one another as they turned to the head of security and said, "Yup! Thanks!" As they entered their cabana, Erick stated, "Fuck it! Let's have some gin!"

Honeymoon Day 4

Erick was completely paranoid the next day. He knew they were being watched. He was on the lookout for undercover security *and* undercover nuns. His eyes darted around his entire surroundings as Maddy said, "Now, Erick, we really *must* be on our best behavior today, all right, dear?"

"Of *course*, darling. We shall not allow one foul word to escape from our mouths. It shall be thus!" Upon entry to their next park, they were asked to check their bags. "Hey! What the f—" Maddy began before demurely smiling at the security guard and saying, "Why of course, sir. Here you are." *These fuckers are so lame. They'll* never *find my hidden pouch with my scalpel and pepper spray.* And they didn't.

They were once again standing in line with the great anticipation of finally being able to go on a nausea-free ride. They were standing there in silence with their arms at their sides, giving each other knowing glances and smirks. They both looked like a cat that had eaten *all* of the canaries when Maddy's burner phone went off.

"What the f—, I mean, I wonder who *that* could be dear?" Maddy answered her phone and said, "Oh, hey, Aunt Blair, wazzup?" "No, we're in line for a ride." "What the *fuck* you say? No, I had nothing to do with—" she then gazed up into the stern eyes of the undercover security employee. "Uh, Aunt Blair, I think I'll have to call you back in a while. We're getting kicked out of the park . . . again."

Immediately after the couple threw their bags down on the bed at a nearby hotel, Maddy pulled out her burner phone, put it on speaker, and dialed her aunt. "Okay, so what the fuck is going on? You're on speaker with Erick, by the way."

"Well, dear, as I tried to explain *ninety minutes ago*, it has just been reported that your ex has perished, and I want to know if either of you had anything to do with it. He comes from a rather affluent family who will want to get to the bottom of this, and I need to know what we're up against."

"No," Maddy stated, "I haven't even thought of that douche in years. I promise you, I had nothing to do with it." She then looked inquisitively at her husband who held a dumbfounded expression. "What?" Erick stated defensively. "No, nothing. I mean, yes, I dug the hole in case I *needed* to do something, but I have done *nothing* to pursue it and had *nothing* to do with this directly, indirectly, or otherwise. I swear to you both!"

Maddy looked into her love's eyes for a moment and then said, "Nope, he didn't do it either. He can't lie to me. So what happened? How did he die?"

"Well, dear" came Blair's calm reply, "He started his car in his garage, and it blew up. I understand that there isn't much left of him." "Wow," Maddy stated as she tried to hide her grin, "I guess *both* of my husbands got blown on this trip."

Honeymoon Totals

- Two very upset religious gun freaks who left early
- Two souvenir shirts, covered in vomit
- One unidentified blonde nun
- One blown-up ex-husband
- Twelve calls from an overly protective Sam

- Thirty-three sets of parents who were offended by the vulgar language
- Nine sets of offended parents who were told to fuck off
- Eighteen rounds played of Real Movie Name to Porn Movie Name
- Forty-eight gin and tonics
- Twenty-six lime wedges (they ran out of limes)
- Eight intimate moments in their cabana
- One semi-public blow job
- Four female character costumes (tattered to shreds)
- 286 pictures taken of Maddy
- Zero pictures taken of Erick
- Three parks attended
- Two parks escorted out of
- Two hotels
- One ride, with vomit
- Zero fireworks displays
- Two enraptured newlyweds

On the plane ride back home, the ecstatic and tittering couple was looking through the myriad of pictures. "Best fucking honeymoon *ever*!" Maddy exclaimed as the parents across the aisle glared at them. "Are you sure you're not disappointed?" Erick inquired. "I mean, you only got to go on one ride and that was . . . well . . . less than enjoyable." "Fuck the rides!" Maddy stated. "I was at the greatest theme park ever with my prince, and that is all that I've ever wanted! Besides, there's always the parks in California!" *Oh, fuck,* Erick thought.

Chapter 33

She Just Wants to Be

The following Tuesday afternoon, the blissful newlyweds were on their customary brown leather couch in the reading section of the bookstore laughing at their customary "that's what she said" juvenile jokes when Maddy caught an approaching petite female from the corner of her eye. She looked at the conservatively dressed Laotian blonde and her facial expression immediately turned from glee to rage.

"What the fuck are *you* doing here?" Maddy bellowed. "Hey, listen," the petite woman began in her meek voice. "I didn't come here to cause any trouble or anything. I just saw that you had gotten married and wanted to say congratulations. That's all." "Oh, really," Maddy angrily countered. "So you saw that I'd just gotten married, and you thought you could see if you could fuck *another* one of my husbands, right? Well, let me tell you something, bitch! This man loves me and would *never* cheat on me! Especially with a skank-ass whore like you. So I said this before, and I'll say it again. Just fucking disappear and leave me alone!"

A slightly confused Erick turned to his wife and said, "Okay, folks, what's going on?" "All right then," Maddy answered as she attempted to calm herself. "Erick, this is Lucy, but you would know her better as The Nameless One. And Lucy, I'm not even going to introduce you to my husband, because you don't *need* to know him. Now that everyone knows what the fuck is going on, how about you go die under a fucking rock or something?" As her defiant words tumbled out of her mouth, Maddy realized that this was the second time that she had recently uttered the name of her former best friend and now sworn enemy and wondered what that meant as conflicting feelings began swirling about in her psyche.

"Hey," Lucy began once again more assertively. "I understand. I really messed up and I can't blame you if you can never forgive me. But there are some things that you don't know about from back then. I'm not saying that I'm completely innocent, but there are just some things that I would like to tell you so that you have a complete understanding of what happened. It's the only time that I will offer. If you want me to just leave, then I will. But I think that you will want to hear what I have to say. Regardless, whether you believe me or not, I will always love you and I wish you and your husband nothing but happiness."

"Oh, for fuck sake," a grimacing Maddy softly stated. "Erick, may I see you for a moment in private?" "Of course," Erick replied. As the pair began walking toward a more secluded area of the store, Maddy looked over her shoulder at Lucy and said tersely, "Just stay there. Or don't. I don't really give a fuck." "Okay," Maddy began. "I don't want you to tell me what to do. In this situation, you're like my consigliere or something, okay? I just want your counsel. Now, please tell me what to do." Erick had to hide his smirk as he gently held his beloved wife's hands and softly said, "Well, I think you are being given a great gift. The one thing in your life that has always bothered you is how your best friend could betray you. And now you may have an opportunity to solve that riddle. I personally see no harm in hearing her out. The worst case scenario is that she tells you a bunch of bullshit and you have even *more* justification for your hate of her. There is nothing but an upside here. And I will, of course, support you in whatever you decide. But if you pass on this opportunity, I fear that it will be something that will gnaw at you for the rest of your life."

"Why do you have to be so fucking reasonable," an outwardly annoyed but inwardly relieved Maddy asked. "Yeah, fine. We'll hear her out. But then that bitch is out of our lives forever, got it?" "Sure," an unsure Erick replied.

Maddy swaggered toward her former friend with her head held high as if to dare her to do or say something untoward. "All right bitch," Maddy stated coldly, "Here's our address. 6:00 tonight. You have ten minutes. If you don't show, then don't bother coming around anymore. See ya tonight, or not. I don't really give a fuck." "No, I'll see you tonight," Lucy retorted in a surprisingly confident voice.

That evening, Maddy was uncharacteristically pacing around the house. She was wearing tight black jeans, a black hoodie, and black boots. She was presenting herself as being ready for battle. "Hey, why the hell are you dressed like that?" Erick asked. "I don't care *what* she has to say, we're *not* killing your former friend. Especially in our home. And that's final." "Yeah, I know," Maddy replied, "I just want this bitch to remember who she's going up against." "Maddy," Erick responded, "I would suggest to you that you open up your heart to the *possibility* that tonight won't be adversarial. And remember, I won't allow *anyone* to hurt you. If she says *anything* that is painful for you, I will *personally* toss her ass out of here. Let *me* be the bad guy. You just focus on understanding and perhaps healing, okay? For this one moment, it is all right for you to let your guard down. I'm here."

At that moment, the clock chimed six o'clock at the exact same time that the doorbell rang. "Oh, fuck she's here, oh fuck, she's here, oh fuck, she's here!" the pacing Maddy exclaimed. "You go answer the door. I need to position myself on the couch. Have her sit over there."

Erick answered the door to find the small-statured woman gazing up at him solemnly. "Good evening, Lucy. Please come in and sit on that couch. I've been informed to tell you that your ten minutes begins upon your being seated."

"Thank you," Lucy stated as she meekly entered the living room and gingerly took a seat. "All right bitch," Maddy began frigidly. "I'm all fuckin' ears. Say what you have to say then get the fuck out. But before you begin, I just want to tell you how much you hurt me. *You* were my sole confidant. You *knew* how I felt about that ex-douchebag and how I thought he was cheating on me. You *knew* all of the fucking mind games he was playing on me. You *knew* how he made me feel about myself. You *knew* how sadistic he could be. And yet, you betrayed me anyway. Of all of the bad shit that happened that year, with the exception of losing my Uncle Joe shortly after, your betrayal was what hurt me the most. And I will *never* forgive you for that. Now, say what you have to say."

The woman looked at Maddy with apprehensive eyes. "Maddy, first of all, thank you for allowing me to speak with you. Secondly, I know it's very late, but I'm so sorry that you lost your Uncle Joe. I know how much he meant to you and . . . well . . . to all of us really." Seeing the immediate look of rage flash on Maddy's face, Erick reached out and grasped her hand. He had to fight to keep from grimacing as she squeezed her anger into his palm.

Sensing that she may have said the wrong thing, Lucy immediately changed topics. The next topic was not pleasant, but it wasn't nearly as sensitive as comparing *her* adoration for Uncle Joe to Maddy's. "Okay, I'm now going to tell you everything that happened and how I became . . . involved with your ex-husband. If you remember New Year's 2017, I had gotten really drunk. And he offered to drive me home. And well, you know how flirty I can be when I'm drunk, and I was like that with him that night. I even asked him to come up and tuck me into bed. And he did come up. And we started kissing. And then I realized what I was doing, and I told him to stop. And he said that it was too late to turn back now. He dragged me into my bedroom, tore my dress, tore my panties off, and he . . . raped me. I kept pleading with him to stop, but he just kept . . . going and took pictures while it was happening. I know I messed up. I should have told you. I should have reported it. But you know that the police wouldn't have taken me seriously. So it's *my* fault that I was flirty. And it's *my* fault that I didn't tell you or anyone else, but that doesn't mean that I deserved to be raped."

There was stunned silence as Lucy began to shed a few tears down her light almond skin before she continued. "After it was . . . over, I asked him why he had done that, and he said that he didn't have anything against me. That I was just collateral damage. That what he was trying to do was to hurt *you*. That he got off on making women subservient to him. He got off on making women feel bad about themselves. That he got off on being a puppet master and making women feel whatever he wants them to feel at any given moment. He said that his first two wives were so damaged, that they never got involved in a relationship again, and that he wanted to damage *you* even more. That he was going to cripple your spirit. And then he laughed. Jesus, Maddy it was such an evil laugh. He wanted you so damaged that you'd be put into a rubber room. And that he would do that unless—"

Lucy's voice trailed off for a moment as her tears began flowing once again before she continued. "Oh god, Maddy, I'm so stupid. He said that he would do that unless I slept with him three more times and he could take pictures of it. He said that if I did that, then he would destroy the pictures and never tell you and that when the time was right, he would simply divorce you and not hurt you anymore. It sounds so stupid now, but I believed him, and I did that . . . two more times. Yes, I did it selfishly so that he wouldn't tell you and I could save our friendship. But I *also* did it because I believed that maybe he wouldn't hurt you anymore. So I did it. In some seedy hotel, I dressed up for him. I let him tie me up and whip me. I let him play out all of his twisted fantasies. And he forced me to smile as he took pictures of it all. He would say, 'Smile for my lovely wife. The more you smile, the less likely it is that she will ever see these.' I'm not perfect, Maddy, but I truly thought that I was helping you. I thought that, in some twisted way, I was protecting you. Just like you had always protected me. It's so messed up, but he actually convinced me that I was protecting you by sleeping with him. And then—"

Lucy looked away from her former friend, attempting to hide her anguish. Erick put his arm around his shocked wife's shoulders. He could sense the combined rage and grief in her soul. Then, Lucy's tear-filled eyes looked upon her former friend once again as she said, "Then came the night that you caught him cheating. The night that he burned your photo album. The night that you beat him up. I thought that it was finally over until he sent me a text that said, *Only twice. Too bad. Deal's off.* And then he sent the pictures to you, and you kicked me out of your life. And I just thought that maybe it was for the best if I just disappear and start a new life. And I did. I can tell you more about what I did later if you want. But that's the whole story, Maddy, and I'm *so, so sorry* that I hurt you."

A stunned Maddy just sat there for a moment before she said, "Erick, may I see you upstairs for a moment?" Upon the closing of their bedroom door, Maddy exclaimed while flailing her arms, "Well, what the *fuck* am I supposed to do with *that*?" Erick looked at his wife and said with the full realization that this was a climactic moment for her, "Maddy. Let's just calm down and process this for a moment. First, do you believe her?" "Yeah," Maddy stated softly. "I can see him doing that fucked up shit. I didn't realize how fucking evil he was until I saw it in hindsight. It was so hard to see while I was immersed in it, y'know? It's like you get brainwashed with the same toxic shit being beaten into your brain day after day, week after week, year after year. And after a while, you almost believe that you deserve it and get numb to it. You just don't feel *anything* anymore. It just becomes normal for you. People always ask how women can stay in abusive relationships. It's not because we're stupid. It's because we get indoctrinated into believing that that is the life we deserve. And it's just so *fucking hard* to get out of that mental quicksand once you're in it. I was lucky. I was with someone so sadistic that he tried to take away the memories of the most important man in my life. And at that moment, it was like I just snapped back to who I truly was. It was almost like Uncle Joe grabbed me and pulled me back from the brink and said, 'What the fuck are ya doing, Buttacup? Let's go fuck up this douchebag.'"

Maddy gave a slight chuckle as a single tear rolled down her lightly freckled cheek. "But most abused women aren't so lucky. I found out that his two previous wives were pretty fucked up after being with him. And knowing how fucking gullible Lucy is, I can see how she would fall for that. And yeah, he fucked with my mind, but he fucking *raped* her *and* fucked with her mind. And she *kept* fucking him. To protect *me*, she kept fucking a man that had *raped* her. We were *both* his victim. So yeah, I believe her. *Now* what do I do? What do I *say*? How can I ever repay her for her sacrifice? How can I make it up to her? All of the horrible things that I've said to her. How do I make that right?"

Erick wrapped his arms around his love and whispered into her ear, "You have been given a great gift. The gift of a reunion with your best friend. The gift of an even greater emotional bond with her. The gift of the two of you being your mutual support systems. Go back down there and just speak from your heart. The words will come to you. All you have to do is speak them. You are about to experience one of the most beautiful and powerful moments of your life. Embrace it."

The pair went back down their metal staircase and re- entered their living room finding Lucy staring blankly at her feet. She looked up. Her eyes met the familiar brilliant green of Maddy's. And Maddy broke down. "Oh, Jesus Christ Lucy, I'm *so sorry*! I'm *so sorry* you went through that! I'm *so sorry* I didn't listen to you! I'm *so sorry* for the things I've said to you and about you!" The weeping pair fell into a long overdue warm embrace and continued their apology and forgiveness tour through tears, smiles, and laughter.

"All right, ladies," Erick stated, his words cutting through the intense emotion in the room. "I don't know about you two, but I'm fucking starving. So I'm going to go out and get us all some sandwiches. I'll be back in an hour." Erick put on his coat and opened the front door. He then peered at the pair and said warmly, "And Lucy, it is *truly* a pleasure to meet you. Welcome to our home. Welcome back to *your* home."

Despite it having been nearly six years, it felt as though the pair of tittering friends had never parted. There was laughter and stories, both new and old, over the feast of sub sandwiches and deli salads, which were also being enjoyed by the relentlessly begging Hunky and Dory. The evening was filled with stories of how Maddy and Erick had met and fallen in love. There were stories from Lucy and Maddy's college days. There were jokes. There was laughter. But most importantly, there were frequent embraces between the once again inseparable friends as a proud Erick looked upon his wife's beaming face. He had seen her happy before, but he had never seen her *this* happy. What he saw in her joyous emerald eyes and constant smile was a woman who was now complete.

There was a moment, however, when he had to excuse himself, go into a private room, and silently weep. Maddy was right. She was one of the lucky ones. She had somehow managed to tap into her own inner strength and escape the grip of this most diabolical fiend. Through the love of her family, she was blessed with the resources, both emotional and financial to break the patriarchal bonds of servitude and emotional despair. But, as happy as he was for her, he was equally despondent over the plight of millions of others.

He wondered, how would all of the other women and girls ever find *their* escape from the sadistic forces of their misogynistic mates and find the peaceful and joyous life that they so richly deserved? And how would their male children ever grow up to be decent and respectful adults? How would their female children ever find *their* personal strength and self- esteem? Or were they all just doomed to repeat the same abusive cycle over and over again for generation after generation? Was there something that *he* could do, to break this cycle for at least a *few* of these battered souls? Erick re-entered the dining room in time to hear Maddy's question to her friend.

"So have you been in New York this whole time, or," Lucy responded, "Ummm, no. I went away for a while. I'll tell you about that later. But ummm, I came back to New York last August. And that was because . . . well . . . I saw that you had gotten involved with someone and I just felt this drive to look over you. To make sure you wouldn't get hurt again. So and I'm really sorry Erick, but I checked you out. I followed you for months to make sure that you weren't . . . y'know . . . an axe murderer or something. At least, not a *bad* axe murderer. I think you may have seen me a couple of times. I was dressed like a nun."

"That . . . was . . . *you*?" an astonished Erick exclaimed. "You see, Maddy? I *told* you! I *told* you a fucking nun was following me! You thought I was crazy, but I'm *not* crazy! She's the one! She's the fucking blonde nun!" "Yeah, yeah, yeah," Maddy stated dismissively, "you were actually being followed.

Whatevs. Don't make a big fucking thing about it. If I had a dime for every time I've been followed I'd be like a bazillionnairre or something."

"Wait!" Erick stated as he stared at Lucy. "Was that you in Disneyworld? Were you following me there?" Lucy sheepishly looked at the couple and said softly, "Yeah, that was me." "But why?" Maddy inquired. "Well," Lucy began explaining, "it wasn't about checking Erick out anymore. By then, I knew he was a good guy . . . for you. But . . . I started thinking about your ex. About how he was so proud of his ex-wives being so damaged that they never got re-married. About how you had humiliated him and how the only thing that he really had was his ego. About how he felt he always *deserved* to win, no matter the cost or who else he might hurt. And I figured that once he found out that *you* were re-married, he might try something to hurt you. To maybe try to hurt you both. So I followed you to Florida to make sure you had an ironclad alibi."

"An alibi? Alibi for *what*?" a confused Maddy asked. Lucy looked up at the pair. Her penetrating dark brown eyes were glinting in the dining room light as her bleached blonde blunt bang hair framed her light almond face which was now twisted by her maniacal smile as she said in a sinister growl, "An alibi for his murder. Because . . . I blew that motherfucker up."

CHAPTER 34

POISON

Maddy and Erick sat with their mouths agape in stunned silence before Maddy broke out into laughter. "Oh, *come on* Lucy! Yeah, good one. I'm not trying to be mean or anything, but you're scared of your own fuckin' *shadow*! But *you* blew the motherfucker up, yeah . . . right."

Lucy looked at her best friend with an iced look of determination and said in a low voice without blinking, "Yeah? Well, let's just say that I've changed more than my *hair* over the last five and a half years."

Her all-too-familiar expression and tone of voice sent a chill down Maddy's spine. "Okay, so I guess I believe you," a hastily retreating Maddy stated cautiously. "So maybe do you wanna tell us how this little transformation happened?"

"Sure," Lucy enthusiastically chimed. *Holy fuck can this bitch turn it on and off,* Maddy thought as she witnessed her friend's dramatic shift in moods. "So the day after our . . . blow up . . . for lack of a better word . . . he started harassing me. So I decided to just disappear. I resigned from the finance company that I had worked for and told them that I had a stalker and that I really needed to relocate immediately. I then took a job with a genetic engineering firm that had been pursuing me, on the condition that I could do my research remotely if they could help set me up. So I shut down all of my social media, got a new phone and number, and moved back to Buffalo with my parents. I converted their basement into my lab and began working with my new firm. I just needed to come back to the city every couple of months or so to attend meetings. I was off the grid, so to speak. And I pay rent to my parents for complete use of their basement because the stuff I was working on was classified."

"During that time, I really didn't do much but hang out with my parents and immerse myself in my work. I just needed to shut the rest of the world out. I had been so hurt . . . so damaged. I just couldn't stand to be around anyone . . . especially men. One night, I came across an old photo album and saw one single picture of a middle age Laotian man. I asked my father about it, and he said, "That is your grandfather. He was a miserable son of a bitch. After he moved us here from Laos in the mid-60s, we hardly ever saw him. He died in 1968, somehow. All I can tell you about that man, Lucy, is that my mother and I shed tears of joy when we learned of his demise and that is all that I will ever have to say about that bastard.'

"About a year into my stay with my parents, I was digging around in the basement and came across an old, locked trunk. I managed to unlock it with an acid I had on hand, opened it, and found several old journals. You guys, what I found in those books was . . . brilliant. They contained some of the most incredibly complicated recipes that I had ever seen."

"Oh yeah?" an even more interested Maddy chimed in. "Sweet! I'm always up for tryin' new cuisine! When are you gonna cook for us?"

"No, Maddy" came Lucy's stern reply. "These recipes aren't for you. Or for Erick. Or for *any* decent human being. These aren't recipes for food. They are recipes of *death*."

"Whatthefuckyousay!" Maddy exclaimed as a pensive Erick sat silently. Lucy then continued, "These are some of the most brilliant recipes of my grandfather's invention. They are recipes for poisonous toxins. Poison gasses. Antidotes for them. And of course, bombs. And I began experimenting with them. Some of the recipes are too complex for even *me* to figure out, and I didn't think *that* was possible. Some are unusable because the ingredients are nearly impossible to find. But some of the recipes I have perfected. There are three recipes for toxins that are made from pretty common stuff. And it isn't the *ingredients* that are necessarily so important. What's *most* important is how the ingredients are *combined*. So I have perfected three toxins. One to knock someone out. One that paralyzes someone for about six hours. And another that kills someone almost instantaneously upon being injected. Then there are the gasses that can pretty much do the same thing. They're absolutely brilliant."

Maddy and Erick looked at each other and transmitted the same thought to one another. *This shit might come in handy.* "So," Lucy continued, "that's another reason why I wanted to talk to you guys. See, I pretty much know all of the murders you've had your hand in, Maddy. I saw you go to the apartment of the guy that watched me getting raped. I was planning on paying him a visit that night as well, but you beat me to it. And I saw you two put the murderer of that doctor into his trunk. I don't know what you did with him, but I'm guessing that he will never be found. And I went back through the murders in the area. You're very smart to not have a pattern. But for those of us who know you, we recognize that having no pattern *is* the pattern. The dismembered guys hanging. The guy with an arrow through his ass. The sliced-up guy left in the alley. And probably a number of others. That was all you, wasn't it?"

Maddy began stammering, "I . . . ummmm . . . errrr . . . well, you see . . . hmmm" Before Erick chimed in. "Yes. And now we're working together. We're not *looking* for trouble, but when someone is being abused, we will sometimes take it upon ourselves to . . . step in."

"Yeah," Lucy stated. "I said it before, and I'll say it again. You two are perfect for each other. So how about adding a third to your little *demented duo*?"

"*Demented Duo*! That's fucking awesome!" Maddy exclaimed. "What's so awesome about it?" Erick inquired. "It's so fucking *cool*! We totally need a cool name like that!" Maddy excitedly responded. "We don't need a fucking name," Erick said dismissively to his wife.

"Anyway," Lucy interrupted, trying to get the conversation back on track, "what do you think? With our combined experience and techniques, we might be able to make a difference in some lives."

"Well," Maddy began, "First of all, *this guy* doesn't *have* any technique. All he has done so far is dig a fuckin' hole. And to make matters *worse*, his choice of murder prep music is just *awful!*" "Oh, for Christ's sake, Maddy," Erick bellowed. "What is the big fucking deal? Why can't I listen to whatever I want without being harassed for it?" "Because," Maddy replied calmly, "you, my love, are *doing it wrong*!"

The pair let out a burst of laughter as they realized the absurdity of the conversation before Maddy began again. "Okay, Lucy. We *might* consider taking you on as a junior partner or something. But first, what are your qualifications? Okay, you've blown up a car. I think that's a very good start, especially considering who was sitting in that car at the time. But we're not really equipped to take on trainees. So how many motherfuckers have you offed?"

"Well," Lucy began demurely, "I don't want to brag, but it's probably considerably more than you." "More than *me*?" an incredulous Maddy exclaimed. "Are you fucking *serious*? I've tortured and killed, like—" she then looked up at the ceiling in order to concentrate and began counting on her fingers.

"Oh, fuckin' hell yes!" Maddy yelled out. "I'm into double digits! I'm up to *ten* of these motherfuckers!" Lucy began quietly snickering and rolled her eyes. "What the fuck is so funny, bitch?" Maddy angrily inquired. "Ten . . . that's cute," Lucy replied condescendingly. "I have 112."

"No . . . fucking . . . way," an astonished Maddy stated before turning to her husband and saying, "Baby, we gotta step up our game!" "Maddy," Erick said in a reassuring tone, "it's not a competition. Plus, we do *our* shit mostly one on one. She's making bombs and gasses and shit. She might be taking out multiple people in one shot. Am I right, Lucy?"

"Yup, you got it, Erick," Lucy proudly stated. "With a bomb or gas, you can take out a lot of people rather efficiently." She then looked at Maddy with a dead calm and said, "And Maddy, you know how *efficient* I was in college." Another chill ran down Maddy's spine before she said, "Yeah, if you're as good at *this* shit as you were at acing tests in college then . . . fuck . . . you could wipe out the eastern seaboard if you wanted to."

"Yes, I could" came Lucy's chilled response before smiling and saying playfully, "But I won't! I only go after bastards that deserve it!" *Alrighty then. Multiple personalities much?* Maddy thought to herself as she had once again witnessed her friend's dramatic transformation.

"So let me tell you both a bit more of my story," Lucy continued. "I spent another year in my parents' house working for the genetics company, saving money and perfecting some of my grandfather's recipes. I made a *lot* of that stuff. I have enough toxins and gasses securely stored in my parents' basement to . . . well . . . wipe out the eastern seaboard. Oh, yeah, and bombs!"

"Wait," Erick interrupted, "you mean to say that you have *bombs* in your parents' *basement*? Aren't you afraid that they'll be blown up?" "Oh, Erick," Lucy stated condescendingly, "they aren't *functional* bombs . . . yet. I put them mostly together but don't attach whatever triggering mechanism I'm going to use until just before I install it. And I've actually only used the one bomb. They're obviously not very safe, and you have to be careful not to hurt anyone else. But with *that* bastard, I wanted to make a bit of a splash. And I did. His blood was splashed all over the neighborhood. Any more questions at this point?"

Maddy and Erick just shook their heads silently before Lucy continued. "Okay, then. So I had all of these toxins and stuff and wondered what to do with them. I recently read an article about the scourge of human trafficking. All of these women and children who were being abducted and sold off for . . . God knows what." Lucy paused as she allowed a shiver to go through her petite frame before continuing.

"So I resigned from the genetics company, and I moved to Iowa." "*Iowa?*" Erick howled. "Why the fuck would you move to *Iowa?*" "Oh, Erick" came Lucy's once again condescending reply. "Not a lot of people know this, but Iowa is a hotbed for transferring the victims of human trafficking. It's because of the two Interstates that intersect. The scum can pull off at a truck stop, make their transaction, load their victims into another truck, and be off on another Interstate to whatever hell hole they're going."

"So I moved there and started hanging out at the truck stops. It was pretty easy to blend in with the prostitutes that frequent those places. I would just hang out and watch and listen and learn. And I did learn. I learned where the traffickers would park in the lot. I learned their knowing glances at the buffet. I learned how to recognize them. Then, I would either take them out in the lot or I would follow them and take them out at their . . . well . . . final destination. Would you like to hear a couple of examples?"

Maddy and Erick silently nodded before Lucy continued. "All right. So for example, when I knew there was a semi that had victims in it, I would break into the cab of the truck and wait for the driver. Once he climbed in, I would inject him with what I call *Toxin C*. It's a *really* fun one. They die violently in about ten seconds. They don't suffer for long, but those ten seconds are excruciating. Then, I would find their money . . . there's *always* a lot of money. I would unlock the back, give the victims some money, and tell them to go to the gas station or restaurant or whatever was around. Then, I would hide and wait until the cops showed up, just to make sure that the owner of the truck stop wasn't involved."

Lucy then flashed a huge smile as she said, "Oh! That reminds me of the one time I used *Toxin X*! So through my surveillance, I found out the owner of a truck stop was actually involved in the ring. He was such a scumbag. And *Toxin X* is like a lotion that you apply to your skin, or in this case, my lips. It absorbs into your skin and then for about six hours you are completely lethal to anyone you might touch."

"Wait," Erick interrupted, "why isn't it lethal for *you* if it's on your skin?" "Oh, Erick," Lucy explained, "if you remember, I spoke earlier of an antidote. So I take the antidote twelve hours before I apply *Toxin X*. Then, I'm completely immune. So I dressed really slutty and asked to see the owner. I came onto him. Then I kissed him with my infected lips and smiled. I began to slowly undress for him. *Toxin X* takes about ten minutes to get into the system. So by the time I was down to my underwear, he began convulsing. He started spurting up blood. Blood started coming out of his eyes, ears, everywhere really. Because you see . . . *Toxin X* attacks every organ in the human body. It just begins tearing the hell out of everything. Every organ, including the brain, is ruptured. His eyes finally just exploded like marshmallows in a microwave! It was *really* cool. When I left him to go unlock the back room, he was laying there in a pool that looked like melted strawberry gelatin."

"I unlocked this back room and . . . oh, Jesus . . . there were these young women and girls in there. Five of them. I don't know how old. Maybe ranging from fourteen to twenty. They were chained and dressed in filthy gowns. And they just stared at me. They were just staring and shivering like they were waiting for me to hurt them or something. It was the most disgusting and heart-wrenching thing that I have ever seen. What sort of *animal* can do that to another human being? What type of *evil* must one be? And how many *other* men are out there right now that wouldn't do the *exact same thing* if they had the opportunity? Your ex was one. *He* could do that. How many others *are there?*"

"Okay," Lucy stated as she wiped a tear from her cheek. "I can't talk about their condition anymore. Talking about it makes me want to . . . do things. So I didn't unlock them because I was afraid they might attack me. After I said thank you and kissed the hand of the dork at the front counter of the truck stop, I called the FBI and I waited until they arrived with the vans to take these poor women and girls away." Then her demeanor snapped back to enthusiasm as Lucy said, "So *that's* a pretty good example of *Toxin X*! Pretty cool huh? Wanna hear another one?"

Maddy and Erick just silently nodded as Lucy began once again. "All right, one more. So if I found out that there were a *number* of these slugs holed up somewhere, I would use gas. I would follow them and hide some-where with my vials and a small compressor. Then, when it looked like everyone was down, I'd pump a sleep gas into the house. Everyone, including the victims, would be asleep. I'd drag the women out away from the building, go back in, and get the money. Jesus, you guys. I can't even tell you how much money I've taken from this scum. Millions. And that's *after* leaving a lot with the victims."

"Then, I would pump the death gas into the house. It has pretty much the same effect as *Toxin X*. It's just that it's in a gaseous form. That's why you need to get the money and stuff out before you use it. Otherwise, you're walking around in red fizzy ooze all over the place. Then, I'd inject the women with something to wake them up. I gave them some money, a phone, and keys to whatever vehicles were there. I told them where they were and how to get to the next town. Then, I'd be on my merry little way . . . just waiting for my next adventure! So am I qualified, or what?"

"Yup, I think you'll fit in fine," Maddy stated flatly. "Yes, welcome aboard," Erick agreed. "But before we do anything, we need to have an official meeting and set some ground rules as to how our little . . . organization will operate, okay?"

Maddy and Lucy both nodded in agreement before Maddy excitedly exclaimed, "Oh . . . my . . . god! Tomorrow's Wednesday, and I'm hosting! Everybody's going to be so excited to see you!"

"Really?" Lucy said with a quiet reserve. "Do you really think that they'll be happy to see me?" "Fuck yeah, they will," Maddy yelled out as she bounded off of the couch. "All of the shit that went down was between *us*! As long as *we're* cool, *they'll* be cool. Nothing has changed, Lucy. *Nobody* has anything to fear if they're cool with Maddy, heh, heh, heh. But we'll have to wait for your entrance for a bit tomorrow. Maybe you can hang out upstairs with Erick for an hour or so. See, we have a new member of our group named Amanda, and tomorrow night is supposed to be about celebrating a possible treatment for her cancer. So we need to wait a bit, so your appearance doesn't upstage that, okay?" "Sure," a tearful Lucy replied as she embraced her redis-covered best friend.

"Oh, and there's one other thing that I've got to do," Maddy said as she pulled out her phone. "Yeah, hey, Aunt Blair. Could you maybe come over for a bit? I think that we need to have another conversation that never happened and will never happen again . . . again."

CHAPTER 35

FRIENDS

On July 3, 2017, twenty-two-year-old Amanda Denhart lost her husband through what was called an "accident." Pieces of his partially eaten body had washed up on the shore of Hampton Beach. His head was never recovered. Investigators were puzzled, however, at why a recovered portion of his wrist seemed to have duct tape residue on it. Regardless, the cause of death was officially determined accidental, with the assumption being that he had gotten drunk, swept out into the ocean where he had drowned, and provided a snack for the various carnivorous aquatic wildlife. *Only the last part of that scenario was, in fact, true,* Maddy had thought at the time through her devilish cackles.

Upon hearing the news, Amanda and her five-year-old daughter Vai held each other and wept. They then screamed with joy and laughed hysterically. The reign of terror was finally over from the misogynistic scourge that had dominated them for so long. The beatings. The rape. The screaming. The lit cigarettes being put out on their arms and legs. The heavy items and bottles being thrown at them. The threats to their other family members. The tyranny was all over, and the pair of giggling females held their heads high and promptly walked down the street to buy themselves some well-deserved cheeseburgers and milkshakes.

But as is true with many women who are able to escape the clutches of abuse, the freedom from the physical and mental anguish is quickly met by the cold reality of a crippling financial situation. Amanda picked up as many hours as she could at the bookstore, but one income wasn't nearly enough to make ends meet. And then there was the additional problem of quality child-care while she was at work.

Amanda talked to Maddy about her financial problems. Maddy did all that she could from the standpoint of wages and work hours, but her efforts fell far short in the money pit that is New York City. So Maddy talked with Kristy and Jason. And by the late summer, the Denhart ladies had moved into the guest home of the upper-middle-class Andersons. Jason, Kristy, Adam, and Aaron welcomed their new neighbors into what was originally intended to be a temporary situation. But within a month, the Denharts had become a part of the Andersons family. This was especially true for the one-year-old twin boys' fondness for Vai, who they bonded with as though she were their biological older sister. And two years later, Alexa would hold that same bond and affection for both Vai and her older brothers.

The only burden that the new family situation presented was that Jason would have to make an additional portion of chicken nuggets and macaroni and cheese on the Wednesday and Friday girls' nights, which now periodically included Amanda unless she was working. The children would eat, play, and watch colorful animation together, week after week as Vai's wounds slowly began to fade from her chest, arms, legs, and psyche. And week after week, Vai's smile would increasingly replace her looks of fear, anger, or self-doubt. Jason and Kristy loved her as though she were one of their own and they basked in the young girl's glow of steadily increasing self-confidence.

Amanda and Vai Denhart had obtained what all women and girls deserve to obtain. They had housing security. They had financial stability. They had freedom from abuse. They had support from an extended family of true friends. And they had love. What they *didn't* have and what no one, not even Maddy, could give them was luck.

In March of 2021, Amanda began feeling run down. When she wasn't working or helping her beloved daughter with her homework, she was sleep-ing. She had difficulty getting in to see a doctor as the nation's health care system was once again buckling under the weight of the Covid pandemic. Only this time it was preventable, as most people that were clogging up the hospital system were those that had chosen not to receive the vaccine due to their belief in wild-eyed conspiracy theories. Therefore, people like Amanda were pushed aside in order to care for the most urgent of cases. She finally was able to see a doctor that fall and was diagnosed with a rare and aggressive form of cancer. She was told that there were treatments that could be tried, but the initial prognosis was that she might have two years left to live.

By the summer of 2022, Amanda was too weak to work. Everyone in the group including the Andersons, Jules, Sam, Monica, Erick, and Maddy chipped in to see to it that the Denharts had food, shelter, clothing, and . . . health insurance. Despite the grim outlook, there were rumors of an experimental treatment that, although quite costly, showed promise in substantially extending both the length and quality of life of people with this rare form of cancer. And if her life could be extended, then perhaps she would live to see an actual cure. Everyone in the group remained eternally hopeful.

And then it happened. In February of 2023, Amanda's doctor told her that the experimental treatment was ready to be tried and that he was recommending her for the first round of treatment. All that needed to be done was to convince the insurance company to pay a portion of the cost, while grants would cover the remainder.

Amanda would sleep most of the entire week so that she could attend Maddy's bridal party and wedding. Although her pain and fatigue forced her to leave early on both evenings, her smile beamed from under her blonde wig that covered her fading patchwork of real hair. So it was under this backdrop that Maddy hosted Amanda, Blair, Patty, Sam, Kristy, and Jules this Wednesday, February 22. This was not going to be a quiet evening of sipping wine, snacking on cheese, and waxing poetic on the latest events in their neighborhood, city, and world.

"This is a fuckin' *party*!" Patty exclaimed as she turned up the living room stereo and cranked, "Jet Boy Jet Girl," by The Damned. "Why the fuck aren't we in the big room for this, anyway?" Patty bellowed. "These tiny speakers suck!"

"I know," Maddy explained, "we'll be up there in a bit. We're going to hang down here and celebrate Amanda's great fuckin' news, then we'll go up there, and Erick's gonna DJ for us."

"Oh fuck, *he's* home?" a surly Patty responded. "I swear, if he plays Christopher Cross one more fucking time, I'm gonna rip his mixer apart. What the fuck is up with *that* kick lately anyway?" "Uh . . . I dunno," Maddy sheepishly replied as she nervously glanced at her Aunt Blair who just smirked and gently shook her head.

Amanda was glowing in the never-ending love and support of her friends. She thought back upon earlier in the week when she had told her daughter of the possible treatment. The eleven-year-old Vai clung to her mother and said, "I *knew* you wouldn't leave me, momma. I just knew it."

There were jokes and laughter and hugs. There were also arguments that came in the form of Sam and Jules. "Jules, would you *please* stop leaving used condoms on my car?" a beleaguered Sam requested. "I know you're upset with me for harassing you about getting married without our having a chance to meet with him. But I'm sorry . . . okay? Please just stop. It's absolutely *disgusting*! I'm now carrying a bottle of cleanser and rags to wipe your man's seed from my windshield every morning. I've apologized, so please stop now, okay?"

Jules, who was sitting slouched down in her overly cushioned chair and wearing all black gave her good friend a condescending smile. Then, without saying a word, she flipped her off, got up, and retrieved another glass of wine.

"Maddy," Sam begged, "Could you *please* do something? *Please*? I mean, it's been almost two weeks now. And it doesn't matter where I'm parked. I came out of a theater the other night with a date, and I had *five* of those foul things leaking all over my windshield and hood. There was even one tied to my antennae that I had to touch to get loose. I walked into work the other day and there was one stuck to my shoe! Please, Maddy. She'll listen to you."

Maddy looked around the room. Everyone was in complete silence and carried the exact same evil grin on their faces. She knew it was funny. She knew that everyone else knew it was funny. And she had no desire to intervene in this battle between the will of the hyper-rigid and the will of the who-gives-a-fuck. Plus, she *really* wanted to see this play out. Would Sam dare to escalate the battle? If so, how? How would Jules respond? Would Jerry get sucked into it somehow? The intrigue made Maddy salivate.

"All right, Jules, you've had your fun. Now knock it the fuck off!" Maddy yelled. "Fine!" Jules angrily retorted. "But one more word from that bitch about my marriage, and she's gonna be *covered* in semen, and I'm *not* talking about sailors!" Sam hugged Maddy and whispered, "Thank you," into her ear. Maddy responded by whispering, "And thank *you* for saving my life. Now just leave her alone, okay?" Maddy looked up and saw a slight nod of approval from the ever-attentive Blair.

The truce had been settled and Maddy maternally watched as Jules handed Sam a fresh glass of wine with an apologetic smile. It was the most contrition anyone would ever receive from her.

After another hour of conversation about Amanda's condition and treatments, she said, "All right! Enough of this blathering on about me. This night isn't about me. It's about friendship. I don't know how this will all end up, but I do know one thing. I've never been so happy in my life as when I met and started hanging out with all of you. And your men. You have all been so gracious to me and Vai, and I know that if something happens to me that she will be well taken care of." With this last sentiment, she reached out and clutched Kristy's hand as a tear rolled down her pale cheek.

"And it is just so incredible to see how powerful of a group of women we are. How intelligent. How accomplished. And despite our petty differences, how much love there is between us all. *That* is what I want to celebrate tonight. I want to celebrate how we as women can overcome *anything* that we put our hearts and mind to. Even the fucking *Supreme Court*! Now let's go fucking party!"

There was a huge roar of approval followed by applause and tear-filled hugs as the seven women turned to begin their determined march up the metal staircase to the awaiting Erick and his ear-splitting monsoon of sound. Upon reaching the party room door, Maddy turned around and said, "Okay, I gotta go in first real quick. I just want to make sure Erick has the first song ready, okay? Plus . . . um . . . well, there's another guest that I want you all to meet. So just hang tight for a sec."

The remaining six women were looking at each other with confused expressions when Maddy opened the door. Patty strutted in and yelled out, "All right . . . so who's this *new* bitch we have to meet?" From behind the darkened bar in the far corner of the room came a small voice. "Well, Aunt Patty, it's not so much that I'm new. It's just that I'm . . . back." As the slight frame emerged from the shadowy corners and into the dance lighting there was a collective stunned gasp.

Maddy walked through the veil of silence and over to her friend, lovingly held her hand, and said, "Everybody, please join me in welcoming our Lucy home." There was a shriek of exhilaration followed by Lucy being immersed in hugs from her friends in a jubilant reunion.

Maddy went up to Amanda and said, "I hope this is ok, on your big night and everything, but *she* just brings this all together." "Who . . . who is she?" a confused Amanda asked. "Well," a smiling Maddy replied, "you would know her as The Nameless One. But as of tonight, she's your newest sister, Lucy."

As Erick began playing the Maddy suggested, "Movin' on Up" by Primal Scream, the group of triumphant women began their joyous gyrations that would not end until several hours later with the final note of Elton John's "Friends." They even danced through not *one*, not *two*, but *three* Christopher Cross selections. Lucy was the final piece of the puzzle, and *nothing* would be able to stop them now. What they did not yet realize, however, was that human frailty has its limits that no amount of love can alter. Especially when that love is pitted against American corporate greed. And they also had yet to realize that Lucy was *far* from the last piece of the puzzle.

———

The following Friday evening, Sam, Jules, and Kristy were on the dance floor of an area nightclub listening to the monotonous beats of electronic "music" while Maddy was watching Lucy put on her crimson lipstick in the ladies' room. "Fuck man, I love that color!" Maddy exclaimed. "Let *me* try it!"

"Uh . . . no, Maddy. This one isn't for you. You haven't taken the antidote." Lucy smiled coyly and exited the restroom with an excited Maddy at her heels like a puppy who was welcoming her owner home. "What the fuck, Lucy," Maddy began, "why are you wearing *Toxin X*?" "I'm not" came Lucy's reassurance. "This is one of my *own* creations. Well, I mean, it's an adaptation of one of my grandfather's recipes. *This*, on my lips, is *Toxin I*."

"What the *fuck* is *Toxin I*?" an overly eager Maddy asked impatiently. "Well, *Toxin I* permanently blocks the chemical reactions in the hypothalamus and prevents any sort of sexual arousal. It doesn't prevent sexual *interest*, it just prevents the *arousal*, if you know what I mean. I don't wear it often. Just when I go out to nightclubs where I'm sure I'll encounter some overly-handsy scumbags. So . . . I just give them a taste of what they want. Just a small kiss. And in about ten minutes, there won't be enough little blue pills in the world to get them hard . . . *ever*. You see, the "I" stands for "Impotence.""

"Fuck, man!" Maddy yelled, "I've been sucking on your straw *all night*, stealing your drinks! I'm fucked!" "No, you'll be all right," Lucy replied. "*Toxin I* can only be spread from human to human. Once it hits any surface other than human tissue, it dies immediately. And the guys that I've kissed tonight aren't contagious either. So don't worry about it."

"*Guys*?" a shocked Maddy asked. "How many fuckin' guys have you *kissed* tonight?" "Oh, I don't know," Lucy replied dismissively. "Maybe four .

. . or five. I'm not sure." "Ummm . . . Lucy," a shocked Maddy gently began inquiring, "How many guys in total have you used that on?"

Lucy looked at her friend with bemusement then began a low chuckle before she said, "Let's just say that there are about two hundred fewer dead-beat dads in the world and leave it at that, okay? Oh, hell! I love this song! C'mon, let's dance!"

And with that, Maddy found herself in a very similar situation to when the pair of best friends were younger. She was there to keep the guys away from her. Only *this* time, it wasn't to protect *her*. It was to protect *them*.

Jules said her goodbyes and left with Jerry about an hour before the quartet of Maddy, Sam, Kristy, and Lucy left the club. As Sam approached her car, she quietly said, "Oh, goddammit. I thought that she didn't hear me bitching about her marriage tonight." Splattered on the windshield was yet another used condom. "All right," a reserved Maddy said. "I'll talk to her tomorrow."

CHAPTER 36

YOO HOO

Maddy, Erick, and Lucy were sitting in the dark corner of a neighborhood bar when Maddy stated, "Okay, welcome to our first official meeting. First order of business is that we need a name for our group." "Why?" Erick inquired. "Ummm," Maddy began explaining, "because it would be cool. We need a cool name." "Why?" Erick asked again. "Oh my god!" an increasingly annoyed Maddy retorted as Lucy looked on with a sly grin, "Every serial killer has a cool name, right? And every vigilante group has a cool name, right? So we need one too so we can be cool!"

"But," a confused Erick replied, "why? To what purpose? Who else would ever know about it? Are we going to take out a full- page ad in *The Times*? *Slashers for hire. Call 1-800-FuckHimUp to get a personal slasher on the phone now. Really fucked up operators are standing by*. I kinda doubt it. There is no purpose for us to have a name and I vote that we don't have one because it's silly."

Maddy folded her arms and began pouting. Seeing this, Lucy tried to find a compromise by saying, "How about we call ourselves *Mel*?" "Why *Mel*?" Maddy asked. Lucy responded, "Well, it's just the first letters of our names and it would be easy to refer to ourselves in public without anyone knowing what we were talking about. For example, if we saw some jerk abusing their kid, we could look at each other and say, 'This looks like a job for Mel.'"

"Or we could just give each other a knowing glance and a nod," a bored

Erick replied. "Okay, Lucy," Maddy began, "first of all, thank you for being the *only one in our group* who is taking this seriously. But I'm afraid I'm going to have to veto *Mel*. It's just not cool enough."

"And that's another thing," Erick chimed in. "Who made *you* president of our twisted little club? Why do *you* have the right to veto something?" "Well," a defensive Maddy began explaining, "it's because *I* would be best for this leadership role. There was a scientific survey conducted to determine who would be best to lead a group of vigilante serial killers, and well, not to brag or anything, but I came out on top. And you, mister, weren't even in the top 500! And that's science! And you can't argue with science!"

"Okay," Erick began as he tried to understand his beloved wife's so-called logic. "So you have appointed yourself president based upon your large ego and made up scientific 'facts' and you have the right to veto any decision that is made, and you can never be removed from power, which makes you a dictator and makes us your servants. Do I have that right? You know who that sounds like, *don't you?*"

"Don't you *even* fuckin' say it!" Maddy exclaimed as she glared at her husband's smirking face. Erick, knowing that he had hit on the intended nerve pressed on. "I mean, you've almost got the right hair color for it and if you'd just excessively tan to give your skin that nice burnt orange hue, you *might* be able to pull it off."

Erick smirked as Maddy's simmering green eyes glared right through him as she tried to find a reply. Finding none after nearly three minutes of complete silence, Maddy found the courage that a certain disgraced and traitorous ex-president couldn't and conceded the argument.

"Okay, mister," Maddy began, "I can see your point. And since *I* do not have the emotional maturity of a toddler and am not a sociopathic narcissist, I shall concede your point. But I would like to nominate myself as the leader of this group because I have family ties to this activity and much more experience. I could outline all of my successes in this area and give you my detailed qualifications if you would like."

"Well," Lucy interrupted. "I mean, if we're being honest with ourselves, all three of us are kinda sociopathic narcissists. I mean, we're all playing judge, jury, *and* executioner which is pretty narcissistic. And the sociopathic part . . . well . . . I don't think I really need to explain *that*, do I?"

"Okay, yeah, yeah, yeah," a defensive Erick began, "so maybe we're a *bit* narcissistic and definitely a *bit* sociopathic, but it's not like we're trying to instigate a coup to overthrow our constitutional democracy. It's not like we're trying to hang elected leaders. It's not like we're terrorizing the victims of school shootings. And it's not like we're using force to silence anyone who doesn't believe exactly as we do. In fact, we're using *our* twisted shit to try to *eliminate* would-be traitors, terrorists, and murderers. And we're doing that because we *don't* completely lack a conscious. Sure, we don't give a *fuck* about the 'chads' because they are worthless blights on our society. But we actually *do* possess a conscious because we're doing this out of our empathy toward the abused people who lack the resources to fight back against the *true* narcissistic sociopaths. We may possess some of their traits, but we are not *them* because *our* motivation is in helping *other* people and not self-aggrandizing *ourselves. We* are other-person-centered. *They*, by contrast, are most certainly *completely* self-centered. So I would consider our diagnosis to be something like *empathetic personality disorder with narcissistic and sociopathic tendencies.*"

"Works for me," a content Lucy stated. "Okay, *thank you* for your contributions to our conversation here, Doctor Freud," Maddy replied dismissively. "But I don't think that's actually a real diagnosis. Plus, I really don't give a fuck about all of this psychobabble. All I know is that when I see or hear about some asshole hurting someone else, then I want to fuck them up. It's that simple. Now, may we get back to the task at hand which was electing me as the leader which will be immediately followed by our choosing a cool name."

"Well," Erick conceded, "you are right about *one* thing here. That *is* a made-up diagnosis. But *all* personality disorders are made up. They're just another way of saying that someone's an asshole in one way or another. And *we* most certainly would be considered assholes by the 'chads' of the world. So I'm sticking with it. I say it's just as valid as any other personality disorder that would be in some shrink's vocabulary. Additionally, I would like to second the nomination of Mrs. Maddy Sommers to be our leader."

Maddy smiled and looked at Erick out of the corner of her eye before planting a big kiss on his lips and saying, "Thanks, baby, for your support." "Yeah, well don't get too full of yourself yet," Erick replied. "I have a list of rules that I believe we need to adopt and pledge to if we're going to work together, okay?"

Upon his female partners in crime's nodding approval, Erick began outlining the rules under which the group would operate.

RULE 1: The president of the group is to *facilitate* decisions made by the group, not to *make* the decisions unilaterally.

RULE 2: If there is substantial disagreement between the parties as to how to proceed with any issue, Aunt Blair would be consulted, and the entire group will abide by her decision.

RULE 3: Only the lives of people who represent a significant threat of physical or emotional harm to someone else who is vulnerable may be exterminated.

RULE 4: Less significant threats may be considered for "minor" injury or malicious pranks as determined by the group. Minor injury is defined as any injury inflicted that does not ultimately cause death. Examples include, but are not limited to: lacerations, bruises, broken bones, loss of teeth, loss of any or all of the five senses, loss of limbs, brain damage, and temporary or permanent paralysis.

RULE 5: Only people who identify as male may be considered to be a "chad" and for retribution at any level.

RULE 6: The group will decide who will carry out the responsibilities of surveillance, acquisition of needed materials, and the actual act of retribution.

RULE 7: The group member who is responsible for carrying out the act of retribution is solely responsible to determine the methodology of the retribution.

RULE 8: Each group member may listen to whatever preparation music that they want without fear of harassment or reprisal by another group member. This includes any song by Christopher Cross.

RULE 9: No conversation about group business between any members of the group will have ever happened. Ever.

RULE 10: The group shall be completely honest with and loyal to all other members of the group.

RULE 11: This is murder folks! So let's just have fun with it!

"Okay, I'm cool with it, although number eight isn't necessary, but whatevs," Maddy began, "but why are there *eleven* rules? Ten would be much cleaner and the eleventh one isn't so much a rule as it is a lifestyle choice." "True," Erick agreed. "But I wanted eleven rules in order to pay homage to *This Is Spinal Tap*." "Valid point!" Maddy exclaimed. "All right then, I hereby move to ratify these rules! All those in favor say *Aye*!" Erick and Lucy both raised their hands and said *Aye*.

"Okay, and does this mean that I'm now the *president* of this little band of misfits, *hmmmm*?" Maddy playfully inquired. Erick looked at Lucy. They both smiled and said *Aye*! "Well," Maddy began in a self-congratulatory tone, "I would like to thank all of my supporters who have put their trust in me. And I want to assure you all that I will fulfill my responsibilities to the fullest. This is truly a humbling experience, and I will—" Erick then interrupted. "Maddy, can we just get on with the meeting? There's a movie on in an hour that I want to watch."

"Okay fuckin' fine," a newly agitated Maddy stated before reclaiming her bubbly disposition and saying, "Then let's get on to the serious business of selecting our name!" "Oh, for fuck sake, Maddy!" Erick exclaimed. "We don't need a fuckin' name! There's just the three of us, and we can't share the name with anyone else anyway. There's simply no point!"

"Ummmm," a hesitant Lucy began, "I'm sorry Maddy, but I have to vote with Erick here. It just doesn't seem necessary."

Maddy let out a measured breath, tilted her head slightly, and said while attempting to mimic the reserve of her Aunt Blair, "I see. Well, I guess we'll just vote to *table* this discussion until you two are thinking more clearly." "Maddy," Erick stated, trying to be understanding of his wife's hurt feelings, "we're not tabling the discussion. We have just voted. We are *not* going to have a name. The decision is *final*. Please understand."

"Oh, I understand," Maddy replied in her lilting voice. "I understand that unless *someone* in this group votes to table the discussion then someone *else* in this group won't be in the mood to wear a certain special outfit tonight, so maybe *that* someone should cast his vote accordingly . . . y'know . . . if he wants. I wouldn't want to *dissuade* anyone from voting their conscious. I'm just sayin'."

Erick looked at Lucy apologetically and said defeatedly, "I'm sorry Lucy, but there's no rule against sexual coercion, and . . . it's a really cute outfit, so . . . I vote to table the discussion of our group name." "Yay!" Maddy yelled out. "Okay, so until the group has the time to take up our cool name, I'm going to refer to us as the *Trio of Terror*, 'cause I think that's really cool and that's probably what we'll be called anyway." Erick and Lucy just looked down at their drinks and shook their heads. They now fully understood just how much of a "democracy" their group would be.

"Alrighty then," Maddy enthusiastically continued, "now for our theme song." "Our . . . what?" a bewildered Lucy inquired. "Our theme song," Maddy assertively replied. "Y'know . . . we need a cool song with a driving beat as we're walking slow-mo down the middle of the street shrouded in fog and dressed in black leather . . . y'know . . . our theme song."

Erick immediately replied, "'You Hoo' by Imperial Teen." Maddy squealed as she jumped up from her seat and said, "Oh . . . fuck . . . yes!" She then straddled herself on Erick's lap and gave him a passionate kiss. "Oh, fuck baby, we're such a great team," Maddy whispered into his ear. "Two sides of the same coin," Erick whispered back.

"Okay, this *has* been a productive meeting now, hasn't it?" a beaming Maddy stated to her "team." "Now that the *important* stuff is out of the way, we can deal with this. So a little birdie told me that there's a fuckin' douche who gets off on beating his wife and kid. He just broke his kid's arm last night, and the wife is too afraid to talk to the police. But she *did* talk to my little bird. And I happen to know that his car is parked about four blocks from here. So who wants it?"

"Shit," a dejected Erick said. "What's wrong baby?" a concerned Maddy asked. "Well . . . it's not that big of a deal . . . it's just that . . . I was really looking forward to watching that movie tonight." "Well," Maddy bellowed, "if you would crawl out of the fucking stone ages and learn how to hit the little record button on the remote you could watch your shit whenever you want. You're so fucking ridiculous."

Lucy then chimed in. "I think, since it's our first one as a group, that maybe we should *all* pitch in on this one." "Alrighty then," an intrigued Maddy stated as she peered at her once again best friend, "What do you have in mind?" Lucy looked up at the pair again wearing her maniacal grin and said, "How about we do *this*."

———

The intoxicated man's car door let out a loud rusted creak as it opened. He crawled into his 1975 Pinto, closed one eye to block out the double vision, and inserted the key into the ignition. It was then that he felt the sting of a needle in the back of his neck. He felt instantly sober, conscious, and completely paralyzed. He felt someone shove him over into the passenger seat as someone else got into the back seat. He began profusely sweating on this chilly early March evening as he felt his car begin to move and heard the following conversation.

"So he's completely paralyzed?" a man's voice came from behind the steering wheel. "Yes, completely" came a female voice from the driver's back seat. "He's completely conscious but can't move a muscle. But the most important part of this particular toxin is that, although he can't move, his nerve endings are very much alive. He'll feel *everything*."

"So tell me again" came a second female voice, this time from directly behind him. "How many of these toxins do you have, anyway?" The first female stated, "I have perfected five, which is probably all that I will ever need. They are made from some pretty common chemicals and compounds that I can readily find. And they work practically instantaneously and perfectly. *Toxin X* is the lotion I told you about. Then, there's another lotion-based one that I'll tell you about later.

Toxin A knocks a person out in about five seconds. They'll stay out for about two hours. You can always shoot them up again if you need them out longer than that. Oh, and they wake up with a hell of a headache. Well," he then heard the most evil laugh before the voice continued, "that is if we *let* them wake up."

"*Toxin B* is what *this* guy has in him. Instantaneous paralysis for around six hours with complete consciousness and live nerves. It's absolutely perfect for tonight's torture scenario." With that, he felt his head being tilted back and a pair of lips kissing him on the forehead followed by evil laughter.

"And then there's *Toxin C*. Lethal in about ten seconds. Perfect for a quick in and out with no mess. There are certain forensic tests that pick up on some of the ingredients, but there hasn't been a test developed yet to put together the entire recipe. That, my friends, is and shall always remain a family secret."

"Cool, we're here," stated the male driver. He heard the car door open and felt himself being grasped by the wrists and ankles and carried. He heard a larger door open, then a bright light revealing an empty, large, and run-down industrial space. He felt the rope around his wrists. Then the sensation of being lifted four feet off of the floor. His mind was screaming for them to stop, but not a sound emerged from his unable-to-tremble lips.

And then he saw them: a blonde Asian woman, a white redheaded woman, and a brown-haired white male. They were all dressed alike in black jeans, hoodies, boots, and gloves. He could do nothing but watch and listen as the red-headed woman with glowering green eyes looked up at him and said, "Hey, motherfucker! You like beating on innocent women and children? Yeah? Well, we love beating on people too!"

He felt the baseball bat shatter his right knee. His psyche was the recipient of the excruciating pain of each blow as each of them took turns battering him. He heard and felt his bones snap. His legs. His arms, his ribs, his chest, his back, his neck. Over and over and over the painful strikes would come from the blur of the never stopping bats. His kidneys. Then, his kidneys again. Then his kidneys again as he felt urine flow down his pant leg.

"Oh, I bet you really punish your sweet little boy for wetting himself, don't you, motherfucker?" the redhead sternly asked. "Yeah, I bet that's why you broke his arm last night. It was because he had an accident. He didn't make it to the restroom on time, so you broke his fucking arm! Snapped it in two, didn't you? Well, motherfucker . . . *this* is no accident!"

Blow after blow after blow on his testicles as all of the beer and cheeseburgers that he had consumed earlier came flowing out of his mouth, dribbled down his chin, and onto his chest before pooling in light brown chunks on the cold cement floor. "Goddam!" the male exclaimed. "This motherfucker's resilient! Hasn't even passed out yet!" "He can't," said the petite Asian. "That's another benefit of *Toxin B*. It has adrenaline in it. No matter how much pain they're in, they simply can't lose consciousness."

"Well" came the redhead's voice, "I guess it's fuckin' party time then!" The blows and the pain and the cracked and broken bones continued for what seemed to be an eternity. Then, it mercifully stopped. The redhead looked up at him and smiled. Then she said, "Okay, listen, mister. I'm feeling generous tonight. Yeah, I'm going to do you a favor. I'm gonna get your sweet little boy a present. But, before I do, I want to make sure that a boy would like it. Erick, honey? Would you come over here please?"

He could see the man approach. His face was beet red as he looked up at him and gave him a mischievous grin before saying, "Yes, dear? What is it?" "Well," the redhead said, "you're a guy so I was wondering if you thought that his little boy would like . . . a pinata?"

The last thing the hanging and battered man heard before the fatal blow to his skull was the man named Erick yelling, "Let's see some fuckin' candy!"

———

"That's what happens when you fuck with a friend of a friend of the *Trio of Terror*!" Maddy proudly exclaimed before engaging in uncontrollable cackling. "I don't like it. It's too cheesy. Sounds like a cheap ass horror movie."

Erick stated flatly as he watched the man's brain secrete out of his shattered skull and down his purple, swollen face.

"What the fuck do you *mean*?" an incredulous Maddy retorted. "That fuckin' name is cool! It's a name to be fuckin' *feared*!" "Yeah, but nobody else will ever hear it, and since this isn't an official meeting, I don't want to talk about it anymore" came Erick's uninterested reply. "God, you two are soooo messed up. I can see how you fell for one another," Lucy stated as the trio (of terror?) exited the industrial building and began a long two-mile trek to the nearest subway station.

As the three dark-clad silhouettes were walking in slow-mo into the dense fog bank, they could feel the rhythm of their cool theme song pounding in their brains. Unfortunately for them, somewhere in the distance, a car radio was playing an all too familiar tune.

"What the *fuck* is the deal with hearing 'Sailing' all the fucking time?" Maddy angrily bellowed. "Just admit, Maddy," an arrogant Erick replied as Lucy just sadly shook her head. "It's a cool fuckin' song."

CHAPTER 37

THE BIG MONEY

The joyous news finally arrived at 4:04 PM on March 21, 2023. The insurance company had finally agreed to pay for Amanda's experimental treatment which held the great prospect of substantially extending the length and quality of her life. And in what the insurance company would *surely* consider to be a win-win situation, the decision was made just under three hours *after* Amanda succumbed to her terminal illness which would save the company and its shareholders nearly $400,000. The jubilant cheers and popping sounds of uncorked champagne bottles from the insurance company's billion-dollar skyscraper in Hartford resonated in Amanda's lifeless heart that was resting in the cold Brooklyn morgue.

Amanda had been placed in intensive care at the hospital five days before her demise. Her medical team had pleaded with the insurance company to grant payment for the experimental treatment, but they had insisted upon another round of a previously tried treatment before proceeding to what they felt was the highly speculative and very costly experimental one. At 1:12 PM, Amanda looked upon her beloved daughter with sunken eyes and said, "I will always love you. Be a good girl for the Andersons. I will always be with you, my love. My child." She then closed her eyes while emitting a final shallow gasp. Vai whispered to her mother's corpse, "I will always love you, momma. And I will *avenge* you."

Everyone in the room, including the hospital staff began weeping. Jason held Kristy. Erick held Maddy. Jerry held Jules. Sam held Lucy. Blair held Patty. And Aaron and Adam held their best friend Vai whose grief-weary face contorted into a rage. She took the hands of her adoptive brothers and silently exited the room with the four-year-old Alexa trailing behind them. The adults in the room were amazed by this display of youthful solidarity. Vai was only eleven at the time. Adam and Aaron were seven. And they marched out of the room together with the grim determination of an army battalion marching off to war.

As the solemn group was preparing to leave the hospital, Adam and Aaron went up to Maddy and said with each toe- headed twin taking turns, "Aunt Maddy, why did they hurt her?" "Yes, why did they hurt Aunt Amanda?" "Why did they hurt our friend?" "Yes, how can we help Vai? Why did this happen?"

Maddy took to one knee and looked at the adorable twin boys in their piercing blue eyes and began her explanation. "Oh, my dears. I . . . I don't know . . . I don't know what to . . . tell you . . . I," She then looked pleadingly up at her beloved husband and said, "Can you please help me? I don't know what to say."

Erick bent down and picked the boys up, one in each arm. He carried them over to where Vai was sitting expressionless and sat them down on either side of her. He got down on one knee before these devastated children and said in a passionately soft voice, "*I'll* tell you why they did this. I'll tell you *exactly* why. And it will make you *angry*. It should make *everyone* angry. They did it for *money*. They did it for *greed*. They did it so they can have another yacht or sports car or third home in Vail. They did it because they have *no regard* for the human life that they profess to care so much about. They don't care about *you*. They don't care about *me*. And they sure as *fuck* didn't care about Vai's wonderful mother. They care about *things*. They care about *stature*. They care about *power*. We are just *meaningless pawns* to them. But we aren't. *We* have the power to do something about it if we have the *balls* to stand up and fight back."

Aaron's brilliant blue eyes looked into Erick's as he said, "We hate them, Uncle Erick." "Yes" came Adam's reply. "We want to do bad things to them." Erick embraced all three of the children and whispered to them, "Never let go of that rage in your heart. There are many of these motherfuckers that you're going to have to fight in your lives."

From directly behind him came the small voice of Alexa who simply parroted, "*Motherfuckers.*"

The Andersons had made up a permanent bedroom in their home for Vai. The adoption papers had already been drawn up and would be signed the following morning making Vai an official member of the family. But Vai would not take their last name, choosing to remain Vai Denhart. Nor would she sleep in her new bedroom that night. She insisted on sleeping in her mother's bed in the guest house. And *The Twins* insisted on staying with her. "We have to be with her, Dad." "Yes, we must be there to protect her." Jason's heart wilted at this solemnly loyal request, and he spent the night sleeping on the short couch of the guest home.

The following morning, Jason went into the bedroom to find the three children already awake and playing with Vai's dolls on the bed. A female doll adorned in her most beautiful dress lay still in the shoebox of her mother's favorite pair of black pumps. They were the shoes that Amanda had worn to go out dancing on the evening that they had found out that her abusive husband had perished. Other dolls were seated around the box, each dressed in their Sunday best. Silently playing on the stereo was the song that Amanda would lovingly sing to her beloved daughter each night. As Paul Simon's "Mother and Child Reunion" soared out of the table-top speakers, Vai wiped a tear from her eye.

Jason's heart was aching. He had no idea what to say at this moment. Should he hold her or just leave her alone? Should he say something, or silently join this lovingly black ceremony? He then saw another male doll hanging from the nightstand lamp by a shoelace. His arms, legs, and head were lying beneath the suspended torso, drenched in red fingernail polish.

"Who . . . who is *this* then," Jason cautiously asked the trio. Adam looked up and said flatly, "That is the insurance man." Aaron then joined in. "Yes, Dad. He did bad things to us, so we did bad things to him. It made Vai smile." Jason then looked at Vai who was just staring at the doll in the shoebox. She was wearing a maniacal smile and lightly rocked as she hummed along to the tender melody.

Jason told Kristy, Blair, Erick, and Maddy about the morbid scene in the guesthouse bedroom earlier that morning. "Ummm," Kristy began, "should we maybe get them a therapist or something?" "Well," Blair responded tenderly, "You may do what you wish. But it seems to me that it is healthy for these children to act out their grief in a manner that doesn't harm innocent others. They have so much hurt and anger in them right now. And that hurt and anger must go somewhere. I believe it to be better that they are taking their wrath out on dolls rather than . . . someone else who does not deserve it. Plus, our Maddy used to have that same form of rage as a child. And you can see how *she* has turned out. I think they will be fine. If you are concerned, Maddy and I can assist you in . . . *directing* their anger as they grow a bit older, isn't that right, dear?"

A hesitant Maddy looked into the bewildered eyes of her husband, then at her aunt's determined expression. "Uh . . . yeah . . . I have a little bit of experience with those types of feelings, so I could probably help them, y'know if they need it. But they'll probably just outgrow it and be just fine."

"Yes, you're probably right, dear," Blair calmly replied. "They will probably outgrow it. Just as *you* did." This final sentiment sent a chill down Erick's spine.

Following the simple but elegantly heart-wrenching funeral service, an emotionally drained Vai was walking out with her newly adopted family when a sharply dressed woman kneeled before her. "Hello, honey," the young brunette said tenderly. "On behalf of our insurance company, I want to express our deepest condolences. We are *so sorry* for your loss, and if there's anything that we can do to help you at this time, please reach out to us."

Vai smiled innocently at the woman and said sweetly, "Thank you for your caring. Yes, there *is* something that you can do for me. You can go back in time and give my mother the treatment that she needs. And if you can't do *that*," Vai's voice then deepened and her face turned bright red as she said through her gritted teeth, "then what I want you to do is fucking *die*, you heartless bitch! Take your *I'm sorries* and shove them up your ass. I hope you *choke* on your next paycheck. I will *never* forgive you. I will never forgive *any* of you." As *The Twins* passed the shocked woman, they said in turn, "Shame on you." "Yes, shame on you." "You have been bad." "Yes, you must be punished." They each put their arm around their beloved sister Vai and proceeded out of the church.

Erick, Maddy, and Lucy were driving to their home where they would host the reception. They were listening to Lou Reed's "Dirty Blvd." as Maddy played on her phone. Her brow furled. The right side of her mouth slinked upward in a serpentine half- smile. She then said, "Baby, we need to pack." "All right," Erick replied, "where are we going?" "Kansas City" came Maddy's immediate and determined reply. "All right, what's in Kansas City?" Erick inquired. Maddy's voice lowered as she looked at a man's pudgy, smug face on her phone and said wickedly, "A health insurance convention."

———

GAAAAAWD! I fucking hate wigs! Maddy thought as she adjusted her new platinum blonde locks and placed her blue contact lenses into her eyes. She exited the lady's room adjacent to the posh hotel lounge and began making her way through the tittering sea of insurance executives, their wedding rings glinting in the dim lighting as they had their arms draped around some giggling "associate" or "niece."

Her hips swayed through the crowd of frequent offers to buy her drinks and subtle whistles. *Not surprised*, she thought to herself. *I damn near look like a fuckin' hooker in this short gold dress, black stockings, black, silk elbow gloves, and black strapped pumps. Now, where's my handsome pimp?* She scanned the bar and found a dour Erick in the corner, casually sipping a tonic with lime and wearing a look of disgust on his face. *Oh, fuck he looks pissed. He sooo hates wearing that fucking suit. And he sooo wanted to help me tonight. But we can't risk both of us being on camera going to this prick's room, so he'll just have to be content with being my driver . . . and back up should I need it, which I fucking won't!*

She found her rotund quarry, laughing, chuckling, and backslapping as she squeezed between the men to take a seat at the bar. She looked up at him, batted her blue eyes, and suggestively said, "Hey, that's a *really nice* tie. Do you ever use it for anything besides wearing it around your neck?" *Oh, this is going to be so fucking easy!* Maddy thought as she noticed a slight trail of drool dribble from the corner of the man's mouth.

"Uh . . . well thank you," the man stammered, "I'm sure we can find some *other* uses for it. It did cost $300, so it better be good for something a bit *more fun*, don't you think?" "Definitely," Maddy purred. "Wow, $300. You must be someone *really big* and important." "Well, I don't like to brag," the encouraged man replied as he felt blood rushing into his penis, "but I *am* the CEO of a *rather large* insurance company."

"Wow, I knew when I first saw you that you were someone *special*. And I bet your company isn't the *only* thing that's *rather large*, is it? Maybe you'd like to show me?" The man's now engorged penis was completely in charge of his decision-making at this moment as he eagerly said, "Why, yes. I'd love to.

Uh, won't you join me in my room for a nightcap?" "Oh gaaawd yes," Maddy whispered breathily into his ear. As she exited with her left arm draped around the man's waist, she looked back and flashed a mischievous smile at her glowering Erick.

Acting as his personal compass, the man's straying penis pointed the couple first to the elevators, then to the penthouse suite then to the luxury bedroom. "Oh, my gaaawd! This place is beautiful!" Maddy exclaimed as she landed back first upon the enormous bed, giving her prey a slight flash of her black lace panties, just to seal the deal.

The man began untying his tie and unbuttoning his shirt with a lascivious look of primal greed. "Tee, hee," Maddy giggled as she got up from the bed and walked to the man's closet. She began stroking the silk ties that were hung there, playfully looked at the man over her bare shoulder, and said, "So . . . I guess you're here for an . . . examination. Should we see what your insurance policy covers? Let's see here, I bet you're here to be tied up with these lovely ties, aren't you? Well, let me just check your policy while you lie down on the bed. And if it *is* covered, I'm gonna need you to sign my form with the . . . *ink* . . . from your *pen*."

The bedsprings strained as the man flopped onto the bed and immediately served up his outstretched arms. "Why yes, sir," Maddy stated softly as she climbed on top of him with ties in each hand. "Your policy *does* cover this procedure. Now just lie still, I promise I *won't* be gentle." She firmly tied the panting man's wrists to the bedposts. "Oooooo, I *really* like this one," Maddy cooed as she began wadding up the tie that was adorned by pink hearts and placed it into the man's eagerly awaiting mouth. "It reminds me of Valentine's Day, which, reminds me of the day I first met my husband and of our wedding day."

The man suddenly looked confused as Maddy climbed up off of him and began speaking in a much more stern and direct cadence. "Yeah, my husband *really* wanted to fuck you up, but I insisted that it was better this way. You see, he *really* hates insurance companies. He *really* hates how they take the money from middle—and working-class folks month after month, year after year, then, when those people actually *need* the insurance, they have to go through all of this fucking stress and red tape if they're not just outright denied. Is that fair, Mister CEO of a big, fancy insurance company with his fancy ties? Is it *fair* that you become obscenely rich over denying people the medical care that they rightfully paid for?"

Now realizing that sex was definitely off of the table, the man began struggling to free himself. "Oh, I'm sorry," Maddy apologetically stated, "But your policy only covers getting tied up. We don't cover you getting *untied*, so I guess you'll just have to lay there and—" Maddy's face became twisted and bright red as she finished her sentence angrily, "*Listen to me!*"

"*Listen to me* as I tell you about a good friend who I just *buried* because *your* fucking company wouldn't provide her with the procedure that her doctors said she needed! *Listen to me* as I tell you how that woman suffered for days while waiting for *your* fucking approval! *Listen to me* as I tell you how she finally succumbed to her ailment *three hours before* your fucking company finally called with the approval. *Listen to me* as I tell you how *your* red tape killed an innocent, sweet woman. *Listen to me* as I tell you how I know that she isn't the only one. How I know that there are probably millions of people out there suffering and dying because of this scam insurance! People are worried about government health insurance because there will be government 'death panels'? Really? When are they going to wake the fuck up and realize that there are *already* death panels! The entire health insurance industry is one big fucking *death panel*! *You* are a death panel! *You* are responsible for my friend's death! And I, motherfucker, am *your* death panel. And it just so happens that your policy has a death benefit. But not for *you*," Maddy then straddled the man once again, her emerald eyes shimmering from behind the blue contacts, "But for *me*," Maddy then leaned forward and breathily whispered into the panicked man's ear, "because I'm *definitely* gonna benefit from squeezing the fucking life out of you."

Her face contorted into a twisted macabre smile as she placed the crimson tie around the man's bulbous neck. She pulled as hard as she could, grunting as she squeezed. The man's face turned bright red, and his eyes began to protrude as tears of anguish flowed out of them. He was violently choking and gagging as he tried to force air into his lungs while staring at the maniacal smile of his platinum-blonde assassin. The enraged Maddy continued to choke him for a full two minutes after he stopped moving.

She casually got up from off of the bed and took her burner phone from her purse. "Hey, you! Yeah, it's done. Yeah, give me fifteen minutes. Yes, I know where the fucking car is! Dark parking lot a half mile east of here. Okay, see ya soon. Yeah, love you too."

Maddy climbed into the car and placed the garbage bag with her wig, outfit, and accessories into the back seat. Erick was listening to "Tie a Yellow

Ribbon Round the Ole Oak Tree" by Tony Orlando and Dawn as he said, "So how'd it go?" "Well," Maddy began quietly, "not so good for *him*. You see, I had to—" she then flashed her beaming smile and exclaimed with glee, "cancel his insurance policy!" "Get it?" Erick just shook his head sadly, started the car, and said, "Jesus, you are so bad at this." The pair of bickering voices faded out as the car pulled out of the dark parking lot driveway and headed toward the interstate that would lead them to Jefferson City. "What the fuck do you mean, *bad at this*?" *That*, mister, was pure fucking gold!"

CHAPTER 38

FIRE

Maddy and Erick's rental car pulled into the parking lot and came to an abrupt halt in front of the stained door of the rundown motel a few miles south of Jefferson City. Maddy leaped from the driver's seat, ran up to the door, and began pounding. "Lucy! Let us in, bitch! C'mon, hurry up! This is a matter of *life or death*!"

Lucy opened the door and Maddy dashed past her as Erick casually sauntered into the room. "Can't talk! Gotta piss!" Maddy yelled out as she slammed the bathroom door. Lucy and Erick then heard her relieved exclamation coming from behind the closed door. "Oooohhh fuck. That feels soooo gooood." Maddy then opened the bathroom door and popped her head around the corner. All that could be seen of her was her bewildered emerald eyes underneath her copper bangs. "Ummm, Erick . . . could you come in here for a moment?"

Her dutiful husband entered the bathroom. A concerned Maddy pulled back the shower curtain to reveal a gelatinous pool of blood and external organs that were intended to be internal filling the bathtub. There was something that resembled a head resting atop the frothy lake of pink fluid. Aside from that, very few people would be able to recognize that this oozing, chunky slime had once been human.

The pair entered the bedroom and cautiously looked at Lucy, who was laying on one of the twin beds in her pink pajamas watching *The Blob*. As the title song filled the room, Maddy began hesitantly, "Hey there, Lucy . . . how are ya doin?" "Fine," Lucy replied without looking up from the thirty-year-old television set. "So," Maddy began again, "you wanna tell us who the guy in the bathtub is?"

"Oh . . . him," Lucy replied uninterestingly. "He was beating on a hooker outside of this diner down the road and—" She then looked at the pair excitedly and exclaimed, "Oh . . . that reminds me! This diner down the road has the *best* cherry Jell-O. They put pieces of fruit and stuff in it! Wanna go?"

"Well . . . maybe a bit later," Maddy replied with continued caution. "So . . . I'm guessing you brought a bit of *Toxin X* with you?" "Yeah," Lucy replied. "This guy was a dirtbag, and I wanted to try my new injectable version of it. I call it *Toxin X+*. It works *way* better than the lotion. He was beating on this hooker, and I was already a little pissed about being left out of Kansas City, so I wasn't in the mood to see that. So I lured him back here and told him I was into bathing together. He undressed and got into the tub. I injected him and within, like, thirty seconds, shit just started pouring out of him. I mean, it was like his skin just ripped open and his organs started falling out and kinda, liquifying. It was *so cool*! Are you sure you don't want to get that Jell-O?"

"Yeah . . . well . . . that doesn't really sound good to me at the moment," Maddy softly replied as her stomach began churning from the very thought of it. "So . . . aren't you a bit concerned about leaving him in there? Y'know . . . about maybe getting identified and caught?"

"Oh, Maddy," Lucy replied with her condescending tone. "We're using fake names. We have this room for two days past when we get back to New York. And I picked *this* slimeball room from hell because this place is known for its . . . discretion. My guess is that they'll just clean it up with a Shop-Vac or something. They definitely *do not* want the cops snooping around here. Don't worry. It'll be fine. Showering will be kinda tricky though."

"Sure, sure, makes sense," Maddy calmly replied. Erick then inquired, "So, Lucy . . . um . . . we're supposed to be a team, right? So we're supposed to decide together who we . . . um . . . take care of . . . right?" Lucy looked up and glared at Erick in silence before he immediately said, "You know what? Not important right now. There's going to be a bit of a learning curve. Why don't we just get a good night's rest and get a fresh start in the morning." Lucy dropped her glare as her eyes lazily moved back toward the television.

The next morning, Lucy came bounding into the hotel room with three bags and cups of coffee. "Hey all!" she exclaimed as she began emptying the bags onto the well-worn round table in the corner of the room. "I brought breakfast!" Erick and Maddy wiped the sleep out of their eyes, scratched their respective asses, and plopped themselves onto the chairs. They carefully inspected their meal. The egg and sausage biscuits were heartily consumed. The Jell-O was discreetly discarded outside the moment Lucy went to the bathroom.

The arrangements for that evening's events were relatively simple. Lucy had already located an empty farmhouse that was for sale well off of the beaten path. Maddy had a vial of *Toxin A*, a mini-skirt, and her infectious smile. And all Erick had to bring was his rediscovered rage. That was until they were getting ready to depart on their various missions and Maddy ordered, "Don't forget the marshmallows, hot dogs, buns, and mustard, mister!" "Fine!" a disgruntled Erick replied as his mind shifted back as to why they were there.

Since they had a job to do in Kansas City, Erick felt that the time was right to take out a certain church cult leader who had brainwashed his wife and hundreds of others into believing all sorts of outrageous claims, including that the COVID vaccine contained government microchips. So when the COVID pandemic hit her church hard, she was vulnerable. And she died like millions of others throughout the world. Except, her death had been preventable. Had he only been able to penetrate through the dense fog of outrageous lies, he may have saved her. His marriage, however, was beyond repair regardless of her vaccination status as he had found out that the cult preacher wasn't against *everything* that penetrated a woman's body, including his wife's. "Why," Erick had proclaimed at the time, "that insurance convention being in Kansas City is like, well, *divine intervention*!" "Oh, my fucking god, that is so funny!" Maddy screamed as the pair rolled around on their disheveled bed laughing.

———

While Lucy and Erick were at the grocery store procuring the necessary items for that evening's dinner, Maddy was floating into an area church, asking for the pastor. She was wearing a tight green sweater with a tan miniskirt that went only mid-thigh over her olive leggings. She looked around the tidy but run-down church. It was reminiscent of the house of cult worship from her childhood and the same fearful chill ran from her shoulders and down her spine as the pastor emerged from his inner sanctum. He was wearing a large, charismatic smile. He was tall and lanky with slicked-back blonde hair. He wore black slacks and a black jacket over his black cardigan. *I hate it when these motherfuckers dress like us,* Maddy thought.

"Yes, how may I help you, my child" came his slithery greeting. "Hi, thank you so much for seeing me" came Maddy's reply. "Ummm . . . my name is Josephine, and I just moved to the area. I just bought an old farmhouse south of town and I'm looking for some . . . *spiritual fulfillment* . . . and I heard that this church may offer what I'm . . . looking for. You see, I just separated from my husband because . . . well . . . he just doesn't *see it,* Pastor."

"See what, my child?" came the cultist's inquiry as he began assessing just how vulnerable his new prey was. Maddy, attempting to channel her parents without becoming nauseous replied pleadingly, "He just doesn't see how he has gone down the path of sin. He doesn't see how the deep state government is trying to indoctrinate us into their world of crime, drugs, and godless fornication. I mean, he has no problem with the blasphemy of men lying with men and women lying with women. He *actually believes* that a woman has the right to murder an unborn soul. He doesn't understand how we all need to take up arms against the tyranny that is coming for us all. How, as a white man, he should be *dominant* over his women and everyone else in society. That it is his *rightful place* to be domineering over *all* of our Lord's creatures. That the deep state is trying to tell us how to raise our children to be ashamed of their *God- given* white heritage. He even . . . oh my lord, please forgive me for staying with him for so long . . . he even received that demonic communion of the vaccine. It was *then* that I realized that he was beyond redemption and that I had to relocate. To find someone who understood me, who understood *us,* who understood the *truth.* And our Lord led me to *you.*"

"Well, Josephine," the cult leader eagerly began as he subtly wet his lips with his serpentine tongue. "I am *so sorry* that you have had to experience that. I want to commend you on staying on the path of our Lord under such blasphemous pressure. And we would like to, of course, welcome you to our most reverent congregation. You will be a most welcome addition to our cause. But . . . and I hope that you understand, we must ensure that any new member is not an interloper who is a threat to us. I must *personally* get to know you so that our Lord may guide me into understanding your true intentions with us. Would that be all right?"

"Well, *of course,* Pastor" came Maddy's immediate reply. "In fact, it would be *my honor* to prepare a delicious meal for you tonight at my new home. Then, we could spend some time together and get to know one another . . . much better. You may ask me *anything* that you desire, and you may open *anything* that I possess."

"Well," the pastor enthusiastically replied, "a home-cooked meal does sound quite tempting. Shall I follow you?" "Ummm," Maddy began sheepishly. "Actually, I got a ride into town with someone because my car just broke down. Would you mind giving me a ride? I'm *completely* helpless at the moment."

As the March air's temperature began to plummet with the setting sun a duo of black-clad figures observed the pair leaving the church and getting into the eager man's brand-new Lexus. He had his gangly arm around Maddy's waist as he opened the car door for her. "Seriously," Erick began to bemoan. "How fucking stupid *are* these people? How can they not see that they're giving their hard-earned money away so that *this* prick can drive a new car?"

"Really?" Lucy inquired. "*That* is what you're upset about? How about the fact that he's all over your wife? Do you not care about *that*?" "Well," Erick stated in a low growl, "there's *a lot* of stuff that I'm upset about. I'm just saving *that one* for later tonight." The dark pair entered the church and disengaged the alarm system before Lucy asked, "Are you sure you don't want to do this when it's full?"

"Naw" came Erick's dismissive reply. "I don't want to hurt the ignorant. I just want to fuck up those that *manipulate* the ignorant into doing their perverted bidding." And with that last sentiment, the pair fell into silence as they completed their work.

The vile pastor woke up in complete darkness. He could feel that he was bound and was resting atop uncomfortable logs as their knots protruded into his legs and buttocks. He tried to speak, but the gag prevented anything but panicked mumbles. Then, he saw the light.

A flashlight, to be exact. It was being held underneath Erick's chin, giving his face the same sinister shadows as children who are telling ghost stories in their tent. There was a look of determination upon Erick's face, followed by a joyous smile.

"Hey there, motherfucker" came Erick's inviting voice. "Remember me?" The nefarious man's face held a look of confusion. Then recognition. Then bone-chilling fear. "Yeah, I'm not going to go into too many speeches tonight. I'm not going to go into how repulsive you pricks are. How disgusting it is that you prey upon the fears of ignorant and vulnerable people just to enrich yourself. Enrich yourself with money. Enrich yourself with self-professed power. Enrich your tender little egos. Enrich yourself with sexual domination . . . oh, by the way . . . I believe you've met my new wife."

Maddy's flashlight-lit face then appeared. "Hey there, Pastor!" came Maddy's gleeful voice. "Listen, I'm gonna have to take a raincheck on that whole one-on-one-get-to-know-me- better thing. You see, I forgot that I already had plans with my friend and husband. We already had made plans for dinner and a show, so maybe some other time. But I doubt it. Better people than you have tried to indoctrinate me in the past. And let's just say, it didn't work out so well for them. Nor will it work out so well for you. But, on the plus side, you get to have yourself a last supper!"

Lucy then approached the man and began dousing him with lighter fluid. The cult leader was sweating profusely as he began his hysterically vain attempts at freeing himself. The three sadistic assassins burst into laughter. "Holy fuck!" Erick exclaimed. "Is that the goofy face you made when you were fucking my ex? Wow. I will never understand what she or anyone else saw in you. But whatever. It's water under the bridge. All debts are paid off in full tonight. You got what *you* wanted. And now I'm going to get what *I* want."

Erick's face then turned crimson as it twisted into an intensely macabre jubilation. "And what *I* want is to see your entire world collapse into fire and fucking brimstone! What *I* want is to see a sneak preview of your pathetic soulless body burning in the eternal flames of hell. But mostly, what I want *right now* is to be nourished. And you, and everyone like you, are the *fuel* for my nourishment."

"But first," a joyous Erick proclaimed, "how about the show? Let's blow the fuck out of his church! Lucy, if you would be so kind." Lucy flipped a switch and there was a tremendous explosion and pillar of flames that illuminated the entire area from several miles away. Maddy, Erick, and Lucy simultaneously began saying, "Ooooohhh," "aaaawww" as explosion after explosion was heard immediately following another flash of brilliant orange and yellow flames and debris being flung into the dark sky.

"That was fuckin' sweet, Lucy," Maddy said in a congratulatory tone. "Thanks. So are we gonna eat or what? I'm starving," Lucy casually replied. Erick then lit a wadded-up piece of paper and tossed it upon the frantic false prophet. Soul- consuming flames began licking around his body as his screams became increasingly voluminous. He was then completely consumed as the wood that he was resting on ignited. Erick watched as his slicked-back blonde hair appeared to melt from the man's skull and his skin began to bubble and pop like bacon frying in a greasy pan.

Maddy went over to her beloved husband and wrapped her petite arm around his waist. "Hey, baby, you okay?" she softly asked. The flames were mirrored in a single tear that was rolling down his cheek as he said, "Nope. I'm fuckin' starving. Let's eat."

By the time they heard the sirens several miles away, they were sitting silently and fully enraptured while watching their hot dogs and marshmallows roast over the popping wood and charred corpse.

The silence was broken when Maddy exclaimed, "See motherfucker? The *Trio of Terror* has a long fuckin' memory!" "Maddy," Erick sternly retorted, "that is *not* our fuckin' name!" "Oh, good!" Maddy exclaimed. "Are you guys ready to un- table the discussion on our cool name? Should I call an official meeting to order?" "No" came the unified response of Lucy and Erick. "Fine, fuck it," a disappointed Maddy stated as she began pouting. Her spirits were immediately lifted as Erick handed her a freshly roasted hot dog covered in mustard.

CHAPTER 39

CREATURES OF LOVE

It was the last Friday in July, and instead of all of the ladies going out, they met at Erick and Maddy's home to try a new lasagna recipe that Erick had discovered. Upon entering the home, Jules flatly inquired, "Okay, what the fuck's going on? Why are we here?" "What the fuck do you mean?" Maddy retorted. "C'mon, why is Erick cooking for us? What's going on? Just tell us so we can get on with the rest of our lives."

Maddy and Erick both wore shocked expressions as Maddy incredulously stated, "Okay, so my *wonderful husband* has worked all day to prepare us all a delicious meal and we get *accused* of shit? What the fuck? Don't eat it if you don't want!" "Okay, okay, sorry," Jules stated in retreat. "It just seems a little weird, that's all."

"Yeah, a fuckin' dinner party's *weird*, I guess. Hey, baby, how long will it be?" Maddy inquired. "Well, the lasagna needs to set for about twenty minutes while the bread is baking, so twenty-five, thirty minutes, something like that," Erick answered. "Cool!" Maddy responded. "Come sit with me, and we'll chat for a while!"

Erick entered the living room and smiled at all of their guests, which included Sam, Jules, Kristy, Lucy, Blair, and Patty. "Oh, and Sam, I made a veggie one just for you," Erick stated. "Thanks, that's really sweet of you," Sam replied. "Soooo . . . what should we talk about," Maddy inquired as she was sitting on Erick's lap with her legs dangling from the side of the chair's arm and swaying her bare feet. "Oh! I know! Why don't we tell them about that thing we found out about!" "What thing?" Erick inquired. "You know .. . that thing we found out about on Tuesday," Maddy responded. "Why the fuck would they care about *that*? I mean, we can tell them but that's only going kill about thirty seconds or so," Erick offered. "Yeah, you're probably right. Let's talk about something else," Maddy conceded.

Blair looked right at Maddy and inquired sternly, "Maddy, Erick, what do you both have to tell us?" "Weeelll . . . it's *really* not that big of a deal," Maddy began coyly through fake snickers. "It's just that we just found out that, well . . . I'm pregnant." She then bounded from Erick's lap and exclaimed, "We're havin' a fuckin' *baby*!"

The reactions were priceless and varied from person to person. Blair said nothing and just wore an expression of knowing satisfaction. Patty started laughing as she said, "Oh, fuck, this should be *really* fucked up!" Jules said, "Yep, I knew they were up to something." Kristy blurted out, "Pregnant? How the hell did *that* happen?" to which Maddy responded, "Um, well, he fucked me. Really Kristy, out of everyone here, I would have expected you to understand how this shit works." Sam just shook her head slowly and muttered, "Oh my god. They're breeding." Lucy sat silently with a detached grin.

"How far along are you, dear?" Blair inquired. "Welp, I'm about eight weeks, so seven more months of this shit," Maddy began excitedly. "And in about eight more weeks, we find out if it's a little boy or a little girl, and I know Erick really wants a little girl even though he won't admit it but he keeps referring to the baby as "she" and "she" I mean the baby was conceived like the last week in May which is weird because that's the week a year ago that we started dating, isn't that weird? But the really weird part is that her, I mean the baby's due date is February 14, which will mark the second-year anniversary of our meeting and our first-year wedding anniversary of course, who knows if that will actually happen, but it's still weird dontcha think?"

"What the fuck did you just say?" Jules snidely inquired. "Well, smartass, what I said was that we don't know the gender yet, but what we *do* know is that we're gonna have a—" Maddy then placed her hands on Erick's shoulders, placed her forehead upon his, stared him into his eyes and with both of them wearing mischievous grins they began chanting, "*Satan* baby, *Satan* baby, *Satan* baby!" before bursting out into maniacal laughter.

"Yep. *This* kid's gonna be well adjusted," Jules said flatly. "Everybody better start locking up their knives." Everyone burst into laughter with the exception of Blair who sat quietly and reflected upon just how prophetic that statement might have been.

Over the next two months, the couple prepared for the baby's arrival. Maddy's closet and sitting room were converted into a nursery, with one-third of the guest room being walled off and converted for Maddy's use. Erick read exactly thirteen books on how to raise children, most of which he still didn't understand. His research only served to increase his anxiety and he began making copious lists of everything that needed to be done and everything that needed to be purchased. So at week twelve, he decided that he had better child-proof the house . . . six months before the due date. Everything in the house was child proofed including the electrical outlets, corners of furniture, doorknobs, and cabinet doors. Maddy attempted to take Erick's unbridled enthusiastic energy in stride until, upon trying to open a child-proofed cabinet above the sink to get a glass of water, Maddy exclaimed in frustration, "Why the fuck did you put one up *here*? Am I giving birth to Wilt Chamberlain? I love you, but you're driving me fucking crazy!" Erick's reply was silent embarrassment.

At week sixteen, the couple found out that they were, in fact, having a daughter. Her name would be Josephine (in tribute to her Uncle Joe and Aunt Blair) Patricia (after her Aunt Patty) Sommers Parker. She would be known as "Josie" and she would be the most cared for and safe child in the history of the world. Erick was driven to see to that.

Shortly after naming their daughter on a chilled October evening, Blair's phone rang. She answered to the emotionally devastated voice of her niece saying, "C—c—can y—you c— come over? T—the w—w—worst t—thing in the h—history of the w—w—world h—has happened!" Upon their arrival, Patty asked, "Okay, Mads, what's the tragedy?" "I—it's only the w—worst thing *ever!*" Maddy began as tears streamed down her beleaguered face. "I—I just f—found out that E—Erick's been sneaking a—around on me b—behind m—my back!"

"Oh, dear," Blair began in her reassuring tone. "That man loves you more than anything. I simply can't imagine him doing that." "No! It's true! I have proof!" Maddy exclaimed as she pried her body from the chair's cushion and began toward the basement door. "Come to the basement and just *look* at what he's been doing behind my back!" The trio cautiously began descending the staircase. The only discernable sound was the eerie creaking of each wooden step as they laid their weight upon it. During their brief journey, Patty and Blair pondered what horrific sight they were about to witness. What they saw upon turning on the basement light was beyond anything that they had imagined.

Covering every wall, corner, and shelf throughout the basement were neatly organized stacks of . . . baby supplies. "See! I *told* you! Look at what he's *done*! He's built a fuckin' *baby bunker* down here without telling me! And my god! If it's like this *now*, how is it going to be when we actually have a fuckin' *baby*! My doctor warned me. She said that he was going to spoil our baby, and that's *exactly* what's happening! He's going to spoil her, and we're going to raise a spoiled little bitch!"

Patty and Blair looked at each other, and upon seeing the other try to hide their respective smirks, failed to contain an explosion of laughter. "This isn't funny!" Maddy protested. "Well, Mads," Patty began, "I can think of about a million things off the top of my head that has happened in this world that are worse than this, so . . . you're kinda overreacting."

"Oh . . . overreacting, am I? Well. Let's just go through the inventory shall we and then we'll decide who's overreacting!" Maddy exclaimed. "For starters, do you know how many diapers are down here? I'll tell you! 7,200 fucking diapers! Why? Because he read, which is *one* of my problems . . . the mother-fucker knows how to read! He read that babies use at least ten diapers per day, so he did the math, and if she's potty trained by the age of two, then she'll go through 7,200 diapers. That we apparently have to have right now because he's all freaked out about the possibility of another pandemic or something so now, we've become psycho fucking hoarders! I mean, look at this fucking thing! He's built the Great Diaper Wall of China!"

"Overreacting? Wanna know how many fucking stuffed animals there are? Fifty! Josie's going to wake up in her bed for the first time, see all these furry faces and think she's about to be mauled by the entire cast of *Sesame Street*! Need a piece of shit plastic light up toy? We got thirty of those fuckers. And, and . . . look at this! We have *five* of every over-the-counter baby medicine there is! We have baby nail clippers and suction things and cough syrup and ear stuff and gum stuff and band-aids and cold medicine and teething rings. Five . . . of everything! We have enough fucking baby medicine to take care of every infant born in the entire New York metropolitan area for the next fucking decade!"

"Overreacting? Do you know a baby that needs *four* sets of top-of-the-line baby monitors? Well, I guess this one makes sense because I know that Josie plans on starting her own private eye agency the moment she comes shooting out of me! We have *ten sets* of baby dinnerware. We have four *cases* of baby bottles and a case of *five hundred* bottle nipples. Which, sure, that'll come in handy when I work on my erotic art project. We have three *cases* of baby powder. Three *cases* of baby oil. We have three *cases* of baby lotion!"

"We have, oh for fuck sake, this is almost as good as the diapers. Listen, if you ever need baby wipes, please, don't buy any. Just let me know. Because we have *twenty fucking cases* of baby wipes! And do you know what he said? He said, 'Maddy, we're gonna need those. She's gonna be a little poo machine!' So I said, yeah, you're probably right. We *will* go through those. Like, when I'm eighty-five years old and I need to use baby wipes to clean myself and Josie's helping me and she says, 'I'm sorry, Mom, but we're out of baby wipes.' Then, I can say to her, 'Don't worry, dear. Just go to the basement. There are still three *fucking cases* that your father bought fifty years ago.' It was at that point that he got pissed and said he needed to go for a walk."

"I mean, I love him more than anything and I know he's just doing this out of the love in his heart for me and Josie, but . . . but . . . we have *seven fucking mobiles*! Need a pacifier? Here have ten. Don't worry about me, I've got ninety more to go along with the twenty rattles, twenty baby blankets, and *four fucking playpens*! We have exactly thirty bibs, thirty socks, one hundred burp rags, one hundred and twenty onesies, and one hundred and twenty pajamas!"

"Overreacting, you say? We have . . . for a baby that's not even going to be born for four months, mind you . . . two changing tables, a walker thing, a swing, and exactly *fifteen* dolls. We have *four* bassinets and *four* cradles! Why? Fuck if *I* know! Ask the crazy person that's been running a shuttle from our house to the warehouse store for the past five months!"

At that point, the ladies heard the opening and closing of the front door upstairs. They heard someone go upstairs to the bathroom and into the shower. Thirty minutes later, Erick joined them in the living room. Patty excitedly exclaimed, "Well . . . *we've* been a busy little beaver now, haven't we?"

Apologies and hugs were exchanged before Blair negotiated a solution. They all went to the basement, took a complete inventory, negotiated on what could be returned (except the diapers. Erick was hell-bent on keeping the 7,200 diapers), and called the store to determine what could be returned with the savings put on a gift card for later use. Maddy dialed the phone and put it on speaker as a young lady answered. "Hey, hi, I have a question. My husband and I are having a baby and he's been coming in there and buying stuff, and I think he may have gone overboard on a few things. So . . . I was wondering that if we have the receipts and the stuff hasn't been opened, could we return the extra stuff and put it on a gift card?" The female employee on the other end of the line enthusiastically said, "You sure can! You must be Erick's wife! He sure is excited about that baby!" Erick looked down at his feet as Maddy just slowly shook her head at him with an annoyed expression.

Before turning out the light and falling into a relaxed slumber, Erick said, "Oh, by the way. I took care of one of the items on our list tonight." "Oh, cool . . . thanks, baby," Maddy appreciatively replied before giving her beloved husband a light kiss goodnight.

CHAPTER 40
————————————

JOHNNY PISSOFF PT. 2

Erick was pissed earlier that chilled October evening. As he walked along the Brooklyn streets toward his intended destination carrying his black duffle and wearing all black, he thought, *Why the fuck am I in trouble? All I'm trying to do is provide for our child. And it isn't like we're involved in a low-risk hobby here. What's wrong with being prepared in case something happens to me? What's wrong with actually being organized and prepared for our child's arrival? Oh sure, maybe I went a bit overboard on a few things, but who cares? Better too much than not enough! And yeah, I maybe should have told her what I was doing. But that would have ruined the big surprise! And maybe I'm starting out by spoiling our daughter a little, but, but . . . well, sure maybe I've denied Maddy the opportunity to have fun picking stuff out too, but, but . . . dammit. Okay. I fucked up.*

In an attempt to elevate his mood and alleviate some of his guilt, his mind then went back to a meeting of their little group in September where it was decided that they would focus on eliminating anyone in their immediate neighborhood that they determined to be a significant threat to their child as she grew. They, of course, knew that it was impossible to identify and remove every threat in the world. But they also knew that there were some obvious ones that they could take care of in order for Josie to live as carefree a childhood as possible.

Maddy's little community birdies began chirping into her ear. There were three neighborhood men identified as candidates. Two of the men required further surveillance in order to determine their worthiness of the trio's retribution. The first man, however, nearly did not make the cut on that September evening. Unfortunately for that man, Erick countered Maddy's objection to him and the group voted to proceed. And also unfortunately for that man, Erick had just had his first argument with his beloved wife and needed to do something to get out of the doghouse. This man's sacrifice would serve as Erick's *baby bunker* redemption.

———

"Here ye! Here ye! Here ye! As duly elected president of this esteemed organization, I hereby declare that this meeting of the *Trio of Terror* come to order!" Maddy exclaimed that September evening as Lucy and Erick rolled their eyes at each other.

"Okay, first item on the agenda. So here's a guy, but I just don't think he rises to the level of being a direct threat to our child, so I vote we move on from him," Maddy stated to begin their now-official meeting. "Well," Lucy inquired, "what's the deal with him?" "Okay, there's no question he's a fucking douche," Maddy began explaining. "He's the one responsible for beating up a number of the gay and trans people in the neighborhood. Everybody's sure it's him, but the cops have no evidence so he's still out there. Regardless, I just don't think that he's a significant enough threat to our child, so I vote to move on to somebody else."

"Hmmm," a pensive Erick began, "I think that we're being discriminatory against our LGBTQ+ brothers and sisters." "How so," Maddy retorted defensively. "Well," Erick continued, "we *do* have a precedent. You yourself dismembered and hung the hicks for beating and raping a trans man, did you not?" "Well, yes I did," Maddy conceded. "And," Erick continued, "we have had no problem with disposing of wife beaters now, have we?" "Ummmm . . . nope," Maddy replied. "So what's the difference?" Erick asked. "Are we saying that it's all right to kill hetero wife beaters but not men who do the exact same thing to our LGBTQ+ friends? Isn't that blatant discrimination? Are we saying that a hetero-female victim is worth more than a gay man or a lesbian or a trans person? Plus, what if our daughter turns out to be gay or trans? Wouldn't that put her directly in this motherfucker's crosshairs?"

"He makes some pretty good points," Lucy stated as Maddy sat silently processing her beloved husband's arguments. "Alrighty then," Maddy stated. "I vote we take him out. You are absolutely right. My initial reaction was to value hetero- female victims more than our gay, lesbian, and trans friends. Isn't it weird how cultural discrimination works? I mean, I consider myself to be one of the most open people to others' lives. I believe that people should be able to live freely as they are as long as they aren't hurting others or forcing others to subscribe to their worldview as the religious and political cults do. I believe that every peace-loving life is equally important. But here I am with that knee-jerk decision that was *totally* discriminatory against multiple groups of people. Thank you, baby, for enlightening me. This just proves why we need to feel free and open to discuss our thoughts and opinions within the walls of the *Trio of Terror*. Maybe our society would be a much better place if everyone just adopted our attitudes, huh?"

"Well," Lucy said reservedly, "there sure as hell would be a lot fewer people." A chill ran down the three spines as they each pondered the ramifications of Maddy's suggestion. The ramifications of everyone in society acting as judge, jury, and executioner. It would be mass chaos with no adherence to formalized norms, rules, or laws that are necessary to ensure the peaceful functioning of our world. It would be the wild west with AKs. And everybody's personal opinion of someone else could qualify them for execution at any time. It would *not* be a world worth living in.

But as is true with all known persons with *empathetic personality disorder with narcissistic and sociopathic tendencies*, they quickly discarded the notion that *they* were doing anything wrong because they had convinced themselves that *their* actions were just. *All* persons who carry that diagnosis possess that feature. And that is a scientific fact. Because the only three people who carry that diagnosis were sitting around this very table.

———

Erick smiled to himself as he turned the corner and began casually sauntering down the darkened street where his prey preferred to hunt. This was Erick's fourth evening of tossing himself as a lure into this asphalt pond in the hopes of getting a bite.

The man he was fishing for cruised this particular neighborhood looking for gay or trans men. He presented himself as someone who was simply looking for a discreet good time. Most men rejected him, for a variety of reasons, but usually because they were happily married or otherwise previously engaged and weren't looking for a one-night stand. Those who fell for the ruse found themselves staring down the barrel of a gun immediately upon their fastening their seatbelt in the late '80s tan Chevy. They would be driven to a secluded wooded area, bound and beaten mercilessly as the man would spout grossly misinterpreted Bible passages. They were then warned against reporting it to the authorities. This was a warning that the men would heed and ultimately did not need as the police force had historically not taken "gay bashing" all that seriously and there was still lingering mistrust between the two groups. So out of this mistrust, the men would not cooperate much with the local police and would not give a description of who their attacker was. They would, however, talk amongst others in the neighborhood. And *some* of those others were little birdies who would talk to Maddy. Now, Maddy's little birdies weren't aware of just *how* she was involved. They only knew that she had the ability to make certain things happen when needed. So the currently pregnant Maddy would then talk to her associates who were then dispatched to conclude the deserving target's final act. Tonight, it would be Erick's turn.

Shit, Erick thought as he unzipped his black duffle to procure his needed tools, *I forgot I picked this up the other night in a shop while I was cruising around here. I'd better not show this to Maddy. At least not tonight.* He then placed the adorable stuffed chipmunk, better known as *Stuffed Animal Number Fifty-One,* underneath the other more sinister items in the bag.

Just as he was placing the desired items into his hoodie pockets, a late '80s tan Chevy pulled up to the curb. The driver reached over to the passenger side of his car and manually rolled down the window. He wore a seductive smile under his greying mustache as he said in a pleasant but provocative voice, "Hey, there. I think I might be a little lost. Would you maybe like to get in and help me find my way? I'm looking for a nice quiet place to just be me. You know what I mean?"

"Yeah," Erick replied wearing a wide smile. "I *do* know what you mean. I know a few spots not too far from here that is good for . . . introspection."

"Well, thanks buddy," the man said as he opened the passenger-side door. "Hop on in, and let's take a ride." The moment Erick's ass hit the well-worn velour seat, he pulled a screwdriver from his right hoodie pocket and violently thrust it horizontally through the man's neck. Blood began to seep out of the two newly formed holes as the man could only grunt his objections through his impaled windpipe.

Erick then got out of the car and sat on his knees on the sidewalk behind the open door. He laid the desperately gurgling man down on his front seat with his face up. He peered down wearing a sadistic grin before plunging a short screwdriver into each of the man's eyes. There was a slight "pop" as the steel heads penetrated the tender membrane into the dilated pupils followed by a red and white trickling discharge.

"So," Erick stated to the trembling man in a casually satisfied tone, "*this* is what happens when you fuck with other people that don't deserve to be fucked with. *This* is what happens when you use violence to shove your fucked up religion down others' throats. *This* is what happens when you terrorize an entire community. *This* is what happens when you put innocent people in the hospital. And *this* is what happens when your holier-than-thou beliefs leave physical and emotional scars upon the blameless. This is what happens. You provide me with the best screw of my life."

With that final sentiment, Erick pierced the man through one of his ears and completely out of the other with a final long, hard screwdriver. The man stopped moving. Torrents of blood were now pouring out of the six holes in his neck, eyes, and ears and being absorbed by the tan velour.

Erick stood and carefully closed the car door. He looked around. He was initially not pleased by what he saw. Through the slight parts between drawn curtains in the immediately adjacent apartment buildings, he could see a number of peering eyes. He began sweating as he lifted his black duffle and began his hasty retreat down the street with his head down. That was until he heard a woman's voice exclaim, "Say hi to Maddy for us!" He lifted his covered head, slowed his cadence, and gave the on-lookers a casual wave as his now-strutting figure disappeared around the next darkened corner.

He went into a small convenience store and asked to use the restroom. There, he removed his wig, hair net, gloves, clothes, and boots and placed them into his garbage bag. He then put on a duplicate set of clothes that appeared identical in every way. Microscopically, however, their fibers were completely different. He wiped the sweat from his brow and exited the restroom.

As he was departing the corner shop, he noticed something that sent a chill down his spine and caused him to hasten his cadence out of the glass doors. He made it about a half block toward the subway that would take him near the river before abruptly turning around. He paced outside of the store nervously. He peered in the window. *It* had seen him. And *it* was just sitting there as if daring him to act. A decision needed to be made. Either he was going to confront his antagonist, or he would leave here with the gut-wrenching feeling of unsatisfied longing. He wondered if this was what heroin addiction felt like. "Fuck it, I just can't help myself," Erick muttered to himself as the door's bell chimed once again. He grabbed it with embarrassed violence and flung it on the counter. His cash was haphazardly tossed to the cashier. "Keep the change," Erick ordered as he marched once again out of the glass door. *Josie's gonna fuckin' love this*, he thought as he stared down at the stuffed manatee before placing *Stuffed Animal Number Fifty- Two* deep into his duffle.

CHAPTER 41

MURDER, INCORPORATED

Two evenings later, Erick was smiling to himself as he waited for Lucy to arrive to assist him with the removal of the body. He watched the man lying in his bed, violently convulsing. Bloody tears were coming out of his eye ducts and dripping all the way down to his chin through the froth coming out of his gasping mouth. "Sorry, Chad. But you're just too big of a fuckin' creep to keep around in this neighborhood. Or anywhere, for that matter. But *definitely* too creepy to be anywhere near my Josie. You see, *this* is what happens when you fondle children. *This* is what happens when you scar them for life. *This* is what happens when you fuck them up so that maybe they do the same thing as adults. *This* is what happens when you abuse your position of authority and the trust that so many have placed in you to molest innocents to fulfill your fucked up desires. And this is *definitely* what happens when your *fucking church* knows all about it and does nothing more than transfer you to a new hunting ground. You holier than thou fucks. You have a direct pipeline to God, do you? Is God into fucking little children? Well, if he is, then God's a fucking prick too."

"But I don't think so," Erick continued to the recently deceased body as he watched the man's clerical collar absorb his expired body's fluids turning it from white to a hellish pink. "I'm not even sure God *is* a man. I'm not even sure that there *is* a God. It can't be proven, so who's to say? But if there *is* a God, then my money's on them being a woman. Makes sense, doesn't it?

Who has the power of creation? Women. Who can create beautiful life out of nothing but a ball of goo? Women. So just seems to make sense that the men who wrote all of these so-called holy scriptures made God a man out of their own pathetic need to be domineering over women. But man, they fucked up. Because most women have the emotional strength and incredible intelligence of ten fucking men put together. Oh, they get a bad rap for being "overly emotional," don't they? Yeah, 'cause it's the *women* of the world who are so ill-tempered and such fucking snowflake babies that they start wars and commit genocide, right? Oh, wait. That's right. That's usually fucking men."

He then started chuckling to himself as he said to himself, "And Lord knows that they are *so* fucking easy to live with." And with that, Erick began thinking about his earlier conversation with his beloved wife as he was preparing for tonight's errand.

"Okay . . . *now,* what the fuck are you listening to?" Maddy exclaimed as she burst into their bedroom to catch Erick swaying his hips as he put on his hair net. "Okay," an annoyed Erick replied, "for starters, I'm invoking *Rule Number Eight,* all right? Secondly, you said you didn't want me to prepare for killing someone by listening to Christopher Cross, so I changed it."

"Uh, yeah . . . I noticed," Maddy replied dismissively. "So what the fuck is *this*?" Erick grasped his wife's expanded frame in his arms and began whisking her around the room as though they were in a ballroom. "This, my dearest—" he began explaining with a beaming smile upon his face, "is '9 to 5 (Morning Train)' by Sheena Easton."

The dancing pair giggled together as they began kicking their legs in unison to the bouncy pop in a vain attempt to mimic the Rockettes, each only able to kick about two feet into the air, but for different reasons. They fell on the bed, laughing together. "Oh, my fucking god," Maddy stated through her chuckles, "You are so fucking *doing it wrong*! But whatevs, Rule Eight. Who am I to say? So how are you offing this creepy motherfucker?"

"Well, you know there's that show on tonight that I want to watch live, so I just borrowed some *Toxin C* from Lucy. Get in, get out, no muss, no fuss, get rid of the body, home in time for my stories."

"Okay," Maddy began, attempting to remain calm. "First, your *stories*? How fucking old *are* you? You're watching the new episode of *Forensic Files,* not fucking *Matlock*! And secondly, really? You're just going to go in, inject him, and get rid of him? C'mon, man! Where's the *ingenuity*? Where's the *creativity*? Where's the *panache*? C'mon, baby! You're better than this!"

"Maddy," Erick began patiently, "first of all, I'm invoking *Rule Number Seven*. And secondly, how come *I* get shit about this, and Lucy doesn't?"

"Well," Maddy began cautiously, "first, it's kinda my job to give you shit, and it's kinda fun. Secondly, I really don't think that I want to piss Lucy off. She's . . . different than she was. And thirdly . . . ummm . . . why don't you just complete the hat trick of *doing it wrong*? *Wrong* prep music, *wrong* method of murder . . . just complete the hat trick and *get caught* while you're at it!"

"Maddy, I'm *not* going to get caught" was the final thought that went through Erick's head before he heard the tell-tale sound of a gun being cocked behind his head. "Mr. Parker," a stoic voice came from behind him. "Please don't move. You will be coming with us. It's time that we all have a little chat."

He just sat there on his frozen knees with his fingers clenched behind his head while listening to another man on his phone. "Yeah, we got Parker." "Yeah, he's going to go pick up the Sommers girl and her friend. We'll be there in thirty."

As Erick was escorted into a room flanked by two large men, his black hood was taken off. His eyes quickly adjusted to the dimmed lighting as they darted around the room in a vain attempt to become oriented.

A slender, sharply dressed elderly man was sitting behind a grand mahogany desk. "Please, Erick, have a seat, won't you?" the man politely invited.

Erick took a seat and looked around the dark room. Six stern faces were staring at him, their hands firmly placed inside their coat jackets. The walls were papered in red velour, with gold accents. Multiple priceless paintings from some of the world's artistic masters adorned the walls. The furniture was all deep brown heavy oak with cushions that matched the walls. The man behind the desk said, "Gentlemen . . . we're all friends here. Please remove your hands from your coats and join us." The men looked at one another, then at Erick. They nodded to the man and took their seats on the adjacent sofas on either side of the desk.

"Listen," Erick began in an attempt to sound much more confident than he was feeling. "I don't know what's going on or what this is. If we've done something wrong, just tell us and we'll stop it, okay? But I swear to you. If you harm my wife or our child, I will rip your fucking heart out with my bare hands, and you don't have enough bullets to stop me in time."

One of the men chuckled and said, "Well, I can see how he ended up with Maddy," as the other men began laughing. "Mr. Parker," the man behind the desk responded delicately, "Please don't misunderstand. I know that your visit here is a bit unusual, but please let me assure you that it is for the safety of all of us that we take such clandestine measures. And please, let me assure you that you, your wife, your unborn child, and your friend are not in any danger. We simply need to have a little chat with you all. And we can begin that as soon as your lovely wife arrives and—"

The man's statement was cut off by the demanding voice of Maddy coming from outside of the room. "Where the *fuck* is my husband, you motherfuckers?" "Oh dear," the man behind the desk said softly. "I do wish that she had a bit less of Joe and a bit more of Blair in her."

The heavy door was flung open and the short figure of Maddy came burgeoning in as quickly as her five-month- pregnant frame would allow. "Hello, Maddy, my dear. It's so nice to see you again. It's been too long," the man greeted warmly.

"What the fuck are *you* doing here?" Maddy exclaimed to the kind smile of the eighty-one-year-old retired Det. Edmund Simmons. "Well, my dear," Edmund began, "that's a bit of a story which I would love to tell you. But all in due time. Please, Maddy, Lucy, won't you have a seat next to your husband?"

"Okay, fuck that," Maddy retorted. "Just tell me what the fuck is going on so that we can get out of here. These two have a fuckin' body to hide, so tick-tock, motherfuckers. Just say your peace, and we'll be on our way."

"Maddy, have a seat," Edmund stated much more sternly. Realizing that she may have overstepped her bounds a bit, Maddy turned up her nose and haughtily said, "Fine. I will. But not because you told me to. My legs are a bit sore, that's all."

"Oh dear, so much like your uncle," a slightly exasperated Edmund began. "Very well, let's get started, shall we? You are in the secret office of an organization whose true name is known only by its members. But we are known generally by laymen as *Murder, Incorporated*. We are a group of hitmen that was established in the sixties. We do not hit people just for the sake of it. Or for petty grievances. We hit people who are a threat to others . . . for a price of course. And there is a group of men who are now a threat to *us*."

"Upon this group's inception, there have been dark forces deep in the organized crime world that have tried to either force us into their service or should they fail at this, eliminate us. They pop up every fifteen years or so and try again. And they are quite active right now. They present a rather serious threat to us . . . and by extension, to all of you. They have no problem using loved ones to get to whomever they are after. You are all in danger. So this little meeting is both a warning . . . and an invitation."

"Ummm . . . boss?" one of the large men hesitantly inquired. "What about Blair? Shouldn't she . . . y'know . . . be here for this? I mean . . . well . . . she is going to be really pissed."

"Yes, I know," Edmund regretfully replied. "I never intended to break my promise to her. You see, Maddy, your aunt never wanted you involved in this. She only wanted us to look over you. To make sure that you didn't get into some *real* trouble. And despite my attempts to explain this new threat to her, she believes that we can take care of this without your involvement. I disagree. Hence, our meeting here tonight. Let me explain what is now happening."

The trio (of terror?) sat silently and listened with the attentiveness of a viewer of the most intriguing who-done-it before Edmund began again in his kindly voice. "Your Aunt Blair has been working as a double agent. She has infiltrated this other group and has been trying to gain their trust. She has been conversing with only one contact, but we believe there are about fifteen others that are involved. She has promised to tell them about our vulnerabilities so that they can take us out one by one. But, as one might expect, they are being quite cautious about placing their trust in her. That is where *you* come in. The three of you are quite well-known in our circles. And this other group has interest in your services. So my idea is to have Blair bring the three of you into their fold, thus cementing the pact. We have plans to have Blair host a little Halloween party to introduce the three of you to them. About nineteen people will be invited to the party. Only four will leave. That would be you three plus Blair. The threat will be eliminated in one swift move. And the message will once again be sent, assuring at least another decade of peaceful co-existence. Now, what do you think of our little offer?"

Erick and Lucy looked inquisitively at Maddy. It was at this moment that Maddy regretted ever installing herself as *president* of their little demented group. "Ummm, well," Maddy began as she tried to find the right words, "so . . . well . . . maybe. I mean, if Aunt Blair's involved, and we're in danger anyway, then why *wouldn't* we lend a hand? I mean, these guys seem like complete douchebags, so yeah, maybe. But y'know . . . the three of us would have to discuss it and vote on it. We're a package deal and we run our group as a democracy." This last statement caused Erick and Lucy to silently roll their eyes at one another.

"Very well," a relieved Edmund replied. "But before we leave the three of you to make your decision, I believe we have a bit of internal housekeeping to take care of between Maddy and Lucy." "Whatthefuckyousay?" came Maddy's immediate defiant reply. "Lucy and I are *best friends*! We get along *great*! And our little group runs like a *well-oiled machine*! So there isn't any 'housekeeping' between us. Erick does most of that shit at home anyway, heh, heh, heh."

"Maddy, please just listen. There is one more piece of information that you need" came Edmund's calm reply. "You see, Joe's father was an original member of this group. He and his wife were assassinated by a hit man. They were blown up in their own home. This group then reached out to Joe, through me, and told him how to find that hit man. Joe, in turn, killed his parent's murderer in his most . . . um . . . unique fashion."

"Uh, yeah. Old fuckin' news, Edmund. What the fuck does that have to do with us?" an impatient Maddy retorted.

"Well, Maddy . . . Lucy . . . you see . . . the man who murdered Joe's parents and was in turn murdered by Joe was . . . Lucy's grandfather."

CHAPTER 42

SECRET AGENT MAN

"Oh, for fuck sakes!" an exasperated Erick exclaimed. Everyone in the room looked at him in shock as he continued. "Seriously, how many twists do we *need* in this story? I mean, first, you have *my* shit of having tragically lost my brainwashed wife then secretly wanting to become a killer. Then we have, of course, Maddy's whole thing. Then there's Uncle Joe's father getting involved in organized crime and becoming a charter member of this hit man thing. Then we have him and his wife getting blown up by . . . who else? Of course, it's Lucy's *grandfather*! And Joe joins the hit man thing so that he can kill Lucy's grandfather . . . or whoever beat up Blair and caused the miscarriage . . . or . . . what fucking ever! The point is that Joe joined the hit man thing. And we have Detective Simmons who has been involved all along and is now the boss with Blair lurking around in the background kinda pulling the strings on everything while ensuring that the hit man thing is watching over Maddy. I mean, *c'mon people*, just how many subplots does this story *need*? Why can't we just have a simple, sweet love story with a few gruesome murders? Why does this shit have to be so convoluted?"

An exhausted Erick slumped back down into his red velour chair before concluding. "Whatever. I'll support whatever my wife wants to do with this. But what else am I gonna find out? That Patty can *actually cook* and that she uses her culinary skills to poison corrupt foreign dignitaries or something? Jesus!"

The entire room then looked at Maddy. The tension was palpable as she said, "Well . . . no . . . Aunt Patty kinda knows that Uncle Joe was up to some shit and she kinda knows that I've been up to some shit and she kinda knows that Aunt Blair knows everything. But she's always been happy never knowing the true depth of all of this, so no she really isn't involved. And no, she really can't cook."

Maddy then began cackling like a schoolgirl before beginning once again. "Oh my god! I almost forgot about this! I remember one time when I was in first grade, and Uncle Joe and Aunt Blair were . . . well . . . this makes sense now. They were in New York for a 'business convention.' And my parents were away at some cult Bible camp thing, probably sacrificing godless whores or some shit. Anyway, I had to stay with Aunt Patty for a couple of days, and she had to make my lunch for me. So I go into the cafeteria and sit down at a table with some other kids and remove the contents of the paper bag. And what it contained was: one piece of bread. One full, raw, unwashed carrot and three snack cakes which were dried out because she had unwrapped them because she didn't think that I'd be able to. Oh, and she had poured some toasted cereal into the bag, so they were just like, y'know, laying in the bottom of the bag."

Maddy began cackling once again, almost to the point of tears, before continuing. "So this kid that was sitting across from me at the table started making fun of my lunch, so I gouged him the eye with the carrot! And that little fucker had to wear an eye patch for like three months! It was so fucking funny! And as Uncle Joe was walking me to the car after we met with the principal that day, he said, 'That's right, Buttacup! Don't take any shit from any of these douchebags!' Then we went for ice cream. Oh, and that kid was called 'patch' for the rest of his school days, and kids would leave carrots in his locker or throw carrots at him as he walked down the hall and laugh at him."

Maddy then became introspective as she said, "Y'know, I think that kid committed suicide when he was in high school. Huh. Kinda makes you think, doesn't it?" She then paused before concluding, "Well, it probably wasn't because of *that*. I think he was fucked up in some *other* way. Whatevs, not my prob. And besides, he *shouldn't* have made fun of my lunch."

Erick then looked at his lovely wife with adoration and said, "Yeah, fuck it. Let's join. She definitely needs an outlet for her viciousness." "Right back atcha, baby!" Maddy exclaimed as she plopped onto Erick's lap and kissed him passionately.

Following their kiss, Maddy gingerly said, "Ummm . . . Lucy . . . are you okay?" "Yeah, I'm fine" came Lucy's immediate uninterested response. "What do I care? My dad said that my grandfather was a bastard. So he had it coming to him. It's actually kinda nice to . . . I don't know . . . keep this all in the family."

"Alrighty then," Maddy exclaimed as she pried herself off of Erick's lap. "As *president* of our little group, I am officially calling a meeting to order and calling for an official vote. All of those in favor of joining forces with *Murder, Incorporated*, please raise your hands and say Aye." All three enthusiastically raised their hands while saying "Aye."

"Very well," a pleased Edmund said. "There is only one more order of business to attend to before you are officially welcomed in. Your group needs a code name. Preferably something cool." "Oh . . . my . . . fucking . . . *god*!" Maddy excitedly shouted as she clapped her hands and bounced around in a circle. "I knew it! I fucking *knew* we needed a cool name! And we have one." Maddy then looked smugly up at her defeated-looking husband and said, "Gentlemen, we are known collectively as the *Trio of Terror*!"

Maddy's anticipatory face waited for the response from the seven men who were staring at her in amazement. They looked at one another with confused expressions before bursting out into laughter. One of the men said through his chortles, "*Trio of Terror*? What the fuck are you? A twisted group of operatic tenors?"

"Hey now," a defensive Erick began upon seeing the embarrassed look on his beloved wife's face. "It's really not *that* bad. And it's just a working name before . . . y'know . . . we un-table the discussion to vote on our *real* name." Lucy then chimed in excitedly, "How about *mel*?" "What the fuck is *mel*? No, not cool enough," another of the men replied dismissively.

"Okay," a desperately searching Erick replied. "Maddy, our meeting is still open, right?" "Yeah," a hurt Maddy replied softly as she looked down at her feet. "Well, then I would like to move that we un-table the discussion of our group name!" Erick enthusiastically stated. "And I would like to propose as a point of order that our cool group name should be *The Unholy Trinity*!"

"Oh, my fucking god yes!" Maddy squealed as Lucy silently nodded with a sly smirk on her face. "All those in favor, say Aye," Maddy yelled out. The trio . . . or mel . . . or the trinity responded with an enthusiastic "Aye," before enveloping each other in warm hugs.

"Yeah, okay . . . whatever" came Edmund's flat response. "We'll just call you *The Trinity*. Now, I need each of you to sign into this book. By signing this book, you are committing yourself to our organization. You are committing yourself to supporting this organization and every *member* of this organization. The rules are quite simple. You may refuse any particular job for any reason, but you must agree to do at least one paid job every quarter. Any job that you intend to do outside of our group must be cleared by me first. This is to prevent any possibility of territorial wars with other actors, including legal authorities. Discussions that are conducted between members are to be kept in utmost secrecy. And finally . . . and this is of the *utmost importance* . . . any betrayal to this group will be punishable by death. Do you three understand?"

"Yes, we understand" came *The Trinity's* response in unison. "Very well then. Upon your signatures, you will be official members," stated Edmund.

Erick was the first to step up to the desk. Upon picking up the ink pen he inquired, "Um . . . do we need to sign in blood or something?" "No" came Edmund's bored response, "we're not a satanic cult. Just sign it in pen please." "Okay," Erick responded, "but is there going to be some sort of an initiation or something?" "No," an increasingly annoyed Edmund replied, "we're not a fraternity. Just your signature will do." "Okay . . . just askin'," Erick replied as he grinned and signed the book emphatically large as though he were John Hancock signing the *Declaration of Independence*.

Lucy then took the pen and silently placed her well- manicured signature into the book. She looked at Edmund with a wry smile and asked, "So . . . do you guys ever do anything internationally?" "Yes" came Edmund's response, "you will have those opportunities." "Sweeeet!" Lucy exclaimed as she returned to her seat.

Maddy took the pen and looked at the signatures of her beloved husband and best friend. She then looked up into the kind eyes of Edmund. She wrapped her arms around him and whispered into his ear, "I know that it was you who ran interference for me all of those years. Thank you."

Edmund delicately replied, "It was all intended to lead up to this very moment. You are most welcome. Your uncle would be *so proud* to see you taking his seat at our table." Maddy shed a tear and said, "My uncle *is* proud of me. I know he's still out there, somewhere, looking over me. He gave me the strength to beat the fuck out of my ex-douche when I needed it. He helped my friends find me the night that I overdosed. He instilled in me my sense of justice against the fucked-up bullies of this world. He sent my soulmate to me. And he led me to this moment. He will *always* be with me. And I, with him." With that, Maddy relinquished her warm embrace from Edmund and placed the pen on the table. Edmund held a look of worry before she picked up a red-inked pen and violently signed her name, "Mrs. Maddy fuckin' Sommers."

"And now," Edmund began as he sat upon the mahogany desk facing his three new recruits, "let me tell you how I became involved in this little operation. Then, you shall be officially welcomed in. And then I think that there's a little matter of a body that needs to be disposed of."

"As you all know, I was a detective in Madison. Through my police work, I stumbled across the knowledge that Joe's father was a hit man. After a little bit of digging, I was able to identify his involvement in this group. I was so intrigued that the father of my best friend was involved in this. And I was also so intrigued by *who* this group killed. They weren't just killing other mob bosses or people who didn't pay their protection money. On the contrary, they were killing people who preyed upon the less fortunate. The innocent. The vulnerable. So I decided to keep my knowledge of them a secret. But *my* knowledge was not kept a secret from *them.*"

Shortly before Joe returned from 'Nam, his father invited me out for dinner. What he did not tell me, however, was that the dinner would be in Brooklyn. We flew to New York, and I was brought into this very room. This room has not changed one bit since then, mind you. Basically, I was told that it would be in my best interest if I were to join them. And to assist them in recruiting Joe once he returned home."

"And I did. Joe didn't want to join. He just wasn't a joiner of anything. He took pride in his independence and not taking orders from other people. Even though this group assisted him with finding his parents' murderer, he wouldn't join. Even though his father had been a member, he wouldn't join. So my role in all of this was three-fold. Keep my ear to the ground with various police precincts and inform them if any cops were getting too close. To provide them with intelligence about people that they might find actionable. And finally, to groom Joe. Most of the people that I referred to Joe were, in fact, neighborhood assholes who had a beating coming to them. But most of the people that I referred to him to be murdered were, in fact, targets by this organization. So by the time of Blair's . . . unfortunate loss . . . Joe was well groomed and ready to roll once he joined up."

"Plus . . . this group actually talked to Blair in the hospital as she was recovering from her beating and subsequent miscarriage. It was because of their influence and their promises to keep them safe that Blair told Joe to call them and to join them in order to avenge their lost child. And Joe was so heartbroken and so in love with his Blair that he would have done anything for her at that moment. Anything. And he did. He joined and became one of the best and certainly most . . . inventive . . . hitmen in this organization. Five years ago, following my retirement from the force and the latest boss's death, I was promoted to lead this group."

"Joe never knew any of this. The most independent man in the world was being manipulated by his loving wife and dutiful best friend on the behalf of a syndicate of hitmen. He never knew, and we never told. And I think that we regret that to this very day. It wasn't wrong to recruit him. But it *was* wrong to keep that from him. And I suppose that I have yet to learn my lesson because here I am with you three. After promising Blair that I would never recruit you Maddy, here I am going behind her back. And I know that once this external war is resolved, the internal war that I have just started will continue to rage between her and I. I hope that she will forgive me for this indiscretion. But what must be done, must be done . . . for the salvation of us all. And with that my new colleagues, we would like to officially welcome you to . . . *Vendetta Degli Oppressi* (revenge of the downtrodden)!"

"Well, isn't this nice?" came an icy female voice from the just-opened door. The thin figure that was wrapped in a black trench coat entered the room. With her hands in her pockets and her jet-black hair with a single silver streak cascading down upon her shoulders, the seventy-year-old Blair sauntered into the room to the greeting of chilled silence. There was an apparent collective gulp as she approached the ten stunned figures.

"I came here tonight to tell you that the setup is complete," an attempting-to-be reserved Blair stated in a calmly quivering voice. "My contact has been successfully set up for a murder of one of their own. In order to prove my trust to them, I need to be the one to eliminate him. Then, the rest will congregate at one of their clubs for our Halloween party, and I am to be officially initiated into their group. The rest will take care of itself. That is why I came here tonight. I did not come here tonight to find . . . *this*."

Everyone in the room avoided eye contact with their matriarch. Clearing her throat and fighting back rare tears, Blair stated, "Maddy, Erick, Lucy, it is time to take our leave now. This life is not for you. This is over, and it will never be discussed again. Edmund, we will have words later. Now, come along you three."

"Blair," Edmund began hesitantly. "I'm sorry, my dear friend. But it is already done. They have joined us. The book has been signed. But it's better this way. Now you can infiltrate them with an even greater credibility. You will bring these three to them as a peace offering and then . . . well . . . *they* can take care of the rest. It's the perfect plan, Blair. Please understand. It's the only plan. I know you don't agree, but it's the only way to assure their safety."

"What I see, Edmund," Blair stated as she slowly walked over to her friend, "is my dearest and oldest friend betraying me. I see someone who made a promise to me and betrayed my trust. This is not over, Edmund. This has only just begun. But that will have to wait until our mutual . . . interests have been taken care of."

"Listen, Aunt Blair," Maddy began in a consolatory tone, "c'mon. I'm an adult now and I can make my own decisions. I mean—" Maddy stopped speaking the moment Blair's slender index finger was raised in front of Maddy's apologetic face. "No, no," Blair's frigid voice stated. "*you* would be wise to not speak to me at this moment." As she looked into her beloved niece's emerald green eyes, Blair then uncharacteristically lost control over her emotions.

As tears began to flow over her slightly wrinkled cheeks she said desperately, "I *never* wanted this for you. I *told* you not to do this. I *warned* you. This will end in tragedy for you . . . for Erick . . . for Lucy and for—" she buried her face into her hands as she sobbed the words, "for our Josie."

The cold silence was interrupted only by the nervous cracking of the knuckles of one of the large men. Blair righted herself once again, wiped the sadness from her face, and said in a controlled voice, "Very well. It is done. I have failed. I need some time to . . . process this. It would be wise for you Madeline Ruth to leave me be for a few days. I need time to come to terms with this before I can face you again."

Blair abruptly turned and strode out of the room with the attempted dignity of a fallen general who had just signed their surrender. Maddy stood there shaking. It was not lost on her that this was the only time that her aunt had ever used her full name. The only other person who had ever done so was her reviled mother. She knew that Blair had done this intentionally. She was sending a message. This was serious.

"Maddy," Edmund began sincerely, "I am so sorry if I have caused a rift between you and your aunt. I promise you that I will work tirelessly to remedy this. It just may take . . . some time."

"Eh, she'll be all right," an unconvinced Maddy stated with feigned confidence. "I'll just turn on the charm. She can't resist it. So how about that body? Let's go get that motherfucker!"

"Maddy, no." Erick sternly replied, "Lucy and I will get the body. You head on home and finish compiling our notes for the next one."

"Oh, my fucking god!" Maddy exclaimed angrily. "I am so fucking *bored* just watching people and compiling notes! I wanna have some fun . . . c'mon . . . *pleeease* . . . just this once?" "Maddy, no" came Erick's stern response once again. "Okay fine, fuck it," a disappointed Maddy replied, " just tell me what you're doing with these bodies."

"Ummm . . . nope . . . sorry, but we can't tell you that," Lucy softly replied. "We voted and decided that it would be best to leave you out of the details of the . . . y'know . . . disposal. We'll tell you after Josie has arrived. Until then, just take it easy. We got this."

"Oh, for fuck sakes, fine," a defiantly conciliatory Maddy growled. "But we *are* playing our cool theme song as we strut the fuck out of here!" Maddy took out her small Walkman cassette player that she had begun carrying with her for just an occasion. She pushed play. She began strut-waddling toward the door. Out of the tiny speaker came . . . Sheena Easton.

"You *motherfucker*! Come back here!" Maddy screamed at her husband as he ran out of the room laughing hysterically.

CHAPTER 43

SCREAM AND SCREAM AGAIN

Maddy entered her former apartment with trepidation and found a stone-faced Blair sitting on the couch in her satin merlot pajamas with her arms folded. "So . . . I gotcha some sour cream and onion chips," Maddy stated with a singsong lilted voice. "That's nice," Blair replied without looking over at her niece. "Sooo . . . wouldjya like to eat some?" Maddy gingerly inquired. "Just place them on the counter" came Blair's cold response. "Sooo. Are ya still mad at me?" Maddy inquired cautiously. "What do *you* think?" came the response as the temperature in the room seemed to plummet.

"Well," Maddy began, trying to sound confident, "*I* think that I've got the most *wonderful* aunt in the world who loves me *very much* and who has forgiven me for *much worse* things than this, sooo . . . nope, I don't think that you're mad at me!" With that, she flashed Blair her silly face.

"Dear," Blair stated coldly, "that little trick only works on emotionally impotent old men." "Really . . . you think so?" Maddy retorted. "Let's try it again!" The full arsenal of Maddy's "silly face" was unleashed on the well-prepared and stoic Blair. "Seeee?" Maddy began again as if she were speaking with a four-year-old. "I can see the corners of your mouth start to move upward. Yes, I doooo . . . there they go . . . you're wanting to laugh at meeeee."

Blair was unmoved. Her lips were tightly held together until a slight chuckle emerged followed by the release of a huge laugh. "Damn you to hell, Maddy! This doesn't change anything! I'm still very cross with you!"

"No, you're not," Maddy arrogantly replied, "but, just the same, I'm sorry I fucked up . . . *again* . . . and I promise I won't ever fuck up, well, at least *not like this* . . . again. I *promise* that I'll consult with you before I make these types of decisions . . . okay?"

"No, it's not okay. It will never be okay. You have hurt me deeply, and I will never rest peacefully again now that you are involved with this." Blair solemnly replied. "But what is done is done. I will need to work with you more intensely now. I must prepare you for all of the threats that your membership has opened you up to. I love you more than anything in this world, my darling niece. But I can't protect you any longer. All I have now for you is my guidance. I would strongly suggest that you take it. And besides, we haven't time to squabble. We have a Halloween party to prepare for."

One of the benefits of being a newly minted official member of *Vendetta Degli Oppressi*, or *Murder, Incorporated* was that you had the full disposal of their resources. All of their various informants and technical experts were at your beck and call. This included Rod.

Rod worked in a dark corner of the basement in the unassuming Brooklyn house that served as the hit man syndicate's headquarters. He rarely left the home and was a complete introvert. His thirty-eight-year-old frame stood well over six feet tall and weighed all of 120 pounds. He wore thick-lensed pop bottle glasses and had stringy greasy hair. He always wore sweatpants and a sweatshirt, regardless of the weather. His avoidance of eye contact was off-putting, especially to the female associates who assumed that he was fixated on another part of their anatomy.

Maddy's first words to Rod upon meeting him were, "Hey, Rod! Yup, eyes up here, buddy. Good boy. Now, I've got this guy that I need you to hack into his computer and see what's going on. He's the old dude that owns the little toy shop. Several years ago, he got busted for having cameras in the bathrooms. It was suspected that he was photographing the kids while they were in there. There was a bunch of controversy, but he got out of it somehow, so he just moved his shop a few blocks from where my Josie is going to live. And *that* shit just ain't cool. So check it out and report back to me, all right?"

Rod's eyes struggled to maintain contact with Maddy's piercing green iris and they drifted downward toward her motherly bosom before he said in a very nasally, staccato voice, "Yeah . . . okay . . . I'll check on it . . . give me fifteen minutes." "Fifteen minutes! Fuck you *are* good! For *that* kinda service you can stare at my tits *all day long*. Who gives a fuck?" An embarrassed Rod stuttered, "Umm . . . I wasn't . . . I mean . . . I wouldn't . . . I'll be right back." "Yeah, yeah, yeah," Maddy replied dismissively. "Whatevs, perv. Just get me my fuckin' report."

Fifteen minutes later, Rod returned to the red velour meeting room as Edmund was watching the proceedings from behind his desk gently jingling the ice in his glass of bourbon. Rod was carrying a folder in his left hand. With his right hand, he wiped the drool from his mouth and snot from his nose before handing Maddy the folder . . . with his right hand.

Maddy gently took a dry corner of the folder and said, "Uh . . . okay . . . thanks. There's still a bit of a pandemic going on so y'know, you might want to . . . oh, fuck it. I've had worse on my hands. Okay, Mr. Toy Man, let's see what we've got here." Upon opening the folder, Maddy's expression went from calm curiosity to mild shock, then to intense anger. "Yup, just as I suspected. Sorry 'chad,' but it's time to hold a meeting."

Later that evening in the warmth of his brownstone, Erick was laying on the couch reading yet another baby book while listening to Mozart. Lucy was there as well. She was sitting at the kitchen table with her laptop running a final analysis of a new toxin that she was trying to complete in time for the Halloween party that was to be held in two days.

The pair was startled to attention as Maddy's beaming voice came through the front door. "Here ye! Here ye! Here ye! As *president* of *The Unholy Trinity*, an official subsidiary of *Vendetta Degli Oppressi*, I hereby call this meeting to order!"

"Oh, for fuck sakes, Maddy," an annoyed Erick responded. "Do we have to go through this every time? Just say we need to have a meeting." "Uh, I can't do that" came Maddy's reply. "Why the fuck not?" Erick angrily retaliated. "Um, 'cause then it wouldn't be an *official* meeting and we have to have an *official* meeting so that our decisions will be *official*," Maddy stated quietly in her "hurt" voice. "But . . . but . . . but," Erick stammered as he attempted to find a reasonable response to his emotionally impressionable wife. "Just give it up, Erick," Lucy dryly stated. "Just let her have her fun. You're not going to win this one, anyway. It's a waste of effort."

"Fine," Erick angrily stated as he plopped down at a seat at the kitchen table between his two colleagues. "So what's the big deal?" "Well, just take a look at this report that I just got from Rod the Wad," Maddy replied sinisterly.

The trio (formerly of terror) went through each page and were aghast at the multiple images of neighborhood children in various stages of nudity as they used the toyshop restrooms or were having their diapers changed. The ages ranged from infants to teens of both genders. Finally, Erick got up from the table and said adamantly, "I can't fuckin' look at this. This is fucking demented. Lucy, tomorrow night. And we do this one *my* way."

"Hey, wait!" Maddy called after him as he hastily left the living room and began ascending the stairs, "we haven't officially voted yet!" "Fucking *Aye!*" Erick furiously bellowed without slowing his pace.

"Well . . . okay," Maddy calmly expressed. "A *bit* out of order, but I suppose it's an official vote. Okay, you two take care of this fucker while Aunt Blair and I take care of the final preparations for Friday's party. Then, how 'bout all of us meet up at the diner around nine-thirty for shakes and burgers?" "*Aye,*" Lucy agreed unenthusiastically as her eyes drifted back toward her computer screen.

———

The sixty-something man's eyes lazily opened and tried to adjust to the dim lighting in his living room above the toyshop. His head was pounding. Then he saw them. A male and a female. They were just sitting there, looking at him with childlike, wondrous smiles.

"Well, *hello* there," Lucy stated in an enthusiastic greeting as the man began to struggle to free his hands which were bound behind him, and softly stammered, "Please . . . please . . . don't hurt me." Erick then began.

"You're very clever. It's really quite clever to use a toyshop to lure unsuspecting parents and children into it. And your cameras are very well hidden. You have quite a talent. It's really too bad that you use it for your fucked up shit. I'll never understand this. I mean, I understand that everybody's got their own kinda kink that they get off on. But I'll *never* understand how men can get off on looking at naked children. Or, God forbid, having sex with children. How could that *ever* be a thing? Oh, I know that it is. I know that there are tons of "Daddys," and "Uncles," and "Friendly Neighborhood Shop Owners" out there who are diddling sweet, innocent children. Oh, and priests. Let's not forget about *those* unholy fuckers."

A slight smile crossed Erick's lips as he briefly recalled the anguished priest's dying face from a few nights earlier before he continued. "I don't know if you've ever actually *fucked* a child, but you want to, don't you? It's just a matter of time . . . and opportunity, isn't it? And what *exactly* goes through you sick fucks' minds as you listen to the helpless screams of children as you are *raping* them? What are you *thinking* as their innocent faces are awash with tears? How do you *feel* as you cover their mouths to muffle their desperate cries? Are you still turned on as you watch them sob as they clean your vile seed off of themselves and get dressed? *What the fuck is wrong with you?*"

Erick turned from the pleading man and Lucy. The horror of the scene that he had just described caused him to begin weeping because he knew that it was impossible to stop *all* of them. He couldn't even stop *very many* of them. He knew that at this very moment perhaps thousands of children were experiencing the brutally vile transgressions that he had just described. And he was powerless to stop them. But he wasn't powerless against this particular sadistic predator.

Regaining his composure, Erick turned back toward the man with a forced smile. "So you like toys, huh? Yeah, me too. And I must admit, you seem to have some quality stuff in your store. I've picked out a few to play with. You see, I'm about to be a father and I want to see just how durable some of these toys are. Let's start with these, shall we? But first, maestro, if you please."

Lucy pushed "play" on the small CD player that they had brought along. As Aerosmith's "Toys in the Attic" poured out of the speakers, Erick pulled down the desperate man's pants and plunged three pick-up sticks into his urethra as far as they could go. The man's excruciated screams were drowned out by the thunderous music as Erick violently pulled the man from his chair so that he was now face down, ass up on the floor.

"Hurts, doesn't it, motherfucker?" Erick sadistically inquired in his deep growl. "Yeah, it doesn't hurt nearly as much as the physical and emotional scars that you leave upon your innocent victims. Not *nearly* as much. But . . . I'm gonna try to rectify that. Or should I say 'rectumfy'?"

Erick then took a six-inch-long wooden toy soldier, complete with sharpened bayonet, and destructively jammed it into the squealing man's posterior over and over and over until a geyser of blood came shooting out of his dark cavity.

"Well . . . that was different," Lucy flatly assessed as the pair gleefully watched the man's final pain-stricken whimper. "Feel better now?" "Yeah, a little," a satisfied Erick replied before saying, "C'mon, let's get this fucker moved. We only have an hour before we're to meet at the diner and I'm fuckin' starvin'. Plus, I'd like to get there early so that I can anticipate Maddy's cravings tonight and plan our order. I swear if she steals just *one more* french fry."

————

"I am *not* fucking eating this!" Maddy declared in the middle of the kitchen of the club that was to host the following evening's Halloween party. "Nope. No fucking way. I don't care *how* fucking pregnant I am or *what* type of cravings I might have! You can smear it in peanut butter and cover it in pickles all you want! I'm *never* going to eat *this*!" her protestation continued as she looked down upon Blair's naked, bound, and gagged former contact from the darkest of the underground organized crime syndicates.

"Oh dear" came Blair's calm reply with a slight chuckle. "You won't have to eat it. I don't know why, but this group is much more demented than their previous incarnations. They have a ritual whereby they cook and eat the traitors to their cause. And in order to prove that we are on their team, we have been tasked to prepare this particular meal. Besides, Thanksgiving is coming up, and I believe that it is high time that you learned how to cook, young lady."

"Why?" Maddy cried out, "*Erick's* gonna cook for Thanksgiving!" "Maddy," Blair softly responded as she opened the kitchen drawer and retrieved the tool that she had been searching for, "a good wife knows how to cook." "*A good wife knows how to cook, blah, blah, blah*," Maddy sarcastically replied under her breath while rolling her eyes.

"Now dear," an unfazed Blair continued, "the first thing that we want to do is tenderize the meat." She handed Maddy the glistening meat tenderizer with short metal spikes protruding out of its square head. "Just forcefully hit the meat with this. And you want to do it all over. You don't want to miss a spot." "Alrighty then," Maddy enthusiastically responded as she grabbed the meat tenderizer and began slamming it into the flesh of the bound man. His muffled screams acted in concert with the percussive *pop, pop, pop* as the metal spikes gouged the wriggling man's skin.

As Maddy was tenderizing the following evening's meal, Blair looked the man into his pleading eyes and said, "First, I want to thank you for allowing us to use your club for our Halloween party. And I must apologize to you for betraying you like this. As you know, one of your colleagues has been . . . eliminated. That was conducted by *Murder, Incorporated.* And they, along with my assistance with some careful editing of our recorded conversations, framed you for his demise. And you know what the penalty is for betraying them. In fact, I know that you yourself have prepared and partaken in such feasts. And my former fake friend, you now know the penalty for betraying *me.*"

Blair glowered at the meat as she continued in a delicately sinister voice, "You assured me that if I joined you and offered information on *Murder, Incorporated,* that you would leave my beloved niece out of this. Now, I of course had no intention of living up to my end of the bargain. But it was still hurtful to me when I discovered that Maddy's involvement was a part of your master plan all along. So you now have your wish. Despite my protestations, here she is. My most precious possession. I hope you enjoy getting acquainted with her."

"Hiya! I'm Maddy! Pleasetameetcha!" Maddy's enthused face beamed as she stuck the tip of her tongue from one side of her mouth and grunted with each subsequent tenderizing blow. "Hey, how about some music?" Maddy asked. "Turn on the radio, won't cha?" The vicious whacking continued as Jimmy Buffett's "Cheeseburger in Paradise" played in the background. "Hey, that was kinda fun!" Maddy stated as she proudly looked at her completed work. The entire man's body from his head to his toes was covered with pinkish potholes as though he had some form of inverted measles.

"Okay, maybe cooking isn't so bad. What's next?" the enthused culinary pupil inquired. "Well," Blair began explaining. "He is too large to fit into the oven whole. Plus, they are only interested in eating the torso and head. So we need to remove his arms and legs, then cauterize the wounds so that he doesn't bleed out. We want him alive all the way up to when we slide him into the oven, which I have already pre-heated to 450 degrees."

"Yup cool," Maddy replied as she began sawing through the man's left leg. His screams became increasingly louder as each appendage was removed, cut up, and placed into a boiling pot. Maddy was then instructed to begin chopping up a variety of vegetables that included onions, garlic, and celery. She burst out laughing as she placed the carrots into the boiling pot along with the other vegetables, parsley, salt, pepper, thyme, and oregano.

"The key to a good roast, dear," Blair continued as if channeling her inner Julia Child, "is to have a rich and flavorful broth. This is your grandmother's secret recipe. The natural flavor of the meat will merge with all of the flavors from the vegetables and seasonings as it is baking. It truly is quite delicious."

The pair of demented chefs picked up the man's screaming torso and placed it into a large baking pan. The sound of his skin sizzling could be heard as the white-hot broth and vegetables were poured over him. "And now, six hours at 450 degrees, and we will have the perfectly cooked medium rare delicacy," Blair stated proudly as the shrieking man was slid into the oven. Maddy watched the dying man's skin buckle and pop through the oven window and began feeling ill before Blair said, "I think I may go to the party tomorrow night as the witch from *Hansel and Gretel*. What are you going as?"

"I don't wanna fuckin' talk about it!" an annoyed Maddy replied as the pair locked up the club and began their ten-block walk to the diner.

"Wassup, buttacup?" Erick excitedly asked as he embraced his wife and pulled her chair out for her at the round table in the middle of the scarcely populated diner. "Hey, you. Uh . . . nothin'," a still queasy Maddy replied. "Everything went okay?" Lucy inquired. "Just fine, dear, just fine," Blair answered, "we will need to go back in a few hours and place the meal in the refrigerator. Other than that, everything for tomorrow evening is prepared. Isn't that right, Lucy?"

"Yep. The new liquid toxin is all set. We'll have to take the antidote around 6:00 AM to ensure we're protected. "Hey," Erick inquired, "so what are we having for dinner tomorrow night? Should I skip lunch so that I'm extra hungry?"

"Oh, fuck," Maddy blurted out as she covered her mouth and made a hasty retreat to the ladies' room. "What's wrong with her?" Erick inquired. "Oh, I think that I'll explain that later. Why don't we just enjoy our meal?" came Blair's dismissively calm reply.

As the waitress was taking their orders, a pale green Maddy slowly closed her menu and said, "Uh, nothing for me thanks. I'm not really hungry." Fifteen minutes later, Lucy knowingly smiled as she watched an exasperated Erick looking on as his smiling wife greedily chewed a large bite of his cheeseburger while grabbing a handful of crinkle fries from his plate.

Chapter 44

Dead Man's Party

"Why the *fuck* are you dressed like a witch?" Patty exclaimed to her sister as Blair adjusted her pointed hat and picked up an old broom. "I have an engagement this evening. You should not wait up," Blair replied earnestly. "Wait, you're going to a fucking *Halloween party*? Why didn't you tell me! Shit! Just give me fifteen minutes, and I can be ready!"

A slight reminiscent grin crossed Blair's face as Patty ran into her bedroom and began excitedly yelling at her sister through the wall, "What should I wear? How about a sexy nurse? No, too on the nose. How about a sexy pirate? Hey, are there gonna be some hot middle-aged chicks there? My girlfriend's outta town. How about a sexy cop? Nah, that one got ripped up three Halloweens ago. Here we are . . . sexy voodoo priestess. This baby's gonna get some mileage tonight, heh, heh, heh."

Blair entered her sister's bedroom and stated sternly, "Patty, my adored sister, you are not invited to this party tonight." "Why the fuck *not*?" an increasingly enraged Patty exclaimed. "I got excluded from whatever the fuck you were doing last night, so I was stuck watching a fucking rom-com with Sam, Jules, and Kristy. I swear, those girls are becoming more fucking boring by the day. Did you know that Jules doesn't even drink now? That Jerry's been a really bad influence on her."

"Patty," Blair began again. "I'm sorry, but you are not invited to this party." "Oh, fuck that!" came Patty's immediate retort. "I'm definitely going. I'm not sitting around here all night while there's a banging party going on. Here, help me zip this. It's gotten a bit . . . tight . . . since I last wore it. Wow, that was a night. That little treat was a screamer!"

Blair stood in front of her sister and stared into her eyes. She gently placed her hands upon Patty's shoulders and stated in a deep voice, "Patty. You are not invited. You are not going. And if anyone ever asks, I wasn't there either. Do you understand?" Patty gulped hard and immediately averted her gaze away from Blair's. There was a familiar chill that ran down her spine. The same chill as when she had found out about what happened to the cult preacher in Madison. The same chill she experienced when she learned about the U-Haul parked behind the Argento's home on the day of Maddy's birth. The same chill as when she had heard muffled stories throughout the neighborhood of vicious beatings and murders. And the same chill that she felt when she heard about similar events occurring in her adopted home of Brooklyn. She did not *know* what was going on. But she *knew*.

"Is . . . Maddy going to be there?" Patty lightly asked. "Yes . . . now do you understand?" "Okay," Patty conceded. "I'll just . . . keep the home fires burning for you, okay?"

Blair kissed her beloved sister on her forehead and whispered, "Thank you, my darling sister. I'll be back in a few hours. Then, we can go out. Then, we can go out without having to look over our shoulders ever again. I promise you that. Okay?"

———

"I look fucking *ridiculous*!" Maddy screamed as she emerged from her room and entered her bedroom to find Erick dressing. "What's wrong?" Erick inquired as he attempted to not burst out into laughter.

"Oh, you *know* what's fucking wrong! Look at me! I'm a fucking orange nightmare!" Maddy was standing there in green tights and wearing a green stem atop her head. The rest of her body was encased in a giant orange sphere. She was indeed an orange nightmare.

"Um . . . well . . . we wanted to make sure that you had enough padding to cover the bulletproof vests. We can't take any chances tonight, Maddy. We have to protect Josie. It's just one night. Then we will come home, and you can take that thing off . . . assuming of course we can get you through the door." With that, Erick let go of his repressed laughter as Maddy stood there annoyed with her hands on the area that should have been her hips and tapping her left foot.

"Yeah, really fucking funny, mister," Maddy stated coldly as she glared at her guffawing husband. "Oh, by the way. What the fuck are *you* supposed to be?"

Erick was standing there wearing a lavender T-shirt, white slacks, white suspenders, white platform shoes, and a brown, white man's afro. He looked at his wife, flashed a huge smile, and proudly stated, "I'm '70s chart-topper and pop icon Leo Sayer!"

"What . . . why . . . why would you wear?" a confused Maddy began stammering as she searched for the appropriate words. All that came out was, "Who is even gonna know what you . . . why can't you just be normal? Why are you so fucking *weird*?" "Well, I don't see anything weird about dressing up as one of your idols on Halloween," Erick retorted defensively. "Well, it is . . . it is weird," Maddy replied with a hint of concern. "It's weird that you're dressed like that. It's even weird that Leo Sayer is one of your idols. Who the fuck has Leo Sayer as an idol? I don't understand—"

Maddy's voice trailed off as they heard Lucy answer the door downstairs and greet Blair. Erick bounced down the stairs to greet his aunt-in-law. Maddy cautiously began placing one size six foot in front of the other before she bellowed, "Hey! Motherfuckers! How about a little help here? I can't even see my feet in this fucking thing!"

Erick immediately rushed back up to the top step, took his wife's swollen but petite hand in his, and guided her down the treacherous staircase.

Upon seeing her niece, Blair burst into laughter. "Oh, my lord. I knew it would look silly, but this is . . . this is . . . just precious. If it weren't such a provocative evening, I would have to take a picture. But I don't need to. This vision will be etched into my brain for as long as I live on this earth."

"*Me?*" Maddy yelled out. "What about *him*? Look at *this* fucking thing that *he's* wearing!" Blair looked Erick over and proudly stated. "My, don't you make a handsome Leo Sayer. Very creative. Very nicely done, my dear. Well now, shall we go?" As they departed their home, Erick said, "See Maddy? I told you that—" "Just don't fuckin' talk to me right now" came Maddy's terse interruption. The petite ninja that was trailing them chuckled quietly to herself before recapping the plan for the evening.

"Okay," Lucy began. "Everybody but Maddy took the antidote twelve hours ago. It's good for another eighteen hours or so, so we'll all be fine. Maddy, even the antidote could be lethal for your child. And since you're pregnant, you'll be excused from drinking the punch. The punch that I have spiked with my newest adaptation, *Toxin D*. *Toxin D* acts much like *Toxin C*, except that because it's in liquid form and not an injectable or gas, it takes ten to fifteen minutes to get absorbed into the bloodstream and take effect. Then, there's the excruciating pain followed by death. It's clean, simple, odorless, flavorless, and highly effective. Any questions?"

The other three silently shook their head as each pondered whether they would ever eat or drink anything in Lucy's home again. They arrived at the club two hours before the underworld syndicate members were to arrive. They knew they were being watched, so every movement was very deliberate and very benign. Lucy mixed the punch with pre-spiked fruit juice, gin, vodka, and a splash of lime juice. "Mix well, and *voila*! A witch's brew!" Lucy exclaimed as she placed the punch bowl on a table in the dance hall.

"Wait, that's our *supper*?" Erick yelled out as he watched a perfectly cooked head and torso being placed into the oven to be reheated. "Just be cool!" Maddy whispered to him before saying, "Yes, dear. Don't you remember? I told you that we have to consume just a little bit of our enemies in order to show allegiance and solidarity with our new brothers. Don't worry. We just need to eat a little. Plus, I brought steak sauce."

Erick then mouthed to his wife, "*I didn't eat lunch*," to which Maddy mouthed back, "*then eat some fuckin' cookies and shut the fuck up*!" Despite the silence of the exchange both understood one another perfectly. Erick went over to the refreshment table, picked up a cookie, and shut the fuck up.

All fifteen expected guests arrived at the same time. Each of them was dressed in all-black suits. "Well, fuck!" Maddy stated quietly, "don't *we* all feel silly now?"

"Hello, darlings," Blair sweetly stated as she gave a slight hug and peck on the cheek to each of the guests. "Won't you all have a seat? Gentlemen. First please allow me to introduce you to your newest and most lethal members. This is Lucy who specializes in bomb-making and other . . . bodily explosives. This is Maddy's husband Erick who . . . well he has yet to find his niche . . . but he has proven to be quite effective at the art of execution."

Before Blair could finish her introductions, one of the black-clad men said, "What the fuck are *you* supposed to be dressed up as?" Erick smiled widely and proudly stated, "Why, *I'm* '70s hitmaker and pop icon Leo Sayer!"

"Who the fuck is Leo Sayer?" came the man's surly reply followed by a room filled with laughter. There was one laugh that was much louder and much more pronounced than the others. Erick looked down disappointedly at his cackling wife. "Sorry . . . but . . . it *does* really look stupid. Oh, Hiya! I'm Maddy by the way! Pleasedtameetcha! And even *more* pleased to work alongside you gents to get rid of all of these goodie, goodie *Murder, Inc.* fucks!"

The fifteen men then introduced themselves. The names went in one ear and out the other of their four-person audience. Their names were insignificant. These *men* were insignificant. And they would be even *more* insignificant in about half an hour.

"Well, now, I suppose I should explain our attire," a blushing Blair began. "You see, following this gathering, we are all going to an all-night Halloween party to let our hair down and celebrate our most joyous union with you all. And you are all invited to come along should you feel . . . up to it. But we didn't think that we would have time to change before our next event, and since it was Halloween, we didn't suppose you would mind our looking a bit . . . flamboyant."

"Yeah, it's fine," a large, tall man sitting in the center of the group began. "Let me explain to you all what you've signed up for. And believe me . . . you are *all* now signed up. *Including* that little yet-to-be-born bundle of joy. We are a part of an international underground network that runs deeper and more powerfully than all of the standard organized crime families combined. We are into money, yes. But we're mostly into power. Specifically, white, male power. But, since you are all very talented, I suppose we can take on a couple of broads too. Even one that's a g**k. Just as long as you all know your place, got that?"

The four slowly nodded their heads and listened in measured silence as their faces became flush from their rising blood pressure. "We're New York's enforcement branch for this international web of ultra-right-wing think tanks and power brokers. *Their* job is to put mostly white men in positions of power in order to slowly corrode the institutions of democracy so that each country will become a dictatorship ran *by* white people *for* white people."

"And they have been quite effective. Russia was among the first to fall and was quite easy. They were a young democracy whose population was already acclimated to life under a strong- man regime. Belarus is yet another example of their success. Great strides are happening in Turkey. And in America, just look at how little time it took them to install enough people in order to make women in this country second-class citizens! Hell, they even installed a *broad* just to make it all look constitutionally legit!" The room exploded with laughter before the man continued.

"That is *their* job. *Our* job is to recruit like-minded and talented individuals and to take out anyone that is a threat to their mission. And *we* have been quite effective as well. With one exception. *Murder, Inc.* has escaped us for decades now. Each generation tries and each generation fails. Until now."

"*Our* generation decided to do things a bit differently. *We* decided to recruit from within their own ranks. And here we are tonight. We are here tonight to celebrate our ushering *Murder, Inc.'s* own into the fold and the ultimate demise of that damned institution. They are going to fall tonight just as the institutions of American democracy will fall over the next two decades!"

"And they will fall not because of *us*. They will fall because of the American people *themselves*! They will fall because *many* of the American people are easily brainwashed into believing in propaganda designed to make them fear and hate the other. They will fall because *many other* Americans are self-absorbed political eunuchs who are so apathetic about everything that they can't even be bothered to spend ten minutes watching the news. All *they* care about is gas prices and taking selfies!"

"In the meantime, our associates are broadcasting their glorious messages into America's homes. They are turning Americans against one another one household at a time. They have *already* created a cold civil war. Neighbors silently hating neighbors. Brothers silently hating brothers. In just a few short years, there will be a *hot* civil war."

"Why do you think that they have pushed so hard to have military-style guns out in the streets and in the hands of ordinary people? Because *they know* that most of the ordinary people that are going to carry those guns are *their* people. They are the ones who are most likely to be indoctrinated into our worldview of fear and hatred of others. They are the ones who so rightly understand that it is their *God-given right* to be in a position of domination over the others. And *they* are the people that will be the most heavily armed once the *hot* civil war begins. And then, my friends, we will all rule supreme!"

Let's have that toast, let's have that toast, let's have that toast, raced through Maddy's mind before she said, "This is a glorious vision of the new world order! And it is such an *honor* to play a small part in assisting you men in achieving this most wonderful eventuality. Now, let's eat that traitorous motherfucker! I'm starvin'!"

Blair, sensing her niece's impatience, and being completely revolted herself said politely, "Yes! Erick, won't you bring out the main course? In the meantime, why don't we toast to this most magnificent union and the destruction of the world order as we know it! Lucy, would you please do the honors?"

As an ill-looking Erick was wheeling a partially carved charred head and torso to the dining table, Lucy was pouring the punch into eighteen ceremonial goblets. One of the black- clad men handed Maddy a can of lemon-lime soda. "Here, baby. You shouldn't be drinking in your condition. Damn. I bet you were really fine before you got that kid stuck in 'ya. If you ever regain your figure, maybe you and I could . . . y'know . . . get together." "I can hardly wait to see you lying underneath me" came a smiling Maddy's unflinching response as Erick reached for the carving knife, then slowly put it back down.

Each of the nineteen participants raised their drinks. Blair excitedly exclaimed, "To us. To how our Lord intended it to be. To our union. And to the brutal destruction of our enemies!"

The fifteen men waited a moment until their four new recruits had guzzled their punch before gluttonously downing theirs. Erick thoughtfully placed the meat on each plate. He took his seat. Everyone picked up their knife and fork. Erick began sweating. Maddy's heart was racing. They looked at one another and silently communicated to one another, *"Say something! We gotta stall for time!" "Me? You're the one that's so fucking great at 'winging' it! You say something!" "I can't! If I open my mouth, I'm gonna hurl!" "Hey! I'm the one that's fucking pregnant, so if anyone's gonna hurl, it's gonna be—"*

And then the slight coughing began. One by one the men began gasping for air. They clutched their throats, then began screaming in agony before falling to the floor. As their insides were being torn apart, the dying men writhed and gagged in their splendid torture. Blair sat in her chair calmly watching the scene as she casually chewed upon yet another bite of her dinner. "I must say, I don't think even my *mother* could have prepared a meal as satisfying as this."

Blair took out her phone and dialed. "Yes, hello. It is done. Peace has once again been restored, but our work is far from over. In fact, it is even more daunting than what we have ever believed. This isn't about money. This isn't about local power. This is about taking over our country. This is about taking over the world. We need to meet, but not tonight. We're going out for pizza, then I promised my sister a Halloween party. And Erick is starving. For some reason, he skipped lunch. Yes, tomorrow afternoon then. Good night, Edmund."

It was 9:00 PM. The plan was laid out. The group text was sent. "URGENT MESSAGE FROM MADDY SOMMERS! BY MADDY SOMMERS! WE NEED YOU NOW! PIZZA PLACE IN 30! DANCE CLUB AFTER! WEAR SOMETHING SCARY! THAT IS ALL! OVER AND OUT! THIS HAS BEEN AN URGENT MESSAGE FROM MADDY SOMMERS! BY MADDY SOMMERS!"

Blair, Erick, Lucy, and Maddy sat at their table casually sipping their drinks and reflecting on the evening's events. They were watching their friends on the dance floor. Kristy and Jason, having left their children in the care of a trusted neighbor, were doing some form of gyration dressed respectively as a doctor and a nurse. Jules dressed as a biker chick was grinding her crotch on Jerry's leg. Jerry was dressed as a biker, so he didn't have a costume. Sam was gliding around the dance floor with a newfound companion. They each thought about how unaware their friends were. How oblivious they were to the war that was being raged beyond the reaches of the conventional institutions of their democracy. How blind and naive even the most intelligent people were of the impending storm. Their solemn thoughts were abruptly halted when Patty came rushing up to them.

"Maddy! You gotta *do* something with that bitch!" "What are you talking about?" Maddy screamed above the blare of the electronic beats. "That bitch, Sam! Look at how she's rocking that sexy Voodoo Priestess outfit! Do something to make her gain weight! She's making me look bad!"

Maddy watched as Erick placed a fifty-dollar bill into a man's hand. She averted her gaze as he turned toward her and strode across the dance floor. He offered his hand to her. Maddy suspiciously placed her hand into his. Her wedding ring shot prisms of colored light across their smiling faces. He led her onto the dance floor and waited. He placed his arms around her green body-suited waist and held his abdomen close to hers. Their child was sure to hear both of their heartbeats. He began delicately swaying with his wife as Leo Sayer's "When I Need You," began playing. Everyone left the dance floor except for two figures who were unaware of anything but their love for each other and their love for their unborn child at this moment. At this moment, there was peace. At this moment, *they* were at peace.

"Okay," Maddy partially conceded. "It's kind of a sweet song. Y'know in a *pukey* sort of way." She looked up at him smiling and batted her copper lashes over her emerald green eyes. He smiled at her and gave her a tender kiss before whispering into her ear, "Maybe we saved our country tonight." She softly replied, "No, we didn't. But maybe we helped a little to give people the time they need to wake the fuck up before it's too late."

Chapter 45

Redemption Song

It was a brisk Tuesday evening, November 7. Erick and Maddy had just finished cleaning up dinner as the scent of homemade nachos still clung in the air. Maddy, now six months pregnant began her labored ascension up the metal staircase toward the shower when the doorbell rang. "I'll get it! Who the fuck could *that* be?" Maddy yelled out to Erick. Maddy opened the heavy oak door and was greeted by the slim, pale face of a sixty-six-looking more like an eighty-year-old man.

"Hello, Madeline. I'm sorry to just drop in on you like this. It's so wonderful to see you. May I come in for a moment?" the man sheepishly inquired. Maddy, wearing a shocked expression on her face paused for a moment as she tried to process what was happening. The seconds that passed in the awkward silence felt like hours until she finally said reservedly, "Uh . . . yeah . . . of course. C'mon in . . . Dad."

The frail man entered the home, looked around, and said, "My . . . what a wonderfully inviting home you have here," then, upon seeing the prominently displayed poster for Hammer's *Dracula AD 1972* let out a slight chuckle before concluding, "it's just as I would have expected it." "Maddy, everything okay?" an inquisitive Erick asked upon seeing the slight man enter. "Yeah . . . uh . . . Erick, this is my father . . . uh . . . Frederick. And, Dad, this is my husband, Erick." "Uh . . . well hello, Mr. Sommers . . . it's uh . . . nice to meet you . . . I guess," Erick very tentatively said as he extended his hand while cautiously monitoring his wife's reaction.

The pair timidly shook hands as Frederick wore a bemused expression. "Won't you please have a seat, Mr. Sommers?" Erick invited. "Thank you. You're both being kind to a fool of an old man who doesn't deserve such graciousness." He then shook his head and with a regretful chuckle said, "Freddie the Fool was what they used to call me. And how right they turned out to be. Madeline, I have come here to tell you something and I hope that you will allow me that honor." "Of course, Dad. It's . . . um . . . nice to see you after all of these years," Maddy sincerely replied.

"Yes, it has been far too long," Frederick said in a regretful tone. "Madeline, I've been such a fool for nearly my entire life. I have never stood up for myself and always allowed other people to dictate to me what I should be and what I should think. That, of course, includes your mother . . . a monstrous *bitch* of a woman if I've ever seen one." If Maddy had been an animated character in a *Looney Toons* cartoon at this moment, her jaw would be laying on the floor.

Frederick continued in the same regretful tone, "I mean, my *god* Madeline! The things that that woman would have me believe. The things that she introduced me to! And damn me to hell for believing in all of that shit! I mean, who in their *right mind* hates people just because of the color of their skin or who they are driven to love, or because they worship differently? How could I have ever come to believe that? Patty, Blair, and I were never raised that way. How was it that I came to believe such hateful bile?" Frederick's voice began to rise, and his cadence began to quicken as he stared at the bewildered pair sitting on the adjacent couch and continued, "I mean, I just sat there, I fucking just sat there, Madeline, as that fucking bitch beat you for all of those years. You stupid spineless fool!" Tears began to stream down Frederick's face as he began to emotionally absorb the weight of his confessionary words.

"Only a fool of a man could have believed what I have believed for so long. Did you know that that bitch and I were *actually there* on January 6, 2021? Did you know that I was so fucked up in my head that I actually was part of the mob that was standing outside of the capitol as it was under siege? That I was a part of an attempted coup to take over our government? And why? Because of the lies of a fucking *game show host*! That's the fucking cherry on the top now, isn't it? That just perfectly illustrates just how stupid we all have been. To take the word of a self-centered fucking *game show host* over the word and warnings of thousands of diplomats, politicians *of his own party*, military officers, psychiatrists, and thousands of others. And now, here we are. And it's happening all over again. A divided nation that can't even agree on vaccinations during a fucking pandemic. A nation that is on the verge of warring against one another because half of the country actually believes all of the bullshit that I used to listen to. It's so ridiculous, a fiction writer wouldn't have been able to come up with this shit. What a sight we have become. And you, Madeline, knew it all along. I am just so glad that I at least was able to give you access to healthier role models with healthier ideals. I am just so grateful to Blair, Patty, and Joe for shepherding you and protecting you through your early life. Because I and your mother were fucking toxic for you."

Silence fell upon the trio. Erick held onto Maddy's ever-tightening hand as he thought, *Nope. I'm not gonna get involved in this. This is their fucking dance.* Maddy, attempting to break the hushed tension began awkwardly mumbling, "Ummm . . . well, okay then . . . so . . . hmmm . . . sooo," Erick, unable to stand Maddy's fumbling any longer finally interjected, "So . . . Mr. Sommers . . . what, may I ask, has brought you to these conclusions?"

"Please, call me by my first name," Frederick corrected. "Um . . . all right . . . Frederick then." Erick replied. "No, not that name. That was the name that that fucking cult called me, and it's tarnished forever. I was always called Freddie until I met that bitch and I intend to be Freddie once again for my final days on this earth. Now, Erick, to answer your question, I found out that I was going to be blessed with a granddaughter. And I didn't want your precious child, my granddaughter, to know me as the person that I've been for most of my life. I wanted her to at least have a few fond stories about her grandfather and to maybe have the opportunity to teach her through my missteps that no one is beyond redemption. Because you see . . . and I'm not telling you this to garner any sympathy . . . it's just that . . . I have cancer, Madeline. It's been recently diagnosed, it's incurable and I only have a few weeks left. And I wanted to make sure that you had a complete picture of who your father was before I'm cast out upon the wind."

Her father's words fell upon Maddy's heart like an anchor. This man who she had loathed and resented for so long had succeeded in finding his way into her heart once again. And just as an ember of hope for a relationship with him began glowing, she realized that she would soon lose him once again. She had sworn to herself, many years ago, that she would never cry over the plight of either of her parents. She had no control over keeping that oath as tears began streaming down her lightly freckled cheeks as she said, "Dad . . . I'm, I'm so very . . . sorry . . . I don't know what to—"

Her father, in an attempt to comfort his beloved daughter, cut her off and said reassuringly, "It's all right, Madeline. I would rather have only a few days left as the person that I am today than live a hundred years as the person that I was. I have said what I have come to say, and I think it's time for me to retreat back to my hotel. I would love to have dinner with you both before I return home in two days if that's all right with you."

Maddy looked pleadingly at Erick who, upon receiving his cue, instinctively said, "Hotel? We will hear nothing of it. You will be staying with us. In fact, if I were you, I would cancel that flight. I think you need to stay with your family for as long as you are able. So I'm going to go to your hotel and retrieve your belongings. Maddy, why don't you call Blair and Patty. I think you all need a family reunion. And, Mr. Sommers, Freddie, it has indeed been a pleasure to meet you, sir."

Two evenings and one missed flight later, the trio was sitting around the dining room table, joined by Blair and Patty trying to eat Chinese takeout through their laughter. After swallowing a bite of egg roll, Freddie said, "That bitch was so insane, that we couldn't ever eat Chinese food again once the pandemic hit because she said . . . now wait for it . . . Chinese food caused the 'kungflu'! How fucking stupid can a person be?" Uproarious laughter ensued and continued as the stories, mostly about a young Maddy flew around the table. "Oh, and this manipulative little child," Blair would recall, "would look up at Joseph and bat her pretty copper eyelashes over her sweet green eyes and say, "Gee, Uncle Joe, I just don't know which dolly to choose. I just love them both so much." And Joseph, being the sucker that he is, would say, "Well then I guess we'd better just get both of them then, buttacup." And she would squeal with delight as he would pick her up in his big strong arms and twirl her around. In those moments, it was as though they were the only two people in the world. It was so damned sweet that I just couldn't bring myself to be cross with either of them."

Tittering immediately turned to reflective silence in the room until it was interrupted by a soft voice saying, "Thank you." Freddie had looked up and was moving his eyes between his sisters' mournful faces as he said, "Thank you for looking after me as I was growing up. Thank you for trying to get me to see the world differently. Thank you for not giving up on me and staying in contact. And most of all, thank you for helping to shape my daughter into the incredible person that she has become. I love you both so much."

He then began to chuckle while turning to look at his beloved daughter. "Oh . . . my lord . . . the look on that bitch's face when she saw . . . what you had done to the pages in the Bible! To use it as toilet paper! And . . . and you put the roll upside down! It was just so . . . perfect!" He was laughing uncontrollably while wiping tears of joy as he continued, "And . . . and . . . oh my lord . . . when you beat the shit out of her . . . it was the most fulfilling moment . . . of my life! It just had to happen, and you had to be the one to do it. It is my prayer that that is my final image before I pass because I know that I will pass with a smile on my face."

At that moment, Freddie's phone rang and the temperature in the home seemed to plummet by twenty degrees. "Madeline, would you get that for me please?" Freddie inquired. "Sure," Maddy stated as she waddled across the room to the sound of the infernal buzzing. "Hello . . . oh, hi Mom . . . yeah, he's here . . . uh, I don't know . . . just a sec. Hey, Dad! Mom wants to talk to you! She wants to know when you're coming home!" Freddie immediately retorted, "Tell that bitch that I *am* home and to *fuck off*! I never want to hear from her again!" "Okeedokee then," Maddy chirped before returning to the phone. "Mom? Yeah, Dad says that he *is* home and that you should fuck off and to not call him again. Okay? So byeeee!" The call was cancelled, and the room immediately returned to its previous coziness.

Over the next few weeks, Freddie Sommers basked in the embrace of his newly adoring family. There were dinners, games, and stories before he would retire to bed, a little earlier each night. And he would join them on two occasions at the karaoke bar. He felt immediately welcomed by Maddy's friends and watched in wonder at their playful and unvarnished conversations. He also reveled in the frisky banter between his spirited daughter and equally spirited son-in-law. "Just fuckin' sing it!" Maddy would order. "No, Maddy, I haven't practiced this one! You know I suck at songs that I haven't practiced!" Erick would reply. "Just fuckin' do it! It'll be fine! You'll sound great! C'mon, it'll be really funny!" Maddy would insist. "Fine! But if I suck, I'm withholding sex!" Erick would pseudo-threaten. "Oh . . . *pleeeease* don't do that! How on earth will I ever have a *baby* then?" Maddy would mockingly counter with an ornery grin.

Upon Erick's return to the table wearing a very annoyed expression following his "performance," Maddy said, "Okay . . . so what have we learned? Well, maybe you really *should* practice before trying 'Surrender' or probably any Cheap Trick song for that matter. Okay, my bad. Sorry." Erick just glared at her before breaking down into laughter as she flashed him her "silly face."

Frederick "Freddie" Sommers passed away on December 21st in the comfort of his daughter's home as his beloved sister Patty tended to his every need during his final days. Just before passing, Freddie motioned for Maddy to come closer. A tearful Maddy leaned her delicate ear next to her father's mouth and listened to his final rasp. "Madeline, my love. I am so proud of you. Please scatter my ashes in the playground you said you would take my granddaughter. I want to spend eternity watching you and Josie play." With that, Freddie closed his eyes forever. He had a smile on his face.

The private funeral service was held at Erick's church and presided over by Pastor Tim on the early morning of December that were to begin. There were no speeches this time. There was only a brief Bible scripture followed by a rendition of her father's favorite song from when he was a child. The Freedy Johnston version of "Somewhere Over the Rainbow" echoed throughout the nearly empty chamber as Maddy, Blair, and Patty embraced. Erick, Sam, Jules, Kristy, and Lucy stood behind them and held hands. Following the service, Maddy silently waved everyone away from her, picked up the urn, and left the church.

She went to the park that was five blocks away and sat on a swing. Her copper hair was motionless until she began pouring the contents of the urn onto the ground, at which point a delicate breeze emerged from the north, tussling her auburn strands and carrying his ashes throughout the playground. In the distance, two birds could be heard singing. She took out her phone and prepared herself for the conversation that she had long been dreading and longing for simultaneously.

"Hey, Mom . . . who the fuck do you *think* it is? How many fuckin' kids do you have? Anyway, I just thought I should call you and tell you that Dad's gone. He passed a couple of days ago, and we just had the funeral. And I also wanted to tell you that I hate you now more than ever. I now realize the man that could have been my father if you hadn't been such a controlling, insane bitch! I will never, ever speak to you again. And if you want to see Dad again, well . . . you know what to do now, don't you, you worthless shriveled up unsubstantial piece of shit of a human being. You were worthless my entire life and you're even *more* worthless to me now, so," Maddy's voice then dropped into a nearly demonic growl as she concluded, "so just do me and everyone else a favor, you fucking hag. Do something right for once in your miserable existence. Just do it. Everyone who is supposed to love you has abandoned you. You have nothing here. You wanna meet your maker so badly? Then just fuckin' do it. Maybe *he* has some use for you because *we* sure as fuck don't. Maybe you'll see Dad again, but I doubt you'll be going to the same place. Fuck you."

The next morning, Maddy, Erick, Patty, and Blair were unwrapping the brightly colored packages that were being exchanged while recapping the amusing stories of Freddie from the previous few weeks when Blair's phone rang. Blair answered and in an emotionless voice said, "Yes, I understand. Thank you so much for calling. Yes, thank you, we will do our best to have a merry Christmas." She hung up the phone, looked Maddy thoughtfully into her eyes, and said, "Maddy, your mother was found dead this morning. She has hung herself. She was found hanging in the dining room. And she was clutching a yardstick and the Bible."

Maddy looked down at her protruding belly which gently carried and protected her own daughter. Her daughter whom she and Erick already loved more than anything in this world. The daughter that the loving couple would soon be greeting. "Oh . . . my . . . god. What have I done?" she said quietly. She then looked up at her family with such a beaming expression it seemed as though her dimples would explode from her face from the intensity of her smile. "Well, fuckin' God bless us all, everyone! It's a fuckin' Christmas miracle! And if anyone hears a bell ring today, it won't be for *that* fuckin' bitch, I can assure you of that!"

Following her exclamation, she looked into the eyes of her beloved husband, batted her lush copper eyelashes over her emerald eyes with her head slightly cocked, and said in her childlike voice, "Hey, baby? You think maybe we could have some French toast and sausage?"

CHAPTER 46

VALENTINE'S DAY

Thursday, February 13, 9:30 PM. Erick and Maddy were at the vacant bookstore as she was completing some final paperwork under his protective gaze before her extended maternity leave. "Ummm . . . hey, baby? I was just *thinkin'* that *maybe* I could come in for a little while tomorrow morning . . . y'know . . . just for a final pep talk to everyone," Maddy tentatively stated with her head slightly cocked while batting her emerald eyes at her husband. "Maddy," Erick sternly began, "You *promised* that tonight was your last night. Sean and your crew have it under control. The place isn't going to burn down. They'll be fine. Tomorrow's supposed to be Josie's birthday. And it's our first wedding anniversary. Please?"

"Okay, fine, but I think she's being stubborn. *Not unlike her father, I might add.* Just give me a few minutes to finish this shit up, okay?" Maddy conceded. "Yup, cool!" a relieved Erick responded. "Hey! Can I go get that huge book of baby stories? I was wanting to read to Josie out of it tomorrow night!" "Jeezus, mister! That thing weighs like twenty pounds! Just get a couple of nursery rhymes or something," Maddy ordered. "Ahhhhh! C'mon!" Erick began pleading in his childlike demeanor. "That thing has like every great story *ever*! I *promise* I won't buy any more books until Josie and I have gotten through every story. *Pleeeeease*?" "Oh, fuck, fine. You're such a fuckin' baby sometimes. I'm gonna be raising two of you little bastards! Just make it quick. I need to finish this paperwork and lock the front door," Maddy retorted while feigning annoyance in order to hide her amusement. "Yay!" Erick exclaimed as he literally skipped back to the children's section of the store.

"What the fuck is taking him so long?" Maddy thought as she grabbed her keys from her purse. "If he brings ten books up here, I'm gonna—" Maddy's thought was interrupted by the buzzing of the front door. A tall man in a grey trench coat and large-brimmed grey hat entered. "Uh . . . hey, hi! Sorry, but we're closed." Maddy stated to the man. "You'll close when I say you'll close," the man countered in an ominous voice. He then lifted his head. Maddy's expression immediately turned to shock as she recognized the face as being that of the third and final man from the neighborhood watch chadlist. He was a man that she and Erick had been closely watching in an effort to determine whether he posed a significant threat or not. In fact, they had been unable to uncover anything so untoward that required him to be eliminated and he was about to be taken off of the chadlist until he said, "Now, bitch . . . why have you been following me?" "Uh . . . hey . . . there must be some kind of misunderst—" Before Maddy could finish her sentence, the man pulled a revolver from his coat pocket and fired, hitting Maddy in her left shoulder. She fell upon her right side heavily, breaking three of her ribs. "Jesus Christ, man! What the fuck! I'm pregnant! Oh, fuck . . . something's wrong . . . with my baby!"

The man stood over her with the revolver pointed at her burgeoning midsection. "*Fuck* you and *fuck* your baby. This will just save me from having to fuck that kid up later." The hammer of the gun could be heard being cocked followed by an intense thud! The man collapsed from the impact of a twenty-pound book of children's stories being crushed onto the back of his head.

"Oh fuck, oh fuck, oh fuck!" Erick began stammering as he immediately grabbed the gun then went to his wife's side while simultaneously reaching for his phone and dialing 911. "Oh, fuck baby, something's wrong . . . I need help," Maddy pleaded. "I know, I know, I'm calling—" Erick stated in a panicked cadence. "Yes, hello, we need an ambulance. My pregnant wife has been shot. The shooter ran out the front door and is out there somewhere! Please hurry and send the police!" Erick gave the address, hung up the phone, and said, "Okay, listen. I gotta . . . put this guy somewhere. I'm not gonna let the police fuck this up. Just hang tight . . . okay? I'll be right back." Erick took his ever-present zip ties from his back pocket, tied the man's ankles, then his wrists behind his back, and dragged him to the basement door. Despite her agonizing pain, Maddy could hear the thump-thump-thumping of the man's head as it hit every step on his final journey to the dank basement.

Erick called Blair who arrived at the same time as the blaring siren of the ambulance. "I'll give a statement at the hospital, officer! I have to go with my wife!" Erick yelled as the ambulance doors were closed with Blair and Erick each holding one of Maddy's trembling hands. As she looked down upon her beloved niece's pain-stricken green eyes, Blair relived her own trauma nearly fifty years prior of having lost her own baby at the hands of a brutal assailant. She gritted her teeth and shed an uncharacteristic tear.

Upon entering the hospital with Maddy's bloodcurdling screams of "Mooootherrrfuuuuckeeer!" bouncing off of the walls, Blair grabbed Erick by the shoulder and said, "Patty will be here soon. She and I can watch over Maddy. You have business to attend to. Call Lucy to help and get back here as soon as you can." "But . . . but . . . I have to—" Erick began arguing. Blair cut off his protestations and said, "What *you* have to do is to do right by your wife and child. There's nothing that you can do to help here. Make a brief statement to the police about how a robber shot Maddy and then immediately left when he saw you. Then, give me your phone. You were here all night. I will call the bookstore when I know anything. One ring for everything's all right. Two rings mean that you had better come quickly. Now go."

Erick and Lucy began descending the rickety wooden staircase to the basement of the bookstore. The only discernible sound besides the heavy breathing of a panicked man was the creaking of the stairs as the pair laid their weight upon them. There was a reason that the police had never found the bodies of the other two from the chadlist. While doing research, Erick discovered that the building that currently housed the bookstore used to house a large butcher's shop. And much of the industrial equipment had been left there. And stored in the currently unused basement. And it was still functional.

Lucy stood behind Erick silently as he glared with an insane intensity at the man who had jeopardized the lives of his wife and daughter. His face was beet red and demonically contorted. He then said in a methodical cadence with a tone resembling a death rattle, "I once made a promise to my wife. I promised her that if anyone ever harmed her or our child that I would rip them apart with my bare hands. And I never break a promise to my wife."

With that, Erick straddled the man's lap, took out a large, serrated butcher knife, and tore the man from just above his groin to his sternum. Blood gushed from the gaping wound as the gagged man's muffled screams grew in intensity. Erick dug into the man's cavity, and upon finding what he was looking for, grabbed his ribs with his scrawny-looking hands and pulled them apart with such ferocity that a geyser of iron-scented crimson erupted from the gaping wound. He looked the man in his eyes as he grabbed his still beating heart, tore it from its chamber, and squeezed the blood onto the man's dying face while saying, "Happy Valentine's Day, motherfucker."

Erick sat on the man, looking at his traumatically frozen face. Erick's clothing was stiff as the iron-scented molasses began to congeal. He was in a post-murderous trance until Lucy said, "You'd better get cleaned up. I can take it from here. Let me know when you know anything. Otherwise, I'll join you at the hospital as soon as I'm done. It's going to be a while, though."

Erick gave a knowing nod, went to another room, stripped his clothes, and threw them in the furnace. He then climbed into the industrial-sized wash basin and scrubbed the remnants of this horrific man from his skin and soul. He was still weeping as he dried off and put on a new set of clothes that he had stored there. He then heard a sound. It was not the sound of the phone ringing to update him on the events at the hospital. It was the sound of labored gnashing of the industrial meat grinder.

———

Maddy's piercing screams echoed off of the sickly green hospital walls as she was rolled down the sanitized hospital hallways on a rickety gurney. She didn't know what hurt worse: the sting of the bullet hole in her shoulder or the constant knifelike jabs from her broken ribs or perhaps it was the emotional scars that once again were being recalled as she feared she may be taking the final ride of her brief thirty-six-year existence.

A kaleidoscope of images and memories was flashing in her pounding brain: the beatings at the hands of her mother as her impotent father looked on; the love of her beloved aunts and uncle; the Friday night dance parties, the smorgasbords of junk food; the cross-country trip to college with her beloved uncle Joe; and the laughing and singing with her friends and babysitting Kristy's delightful children. This last image put a slight smile on her tortured face.

The smile quickly faded as her thoughts turned to her mentally sadistic

ex-husband and the execution of her uncle. Intense outrage replaced hopelessness as she relived her brand of justice that she had applied to the insignificant
deplorables that found their way into her world. The white trash that had
murdered her uncle leading her to cut his brakes and plant his head into a
pole. The wife and child beater that discovered that fireworks in the right
hands could be quite deadly. The deadly overdose that she injected into the
arm of the man who was grooming her to be a sex slave and who had nearly
killed *her* with the same intravenous venom. The would-be date rape druggist
who she ripped to shreds in a dark alley. The black- market pandemic profiteer of essential goods who has eaten his last hot dog. The serial rapist and
murderer of children who received a righteous arrow through his rectum.
The pair of redneck rapists who she publicly left dismembered and hanging.
The voyeur of her best friend's rape that she eliminated in a most sado-
masochistic manner. Her work couldn't be over yet. She and Erick had so
much more to do.

Then her prince's face flashed before her eyes. She looked up at her aunt
Blair who was gripping her sweaty hand as the gurney rumbled along. "Erick!
Where is Erick? I need him now more than ever! Where is he?" Maddy
screamed. "He'll be along dear," Blair replied in as soothing of a voice as she
could muster. "You're in good hands. I'm here. Patty's here. The doctors will
take care of you. Erick will be here as well. Please don't worry. Just try to relax.
We are all here to take care of you and—"

At that moment, the gurney turned a sharp corner and entered an operating room. Maddy could hear voices say, "We have to take her now!" "But,
Doctor, she's in too much pain!" "I know, but dammit, it has to be now if
she's going to make it through!" She was transferred onto a bed and the
bright lights shone down upon her, immediately dilating the pupils of her
fading emerald, green eyes. Something was being injected. Her aunt's grip was
steadfast. And the only thought in her mind was "Erick, where are you?"

"Okay, now Maddy, this isn't going to be a walk in the park, but I need
you to push now dear," the doctor demanded as soothingly as possible. "It . . .
hurts . . . too . . . fucking . . . much!" Maddy screamed. "I know dear, I know.
But there's someone who wants to come out and meet you and she needs
your help. Now just breathe deeply and push."

Erick arrived at the hospital shortly after 12:00 AM, Valentine's Day. He
demanded to see his wife, but the obviously distraught and near hyperventilating man was refused entrance. Defeated, he stumbled to the waiting room,

sat on a hard plastic chair, and accepted the attempts of a comforting embrace from Sam, Jules, and Kristy. He sat there, with his head in his hands, and wept profusely as he imagined the worst possible outcome for his endearing wife and beloved daughter.

By now, after two previous runs, Lucy knew the drill. Dismember the body into smallish pieces with a sharpened axe. Put the pieces into the meat grinder. Put the ground meat into Tupperware containers. Put the containers into the large refrigerator. Lock the refrigerator door, the key to which only she and Erick had. Then, the "fun" part. Clean, sanitize, and bleach everything three times over. Burn the clothes. Bathe. Change. Get to the hospital. On the way to the hospital, Lucy began the distribution process of the ground meat. In dark alleys throughout this Brooklyn neighborhood, stray cats, dogs, and other furry creatures would be delighted once again to find a special treat for dinner that night.

Fighting through the unimaginable torture that her body and psyche were enduring, Maddy gave one final push. Her bloodcurdling wail was joined in unison by another before she collapsed in exhaustion.

Josephine Patricia Sommers Parker entered the world at 2:14 AM on February 14, 2024. Maddy awoke to find her prince delicately holding a blue blanketed bundle that was making content cooing sounds in the arms of her loving father. "E— Erick? Is, is she . . . okay?" Maddy hesitantly asked. Erick stopped whistling the tune of "Build Me Up Buttercup" and turned around to face his cherished wife. His tears were flowing down his cheeks from his hazel eyes, and he wore a beaming, prideful smile as he said reverently, "She's better than okay. She's perfect. Jeezus, Maddy, she has *your eyes*."

Song Reference List

The author would like to thank the countless musical artists that have enhanced his entire life. In particular, the author would like to give a heartfelt thank you to the following artists for enhancing the experience of both writing and reading this book.

Jackie Wilson: "(Your Love Keeps Lifting Me) Higher and Higher"
Oingo Boingo: "Weird Science"
Belly: "Feed the Tree"
Link Wray: "Rumble"
Beatles: "In My Life"
Blondie: "One Way or Another"
The Young Rascals: "Groovin'"
MC5: "Kick Out the Jams"
The Archies: "Sugar, Sugar"
The Cowsills: "Hair"
The Monkees: "Pleasant Valley Sunday"
Alice Cooper: "Only Women Bleed"
The Mindbenders: "A Groovy Kind of Love"
The Angels: "My Boyfriend's Back"
Ray Anthony: "The Hokey Pokey"

Fleetwood Mac: "Never Going Back Again"
Tragically Hip: Long Time Running
The Cramps: "Hot Pearl Snatch"
The Cure: "The Baby Screams"
The Foundations: "Build Me Up Buttercup"
Talking Heads: "Stay Up Late"
The Everly Brothers: "All I Have to Do Is Dream"
Marcel Bontempi: "Dig a Hole"
Billy Idol: "White Wedding"
The Cramps: "The Crusher"
Christopher Cross: "Sailing"
Echo & the Bunnymen: "The Killing Moon"
Marvin Gaye and Kim Weston: "It Takes Two"
David Johansen: "Bohemian Love Pad"
Macy Gray: "I Try"
Dion & The Belmonts: "When you Wish upon a Star"
Lindsey Buckingham: "Holiday Road"
REM: "She Just Wants to Be"
Alice Cooper: "Poison"
Elton John: "Friends"
The Damned: "Jet Boy, Jet Girl"
Primal Scream: "Movin' on Up"
Imperial Teen: "Yoo Hoo"
Rush: "The Big Money"
Paul Simon: "Mother and Child Reunion"
Lou Reed: "Dirty Blvd."
Tony Orlando and Dawn: "Tie a Yellow Ribbon Round the Ole Oak Tree"
The Crazy World of Arthur Brown: "Fire"
The Five Blobs: "The Blob"
Talking Heads: "Creatures of Love"
The Fugs: "Johnny Pissoff Pt. 2"
Bruce Springsteen & the E Street Band: "Murder, Incorporated"
Sheena Easton: "9 to 5 (Morning Train)"
Johnny Rivers: "Secret Agent Man"
Screaming Lord Sutch: "Scream and Scream Again"
Aerosmith: "Toys in the Attic"
Jimmy Buffett: "Cheeseburger in Paradise"

Oingo Boingo: "Dead Man's Party"
Leo Sayer: "When I Need You"
Bob Marley: "Redemption Song"
Cheap Trick: "Surrender"
Freedy Johnston: "Over the Rainbow"
David Bowie: "Valentine's Day"

ASCENSION

HANGING CHADS BOOK III

PROLOGUE

She had to pause for a moment. The pressure of her heartfelt eulogy fell upon her soul like a ten-ton weight, helplessly splashing into a dark ocean of despair. The silence of the mourning congregation was deafening as her mind raced. She felt dizzy and heard a slight ringing in her ears. She held her head down so that her lush copper locks covered her tear-filled emerald-green eyes.

This was not supposed to happen. This was a travesty of justice. She had already lost the man who had taught her how to trust and love. Now she had lost the strongest woman in her life. The woman who had nurtured her from birth. The woman who had fostered her own sense of self-worth. Her own sense of being. Her own sense of justice. She had taught her about the power of the feminine spirit and the power of female bonding. And now, without her, she felt utterly powerless.

This was not supposed to happen. They had all been so careful. They had meticulously identified their threats and then took them out one by one. There were no clues. There wasn't supposed to be anyone left. There wasn't supposed to be any further threat to the syndicate or her friends. And, most certainly, there wasn't supposed to be any further threat to anyone in her family. She and the younger generation were sure that they had seen to that.

And yet, there she was. Right in front of her. Lying still. Her spiritless corpse painted like an obscene mannequin in the window of a trendy shop in a strip mall. Her beautiful yellow gown covering the fourteen bullet holes that had ripped her life away. It was all over. There was nothing left.

She crouched even farther, trying to become invisible behind the dark-mahogany altar. She could not bear this. She had been raised to bear anything. But she could not bear this. Not again.

And then it came. Breaking through the silence was the spirited chirping of a little bird from outside a cracked window. The song penetrated her soul. Buoyed by the hopeful sound, she looked up at the solemn faces of her congregation. This *wasn't* over. This was now *her* responsibility. This is what she had prepared her for. It was now *her* time to ascend.

She gave a comforting and confident smile and then a slight nod to the musical director. He pushed play. As the opening metal riff of AC/DC's "Thunderstruck" boomed throughout the hall, her lithe frame began the confident trek down the church's steps. Her pace quickened, and her stride transformed into a strut as she glided down the middle of the on-looking well-wishers and mourners. When the enormous opening lyric to the song came thundering through the speakers, she tore off her conservative black dress, revealing a skintight green faux-leather cat suit. She kicked open the church's doors and screamed to the universe, "Here I am, motherfuckers! Time to fuck some shit up!"

Chapter 47

The Rain, the Park, and Other Things

She lay there and stared up in fear at the two pairs of piercing eyes that were gleefully staring back. She was outnumbered, and at this moment, she instinctively knew that she was powerless to stop their inevitable attack. All that she could will her body to do was lightly kick her arms and legs. *This isn't much of a defense,* she thought to herself as the ominous eyes inched closer to her face. *Do something!* she screamed to herself. Her bottom light- mauve lip began puckering as she let out an anguished, defensive wail.

Then, as quickly as the attack had begun, it was over. Her two feline nemeses were unceremoniously lifted into the air as though being retracted by some divine being. She heard two voices. "Hunky, come on, you leave Josie alone."

"Yes, you too, Dory. Josie is just a baby and doesn't want to play with you right now."

"Thank you, Aaron! Thank you, Adam! You boys are sweet!" came her mother's familiar voice from a distance.

"You're welcome, Aunt Maddy," came the voice of an eight-year-old, whose name was Adam.

"Yes, you're welcome, Aunt Maddy," came his twin brother Aaron's reply.

"Aunt Maddy, we will always be there to protect Josie." Adam stated, which was quickly followed, as always, by Aaron's contribution to the discussion, "Yes, Josie is our friend. No one will ever harm her. If anyone ever tries to harm her, we will harm them."

"Hey, guys," their father, Jason, began tentatively inquiring to his pair of toe-headed sons, dressed identically, as always, in white slacks, white shirts, and white ties, "how would you . . . ummm . . . harm them?"

"Well, Father, Mother, that would depend," Adam replied, followed by his brother, "Yes, it would depend."

"Yes, it would depend," their twelve-year-old adopted daughter Vai interjected remorselessly. "It would depend on what they tried to do. We would counter them. We would do to them ten times worse than what they would ever try to do to our Josie. She is our friend, and we will stop at nothing to defend her." She then looked down at the settling infant who was lying on a blanket on the living-room floor of Josie's home, her tears drying from her brilliant emerald-green eyes as her growing copper locks were beginning to display a slight curl. "You will never have to worry about anything, Josie. You will never have to fight. We will always be with you. We will always be there to fight for you."

A familiar chill ran down the spine of the observing Patty as her beloved sister Blair entered the room with chips and salsa and stated calmly, "Oh, don't worry about it, my dears. Children instinctively have the urge to protect their own. I'm sure that they would never do anything to harm another."

"Yes, we would," came the unified solemn reply of Vai, Adam, and Aaron before returning to the other side of the room to innocently play with their five-year-old sister Alexa.

Trying to change the subject, Erick asked, "Hey, boys . . . how come you always wear white? And why don't you wear different clothes? It would make it a lot easier to tell you two apart. Aren't you tired of people confusing you?"

"We like white, Uncle Erick," came Adam's emotionless response, followed by his brother's, "Yes, we like white. Good guys wear white. And we don't mind if people are unsure of who we are. We are one, so that doesn't really matter. We think as one, and we act as one. We don't even have to speak to understand one another. And it is fun to play this game with adults. They care much more about our names than we do. It is funny to us."

"Okay, then," came Erick's concerned reply, followed by his asking, "Say, Maddy, Lucy, Blair, could I maybe see you three upstairs for a moment?" Upon shutting the soundproofed door of the third-floor party room, Erick began his earnest discussion. "Listen, I'm really concerned about something."

"Okay, baby," Maddy calmly replied, "I know *exactly* what you're concerned about. There are three of *them*, and there are three of *us*, and you're worried that they might try to take our cool name. But don't worry. We are and shall always be the Unholy Trinity, an official subsidiary of Vendetta Degli Oppressi. Those little fuckers will just have to come up with their own cool name."

"No, Maddy, that's not what I'm—" Erick attempted to interject before his beloved wife cut him off.

"And no, they don't get to use our cool theme song either." Maddy looked around the party room at the vast collection of music on display there and concluded, "I'm sure that you can help them find their *own* cool song to walk down the street in slo-mo to."

"Maddy, that's really not what—" an increasingly frustrated Erick began before being cut off once again.

"And they'll just have to find their own way of killing people. Y'know, we really should copyright our shit or something."

"Maddy!" a boiling-over Erick interjected. "Would you please listen to me? Please stop cutting me off! I don't give a *fuck* about names or songs or copyrights! What I care about is that they are *children*! We are going to teach *children* how to be assassins and serial killers! Isn't that fucked up? Aren't you three the least bit disturbed by that?"

Maddy, Lucy, and Blair looked at one another silently and just shrugged before Blair stated, "Erick, we understand your concerns. But they are unwarranted. These three are destined for this. They are the next generation. You know the fight that all freedom-loving people are up against. It isn't just a fight against random sadistic neighborhood bullies any longer, although that fight shall continue. This is a fight against fascist oppression. We must take up this fight because there are so few others who are willing or able to do so. And you know that this fight will rage on from one generation to the next. It is for their benefit that we get them started as early as possible so that they are prepared. And it is to Josie's benefit because this will *not* be her fight. I already failed to keep my beloved niece out of this. I *will not* fail again. Josie *will not* be a part of this. Ever. Josie will be protected from this life. Do you understand now, dear?"

"Yeah . . . I guess so . . . but," a confused Erick replied. "but . . . they have parents! What about Kristy and Jason? And Alexa? Is that sweet little girl going to be a part of this too? Shouldn't we feel bad about betraying their parents?"

"Yeah, that part kinda sucks," Maddy answered solemnly. "We're really not sure about Alexa yet. We think it might be best to leave her out of it. And I'm afraid that there might come a time our friendship with Kristy comes to an end. I'm afraid that at some point, she'll figure it out. And by that time, the die will have been cast, and Vai, Adam, and Aaron will make their final decision to come with us. That will be a really sad day. But until that happens, we *still* have a dinner party to throw, and we're being rude and leaving our guests unattended. So hop to, mister! Let's go downstairs and be pleasant or some shit!"

The solemn expression on Erick's face immediately disappeared and transformed into a prideful smile the moment he lifted his one-month-old daughter off her blanket. She squealed in delight as her father spun her around, her yellow flowered dress floating above her diaper as the air hit her pudgy legs. She furiously batted her copper eyelashes over her vivid green eyes, and her slightly curled auburn hair drifted in the breeze like brilliant autumn leaves. He beamed at her, and she beamed back. Erick looked over to his wife and stared at her as a tear formed in his eye. It was just the two of them silently communicating with each other. And what he was saying to his adored wife was "I understand."

"Jules, have a fuckin' drink!" Maddy ordered as the dinner party was greedily consuming their homemade chicken enchiladas. "C'mon! I made the margaritas myself!"

"Naw," came Jules's flat response. "Jerry's in recovery, and I like—oh fuck —love him and shit, so I'm trying to be understanding and supportive. Besides, drinking wasn't ever that big of a thing for me. It was just something you did when you went out looking to get laid. And, well, I've got Jerry for that. And fuck is he huge! That fucker makes me cum buckets!"

Erick just sat there with a hint of regret as he silently admonished his designer for the somewhat-adequate manhood that he had been "blessed" with.

"Jules! Maddy!" Kristy exclaimed. "Will you *please* watch your language? We have children here!"

"Uh . . . yeah . . . sorry," Maddy conceded as she thought about the worse things that her children would hear from her in the coming months and years. *I'd better be really fuckin' nice to her,* Maddy thought. *It's the least that I can do for stealing her children away. Oh, fuck it.*

"Hey baby, are you gonna finish your enchilada . . . hmmm?"

"Oh, what?" Erick angrily exclaimed as he got up from the dining room table. "Yours not *big enough* for you? Fine! Just take it!"

"What is *his* problem?" Sam inquired.

"Oh, he just gets that way anytime Jules talks about Jerry's dick size. He'll be all right . . . y'know . . . later tonight," Maddy replied through her chuckles.

"You wanna know the funny part about that?" Jules interjected. "For a really tall man, Jerry's really not all that . . . y'know . . . endowed. I just like fucking with Erick."

As Erick was upstairs putting on his hairnet and black hoodie, he heard a roar of laughter over his preparation theme song of Stephen Bishop's "On and On." *Yeah, probably laughing about my dick size. Really fuckin' funny. I am sooo in the mood for this shit tonight.*

———

Erick and Lucy waited quietly inside the one-bedroom apartment of the man who had provided the neighborhood strays with their latest special treat. They were awaiting the brother of the man who had nearly murdered his wife and unborn child. The brother had not heard from his sibling in over a month. Through the monitoring of his email and social media correspondence by Rod (the Wad), the Unholy Trinity had learned that the brother was at least aware of his sibling's grotesque deeds of raping and murdering children throughout the United States, Canada, and especially Mexico. He had been doing it for years, and his brother had at least been aware of it, if not complicit in it. And now he was coming to retrieve his brother's belongings before the police had a chance to. He had correctly assumed that something sinister had befallen his brother and was determined to discard anything in his brother's belongings that might implicate *him* in the horrific transgressions. And through Rod's diligence, they knew when he was coming, what flight he was on, and when he would be arriving with a U-Haul.

"So," Erick began whispering to Lucy as he was losing control over his impatience, "why do you ladies call Rod, *Rod the Wad?*"

"Oh, that," Lucy dryly replied. "It's because he always stares at our chest. It's really creepy. Plus, it rhymes."

"Yeah, but I don't think that he's doing that on purpose," Erick replied in a hushed tone. "I think that he has really bad vision and is socially awkward, so that's just where his eyes unfortunately land when he's talking to someone else. I mean, he stares at *my* chest too, and there's really no reason to do that. I really think that you ladies need to cut him some slack and—"

Erick's thoughts were interrupted by the sound of a truck pulling up from three stories below. "It's showtime," Lucy stated as the pair took their places on the set of their most recent kill scene.

There was the clinking of keys before the rusted door hinges created an ominous creak. A dark silhouette entered the room. The dark silhouette immediately hit the floor with a heavy thud, following being struck in the head by Erick's impressive bat.

"Well, hello there!" Lucy excitedly exclaimed as the bound brother regained consciousness to find two smiling faces looking at him.

"Hey, chad," Erick began as the man began struggling against his restraints in a metal chair. "So I haven't much time tonight because I need to get home to my wife and baby. So, I'm gonna keep this short. We just thought you'd like to meet the people who are responsible for your brother's death. My name is Erick, and this is my colleague, Lucy. And we murdered your brother because he nearly killed my wife and unborn child. So, he nearly killed two people, and we have only killed one so far, and that doesn't seem quite fair. So, you're the second. And then, the score will be settled, and we can all just go on our merry little way. We will go on to live our lives, and you will join your brother in the fiery pits of hell . . . God willing."

"So . . . wouldja like to know what we did with your brother?" Erick inquired of the man as he began his muffled screams. "Well, after he shot my about-to-give-birth wife, I clocked him with a heavy book of children's stories. I then dragged him to the basement, cut him from his dick to his chest, ripped open his rib cage, and tore his heart out. It was still beating as I squeezed the blood from it over that prick's face. Then, we dismembered his body and ground him up like hamburger. He was then fed to all the sweet little furry creatures throughout the city. Pretty cool, huh?"

Erick began maniacally cackling before continuing, "Which brings us to *you*. Why would we kill *you*? Well, because *you* at least knew what your brother was up to. I don't know what is worse. The fucking scum who does this twisted shit to innocent children or those who know about it, have the power to stop it, and do nothing. How many children could you have saved if you had just reported your brother's fucked up shit? How many families would be tucking their sweet little kids into bed tonight instead of crying themselves to sleep? *You* had the power to stop it, and *you* did nothing. We had the power to stop your brother, and we acted. And *now*, we have the power to stop *you*, motherfucker!"

The bat was swung and repeatedly crushed the face and skull of the man. Blood, flesh, teeth, cartilage, and bone were strewn throughout the room, covering himself and Lucy. Erick flashed back to the evening only a few years prior when he had exacted the same revenge upon the tools of propaganda that had taken his first love from him. He was in a bat-wielding frenzy before Lucy finally said, "Hey, I think that's probably enough."

Erick looked at his friend. She was covered in blood and bodily fragments. Blood was dripping down off her bottled-blonde hair and pooling on the tile floor.

"Yeah, okay," Erick breathily stammered before taking one more swing of his gargantuan bat, crushing the man's skull entirely and forcing one eye to pop out of the socket.

"Shit, man," Lucy stated as she looked in dismay at the crimson carnage throughout the room, "this is gonna take forever to clean up."

"Naw," Erick replied, "let's just clean ourselves and get changed. Let's leave the mess for the cops to try to figure out. There are going to be some great crime-scene photos! Maddy is going to be so proud of me!"

———

An exhausted Erick entered his bedroom to find his lovely wife feeding their near-slumbering child. "Hey, you," Maddy whispered as she smiled up at him and batted her green eyes. "Wassupbuttacup?" Erick replied. "Aw, nothin'. It's just that I think that she might have her mother's appetite," Maddy playfully responded.

"Aw, fuck," Erick responded with resignation.

"Hey, what's wrong?" Maddy inquired in a concerned tone.

"It's just that," Erick began with his head down as he was taking his socks off at the edge of their bed. "I've just been thinking, Maddy. If she has *your* appetite, then in a couple years, I'm *never* gonna be able to eat a french fry again!"

He then flashed his mischievous smile at his adored wife as she replied in a hushed tone, "Yep, you're fucked. Bitches gonna get *all* the fries, heh-heh-heh."

He picked his daughter up and began patting her back as he bounced around the room with his cherished, blue-blanketed bundle. Upon the telltale sound of her gas being released, he took her to her room, changed her diaper, and returned to gently lay their child on the bed between the two of them.

"Awww, c'mon, man!" Maddy said in a hushed but pleading voice. "You're gonna spoil her! She's gotta get used to sleeping by herself! Plus, she's sweaty as fuck!"

"Just one more night, Maddy," Erick thoughtfully stated while placing a stuffed manatee next to his daughter's cheek and a pink flower in her curled copper locks. "I promise. Tomorrow she will sleep in her own bed." "Yeah, I've been hearing that for two fuckin' weeks!" a disgruntled Maddy replied as she rolled over and closed her eyes.

She opened her eyes. There they were again, just staring at her. Only this time, instead of fear, she felt comforted. She smiled and began to lightly coo as a pair of purring, fuzzy heads nuzzled themselves under her soft chin. Josie was with her pussycats, and Josie knew that she was safe. Josie knew that she was loved. Josie knew that she was home.

CHAPTER 48

TOILET LOVE

"What the fuck? Why aren't you dressed yet?" an astonished Maddy inquired of her husband as he was twirling their three-month-old Josie around. She was cackling and squealing hysterically as her green eyes locked onto those of her father.

"Well," Erick began sheepishly, "I was just thinking that maybe I would stay home tonight. I know Abana's a wonderful mother and will take good care of Josie, but she's just so small. What if she gets scared? What if she misses us? What if she *doesn't* miss us? What if something happens? I just think that you should go out and have a wonderful thirty- sixth birthday celebration with your friends, and I'll just hang with Josie. Besides, there's really no reason to put Abana and her little boy out."

Maddy had mixed emotions. On the one hand, she absolutely cherished how much love her beloved husband had in his heart for their child. To her, he was the perfect father who would do anything for their Josie, and this was a quality that she did not want to extinguish. On the other hand, she really needed to get out of the house and was annoyed by his reluctance. She needed to walk a fine line here and not fuck this up. She fucked it up.

"Okay, listen here, mister!" Maddy roared, causing Josie to look at her mother with a shocked expression. "For starters, we're not putting Abana out. As you know, her husband, Henri, has just returned from visiting his home country of Cameroon following his discharge from the army. So, he's home to take care of their three-year-old boy, leaving Abana free and clear to spend the night here with Josie!

"Secondly, we have not been out in months! C'mon, it's my birthday! I need to go out and get all hot, sweaty, and fucked up! So there is no debate here. Put the baby down and get dressed! We're leaving in ten!"

As soon as her final thoughts came tumbling out of her mouth, Maddy realized that she probably had just triggered her husband's anti-authority streak. He did not mind suggestions. But orders were an entirely different thing.

"Well, if you're going to be *that* way about it, then fuck it! I'm *definitely* not going!" Erick bellowed back as he caressed his child.

Maddy knew that she had to make a hasty retreat. "Okay, baby, I'm sorry. Listen . . . I know how much anxiety you are having. It's our first night away from Josie. I understand that, and I love that about you, okay?" She saw the slight anger melt away from his face and become replaced with haughty satisfaction. It was working. Now, for the humor. Her mauve lips curled upward in a mischievous smile before she said in a slow, calm cadence, "Just put the baby down, raise your hands in the air, and slowly walk away."

"But Maddy," Erick attempted to interject.

Maddy once again stated calmly, "Just put the baby down . . . raise your hands in the air . . . and walk away. We don't want any trouble tonight. Just put the baby down and walk away." To cement the manipulation, she then flashed her "silly face" at him.

Erick, now understanding the absurdity of the situation, burst into laughter as he gently laid his beloved child into the kind awaiting arms of Abana, who had just entered the room.

"You have nothing to worry about, Erick," Abana softly stated as she smiled upon the cooing treasure resting in her arms. "I will care for her as if she were my own."

"I know you will, Abana," Erick sincerely replied before grabbing his best jeans and T-shirt and bustled into the bathroom.

On their way out the door, Erick continued to bark orders, "And she needs to be fed at seven and again at nine. And she needs to be burped. She may need up to four diaper changes before you put her down to sleep. And she goes to bed right after her nine o'clock feeding. And no loud sounds on the TV. And keep Hunky and Dory out of her room. They like to sleep in her crib, and I'm afraid they're going to smother her. And make sure all six baby monitors are turned on, just in case. There's one in the basement, one in the laundry room, one in the living room, one in our bedroom, one in the upstairs bath, and one in the party room. And—"

Erick's anxious demands were finally cut off as Maddy impatiently stated, "Oh, for fuck sake! C'mon, it's all written down. Let's go!"

Abana just chuckled to herself as she heard Erick's voice fading out as he and his wife made their way down the street in the unseasonably warm mid-May evening air. "And we'll have our phones on us, so call if anything—and I mean *anything*—happens!"

Maddy and Erick entered the dingy punk club and made their way to a table near the front of the stage to join Patty, her girlfriend, Jerry, Jules, Kristy, Jason, and Sam. Lucy and Blair could not attend as they had other engagements that only Maddy and Erick knew about. Piercings and spiked hair could be seen glinting in the subdued multiple-colored lighting throughout the club as Green Day's "American Idiot" boomed into their ears. And the sexual tension was palpable.

Over the previous several months, the couples and members of the group had experienced a drought of sorts in their love lives. Jason and Kristy spent most of their free time attempting to work with Vai, Adam, and Aaron on finding healthy outlets for their anger. The seemingly futile actions left them emotionally exhausted, and they would fall into a deep slumber as soon as their respective heads would hit their pillows.

The thirty-seven-year-old Sam faced increasingly greater odds at satisfying her carnal pleasure as younger women were beating her out at her conquests on a more consistent basis. It was not so long ago that she was the hit of the clubs and felt confident that she could bed any male that she set her sights on. She now felt increasingly invisible and more like a novelty in an increasingly younger sea of makeup, short dresses, and cleavage. It did not help that her hunting grounds continued to be the same ones as when she was in college. So, she was torn between battling against the younger competition or settling for her rather pudgy and uninteresting middle-aged male counterparts. She had decided to take up the challenge on this evening and began to eye a mid-twenties strapping young punk in a Black Flag T-shirt and facial piercings.

Jerry still had a defined limp from falling off his motorcycle after he had an evening of falling off the wagon two months prior, which had left him laid up in bed until just recently. Jules, having newfound compassion, at least for this one man, catered to his every need during his recovery, even though he had been incapable of catering to hers.

And Erick and Maddy were simply exhausted from raising their newborn. To make matters worse, Erick hovered over his daughter and frantically responded at the slightest cough, gag, or hiccup. Maddy, attempting to calm her husband's nerves and reclaim her previous sexual glory, would dress in provocative outfits, only to come to bed and find her husband reading to their daughter with a delighted expression on his face. Although Maddy wouldn't trade her husband's affection for their child for anything in the world, it did not keep her from feeling slightly dissatisfied. Hence, her idea for tonight's gathering. She mentally developed a foolproof plan.

MADDY SOMMERS'S PLAN TO FUCK MY HUSBAND
BY MADDY SOMMERS

Step 1: Get him to put the baby down.

Step 2: Get him out to a club with loud music that he loves.

Step 3: Get him just drunk enough to ease his anxiety but not so drunk that his dick goes limp. If the latter happens, encourage him to use his tongue.

Step 4: Get laid.

All the evening participants had similar libidinous plans in their minds. With the notable exception of one. The seventy-two-year-old Patty was consistently face-deep in her fifty-nine-year-old girlfriend. And her girlfriend would eagerly reciprocate. From the moment that Patty had met Jacklyn at Maddy's bachelorette party, the two had become nearly inseparable. For the first time since her teenage liaison with her high school teacher, Patty was in love. And the pair made the most of their later-in-life union. Nightly. Including tonight, which offered multiple opportunities for straying fingers under the table as they stared into each other's eyes while lasciviously sucking on the straws of their drinks.

About an hour into the evening's proceedings, Maddy turned to her husband and said bluntly, "Okay, give me your phone."

"Why?" Erick replied, feigning ignorance.

"You fuckin' know why. Abana just texted me and said you've been texting her like every five minutes. You're driving her fucking nuts. Now give me your fuckin' phone."

"Okay," a resigned Erick replied as he watched his phone being placed into Maddy's faux black leather purse.

"Good, now, let's go dance!" Maddy excitedly exclaimed.

But instead of the dance floor, she took him to the men's room on the second floor of the club. "Maddy, what are you doing?" Erick excitedly inquired as she pushed him into a stall, slammed the door, and began passionately kissing him. Their pants of passion were interrupted by the hyperventilating voice of Sam from two stalls down.

"Maddy . . . is that you?"

"What?" Maddy replied breathily. "No, I'm not Maddy. I'm—" She then made her voice three pitches higher and in an overexaggerated falsetto said, "Ummm . . . I'm not Maddy . . . I'm . . . ummm . . . Maggie."

Sam then heard Erick's voice say, "Maggie . . . I like that. That's fuckin' hot."

"Okay, cool, then fuck me!" "Maggie" ordered. So, he did.

Two sets of couples came out of their respective stalls at the same time. The only one who made eye contact with the others was a twenty-something strapping punk who excitedly proclaimed before exiting, "Fuck, man! I love this fuckin' club!"

Sam, looking down at her soiled shoes, just said flatly, "This never happened, understand?" before regaining a bit of her dignity and strolling out of the men's room as "Toilet Love" by Wayne County and the Electric Chairs blared through the newly opened door.

The three separately made their way to three different bars and returned to the table with drinks. "Oh, there you are!" an overacting Erick said to his wife. "I was wondering where you got off to!"

"Oh . . . well . . . I just went to get a drink!" Maddy stated unconvincingly.

"Yeah? Me too!" Erick replied as if he were acting in a low-budget film.

"Hi, Sam, where have you been?" Erick and Maddy jointly inquired as Sam returned to the table with a drink of her own.

"Oh, I just went to get a drink!" came Sam's exaggerated reply.

At that moment, a disheveled-looking Kristy and Jason returned to the table. They immediately looked down at their drinks so as to avoid eye contact with the others. Their faces were flush, and it was quite obvious that

Kristy's bra had been removed. There was also a rather obvious stain on the crotch of Jason's pants.

Finally, Jules and Jerry took their rightful places. As Jerry nonchalantly looked around the bar while whistling, Jules looked at her colleagues lewdly and wiped her mouth with the back of her hand.

Patty looked around the table. "Hey, fuckers, look at me!" she ordered. Each of the friends around the table looked awkwardly into Patty's elated eyes briefly before darting down once again. "Son of a bitch!" Patty gleefully exclaimed as she began laughing. "You've all been fucking in the bathroom! Damn, kids! I'm fuckin' proud of you! Cheers!"

———

"Shhhhh," a shout-whispering Erick said to his staggering wife as they entered their darkened home. "We don't want to wake anybody up! I just want to go check on Josie and then we'll—"

Maddy heard Erick slip and fall on his back and began laughing. "Jesus, baby! How fuckin' drunk are you?"

"Not *that* drunk. Somebody spilled something on the floor. Turn on the light," Erick requested.

The light came on, and Maddy saw her husband sitting on the floor in a pool of blood between a headless body and the head of Abana, her face permanently frozen in an anguished scream.

"Oh, fuck . . . Josie!" Erick yelled out as he bounded up the stairs to his daughter's crib, followed hastily by Maddy. With their hearts pounding, they turned on the light, looked into the crib, and found the content sleeping bodies of Hunky, Dory, and Josie. They then looked at the wall behind the crib. Written in Abana's blood were large letters that spelled out Back Off Pigs Or She's Next!

Chapter 49

Seven Nation Army

"This means fuckin' *war*!" came Maddy's bellowing battle cry as Erick sat in the corner, gripping his blue-blanketed bundle with desperation. "Oh, they thought we were coming after them *before*? Now, we're taking them *all* out. I don't give a *fuck* where they're at or who they are. All these murdering autocratic fucks are going down!"

Edmund and Blair sat silently as they watched the cleanup crew wipe and carry away the last remnants of the unsuspecting babysitter, Abana. Her husband, Henri, sat next to them, seething in anger as his three-year- old son, Lionnel, slept upstairs on a guest bed. He had been contacted by Maddy and told to come right over. There had been a devastating tragedy. He arrived to find not just Maddy and Erick but also Blair and Edmund. They explained what had happened. They explained why it had happened. They explained the international war that had been waging and was now escalating between the forces of freedom and the forces of autocracy. They explained how they were now recruiting. And they suggested that he could make a difference in seeing to it that something like this never happened again. That he could weaponize his anger and use it as a force for freedom. It was an invitation that Henri found comforting. He was a highly trained sniper in the United States military. And although now out of the service, he felt his oath to defend the United States Constitution pounding in his thoughts as he watched his murdered wife's severed head being placed into a plastic bag.

While the cleanup crew was completing their morbid work, a second crew was installing a new security system in the home, complete with metal shutters for the windows, alarms, and heat and motion sensors. The Parker home was being converted into a fortress. Lucy was hastily bringing boxes in and immediately taking them to the basement. On one side of the basement, there was the baby bunker, which contained the laughably obscene number of diapers, toys, stuffed animals, and every other baby- related item that one could imagine. It was a toy store on steroids.

On the other side would be Lucy's new lab for the development, production, and storage of her toxins and bombs. She would now live in the guestroom. Erick and Maddy would take Josie into their room so that the nursery could be used by Henri and Lionnel.

And walls were being put up in the third-floor party room. It was being converted into a suite of small bedrooms, with the stereo and music collection being walled off. This was no time to party. This was no time for celebration. *This is a time for solemn preparation,* Erick thought as he wiped a tear from his eye and played one final song before the area was walled off. As he clutched Josie's innocently slumbering, limp body, he softly played "There Is No Time" by Lou Reed.

Upon the song's conclusion, the stereo components were sorrowfully turned off and the light switch flipped. As he descended the metal stairs, he heard the buzzing of electric screwdrivers closing off the area that had been used for some of his most cherished memories. The dance parties. The birthday celebrations. The drunken laughter over booming rhythms. Their wedding reception. *We'll do it again, I pray,* he thought to himself as he reentered the tense discussion downstairs.

Rod had arrived and was uncomfortably staring at Blair's chest as he gave his reconnaissance report. He reviewed the security camera footage and cross-checked the images with stored images and information from databases throughout the world. He knew the man's name. He knew the man's address. And he knew the man's past. He was a highly trained and especially brutal assassin who originated in Russia but was silently granted United States citizenship in 2019. He had been working with a self-proclaimed "militia" group in the American Northwest but had been recruited to rebuild the group's presence in New York following their fateful demise the previous Halloween. All this information was relayed to and heard by the members of Murder Incorporated.

And all this information was relayed to and heard by four more sets of ears, who were eagerly listening in Josie's bedroom. The assassin was unaware that Abana was also babysitting Vai, Adam, Aaron, and Alexa on this fateful evening. While he was decapitating an innocent woman and painting his vile warning above the bed of a slumbering infant, four other children were fast asleep in the adjacent bedroom. Actually, only three of the children were asleep.

"So, Alexa," Vai flatly inquired, "did you get a good look at this guy?"

"Yes, I did," came the adorable five-year-old's response as she lay on her stomach, drawing a perfect rendition of the crib and wall with the threatening words painted in crimson.

"Can you draw him?" Vai asked.

"Of course," Alexa responded as she turned to a blank piece of paper and began her earnest work.

"So, we have a name, an address, and soon a face," the plotting Vai stated aloud.

"They really should try to remember to turn off the baby monitors when they are having these discussions."

"Yes, they should," came Adam's reply, followed immediately by Aaron stating, "Yes, we now have the information that we need. He hurt Abana. He threatened to hurt our Josie, so now we must hurt him. And quite badly at that."

"Yes," Vai replied as her wheels were turning. "We should see what Aunt Lucy is bringing into the house. I bet it's toys for us to play with."

"I like toys," Adam replied, followed by Aaron's, "Yes, we love toys, in fact. Especially toys that hurt bad men. Let's play with Aunt Lucy's toys."

"What the fuck, Edmund?" an exasperated Maddy pleaded. "I thought that once we took care of all these fucks last Halloween that there would be peace. What the fuck is *this* all about?"

A resigned Edmund replied, "We have overstepped our bounds, Maddy. I think that they would have left us alone. They realize that, although much smaller than them in numbers, we are too formidable to continue this tit for tat. But we were the ones who decided to try to derail their conspiratorial plans. We were the ones who had developed the Europe mission. And they must have found out about that somehow. So, they decided to send *their* message before we had a chance to send *ours*. If we want any hope to regain the peace, this is what we must do."

"First, you will take care of the assassin. They will be expecting that, and it will be understood by them. We then send them a message that we will leave them be if they do the same. We will continue on in our original work and not interfere in their plans of overthrowing some of the world's greatest democracies. We will be out of it, and the fate of these nations will rest solely in the hands of those nations' people."

"Well, I guess they're fucked then," came Erick's sarcastic retort. "It is the *people* who have allowed this country to deteriorate to this point. Too many simply don't care, and too many actually support an autocratic government, complete with their cult-of-personality figurehead. And too few realize what is happening and are prepared to fight for their freedom. The information and propaganda war is being won by the autocrats. It is Germany 1934 all over again. And we all know how that turned out. Only this time, *we* are the ones who are going to be marched into the gas chambers. It seems to me that we have the resources and skills to at least slow this down and buy some time for the pro-democracy forces. I suggest we do that."

"Erick," an understanding Edmund began, "it is simply not the wise move. At least, not now. Let us just take a step back. Be patient. The time will come, but it is not now."

Blair simply sat in reserved silence and observed as Maddy entered the fray. "Yeah, that assassin is as good as dead, but Europe is fuckin' on! Then . . . maybe we tell them we'll back off. But not before we make a *huge* fuckin' statement in Europe. They murdered our friend and threatened to murder our fuckin' kid! Thank god, he didn't know about the other four children being here. Vai's right. For every indiscretion, we must counter it tenfold! Let them know that Europe is the retribution for this. And if they want to up the ante, then we're going to fucking war! And now, as president of the Unholy Trinity, I'm calling for a vote. All those in favor of blowing some pricks up in Europe, say aye!"

Erick and Lucy looked at each other with wry smiles and in determined voices said aye in unison.

"Maddy," Edmund began explaining, "you know that this isn't how this works. All projects must be approved by me, and you will not be granted that approval at this time. Please. Be patient. I am ordering you to stand down."

"And just what do you plan on doing about this, Edmund?" came Blair's chilled voice as she lovingly stared at the portrait of her smiling Joseph holding their infant Maddy. "You recruited Maddy, Erick, and Lucy into this.

You knew who they were, and now you shall reap what you have sown. Just what are you going to do to stop them? I'll tell you what. Nothing. Absolutely nothing. You will grant this operation, and you will do it now. If you fail in this, then you and I are going to have words, my old friend. If you do not do this, then I shall view you as part of the problem and not as a part of the solution. Do you understand?"

Edmund understood perfectly. As soft-spoken as Blair was, he knew that she wielded even more power and influence over Murder Incorporated than he. He also understood that she still had yet to forgive him for betraying her and bringing Maddy into their fold. And finally, he understood that this was not a veiled threat. He knew that, for Blair, alliances were transactional. She had no regard for personal history or emotions when it came to doing what she felt needed to be done. And he knew that opposing this force that was capable of cooking and eating another human being would result in his own demise. So, he reluctantly agreed.

"But only the Europe plan, understand? I will personally handle the . . . diplomatic fallout. And all other plans must be approved by me, agreed?" There was a quiet nod throughout the room. No one noticed that Maddy had her fingers crossed behind her back as she made her silent pledge.

"Very well," Edmund began again solemnly. "But first, we need to find out how they knew we were planning something in Europe. We cannot afford another misstep."

At that moment, a member of the security installation team nervously dropped a large vase that he had moved to install a motion sensor.

"Oh . . . uh . . . sorry. It just slipped . . . sorry . . . I hope it wasn't valuable," the man stammered as he avoided eye contact with the rest of the group.

"Oh no . . . it wasn't valuable," Maddy haughtily replied. "Nope, not valuable at all. That vase has turned out to be *invaluable*. Why don't you come over and take a seat? It looks like you could use some rest."

"Ummm . . . no . . . no . . . I'm fine. I'll just finish up my work here and be on my way," the man replied as a circling Maddy was joined by her now-suspicious husband.

"Now, what kind of guests would that make us?" a smiling Erick inquired. "Please . . . take a seat . . . we need to get to know you a bit better . . . chad."

"Sooo . . . tell me," Maddy playfully began her inquisition, "where all have you put sensors in here tonight? I'm just a little paranoid, and I want someone to double-check all the work."

"Ummm . . . just here and in your bedroom," came the man's nervous reply. Maddy nodded at one of the technicians, who immediately went upstairs with Rod to inspect the work. Blair, Edmund, and Lucy watched with intrigue as Maddy continued, "Gee . . . that was an unfortunate mishap. You technical guys aren't usually that clumsy. And you're kinda new here, aren'tcha? Soooo . . . how's about you just go ahead and tell us what you told them, and we can just move the evening along?"

Erick handed the still-sleeping Josie into the loving arms of her great-aunt Blair. She stretched and let out a soft sigh before returning to her blissful slumber. Erick then stood directly behind the man and took out a six-inch pocketknife. The man looked up behind him with trepidation before saying, "I . . . I don't know what you're talking about. I haven't said anything. I swear. I'm totally loyal . . . I—aaaaaaayyyyyyyy!"

"Wrong fuckin' answer!" Erick angrily exclaimed as he jammed the pocketknife into the man's right ear and twisted it mercilessly. Blood oozed out of the ear canal and down his lobe and began pooling on the shoulder of his gray workshirt.

"Soooo," Maddy began again, "you may have noticed that my husband is a bit . . . wound up tonight. Having his daughter's life being threatened and discovering our friend has been murdered has that effect on him. He's kinda silly that way. Oh, believe me, I have tried to reason with him in these situations before, but he's just kinda headstrong, as you're about to notice."

The pocketknife sliced through the man's right nostril as the screams continued.

"You see?" Maddy continued through her light chuckles. "I mean, a wife only has so much influence. After all, boys will be boys!"

The pocketknife was then jammed into the man's right eye. Pus and blood combined into a putrid pink cream that ran out of the eye socket and down the tortured man's face.

The pair of Rod and the other technician entered the room. Rod awkwardly stared at the bleeding man as he began in his staccato cadence. "Well . . . we tested it. It works fine. But it's also a bug. We've de-installed the bug, and it wasn't activated yet, so nobody will have heard anything tonight. We'll check the one down here next, but he wasn't done with it yet."

"Okay . . . okay . . . okay," the man began pleading as colorful tears, blood, and pus cascaded down his face, making him look like a nineties female tele-vangelist. "I'll tell you anything. Please . . . please don't hurt me anymore."

"What the fuck did they know?" Maddy screamed.

"Not much . . . I swear . . ." the man stated pleadingly. "I wasn't able to get any bugs into the headquarters. It was just what I overheard. All I told them was that there was something planned for Europe, and you said that it was going to shock the fuck out of them. I didn't know who the target was or how it was going to be done or who in Murder Incorporated was going to do it. I swear. They did this just to send a message and have you back off once and for all. I swear . . . that's all they knew . . . please . . . I'm so sorry . . . they threatened my wife and kids . . . I had no choice . . . Please let me go, and I'll just disappear. I'll just take off by myself and disappear."

Henri got up and stood in front of the man. He was holding a machete that Lucy had handed him during the discussion. "What about your family?" Henri inquired of the quivering pool in front of him.

"W-what?" the man asked as he looked up with his one good eye.

"You said you had a wife and kids," Henri began again. "But you just said that you were going to leave by yourself. Are you going to just leave your wife and kids here? Oh, but that makes sense now, doesn't it? You have no problem creating a single-parent family. After all, my wife is dead because of you. And I'm the single parent of a little boy who will always regret not having known his mother. And you, motherfucker, are going to regret not having a fucking head!"

The machete was swung by Henri's massive right arm and sliced through the man's neck. The head was flung off the shoulders and hit the portrait of Joe and Maddy on the wall. Blood dripped from the round bloody stain on the portrait. And Henri stood over the headless corpse, covered in his crimson stickiness, with his head down, weeping.

"GAAAAWWWWD!" Maddy yelled out. "Now we've gotta get the cleanup crew back over here! And look what they did to my picture!"

"It's all right, dear. It's only the glass in the frame. We'll get another one tomorrow," came Blair's calm reply as a cooing Josie clung onto Blair's index finger.

The tittering threesome of Vai, Adam, and Aaron returned to Josie's bedroom from their vantage point on the stairs. "Oh my, boys, wasn't that fun?" Vai exclaimed while clapping.

"Yes, it was great fun," Adam replied, followed by Aaron's, "Yes, great fun, indeed. Our aunts and uncles play fun games. I want them to teach us how to play those games."

"Here ya go," Alexa stated matter-of-factly as she handed Vai her completed drawing of the assassin. Vai and the twins stared at the picture with twisted little smiles.

"We're going to have fun playing a game with him," Adam stated, followed by Aaron, "Yes, he looks like he will be fun. We know how to play games too. Aunt Maddy and Uncle Erick will be so proud of us."

CHAPTER 50

THE JET SET

"Welcome to London, sister," came the perky British-accented voice of the smiling, attractive flight attendant.

"May peace be with you," came the meek reply of the blonde Laotian nun as she departed the aircraft and began her purposeful trek into the airport terminal.

Upon reaching the terminal, she pulled out her phone and placed the call. "Yes, I'm here. Bring me a car to take me to the flat. I trust that you have procured everything that I require. Very well then. Fifteen minutes. I'll be waiting."

Lucy had never been to London before. She was excited to see the sights and discover new adventures in this bustling Western European metropolis. But that would have to wait. She was not here as a tourist. She wondered if she would be able to do what she intended to do. She had no concern about the mission. That would be easy, although she had never been skydiving before. The thought of it filled her with euphoric anticipation.

The anticipation heightened as she thought about how she intended to entertain herself for the next two days before she completed her assigned mission. Although she had murdered many more people than Maddy or Erick combined, they were all committed passively. The injectables or gaseous toxins. The occasional bomb. Yes, she had dismembered bodies, but they were already deceased. She marveled at Maddy's ability to tear vile men apart with her bare hands as they were still breathing. She wanted to feel what that was like. She *needed* to feel what that was like. She needed to feel what it was like to bathe in the blood that was sprayed on her from a still-beating heart. It was most appropriate that the flat that she was borrowing from a member of Murder Incorporated was located in White Chapel, she thought. A slight smile crossed her flawless almond face as she fantasized about what her potential victims might look like as she resumed her revenge tour, this time as the Anti-Ripper.

It would not be the helpless and innocent working ladies of the night who would need to fear her. It would be the brutally misogynistic males in the area that she would unleash her fury on. The same type of men who had raped her, both physically and, in the case of Maddy's ex-husband, mentally. He had not only physically raped her when she was intoxicated and vulnerable but had also repeatedly mentally raped her. He had forced her to continue to have sex with him. But this wasn't just sex. This was being forced to engage in a wide variety of demented and demeaning sexual acts to service his twisted fantasies.

She remembered the maniacal smile upon his face as he stood over her laughing as she helplessly hung from the wall that she had been tied to in the seedy hotel, her body bruised and bleeding from the lashes of the whip and the beatings of the paddle. He proudly laughed as globs of his demonic seed lazily dripped down her defeated face. And he continued to rape her mind as he shared pictures of their entwined bodies with her best friend, needlessly causing mental anguish for both Maddy and her. He forced her to end that friendship and disappear so that she might protect her friend from his never-ending campaign of psychological torture. He had ruined her. She lost all her appetite for sexual gratification. It had been physically and psychologically beaten and fucked out of her. But now, as she thought about her potential conquests, a familiar feeling began stirring. Yes, she had blown him up. But that single act felt unsatisfying for her, and she had begun craving satisfaction. It was almost achieved as she dismembered and ground up the bodies in the bookstore basement. Almost. But not quite. Perhaps her little adventures in London would provide the climactic release that her body and soul cried out for.

She entered the small one-bedroom flat on the second floor and looked around. The bathroom and tub were adequately sized. All her requested items to complete her mission and perform her chosen extracurricular activities had been procured and were lying on the bed, eagerly awaiting their master's skilled hands and mind to put them to use. She carefully disrobed from her full-length nun uniform, stepped into the shower, and let out a sigh of satisfaction as the hot water began pelting her tingling skin.

She dried off and sauntered into the bedroom. Sitting stark naked on the bed, she began assembling the two devices that would send a shockwave through the scourge of the white nationalist autocratic underworld. It would not take long. They were simple but quite effective devices. She completed her work as the sun began setting over the unsuspecting villagers of White Chapel. The devices were lovingly placed into her flight bag. She was prepared for her mission. And she still had plenty of time to play.

The men from Murder Incorporated had furnished her with the perfect collection of slight dresses and provocative shoes and stockings. Her instruction to her male colleague from across the pond was quite simple: "Dress me like your fantasy." He had not failed, she thought as she slid into the black lace panties, pulled up the black fishnet stockings, and placed the black sequined minidress over her taut frame. Makeup was applied, and cleavage was appropriately adjusted to achieve maximum effect. Black strapped pumps were placed upon her dainty feet. The ensemble was complete with the placement of a gold anklet resting suggestively above her left foot.

She had done her research and knew exactly which back-alley taverns and pubs she would find her quarry. She was quite disappointed at the first pub. The travel guide had apparently not been updated. It turned out to be an electronically loud pickup joint reserved for White Chapel's gay and lesbian community. *Not interested,* Lucy thought as she finished her virgin drink and departed down the dark alley to her next hunting ground.

The second tavern was awash in activity. There was a birthday party for someone's officemate going on in the back. A few frat-looking boys were harmlessly guffawing as they played darts. Several married or otherwise engaged couples were gazing into each other's eyes as they softly spoke to one another while sitting at their small round wooden tables. The couples were of a variety of ages, ethnicities, and sexual orientations. But they all held the same looks of admiration upon their candlelit faces. *Maybe there is some hope for the world, after all,* a somewhat disappointed Lucy thought to herself as she departed and once again began her hopeful journey to the next pub.

As Lucy approached the entrance to the third pub, a man's body was flung out the door. "And don't come back until you've sobered up, you fuckin' lout!" was heard followed by uproarious laughter and the clinking of glasses. *Mommy, I'm home,* a smiling Lucy thought to herself as she entered the bar with a hip-swiveled strut. She surveyed the tightly packed den of sweat and testosterone as pairs of eager eyes lasciviously toured her provocatively dressed figure.

She overheard a pudgy middle-aged businessman inquiring how much it would cost for him to exact some S&M on a local working girl. *There's one,* Lucy thought to herself as she suggestively sauntered over to the man and whispered into his ear, "Hey, you don't have to pay for it tonight. I'm throwing a party at my flat. I'm looking for three fun guys who will punish me for being a really, really bad girl. Wanna . . . come?" The man nearly choked on his drink and feverishly nodded as Lucy giggled lightly and said, "Good. Just stay right here. I'll go find our other playmates."

A young man in a well-worn football jersey was seen slapping his girl-friend. "Blimey, bitch! I'll go home when I feel right up to it!" The girl left crying, and a seductive Laotian could be seen whispering into the hooligan's ear as a wide smile crossed his face.

Two down, one to go, an energized Lucy thought as she approached a third man. He was wearing a T-shirt with the Nazi flag, and his arms were adorned with multiple hate-and ignorance-fueled tattoos. She whispered to him. He nodded and smiled. She took him by his hand.

As she passed the football hooligan, she took him by her other hand, smiled, and continued walking. She stopped at the businessman's table. He looked up and gulped as she gave him a sly wink. He rose as though he were a reanimated corpse crawling from the grave and thoughtlessly followed the petite seductress to his hopeful fate.

Upon reaching the f lat, with the three hormonally charged men circling her, Lucy began to explain the rules for the evening. "Welcome to my party, boys," she began with a voice dripping with hushed seduction. "I'm in the mood to fuck. I'm in the mood to fuck three men . . . three *gladiators.* I'm turned on by a little violence. So, strip down to your skivvies, and start wrestling with one another. The more violent you are with one another, the more turned on I'll get. The more turned on I get, the more of my clothing will be removed. And the more turned on I get, the more ports of call will be opened. I want you hot, sweaty, and bloody. And then, I'll take each of you into the bathroom where we will shower together. And then, the *real* fun will start. And that fun will only be limited by your imaginations . . . and stamina."

The three dupes just stood there frozen with their mouths agape. "I see," Lucy stated disappointedly as she began to put on a rather large and unattractive robe. "I guess you're not interested."

The men immediately began undressing and flinging their clothing throughout the bedroom. They then began tackling and punching one another in a randy frenzy as Lucy took off the robe, bent over, and began unbuckling her shoes. The men had one eye on each other as they braced themselves for another blow or prepared to launch their own fists and one eye on Lucy as she slid out of one fishnet stocking at a time. Sweat, blood, and the occasional tooth went flying as Lucy thought, *Oh my god, they are barbarians. They would kill each other just to get laid. This is so disgusting. This is soooo what I was hoping for.*

Lucy, now clad in only her black lace panties and bra, shouted, "Enough!" The three entranced men immediately stopped. Blood was dripping from gashes on their faces, and tears were beginning to roll out of their swollen eyes as they relinquished their sweaty grips upon one another. "Oh, boys, that was even better . . . even *hotter* . . . than I had imagined," Lucy breathily sighed. "Oh god, let's get you three cleaned up . . . and quickly. I need you all so badly. You first." She pushed play on her phone and turned up the volume, and Patsy Cline's "I Fall to Pieces" began playing on a continuous loop.

She pointed at the atrociously tattooed, panting man, and they entered the bathroom. Lucy shut the bathroom door, reached under the sink, and in a flash plunged a scalpel into the jugular of the man, his eyes going from lechery to panic in a brief instant. She threw the gagging man over the tub, picked up a hacksaw, and began meticulously severing his head from his torso. Torrents of blood began filling the tub as the lifeless, headless body slid its way to its resting place on the cold white ceramic tile.

Lucy's heart was racing. She could feel it building. But she wasn't there yet. She wiped the blood from her body, opened the door, and said, "How about you next?" while pointing to the hooligan. The man eagerly bound into the room and, upon closing the door, was immediately met with the scalpel through his throat. His blood poured onto Lucy's face as she dragged him to the edge of the tub and began sawing. The severed head made a slight sloshing sound as it plopped into a thickening pool of blood in the tub.

"Oh jesus!" Lucy exclaimed. Her legs were quivering, and her panties were beginning to dampen. She wiped herself off once again, opened the door, and silently motioned for the businessman. His trancelike body dutifully followed her instructions. He entered the bathroom as Lucy was standing behind him while grabbing a butcher knife from under the sink.

"Wha . . . wha . . . wha . . ." the man began stammering in a hyperventilating staccato.

"Hi, baby. I heard you like it rough. Welcome to my party," Lucy stated in a low, sinister voice as she began plunging the butcher knife into the man's rolls of back fat repeatedly. He fell to the floor screaming. Lucy jumped on top of him and continued her brutal knife-wielding assault while humping his back and cackling deviously. With each violent gouge, she was being showered by sprays of his blood until her entire body was dripping with the man's crimson life. She looked down at her work and tenderly began licking the blood from her fingertips. By the time his body was dragged over the tub and his head removed, he had sustained eighty- six knife wounds. This was an exact figure. Lucy had gleefully counted each one of them.

Each of the bodies was dragged out of the bathroom and haphazardly discarded in the hallway. Lucy drilled holes in the tops of the heads, placed them on a shelf overlooking the bathtub, and inserted a four-inch-long white lit candle in each.

She finished undressing, lay in the tub, and completely encased her body with the sticky, iron-scented substance. She lay there enthralled with her achievement as she watched the candle wax drip down and become entwined in the blood-matted hair of the heads. *Those flames can't burn forever,* she thought to herself. *I wonder which of the three flames will be extinguished first.*

She again pressed play on her phone and smiled deviously as the opening line of Alice Cooper's "Welcome to My Nightmare" was sung in his sinisterly seductive voice. When the second programmed song came on, she searched the bloodbath for her required tool. Finding one of the three severed floating penises, she recreated the evening in her mind while watching the dancing flames on the top of the three horrified faces as "Closer" by Nine Inch Nails roared out of the tiny speaker. She took the limp phallus and used it to rub herself with wild abandon, sploshing blood out of the tub and onto the tiled floor as her pace quickened to a frenzy. She screamed out in psychotic ecstasy as she finally achieved her first orgasm in over seven years. She lit a cigarette and took a satisfied drag as the dancing flames were reflected in her jet-black pupils.

The tub was drained, and she showered. She put on the tightly fitted flight attendant uniform and picked up her phone. "Yeah, it's me. I'm ready to go to the airport. You're gonna need a cleaning crew over here. Sorry about the mess." The three flames continued to burn brightly as Lucy strode out of the flat.

A sharply dressed Laotian flight attendant walked across the tarmac toward the private luxury jet, carrying an unassuming travel bag. She walked up the stairs and gave a knowing nod to the six-foot thirty-five- year-old blonde pilot. She smiled at her new crewmate and said in a heavy British accent, "Welcome aboard."

"Thank you," the flight attendant replied as her eyes locked onto the intoxicating pools of blue floating on the pilot's beautiful face.

The charter flight crew had been completely vetted and cleared. They were both deemed sympathetic to and members of the conspiratorial auto-cratic cause. Rod had seen to that. The passengers arrived. To protect their conversation, they decided that they would converse while in the air. Murder Incorporated, as well as other governmental agencies throughout the world, had eyes and ears everywhere upon them. And these were three of the most important men in the white-male-dominated international autocratic movement. They would conspire in private as they devised their next phase of the takeover of American democracy. Florida would be discussed at length. And then, upon reaching the appropriate altitude, the chauvinistic men would invite their attractive pilot and flight attendant for a drink and perhaps a bit of harmless cavorting. It would be a glorious flight.

The pilot, Jennifer, and the flight attendant, Lucy, tittered at the sugges-tion that the plane be put on autopilot so that they could join them in a little mile-high-club party. "But of course, sirs," Jennifer replied coyly. "Just let me set the autopilot, and we'll be right back. It shouldn't take but a moment or two."

The altitude was checked, and the autopilot was set. They were almost at the desired altitude, and they needed to make their retreat. One package had been left in the tail restroom of the plane. The other was being left in the cockpit. The flight crew, hidden away behind a security door in a space behind the cockpit, hastily put on full flight suits and parachutes. The emer-gency exit door was disengaged, and two lithe figures could be seen tumbling toward the English Channel from the plane's window.

"Where the fuck are they—" were the final panicked words uttered by the international right-wing propagandist.

———

Instead of their normal preparation music, Maddy and Erick's attention was glued to the television as they were donning their murderous black garb. Then, the report came. A plane carrying an international media mogul, a gas and oil oligarch, and a high-profile financier with links to neofascist movements had exploded in midair just off the coast of France. There were no further developments. The fate of the crew was unknown. "Fuckin' cool, Lucy!" Maddy exclaimed as she bounced around the room, clapping. "And nice job getting them on that plane, Rod!" Erick shouted.

Rod came into the bedroom, holding a cooing Josie while lightly shaking a rattle in front of her bewildered green eyes. "Ummm . . . thank you," Rod stated as his insecure eyes immediately averted to Maddy's chest.

"Goddammit, Rod! Eyes up here! How many fuckin' times do I have to tell you?"

"S-sorry, Maddy . . . it's just . . . a force of habit, I guess," Rod stuttered in response.

"It's okay. I understand. Just take good care of our Josie while we're gone, okay?" an understanding Maddy replied.

"Of course, Maddy . . . Erick . . . I will care for her. And Henri is going to be on the roof the entire time you are gone. We don't anticipate trouble," Rod said reassuringly.

"Yeah?" Erick chimed in. "Well, it's not going to take them fuckers too long to figure out that we're the ones responsible for assassinating three of their biggest names. We know that this won't stop them. We know that another head will grow immediately after we chop one off. But they are going to know that there are people who are willing to fight. There are people who are willing to stand up to them and take them down to preserve the greatest democracy the world has ever known. And they will know not to fuck with us ever again. Now, darling, let's go fuck up that assassin."

"Yes, my love," Maddy snickered as she batted her copper eyelashes over her effervescent eyes. "Oh, hey, Rod," Maddy bellowed as they were leaving home, "if you see Vai, Adam, and Aaron, send them back home. Kristy just called, and she's not sure where they've gotten off to."

As two-thirds of the Unholy Trinity were walking down the street in slo-mo, shrouded in darkness, Erick inquired aloud, "I wonder if Lucy had a chance to do anything fun on her trip."

"Doubt it," came his wife's immediate reply. "She probably just buried her nose in her boring science shit. Man, that chick needs to get laid!"

———

"Welcome to New York, sisters!" the flight attendant stated enthusiastically.

"Thank you," stated a tall blonde nun with piercing blue eyes.

"Yes, may peace be with you," came the reply of the blonde Laotian nun who suspiciously wore a devious smile.

Chapter 51

The Kids Are All Right

Erick slowly opened the window at the rear of the assassin's home. Rod (no longer the Wad) had hacked into the assassin's security system, disengaged it, and unlocked the windows. And he had done so while gently bouncing a giggling, copper-headed three-and-a-half-month-old infant on his lap. Erick crawled into the entrance, followed by Maddy, who did a somersault upon her landing and stood up with her arms proudly thrust into the air as though she had just completed a gold-medal-worthy gymnastic routine.

"Knock it the fuck off!" Erick whispered-shouted at his chuckling wife.

"C'mon, man, I haven't done this shit in so long," Maddy playfully retorted quietly. "I'm soooo fucking excited to fuck some shit up!" "Let's just find this fucker, do him in, and get the fuck out. He isn't someone we want to play with," Erick demanded as the beam of his flashlight swept into the living room, catching some movement. They braced themselves. They were ready for anything. Well, *almost* anything.

"Ooooohhhh, fuck," a deflated Maddy stated, "what the fuck are *you* guys doing here?"

"Hello, Aunt Maddy . . . Uncle Erick," came the sweet monotone voice of Adam followed, as always, by Aaron's, "Yes, hello. We are playing operation. Would you like to play?"

Maddy looked at the scene. The two eight-year-old boys were covered in blood, sitting on either side of a still-alive man whose chest and abdomen were cut completely open, the skin stretched and nailed down on the floor next to him, leaving his internal organs completely exposed, including his rapidly beating heart.

"Well, yeah . . . kinda," an intrigued Maddy began before catching herself and exclaiming, "No! We are not here to play with you. How the hell did you guys get in here anyway? Did you know that your parents are looking for you? I mean, you could have at least called."

"We're sorry," Adam began.

"Yes, we're sorry," came Aaron's contribution. "But you were late. We thought you would be here earlier, and we just got so caught up in our game that it simply escaped us to call. We are sorry, and it won't happen again. Are you sure you don't want to play? It's quite fun. Here, we'll show you the rules."

Vai's chilled voice then emerged from a darkened corner of the room. "Gallbladder" was all she said. "Ah . . . yes . . . the gallbladder. What an interesting choice, Vai," Adam stated.

"Yes, quite interesting. And I believe we shall find it here." Aaron then reached into the man's torso and pulled the gallbladder from its cavity. He squeezed the warm organ over the man's petrified face, covering it in bile. "Oh, look at him, Aunt Maddy . . . Uncle Erick! Just look at him," came Adam's unusually excited response.

"Oh yes!" Aaron gleefully echoed. "Just look at the funny faces he makes as we cover him in his own bile. Oh, Aunt Maddy, he is such a funny man and is so much fun to play with! Please, won't you play with us?"

"Fuck," Erick whispered into his wife's ear. "I mean . . . it does look kinda fun, doesn't it? And since we're here and all . . ."

Maddy looked at her husband with an annoyed expression before bursting into laughter. "Yeah, okay. But just a couple rounds while you guys explain how you did this. Then we gotta kill the fucker and get out of here. Oh, fuck! I gotta call Kristy!"

Maddy placed the call while watching her friend's blood-soaked twins gaze into the eyes of their dying prey with fascination. "Uh . . . hey . . . it's me. Yeah . . . uh . . . I found them. They were just . . . um . . . playing at a friend's house. Ummmm . . . they kinda need to get cleaned up, so why don't you just pick them up in a couple of hours at our place, okay? No, you don't need to bring—fuck," Maddy angrily stated.

"What's up?" Erick inquired.

"She's bringing Sam and Jules over too. This is gonna be a fuckin' shit show. All right, Vai, what's the next one?"

As the assassin's organs were being identified and pulled out one by one, the children began their earnest answers to Maddy's interrogation.

"Okay," Maddy began, attempting to remain calm, "how the *fuck* did you know about this guy? How the *fuck* did you know we were going to be here? And how the *fuck* did you get in here and do this?"

"Well, Aunt Maddy," Vai calmly began explaining as yet another organ was being inspected by two sets of elated blue eyes, "first of all, we would appreciate it if you would watch your language. We are children."

"Yes, Aunt Maddy," Adam replied without looking up from his work of pulling out the long trail of intestines, "you really shouldn't use bad language in front of children."

"Yes, that is correct," Aaron contributed as he began helping his brother wind the intestines around the legs of the living room furniture. "We are just children. And children are impressionable. You wouldn't want us to pick up any bad habits now, would you?"

"Uh . . . nope. Sorry. I'll try to watch my language. Now . . . would you *please* answer my fucking questions?" Maddy roared back.

"Well," Vai responded calmly, "the first two questions are very easy to answer. I have two words for you: *baby monitors.*"

"Yes, we hear everything from the monitors!" Adam exclaimed followed by Aaron's statement of "Yes. We can hear everything. We had all the information on who killed Abana and threatened to harm Josie. We knew when you were coming here and that Rod would help you. We also knew about where Aunt Lucy was and that she would blow up the bad man's airplane. We knew all that by listening to the baby monitors. Oh my! How wonderfully slimy these intestines are! They may be my new favorite toy!"

"Uh . . . yeah . . . that's fuckin' gross," a squeamish Maddy responded before asking, "Okay, so if you knew we were taking care of this, then why did *you* guys come here? We had it handled."

Vai responded once again as if she were a well-polished politician in the midst of a press conference, "We wanted to make you proud. We wanted to prove to you that, although we are children, we are up to the task of protecting our Josie. So, we knocked on this man's door and asked him to use a phone as we were lost. We correctly figured that he wouldn't expect children to be his undoing. Upon entering his home, we injected him with the *Toxin B* so that he would be paralyzed but awake as we played operation with him. It was really quite easy."

"Yes, it was. It was quite easy indeed. And yes, it is all about protecting Josie," Adam responded followed by Aaron's "Yes, Josie is our friend. In fact, Josie is not only our friend, but Josie is our future just as you and Uncle Erick and Great-Aunt Blair are our future. We have seen it. It is time for us to take our leave from our parents and join you. We wanted to make you proud so that you would welcome us into your home. We want to learn your games and have fun with you."

"Whoa, whoa, whoa, fuckin' whoa," a shocked Erick blurted out as Vai began jumping over the intestines that the boys were holding at either end and using as a jump rope. "Hey, guys, you have parents. We're not equipped to take you on . . . at least not now. We thought maybe when you were older that that would be a possibility. But you can't leave your parents now. It would devastate them."

Vai stopped jumping, and the twins stopped twirling the intestines as the assassin was heard uttering his final gurgle. The trio (of definite terror) walked in slo-mo toward Erick and Maddy, stopping just inches from them. Vai looked up with unblinking eyes and held her index fingers in front of the twins to hold them at bay. Erick and Maddy had simultaneous chills run up their spine. They had been prepared for anything this evening. But they had not been prepared for this.

Vai flashed her sweet twelve-year-old smile, revealing her adorable dimples, and began her dissertation in a lovable voice, "Mr. and Mrs. Anderson have been wonderful to me. And they were wonderful to my mother. They gave us love and caring and shelter when nobody else would. But they do not understand me. Nor do they understand the twins. The twins do not belong to them. The twins do not belong to anyone. The twins instinctively go where they are most needed. The twins sense the danger that is here and the danger that is coming. The twins understand that Josie must be protected. It is in your home that the twins are most needed. And the twins need me to assist them in finding their direction and planning for their games. The Andersons simply do not need us. You do. Great-Aunt Blair does. Josie does. Murder Incorporated does. It is as simple as that. Beginning this evening, we will be residing in the bedrooms that have been constructed on the third floor of your home. Aunt Maddy, you must convince them to let us go. You know this to be true. If you don't, then we will be forced to, and that will be unpleasant for us."

"Yes, quite unpleasant," Adam began as Vai's index fingers began lowering.

"Yes, we care for our parents," Aaron responded. "They have nurtured us and are quite nice. But they are in danger as long as we are with them. All of them are in danger as long as we are with them. Aunt Sam, Aunt Jules, Uncle Jerry—they are all in danger as long as any of us are involved with them . . . including you, Aunt Maddy."

"All right," Erick responded, feeling defeated, "all of you kids go jump in the shower and change your clothes. While you're doing that, I'm going to run down to the market and get some late-night snacks and some tissues." He looked at his beautiful wife's bewildered and regret-filled face. "We're *definitely* gonna need a lot of fuckin' tissues tonight."

"Oh my god! Don't you three *ever* run off like that again! Your father and I were worried to death!" came Kristy's motherly reaction upon seeing her three squeaky-clean children and enveloping them in a group hug. "Where *were* you?"

"We were playing games, Mother," Adam replied followed by Aaron's elaboration. "Yes, we were playing operation. We were playing with the man who murdered Abana and threatened to harm Josie. We cut him open and pulled out his internal organs until he was dead. Then, Aunt Maddy and Uncle Erick came and found us. They were there to play with the assassin too. But we beat them to it and played with him first."

"Wow! Whaaaat an imagination kids these days have, huh?" Maddy cheerfully responded. "Well, kids, I guess maybe you should just go home now and—"

Vai stood and lifted her index finger to silence Maddy. Blair took special notice of this child's harsh, manipulative abilities. "Aunt Maddy, we have discussed this. Shall *you* explain this, or shall *we*? It will be less . . . unpleasant if you do it. Abana is dead because of her involvement with you. Is that what you wish for them as well?"

Blair stared at her niece. They both knew what had to be done at this moment. The question was whether Maddy would be able to summon the courage to make her nearly lifelong friends hate her. To curse her. To loathe her. Whether she could find the strength to drive her most cherished friends away from her to never be in her life again. Blair righted herself in her chair and prepared herself in the event that her beloved niece failed in this most important moment.

"Well . . . here's the deal, bitches," Maddy began with fake pomposity. "We're in an international hit-man group who are trying to stop the fascist takeover of the world's democracies, including ours. Oh, my killing career started innocently enough. It's a well-worn story that's been told throughout the ages. Y'know, just the run-of-the-mill murders of the man who killed Uncle Joe. And then the wife-beating father of Vai. And a sweaty fat black-market peddler who wanted me to give him a blowjob. *Yech!* And an attempted date rapist outside of a club. And the douchebag who overdosed me. And a child rapist and murderer. Oh . . . and those two hicks who beat Robbie nearly to death. And also, the guy who watched Lucy get raped. *And nooooo* . . . before you even ask, I was *not* the one who blew up my ex-douchebag. That was all Lucy's doing, so leave me out of that one! What else? Oh yeah. And then there's the religious nutjob who murdered our doctor, Kristy. And Erick's former wife's lover and cult leader. And yet another child abuser. And a pedophile priest. And a pedophile toy store owner. Oh yeah, and the CEO of a greedy insurance company. Plus, Erick took out a homophobic fucker and, of course, the jerk-off who shot me. Plus, his brother. But that was just child's play. All that was just a fuckin' warm-up.

"Since then, we have been taking out misogynistic white supremacist fascists. It's a much bigger game, and we need all the help we can get. We didn't choose your children, Kristy . . . Jason. In a way, they chose us. So Vai, Adam, and Aaron will be staying with us from now on. We need to prepare them. And everything that they just told you is true. They just murdered the fuck out of Abana's assassin. They still have his *blood* under their fingernails.

"So you see . . . your time as their parents is over. And our friendship is over. It's been fun, bitches, but I simply have no use for any of you any longer. I now have use for your *children*. And I am going to *train* them and *manipulate* them and *use* them as I see fit!"

Jason turned beet red and punched Erick on the side of his face. Erick had seen it coming. Erick did not make a move to defend himself. "Over my dead body will you take my children!" Jason roared.

"Oh, c'mon, fuck nut," Maddy dismissively replied as her husband rubbed his chin and pulled himself off the floor, "you have no *fucking idea* what you are up against. But you three girls do now, don't you? You've seen me. You've seen the *real* me. You just didn't want to admit it to yourselves that your best friend was a cold-blooded killer. But you've seen it. And you know what I'm capable of. I *will* get your children one way or another. Or else, my name isn't Maddy *fuckin'* Sommers! And *that's* my name, so *that's* just how it's going to be. One way or another. The easy way or the hard way. Don't make me spill your fuckin' blood. Just turn around and walk the fuck out of my life and never look back!"

A shocked and hyperventilating Kristy looked at Blair and said pleadingly, "A-a-aunt B-blair! Please don't let her do this! How can you sit there and let her do this? Please help me!"

"Oh, my dearest Kristy," Blair coolly remarked as she walked over to her blonde "adopted" niece, "I love you, dear, but I love our freedom even more. I love our liberty. I love ridding the world of bad men. And I love the fact that none of you have seen this coming. My dearest Kristy, my most naive darling, don't you yet realize that this was *my* plan all along?"

All the blood rushed from Kristy's face, and she began violently shaking as she stared into the cold eyes of the woman who she had adored for so many years. She then gazed pleadingly at the expressionless but content faces of her eight-year-old twin boys. And then the reality of what she was dealing with sank in. It sank in through her skin, through her tendons, and through her bones. It finally penetrated her very soul. "This isn't over!" Kristy screamed. "We'll be back. And we *will* take our children. We will be back with the authorities, and we'll—"

Kristy's exclamation was interrupted by Maddy. In a deep growl, she tersely stated, "You gonna come here with the cops, bitch? Really? Don't you know what we're *capable* of? If we're capable of blowing a *fucking jet* out of the sky, then we're *sure as fuck* capable of planting all kinds of incriminating evidence against *you*." Then in a mock-innocent voice, Maddy began again, "Oh, Officer, thank goodness you are here! We're just trying to keep these darling children safe! Look at all the drugs that they have! Look at all the weapons! Listen to these messages of them talking with terrorist groups!" Then, her voice once again transforming into a deep growl, Maddy concluded, "Listen to them, Officer, as they are mercilessly beating their children. Listen to their children's anguished cries as their mother beats them viciously as their impotent father just watches. Just *listen* to *this*, Officer. Then *you* tell *me* where these children belong."

Kristy's body fell limp into her husband's awaiting arms. "C'mon, dear, we need to go home. We need to regroup and think this through," Kristy's adoring husband Jason said to her. "Sam, c'mon, let's just all go now. C'mon, Jules. Let's get out of here."

"No," came Jules's regretful but determined reply. She looked up at her friends with uncharacteristic tears in her eyes and said, "I'm staying here. They're right. It may be fucked up and twisted, but they're right. I'm sorry to say this, Kristy, but your boys are . . . abnormal. And this whole world is abnormal. Everything is upside down. And all the so-called normal people are just sitting there, playing on their phones, looking for constant entertainment and distraction, while the fascists are methodically brainwashing the willfully ignorant and taking over. So, I figure if the normal people aren't going to do anything, then maybe it's up to those of us who are *abnormal* to take up the fight. And if there's one word that you would use for Jerry and me, it would be *abnormal*. Just like Maddy. Just like Erick. Just like Aunt Blair. Just like these sweet children. We are abnormal, and we must do what we must do now. The stakes are too high. I know what this means. I cherish our friendship, and I love you both. But my allegiance is here. I'm staying, and I'm going to bring Jerry along with me. I'm sorry."

Kristy turned her gaze from Jules and glared at Maddy. The intensity of her hatred was being projected out of her blue-flamed eyes as she said in a sinister voice, "Maddy Sommers, I will never forgive this. I will hate you until my dying breath. And I will have my revenge upon you. That is not an idle threat. That is a fucking promise. You . . . fucking . . . heartless . . . bitch!"

"Mother . . . Father . . . would it help if we gave you a hug?" Adam inquired.

"Yes, a hug would be appropriate at a time such as this," came Aaron's agreement. "We promise to visit you, and we will be safe. Thank you for giving birth to us and nurturing us. You have Alexa to care for, and she will love you. We have seen it. We are sorry that we are not capable of giving you the love that you desire from your children. But we are incapable of it. Our allegiance is to those who need us. You don't need us. We are now where we are needed. We are home."

Kristy burst into tears and fled out the door followed by a shell-shocked Jason and a completely disheveled Sam. Before leaving the room, Sam looked back at Maddy and said with sincere morbidity, "I regret having saved your life. I should have left you to die that night." Kristy's devastated wails could still be heard from two blocks away until mercifully dissipating into the sultry night air.

"Okay," Maddy began in a slow controlled cadence as she fought back the inevitable onslaught of tears, "Aunt Blair, please get the children settled into their new rooms. Henri, would you please check and ensure the security system is on? I need my husband, and I need my baby right now. Please do not disturb us unless you have to. Thank you." As Maddy began leaving the living room, she picked up a large box of tissues resting on the TV stand. The entire group heard her pronounced sobs as she and Erick dutifully transcended the staircase to join their unaware child. Maddy thanked Rod and asked him to leave the bedroom. She peered down at her daughter, who was slumbering innocently with her pussycats. A tear fell from her green eyes and landed on her beloved daughter's cheek. Josie woke up and, upon seeing her mother's sorrowful expression, instinctively stuck out her tongue and smiled as she crossed her emerald eyes.

CHAPTER 52

SUNSHINE DAY

"A tentative truce has been reached," Edmund solemnly stated to the members of Murder Incorporated. In attendance were Blair; the seven permanent hit-man members of the Executive Council; and the heads of the Tech Support, Reconnaissance, Clean-Up, Weapons Procurement, Recruitment, and Security Departments. And, of course, the Unholy Trinity, who sat on either side of Edmund at the head of the table.

"The Underground Autocratic Movement, or UAM as they are informally referring to themselves, have pledged to stop in their attempts to take us out. In fact, they are encountering resistance from a number of organizations and governments throughout the world, so they are withdrawing from major cities, such as New York, and concentrating on their more rural grassroots efforts to continue their creation of a populist uprising that would ultimately topple our and other democracies and install autocratic puppet regimes. They and we have mutually agreed that the fate of these nations' democracies is now in the hands of the populace, and they will leave us be if we will leave them be."

"Fuck that!" Maddy exclaimed. "We got them on the fuckin' ropes, Edmund! I say we hook up with these other democratic resistance groups, coordinate our efforts, and take these motherfuckin' douchebags out once and for all! UAM, huh? Well, to me, that shit stands for U Are Mine! Get it? Pretty good, huh?"

Maddy's attempt at a joke was greeted with bewildered eyes and slowly shaking heads followed once again by Edmund's soft but forceful voice. "No, Maddy, that is not the right move at this point. But there is a caveat. If anyone who is directly or *indirectly* linked to their autocratic, neo-fascist movement ever makes a move against any citizen or group in our territory, then I have assured them that our retribution shall be swift and quite brutal. So, I have strongly encouraged them to tamp down their violent rhetoric and stop encouraging their followers toward violence. Otherwise, their self-proclaimed 'militias' and lone wolfs will be decimated."

"But they are going to have a problem with this. We forecast that the population that they wield influence over through their radical propaganda and science-fiction conspiracy theories on television, radio, and the internet will begin to splinter. They will begin to wage war against themselves as their brainwashing indoctrination leads them to ever more radical ideologies. We are already seeing this as they are beginning to purge their own members who are seen as being not radical enough from their political parties and local election boards. Our task is to protect our own while we simply sit back and watch them implode from their own frenzied power grab."

"Okay, fine!" Erick exclaimed. "But I'm with my wife. If any of these motherfuckin' phobists ever fuck around in our neighborhoods, then their ass is ours! Without exception! And we *will not* seek the approval of this council. We will act, and we will act swiftly!"

"Ummmm . . . baby?" Maddy quietly whispered into her beloved husband's ear. "What the fuck is a *phobist*?"

"Oh . . . yeah . . . maybe I should explain that" a slightly embarrassed Erick began as he sheepishly looked into the eyes of the surrounding group. "A phobist is anyone who has an intense fear of anyone who does not completely agree with their fucked-up worldview of white straight Christian men being dominant over all others. And that fear turns to resentment. And that resentment turns to anger. And that anger turns to violence. And that violence becomes increasingly intense and deadly to the point that it spirals out of control and our society is faced with exactly what we are facing now. A large group of hate-filled people who proclaim that they are patriots. But their so-called patriotism only extends to people like themselves. People in their own tribe. *They* are the only ones who should receive government benefits. *They* are the only ones who should have rights. *They* are the only ones who should have freedom. Freedom to *them* is having the freedom to take the rights away from *others*. All others, in their view, need to be dominated or eliminated. They are the xenophobes. The homophobes. The transphobes. The sexists. The racists. The rapists. They are the phobists.”

“Oh . . . cool,” Maddy gleefully replied, “that makes sense. Thanks for the explanation. Y’know, you’re really starting to get good at coming up with cool names. All right, so I guess I’ll stand down and stand by, but—”

Maddy was immediately cut off by her loving husband, who suggested, “Ummm . . . Maddy . . . I really think you should rephrase that. You *kinda* sound like a douche when you say that.”

“What? Oh, fuck!” a hastily retreating Maddy stated. “I mean, I guess I’ll just go back to offing your random date rapists, pedophiles, and wife beaters then and leave the international intrigue up to others. But I’m going to be ready if they start some shit again!”

“Fine, Maddy. That will be fine,” Edmund said while wiping his brow in a release of tension and anxiety. “This is for the best. Embrace our newfound peace. Embrace your daughter. Just think of Josie.”

———

Josephine Patricia Sommers Parker had entered the world on February 14, 2024. Even as a newborn, her smile was infectious. But not as infectious as when she would give an unknowing recipient a flash of her emerald-green eyes. Then, to seal the victory over her adversaries’ emotions, the batting of her sandy-red eyelashes, leaving her worthy combatant immobilized by her charms and completely at the mercy of the child’s whims.

Josephine, or Josie as she was known, was an adorable and good- natured child. Her effervescent eyes would scan the room with intrigue as she keenly observed the actions of her parents and the other large people in her midst. She hardly ever fussed and would immediately calm down the moment her overly attentive father would come rushing to her side with a toy, fresh diaper, bottle, or the comfort of warmth in his loving embrace. She slept through the night and adored her two pussycats that were constantly at her side. And she laughed. Constantly. Everything was funny to her, from seeing a silly face made by an adult to being catapulted into the air. She would squeal with delight as she was spun around, danced with, or “dropped” only to be miraculously caught just before impact with the floor.

Her spirit seemed unbreakable, and her smile was constant. She loved to entertain and be entertaining. One little trick that she discovered at the ripe old age of four months that would illicit the desired response of uproarious laughter from her "audience" was crossing her eyes while smiling and sticking her tongue out from the right side of her mouth. Her loving family members called this her "silly face." Her mother would laugh hysterically and then mirror her daughter's expression. It wasn't only when the loving pair was making their "silly faces" at each other that they looked alike. In fact, Josie looked identical to her mother at that age. With the exception of her auburn-copper locks having a pronounced curl to them.

While her father would immediately attend to her every need without question, her mother would attempt to allow her to fuss a bit before providing her with the immediate comfort that she desired, as Erick paced around the bassinet nervously. Her mother would sit and smile at her while reading books aloud or just conversing with her about the latest world events that she was watching from her rocking chair. From the day of her birth, her mother began teaching her not only about love and trust but also about the importance of self-confidence and independence. Her father would be the one to shower her with unconditional love. Her mother would show her love by showering her with the tools that she needed to make it as an independent woman in her male-dominated society. Maddy's affection went beyond warm embraces and presents. Maddy's affection included giving her daughter a sense of worth. Maddy's affection included giving her daughter the freedom to be whoever she wanted to be. And both of Josie's parents' affection included unconditional support and pride while watching their daughter grow to become . . . Josie. She wasn't *their* Josie. She was everyone's Josie and nobody's Josie simultaneously. She was loved and claimed by everyone who crossed her path, but her spirit belonged to no one. She was just Josie.

It did not take long for Josie's parents—and everyone else in her tight circle—to recognize the precociousness of this child. She was walking at nine months, to which Erick noted, "Good thing that I babyproofed the house early, huh?"

"Yeah, what fuckin' ever," a disgruntled Maddy replied.

At seven months, she uttered her first word, which was, regrettably, *douchebag*. That little gem was followed up two days later by words *two* and *three*.

Upon hearing their daughter mutter *fuckin' fascists* while playing with her beloved stuffed manatee, Erick stated in a slightly cautious tone, "Ummm . . . maybe we need to watch our fuckin' language around her."

"Yeah," Maddy replied in the same tone, "she's picking up our bad fuckin' habits."

Josie was then heard in the corner of the room saying, "Bad fuckin' habits."

Josie was putting complete sentences together by the age of one year. She learned her alphabet at the age of three and was reading at the age of four. Erick scoured through all the baby books that he had read before Josie's birth. "I'm telling you, Maddy, I just don't think this is normal! We need to get her tested and find out what we're dealing with here!"

So at the age of four, Josie was administered an intelligence quotient test. Although they understood that IQ scores at that age were suspect at best, they still looked at each other with wide, bewildered eyes when they were told that their daughter's IQ was 152.

Also, at around the age of four, Josie began the construction of a shelter for stray animals, especially cats and dogs, in the fenced-in back drive of the Parker residence. With the sometimes help of her father, but usually one of his father's more mechanically inclined associates, she constructed a wood-insulated habitat that would shelter the strays during inclement weather. She adored animals, especially the cute, furry kind; and they, in turn, adored her. She would go outside and immediately be followed by at least one, but frequently more, hungry and affection-starved creatures. Her heart would melt, and she would say, "C'mon, Mom, let's go back home and get these little guys settled in."

"Dammit, Josie," Maddy would reply before looking down at her daughter's pleading expression and say defeatedly, "Yeah . . . okay . . . but these are the last ones, okay?" This conversation happened at least weekly throughout Josie's childhood.

From there, Josie and her father would begin the public relations campaign in the form of flyers that would be distributed throughout the neighborhood. Josie's opening line to the flyer was designed to grab the attention of any passerby.

THIS IS AN URGENT MESSAGE FROM JOSIE PARKER!!!!!!
BY JOSIE PARKER

This adorable [cat, dog, etc.] is looking for just the right person to give their love to in their new forever home. Could that lucky person be you? If so, please call the Joe Argento Pet Shelter and ask for Josie at XXX-XXXX.

There would then be a picture of a wide-eyed and smiling Josie holding the animal in question. The level of cuteness was off the charts and proved to be irresistible to many who had read the flyer. Maddy's phone began ringing off the hook. "Goddammit," Maddy would utter under her breath before shouting out, "Josie! It's for you . . . again!"

Josie would take the phone and say excitedly something like, "Yes . . . tomorrow at three would be just perfect! Thank you for taking the time to open up your heart and home to this wonderful [cat, dog, etc.]." Josie had her own basic flip phone by the age of five.

Josie was not just raised by her parents. She had the benefit of an adoring extended family as well who would watch over and entertain her whenever her parents needed to leave for "business meetings." By the age of three, Josie noticed that sometimes when her parents left, they would be wearing their normal clothes while carrying briefcases. On other occasions, they would be clad in black and carrying black duffel bags. She also thought it curious that her parents would always be giggling as they left the house on those evenings.

Frequently, it was Rod who got that evening's babysitting assignment. He would bring a laptop to complete whatever tech-related assignments he had for Murder Incorporated or the Unholy Trinity. Josie would sit on his lap or beside him and watch in bewilderment at the flashing images on the screen as Rod typed furiously.

But Rod would not work in silence. One of the reasons that Rod loved this child was because her kind nature allowed him to feel comfortable around another human being. He never felt he had to fear being judged by Josie; and he would explain, step by step, exactly what he was doing and why he was doing it, all the while smiling and maintaining eye contact with Josie's brilliant green eyes.

Josie would sit there and coo. Later, the coos became giggles, which then developed into repeating words or phrases that Rod used. By the age of five, the advanced young girl would pepper Rod with questions about what he was doing. And Rod would proudly answer her advanced inquiries. And Josie would mentally note every answer.

Henri and Lionnel moved out of the Parker home when Josie was a year and a half, and it was deemed safe to do so. But Lionnel was frequently watched over by whoever Josie's caretaker was at that time when Henri was away on "business," which usually meant performing as a hit man for one of Murder Incorporated's higher-priced clientele. These excursions abroad were also usually attended by Lucy, and the pair was typically flown on a rented private jet by Lucy's British girlfriend, Jennifer.

Jules and Jerry would interact with Josie only on Wednesday evenings as Maddy and Jules were determined to continue that tradition, although the meeting locations were held in private. Maddy had explained to Jules and Jerry the danger of being associated with her and vowed to never involve them in her activities. But they *could* provide a valuable service by becoming one of her neighborhood "birdies." When available, Lucy would also attend these traditional gatherings. Sam and Kristy were never mentioned. It was as though they never existed, except that Maddy would frequently wipe a tear from her eye as she was packing Josie up to go home.

In early 2026, Patty, at the ripe young age of seventy-five, and her sixty-one-year-old wife, Jacklyn, bought the punk club. They named it LOHAD, which stood for Land of Hope and Dreams. It was designed to be a sonic oasis for anyone and everyone. They wanted it to be a politics and religious discussion-free zone for music and libation lovers to come together and find common ground and mutual respect through having a sweaty good time with one another. They envisioned it being a true melting pot of ethnicities, genders, gender identities, sexual orientations, and cultures. There was a strict No Drugs! No Guns! No Assholes! policy that was displayed prominently on the front door. The definition of No Assholes! was subjective and changed based on Patty's whims on any given evening.

On one such evening, Erick was denied entry. While arguing with Patty as to why he couldn't come in, Patty invoked the No Assholes! policy. "But what the fuck did *I* do? I'm the same person who was in here last night!" Erick bellowed as "Trendy" by Reel Big Fish blasted in the background.

"No, you're not!" Patty yelled back. "Last night, you weren't wearing a fucking Barry Manilow T-shirt!" Erick went outside, turned his T-shirt inside out, and reentered the bar as he flipped Patty off.

After Kristy's children were relocated, Blair gave Patty and Jacklyn a full explanation of the past, present, and future activities of her family. Patty's reaction was to continue living and loving as though she had never been told, although she very much missed the loss of two of her "adopted" nieces. But that void was more than filled when Patty and Jacklyn would watch over their Josie in the afternoons while preparing to open the club that evening. As the Parkers' party room was still shut down, it was at Patty's club that Josie was first introduced to a sonic smorgasbord of delight. When Josie would ask her Great-Aunt Patty what it was that they were listening to, Patty would kneel attentively in front of her inquisitive niece and say in a soft, maternal voice, "Josie, my love, what we are listening to is"—Patty would then purposefully contort her voice into a deep, demonic growl—"the music of the gods." Patty, despite her slightly arthritic back, would then throw the unsuspecting child to the floor and blow on her belly, eliciting squeals of laughter from her delighted niece. Patty would then play "My Girl Josephine" by Fats Domino, and the pair of giggling figures would sway together on the sticky and beer-stained cement floor. Maddy would always ask Erick following one of these visits, "Why is Josie always so *sticky* when she comes back from Patty's club?" Erick would just shrug. But regardless of who was Josie's official caretaker at any point in time, she was never far away from the protective gaze of Vai, Adam, and Aaron. They loved playing games and delighted in teaching Josie new games to play as she grew. And the twins loved to make their own game pieces . . . out of spare parts from a human body. Whether it was carved dried flesh, preserved eyes, bone fragments, or teeth, these homemade pieces would frequently find their way into most any innocent childhood contest, whether it be a board game, hopscotch, building blocks, or pick-up-sticks.

Maddy put a stop to this when she discovered the twins attempting to dry out flesh to create their own deck of playing cards. "Okay, boys . . . I love you. But stop using fuckin' body parts when you play with Josie!"

"We're sorry, Aunt Maddy," came Adam's sincere apology, followed by Aaron's contribution of "Yes, we're sorry. We will only use them when we're playing without our Josie. It just makes the games that much more interesting."

"Yes," Adam replied. "As we play our game, we get to think about the game we played with the man who supplied us with these most fun game tokens. It is something that we think about often. We do so love playing games."

And because of this younger version of the Trio of Terror, it was very quickly known around the neighborhood, especially at the nearby parks, that it would be wise to be "cool with Josie." On one sunny afternoon, as Maddy was buying ice cream from a nearby vendor in the park with the sunshine beaming down upon her playing daughter, a six-year-old boy intentionally pushed the three-year-old Josie to the ground, who got up crying and showed Vai her skinned hands. The fifteen-year-old Vai silently nodded at the eleven-year-old Twins, who went up to the boy and said, beginning, as always, with Adam, "You hurt our friend. That wasn't nice."

The boy began backing up as Aaron walked up to him and stared into his sweaty, fearful face and said, "No. Not nice at all. Josie is our friend. Nobody is allowed to hurt Josie. You must be punished."

The twins then grabbed the boy by each arm and marched him up to a large oak tree. They then slammed his face into the tree ten times, leaving blood and multiple teeth lodged into the brittle and jagged bark.

"Oh, we don't want you to benefit from this," Adam stated, followed by Aaron's "No. You shall not profit from this. You do not deserve to be visited by the Tooth Fairy." The boys then dislodged the teeth from the trunk and placed their latest game pieces in their respective pockets as the boy ran past Maddy while screaming for his mother.

"What the fuck is *his* problem?" Maddy inquired of the children.

Vai's cold voice answered, "He fell down. Repeatedly. Against that tree."

"Oh, fuck," a resigned Maddy sighed. "Let's get the fuck out of here before his mother shows up with the cops." No child at the park ever picked on Josie again.

———

In 2029, Josie was five years old. For the past five years, she had been encased in a cocoon of safety, love, and support. In 2029, Josie's parents feared that her idyllic childhood was in jeopardy as Henri entered their home and asked for an official meeting of the Unholy Trinity.

"Here ye! Here ye! Here ye! This meeting of the Unholy Trinity, an official subsidiary of Vendetta Degli Oppressi, is now officially called to order!" Maddy announced to the eye rolls of Lucy and Erick and the confused expressions of Henri and his guest.

"Okay, first order of business," Maddy continued while ignoring her colleagues. "We have a new person at this meeting. For the record, please state your name, sir."

The sweating man looked up with a fearful and beleaguered expression on his face as he stammered, "Umm . . . m-my name is Ch-Ch-Chad."

"Well, *that's* not gonna fuckin' work now, is it?" Maddy declared as Lucy and Erick burst out laughing.

"Okay, listen, man," a snickering Erick chimed in, "that name's not gonna work, so what's your middle name?"

"Well . . . I guess you can call me Gregory," the man replied before hastening his cadence and in a pleading voice said, "You don't understand. This isn't a time to make jokes! This isn't a time to laugh! You just don't understand! CHARLIE is coming! In fact, CHARLIE is already here! You have to get prepared!"

CHAPTER 53

HELTER-SKELTER

The year 2029 was also the beginning of Josie's life away from her home and loved ones for part of her day. It was the year that Josie began public school after five years of homeschooling with her loving father. She would be walked seven blocks to her school with the seventeen-year-old Vai directly behind her and flanked by the nearly thirteen-year-old twins. Each morning, Vai would bend down to her beloved adopted sister and say, "Josie . . . if anyone messes with you, you will tell us, correct?"

"Yes, Vai," came Josie's almost-dismissive response, "I'll tell you. But nobody will mess with me. I absolutely adore everyone here! They are all so nice to me!"

Which was true. Josie's sunny demeanor and constant smile made it nearly impossible for anyone to dislike her. She would befriend anyone, especially those children who sat by themselves. Once Josie would join a loner child at their lunch table or in the playground, that child immediately became accepted by the rest of their class as well. If you were cool with Josie, then you were cool with everyone. She would read to the less- advanced children. She would tell bad jokes and laugh hysterically while sitting in the middle of a circle of attentive children, her copper curls bouncing with each joyous release. She would design and make clothing for her classmates whose families could not afford a nicer wardrobe for their child, as clothing design became one of her hobbies starting at the age of four, along with her pet shelter and adoption service. A third hobby was archery as she became enamored by the exploits of her favorite green-clad archer superhero from the comic books that she read voraciously. Actually, *he* wasn't her favorite, but she was unable to locate a green power ring and lantern, so she settled.

And she assisted her teachers by volunteering to tutor any of her classmates who might be struggling. On day one of school, her classmates were in kindergarten. By the third week of school, Vai and the Twins were escorting her to her new first-grade classroom. Two weeks after that, Josie was welcomed by her new second-grade classmates. At the parent-teacher conference that ended the first quarter in October, Maddy and Erick sat with wide, bewildered eyes as it was decided that it would be best for Josie to begin her formal education in the third grade. At the age of five. And even *that* would prove to be somewhat remedial for her.

While Josie was basking in her achievements and popularity at public school, Vai, Aaron, Adam, and Lionnel were being homeschooled by their great-aunt Blair, who was frequently joined by guest instructors. They were taught all the basics of arithmetic, science, reading, and writing. They were taught that the United States of America was the greatest nation that the world had ever known. But their history lessons weren't whitewashed. While being taught about the beauty of the United States Constitution and all the freedoms that that document attempted to guarantee to its citizenry, they were also taught about how many of the historical leaders of their nation were flawed and that rights for certain groups of people had to be fought for over decades. They were taught that their beloved nation was built upon sexism and racism, especially for its black citizens who continued, as a demographic group, to feel the societal and economic weight of the repugnant institution of slavery and only slightly less repugnant institution of segregation.

The children's guest speakers included a potpourri of individuals associated with Murder Incorporated who taught the children the multiple arts of self-defense. They were also taught about situations where the best *defense* was a good *offense*.

Weekly "field trips" were arranged as neighborhood men who were abusive to others in one way or another were identified. The field trip would consist of the four children approaching the phobist's home, usually dressed as scouts, under the nearby watchful eye of their teacher, Blair. They would ring the doorbell, and Blair would frequently see a devious smile cross the man's face as he invited the seemingly innocent children into his home. His smile would be quickly erased and transformed into an anguished grimace as his throat was sliced open by Vai, and he lay on his filthy floor, gasping as his body was being harvested for new game pieces by a pair of enthralled and giggling toe-headed boys. The children never failed to receive an A for their diligent work. Extra credit was given to any piece of flesh retrieved that contained sexist, racist, white supremacist, or anti-Semitic "art." They almost always received extra credit, usually because of the skilled hands of an eight-year-old Lionnel, who would meticulously remove the violated skin from the dying man's body with a scalpel. Upon their return to their classroom, Lionnel would stick the blood-soaked patches of tattooed f lesh on his bare chest and declare, "Look, Aunt Blair, I'm a fuckin' racist!" Lionnel would then be scolded by a smirking Blair for his language before receiving a loving embrace and a light kiss upon his tan forehead.

And they were taught that the struggle for human rights and equality was never ending. They were taught that the current state of events in the year 2029 posed a significant threat to them and all freedom and democracy-loving people. And they were taught that they had the power to do something about it.

By the year 2029, the United States government had become completely paralyzed by radical partisanship on both sides. Following each election, one side or the other would have slight advantages by controlling either the executive branch or a chamber of Congress, but neither would have a substantial majority, and governmental institutions deteriorated into nothing more than partisan bickering. Each side would attempt to impeach the other's leaders out of spite and political gamesmanship for the sole purpose of tossing red meat to pacify their increasingly fervent, but dwindling in numbers, "base." Political appointees, including judges, were rarely granted confirmation as the extremes of both sides would block their nomination.

On the left, political candidates or appointees would be screened through an impossible litmus test of "wokeness." One off-color joke (to them) told twenty years prior or wrong use of the wrong pronoun was grounds for disqualification, if not outright cancellation of their careers. Their calls to eliminate, rather than reform, required societal institutions were nonsensical with no proposals as to what to do with the void that their extreme policies would leave. Their far-reaching proposals for the overregulation of industry created impossible bureaucracies to navigate, which resulted in unnecessary economic burdens for employers, employees, manufacturers, and consumers.

Their supporters were fervent. But their supporters were small in numbers compared to the voting citizenry that was somewhere in the middle of the political spectrum. And their supporters did *not* advocate political violence. Their supporters were *not* antidemocratic.

This was not true on the radical right, whose leaders continued an assault on basic constitutional rights through voting restrictions and takeovers of local election boards. In pockets of counties throughout the United States, political candidates were vetted through an impossible litmus test of belief in a white male autocracy. Those who advocated for right-leaning but prodemocracy policies were driven out of their tribes as candidates, party members, and election officials. In county after county, election results began resembling those of supposedly democratic Russia, with the candidates with the most extreme rhetoric garnering around 90 percent of the vote.

Their supporters were fervent. But their supporters were small in numbers compared to the voting citizenry that was somewhere in the middle of the political spectrum. And their supporters *did* advocate political violence. Their supporters *were* antidemocratic. And their supporters were driven into their politically violent frenzy by whoever happened to be their cult-of-personality "golden calf " at the moment. This individual, with the assistance of radical right-wing media, would whip their baaing followers into vicious actions by inventing or regurgitating obviously fantastical lies about whoever was the most convenient "enemy of the people" at that moment.

Terrorist attacks increased to the point of becoming commonplace in multiple counties throughout every region of the country. For those who were deemed to be "nonbelievers," societal and political ostracism wasn't enough. The nonbelievers were to be destroyed. Homes were firebombed. Crops were burned. Horrendous beatings and lynchings became weekly, if not daily, occurrences. It was all intended to send a message, and that message was received loud and clear by a bewildered and informationally challenged citizenry. If you do not succumb and support a white-male- dominated autocratic takeover of the United States of America, then your livelihoods, if not your very lives, are at significant risk.

But just as had been predicted by Edmund, Murder Incorporated and both liberal and conservative prodemocracy think-tanks, this extremism and terrorism took their toll on the autocrats' numbers, which impacted their overall political influence at the state and federal levels. Politically moderate people who were able to flee the autocratic counties began doing so—in droves. Suburban, urban, and rural households in prodemocracy counties swelled in numbers as terrorized relatives began living with their siblings or other extended family members. They were refugees in their own country who were forced to flee the extremist political violence from their cherished homeland. The irony was not lost on many of these refugees as they considered their own anti-immigrant stance from just a few years prior. It had now happened to *them*, and *now* they understood the desperate plight that millions of people face every day. Flee to safety or die at the hands of fascists.

There were two other significant contributing factors to the heating civil war that was beginning to simmer. First, the Underground Autocratic Movement had significantly misjudged the advantage that their believers would have in firearms and weaponry. As the antidemocracy forces made gains in the territory that they controlled, people in prodemocracy counties, cities, and regions began purchasing guns and ammunition for their own protection. Although there were many more hoops to jump through to obtain firearms in those areas, the hoops *could* be jumped through, and the weapons *could* be purchased and possessed. And they were. The CEOs and major shareholders of the gun manufacturing industry could be heard bellowing orgasmic exaltations as they shot their cum over each morning's sales reports.

The second significant factor was climate change. Regardless of the reasons, the fact was that the earth was warming. And the weather was becoming more extreme. Heat waves caused rolling blackouts. Extreme winters in some regions caused shortages of heating fuel. Droughts in some areas and extreme flooding in others created significantly reduced crop yields. Which impacted the farmers. Which made them even angrier. The autocrats were angry at the "liberals" for not giving them more money (also known as welfare) during their time of economic crisis and at the scientists who they were convinced were now controlling the weather just to harm them (because that is what *America's most trusted news source* was saying. Without evidence, naturally). Prodemocracy farmers were angry at the autocrats and science deniers for blocking reasonable policies that would mediate the effects of climate change, thereby improving their livelihoods.

All these societal and natural conditions then combined into two significant movements by 2029. One was the onset of the Great Agricultural War that involved the hijacking of trucks that were delivering their wares throughout the country. It also involved the murder of fellow farmers and the declared-legal takeover of that farmer's property by the autocratic sheriffs and county attorneys who would then appoint a hand-selected county agriculture czar to oversee the operation of the newly acquired land. One of the major battlegrounds in this struggle to control the production and shipment of agricultural goods became a long section of Highway 61 from just north of St. Louis to just south of Duluth.

The second movement was the creation in some areas of the country of an autocratic-county, government-sanctioned "police" force. They were exclusively white. They were exclusively male. They wore blue jeans and brown shirts and proudly displayed obscenely vile tattoos. They were known as CHARLIE.

———

"Okay, Gregory . . . *if* that is your real name," Maddy began suspiciously, "who or what the fuck is CHARLIE, hmmmm?"

As "Sheep" by Pink Floyd played in the background, Gregory hesitantly began his explanation, "Okay, I'm sure you're aware of some counties in the country falling under autocratic control. I'm sure that you've heard about good, hardworking families being driven from their homes, if not outright murdered, for their political ideology, race, religion, or land. I'm sure that you've heard about the Great Agricultural War that is now being fought, primarily in the Midwest."

Maddy, Erick, Lucy, and Henri just sat there, nodding with their eyes widening at each passing sentence.

"What you have *not* heard about is CHARLIE. CHARLIE is a recent development in some autocratic counties. They are called a police force, but what they *really* are is a local government-sanctioned fascist militia who do all the dirty work of the county bosses and farm oligarchs. It is in *these* few counties that a new strategy has emerged to regain momentum in the overthrow of American democracy. It is their intent to start a race war. To commit horrendous acts against white people, especially those they consider to be elites, and blame them on various minority groups. They believe that this will create fear and anger in more white people.

And those people will then be ripe for recruitment. Then, as more white people become vulnerable to their insidious indoctrination, their ranks will swell. And as their ranks swell, minority groups will be unable to vote . . . either because of local intimidation or outright genocide. And then, the

Underground Autocratic Movement will be able to take over the government . . . district by district. State by state.

"They are now beginning to infiltrate some of America's major cities. Including New York. All the CHARLIE counties, which currently count six to the best of my knowledge, are a loose confederacy. Each county and each CHARLIE unit can do anything that they deem fit just so long as the end to their means is a race war with increased white enrollment.

"There is a CHARLIE county in upstate New York. They control the state penitentiary there. The warden. The guards. The doctors. Everybody is controlled by CHARLIE. They are about fifty-men strong at the moment, and they originated with the UAM's New York City enforcement members who escaped being killed several Halloweens ago. There were three who survived that night because of being away on assignments. They make up the core of this area's CHARLIE, complete with their . . . traditions. They live on a farm complex about five miles from the prison. And with each white male inmate who is released, they get a new recruit. With each white female who is released, they get another concubine. With each minority male who is released, they get that evening's dinner after they are shot in the back of the head the moment they step foot outside of the prison walls. And with each minority female who is released, they get slave labor in the fields . . . and in their bedrooms."

Lucy's eyes began glowing with rage with this latest revelation as she got up and lit three white candles to calm her nerves. Erick's face was beet red. Henri looked down at the table sorrowfully. And Maddy just stared with unblinking forty-one-year-old emerald eyes. "So how do you know about all this?" Maddy bluntly asked as she leaned forward. "Why should we trust you? This could be some wild goose chase designed to expose us. This could be a trap."

"Yes, it could," Gregory replied in a soft voice. "But it isn't. After I served with Henri in the army, I joined another . . . ummm . . . government group. This group sent me undercover to this prison where I worked as a guard. I have seen all this with my own two eyes. I have been to the farm and seen how those poor women are treated. I was then exposed. I'm not sure how, but I suspect it is from a mole in the government group that I work for. I got out of there and came running to the city where I found Henri . . . where I found you. I'm not asking you to do anything that I'm not willing to do myself. I just need your assistance . . . please. If we can stop this group, it may send a message to the other autocratic counties that this strategy will be fruitless. And if not, if nothing else, we can kill some really bad men and save some people's lives."

Erick leaned back and let out a deep exhale before saying, "Well, we need to talk to Edmund about this. This operation needs to be sanctioned."

"Fuck that," Maddy immediately retorted. "Edmund's too big of a pussy to do anything about this. This is on us. And as president of the Unholy Trinity, I'm calling for a vote. All those in favor of fucking CHARLIE up, say aye!"

The vote was unanimous. Before the five co-conspirators began hatching their plan, Maddy asked Gregory, "What the fuck does CHARLIE stand for anyway?"

Gregory replied solemnly, "It stands for Christ Hails America's Ruling Leaders Inherently European."

"Well, that's stupid," Josie stated matter-of-factly as she strode through the living room to the downstairs bathroom carrying her newfound kitten that needed a flea bath.

"We *really* need to start having these meetings upstairs," Erick stated to a nodding Maddy.

Chapter 54

Wreckin' Crew

"Ow! Ow! Ow!" a grimacing Erick declared to the eye rolls of an increasingly exasperated Jerry.

"That was just the rubbing alcohol."

"Oh yeah? Well, it really stings!" Erick retorted.

"Well, not nearly as much as this is going to. Now lie still and try to relax. This should be over in several hours," an unsympathetic Jerry responded just before the buzz of the tattoo pen began sticking Erick in his right upper arm. Erick screamed in "agony" as the pen began drawing the very discernible image of a black swastika.

"Wow," the observing Jules stated in her customary dry delivery, "for a serial killer, he sure is a pussy."

"Yeah," a slightly embarrassed Maddy replied meekly, "he really doesn't care for needles."

Erick then let out a high-pitched squeal as the black ink began forming the lightning-shaped SS symbol on his right forearm. "Nope," Maddy concluded, "this is *definitely* not one of his finer moments."

After four hours of torture, Erick finally got a reprieve. He looked at his right arm and screamed, "Jesus Fucking Christ! I look ridiculous! I'll *never* be able to show my arms again! What if *Josie* sees this shit?"

"I know, baby, I know," Maddy replied in an attempt to comfort her husband. "Listen, you *have* to do this. You *have* to look the part. Otherwise, you won't be able to infiltrate CHARLIE's farm, and all those abused women are going to die. Plus, they'll continue their fascist stranglehold on that county. The only way to give our state a chance at reclaiming individual rights in that county is for us to get rid of their American gestapo. You *have* to do this. Don't worry about it. We'll get them removed right after the mission, okay?"

"Oh yeah? Well, what if they won't come off?" Erick angrily inquired. "Weeeelll," Maddy began slowly as she searched for an answer, "maybe we'll like cover them with flowers and shit so that nobody will know what it was." Then, in her provocative tone while batting her copper eyelashes over her emerald eyes, she said softly, "And I just think you're being *soooo* brave today. I know how much you hate needles. So for you to do this is *really manly* of you. It's *really* turning me on."

Erick, always a sucker for his beloved wife's sly manipulations, said with renewed swagger, "Oh yeah? Well . . . okay . . . let's get the last one over with then." The buzzing of the pen began anew on Erick's left forearm, which was quickly followed by the overly exaggerated shrieks of the pained wannabe hero.

"I can't fucking watch this. This is too pathetic," Jules stated as she left the room. Maddy, however, *needed* to watch this. She *needed* to see this vile face come to life on her husband's tortured flesh as she imagined what she was going to do to CHARLIE.

It became the face of a deplorable little white man who was the perfect inspiration and symbol of the deplorable little white men of CHARLIE. A narcissistic small-statured hippie from the late sixties who had felt aggrieved. In *his* mind, he was entitled to anything that he wanted. All the women that he wanted. All the fame that he wanted. All the hit records that he wanted. And having no real talent to speak of, he appointed himself as a flower-power guru who manipulated young men and women into doing his deadly bidding of murdering a married couple and an actress who was over eight months pregnant. She was brutally stabbed eighteen times, and both she and her unborn infant perished. This abomination of violence was done for no other reason than to pacify the lunacy of a self-absorbed man-child who believed his claim to fame and power would be to start a race war in the United States. This was the philosophy that CHARLIE adopted.

It was all that anyone needed to know about this group's lack of character, intelligence, and self-esteem. They were as small and pathetic as their namesake. This was why they had to travel and live together in packs. Deep down inside, they realized that they were absolutely nothing as individual men. They knew that *real* men possessed an inner strength that drove them to provide for and protect others. These fully grown toddlers did not possess that inner fortitude, so they congregated together in their brown shirts to bully the world into giving them whatever it was that they believed they were entitled to. They were, both individually and as a group, repellent. To Maddy, they were the perfect representation of "chads." They were insignificant scum who were causing significant damage.

"Okay, man," an exhausted Jerry stated, "one last thing. Time to shave your head." All Maddy could do was wince as she heard her husband's reaction.

————

Erick sat in a dingy corner of the local diner in Upper State New York, attempting to fill his queasy stomach with at least half of his cheeseburger and fries. The overhead fan caused a cool breeze that only served to remind him of his shaven head as he felt the sting in his flesh surrounding the repugnant images on his arms. He peered over the drawing of the farm that Gregory had provided, concluding his memorization of the layout. He checked his bag once again for his bottles of insulin. They were all there, present and accounted for and looking like little soldiers awaiting their orders. Only they did not contain insulin. He adjusted his glasses and recalled what Rod had told him.

"These glasses won't affect your vision. They are connected directly to my network, and we will be able to see and hear everything that you are experiencing. All the electronics are very subtle. They won't be able to detect them . . . ummm . . . I think." Rod then concluded his statement as his eyes drifted away from Erick's chest and onto that of Lucy. "Ummm . . . Lucy . . . did you have something to say?"

Lucy, attempting to ignore Rod's seemingly lurid stares, began, "Yeah . . . at your earliest opportunity, give the antidote to *Toxin X* to yourself and the innocent women. Mix it into their food. It's contained in the insulin bottles. Then, twelve hours later, we'll come and do our thing. It will be messy. It will be brilliant. It will be our greatest statement yet."

Erick then smirked to himself as he heard his lovely wife's voice in his head. "Yeah . . . let's fuck some fascist pricks up!"

As if on cue, three bald young white men wearing tattered blue jeans and brown shirts entered the diner. Erick made direct eye contact and made his arms conspicuous as one of the men approached. "Well, hey there, man, you're new around here, aren'tcha?"

"Yeah," Erick replied confidently while leaning back in his cracked red vinyl seat. "I had nowhere else to go. You see, the fuckin' commies drove me out of my home in Brooklyn. Don't know why. Alls I was tryin' to do was rid my neighborhood of vermin . . . you know the types . . . the fuckin' gays and, well, you know, those who don't look like us." Erick, despite having rehearsed his speech, just couldn't bring himself to use the deeply offensive racial terms that he had intended. He hoped that their omission didn't end his mission before it had even begun.

The brownshirt didn't have any such qualms as he proudly went off on a racially charged diatribe about how "they" were destroying our country and taking it away from the true white red-blooded patriots that God had given this land to. Erick outwardly grinned. Inwardly, he wanted to vomit as he prayed for the moment that he would see just how red their blood was. He glanced around the room. The eight other people there, all white, just looked down at their plates and continued chewing. *These motherfuckers are either complicit in this shit or too fucking scared to do anything,* Erick thought to himself.

"So," Erick began again, "I heard that there was some cool shit happening up here, and I thought I'd come up and check it out. See if maybe you'd all be a good fit fer me. And I like how you talk. So if you're interested, I'd like to sign up with ya'll. It's been some time since I had me some fun."

The three brownshirts looked Erick over and began chuckling. "What's so fuckin' funny?" Erick sternly asked as he began rising from his seat.

"Hey, hey, now, fella," one of the brownshirts began through his laughter, "no offense now, boy, but you just seem a bit old to be joining us. What we do is . . . a young man's game."

Erick did, indeed, take offense. Not as much offense as the other repugnant things that he had just heard, but offense just the same. Although now fifty-three, he had always held a vain self-image of being perpetually in his mid-twenties. This was despite his slight aches and pains here and there and the increased frequency of his naps. He *was* offended. And he *was* pissed.

"Fine," Erick began haughtily. "I'll just move on. Didn't realize that I was dealing with fuckin' amateurs who have no respect for experience. Fuck it. There are other groups who will gladly let me join 'em. Now, get the fuck out my way . . . junior."

The false bravado worked on the intellectually challenged men, and Erick was taken to the farm. It was laid out exactly as Gregory had drawn. He met the other forty-three "men" and was shown around. All his belongings were searched, including his glasses. Upon their removal, Erick began squinting as though he was struggling to see. His glasses were immediately returned as were his bottles of insulin following a perfunctory once-over.

His social media pages that had been set up by Rod were viewed by CHARLIE's leadership. He was easily cleared as they contained what to them were glorious manifestos about white supremacy and the need to take the country over from the "woke" commies. They were filled with radical conspiracy theories that were so inane that a child would have suspected their validity but that grown adults eagerly ingested on a nightly basis on their favorite radical right-wing state TV propaganda networks. Following being checked out, Erick was delighted to learn that as a newcomer, he would be in charge of taking care of the livestock. *The sooner we get this shit over with, the better,* Erick thought to himself. *I can't wait to see these motherfuckers' guts all over the ground.*

His delight immediately turned to horror, and he had to bite his lip to fight back his tears as the barn doors were opened to reveal the most disgusting sight that he had ever seen. There were thirteen women of all various races, except white, chained to the walls. They were lying on filthy mattresses and wearing filthy gowns. Some were just staring blankly ahead. Others were feigning sleep. And the remaining four were quietly weeping as they balled themselves up into a tight fetal position.

"So," the brown-shirt tour guide began cheerfully, "this is our livestock. We take 'em out, and they work the farm, clean the house, y'know, slave shit. You're gonna feed 'em once a day. They look like fuckin' animals when they eat. If one of 'em doesn't eat, hit 'em like this." While wearing a devilish grin, the man then shocked one of the despondent women with a cattle prod. She just shook violently and fell over without making a sound. She was numb to it at this point.

The brown-shirted men began laughing as one of them said, "And . . . you can have whatever kind of fun you want to with 'em. You just may want to do it after their daily hose down. They can be smelly bitches. And it'll be feedin' time at nine o'clock. So you've got two hours to get settled in, get in your new uniform, and then we'll take you to the kitchen to get their feed." Erick was shown to his small, dank bedroom, and he closed the door.

He stifled his cries by clasping his mouth with both of his hands. He took out a small piece of paper and a pencil. He wrote, "9:30AM tomorrow. BE HERE." He stared at the paper for ten seconds through his glasses before wadding it up and eating it.

Just before nine o'clock, Erick was taken to the kitchen and given a large pot of white rice. "Just throw it on the barn floor next to their beds. Them bitches will gobble it up like the little piggies they are" were his only instructions. He was being accompanied and closely watched. "Hey, man," Erick stated to his "trainer," "get me some gloves, all right? I don't want to catch any diseases from these bitches if they try to bite me." The dullard dutifully left to retrieve a pair of gloves as Erick took four insulin bottles out of his pocket. Three of the bottles were hastily poured into the rice and stirred, while the fourth bottle was consumed by himself. He returned the bottles to his jean pockets just before the gloves arrived. "All right then," Erick said while smiling, "let's feed some little piggies."

The rice was splattered upon the floor, and the women began eagerly consuming it with their hands. With the exception of one Hispanic American woman who just stared at it with dead eyes. "C'mon now, eat up, bitch!" Erick yelled at the beleaguered woman. "If they don't eat, just shoot 'em," the brown-shirted guard stated dismissively.

"Naw, c'mon, man, let me have some fun," Erick replied before going over to the woman, grabbed her by her oily hair, forced her mouth open, and began shoveling rice into it. He held her mouth closed until the defiant woman swallowed each bite.

"Damn, man! I like your style! Never thought of that before. Now we can get another day of work out of her!" the wicked man exclaimed before taking his leave. Erick held the woman's head next to his and whispered, "I'm so sorry. Please forgive me. I'm here to get you all out. Don't say anything to anyone. It's happening tomorrow morning. I promise." The woman looked into Erick's kind hazel eyes and realized that he wasn't playing a mind game with her. She managed a slight smile and a knowing nod before silently curling up on her dirt- and flea-ridden mattress. It was the first time that she had felt hope in months.

The midmorning sun was beaming down brightly as Henri and Gregory looked through their respective binoculars from a grove of dense trees and brush fifty yards away from the gated entrance to the farm. The women were in the field being overseen by a yelling Erick, who was holding a whip. Every now and again, he would crack it near one of the terrified women, being careful not to actually strike them. He was observed looking around and then going up to one of the Hispanic women and whispering into her ear before screaming at her and giving her a fake slap across her face. The woman pretended that she had been struck by crouching over and holding her "pained" face. As she continued her performance, she began going up to the other women, who in turn began congregating together in a tight circle.

The other forty-six brown-shirted fascists were located. One was at the gate. *Easy enough,* Henri thought. *He's the only one who's gonna get off easy today.* The rest were either staying in the main boarding house or mingling about near the front porch, holding cans of cheap "American" beer that was actually produced by a Russian company. "Two upstairs windows, two downstairs windows," Gregory stated to his friend in a calculating voice. "We have three mortars. I'm gonna aim for the left upstairs window, the right downstairs window, and right in front of the front porch." Henri nodded just before crouching into his position with his sniper rifle.

Henri heard a slight pop from his rifle just before he witnessed the guard's brains exploding out of the back of his head through his viewfinder. A few seconds later, he could hear the shattering of glass and see deep purple clouds of smoke emanating from the house's windows and just in front of the porch. He saw a flurry of activity from the brownshirts. Erick was heard yelling, "We're under attack! I'll get the piggies back in the barn!" Erick and the women were seen scurrying into the barn. Erick emerged, locked the barn, and just stood there with a maniacal smile upon his beet-red face with his fists clenched tightly.

A pudgy bald middle-aged brownshirt with an eye patch emerged from the purple haze and picked up one of the canisters. "Boys! It's just a smoke bomb. Some motherfuckers are playing games with us! Find them! And grab that new motherfucker! This ain't no coincidence!"

A brawny tall brownshirt hastily approached Erick. He grabbed Erick by the front of his shirt and screamed, "You're comin' with me!" There was then a look of anguish upon the man's face as his brownshirt turned to a dark crimson, and his intestines fell to the ground with a discernible "plopping" sound. Throughout the complex, there were high-pitched wails of agony as the brownshirts became transformed into oozing dark-pink pools of blood and internal organs. Their eyes began popping out of their sockets and were just hanging down over their blood and pus-soaked cheeks. There was a putrid smell of guts and death hovering over the complex.

"Awww, man," Lucy was heard lamenting behind the steering wheel as she watched the scene unfold through her binoculars.

"What's wrong, Luce?" Maddy responded in a concerned voice.

"Awww . . . it's nothing . . . it's just that . . . well . . . now I'm craving that delicious cherry Jell-O from that diner in Missouri." Lucy and Maddy burst into laughter as the bus's engine roared to life.

The bus stopped one hundred yards away and picked up Henri, Gregory, and their tools of liberation before crashing through the gate. You could hear the pounding chords and beat of The Meteors' "Wreckin' Crew" before you saw the black school bus with its windows and front end fortified by steel bars come flying into the complex and screeching to a halt. The ebony behemoth looked rightfully like something out of a futuristic apocalypse movie.

The door of the bus opened, and the volume of the frenetic psychobilly music became deafening. A black faux leather catsuited Maddy came strutting out and was enveloped in the dense purple shroud while holding a plastic bag and wearing a devious smile so wide that her dimples nearly exploded off her face. She went bouncing up to her husband and enthusiastically yelled, "Hey, you!" before wrapping her arms around him and giving him a big kiss.

"Wassupbuttacup?" came the smiling Erick's customary reply as he gazed deeply into his beloved wife's sparkling green eyes.

They were both standing in repugnant chunky pink slime as Maddy replied playfully, "Ohhhh, nothin'. Just watching my prince save the world . . . nothin' big." They then burst into laughter before Maddy yelled with elation, "Oh, I brought something for you!" She reached into the plastic bag and pulled out Erick's brown afro wig from his Leo Sayer costume. He immediately put it on and stood with his hands proudly on his hips, posing like a conquering hero at the end of a comic book. "So what do you think?" Maddy rushed up to him and embraced him once again before whispering into his ear, "You've never looked sexier in your life."

Lucy unlocked the barn. Standing there in her own black faux leather catsuit, she said in a reserved but kind voice, "Okay, ladies, please just listen. We know that you've been through a lot that . . . well . . . I can't even imagine.

We're here to get you out, but we need to leave right now. So, if you're coming with us, get on the bus—now."

The ladies just stood there and looked at each other with bewildered expressions. "Fuckin' now, ladies!" came Maddy's bellowing voice from outside of the barn, and the confused women began shuffling toward the bus obediently.

Henri was behind the steering wheel as the women began climbing the steps into the bus and was greeted by Maddy, who was standing just inside the front seat. "Okay, ladies! Keep it moving! Get to the back of the bus!"

Erick grimaced and said to his wife, "Ummm . . . you might want to rephrase that."

"What?" Maddy exclaimed, "What do you—oh fuck. I didn't mean it like *that*, ladies! It's just that . . . well . . . just sit wherever you want."

As the fortified black nightmare rumbled out of the purple fog and onto the highway with Gregory scanning the horizon out of a side window for signs of trouble, Maddy began addressing their newfound friends, "Okay, ladies, here's the deal. We're taking you to Brooklyn. We're a part of a kind of underground freedom-fighting vigilante serial-killer group. Now, please don't be frightened. We have no desire to kill *you*. That would be *silly*. We take out the motherfuckers like the ones who beat and raped you. And we're gonna take *more* of them out. Once we get to Brooklyn, you're welcome to leave and go do your own thing. Or . . . you can hang with us. We'll train you, and you can help us in fighting for *everybody's* freedom by beating back the oppressive forces of fascism. The choice is yours. In the meantime, me and Lucy— ummm, this is Lucy—are going to tend to your wounds and get you cleaned up. And there's sandwiches and soft drinks in the coolers. Help yourselves."

The women immediately opened the coolers and began passing sandwiches and cans of soda to one another. Before eating, they looked at each other and began sobbing while embracing whoever they were sitting beside. Several women said a silent prayer before taking their first hope- filled bite.

Two hours into their trip, the women were heard huddled together and speaking in soft, secretive voices behind the privacy curtain that Lucy had put up so that the women could be examined, treated, bathed, and dressed in clean clothing. Maddy had yelled out, "No lookin', you pervs!" as the barrier was being hung. An hour later, as the bus was nearing New York City's northern suburbs, a Hispanic American woman stood up in the aisle, took down the curtain, and said, "We have something to say to you all."

Henri continued driving; and Maddy, Lucy, Erick, and Gregory looked at the thirteen women, now freshly washed and wearing black jogging suits. They listened with great attention as the women's spokesperson began.

"My name is Rosa . . . Rosa Alvarez. First, I need to personally thank you, Erick, for making me eat last night. We obviously weren't affected by that gas because you put something in the rice. Thank you." Erick had to turn away and look down to hide the tears that were forming in his solemn eyes as the weight of the women's plight fell upon his soul.

"And we have to thank all of you for helping us escape. Yes, we were tortured. Beaten. Raped in so many ways. Belittled. We were treated worse than animals. It would have been more merciful if they had just shot us. And we know that there are more groups of men out there like them. We have heard them talking about it. And we have all decided that as long as we have one breath left in us, we would do *anything* to stop this violence. To stop this oppression. To stop this hate. To stop this minority of evil, insane people from terrorizing their way to power. In short, we have decided to join you, if you will have us."

Thirteen pairs of raging, determined eyes looked up and stared at Gregory, Henri, and the Unholy Trinity before Rosa concluded in an ominous voice, "Collectively, we will be known as the Coven."

Chills went up the spines of Erick, Maddy, Lucy, Henri, and Gregory as, at that very moment, "Witch" by The Sonics began playing from the bus's sound system. The tension was broken as Maddy gleefully exclaimed, "Cool fuckin' name, ladies! Welcome aboard!"

———

Hunky and Dory were purring contently as they snuggled under the slumbering Josie's chin. She was smiling, as usual, as her colorful utopian dreams pranced around in her subconscious. The new women were bedded down temporarily on air mattresses in the third-floor bedrooms of Vai, Aaron, and Adam, who were waiting to speak to Erick in the living room. Vai began the discussion. "Uncle Erick, it was a wonderful game that you played with those bad men, but we feel awful about how you had to defame your body to do it. We believe we may have an answer to your problem."

"Yes, we believe we have come up with the perfect solutions," Adam replied followed immediately by Aaron, "Yes, we were going through your musical records, and we believe we have found the perfect images to transform those ugly symbols on your right arm into something you can be proud of. Your left arm was a bit more difficult, but we feel as though you may like this."

Adam handed Erick a piece of paper with crude drawings of his future ink. "Maddy, call Jerry please. These are perfect boys . . . Vai . . . thank you."

Erick sat in contemplative silence as Jerry completed his refurbishing work on both of Erick's arms. When it was complete, Erick looked in the mirror. The abominable swastika was now a majestic blackstar. The SS symbol of genocide was transformed into a perfectly colored and shaded *Aladdin Sane* lightning bolt. His left forearm still projected the disgusting image of CHARLIE's namesake. Only now, it had bright-red crosshairs superimposed over it. *It is perfect,* Erick thought to himself as he took his loving wife into his arms and quietly began releasing his pent-up emotions through his tears.

CHAPTER 55

PEOPLE HAVE THE POWER

There was a frigid bite to the late-October air as Edmund slowly made his way up the staircase to Blair's apartment building. She buzzed him in, and he went up the one flight to the second-story apartment that Maddy had once lived in. He knocked meekly, and Blair answered the door. He was about to have the conversation that he had long dreaded. Something had to be done about Maddy.

"Thank you, Edmund, for coming. We need to discuss the Maddy . . . situation," Blair stated in her customary politely cold tone. "Please, have a seat."

Edmund took a chair to the left of the coffee table. He looked around the apartment. It was filled with cheap flea-market ceramic knick-knacks. All the end tables had hand-crocheted doilies. There was plastic on all the furniture and throw pillows. The chicken-shaped candy dish in the middle of the coffee table held mint-flavored jellied candies. It looked exactly as it was supposed to look. It looked like the home of an elderly grandmother.

He then looked at Blair, who appeared far from an elderly grandmother or, in her case, great-aunt. She was sitting cross-legged on the couch, slim as ever. Her bare toes were peeking out from under her bell-bottomed faded blue jeans, and her raven-black hair with one two-inch silver streak to the left of her face cascaded down upon the shoulders of a Men Without Hats concert T-shirt. *My lord,* Edmund thought to himself, *she recently just turned seventy-six, but she looks closer to fifty.*

"Blair," Edmund began reverentially, "I know how much you love Maddy. You know how much *I* love Maddy. But this latest caper with CHARLIE. We simply cannot do this, Blair. We cannot have our operatives flying off half-cocked, starting wars with powerful forces. She and the others knew that there was a chain of command. And she chose not to follow it because she knew that I would never agree to such a cockamamie scheme. I'm sorry, Blair, but I have made my decision. Maddy, as well as Lucy, Erick, Henri, and this new guy, Gregory . . . they are out. They are out of Murder Incorporated. They are out from using our resources. And they are out from under our protection. My decision is final. I know that I was the one to bring her in. This is my responsibility, and I am now righting what I have done. I'm sorry, my old friend. I hope that you understand."

"Yes, I understand," came Blair's dry, unblinking response. "I understand completely. I am going to go over exactly what it is that I understand. Then, my old friend, you and I are going to come to an . . . agreement."

A frigid chill ran down Edmund's spine upon hearing her last statement before Blair continued, "Here is what I understand. I understand that the Underground Autocratic Movement once again violated their agreement with us by beginning to send their CHARLIE operatives into our territory. I understand that my beloved niece and her colleagues identified the threat, developed a plan of action, and executed that plan to perfection. Not only did her plan wipe out this CHARLIE unit, but it also freed thirteen innocent women. Women who we now have as a talented and determined resource for our endeavors. I also understand that because of Maddy's actions, the state forces have been able to return to that county. They have retaken control of the prison and are making the living conditions of the inmates . . . well . . . at least not tortuous. I know that they can now begin investigating the autocratic county leaders and oligarchs and hold them legally accountable for their treasonous and murderous actions. I know that the farmers who had been driven from their land are now returning to reclaim their lives. To reclaim their livelihoods. To reclaim their dignity. I understand that this was made possible because of Maddy's instincts, leadership, and tenacity. And, my dear friend, I understand that for some reason, you have been very hesitant to take on the UAM. I further understand that it is now Maddy's time to ascend to the leadership of Murder Incorporated, which means that your time must come to an end. Vai, dear, would you please bring out the tea?"

Edmund began sweating as the seventeen-year-old Vai entered the room and placed the flowered antique porcelain tea set in front of him. She also was barefoot and wearing blue jeans. Her light-blonde hair cascaded down over her White Stripes T-shirt. Edmund could not help but notice that she had added a silver streak on the left side of her lemon-colored strands. Vai looked at Edmund with her uncaring blue eyes and said, "Would you care for cream and sugar in your tea?"

Edmund's eyes widened as he looked at Blair and stated in a pleading tone, "Blair, please don't do this. You will create a mutiny within our organization. They will never accept Maddy as their leader. My god, Blair, what would *Joe* say?"

"Ah, yes," Blair began as she lifted an eight-by-ten framed picture of her Joseph holding a delighted two-year-old Maddy in his arms. As she looked upon the beaming faces of her cherished ones, she felt a slight tear form in her right eye. The tear quickly dissipated as she looked at Edmund once again and began, "Yes, I thought that you might ask that of me. What would my Joseph think of this? I believe that my Joseph would be quite saddened today. I believe that he would be quite saddened to learn that it was you, *his best friend*, who set him up to be murdered. That it was *you* who attempted to make an unholy pact with that early incarnation of the UAM. That it was *you* who told them about his weakness for needing to play the hero to battered women. That it was *you* who would tell them where to find him so that they would send one of their dullard pre-CHARLIE hicks to stage that violent scene and then execute him. He would also be quite saddened that you knew that his murder would trigger Maddy's more . . . violent impulses. And his sadness would turn to rage if he knew that it was your plan all along to bring his beloved niece into this madness. And then, Edmund, my Joseph would have torn you to shreds with his bare hands."

"How . . . how . . . how . . ." Edmund began stammering, "how do you *know* all this?"

"Oh, I've known for some time now, my friend," came Blair's immediate response. "I've known ever since the night before the Halloween party in 2023. Before Maddy arrived, I took the opportunity to have a chat with our main course. He, of course, pleaded with me not to prepare him for dinner and told me about how you had been working behind the scenes to try to ensure peace between the two groups. That you had offered my Joseph up to them as a token of goodwill. That you had promised to bring Maddy into *their* fold. And he told me how they had fooled you. How they never intended to stop coming after Murder Incorporated. You see, Edmund, these . . . people . . . are liars. They are con men. They say whatever it is that they have to say to pacify so that they can then get whatever they want. They pander to the dim-witted. And you, Edmund, proved yourself to be dim-witted when it came to them. You trusted the untrustworthy. You played into their hands and were complicit in their fascist con game. This is why you have always been hesitant to go too far with them. The Halloween party was my deal. And you knew that if they were tipped off about it that everyone would know that it was you who was the mole all along. My god, Edmund, *you* are directly responsible for the murder of that sweet Abana and my Josie's life being threatened".

"So once Murder Incorporated learns all this, I am quite sure that they will welcome Maddy's leadership with open arms. Erick and I will serve as her consiglieri, and Murder Incorporated will rise to become a truly feared force for freedom in our country. Please, Edmund, it will do you no good to fight this. Just drink your tea. Go to sleep. I assure you that it will be quite painless. Or . . . do you want me to call for the twins?"

"Th-the t-t-twins are h-here?" a hyperventilating Edmund blurted out. "Why, yes," came Vai's cold response, "they are in the guestroom playing a game. I'm sure that they would love to be invited to play a game with *you*. But they have never enjoyed tea parties, so I suggest that that is the game you choose to play."

Edmund closed his eyes and said a silent prayer to himself. The shaking teacup chattered against the porcelain saucer as he lifted it from the serving tray. He placed the cup up to his lips and drank deeply. He closed his eyes. He then clutched his throat, collapsed onto the hardwood floor, and began violently flailing about while screaming in agony through his frothing mouth. Blair and Vai looked on emotionless as Detective Edmund Simmons exhaled his excruciated final breath. Blair stood over the corpse, spit on it, and said in a dark, gravelly voice reminiscent of her Joseph's, "Hmmm . . . I guess that wasn't painless after all. How does it feel to be lied to, you motherfucking douchebag?"

Blair picked up her phone and placed the first call. "Yes . . . it's me. Yes . . . it is done. Please send a retrieval crew. They are to take the body to our crematorium. No . . . there will *not* be a memorial service. Call the seven hit men and the department heads. Tomorrow evening, we are to have a coronation."

The second call was then placed. "Maddy, my dear . . . something terrible has happened. Edmund has suffered a heart attack, and since conditions are quite dangerous right now, we cannot risk congregating for a service. You and Erick need to come at once. We have preparations to make. Yes . . . you may bring Josie, but she must stay in the bedroom and play with the twins. Yes, dear, one hour will be fine. I'll be waiting."

"Aren't you going to tell her?" Vai inquired of her mentor.

"No," Blair responded, "it would serve no purpose for Maddy to know all this. It is best that someone holds some fondness in their hearts for Edmund. And besides, Maddy can be a bit . . . emotional. Hearing this may be counter-productive, and she may fail as a leader. We need her to be emotionally stable, dear. To hear about a loved one's betrayal of her beloved uncle Joe would send her over the edge. I only pray that nothing untoward ever happens to Erick. That is a crossroads that I never wish to witness."

The five-year-old third grader came bounding into the apartment with her ever-present smile and bouncing copper curls. "Hiya, Aunt Blair!" Josie squealed as she was picked up and twirled by her giggling aunt.

"Hello, my dearest! It is so good to see you! Have you found any homes for your cherished pets this week?"

"Oh my, yes, Aunt Blair! Two adorable tortoise-shell kittens, one black kitten, and one fluffy gray kitten have found their forever homes! I'm just so *thrilled* for them! And Mom said that we can take in the mother and the final fluffy gray kitten . . . right, Mom?"

"Yeah . . . fuck . . . yeah," Maddy said in an exasperated tone as Erick stood off to the side, wearing a brown rug over his head stubble and snickering behind his hand. "Not fuckin' funny," Maddy stated sternly while glaring at her amused husband.

"Boys, come in here!" Maddy ordered.

"Yes, Aunt Maddy?" Aaron inquired upon entering the room, followed by Adam's "Yes, how may we be of service?"

"Okay," Maddy began while looking at the identical nearly thirteen- year-old boys, " jesus . . . when are you guys gonna start dressing in something —*anything*—other than those fucking ice cream vendor outfits? You know, one of these days, you're gonna want to pick up chicks, and I'm tellin' ya, *that* shit just isn't going to cut it!"

"We really have no interest in picking up . . . chicks . . . as you so callously refer to girls," Adam replied, followed by Aaron's, "No, nor boys. We really don't believe we will have much interest in that. Those aren't the types of games we like to play."

"Well . . . kinda creepy as fuck, but that *would* solve a lot of problems later," Maddy pontificated before coming to her point. "Okay, listen. We need you to play with Josie in the other room for a bit. What game are you playing tonight?"

"Oh, we are playing cards tonight!" Adam excitedly exclaimed, followed by Aaron's "Yes! Oh, Aunt Maddy, you know how we so love to play cards! And Josie is getting quite good at it herself!"

"Uh-huh," Maddy replied while looking at both of them suspiciously out of the corner of her eye. "Go get the game. I wanna see it."

"Very well then," the boys cheerfully said in unison.

Upon reentering the room, Maddy looked the game over. "Yep, just the standard pieces here . . . *right*? There aren't any *other* pieces to this game, are there?"

"Oh no, Aunt Maddy," Adam answered, followed by "Indeed not. Any extra pieces to this game are reserved for only our enjoyment. They are not for Josie to play with. We promised you that."

"Yeah . . . all right," a satisfied Maddy replied. "Okay, you three go in the bedroom and play your game. And turn the TV on . . . loud."

Once the children's TV was heard, Erick, Blair, Vai, and Maddy sat down on the plastic-covered couch and the matching chairs at either end of the coffee table. Maddy put her size-six checkered sneakers up on the coffee table and popped a mint-jellied candy into her mouth. She immediately spit it out. "*Blech!* Why do you always have this old-lady candy? Why don't you spring for some good shit?"

"Maddy," Blair tenderly replied, "the candy isn't important. You need to listen to me now."

———

"Here ye! Here ye! Here ye! As the new president of Vendetta Degli Oppressi, I hereby declare this meeting come to order!" came Maddy's opening declaration to the bored eye rolls of Erick and Lucy.

"Okay, first of all, I know that we are all mourning the loss of our longtime leader and my family's personal friend Edmund. His wisdom, leadership, honesty, and conviction for our mission will be missed. And I thank you all for putting your trust in me. And I pledge to lead our organization fairly and with the same steady hand that you have been accustomed to. As you may know, my boss Monica retired a year ago, and I bought the bookstore. That will *not* interfere with my responsibilities here. I have put my long-time assistant Sean in charge so that all I will need is a few hours a week to provide oversight. Sean has my deepest trust as do all of you.

"Now, just because I'm now the *president* of our little hit-man group doesn't mean that you have to refer to me as that. I'm just plain old Maddy, just like before. Except that *now* I can order you all around, heh-heh-heh. Just joking. And please, it is *not* necessary to heap praise upon me at the beginning of every meeting. But if someone is so *inclined*, I certainly wouldn't be *opposed* to a few kind words about my leadership or intellect or cunning or whatever you might feel is appropriate. You know, just to break the ice and get things rolling,"

"Oh, for fuck sakes!" Erick exclaimed.

"What the fuck is wrong with *you*, mister?" Maddy retorted.

Erick immediately replied in a lecturing tone, "So . . . you want everybody to go around the table and sing your praises before every meeting? Does that remind you of someone? Is there anyone *else* who expected his cabinet to gush over him so that he could fill his overinflated daddy-issues ego? Anyone come to mind? Anyone at all?"

"Okay, gang!" Maddy replied with her face red from embarrassment, "New plan. We'll just open each meeting with introductions followed by an overview of the agenda and then just get to work. No need for any dramatic praise or anything like that. I'm still just Maddy, and I am here to work along-side you folks not above you.

"And now that the pleasantries are out of the way, I want to talk about our new direction. Yes, the seven primary hit men will still be our cash cows and handle the pay hit-man service. That is their specialty, and I see no reason to shake that up. Every department will have the same responsibilities. But when it comes to the UAM . . . well . . . I, for one, am tired of sitting on my hands and playing defense. We're going to go on the offensive. They *started* this shit by sending their CHARLIE units into *our* territory. And as far as *I'm* concerned, *all* the CHARLIE units around the country are one and the same. So, they want to fuck with *us* in *our* territory? Fine. But now, we're gonna fuck with *them* in *theirs*. We are going on a mission to destroy their terrorizing gestapo wannabes. We're going to give the people in those terrorized counties a chance to fight back. We're not going to fight their battles for them. We're just going to put our thumb on the scale so that they have a fair fight so that those people have the power to stand up against their oppressors. It's still up to the American people to believe what they want and to vote how they want. But believing in something strongly and encouraging civil discourse is one thing. Using your beliefs as a weapon to stoke fear and anger or actually *commit* violence against innocent others is quite another. These are the types of people— these chads—that I swore to fight back against many years ago. And it is a battle that I shall continue. It is a power that I shall wield and give to other people. Or else, my name isn't Maddy *fuckin'* Sommers. And that's my name, so that's just how it is. Thank you for coming. Your new assignments are in the envelopes that have been given to you. Long live Vendetta Degli Oppressi!"

The meeting attendees began picking up their belongings and preparing to leave before Maddy added, "Oh! One more thing! If *any* of you motherfuckers ever double-cross me or this group, I will fucking *kill* you in as painful of a way as I can imagine. And I have a pretty vivid imagination. So . . . don't *fuck* with me. Okay, thanks, everyone! Great meeting! Call me if you need anything!"

"Well," Erick began as he placed his arm around his wife's shoulder, "a bit of a rough start, but you nailed the landing. I'll give it a 9.8."

"Thanks, baby," Maddy playfully replied before giving her beloved husband a kiss.

Chapter 56

Highway 61 Revisited

The carnage was indescribable. Even the most visually verbose fiction writer would have difficulty in painting the picture that lay before Henri and Gregory on the frigid asphalt of Highway 61. Agonized squeals of pain were coming from brown-shirted bald white men who lay strewn about in impossible angles with their limbs torn from their bodies. The blood had almost immediately frozen to the pavement as had internal organs, lying hard and stiff and permanently affixed to the roadway until the next spring thaw. Some of the men were already dead, having been completely blown apart. Others were anguished as they desperately tried to move limbs that they no longer possessed.

No clean-up crew would dare come to this stretch of Highway 61, which traveled through the northeastern most county in Missouri and southeastern most county in Iowa. Those counties were controlled by the local autocratic oligarchs and enforced by their respective counties' versions of CHARLIE. All traffic steered a wide berth around this area of land, usually taking a long detour through Illinois. The local CHARLIE units would coordinate and surround desired vehicles in their ridiculously adorned "convoys" with heavily armed brownshirts in the back of pickups and vans. They would pull the vehicle over, execute the driver and passengers, and confiscate the vehicle and its contents.

That was what happened to the lucky ones. The unlucky ones, frequently white families, were taken into the woods; stripped naked; and hunted for sport by the local oligarchs, election officials, and sheriff's departments. Men, women, and children would be sent screaming and naked into the heavy timber. After fifteen minutes, the horrendous posse would be dispatched. They would quickly find their desperate quarry and brutally murder them with axes. Over a nine-month span from June 2029 to February 2030, it was estimated that 165 people were murdered at their hands. The ages ranged from infants to the elderly. This was one area that they did not discriminate in. The more helpless the victims looked, the easier it would be to raise outrage in the white community.

There were black men who they had unjustly incarcerated to pose with the bodies. The right-wing Internet propaganda sites would be set abuzz as a picture of a hanging and bloody black man would be shown with the sacrificed white family lying beneath him. There would be a headline on the story, such as "Local Patriots Capture and Kill Black Lib Monster." There would then be a link for donations and information on how to join the movement. And the true believers would salivate as they looked upon the horrendous carnage.

The theory was ludicrous. The vast majority of people, regardless of race, were not going to engage in a race war. They were far too intelligent and kind to be indoctrinated into believing that an entire race of people had suddenly become murderous savages. The only soulless people who believed in it had already been recruited. Those who did not believe in it were sent running from their homes, farms, and shops by the brownshirts. Those who fled fully understood that the *true* terrorists were the white fascists who enforced the autocrats' rule over their county with an iron fist and guns and knives and beatings and rape.

Henri and Gregory just silently watched as vehicles carrying the displaced county residents arrived. They had been located and contacted by Rod, who had invited them home to this party. The men and women who would once again be the backbone of their counties' livelihood, strength, and culture exited their vehicles with purpose and meticulously shot each surviving brownshirt in the head. They gave a respectful nod to Henri and Gregory; got back into their vehicles; and made their way back to their homes, farms, and shops. The Unholy Trinity had put their thumb on the scale, and the residents were indeed taking back their lives. Their livelihoods. Their dignity.

And it had been so easy. A simple message board advertising a very valuable shipment that would be carried by two semi-trailer trucks.

Because of the value of the shipment and the time limitations, they would have no choice but to travel this treacherous stretch. It was a shipment of treasure and armaments bound for a county in southern Minnesota. It was a shipment bound for the CHARLIE unit there. The Unholy Trinity correctly predicted that the Missouri-Iowa CHARLIE units would not care that it was their brothers in cause who were the intended recipients. They correctly surmised that they had no loyalty or regard for anyone other than themselves and took actions only for their own enrichment. After all, they were willing to steal from, terrorize, run off, and murder their own supporters. Of course, they would steal from their brothers. It was their natural, deplorable state of being.

And they had correctly surmised that the value of the shipment would bring out nearly every brownshirt in the area, as each county's oligarchs would want their fair share of the bounty. So as the two semis were approaching the Missouri-Iowa border, they were surrounded by nearly thirty vehicles each. They were ordered to pull over. Henri was driving the front semi and flashed his lights. Gregory, driving the second semi, flashed his lights in understanding. The ceilings of the cabs popped opened, and the makeshift ejector seats catapulted the two men one hundred feet into the air. Upon seeing their parachutes open, Lucy pushed a button and said, "Boom."

The two semis, which were packed full of explosives, exploded with a deafening roar that was heard for miles away. The surrounding vehicles and men were immediately engulfed in cleansing flames and flying pieces of metal, which had been packed into the explosives. The flames immediately scorched the skin from their bones. The shrapnel sliced them to shreds. Only the vehicles that were farthest from the explosion contained any survivors. And that would be short-lived. The newly arrived caravan of residents would see to that.

As Henri and Gregory approached their rendezvous point, they found a flushed and weak-kneed Lucy. "Hey, Lucy," Gregory inquired with concern, "are you all right?"

"Yeah," Lucy breathily responded, "it's just that . . . well . . . that was fuckin' hot. All those bodies. All that blood. All the limbs. It was . . . just really fuckin' hot."

"You really need to get laid," came Henri's uninterested reply as the trio climbed into their minivan.

———

The county oligarch received a call from a deputy sheriff. "Th-they're all gone!" the deputy screamed into the phone.

"Who is all gone? What are you talkin' about?" the middle-aged oligarch screamed back.

"The brownshirts! They're all over the highway! They've been destroyed! And the people that we scared off—they're all back! They're coming *here*! We need to get whatever is in that safe and get out of here!" The phone then went dead.

Three well-dressed white men urgently entered the sheriff's office. The sheriff, the head of the county election board, and the local oligarch looked around in horror. Their three deputies were lying on the floor in their own blood. Each of their throats had been sliced open. There was the sound of a drill coming from the back room where the safe was located. And there was a figure sitting with their cowboy boots crossed upon the dispatcher's desk, dressed in the sheriff's uniform with their wide tan hat pulled down over their face.

"What the hell is going on, and who the hell are *you*?" the election board official yelled. The figure at the desk casually lifted the brim of their hat so that it was now sitting back on their head and looked up. They were greeted by a beaming smile and glowing green eyes as she said, "Well, howdy there, I'm just here to tell ya'll that . . . well . . . there's a new *sheriff* in town, heh-heh-heh. Hey, baby, did you hear that when I said that there's a new sheriff in town? Did you hear that? Pretty funny, huh?"

"What?" Erick bellowed back impatiently. "I can't hear a fucking thing that you're saying over this drill! What did you say?"

"Oh, fuckin' never mind! Only the greatest joke in the history of the world, that's all!" Maddy yelled back as the three men began reaching for their handguns. "Yeah, I wouldn't do that if I were you," Maddy cautioned.

"W-why the h-hell not?" the newly retired sheriff asked.

"Um . . . 'cause those folks behind you won't care for it much."

Over twenty of the newly arrived residents were standing behind the men with maniacal looks of anger on their faces. Three female residents came up from behind the men and relieved them of their guns. "Now, just stay calm," one of the farm wives said coldly. "There's nothing to worry about. We're just going to take you three hunting."

"Got it!" Erick declared before bounding into the room with two large sacks of money. "Here, folks!" Erick said while handing the bags over. "I don't know how much is in here. Spread it throughout the community, okay? Hopefully, this will help you all to get reestablished until the states can regain control and sanity over this area."

One of the women began crying and gave Erick a thoughtful embrace. "How can we repay you?" she asked.

"*Him*? This was *my* fuckin' plan! What the fuck!" Maddy yelled out. "Well," Erick answered softly, "how are you at baking pies? My wife *really* likes pies."

As the Unholy Trinity, Henri, and Gregory were savoring their freshly baked apple pie in the most charming kitchen this side of the Mississippi, Maddy's phone went off. "Yo, bitch, wassup?" Maddy answered casually.

"What? You're fuckin' *done* already? Shit, man, you chicks are efficient. Nice job. See ya back in New York."

"And," Erick chimed in as pieces of flaky crust flew from his mouth, "as soon as we get back, we need to pack. It's Josie's sixth birthday in two days, and she's so excited about this trip. We just need to . . . watch our behavior this time."

Maddy flicked a partially eaten piece of crust from her cheek with disdain and stated back to her husband, "I hope they don't remember us. Otherwise, this is gonna be a fuckin' shit show."

———

Rosa Alvarez always knew she was special. Even as a small child, she always felt a strong connection to nature. She felt as though she could almost communicate with the flowers and fauna that she happily would saunter through. She felt as though she could actually *feel* their energy. She had a very pleasant and nondescript childhood. She was adored by her parents. She had decent grades in school and excelled in athletics. It was almost as though the softball would be in slow motion as it approached her bat. She had an incredible batting average that landed her a scholarship at a college in upper state New York. While there, she found that she could communicate with her teammates through a slight glance and thought. She could have them visualize what pitch was coming or when to run. She never thought of this as abnormal. It was what she had always experienced. Then, as a sophomore in college, she made the mistake of speaking about her ability to connect and communicate with other forces in nature, whether they be people, animals, or plants. She became convinced that her abilities were not abilities at all but figments of her imagination that were enhanced through random coincidences. She became convinced that she wasn't special. She became convinced that she was mentally ill.

And she was placed on antipsychotic medications. Her entire demeanor became dulled. She could no longer feel the energy of the other life around her. Her grades plummeted as did her batting average. To combat her depression, she became involved with a man who turned out to be a petty criminal. For her contribution of driving the car at a convenience-store heist, she was awarded a six-month prison sentence despite having no previous criminal record. She suspected that her last name and complexion might have played a part.

At the age of twenty-two, she was released from prison and immediately thrown into a van filled with men wearing brownshirts. She was stripped down, gang raped, then dressed in a filthy gown, and chained to a wall near a stained mattress. She endured weeks of hard labor, rapes, and beatings as did an increasing number of other enslaved women in the barn. Following the public execution of three of her sisters for being too emaciated and exhausted to work, the number of women chained in the barn settled in at thirteen.

But now that she was no longer taking antipsychotic medications, she was beginning to experience familiar sensations once again. She realized that her abilities were being restored when she was able to feel and connect with the kindness of a new brownshirt who, ironically, was brutally forcing her to eat. Upon experiencing this feeling, she succumbed to his efforts and ate her rice dutifully. And she allowed herself to believe him and be comforted when he told her that he was there to help.

Her parents looked for her but were told that it would be unwise to go into that county. They were desperate and reported their suspicions to a governmental agency which, in turn, placed a mole in the prison. That man's name was Chadwick Gregory Davenport III.

Despite his fancy name, Chadwick (or Chad, as he was known) was raised in a hardworking middle-class family in the suburbs of Philadelphia. He was very popular in school and had a natural charisma, which enabled him to make friends easily. He could naturally move from one clique to the next and find common ground with disparate groups of people. He used this charm to assist other schoolmates who were viewed as being "different" from being bullied by their less-evolved classmates.

He immediately enlisted in the United States Army following his graduation and displayed great analytical and diplomatic skills. In 2028, he was offered the opportunity to enlist in a special antidomestic terrorism task force, which he eagerly joined. Shortly after his training ended, he found himself in the appallingly torturous conditions of a prison in upper state New York to investigate and report back the strength of the local brown-shirted militia there that had recently risen to power. He nearly wept when he was given a tour of the farm and witnessed the condition of the enslaved women. One Hispanic American woman looked at him with pleading eyes as the barn door was shut, ending their brief gaze.

One morning, as he was in the locker room changing into his prison guard uniform, two fellow guards came up to him and said that his presence was requested in the warden's office. Chad instinctively knew what that meant. He had been exposed; and assuming it was someone within his own government agency that had exposed him, he escaped through a seldom- used employee back exit and went to Brooklyn to find the one man he felt he could trust.

Henri Hamadou was a legal immigrant from the nation of Cameroon. He and his wife, Abana, were expecting their first child when he met and became close friends with Chad in 2019. Henri was always a wise and prudent man. He carried a muscular build upon his six-foot-five-inch frame. He was also very proud. That pride led him to refuse involvement in a local gang, which, in turn, led to the gang brutally murdering his parents. His recently married wife would be next, so he escaped looking for asylum and safety in the United States in 2017.

He was granted asylum despite being from what one phenomenally ignorant person called a shithole country and enlisted in the United States Army. He became a superb sniper and reveled in the fact that he was a patriot on the front lines of protecting the United States Constitution.

But the lure of being with his wife and young son led him to leave the army with an honorable discharge in 2024 at the age of twenty-seven. Shortly upon his return home, he was devastated by the decapitation of his wife by antidemocratic forces, and he joined Murder Incorporated as a pro-democracy assassin. Five years later, his good friend from the army found him.

As Rosa was dressing for her evening's mission, her mind wondered about all the improbable coincidences that led these three—herself, Gregory, and Henri—into this unlikely and quite violent situation. Could it be that she was somehow responsible? Could it be that she had somehow called them together so that they could then join up with Maddy's crew? Could it be that she possessed skills beyond what she had previously known? Could it be that she had the power to manipulate destiny itself?

There wasn't time to ponder that any longer. All that was important at *this* moment was that she knew that she had the ability to fulfill her mission. She with the inner strength of her twelve sisters in the Coven. The bus pulled up outside of CHARLIE's Minnesota compound just off Highway 61. Thirteen ladies dressed in black hooded gowns and combat boots disembarked into the subzero darkness of the hour. They held hands. "Just focus on me. Just focus on heat. The most excruciating heat that you can imagine. Focus all that heat on me. Now, let's wake them up" were Rosa's instructions to her sisters.

The driver of the bus pushed play on the bus CD player, and Santana's "Black Magic Woman" came blasting through the PA system on top of the bus. Forty-plus men came scurrying out of the main complex, hastily putting on their coats and clutching their guns. They saw thirteen dark silhouettes in the distance. The shrouded figure in the middle began glowing an eerie red as she stared at them. They immediately raised their guns in fear and pointed them at the thirteen ominous figures.

Then, the screaming began. The men threw down their guns and began wailing in pain as they began disrobing, leaving their coats and pajamas strewn about the snow-covered ground. Rosa's eyes glowed with burning intensity as she watched the naked men run to their well and begin futilely dousing themselves with water. The tortured men felt as though they were being bathed in blistering lava even though the water immediately froze on their skin in the negative-ten-degree wind chills. One by one, the human popsicles fell over as their bodies succumbed to the bitterly arctic conditions. Their faces were quite literally frozen in tortured anguish.

"Well . . . that was easy," Rosa stated matter-of-factly as her sisters let go of one another's hands and relinquished their psychic connection with her. "I'll call Maddy and let her know it's done and then let's get back to New York. I've got a *hot date* with Gregory tomorrow night. Pun intended."

The thirteen women began laughing and high fiving as they ascended the stairs of the bus, took their seats, and opened several well-earned bottles of champagne. One of the women yelled out, "Hey, driver, turn the heat up a bit will ya? It's fuckin' freezing out there!"

CHAPTER 57

I'VE BEEN EVERYWHERE

"It's intermission time! Time to go to the snack bar for your favorite cold drinks and tasty treats!" Erick bellowed in his best announcer voice as he brought in a tray with a fresh soda, hot dog with ketchup, ice cream cup, and roll of sour candy. Josie giggled in delight as she sat on their parents' bedroom floor in front of the TV, surrounded by suitcases, and put a new animated DVD into the player.

"Ooooh, that looks good," an intrigued Maddy stated to her daughter as she began salivating. "Can I have a bite of your hot dog, hmmmm?"

"Mom," Josie replied in a lecturing tone, "there are *plenty* of hot dogs downstairs. Plus, a bite for you means that I won't have any hot dog left. And finally, you need to finish packing. Dad and I were done last night."

"Oh, what fuckin' ever," the disappointed mother replied, "you don't fuckin' do it right anyway. You're supposed to put mustard and relish on a hot dog. *Not ketchup!*"

"Mom," Josie replied as she looked up at her mother, mirroring her emerald-green eyes, "you enjoy your hot dogs *your* way, and I'll enjoy mine the way that *I* like them. Please don't be so judgmental. Jeeez . . . it's *only* a hot dog."

Erick chuckled to himself under his breath as he began picking up the suitcases and taking them to the car. Maddy just shook her bemused head, causing her straight copper strands to sway like windblown grain in a field, and thought about the conversation that she had had with her daughter a few months earlier as they were sitting at the breakfast table.

"Mom," Josie began in an overly innocent and manipulative voice while looking up at her mother and batting her auburn lashes, "I've been pretty good this year . . . right?"

"Yeah, you've been a fuckin' peach. What's your point?" came her mother's not-so-delicate reply.

"Well," Josie began again with demure drama, "I was just thinking that my sixth birthday is coming up, and *that* means that I'll *practically* be pushing ten! I'm starting to get *old*! And there's only *one wish* that I have before I say goodbye to this world. My only wish is to go to a theme park in Florida."

Erick gagged, causing his oatmeal to fly out of his mouth and onto the table. Maddy responded in as sweet of a voice that she could muster, "Well, that's really sweet, but numero uno, you're not going to die for, like, eighty years or something, so I think you've got some time to play with, and numero two-o, wouldn't you rather have a pony or a car or something? And numero three-o, your father and I have already been there. It's . . . umm . . . overrated."

"Mom," Josie retorted, "where would we keep a pony? Besides, I was thinking that would be for my *tenth* birthday to keep me from falling into a midlife crisis. And the car, *obviously*, would be for my sixteenth birthday. I can't use it until then. And I'm sure they've added all kinds of attractions since you were there. *Please*, Mom . . . Dad . . . *please*? Going to that park will be my most vivid memory ever!"

"Well . . . she has *that* part right," Erick muttered under his breath before saying, "You know what, I think that's a great idea! If my little girl wants to go to that park, then my little girl is going to that park! C'mon, baby . . . let's book it."

"Oooookaaaay . . . we will. If we can," Maddy replied hesitantly.

She looked down and smiled as her daughter was sitting there wearing her large-eared novelty hat while chewing on her improperly dressed hot dog and watching the animated flurry of colors. She thought back to how she had dreamed the very same thing as a child. It wasn't until she had met and married her prince that she was finally able to fulfill that childhood dream. It was the most wonderful honeymoon in the history of the world, and this would be the greatest birthday in the history of the world. They would just have to stay out of theme park jail this time. Maddy dug into the top shelf of the closet and found the final item that needed to be packed. "Well . . . hello there, old friend," Maddy said reverentially as she gently placed her own novelty hat into her suitcase and shed a single tear of joyful anticipation.

Josie's Birthday Trip, Day 1

Josie came bounding into the vast lobby, dragging her animated- character-adorned pink suitcase behind her, followed by an equally exuberant Maddy, carrying only her purse. Erick brought up the rear wearing an exhausted, sweating face while carrying two overly packed large suitcases.

"Okay, here we are!" Maddy exclaimed as she picked up her delighted daughter and twirled her around, nearly knocking Josie into a family who was patiently waiting for their turn in line. "I'll just go check in, and then, my loves, it will be time for some fu—fantastic theme park magic!"

Erick stood and listened to his wife's conversation with the check-in clerk in anticipation. He could only hear one side of the conversation as the clerk was protected behind bulletproof glass. This had been made necessary because of the mass shooting in 2027, one of many throughout theme parks that year. A deplorable and evil man came in armed with an AR- 15 and murdered twenty-three adults and seventeen children in a vicious and cowardly hail of lead that tore people's limbs from their bodies and ripped their heads and torsos apart. Novelty hats were seen strewn about everywhere, covered in bullet holes, blood, and gore. The mass shooting was the direct result of radical social media sites and "mainstream" right- wing television networks promoting the latest tin-foil-hat conspiracy theory that Jewish people were indoctrinating children to become "gay" through subliminal images in animated movies and signs throughout family theme parks. There were five such shootings that year. The summer of 2027 became known as the year that children's dreams died.

Erick listened attentively and then winced as he heard his beloved wife bellow, "What the *fuck* do you mean you've canceled our reservation? That was fuckin' seven years ago! You can't hold that against us *now*! I promise! We'll watch our fuckin' language and be on our best behavior! Oh, fine . . . *fuck you*! This place is infested with rodents anyway!"

Maddy kneeled before her daughter, took off the headphones that she was wearing, and said, "Hey, sweetie . . . you wanna see California?"

The Sommers-Parker family was then escorted out of the building by two security guards. "Wow, you guys are much bigger than the ones a few years ago," Maddy stated to the unamused security detail. As they were being led out, Josie broke away and laid her novelty hat on the memorial for the shooting victims and said a silent prayer. "We will never forget you," she whispered sincerely to the forty engraved names on the shining black granite.

On the cab ride back to the airport, Josie looked at her parents sternly and said, "Okay, I'm not going to get upset. Just tell me what you did that has gotten me barred from this park."

"Well," Maddy began cautiously, "you need to understand, sweetie, that your father and I were much younger then and not nearly as mature as we are now, so . . . we just got into a little trouble, and they *totally* overreacted. That's all. But all is not lost because a great park in California awaits us!"

"Mom . . . Dad," Josie patiently replied, "you were both adults seven years ago, and I *highly* doubt that you have matured all that much. And I doubt they overreacted. If you acted then like you act now, then I can understand why they kicked you out. So please . . . *please* don't embarrass me in California . . . okay?"

"We won't, sweetie," Erick promised as he kissed his beloved daughter on her slightly freckled forehead. Josie's official birthday was celebrated while eating a snack cake on an airplane bound for Los Angeles.

Josie's Birthday Trip, Day 2

"What the *fuck* do you mean we can't come in?" Maddy yelled at the quivering teenage girl behind the bulletproof glass at the theme park in California. "We haven't even been here! We're on what? What fuckin' list? You mean *everywhere*? Every park in the fuckin' *world*? Oh, fuck this!"

Josie was playing a game on her device and wearing headphones, attempting to not be involved as Maddy approached her husband and said, "Well, fuck. We can mass murder fascists, but we can't get into a theme park? Really? Good thing the Twins aren't here. One disappointed look on Josie's face, and this place would be rubble. Okay, I have an idea. Let me make a call."

Erick stood beside his wife nervously as she said into her phone, "Hey there, it's Maddy. Oh . . . *that* isn't necessary but thank you *so much* for your support. It really means a lot. Anywhooo . . . do you have any connections with your local theme park? Yeah? Well, there seems to be a bit of a clerical error, and I've been told we're on some sort of a list. I know, right? It's like we're fuckin' international terrorists or something! So, can you get us in? Okay, cool! We'll be there tomorrow! Oh, one more thing. How did that . . . umm . . . thing go the other night? Yeah? He's not gonna wake up? Okay, cool. Nice job and thanks!"

Maddy gave her husband a grin and a nod before kneeling once again before her daughter and taking off her headphones. "Hey, sweetie, I was just thinking. You know, *any* little American girl can celebrate her birthday in her home country. So . . . you wanna go to Paris?"

"Oh, mon oui!" Josie shrieked as she hugged her mother. "Maintenant je peux pratiquer mon français!"

A bewildered Maddy looked up at her husband and then back at her daughter. "What did you just say?"

"I said," Josie explained, "'Oh my, yes! Now I can practice my French!'"

"Wh-what?" a confused Maddy inquired. "Whe-when did you learn French?"

"Right after I learned Italian . . . *duh, Mom*," came Josie's dismissive reply.

"Wait a second," Erick chimed in. "Are you telling us that you know *three languages*? How is it that you know three fuckin' languages? Why didn't you tell us?"

"Well, Dad," Josie began once again, "actually, I know four. English, of course. Then I learned Spanish, Italian, and now French. But I wouldn't call myself an expert. I'm still not very well-versed in the particular regional dialects, but I know enough to get by. I teach myself by taking my most- read comic books and then translating them into whatever language I'm studying. Then, I reread those comics over and over in my new language. It usually takes about twenty comics before I get it down pretty well."

Maddy and Erick just shook their bewildered heads at their amazing daughter before Maddy said, "Okay, security's here. We'd better just go now."

Josie's Birthday Trip, Day 3

As the cautiously optimistic family was on their transcontinental flight to Europe, Erick was reading an article and exclaimed, "Those fuckin' fascists. Now they're trying—again—to take over local school boards. I swear, if they try to indoctrinate *my* kid into their fascist bullshit, I'm gonna—"

"Dad," Josie calmly interjected as she innocently looked up and batted her eyelashes at him, "violence is never the answer. If we can just show people how much more powerful love and understanding is, then they will be all right. If we can just have them see how beautiful the world can be and how they can make it an even *more* beautiful world, then they will be all right. We just need to show them how to open up their heart. Violence begets violence and is never the answer."

Maddy looked at her husband and whispered to him, "Are you *sure* this is *our* kid?" before addressing her daughter, "What about people who *can't* understand love and understanding? Who *don't* care about others? Who only care about themselves?"

"Oh, Mom, there's *nobody* like that in the world. *Everybody* can understand love in their own way. It's just up to the rest of us to reach out and *teach* them how to love."

"Oh really?" Erick replied as he was now eager to engage his brilliant daughter in this debate, which would have been far too sophisticated for most any other six-year-old. "How about the Nazis who marched over *six million* innocent people into gas chambers? Shot them in cold blood with firing squads and watched as their dead bodies fell into mass graves? Used their flesh for soap and lampshades? Should the world have just laid down their arms and allowed the fascists to continue their murderous rampage? Should they have been allowed to take over the world? What about the people who are murdering and running innocent people off their land and homes and jobs in our own country *right now*? What about them? What about the man who gunned down those forty men, women, and children you just paid tribute to? Are you saying that *they* have the capacity to love? To understand? To be empathetic to others? Are you saying that they have a soul? Because if you are, then I am going to have to strongly disagree with you. I'm sorry, sweetie . . . but there *is* evil in this world. True evil. And sometimes the only way to combat true evil is through violence. It had to happen in World War II, and it has had to happen at other times too. Yes, there are probably many more examples where violence was unnecessary. But if you are confronted with someone who has no soul, who has no capacity to be empathetic toward others, who delights in watching other people suffer . . . then violence may be the only alternative to stop them from brutalizing innocent others. I'm sorry, but that's just how the world is. I wish it weren't. I wish that I could see the world through *your* eyes. But I can't. I've seen too much to convince me otherwise. They can believe whatever they want to believe, but when their beliefs become a call to action and they begin terrorizing, beating, and murdering innocent people, well, then it is up to society to take a stand. Otherwise, they won't *ever* stop. They won't *ever* be satisfied. We can sit here and talk about butterflies and rainbows and unicorns—all that we want. But while we're doing that, they are putting a fucking bullet into their neighbor's head. They kill their neighbors because they look different. Because they love different. Because they worship different. Because they vote different. They will murder people *just because* they are *different*."

Josie sat there in reflective silence for several minutes. She then said, "Well . . . I have yet to meet anyone like that. But if what you are saying is true—if it is *true* that there are truly evil people in our world— well . . . *maybe* the use of violence is justified. Maybe. But not before we do everything that we can to show those people the power of love. That is what I believe now and shall always believe."

"And we love that about you," Erick softly stated to his beloved daughter as he placed a delicate kiss on the top of her auburn curls. "I hope that you can always believe that. I truly do."

As the plane was taxiing at the Paris airport, Josie was gazing out of her window and reflecting on her earlier conversation with her parents. She was thinking about the six million innocent people who perished at the hands of the Nazis. She was thinking about the people who were being murdered and terrorized in some counties throughout her country. And she mostly thought about the innocent families who had been mowed down by gunfire at theme parks throughout the United States in 2027. A small ember began glowing in Josie's soul as she thought to herself, *Well, maybe* that *douchebag deserved to die.*

Josie's Birthday Trip, Days 4 to 7

"That's what I'm fuckin' *talkin'* about!" Maddy yelled out as she took her park tickets and resort reservations from the check-in clerk at the latest theme park. Erick picked up his daughter and spun her around as she squealed and cackled in delight.

For the next four days, the elated family rode rides, bought souvenirs, and ate *way* too much junk food. Following a carb-and-sugar-infused lunch on day two, Maddy held her stomach and said, "Oh, I don't feel so well. I think that maybe I should take a break from the rides for a while."

"Yes, I think that is a very good idea," came Erick's relieved response. "Oh, come on, Mom!" Josie screamed out. "Don't be a wimp! This ride is going to be incredible!"

"Wimp, huh?" Maddy barked as she got up from her park bench.

Erick immediately stood in front of her and said, "Just sit down and settle your stomach. You don't need to prove how tough you are to a six-year-old."

"Yeah, yeah, yeah," Maddy replied as she looked down at her daughter out of the corner of her eye, "but she'd *better not* call me a wimp again. I'll take her on so many fuckin' rides that she'll *never* get her equilibrium back!"

"I know, dear, I know," a pacifying Erick stated before saying, "C'mon, your mom's being a wimp! Let's go have some fun!"

Maddy burst out laughing as she saw her cherished family exiting the ride. "Sorry, Dad," Josie expressed regretfully to her father, whose shirt was covered in vomit, "I guess maybe I ate too much."

"Yup," an exasperated Erick responded, "you are definitely your mother's daughter."

Pictures were taken with every mascot, at every restaurant, at every shop, and at every attraction. When Maddy wanted to take her picture by herself, there was almost always the smiling image of a photobombing Josie in the background or to the side of the frame. When Josie wanted to take her picture by herself, there was almost always the smiling image of a photo-bombing Maddy in the background or to the side of the frame. Josie went on every ride that there was. Maddy went on all but one. Erick became exhausted by day three and ended up going on only half of the rides. He was then begrudgingly demoted to holding the bags that were full of stuffed animals, shirts, toys, and various souvenirs.

While Josie was playing in a well-monitored play area and speaking near-fluent French with her new friends, Maddy nudged her husband in the ribs and said in her mischievous voice, "Hey, there's a men's room over there!"

"Yeah, so?" a confused Erick responded.

"C'mon, let's go in there. It'll be . . . y'know . . . fun, heh-heh-heh."

Erick, now realizing what his ornery and somewhat-randy wife was suggesting, simply said, "Nope. We can't get kicked out, especially for *that* and especially with Josie here."

"C'mon! We *won't* get caught, and we *can't* get kicked out. I've seen to that," Maddy countered pleadingly. She then cocked her head, stared into his eyes, and began furiously batting her copper lashes as she said suggestively, "Remember the punk club a few years ago? *That* was fun, wasn't it?"

Twenty minutes later, the giggling pair could be seen exiting the men's room arm in arm to the appalled glares of several other park attendees. "C'mon, sweetie!" Maddy exclaimed to her daughter. "Let's go to another park. We've done just about everything that we can here!"

On the final night of the trip, a blindfolded and giggling Josie was taken into a large dance hall and seated at the head of the table. As "Birthday" by the Beatles began playing, her blindfold was taken off, and what she witnessed overwhelmed her young soul with absolute joy. There was a huge three-level white cake with pink frosting. There was every theme park mascot, including every princess, prince, and nonhuman-animated character whose image had ever flickered on a movie screen. There were loads and loads of brightly wrapped packages. But most importantly, there was her great-aunt Blair. And her great-aunt Patty. And Patty's wife, Jacklyn. And Jules with her husband, Jerry. There was Lucy with her girlfriend, Jennifer. There was Rosa and her new boyfriend, Gregory. There was Henri and his son, Lionnel. There was even a very awkward- looking and sweating Rod. Even her more extended family that she did not see as often were there. Sean from the bookstore. Pastor Tim and his husband, Jeremy. Charlie and Rosetta, who would come over to the house every other week and sing with her father. And standing in the middle of them all were her beaming, tear-filled, and proud parents.

As Josie tore through the cornucopia of presents under the ever- watchful eyes of Vai, Adam, and Aaron, she exclaimed, "This is the best birthday party in the history of the world! Thank you all so much!"

There was one final gift to be opened. As Adam handed Josie the medium-sized box, he said, "Here, Josie. This is from Vai, Aaron, and me. We made it ourselves. We hope that you like it."

"Whoa, whoa, whoa!" Maddy immediately exclaimed as she got up from her chair.

Blair put her index finger up and said softly, "It's all right, dear. There is nothing to be worried about. I helped them with it myself."

"Well," Maddy replied suspiciously, "there'd better *not* be anything to fuckin' worry about."

Josie ripped the package open and lifted the lid of the box. She took out its contents, and tears began streaming down her tender face as she looked at page after page of photographs of herself with all her most cherished people from her life. "We made you a photo album," Adam stated, followed by Aaron's, "Yes. We have taken a picture of you every day that we have been with you since you were born. There are pictures of you with everyone that you love. We wanted you to have this because we love you. We hope that you like it."

The overwhelmed little girl couldn't speak. She got down from her chair and enveloped her three best friends and guardians in the warmest embrace of her life. Josie knew that she was safe. Josie knew that she was loved. Josie knew that she was home.

Following the party, Maddy went up to Vai and the Twins and said, "Ummm . . . sorry that I doubted you, but . . . that was pretty fuckin' sentimental coming from you three."

"Yes. Quite sentimental indeed," Adam replied, followed by his brother, "We are misunderstood. People don't believe that we are capable of loving someone else, but that is not true. We are capable of loving those we deem worthy of our love. We simply have not encountered very many of these people because many people are—as you would say, Aunt Maddy—fuckin' douchebags."

Birthday Trip Totals

- Two cussed out check-in clerks
- Two parks refused entry to
- One park entered
- Three very long flights
- One family nearly knocked over by Josie being twirled
- One novelty hat donated to a memorial
- Two states visited
- Two countries visited
- Four languages identified that Josie is fluent in
- One moment of disillusionment followed by an epiphany
- One shirt covered in vomit
- Fifty-four rides
- 226 pictures of Maddy photobombing Josie
- 318 pictures of Josie photobombing Maddy
- Zero pictures of Erick
- One semi-public intimate encounter

- Four fireworks displays
- One best birthday party in the history of the world

As Erick was driving his fatigued family home from LaGuardia Airport, Josie yelled out, "Stop the car, Dad!"

Erick immediately put on his brakes and pulled over. Josie jumped out of the car to his father's protestations. "Josie, where are you going? Get back in here!"

Josie immediately returned holding a food and affection-starved Beagle puppy. "Look, Dad. He's homeless. We need to take him home . . . *please*?" Erick looked at his drowsy wife, who simply said, "Fuckin' whatever. Why should today be any different?"

"Yay!" Josie squealed out as she fed the puppy the remainder of her ham sandwich.

Birthday Trip Totals: Updated

- One saved puppy

CHAPTER 58

iPhone

"Do you remember the good old days when we just went out and murdered individual scumbags?" Erick asked his wife as the pair lay in bed watching *I Spit on Your Grave*.

"Uh-huh," Maddy replied lazily.

"Well, wouldn't it be nice to just do *that* again for a while? I mean . . . it's New York. There *must* be some worthy candidates lingering around just under our radar. We could reconnect with our community network of little birdies and . . . y'know . . . have some fun for a while."

"Well," an intrigued Maddy replied, "that *would* be fun, but I think we need to keep an eye on the prize here. We have fuckin' CHARLIE on the run. After we took out their operations in New York, Minnesota, Missouri, and Iowa, there were only two units left in the country. And after I sent my message that said, 'You got the picture now, motherfuckers?' the units in Texas and Kansas just split up without a fight like the little pussies that they are. They disappeared, and the citizens of those counties have been able to run out the fascist oligarchs and reclaim their lives."

"Exactly," Erick replied. "There is *still* a grave threat from people being indoctrinated in bullshit propaganda, but the militarization of UAM's operation is over. It's up to the *people* now to decide their own fate, which frees us up to do what we do best. Hide in dark corners, jump out, and fuck some pricks up!"

"Okay, you're right about one thing," Maddy responded as she sat up and looked at her beloved husband. "They aren't *nearly* as organized anymore. But they *are* still a danger. They have broken up into really small packs and are planning terrorist attacks in major cities. They still believe that they can start a race war. We definitely put a dent in their operations, but they aren't done yet. I think that we need to focus on these smaller units, especially if they show up here. We take them out, then I promise our life can get back to normal. We can just focus on being small-time vigilante serial killers without all the international intrigue . . . okay?"

"Well . . . I suppose you're right," a pouting Erick replied. "But if I can't do *that*, then I want some ice cream!"

"Well, *now*, you're fuckin' talkin'!" Maddy exclaimed as she jumped out of bed and made her way to the kitchen. She returned a few minutes later with a disappointed look on her face.

"Hey! Where's the ice cream?" Erick urgently inquired.

"Well . . . I don't know how to break this to you but—" Maddy began explaining while looking down at her shuffling feet. "I kinda forgot that Josie and I finished it last night . . . sorry."

"Well, that's just great!" Erick exclaimed angrily. "First, I can't take out any chads, and now I can't get any ice cream. Fuck it. I'll just go to sleep then!"

"Fine!" Maddy bellowed back. "I'll just play on my phone and check my likes for a while!"

"Yeah, what else is new?" a disgruntled Erick muttered under his breath as he rolled over.

The following morning, Erick was greeted by a surprisingly alert and chipper Maddy, who was in the kitchen, attempting to make breakfast for her family. "What's all *this* then?" a surprised Erick exclaimed as Vai, Adam, Aaron, and Josie looked up from their phones and then looked down with dread at what was supposed to be scrambled eggs.

"Well, I got up early, and I thought that I'd treat my loving family to a home-cooked breakfast! C'mon, everybody! Eat up!"

The children looked pleadingly at Erick, who just gave them a resigned nod and took a bite. "Pretty good, huh? You didn't know I could cook, didja?" a beaming Maddy exclaimed to her brood, who were attempting to force smiles upon their faces as they were forcing the overly salted and undercooked meal down their resistant throats. Adam and Aaron were heard choking before Adam spat out a portion of a shell.

Then in her singsong voice Maddy stated to her husband as she plopped upon his lap, "And I have a *very special* surprise for you." She handed him an envelope and then noticed the children looking on with curious little faces. "Hey, this is adult shit! Eyes back on your plates!" Maddy bellowed at the children as Erick opened the envelope.

"Really? You got this for me?" a moved Erick stated while gazing into his beloved wife's emerald eyes. "This is one of the nicest things that anyone has done for me. Thank you for understanding."

"You . . . are . . . welcome! You have earned this!" Maddy stated excitedly. "Now, go take your hall pass and have a good time tonight!"

Oh my god! I can't believe she's allowing me to do this! I'm so excited! Erick thought to himself as he sat on the corner of a strange bed in anticipation. Now at the age of fifty-six, he was concerned that his time was running out on these types of exploits, and he wanted to savor every instant of this upcoming encounter.

He was visibly shaking with excitement as he saw the doorknob in the bedroom begin turning. The figure entered the room and saw Erick. "Hi there!" Erick exclaimed. "Oh, thank you so much for doing this. I can't tell you how much I need this right now!"

Erick then pulled the crowbar from behind his back and lodged it into the unsuspecting man's temple. The man fell to the floor, screaming in agony as blood began oozing out from around the metal in his head.

"Oh god, that felt good," Erick stated with a hint of relief. "I've needed to fuck up one of you fucking rapists for *so long*. Sure, I've helped in taking out pseudo military fascists, but there's just nothing like a good old-fashioned thrill kill!" He violently pulled the crowbar from the man, sending small chunks of skull shrapnel flying about the room. He then proceeded to bash the man's face repeatedly with the crowbar in a blind rage until it was an unrecognizable oval of ground meat.

"Wow, that was fun. That was good. I needed that," Erick said aloud to himself with a spent satisfaction as he began disrobing and entered the hot shower.

Later that evening, Erick stepped into his own bedroom to find his beloved wife and daughter watching *Cinderella*—again. Only this time in

French with English subtitles. "Hey, you! How was your evening?" Maddy inquired in a bubbly voice.

"Good," came Erick's satisfied reply. "Really good. Thank you."

"No prob . . . I know how to take care of my man," Maddy responded before they both broke down into hysterical laughter.

"Excuse me," an annoyed Josie stated. "Could you *please* keep it down? I'm *trying* to watch the movie."

"Oh, shut up," a disregarding Maddy stated flatly before shoving her beloved daughter off the bed.

———

It was the first day of school in 2034, and the ten-year-old Josie hugged the twenty-two-year-old Vai and the nearly eighteen-year-old Twins goodbye. "Yes, Vai," Josie stated to her eldest guardian, "I will tell you if anyone messes with me. But nobody will. All you have to do to make friends is to see the kindness in other people. It's really quite simple. You three should try it sometime. And could you *please* get this kitten that followed us settled in at home? I'll give her a flea bath and put the flyers up later."

As Josie bounded with her clear backpack through the impenetrable steel doors with bulletproof glass windows toward the bank of metal detectors, Adam said as he caressed the kitten, "I do wish our Josie could always believe in that."

"Yes," Aaron responded. "Her optimism is so very nice. But unfortunately, she won't. She will see the world through our cynicism someday. It will change her. We have sadly seen it."

"But until then," Vai interjected, "we will see to it that Josie has the happiest childhood possible. C'mon, Aunt Maddy has an assignment for us."

"Oh, joy!" Adam exclaimed, followed by Aaron's "Yes! What great fun! An assignment! Oh, how I wonder what fun game we will be playing today!"

Josie enthusiastically took her seat in the front row of her new seventh-grade classroom and immediately began gleefully introducing herself to her neighboring students. The teacher entered the room, and the students dutifully pulled out their EATs (Electronic Academic Tablets). They turned them on. And nothing happened.

Panicked exclamations were heard throughout the building. "What is going on?"

"My *phone* doesn't work either!"

"My feed—I *have* to check my feed!"

"OMG! How will I *ever* LOL again?"

"My pictures of myself . . . of all my dinners . . . they are *all gone*!"

"How can I see how many *likes* my new selfie got?"

Tears began streaming down the faces of Josie's classmates as there was an announcement over the school's intercom system. "Children . . . this is your principal speaking. Please put your phones down and listen to me. Please try to remain calm. There has been an unspeakable tragedy. There has been an evil hacker who has taken out all the wireless communication systems. The only way that we can access the internet is [*gulp*] through old-fashioned phone lines connected to big, bulky laptops. We can't—I mean . . . I can't— oh my god, this is horrible!" The intercom turned to static as the principal broke down in tears. The children sat staring in shocked silence without any direction. They had no idea what to do.

"Sooooo," Josie stated as she got up from her desk and addressed her classmates, "so okay, gang, glass is half full here! Now we can actually spend some time getting to know one another, y'know, face-to-face! This is going to be a good thing, I guarantee it! Or else, my name isn't Josie Patricia Parker! And that's my name, so that's just how it's going to be!"

"Well, *that* should put a kink in the radical propagandist's plans!" a cackling Erick yelled out to Rod, Rosa, and the other twelve Coven members in the basement of a modest home in Brooklyn. "Wow! I knew you could do some shit with nature and everything, but jeezus, Rosa, you have completely outdone yourself!"

"It's all about focus and energy, Erick," Rosa explained. "Everything is energy. Positive energy and negative energy. And positive energy will *always* trump negative energy if it is used wisely and with a purity of spirit. Some people call me a witch. I am *not* a witch. I *do not* cast spells or boil up concoctions with herbs and eyes of newt. I simply have the ability to absorb and direct the energy of other living beings. And my ever-evolving twelve sisters have provided me with that endless energy. Women—*all* women—have this ability. We have been blessed with the power of creation. And when we *bond* . . . when we come together as *one* . . . we can be an unstoppable force. I have just been blessed for some reason to be more advanced in this. I don't know why. I have just always been able to reach out and *feel* and *absorb* and *direct* others' energy. This has been especially true when I form a close bond with other women. My strength carries them. And their strength carries me. Our energy is drawn together, and we become one.

"All we needed to do to overload the wireless systems and cell towers was the technical expertise of our sweet Rod to help me focus our energy on each system . . . one at a time . . . throughout the world. They will be repaired, and then . . . we will do it again . . . and again. This technology can be used for such great and beautiful things. But it has been bastardized. It has been used for our most narcissistic and immoral tendencies. To solicit *money* and *things*. To solicit *attention*. To *indoctrinate* others into hating their fellow neighbors. To *indoctrinate* others into evil, ideological cults through exploiting their loneliness and fear and sense of self-entitlement. To lure innocents into abhorrent situations of beatings, rape and murder. Our technology has outpaced our humanity, and this little trick will significantly slow down the spread of toxic, self-absorbed garbage and calls for violence by grandiose and small-minded infidels.

"Our technology has been hijacked by the lowest common denominator in our world. So if we can't *persuade* them and we can't *stop* them, then I thought that perhaps we could take away some of their tools. People will no longer be mindless zombies just staring at their screens in search of validation. They will have to *actually connect* on a personal basis with other human beings. They will not be able to find immediate gratification by sweeping left or right or whatever that is. They will actually have to go out on dates and get to know one another. They will have to form an actual personality and not present some figment of their imagination online. They will have to become a part of a real physical community again. They will not be perpetually connected to the false realities presented in these vile little electronic devices. They will have to become human again. They will have to become *humane* again.

"This won't completely stop the spread of vicious lies and brainwashing tactics by the forces of evil in this world. But it *will* slow them down. Phone lines will have to be restored. Old-fashioned modems will have to be located and dusted off. And these mental poisons will never again be conveniently held in the palm of our hand or carried on our wrist. Plus . . . as an *added* benefit . . . some of the wealthiest men on this planet who have controlled our society's discourse and self-esteem for two generations have just had their empires collapse. It will be amusing to watch them shopping with coupons at the supermarket."

"Hey! What *the fuck* did you guys just *do*?" Maddy yelled down the stairs. "I was in the middle of sending a picture out of my latte, and my screen just went blank! People *look forward* to seeing what I'm drinking every morning! I get *tons* of *likes*! Did you guys do something to fuck up the Internet service here? Rod? Erick? *GAAAAAAWD*! Would somebody please answer me!"

"Uh . . . I'll *text* you the answer, LOL!" Erick yelled out before the entire group in the basement laughed out loud.

Chapter 59

Land of Hopes and Dreams

"Well, I must admit that I wasn't a big fan of you guys knocking out the wireless systems two years ago, but . . ." Gregory admitted to his adored wife, Rosa. The Alvarez-Davenport union was at the Sommers-Parker home, getting ready to go to Patty's combined retirement and eighty- fourth birthday party at her recently sold nightclub LOHAD on this now-seasonable thirty-eight-degree January evening. The club had been purchased by Sean, now thirty-eight, and the sixty-nine-year-old pairing of Charlie and Rosetta.

This new business partnership was to continue the tradition of what LOHAD was meant to represent. A white gay man in partnership with a straight black married couple to continue the tradition of a politics- and religion-free oasis in the middle of Brooklyn that fostered the acceptance and embracing of differences in everyone in society. Gay, straight, trans, black, white, hispanic, asian, indigenous, male, female, nonbinary, blue collar, white collar, old, or young. It didn't matter. Everyone was welcome to get fucked up, listen to Patty's raucous playlist, and gyrate in a sweaty frenzy as the party's architect joyfully watched over the proceedings with her wife, Jacklyn. Everyone was welcome except one group of people: assholes. Not assholes who wore Barry Manilow T-shirts. *Real* assholes.

Assholes who attempted to bully others. Who attempted to abuse others. Whose worldview and sense of self-entitlement was so warped that they believed that they and they alone had the freedom to take freedom away from others through any means necessary, including violence. *Those* types of people were persona non grata. Upon spotting one, Patty would bellow out in her deepening voice, "Get this motherfucker out of here! Did you not read the sign? No Assholes Allowed! What about that do you not understand?" She would then personally shove the offender out onto the street to a roar of applause and laughter. The party would be rejoined as soon as Patty would turn up the volume and play "Let's Get Fucked Up" by The Cramps.

This particular evening would be a jubilant celebration of Patty's life and accomplishments. Her lifelong career as a nurse at an assisted-living facility. Her tireless efforts to save lives during the tragic pandemic of the early 2020s. Her love and adoration for her family, especially her sister, niece, and great-niece. Her love of wine, women, and song, not necessarily in that order or with equal frequency. There would be guest speakers and a slideshow complete with a musical accompaniment of some of her favorite punk rave-ups. It would culminate in the passing of the torch, represented by the micro-phone from the DJ stand, to Charlie, Rosetta, and Sean, who would then sign the purchase agreement. Then the real party would begin with food catered by Blair. There would be free-flowing drinks, music, and, for the first time in a *very* long time, karaoke.

"Yeah . . . it's real fuckin' great!" Maddy angrily exclaimed in response to Gregory's observation. "*Reeeaaal* fuckin' great. I haven't sung karaoke in fuckin' years. And what songs do I have to choose from? Well, thanks to *you*, motherfuckers"—Maddy then glared at Rod, Rosa, and her beloved husband before continuing—"*now* my song selection is limited to whatever lame shit Erick has on those fuckin' CDGs. It's fuckin' 1995 again because most of the phone lines around the country are still not up, and it's nearly *impossible* to find a working modem! Yeah . . . *real* fuckin' great."

"Maddy," Erick responded in a scolding tone, "chill the fuck out. *So sorry* that you are slightly inconvenienced at not having every song at your finger-tips but look at what has happened over the last two years. Because people now have limited access to the internet, they aren't constantly *inundated* by brainwashing bullshit, whether that be ads from so-called influencers trying to get you to buy some bullshit that nobody needs to ads from white nation-alist fascist fucks who indoctrinate the vulnerable into engaging in violent frenzies.

"Look at how many people have woken up from their haze and realized that they had been duped by an idol-worshipping cult, just like your father had done. Look at how communities are coming together again. How people are now a part of their actual community because their fake online community isn't available as easily. Look at how weakened the UAM and splinter CHARLIE units are throughout the world and at how people, regardless of their political ideology, are voting and accepting the results of the fair elections. People once again are putting out their yard signs in support of their chosen political candidates, and once the election is over, they pull up their yard signs, walk across the lawn, and invite their neighbors over for dinner. There aren't any more political 'caravans' rumbling down the roads terrorizing innocent people and families just because of a political sticker they have on their bumper. The world is saner now. It isn't perfect. The UAM and their hard-core followers are still a threat. But those types . . . the self-entitled fascists . . . have *always* been a threat. And they always will be. So it isn't perfect . . . but it *is* saner. More compassionate. More empathetic. More humane.

"Not only that, but look at the reduction of suicides, especially among teenagers, because of the decline in online bullying. Look at the reduction in online sexual predators. Look at the reduction in people diagnosed with depression because they can now be a part of a supportive community and not be subjected to constant images of what a perfect person is supposed to look like or possess or believe. People are working again and not just wasting their time with their silly computer games. People are taking pride in being productive again. People are taking pride in the journey of discovering who they *truly are* without a little box constantly telling them who they *should be*. Yeah . . . it's fuckin' 1995 again, and 1995 was a pretty good year, so I have no regrets."

The forty-eight but looking-closer-to-thirty-five-year-old Maddy stood there with her arms crossed and tapped her foot while wearing an annoyed expression on her slightly befreckled face. She looked at her sixty-year-old but looking-closer-to-sixty-year-old prized husband of nearly thirteen years. She cocked her head back as though she were a cobra ready to strike. She opened her mouth and then realized that she had no venom.

"Yeah . . . well . . . I suppose you make a few good points . . . maybe. . . but . . . well . . ." Maddy, not ready to *completely* concede the battle, concluded, "but I *still* need to communicate with walkie-talkies when we're out on a mission! That's not real convenient now, *is it*? And my adoring public *still* doesn't know what I'm drinking each morning! And then there's still the little issue of my song selection tonight! So what are you going to do about *that*, Mr. Know-It-All?"

Erick went up to his wife and took her in his arms. He looked deeply into her emerald-green eyes and smiled before saying, "Nothing. I'm not going to do anything about that. I'm going to just sit in the audience and cherish every note that comes out of your beautiful mouth."

"Okay," Maddy stated in a defeated voice, "you fuckin' win." The pair held each other and exploded into laughter. This kittenish war had been waging for thirteen years, and neither of the combatants was prepared to lay down their arms anytime soon.

"Are you two ready to go yet? We're going to be late," came the chilled and flat inquiry from Jules. "Just knock off the love fest. It's been over thirteen years. This shit is getting old."

"Yeah, it's time to get going. We're going to be late," a graying Jerry dutifully agreed with his wife.

"Yes, dear, I have so much food in the refrigerator there that I need to put out. We really need to go," came Blair's contribution as Henri began helping Lionnel put on his coat.

"Nope . . . not yet . . . right, Josie?" Maddy replied.

"Right, Mom!" the nearly twelve-year-old Josie enthusiastically declared as she was being flanked by Vai and the Twins. "We're going to show up fashionably late. We're going to make a *statement* when we go to this party. Just imagine all the eyes that will be on us as we strut into the room in our party dresses as my mom and I's cool song plays! It will be so fun! Aunt Patty will love it!"

"What's your cool song?" an intrigued Erick inquired.

"You'll just have to wait to find out, Dad," came Josie's coy response in a singsong voice while wearing a mischievous smile.

"Fuck . . . you're so much like your mother it's scary," Erick replied as he smiled and shook his head at his daughter.

"Yes, very much like her," Adam stated, followed by Aaron's, "Yes. More than you know. We have seen it. We have seen—" Vai immediately put her index fingers in front of the pair, and they became silent. A chill of dreaded resignation fell over Blair as she watched the scene.

As the large party limousine was pulling up to the home, Rosa began violently shaking. "Rosa!" Gregory yelled out as he grabbed her and gently laid her twitching body onto the couch. "Sh-she's having one of her seizures. I'm sure she'll be fine. I've seen her do this before. She just needs time to come out of it. Henri, could you please stay with us? We'll get her settled and join you at the party in a while. You, folks, just go ahead. I'm sure she'll be fine."

As the rest of the group made their way into the limousine, a sweating Rosa began softly stuttering out of her frothing mouth, "It's horrible. It's horrible. It's horrible . . ."

The limousine turned the corner a block away from the bar, and all the jubilant faces were immediately illuminated in flashing red and blue. LOHAD was completely surrounded by police cars and ambulances. "Wow! What's with all the lights?" Josie innocently inquired.

"Don't fuckin' look! Vai . . Twins . . . keep her in the car!" Maddy screamed out before flying out of the limousine with her husband directly behind her. The pair was a blur that the police had no chance of stopping. They entered the front door of the bar, and what they witnessed was a war zone.

It was a massacre. Everywhere that the eye could see was absolute carnage. There were over forty bodies that had been ripped apart by multiple gunshots, lying in pools of their own blood. Sean's lifeless frame was hanging over the bar. Charlie and Rosetta were clinging to one another. Their faces were unrecognizable. Maddy and Erick were only able to identify them by their blood-soaked wedding rings and the telltale love that their body positions conveyed for one another. Jacklyn was lying on the dance floor with many of the other party attendees, with her intestines sliding out of her abdomen. The rain of bullets had nearly sliced her in two. And the guest of honor, Patty, was lying face down behind the DJ stand. It was obvious to the pair that she had been forced upon her knees and executed in the back of the head. Her skull earring dangled out of her matted gray-and-crimson hair. She was clutching a Bruce Springsteen CD that was completely saturated with her blood. The opening song for the evening would have been "Land of Hope and Dreams."

"M-mom? D-dad?" Josie's weakened and confused voice came from behind them. "W-what is g-going o-on? Wh-why?"

Maddy gave Vai and the twins a look of disappointment before kneeling before her daughter. "Okay, sweetie, we have some work to do to figure this out, okay? I need you to go with Vai and the twins now." She then turned to Vai and said, "Get the emergency evacuation bags and get to the airport. I don't give a fuck where you go. Just get her out of here—now. Don't call us. We'll get in touch when it's safe. Now go!"

"Of course, Aunt Maddy," came Vai's dutiful reply as she took Josie by the hand. The foursome made their way past Blair, whose drawn face was frozen in despair.

"And, Vai," Erick interjected before they exited the shattered doors of the morbid building, "you three be prepared . . . understand?"

Vai gave a nod of acknowledgment and went to the limousine with Josie's bewildered face looking back at her parents.

Josie went into her bedroom to retrieve her emergency evacuation bag. It was a black duffel, just like her mom's. Only Josie's bag contained many different items. Flower-adorned tops, pants, and skirts, many of which she had designed and sewn herself. A wide assortment of snacks. A modest makeup kit. Hair and personal hygiene products. Her stuffed manatee. A large assortment of brightly colored comic books. And as many animated movies that would fit. The only item that might have been welcome in her mother's bag was a small bow-and-arrow set.

She grabbed her bag and looked at her bed. Her pussycats, Hunky and Dory, were lying there peacefully. She went over and stroked their fur. She then discovered that their bodies were stiff. The fifteen-year-old siblings had passed away quietly earlier in the evening. They died the way that they had lived: together. Josie just stared at them in sorrowful disbelief. She had not been there to say goodbye to them. Just as she had been unable to say goodbye to Charlie. To Rosetta. To Sean. To her great-aunt Patty. They were all gone in a blink of her tortured green eyes. There was no warning, and Josie realized just how fragile and fleeting life could be. She took a flower out of her hair and laid it between her two precious friends. She said a silent prayer for all the pain in the world to go away. She petted her latest adopted cats, the mother-daughter combo of Ziggy and Stardust. She walked to the door in silence and turned the light out on her childhood at the age of nearly twelve.

"B-baby?" a shocked and stuttering Maddy stated to her beloved husband as he was tightly holding her in the middle of the blood-soaked devastation that had been their oasis. "T-they will never s-stop. They w-will never s-stop until we're all dead. E-everyone who d-disagrees w-with them. They will k-kill us all. We can't stop them. I-I-I c-can't s-stop them. I can't d-do this anymore. It's too p-painful. P-please just h-hold me. Never l-let me go. P-please."

Tears were streaming down Erick's beleaguered face as he lightly kissed his cherished wife on top of her copper locks and softly said, "I'll never leave you. Even when I'm gone, I will always be with you. I promise you that."

The harvest-gold rotary phone behind the bar then rang. Maddy walked over and picked the receiver up from its carriage. "Hello? Y-yes, Aunt Blair? Are you home?"

Chapter 60

Darklands

"Hello, dear. Yes, I made it home. I need to speak with you now," came Blair's methodically calm voice over the end of Maddy's phone. As Blair was speaking to her cherished niece, she was staring at framed pictures that she had laid out on her coffee table surrounding the gaudy chicken-shaped candy dish. There was a wedding photo of herself with her Joseph. A ridiculous wedding photo of a laughing Maddy and Erick, covered in gooey cake. A group picture from Maddy's college days with her adopted nieces, Sam, Jules, Lucy, and Kristy. A picture of a photobombing and smiling Josie behind her proud parents. A slight smile was allowed to penetrate through the darkness before she began addressing her niece.

"Please listen to me. I'm too old and tired and torn apart to continue this, so I am . . . retiring. It is up to you now. Do not get caught up in your emotions. Do not act irrationally. Use Erick as your support. As your anchor. And if you need further guidance, just listen to the birds singing in the trees. My Joseph will be watching over you and will carry you in your darkest times. Just open up your heart, and he will be there. Protect our Josie. She is our future. Yes, dear. Please talk to me tomorrow. I very much look forward to hearing your voice. Try to sleep well tonight, my dearest. I love you . . . goodbye."

Blair picked up the photo of her adored sister Patty and held it over her heart. She reached up and ran her fingers through the lush long raven strands atop her head. She pulled the wig off, revealing a completely bald head. No one but Patty had known about the battle that she had waged with terminal cancer for the previous two years. It was only Patty who had been there to nurse her through her most difficult days of gut-wrenching vomit and excruciating pain that felt like knives slicing throughout her entire body. With Patty's selfless assistance, Blair was able to continue to play the part of the emotionless matriarch. She *had* to be strong for the others. She could not allow herself to be viewed as weak. Otherwise, her cherished family might be placed in further jeopardy. And now Patty was gone in a most merciless fashion.

She chuckled to herself as she thought about how naive she and her Joseph had been to think that they could abandon Patty after stealing their newborn niece away. They had never spoken about it, but they both knew that Patty would have been sent for at the appropriate time. She knew in her soul that she would be unable to live without her cherished sister by her side. Blair then began laughing out loud as past bawdy statements from her sister echoed randomly through her consciousness.

C'mon, Blair, I don't give a fuck how much you hurt! You've gotta eat! Now open your mouth and take this fuckin' soup!

Sorry, Dad! I'll turn it down!

What we are listening to, my dearest, is . . . the music of the gods!

I think this paper doll looks prettier in just her underwear.

Oh, Blair, you should have seen this giggling little piece that I picked up last night!

Leave my fuckin' brother alone, or I'll fuckin' kill ya!

Why didn't I get sicker from COVID? Clean fuckin' living!

Just fuckin' trap him, Blair! It's almost winter. He's a handyman, right? Who loves to play the hero, right? Wait for a really fuckin' snowy night. Do something to a water pipe and call him to come over. Sound really fuckin' desperate. Answer the door with the shortest bath towel you've got. Once he's fixed your pipe, comment on how bad the snow is outside and invite him to stay over to, y'know, fix your pipes.

She put the picture back down in its resting place on the table and picked up a flowered porcelain teacup. She laid her stiff body down upon her plastic-covered sofa, raised the cup to her dry lips, and drank deeply. She placed the cup back upon its saucer, closed her eyes, and in a peaceful resignation said, "I'm coming home, Joseph." The last sound that Blair heard was the cheerful chirps of a small bird outside of her frost-covered windows.

———

"Josie, c'mon, please eat something," Vai pleaded in a shabby hotel room in an undisclosed location. "C'mon . . . it's your favorite. Hot dog with ketchup and tons of fries with a chocolate shake. *Please*?"

Josie just looked up at her three guardians and asked flatly, "Why did you take me in there to see that? You said to come with you. That I needed to see it. Why?"

"Josie . . . please listen to me. We didn't want for you to see that . . . but —" Vai began explaining in as tender of a manner as she could. "You are on a journey. You are like a caterpillar that has been in its cocoon. And now, you are beginning to emerge as a butterfly. You *needed* to see that. You *needed* to see what this world truly is. You *needed* to see the true evil that exists. You needed it because—"

"Because you are the one to lead us, Josie," Adam interjected.

"Yes," Aaron continued, "We have seen it. You shall be the one to lead us all. And to do that, you must understand. You must understand something about the bad men in the world. And then, Josie, we can teach you new games to play. Fun games like your parents play."

"Awww, shit," Vai muttered under her breath before Josie said, "My parents? What about my parents? Listen . . . I've seen *a lot* in the last twenty-four hours. I've *lost* a lot in the last twenty-four hours. *Why* did this happen? *Who* did this? *Why* are we in hiding? And *how* are my parents involved? I'm asking you nicely to answer me because for the first time in my life, I'm getting a not-so-nice feeling, and I don't think that you want to see that side of me. So spill it!"

Vai looked into Josie's determined green eyes, let out a resigned sigh, and said, "Okay. Your parents are going to kill me, but . . . here it goes."

Following Josie's hearing every detail of her parents' violent exploits, she sat on the corner of her bed in wide-eyed disbelief. Her mind was racing. This couldn't be true. Her parents, although a bit immature with atrocious language, couldn't be murderers. They couldn't be involved in an underground hit-man syndicate that has been taking out fascists. But why would Vai and the Twins lie? What would be their motive? And it made so much sense now. Her parents' clandestine meetings in the middle of the night dressed all in black. Her mother telling her to never look in their black duffel bags. Her being restricted from the basement because that was where Lucy kept her "toys." The knowing glances between them as news reports of a gruesome murder came across the television screen. It all made sense. And it made no sense at all. Simultaneously. Josie's emotions and intellect were overwhelmed, so she simply said, "All right. So my parents are serial killers. Sure. That makes sense, I guess. I'm just going to go to sleep now."

Josie crawled into bed wearing her smiley-face pajamas and pulled the covers up over her face. Then, Josie wept. For the first time in her life, Josie shed true tears of pain. She shed tears of loss. She shed tears of disappointment. She shed tears because her idyllic life had been a lie, and she knew that her life would never be the same again. She took her previously beloved stuffed manatee and threw it onto the stained carpeted floor and continued weeping until she fell into a dark slumber of despair.

———

Henri clung to his fourteen-year-old son, Lionnel, in tears. He was thankful that he had not been there to witness the carnage at the bar, but just the thought of it brought back tragic memories of finding his parents slaughtered at the hands of thugs and his cherished wife's severed head at the hands of different thugs.

Since his wife's murder, Henri had been focused solely on two things. Raising his son as best he could as a single parent and fighting for freedom against the violent forces of fascism. For the past several years, he had used his honed skills as a sniper to take out many deplorable men throughout the world. He had thought that his time in that fight was nearing an end. He had hoped that the international forces of evil had been beaten back enough that he might now be able to take his son and go away somewhere—anywhere. Perhaps purchase a nice cabin on a lake. Go swimming and fishing. Hiking in a dense forest. And perhaps the time was nearing to try to reconnect with his more romantic side. His passionate side. Patty's party, he had thought, would privately serve as his personal emancipation from this despicable war.

Those dreams came to a tragic close when he received the phone call from Maddy. As he watched Gregory's wife, Rosa, continue her trancelike chanting of "it's horrible," he listened to Maddy's grisly report. His heart sank for the needless loss of so many of his friends, acquaintances, and loved ones. And his heart sank once more as he realized that this phone call was also a renewed call to arms.

He looked at his son, who was becoming a strapping young man. His son who had dreams of using his precise motor skills to become a surgeon someday. He wondered if his Lionnel would have that chance. "Lionnel . . . you know what this means, don't you?" Henri asked his son as he clenched him on both sides of his adolescent face.

"Yes, Father," Lionnel answered in a voice that was suddenly deeper than it had been the day before. "It means that you have more work to do. And it means that I have more games to play with the twins. It's okay, Father. It is what we are here for. We are here to support our family. And I will stand by your side and help you with that until we are no longer needed . . . or until my dying breath . . . whichever comes first."

Henri clutched his son once again and prayed for the end of the darkness.

———

Lucy and Jennifer arrived at their flat and listened to the message on their corded answering machine. Their latest paid assassination had taken longer than expected. Plus, there was inclement weather in the Midwest that forced them to take a longer route to New York. Therefore, they missed the party, which meant that they were fortunate to be alive.

"I've got to go to Maddy's," Lucy stated bluntly to her girlfriend. "Yes . . . you go and comfort your friend," Jennifer replied in her subdued British accent.

"Yeah," Lucy responded, "there's that. But I need to check my supplies. Something tells me that I'm going to need a lot more toxins and bombs. You might want to make sure the private jet is fueled and ready to go at a moment's notice. Maddy's going to go ballistic."

Lucy gave her paramour a light kiss on the lips, put on her jacket, and walked out into the chilled evening air with vivid thoughts of her beloved adopted Aunt Patty streaming through her mind. *They really fucked up this time,* Lucy thought as she wiped a tear from her eye and strode down the darkened street.

———

Rod returned to his basement corner office/bedroom in the unassuming Brooklyn home. He fired up his computer and watched as the modem's lights began to dance. He knew the drill. He had worked with Maddy for several years now, and he knew exactly what her orders would be, so he thought he might as well get a jump on it. Plus, he needed to take his mind off how much his dear friend Josie must be hurting at this moment.

Security cameras were hacked into. It took a bit longer now without the wireless networks but not by much. Not for someone as skilled as he. He leaned forward so that his pop-bottle lenses were just a few inches from the screen.

"Yes . . . there you are. Three of you. Wearing brown shirts. Ah, and those are your names . . . I see. Lengthy criminal records . . . not surprising. Armed robbery, vandalism, battery, rape. Yes, the typical brownshirt résumé. Now, are we stupid enough to be using our credit cards? Why, yes, of course, we are. You must have some money. That's a rather nice hotel. Someone is bankrolling you. Well . . . let's just check out your bank records, shall we? Let us see just who is giving you all your money. Oh my. That is interesting. He has been quite clever flying under our radar for so long. He will be difficult to get to. But not for Murder Incorporated. Not for Maddy. You have all made a very large mistake."

Rod printed out the information for the report that he would present to Maddy upon her request. He put on his sleeping sweats, stretched, and turned his computer off. He watched silently as the screen went dark.

———

"It's horrible, it's horrible, it's horrible . . ." was all that Rosa had repeatedly been saying over the last fourteen hours. She was surrounded by a concerned Gregory and her twelve sisters. The morning sun was darkened by ominous black clouds that were foreshadowing an oncoming storm.

A sleep-deprived Maddy came downstairs, looked at the continuing scene, and said, "Fuck. *Now*, what's horrible? I think we've been through enough, Rosa! Time to fuckin' snap out of it! Oh, let me tell you about Josie's cats while we're at it. Yeah, they're dead too . . . so just knock it the fuck off and come out of your weird witch trance. Oh, fuck it. I'm going to go check on Aunt Blair. She sounded weird last night. I'll be back later."

An hour later, Rosa continued to say, "It's horrible, it's horrible, it's horrible . . ." until she let in a huge gasp of air. Her eyes rolled back to their normal position, and she urgently said, "Sisters, take hands. Maddy is broken. She has been devastated. She has lost all her energy. All her will. All her fight. We must fix her now. We must *save* her now. Focus all your will to live upon me, and I will focus on Maddy's image on the wall. And then, we'll just see what happens."

Maddy and Erick entered Blair's apartment and found her lifeless and bald body lying on the plastic-covered sofa. "Oh, Jesus Christ . . . I guess *this* was what was horrible." Maddy desperately exhaled as Erick tenderly wrapped his arms around his beloved wife once again. There was a note. Maddy opened it. Her eyes poured out tears as she read the words contained on the dampening cardstock:

Maddy, my love, this is no one's doing. It is my time. Please do not mourn me. I have had a wonderful life. I have lived and loved and drunk and sung. And I was never happier than I was with you and my Josie. It is now my time to say goodbye. And it is now your time to ascend. To protect those that you have brought together. To protect your prince. To protect your precious Josie. Protect them all, my cherished one.

And do not have a ceremony for either Patty or me. After Joseph's ceremony, Patty and I decided that we did not want anyone to make such a fuss over us. We know that you will celebrate our lives in your own way, but we do not want any public ceremony, especially now during such a dangerous time. Patty wishes her ashes to be spread upon the graves of our parents and brother. I wish my ashes to be spread upon the grave of my Joseph.

There is a note for Josie. Please give it to her should you ever decide to tell her about her legacy.

I must go now. It's teatime, my darling niece. Patty, Joseph, and I will always love you and will always be looking over you. Just listen for the birds.

PS: Stay out of my sour cream and onion chips. They are still just for me. You may have as many "old lady" mint candies as you would like. It feels good to laugh again. You too shall see that in due time.

Maddy looked at her beloved husband, gave him a slight forced smile, and immediately passed out into his arms and into her own personal darklands. The anguish of all the losses over the past day was simply too intense. She had nothing left to give. Her will to fight was over. She would pass the torch to

Lucy or someone else in the organization and just sell books for the remainder of her days. She would live until her final breath in constant grief and turmoil. She was resigned to this. Her life as she had known it was over. Her days of fighting were over.

Erick was lightly slapping his wife's flushed cheeks and yelling her name when Maddy inhaled with a huge gasp. She felt as though white-hot adrenaline had just been injected into her very soul. She looked up at him and said, "What the fuck are we doing wasting time for? We got shit to do! Please hand me that phone, baby."

She dialed the first number on the avocado-green rotary phone as she was shoveling jellied mint candies into her mouth. "Fuck . . . it takes forever just to dial a number on these fuckin' things, and I really hate this old-lady candy . . . Yeah, Rod! Listen, I have something for you. *What* did you already do? Already? Fuck . . . you are good . . . kinda creepy, but you're fuckin' good. Okay, Mr. Know-It-All, I bet you didn't guess that I was going to ask you to do *this* . . ."

"Lucy . . . you know the drill. My house in an hour. Bring Jennifer. I hope you have a lot of fuckin' gunpowder because we're gonna need it."

"Henri . . . yeah, it's me. Can you and Lionnel be at our place in like an hour? Yeah? Okay, cool . . . see ya then."

"Pastor Tim . . . it's Maddy . . . yeah, thank you so much. It's a helluva time. Listen . . . I need a huge favor from you and Jeremy . . ."

"Hey, Rosa . . . cool . . . you answered the phone. Are you done with your creepy fuckin' chanting yet? Yeah? Good. Stay there with Gregory and the rest of the Coven. We'll be there in an hour. We've got some shit to do."

Rosa hung up the phone, smiled at her sisters, and said, "Well, ladies, I guess we can do *that* shit too. Maddy's back. Maddy's back to lead us all out of the darkness."

CHAPTER 61

BLACKSTAR

"Okay, everybody, thanks for coming," Maddy began in a businesslike tone. "I don't have time for all the pomp and circumstance today, so please just keep your praise for me to yourself. You can tell me later if you would like. Okay, so the first thing that we need to do is to get these fuckers who gunned down our family and friends. Then, they will be taken to my new office in the basement of the bookstore.

"I'm converting the huge space right under the record building into a new office for the exclusive use of the Unholy Trinity. No one else is allowed in there without an invitation, got it? Rod, I have given you a list of everything that I want in there, and I trust that it can be completed in three days, yes?"

"Of course, Maddy," Rod awkwardly replied to her chest, "I have everything on order, and the work crew will begin tomorrow. It won't be a problem."

"Okay, good . . . thanks. Just remember, eyes up here," Maddy scolded before continuing. "Here's the plan, gang. We're going to capture these pussy motherfuckers alive. And I mean *alive*! I want them to be *conscious* and *able to talk*! Then, we'll get the names of everyone who is bankrolling the splinter CHARLIE groups. We're not fucking around with the small fish anymore. We're going after the *big* fish with the money and the connections. It will *most definitely* send a statement, and once the money dries up, then these little murdering fascist pricks will have to get a real job or something—if anyone will hire them with their racist fucking tattoos— but that's their problem.

"Then, hit assignments will be handed out to everyone here. I don't care how you do it. Just kill the fuckers. Gregory, I am putting you in charge of the bookstore."

"But . . . I don't know anything about running a bookstore. Why are you taking me off the field?" Gregory inquired in a disappointed voice.

"I'm not," Maddy began explaining. "Listen, I have three great assistant managers who *really* run the place. It practically runs on autopilot. I need someone there with your diplomatic skills, who will be able to calm everybody's frayed nerves after the tragic loss of Sean. I need someone there I can trust to provide oversight. And I need someone there I can trust who will keep everybody out of the basement. But most importantly, the bookstore is now going to become the conduit for all the information that we need to process. You will be responsible for taking information in and then working with Rod on obtaining the final details. You will give me a report, and then I'll pass out the assignment . . . if I don't decide to handle it personally, heh-heh-heh. Your new title will be Chief Knowledge Officer, okay?"

"Ummm . . . no . . . that isn't okay," Gregory defiantly replied. "That is a stupid and conceited title. I don't want or need a title. I understand my role. Everyone else understands my role, and that is enough."

"Yeah, fine . . . whatevs . . ." Maddy dismissively replied before continuing. "Now, Jennifer, is the plane ready to go?"

"Yes, Maddy. It has enough fuel to get you anywhere you may need to go in the Continental United States," Jennifer affirmed. "Good . . . I need to introduce Gregory at the bookstore and then pick up my—" Maddy's voice began to crack, and she looked down and wiped a tear from her eye before continuing, "I need to pick up my beloved aunts' ashes. Then, we're going to pick up Josie, Vai, and the twins before heading to Madison to spread the ashes. Finally, in three days and despite Aunt Blair's wishes, we *will* have a ceremony to celebrate Aunt Blair and Aunt Patty. It will be a fitting celebration for this moment, okay? Everybody clear?"

The entire room nodded, and Maddy concluded, "Good. I know that I don't say this often enough but thank you, everybody. Thank you for your commitment to our mission. And thank you for your commitment to me. I promise you, it doesn't go unnoticed. Long live, Vendetta Degli Oppressi!"

———

Four sullen figures walked across the barren tarmac on the upper peninsula of Michigan on a pitch-black evening.

They trudged up the stairs and entered the airplane's cabin where they were greeted by Erick, Maddy, and Lucy. "Hey, sweetie, give your dad a big hug!" Erick exclaimed as tears began streaming down his face as he embraced his beloved daughter.

"Hello, Father . . . Mother . . ." came Josie's chilled greeting.

"What's with the formalities. What happened to *mom* and *dad*?" a puzzled Erick inquired of his daughter. He looked into her determined green eyes, then immediately turned to Vai, and stated in a panicked voice, "What the fuck did you tell her?"

"U-uncle Erick . . . A-aunt M-maddy . . . I'm so sorry," a fearful Vai began explaining. "I-it's all my fault. It just slipped out and . . . well . . . you know how smart she is. We told her. We told her—"

Vai was cut off by the coldness of Josie's preadolescent voice. "*Everything*. They told me *everything*. I cannot express just how hurt and disappointed I am in both of you right now."

"Okay, sweetie?" Maddy began in a soft voice as she kneeled in front of her befreckled daughter. It was as though she were looking into a younger reflection of herself. "Let me try to explain."

"No," came Josie's curt response, "no . . . not right now. I need time to process all this. I just want to focus on taking Aunt Patty and Aunt Blair to their final resting places. Then, I assure you, we three *will* be having a little chat."

Josie took a seat in the front of the plane, pulled her hoodie over her face, and closed her eyes. Maddy sat next to Vai and the twins and said, "You know . . . I am disappointed, but . . . this isn't your fault. We never should have asked you to carry such a heavy burden . . . such a dark secret. It was bound to come out sooner or later. This is our mess. We'll take care of it, okay?"

Vai uncharacteristically broke down into tears and hugged her aunt. The tears flowed not just from the relief of guilt that had just been granted but also at the realization that her cherished mentor Blair was gone forever. She had lost her mother at the hands of a greedy insurance company. She had lost her adopted mother through a call of duty. Now she had lost the closest thing that she had to a family on this earth. Vai was clinging to Maddy out of desperation. Vai was clinging to the only emotional lifeline that she had left in the world.

Maddy and Erick began softly conversing with one another. "So . . . we're in fuckin' trouble," Erick began as though he were talking to a co- conspiring classmate sitting outside of the principal's office.

"Yup . . . this *is* a problem," Maddy replied. "I mean . . . we knew this day would come, but I was just hoping that we could squeeze a few more years of innocence out of her before she found out. And now . . . I don't know what to do. She's so fuckin' smart. If we try to convince her that what we're doing is right, then we run the risk of her wanting to get involved. We run the risk of shattering that wonderful joy that she has in her heart for humanity. We run the risk of placing her in grave danger."

"Yes," Erick agreed. "And if we *don't* convince her that what we're doing is right, if we allow her to believe that we're just murderous monsters, then . . . then—" Erick looked away from his wife and out the plane's window, unable to finish this unthinkable thought.

Maddy finished it for him. "Then we run the risk of losing our daughter forever." The pair fell into a black silence for the remainder of the short flight.

Jennifer sat in the car and scanned the black horizon for any signs of danger as Maddy, Erick, Lucy, Josie, Vai, and the twins walked toward the first gravesite in the chilled January-night air. There was no snow on the ground, which was common now in Wisconsin for January as the temperature hovered just under forty degrees.

"Hey, Grampa Hank, Gramma Betty, it's your granddaughter Maddy. I wish that I had had the chance to get to know you. And I wish that I was visiting under better circumstances. But I'm here to return your daughter to you. Please take her and protect her."

Maddy turned to another headstone and said reverentially, "Hey, Dad, I wish I had known the person that you became for my entire life. But I want you to know that I absolutely cherish those final weeks with you. I absolutely cherish knowing that my father truly loved me. Thank you for that. In your own fucked-up way, you taught me about the person that I wanted to be. And for that, I will always love you.

"Okay, Aunt P-patty," Maddy's trembling voice stated with hesitation as she opened the urn, "it's time to say goodbye now. It's time for you to join your loving family. Just give 'em hell up there, okay? And don't be hitting on any hot angels! Your wife is right there with you for fuck sakes! Show some class, heh-heh-heh. But seriously, thank you. Thank you for showing me how strong a woman can be. How caring. How compassionate. How understanding of others. Despite your gruff exterior, you were such a fuckin' pussycat just under the surface. You taught me how a woman's greatest strength was in her compassion and caring for others. Now, go smoke some dope and rock out with Hendrix. And Mama Cass. And Lux Interior, of course. And Lennon. And Keith Moon. And Bon Scott. And all the other rock gods who you are going to party with. I will honor you every time I play a song . . . and I'll try to keep Erick from playing his pussy shit."

Maddy scattered the ashes upon her family's graves, and a slight breeze tussled her copper strands. Two birds flew and sat on the branch of a tree and began singing. Maddy looked up and gave them a knowing wink before proceeding to the next gravesite.

"Well . . . since I'm here, I thought I'd place a flower on Edmund's grave. Y'know . . . out of respect," Maddy stated.

"No . . . don't," came Vai's abrupt response. "Aunt Blair didn't want you to know this, but I think that you should. Edmund was the one who set your uncle Joe up to be murdered. He did a lot of other stuff too. I know. I was there when Aunt Blair confronted him about it just before she . . . poisoned him." Josie's eyes were as wide as saucers as she awaited her mother's response to this revelation.

"Sure, sure," came Maddy's resigned reply. "Yep . . . makes sense. Why *shouldn't* everybody be a fucking backstabber? Okay, you'll just have to fill me in on that a bit later. Let's move on, shall we?"

They approached the final gravestone. Maddy pulled out the urn, a container of Butter Ripple ice cream, and a can of sour cream and onion chips. "Well, here we all are again. I thought that maybe we'd eat a little junk food, just like in the old times. Hell, Uncle Joe. My god, how I miss you. I'm here to . . . well . . . I suppose you know, but . . . I'm bringing Aunt Blair back to you. I'm not sure you're gonna want her, though! She's been kind of a pain in the ass lately! I'm just kidding. I know that you two are now going to dance for all eternity. And laugh. God, how I miss you both laughing with each other. Thank you both for showing me what true love between two people looks like. How it is possible to find someone to put all your trust in. That relationships are built not just on love but on mutual respect for one another. All the little things that you used to do for one another. Taking care of each other when you were sick. Cooking or doing the dishes even if it wasn't your turn. Buying each other little trinkets just to show your appreciation.

"Thank you for teaching me that. Thank you, Aunt Blair. Thank you for pulling me out of my personal hell and not allowing me to wallow in self-pity. Thank you for allowing me to manipulate Uncle Joe into buying me shit. I know that used to piss you off. I'm sorry, Uncle Joe, if that got you into trouble, but . . . we had some fuckin' fun now, didn't we? Thank you, Aunt Blair, for showing me when I needed to be soft and when I needed to be hard. Thank you for teaching me how to be a strong, independent woman in this patriarchal world. And thank you *both* for teaching me not to *ever* take any shit from the *motherfuckin' douchebags* of this world. I *promise* you, that is a lesson that I will *never* forget."

The ashes were poured out, and four birds sat chirping on a nearby branch as the funeral party began eating junk food and laughing through their tears.

"One more stop to make," Maddy stated as she approached a barren area of the cemetery. As she approached the unremarkable and small weathered headstone, the temperature seemed to drop by twenty degrees. "Okay," Maddy instructed, "the rest of you go to the car. I really don't want you to watch me do this. Erick, hand me that toilet paper from my bag."

As she watched her beloved family's silhouettes go over a hill in the black distance, Maddy stated in a deep growl, "Hi, Mom, you didn't think that I'd forget about *you* now, did you? Oh no. I'll *never* forget *you*. I have something *really special* for you, you heartless fucking bitch."

As they were walking to the car, Josie looked up and said, "Father . . . you realize that she isn't completely right in the head, don't you?"

"Well," Erick began through slight chuckles, "your mother *definitely* has her little idiosyncrasies."

Maddy bounced back to the car, and Erick asked, "Do you feel better now?"

"Sure do!" Maddy gleefully exclaimed. "I feel like I've just dropped twenty pounds! There's nothing like bitter hate to keep the ol' system regular!" She then stared into her daughter's emerald eyes and said, "Just remember, sweetie. Keep your friends close . . . and *fuck* your enemies. Fuck them *hard* and at *every opportunity* that you have! Now, let's get back to New York and see how the funeral arrangements are coming."

Four birds were sitting on a nearby branch, watching over the scene. One of the birds was squawking uncontrollably as though it had been hit by a fit of laughter.

———

"Mother . . . Father . . . I believe that it is time for us to have our little chat," Josie stated in a calm but determined voice. Her parents gingerly sat on the sofa with trepidation as their beloved daughter put down her archery set, approached them, and stopped three feet away. She picked up the fluffy gray Stardust and kissed her on the top of the head before placing her onto the floor tenderly.

"Okay, I'm just going to come out with it. I *will not* be taking questions or comments until the end, and what I am about to say is absolute. This is *not* a conversation. This is *not* a discussion. This is a *declaration.*"

Maddy immediately flashed back to a similar scene that she had had with her own parents upon her high school graduation. She now realized the dread and powerlessness that her parents had felt as her daughter's lithe frame stood before them, projecting the strength and determination of an invading army.

"I still don't know what to make of all this," Josie began in a matter- of-fact tone. "I'm having difficulty wrapping my head around how two people who truly love and care about other people can do such abhorrent things to other human beings. How you could *murder* other human beings. I have always believed that all people have goodness inside of them, and I now have to question that. I have to question that about *everybody* in our society. I have to question that about *you.* I have always believed that violence begets violence. It is because of *your involvement* in all this that Aunt Patty and all our other friends are dead. They are dead because of your constant escalation of violence. But now, I have to question *that* as well. When did this all start? Who started it? If there aren't people who are willing to fight back, what does that mean? If there truly *are* evil people in the world who want to dominate the defenseless, then how are they to be stopped without people like *you*?

"I don't know. I may be a genius, but I'm also a twelve-year-old little girl who hasn't experienced much. You have kept me in an idyllic bubble for my entire life, so the presence of evil in this world is completely foreign to me. So . . . I simply don't have enough data to make my final conclusions yet. So here is my plan for going forward."

Josie took out a piece of paper from her jeans pocket and unfolded it. "Okay, here it is."

JOSIE PARKER'S PLAN FOR THE IMMEDIATE FUTURE BY JOSIE PARKER

STEP 1: I will finish both high school and college by the age of fifteen. As you know, I'm taking all advanced- placement college courses while in high school, so I'll have enough credits to obtain my bachelor's degree at the same time. I'll decide on my future education or employment at that time.

STEP 2: I am going to restore LOHAD. Aunt Patty's will bestowed either the property or the proceeds from the sale of the property to me. And since it was never sold because, well, Aunt Patty, Sean, Rosetta and Charlie were all *murdered,* well, now I own it. I am placing legal control of it over to Vai until I turn eighteen, and we are going to restore LOHAD to the original vision that Aunt Patty and Jacklyn had for it, except this place will be for kids.

STEP 3: I get to buy as many comic books as I want, including *scary ones* that you haven't let me read, which is *really* ironic if you think about it! I feel as though I have some leverage here, so I'm going to get something out of it.

STEP 4: This is the most important one. You are going to tell me *every detail* of *every murder* that you commit. You are going to tell me *how* you did it, and most importantly, you are going to tell me *why* you did it. It is my hope that I will then be able to obtain a better understanding of your motivations. I will hopefully be able to determine whether this is some twisted form of the battle between good and evil or if it is a battle between two different *versions* of evil. That, then, will form the basis of my decision as to how close I will be to both of you in the future.

"And one last thing so that you do not misunderstand me. I love you both, and I always will. I have seen the love and caring in your eyes as you helped another person or said goodbye to a loved one. You can't fake that. I know that there is good in you. But I'm also afraid that there is unbridled *evil* in both of you. So, I will always love you. I just don't know if I will *like* you. And if I don't *like* you, then I don't know what impact that will have on our relationship for the rest of my life. I cannot describe to you how tormented I feel at this moment. So, I'm going to try to take my emotions out of it and look at this as analytically as I can. That is all that I have to say. Are there any questions, comments, or concerns?”

The befuddled Maddy and Erick looked at each other and began stammering. “Ummm . . . nope . . . honey, you got anything?”

“Uhhh . . . no . . . I think that I’m good.”

“No . . . I think we understand . . . but—” Erick then began crying as he pleaded with his daughter, “Could we *please* just have a hug?”

“Of course, you can!” a relieved Josie declared before jumping in between her adoring parents. They were nearly squeezing the life out of her as Josie realized that there was an ember burning inside of her that was telling her where her relationship with them was heading. But just as she would learn from them, perhaps they could learn from her as well. Maybe her parents could learn to be less judgmental and more discerning over those they served their own brand of justice to. If she couldn’t *change* their behavior, perhaps she could *moderate* it. But in the meantime, she was going to punish them for a while. After all, she had an entire list of comic books that she wanted to buy. And she now had a better understanding of the situation after she had read the note from her aunt Blair just an hour before her declaration to her parents:

My most darling Josephine, it has been my singular joy to watch you grow, and it shall be my singular joy to continue watching you from above. Yes, from above. That is where I believe that I will meet up with your aunt Patty and my Joseph. You may or may not agree with that assessment, and we will never truly know until we have all been taken from this life.

If you are reading this, then you have been told about your parents’ . . . exploits. You are probably aware of all our exploits. I do not ask that you understand. What we have done and what we do is incomprehensible. We also believe that it has been necessary. But regardless of what you might think about all this, please know this.

This life is not for you. You are not to become involved in this in any way. You are to lead in a much different way. This is why I asked Vai and the twins to look over you. You have people to protect you just as your parents and all the others have been put in place to protect the abused and downtrodden. Please understand that. You may not agree with their methods, but please do not question their motivation. Your parents are truly good people. We all are. It’s just that, in our mind, we believe that we are justified in what we do. Perhaps we are wrong. Perhaps our judgment will be much blacker than we think.

Or perhaps not. Perhaps we will all be reunited at some point in a place of joyous redemption. Be well, my darling. I will always love you.

———

As David Bowie's jazz-infused masterpiece that served as his final opus majestically glided from the church's speakers, a single black upright coffin could be seen by the silent congregation just behind the modest altar, which held the picture of an embracing and smiling Blair and Patty. The silence was broken as the church doors were kicked open. There were the repeated loud popping sounds of machine guns as a torrent of bullets went flying through the cavernous space. The church pews were torn apart as were the inhabitants sitting upon them.

Shards of wood, glass, skull, bone, tendons, and organs were whipped around the room as though being twirled by a mini tornado. A fine mist of blood hung in the air over the proceedings like an ominous crimson cloud. Anguished shrieks of pain emerged from the congregation as their bodies were subjected to the repeated tortuous devastation of the malicious weaponry.

An electrified net was then dropped upon the three brown-shirted assailants from the balcony. They writhed and seized in amped-up pain as the rubber-suited Erick and Henri pulled them from under the net and bound their convulsing hands behind their backs. The final notes to "Blackstar" faded out into the universe, and the black coffin opened. All that could be seen from the black opening was a pair of glowing emerald-green eyes until a petite figure dressed in a full-length black gown dramatically emerged.

The figure stepped out of the coffin and around the bulletproof glass in front of the altar. She strutted down the aisle before standing before them while glaring with a sadistic intensity.

"Hey there, motherfuckers," Maddy stated with a devilish grin on her face. "Thanks so much for taking care of this trash for us. You see, the people you just shot up aren't mourners of my beloved aunts. They are *your* people. These are brownshirts and other members of the murderous fascist movement that we located and kidnapped. We then bound their hands and legs, gagged them, and made them just sit in this church and wait. Wait for their brothers to arrive. But not to save them. No, to rip their *fucking bodies* apart the same way you did to *my* loved ones! We knew that you couldn't resist another shot at us. You're all so fucking stupid. So . . . I guess we all know how this is going to end. It will be up to you just how much anguish you experience before I fucking kill you. But not here. This is a house of God, and I *will not* blaspheme it in such a way. No . . . we have a *new* place to take you."

The three struggling men were taken out of a back exit and loaded into a van. Pastor Tim and Jeremy stood in the middle of the blood- soaked destruction in dumbfounded shock. "Thanks so much again, Pastor Tim . . . Jeremy," an appreciative Maddy stated as she shook the couple's hands. "I know we've made a *bit* of a mess but not to worry. There will be a clean-up crew here in just a few minutes. Oh, and as an *added* bonus, we are going to *completely* renovate this place just like you've been wanting to do—free of charge—and *noooo*, I will *not* accept any payment or naming anything after me. It is my *absolute pleasure*, and that shocked look on your faces is gratitude enough. Anyway, I gotta go fuck these guys up now, so . . . see ya Sunday!"

"What the hell have we gotten ourselves into?" Jeremy flatly inquired of his unblinking husband, who simply responded by slowly shaking his head in disbelief.

"Okay, Josie!" Maddy yelled out as she entered the front door of their home. "It's story time! You fuckin' *wanted* this shit, so now you're gonna get it! Just don't say that we didn't try to do you a favor by *keeping* this shit from you for all these years. And no, you're *not* going to sleep with us if you have nightmares. You're just going to have to deal with it."

Josie sat and politely listened as her parents regaled her with very visceral descriptions of that evening's events, complete with hopeless attempts at humor. "Oh, when I came out of that coffin, I looked like a horror movie host on TV, except *this* shit was real! We don't *need* no stinkin' special effects, heh-heh-heh!"

Following her parents' merciful conclusion, Josie simply said, "Thank you for sharing that with me and for your honesty." She went to her bedroom and crawled into bed as Ziggy and Stardust curled up next to her, purring. She opened her new scary comic book and read the first three pages. She tossed the book across the room, nearly making it into her peace sign decorated garbage can. *That isn't scary . . . not compared to what* my *life has just become. How disappointing,* she thought to herself before turning off her lamp and immediately falling into a deep, satisfying slumber.

CHAPTER 62

TWO TRIBES

The three bound, hooded struggling men were dragged to the dark basement. There was the sound of iron keys clanging and then the rusted creek of a heavy door. They were thrown upon the middle of the cold floor, and their sweat-soaked hoods were taken off to reveal a smiling Maddy, Erick, and Lucy.

"So," Maddy inquired of her partners in her singsong voice, "what do you think about our new office? Pretty cool, huh?"

"Uh . . . yeah," Erick replied as he looked around. There were various black-and-white pictures arranged haphazardly on the wood-paneled walls depicting the history of New York City. The floor was now a dark-gray marble, and the furniture was made up of a variety of midcentury modern plastic and vinyl couches and chairs in a kaleidoscope of clashing colors in front of a large traditional oak desk. There was a large assortment of lamps resting upon unmatched end tables. Blair's chicken candy dish was prominently displayed on one of them. The entire room looked as though a failing interior design student had vomited up every bad idea that they had and combined them into this monstrosity of ill-fitting bad taste. "It's . . . um . . . it's—" Erick stammered as he struggled to find the right words to say to his beloved wife's anticipatory face. "It's . . . *eclectic* . . . yep . . . that's the word —*eclectic*! But what's with the giant fish tank?" Erick, attempting to change the subject, inquired about the six-foot-wide and four-foot-tall fish tank covering the wall behind the desk.

"Oh, that!" Maddy excitedly responded. "That's the best part! That's our new fish tank that holds our new cool mascot: the piranha!"

"Oh, fuck," Erick muttered under his breath as he gazed at the nearly two dozen hideous fish swimming around the various colored pieces of coral and cheap ceramic aquarium decorations. "*Why* do we need a mascot?" Erick asked in an exasperated tone. "Are we going to put some high school kid in a piranha costume and have them hand out T-shirts outside of the house that we're committing murder in?"

"No, don't be silly," a smirking Maddy replied, "although T-shirts aren't a bad idea. I was just thinking that *any* group of serial killers can have a cool name. And we've *definitely* upped the ante by adopting a cool theme song. But *no* group of serial killers has a cool *mascot*, except for us! And the piranha is perfect! It's tenacious. It's malicious. It's deadly. And it does just what it needs to do to stay alive in a really cool, bloody way. So, it's perfect. And it's just beautiful. Plus, sometimes when we have *guests* over . . ." Maddy trailed off to then glower at her three shaking captives. "*Then* the piranha might get some new playmates," Maddy concluded before breaking out into a forced and comically maniacal "MMMWWHAAAHAHAHAAAAA!"

"Give it up. You're not going to win this one," Lucy whispered to a solemnly nodding Erick.

"Okay, that's fine . . . I guess," Erick replied. "But . . . what's underneath the sheets?" Erick inquired of three large items in the back of the room covered in white sheets.

"Well," a chuckling Maddy began, "I'm not really *sure*. This will be a pleasant surprise for *me* as well. I just asked Rod to try to locate some cool items to . . . round out the *rest* of the cool decorations in this space. Rod, I'm *so excited* to see what you have found. Would you please take the sheets off them?"

"Of course, Maddy," a visibly nervous Rod replied. "I was able to locate three authentic medieval torture devices just as you had requested. I could locate more if you wish, but I had limited time. Ummm . . . I hope that you like them." Rod pulled the sheets from all three antique devices to the *oooos* and *aaaaaaws* that came out of Maddy's, Erick's, and Lucy's enthralled mouths.

"*Like* them? I fuckin' *love* them!" Maddy yelled out as she bounced in a circle clapping, causing her lush copper strands to flail. "We have a fuckin' *rack*? Awww, fuck, Rod! You'll be staring at that fuckin' thing all day, heh-heh-heh. Just kidding, you wonderful perv. How does it work?"

"Well," a relieved Rod explained, "as you can see, it is a rectangular wooden frame, just a few inches off the ground. It has a roller at both ends. Our guest's ankles are chained to one roller, and the wrists are chained to the other. Then, a handle-and-ratchet mechanism attached to the top roller is used to very gradually retract the chains, slowly increasing the strain on their shoulders, hips, knees, and elbows. I have been told that this is quite painful. This can be continued until the joints are dislocated and eventually separated."

"So fuckin' cool," a surveying Maddy replied in awe as she stroked her chin. "So . . . what's this next one?"

"Ah, yes," Rod replied in an increasingly excited voice. He adjusted his pop-bottle lensed glasses and stated proudly, "This is called a Spanish Donkey."

"The Spanish Donkey? What the fuck is *that*?" Maddy squealed in delight. "It sounds like a date-rape drug that you take up the ass!"

"No, Maddy, let me explain," Rod replied. "I believe you will find the Spanish Donkey to be quite enjoyable for you. It looks much like a standard sawhorse, but instead of being flat on the top, it is quite pointed and has these little spikes upon it. The guest has to sit astride it in the form of an inverted V. He then has weights tied to his feet, and he very slowly slides down the structure until he is cut in two."

"Wow!" an elated Maddy yelled out. "*That* little bitch is going to provide *hours* of family fun! What's this last one called? I've seen this in the movies."

"Ah, yes," Rod began again, "I really looked hard for this one. We had to trade a free assassination to get it into your collection, but I believe you will agree that it was worth it. This, Maddy, is called the Iron Virgin."

"The Iron Virgin?" Maddy replied with intrigue as she wiped a drop of drool from her salivating mouth. "No wonder it's called that. How the fuck is an *iron* bitch supposed to get wet? Heh-heh-heh. Get it? Hey, everybody get it? Because a chick has to get wet to have sex, and if she's made of iron—oh, never mind. You fuckers have no sense of humor. This might be the coolest thing that I've ever seen. How does it work?"

"Well," Rod explained in a prideful voice while standing straight up with his chest puffed out in a rare display of confidence, "as you can see, it is shaped like a full-sized iron human. The guest is placed inside, and the door of the device has very long iron spikes. The door is closed very slowly, and the spikes eventually begin penetrating the guest's flesh from head to toe at an excruciatingly slow rate until they are completely impaled. It is quite fun and provides a stylish focal point for most any torture room. I daresay that you will be *quite* the talk of the hitman and serial killer community once it gets out that you have *this*."

"You got that right, Rod!" Maddy exclaimed. "This is just fuckin' *perfect*! *Exactly* what this room needed to round it out. You've outdone yourself. Thank you so much. You can expect to find a little *spike,* heh-heh- heh, in your pay envelope this week. Wow . . . so cool. But I don't think that I want to waste our first attempts with our new toys on *these* pieces of garbage. No . . . I would rather wait and build up the anticipation. And besides, I haven't fed my *pets* today."

The three men had their clothing cut off them, and their naked frames were bound to cold metal chairs in front of the aquarium before Maddy addressed them in a matter-of-fact tone, "Okay, you little pricks, I told you before it's up to *you* how much pain you go through before you die. Just tell me the following. Numero uno, who paid for and ordered the hit on LOHAD? What's the fucker's name, and where can I find him? Numero two-o, what are the names and locations of all the other rich fascist assholes who are bankrolling the attempted overthrow of the world's democracies? I'll give you thirty seconds starting . . . starting . . . starting . . . now!"

"Fuck you, cunt!" the middle brownshirt yelled out. "We're ain't tellin' you sheet!"

"Oh god, how I was hoping one of you would say something like that," Maddy stated in a satisfied voice. "I was *soooo* hoping that I could make an example of one of you. Lucy, would you like to do the honors?"

"Oh god yes! Thank you, Maddy!" Lucy exclaimed excitedly as she picked up the electric carving knife.

Blood began pouring as the buzz of the carving knife harmonized with the anguished screams of the tortured man. Pieces of flesh were meticulously carved off his arms and legs until the bone was showing on all four of his extremities. He looked like a half-eaten carcass on Thanksgiving as the generous helpings of meat were placed in the fish tank. The piranha began buzzing about the tank while viciously gorging themselves upon the man's discarded flesh.

"Oh, fuck, man," Maddy stated with disappointment as she watched the growing cloud of crimson in the tank, "I may have to get a better filter. That's gonna be a *bitch* to clean. Way to fuck up my brand-new tank prick! Lucy, finish this fucker off!"

Lucy wiped the blood from her eyes and leaned over the pleadingly weeping man with a devilish smile as she suggestively licked her lips. "I know this won't be good for *you*, but it's going to be *really* good for me," she cooed just before giving him a light kiss on his lips. She then smiled and bit the man's lower lip off before spitting it into the fish tank.

"Oh, sweet jesus!" Lucy cried out as she sawed segments of flesh from the man's face, neck, and torso. Grotesque pieces of tissue hung from the man's screaming body as Lucy's blood-soaked black catsuit began to visibly dampen. She let out one final wail of ecstasy as the man mercifully exhaled his final breath. "Oh . . . my fucking god!" Lucy cried out as she threw the knife down and immediately left the room on her trembling legs.

"Welp," Maddy observed, "I guess we know *that* bitch isn't made of iron. Man, she's getting weirder all the time. Oh well . . . whatever gets you off, I guess. Take this fucker's corpse to the fridge. We'll save it for a later feeding. One down, two to go. Whadayasay, boys? You got something to tell me?"

"Okay, listen, we'll tell you everything that we know!" one of the brownshirts began in a frenzied, stuttering cadence. "The man who hired us and paid for us . . . he has lots of names and lives in a lot of houses. We really don't know where he is!" The man heard the buzz of the knife begin again as Erick approached his quivering frame. "No . . . please . . . really! We don't know!"

"He's telling the truth," came Rod's blunt voice. "The man who paid for this massacre is an enigma. I have been able to track down twelve different names with at least double that of addresses. He is a chameleon. He changes his identity frequently and works through underlings. Very wealthy and connected underlings but underlings nonetheless. He will be difficult to find. Not impossible. Just difficult, and it may take some time before I am able to establish a pattern of his movement through his financial transactions. But perhaps our guests know the names of the underlings?"

"Y-yes!" the other panicked brownshirt yelled out. "We know of six of them! And we are to call a middleman to tell them how things went at the church. We also know that they are planning on getting together in Miami to meet about the future once you're out of the way. Please! We can help you! *Please* just don't feed us to your fish! *Please* don't hurt us!"

"Well, *now* we're getting somewhere!" Maddy gleefully exclaimed before giving her beloved husband a quick peck on his lips. "It really is helpful that you bullying murderous fucks are little pussies just under the surface. Okay, boys, here is what you're going to do. You're going to call your middleman. You're going to tell them that the church massacre was a success. I'm dead, Lucy's dead, Erick's—no, I can't even say that. You know what I mean. Tell them we've been taken care of. Offer to send them some . . . entertainment. I'm sure that these sexist pricks get off on dominating hot chicks. Tell them you can send them a baker's dozen of the hottest and most fun chicks to help them celebrate. All you need to know is *where* and *when*."

Following the phone call, Maddy looked at the men and said, "Thank you. I truly appreciate your assistance in this. Perhaps there's some hope for you two. You've done me a favor, and as promised, I shall now do you a favor. Hey, Rod!" Maddy yelled out while continuing to grin at the men who were beginning to wear a glimmer of hope upon their beleaguered faces. "Do you think we can get a guillotine? We'll just stash these two in the holding cell until we can get one and then *WHOMP*! Off with their heads! No muss, no fuss. Well . . . maybe a little muss but . . . instant death, just as I promised." The screaming men's begging voices trailed off following the loud slam of the heavy metal office door.

———

The six guffawing men sat around the meeting room table in an abandoned office overlooking the majestic site of what was left of Miami Beach. Three miles of coastline had been claimed by the rising tides over the last several years, and they looked at the new beachfront with greed as they watched their latest overpriced properties being constructed. "This is so fuckin' great!" one of the portly men exclaimed following a puff off his cigar. "Global warming is the greatest thing that has happened in the real estate business! Every few years, properties get flooded out, and we get to build and sell new units to the stupid fucking lemmings who have no idea what is going on! And since the wireless service was knocked out, they have an even *harder* time getting information. They actually have to give a slight amount of effort to get the news, which makes it the perfect condition to reinstall CHARLIE units throughout the country. Now that that bitch from Brooklyn and her gang are finally gone, *nobody* will be able to stop us from taking over the rural areas once again and starting our race war! Now, bring on the entertainment! Where are those whores those stupid hicks sent us from New York?"

Thirteen black-robed women were shown into the room. The men sat mesmerized as their urges began to grow. They immediately began cheering and hollering as the robes were flung off, revealing glistening skimpy black dresses, high heels, and stockings. "Well, hello, boys," Rosa stated in an intoxicating voice. "We're here to put on a little show for you. So just sit back and relax and enjoy our little . . . performance. And if you're *really good* boys . . . *maybe* we'll show you what your great big *heads* are for." The men began applauding, laughing, and nudging each other as the women encircled the table and held hands. The woman standing at the head of the table began chanting in a language that only the other twelve women understood.

These are the men, my sisters. These are the men who ordered us to be humiliated. To be beaten. To be raped. These are the men who treated us like livestock. These are the men who would do that to every woman on this planet. Feel your rage, my sisters, and send it to me. Send your rage and allow it to swell. Yes, I can feel it now! Make your rage swell, my sisters! Allow it to grow!

As the men stopped their knee slapping and looked at the enticing women with confused expressions, they each began feeling a slight headache. The headache began to swell. They began clutching their heads and screaming in agony as blood began to ooze out of their noses, ears, and mouths. There were then six simultaneous loud popping sounds; and the men's brains, blood, and skull fragments flew upward off their torsos in a crimson geyser before cascading down upon the lasciviously grinning women.

"Well," Rosa stated bluntly as she wiped blood and bone from her eyes and face, "I guess we give *really good* head. It didn't take long at all for them to pop off. Typical men. They get off really fast, and *we* have to clean up the mess." Thirteen women exploded into laughter and tear-filled hugs as they celebrated the demise of these horrendous predators.

———

"Hey, Josie, get your little ass up here! It's story time!" Maddy ordered. Josie came bounding upstairs and into the space between the upstairs bedrooms and the walled-off sound system in the area that had been the dance floor in the party room.

"Okay, sweetie, take a seat, and we shall regale you in just what we've been up to for the past few days since the church massacre," Maddy began. Josie sat there entranced as her mother and father, with glee and frequent laughter, recounted the feeding of the man to the piranha, what the Coven had accomplished in Miami, and what was about to happen to the other two brownshirts once their special order had arrived. Josie's only question to them was "So the other two are still alive?"

"Yes, they are. And now, my beloved daughter," Erick stated as he got up holding an electric screwdriver, "we are going to show you how we celebrate." He began removing the screws from the plywood barricade that had shielded his sound system away for so many years. He scoured his music collection and found the song that he was searching for. He delicately placed it into the CD player and pressed play. He took his beloved wife into his arms, and the inseparable pair began swaying together to Julian Cope's "Beautiful Love."

Josie watched her parents gazing into one another's tearful eyes with adoring faces. She watched as the loving pair held one another and moved to the music as though they were one. Josie was joined by Vai and the twins. All four of them gazed in wonder at this display of unconditional love and affection for one another.

"Man . . . this all so confusing," Josie stated flatly. "I mean . . . they just fed a guy to a carnivorous fish and arranged for other guys to have their heads blown off. And yet . . . just look at them. As though it had never happened. As though they don't have a care in the world. As though their love is the only thing that exists right now. How can *both* of those things have life in the same person? I need to do some more research. C'mon, you guys, let's go for a walk."

Josie sat in front of the iron bars of the holding cell surrounded, as always, by Vai and the twins. "Hello . . . my name is Josie, and I am the daughter of the people who put you here. I am the daughter of the people who are planning on beheading you. And I am the only person in this world who has any influence over them. So, if you do me a favor, then perhaps I can do one for you and talk them out of what they have planned." "Y-yes, little girl— anything! We'll do *anything* if you could just help us!" the brownshirts began pleading.

"Okay," Josie continued, "it's really not complicated. I simply need some information from you. And you must be honest with me."

"Yes, honesty is quite necessary for this situation," Adam stated in his calm, flat voice, followed by Aaron's, "Yes, you must be honest with our Josie.

And we will know if you are not. Otherwise, we may have to play games with you. We do so enjoy games. Oh my, how I wonder what your intestines smell like. I would so love to find out."

"What? *Ewww!*" Josie shrieked as she looked up at each twin with a look of disgust on her face before addressing the brownshirts once again, "I need you to tell me every bad thing that you have done. And I do mean *everything*. And I need you to tell me *why* you did those things. I have all night. If I'm satisfied with your answers, then I may be able to help you get out of this."

"Yeah . . . yeah . . . okay," the shaking men stated. "I don't know if a little girl should hear all this, but here it goes . . ."

Josie sat wide-eyed as she listened to the men vividly describe every murder, including that of her aunt Patty. Every beating. Every rape. And every hunting trip of innocent families who were slaughtered at their tiny hands. Her widened eyes began to narrow and burn as she was told *why* they had committed these atrocities. The burning intensified as she learned that these sadistic acts were committed to destroy democracies and making white males dominant throughout the world. It was an effort to make women subservient to men. It was an effort to dominate, if not eradicate, people from different ideologies, different races, different religions, and different sexual orientations. It seemed to Josie that these men were, at a minimum, glib about their deplorable acts, if not downright proud of them. The men concluded, "So that's everything, little girl. We done told you everything. Now, can you *please* help us? Can you *please* just let us out, and we *promise* you'll never see us again."

Josie sat looking at her not-quite-yet size six pink high top canvas tennis shoes. She pondered what she had just heard for several minutes. The tension in the silence was suffocating. Josie then looked up at the men and said in her sweet preadolescent voice while smiling, "Thank you. Thank you for telling me all that. Unfortunately for you, it seems to me that my mom and dad—I mean my *mother* and my *father*—may be letting you off easy. What you have done is disgusting. It is atrocious. It is . . . pure evil. So no, I cannot help you. And it seems as though my friends here are eager to play a game. So, Adam, Aaron, have your fun."

"Oh joy!" Adam exclaimed as the pair began retrieving butcher knives from underneath their snow-white jackets. "Did you hear that, Aaron? Josie is going to let us play a game with them!"

"Oh my, yes!" Aaron countered. "What fun we shall have! Josie, would you like to play with us?"

"Naw," Josie replied flatly, "you two have fun. Vai, could you take me home now?"

As Josie heard the excruciated squeals of the men who were beginning to be butchered by the enraptured twins, she looked up at Vai with steely green eyes and said, "Do you think that I did the right thing, Vai?"

Vai looked down at her adopted sister and said with a cold calmness while stroking Josie's copper locks, "Yes, my dearest, you did *exactly* the right thing."

CHAPTER 63

I BELIEVE YOU

Erick stood and looked at the carnage that was once his cherished music area in anguished horror. "Josie, oh my *god*! W-what have you *done*?" Josie came bounding upstairs in her flowered dress and said cheerfully, "What's wrong, Father?"

"M-my CDs," Erick replied in a trembling voice, "th-they're missing. There are so many *missing*. There are so many *holes*. Half of my REM discs are missing. A-and . . . the Bowie collection—what happened to my Bowie discs?"

"Oh. . .that," Josie replied matter-of-factly, "I needed some CDs for my CD jukebox at LOHAD, so I took a few from your collection. Oh! And your organization system really needed an upgrade, so I've reorganized everything as well."

"Y-you did *what*? I have a *system*! Why did you fuck with my *system*?" Erick cried out in confused despair.

"Father," Josie replied in a slightly condescending tone, "I believe that you will see that this system is far superior. Just give it a few days, and I think that you will like it."

"But . . . but," Erick stammered, "there are so many *missing*. What if I want to play a song from some of them and they're *not here*? My god, Josie, what have you *done*?"

"Father," Josie began again as she surveyed her father's wall of CDs and records, "I think you have *enough* songs to choose from. And besides, CDs are expensive collector's items, and I needed them for LOHAD." She then looked down at her shuffling feet and said innocently, "I just want LOHAD to be successful, Father," before gazing up at him with her head slightly cocked while batting her auburn lashes over her emerald-green eyes as she said with a childlike demeanor, "You want me to be successful . . . *don't you?*"

Erick's defenseless heart melted as he stared down at his beloved daughter. "Yes . . . of course, I want you to be successful. Okay, I'll just have to get used to it. I'm sure it will be fine."

"Yay! Thanks, Father!" Josie squealed as she kissed her father on the cheek and went skipping out of the room.

"This just isn't fair," Erick muttered to himself as he shook his bewildered head. "They *both* know that I can't resist their fucking green eyes. It should be illegal the way they both manipulate me." Erick then began chuckling to himself as he realized that he had been a more than willing participant in this dastardly manipulation for years. He let out a sigh of resignation and began taking inventory of all the missing music. "But these records and CDs *will* be organized the *right* way!" he bellowed to the universe to retrieve a small portion of his dignity.

Following a year of carefully planned renovations, LOHAD reopened on Josie's fourteenth birthday on February 14, 2038. The wooden DJ stand remained just as it was left, except that Josie put a fresh pink rose in each of the bullet holes every evening before opening while listening to the song that was intended to open the club on that fateful night. As Josie listened to Springsteen's "Land of Hope and Dreams," she would say a silent prayer through her tears as she delicately placed the roses in each hole and then blew a kiss toward the mural of her beloved embracing aunts that had been painted behind the DJ stand.

The bar had been completely refurbished and was now a glistening silver heavy aluminum that curved at the end, making it look like a bumper off a vintage 1950s muscle car. There were bright neon flowers and peace signs thoughtfully placed on the walls. The backseat area held red vinyl booths that slinked around veneer tables that contained yellow smiley face inlays. The walls of this area held brightly colored paintings of some of Josie's personal heroes. Ruth Bader Ginsburg, Nelson Mandela, Malcolm X, Martin Luther King Jr., Harvey Milk, Greta Thunberg, and John Lewis were just a few of the dignitaries who held the privilege of being featured in this caring oasis of acceptance and peace that was intended to be a safe hangout for the teenage sect.

Just before opening the club on the first night, Josie unlocked the door and stepped outside to roaring applause from the line of waiting friends and patrons. She smiled and waved before adding the final touch on the front door. The sign said No Drugs! No Guns! No Assholes! The sign received an additional round of roaring applause. As would happen from that night forward, Josie would open the evening by playing Todd Snider's anthem to acceptance "I Believe You." Each evening, "last call" for sodas or milkshakes would be announced by REM's "I Believe" thundering through the ceiling's speakers. And each evening, a seventeen-year-old Lionnel would dutifully assist in the clean-up while glancing bashfully at a bustling Josie from the corner of his eye. "Thanks, Lionnel, for all your help tonight! You're a sweetie!" Josie would innocently and sincerely exclaim before kissing Lionnel on his warming cheek and being escorted out of the club by Vai and the twins. Lionnel would then watch Josie's perfectly feminine figure walk down the street as he put his headphones on and pushed play on his vintage portable CD player. As Freedy Johnston's "There Goes a Brooklyn Girl" enveloped him, he would think to himself, *I'm going to marry that girl someday.*

And each evening, Adam and Aaron would present Josie with the same request. "That was quite fun this evening, Josie," Adam would begin, followed by Aaron's, "Yes. Quite fun. But perhaps it would be more fun if we were allowed to play some games. Perhaps the basement could be our private game room."

"For the *bajillionth* time, guys!" Josie would roar back. "LOHAD isn't for those types of games! You do what you need to do for my parents, but LOHAD is off-limits. I allowed you to play your games once, and I hope that I never have to do that again. I *never* want to be involved in taking another person's life *ever again.* Aunt Blair told me that I was destined to lead in a different way. And that's just what I'm going to do, or else, my name isn't Josephine Patricia Sommers Parker! And that's my name, so that's just how it's going to be!" Josie was unable to see the slight knowing smirk of the trailing Vai.

LOHAD became exactly what it was intended to be. It was truly a safe oasis for all the teenage children from the area. They could dance, sing, laugh, and gossip while sipping milkshakes or devouring burgers, fries, or home-made pizzas. Neighborhood patrolmen would frequently walk through. The children's eyes would slowly gaze up at the towering officers and... smile. There would be frequent handshakes or hugs with the police officers as they would join a group of teens at a table and playfully steal a handful of fries. LOHAD was a place where all your cares, concerns and prejudices could melt away simply by walking through the door and playing a song off the jukebox. LOHAD represented understanding. LOHAD represented acceptance. LOHAD represented love. And LOHAD represented that which we all long for: peace in our time.

That's where that fucking CD went, Erick would frequently think to himself as a new vintage song was selected by a giggling teenage girl or posturing teenage boy. At the first sign of trouble, Josie would bellow, "Hey! Do I have to take you outside to read the sign? No Assholes!" The trouble almost always would cease immediately. Those who did not take the hint on the first warning were roughly escorted out of the club by a pair of light-blonde-haired twins dressed in all-white suits and ties. The offender was placed on a list and would not be allowed back in without a written apology addressed to Josie. She would read the note, smile, and hug the embarrassed young person before saying, "It's all okay! Welcome back! We love you, and we've missed you! Fries are on me!"

Josie's parents would typically eat there one evening each week. Maddy would always order the same thing from her waiting daughter, who would be dressed in a classic light-blue-skirted car-hop uniform. "Hot dog, fries, gin and tonic, heh-heh-heh. And make it snappy! I know the owner!" Maddy's order would arrive with the tray containing her hot dog, fries, and . . . root beer. The only condiment that would be on the tray was a bottle of ketchup. "Where's the fuckin' mustard? Why do I have to special order mustard every fucking time?" Maddy would yell out, which would initiate the twins to come and stand over the table. "I mean," a retreating Maddy would say softly, "may I please have some mustard?"

"Coming right up, Mother!" a cacking Josie would yell out.

Following Maddy's third appearance at the club, the teenagers would always move as far away as they could from where the Parkers were seated to protect their own precious dinner from the never-ending onslaught of Maddy's appetite. This ritual ended following a visit by Jules. The teens held their ground and stared directly at the Parkers' table, daring Maddy to try to steal a bite of their food. Maddy understood the game that was afoot, defiantly stood up, and took one step toward her pimply culinary adversaries.

Jules folded her arms and silently smirked as every teen in the room held up their fork, and Maddy cautiously retreated back to her seat while rubbing her right hand, which had been "wounded" many years prior. "Jeez . . . these little fuckers are turning into little pricks," Maddy whispered to her amused husband, who was biting his lip to keep from laughing.

In May of that year, as Josie was feverishly blending milkshakes and taking additional orders, a new boy sauntered into the club. He was dressed in sharp blue slacks with a white short-sleeved pullover shirt that clung to his chest and biceps. He looked toward the bar, and the disheveled and sweating Josie blushed and ducked under the counter. Her heart was racing as she heard a smooth male voice say, "Excuse me, miss, may I place an order?"

"Uh . . . yeah . . . just a sec!" Josie responded as she looked at her reflection in a large serving spoon while frantically doing what she could with the sweaty mop of copper curls on top of her head. She bounced up from behind the counter and said, "Hey there . . . sorry about that . . . um . . . café emergency . . . or something. How can I help you, sir?"

Josie's heart continued to race as the sixteen-year-old's deep-blue eyes gazed tenderly into Josie's brilliant green iris and said, "Yeah . . . I want something light. I have a swim meet coming up, and I need to . . . y'know . . . stay in shape. So how about a small salad with a light dressing, a diet soda, and . . . your phone number?"

"Weeelll," a blushing Josie replied through awkward adolescent chuckles, "I *suppose* I could do that. Ummm . . . yeah, that would be fine. Just a *fine* order. Perfect really. Y-yes . . . I'll just go and *get* that for you . . . and—I mean your *food* and everything and my . . . um . . . phone number. Yes, that is just fine. Just perfect. That will be up in just a moment."

By mid-June, Josie and the strapping young man had become an item. Lionnel would glance over and wince as he would witness the pair laughing and joking around together. He needed to go on a much-needed break one evening as he witnessed an enraptured Josie receive her first kiss. Following that event, he became much more violent as he cut open the hamburger and hot dog rolls for that evening.

While walking her home for the first time, his left hand gently wrapped around her right, the boy asked, "So . . . what's with the bodyguards?" as Vai and the twins lurked a few feet from behind. "Oh, *that*, um . . ." Josie bashfully began as her palms began sweating, "they're like my adopted older sister and brothers . . . um . . . my parents are a bit . . . um . . . overprotective. They

were taken in by my parents a number of years ago after their mother . . . um .
. . disappeared, I guess. Don't worry about them. They're pussycats . . .
usually."

"They're also a little . . . creepy," the boy whispered into Josie's delicate
ear just before the front door of the Parker home opened. Erick was standing
in the doorway, his menacing figure backlit by an ominous white entryway
light. He was holding a butcher knife in one hand and a cucumber in the
other. He looked at the shocked pair and said, "Ah, you must be the young
man in our Josie's life. Please, won't you come in? I was just preparing you a
salad. Josie said that you were fond of . . . salads."

"Erick!" Maddy was heard yelling from the living room. "Just let him in!
Don't be a dick! You're embarrassing our daughter."

Josie glared at her father as she walked by him and mouthed, *Just stop it!*

"Hello, Mr. and Mrs. Parker," the boy stated confidently as he presented
his right hand for a cordial greeting.

"Actually," Erick replied as he firmly grasped the boy's hand in a death
grip, "her *mother* is Mrs. *Sommers*. The women in our household are quite
independent. They do not do *anything* that they do not *want* to do. You
would do *well* to understand that up front. Understand?"

"Oh, of course, sir!" the boy replied. "My intentions with your lovely
daughter are nothing but pure. I really like her, and I just want to make her
smile. I hope that is satisfactory, Mr. Parker and . . . Mrs. *Sommers*." He then
reached out and lifted Maddy's right hand and placed a light kiss upon it. "It
truly is a pleasure to meet the parents of the girl I am so fond of."

"Yeah . . . okay, come on," Erick replied with a suspicious tone in his
voice. "You can watch me make the salad."

Mom! Do something! Josie mouthed to a shrugging Maddy as the men
went to the kitchen island. *WHACK! WHACK! WHACK!* could be heard
throughout the home as Erick slammed the butcher knife through the
cucumbers and carrots. The salad consisted of *nothing* but greens, cucumbers, and carrots.

"Ummm . . ." the boy began to inquire, "my father would like to meet
Josie as well, so . . . would it be all right if she came over for dinner on
Saturday night? We have a *really* rad pool. It would just be swimming and
dinner, and I would have her home by ten."

"Oh, Mom, *please* can I go?" Josie pleaded as she avoided the glares of her
father. "*Please*? Can I go . . . and *without* the escort?"

"Well . . . all right," Maddy replied as Erick retrieved another carrot from the refrigerator and violently cut it in two while glaring at the teenage interloper.

The evening ended with Josie receiving a light kiss good night from the boy. She dreamily gazed out of the curtains and through the iron bars of the window as she watched his perfectly masculine frame saunter down the street and disappear into the sultry June evening air.

"Okay, Josie . . . have a seat," her mother demanded. "Before you go out on this date, we're going to have a talk."

"What talk?" her husband fearfully asked. "*The* talk," Maddy replied.

"Oh . . . *that* talk. Good. Yes, I suppose it's about time for that. I'll just go upstairs and organize a few things. Let me know when you're done," a sweating Erick replied as he began toward the staircase.

"Sit the fuck down, mister!" Maddy ordered. "You're helping me with this shit!"

"Fuck!" a trembling Erick muttered under his breath as he took a seat in front of his wide-eyed daughter. Erick had never been so frightened in his life.

"Don't worry," Maddy stated to her profusely sweating husband, "*I'll* start, you big pussy." This was a major moment for the family. Maddy had to use the *exact* words to impress upon her daughter the importance of this situation. Maddy could *not* fuck this up.

Maddy fucked it up. "You see, sweetie, when two people . . . *like* each other, then they . . . *sometimes* want to rub their *naughty* bits against each other and make each other *cum*."

"Oh . . . my . . . god . . . *gross*!" Josie screamed out. "Okay, let me just stop you two right there. I know all about sex. I know all about sexually transmitted diseases. I know all about pregnancy. And I know all about the emotional pitfalls of having sex too young. So let me just reassure you that I am in *no way* ready for that. I am too young. I just want to enjoy having a boyfriend. And if he were to try to pressure me into anything, then I would lose all respect for him because I would then know that that is all that he is interested in, okay?"

"Yup! Works for me!" Erick immediately shouted out. "Great talk, sweetie. Thanks so much for hearing us out." Josie just shook her beet-red face in silence as she made her way up the stairs to her bedroom.

"Well!" Erick proudly proclaimed. "I think that I handled that rather well, don't you?" A bewildered Maddy just stood and stared at him with her arms folded while tapping her size-six foot. "So . . . what do you think of Josie's . . . um . . . *boyfriend*?" he inquired of his wife as he rolled his eyes and pretended to try to make himself vomit.

"I'll tell you *exactly* what I think of him," Maddy bluntly answered. "He reminds me of my douchebag first husband. We're *definitely* sending Vai and the twins."

"Oh good!" a relieved Erick exclaimed as he flopped his emotionally drained body down upon the sofa.

The following Friday evening, the boy gave Josie a tender good-night kiss and strutted out of the club. Josie let out a deep satisfied sigh as Rosa approached her. "Hey, Josie, can I talk to you for a moment?"

"Of course, Rosa! What's up?" the carefree Josie chirped.

"Yeah, hey, listen," Rosa hesitantly began. "I know this is your first boyfriend, and I know how exciting that can be, so I *really* don't want to be a wet blanket here but . . . something just seems *off* about him. The energy that I feel from him is—well, I just want you to be careful, okay?" "Okay, I understand," Josie replied before asking, "Just *please* don't tell my parents, okay? Maybe you're just picking up on somebody *else's* bad vibes or something. Please, Rosa. I *really* like him, and I *promise* that I'll be careful, okay?"

"Of course, sweetie," Rosa replied as she gave Josie a hug. "And if you need anything, just let me know."

"Actually," Josie responded, "could you give me a lift over to Rod's office?"

"Oh my, Josie," Rod began in his nasally staccato voice as Josie peered at the computer screen from over his shoulder, "this security system is quite sophisticated. This is a man who does not wish to be found—ah, here we are. They are in the living room. Is that your boyfriend?"

"Yep, that's him," Josie replied. "And that man sitting with his back to us must be his father. Can you turn it up? I need to hear what they're saying."

The adult man on the screen got up from his seat and turned toward the bar. Rod's widening eyes were magnified in his pop-bottle lenses as he looked upon the man's face. "Oh my, Josie. It's *him*."

Chapter 64

I Wanna Be a Lifeguard

"Hiya!" Josie squealed just before throwing her arms around her sixteen-year-old boyfriend's neck and giving him a long kiss. "I've been looking forward to this all day!"

"Uh . . . yeah . . . me too," the boyfriend replied before asking, "Ummm, what's up with the archery set?"

"Oh, well, you and your father were going to show *me* such a wonderful time tonight that I thought that I'd entertain you two and show *you* both something cool as well."

"Yeah, cool," the boyfriend replied before inquiring further. "And what's in the big cooler?"

"Oh," Josie responded coyly, " just a little something to add to our dinner party . . . I think it's *really* gonna be enjoyable."

The boy's father emerged from the sliding glass doors of the house and onto the marble patio that surrounded the brilliant teal ripples in the pool. "So, this must be the infamous Josie Parker, the beautiful young lady who has stolen my son's heart!"

"Yup! That's me! I'm Josie, but my friends call me . . . Josie!"

"Oh, what a marvelous sense of humor you have, my dear. Son, I do believe that this one might be a *keeper*," the boy's father said with a sly grin. The boy responded, "Yeah, Dad. I don't plan on her going *anywhere*."

"Yeah, I'm kinda *full* of surprises. Anywhooo," Josie began again while chuckling, "it's so *super nice* of you to invite me to this dinner and pool party! So, let's get the party started!"

Following her declaration, Josie immediately began pulling arrows from her quiver in a blur and launching them into each of the men's legs. They fell onto the marble screaming as Josie launched four more arrows, one for each shoulder. "Wh-what the hell are you *doing?*" the father screamed as he was ineffectually attempting to pull an arrow from his left leg.

"Oh well, I just thought it was *supersweet* of you both to invite me to dinner. I was *really* looking forward to it. But it *kinda* pissed me off when I found out that you were planning on kidnapping me and keeping me to be this little douche's plaything. And it *kinda* pissed me off when I found out that you were going to keep me *locked up* and *beat me* and *rape me repeatedly* just to try to take down my parents. And it *kinda* pissed me off when I found out that *you* were the one responsible for the massacre at LOHAD and the execution of my aunt and many of our friends."

Josie's eyes began burning like emerald embers as she continued, "It *really* shattered my world. This young man who had been so nice to me. Who had brought me flowers. Who gave me my first kiss. Who had said such sweet things to me. I can't say that he was my first love, but he *was* my first boyfriend, I thought. I thought that he was the nicest person in the world. And then I found out that it was all an act. It was nothing more than a manipulation. I was just disgusted with myself when I found out that I had been duped by this . . . this . . . *person* who was laughing with his father about all the *horrible* and *tortuous* things that he was planning on doing to me.

"So, I guess I should thank the two of you. Thank you for giving me the final piece of knowledge that I needed to make sense of this world. I've always known that there is true, pure love and kindness in this world. And I now know firsthand that there is also *true, pure evil* in this world. I now know that purely evil people have no soul. And if they have no *soul*, then they are not entirely *human*. They may be biologically *homo sapiens*, but they lack the *humanity* that is required to be considered *human*. And I now know that there is nothing *wrong* with eliminating those who have no soul. Those who mercilessly prey upon others. Those who ruin others' lives for their own greed or pure enjoyment. Those who *beat down* others in the most *deplorable* ways just to satisfy their fragile little egos. I now know that *you two* aren't human, and therefore, eliminating *you two* is not wrong. So, I thought I'd throw my *own* pool and dinner party. C'mon! Let's start with the pool!"

Josie pushed her former beau into the deep end of the pool, causing clouds of crimson to swirl around his thrashing body. "Huh," Josie observed, "I really thought a well-built kid like that would be a better swimmer. C'mon, Pops, show junior how it's done!"

Josie launched herself shoulder first into the man's side. He fell into the pool and immediately began helplessly flailing his impaled extremities. "Well, now," Josie began again, "I think the pool party was rather successful. You gents are fun! Now, for the dinner part. I hope that you don't mind, but I took the liberty of inviting a few of my mom's friends over for dinner. Bon appétit!"

Wearing a devilish grin, Josie opened the large cooler and poured several of her mother's prized piranha into the pool. The malicious fish were immediately attracted to the blood and began feasting on the hopelessly flailing and screaming men. Their razor-sharp teeth tore through their soft flesh, muscles, and tendons in an unholy frenzy of gluttony. The tranquil teal waves transformed into a morbid dark scarlet whirlpool of gore. Josie observed the hideous scene as her adolescent befreckled face smiled with glee. She watched with great anticipation as one of the piranhas devoured a severed penis in one bite. "Cool!" Josie squealed out. "I saw that in a movie once! I guess I'll call you *Deep Throat*, heh-heh-heh."

As the floating lifeless carcasses were being picked clean, Josie yelled out, "Okay, guys, c'mon out! I know you're out there!"

Vai and the twins emerged from the surrounding woods and began approaching the iron gate that surrounded the pool area. "She has arrived, my dears," Vai dryly said as they opened the gate. "She is now complete and ready to assume leadership."

"Yes, you are correct, Vai," Adam stated, followed by Aaron's, "Oh my, yes. And what a wonderful game she played with them. I do believe that she can teach us just as many games as we can teach her! What a glorious, sunny day!"

"Yep," Vai replied coldly, "you can take that to the bank. She's going to be tenacious."

"Well, guys," Josie stated as her guardians approached, "I don't see any reason why we should let their wonderful dinner go to waste! Let's go see what's for eats!" Josie took two pink roses from her auburn locks and tossed them into the churning bloody waves before skipping toward the sliding glass door while singing Tiny Tim's "Tiptoe through the Tulips." As she entered the home, Josie stopped singing, looked up at the camera, and said, "Hey, Rod! Could you make a copy of all this so that I can show my parents before you delete everything?" There were two flashes of the red light above the camera before Josie said, "Thanks, Rod! You're a sweetie!"

"Oh . . . my . . . god," Josie softly stated with exhaustion as she sat back in her chair and rubbed her full belly, "*that* was the most satisfying meal that I've ever had!" She then leaned over the table and stared at the twins with glowing emerald eyes while wearing a maniacal grin. "Boys, maybe it's time that we have a little chat about what games we can play in the basement under LOHAD."

———

"Uh-huh, uh-huh," Erick casually stated as he stroked his chin while watching the full-color footage from the security camera. "Very nice control. The arrows were perfectly placed," he continued as though he were presenting a book review. "Yes, very nice speech. I really like the way that you fully explained the reasoning behind your actions. It was a complete succinct explanation without being overly cumbersome. That is the key to these speeches. Just give your audience enough information so that they have an understanding of your motivation but not so much that you become boring and preachy.

"Oh . . . very creative, Josie. Disable their extremities and then throw them in the pool. And the transformation of the calm blue water to the swirling dark clouds of crimson blood is just a masterful visual. And it also serves to inform your audience of the transformation that is occurring within you. From a calm, carefree, and innocent pool to a troubled, violent storm. It's really quite good work and wonderful use of symbolism."

"Yeah . . . I wasn't really going for that. I just thought it would be cool," Josie sheepishly responded before being cut off by her father.

"Okay, now *here's* a little problem. I would suggest that you try to lose your attempts at humor. I'm sorry, but your jokes just have never really been all that funny, and that quip about *Deep Throat*, which is a reference that you *shouldn't* even know about, takes the scene from malicious revenge to cheese-ball seventies sitcom fare. All that you're missing there is the contrived laugh track."

"Are you about done with the fuckin' book report, mister?" Maddy yelled out at her husband. "And what do you mean *lose the humor*? That was a *great* fuckin' line, Josie. Don't listen to him. He's like humor-impaired or something. It's really fuckin' sad, and I've had to deal with this shit since we met. A simpleton like him just can't comprehend the masterful comedic minds of geniuses like us!"

"But I do have a question. What's up with throwing the roses into the pool?"

"Oh, that!" Josie excitedly responded. "The pink roses are my cool calling card!"

"Whatthefuckyousay?" Maddy cried out with a look of delight upon her face. "*A cool calling card*? Why the *fuck* didn't *we* think of that, mister?"

"Because we aren't *geniuses*," came Erick's dry and somewhat sarcastic response.

"Whatevs . . ." Maddy dismissively replied. "Now, for the important part. What was for dinner? Was it good? Could you make it for us?"

As the footage concluded, Maddy looked at her daughter. She was the perfect reflection of herself at that age. Now physically fully grown as she ventured to the edge of adulthood, Josie stood at a less than imposing five feet four and a half inches. Her petite slender feminine body remained constantly toned despite the carb and sugar onslaught that it was forced to endure through Josie's voracious appetite. Her modestly freckled round face presented a small slightly turned-up nose above her delicate naturally mauve lips and was framed by her flowing curled blunt-bang auburn hair, cut straight at the eyebrows and slightly curled inward at the ends just above the shoulder, giving the appearance of a churning molten copper waterfall. Showcased within this kaleidoscope of perfect facial features were her fierce emerald-green eyes that flickered through the constant batting of her lush sandy eyelashes.

"Now, we have to have the speech," Maddy said solemnly.

"Speech? *What* speech?" Erick anxiously inquired. "She already *said* that she was *too young* to have sex! That's been *settled*! She's probably not going to do that until she's like thirty or forty or something! Why do we have to talk about *that* again?"

"No, baby," a bemused Maddy replied, "not *that* speech. *The* speech."

"Oh, *that* speech. All right. Good. I don't think that I can handle that *other* speech again," a relieved Erick replied as he wiped his sweat from his brow and slumped into the cushions of the couch.

"Okay, Josie, you need to listen to me *very carefully*. When one starts down the trail of . . . *justice*, shall we say, there are certain rules that must be abided by. When one engages in these . . . *practices*, it must be for the right reasons. It must be someone who has done something terrible or is a significant threat to someone else and who is out of the reach of conventional . . . *punishment*. It must never be done for petty infractions or differences and must *never* be done solely for our own gratification. There are many bad women out there as well, but I have *never* believed that any one of us should ever do anything to permanently harm one of our sisters. For them, I believe that *their* punishment, if deserving, shall come in its own natural due course.

"Now, if someone is to *do* something to another person, then that someone needs to be careful about it and take others' safety into consideration. There is to be no harm to anyone other than the target. I want to leave you with this. If someone is going down this path, then it would be wise for that person to *never* keep any souvenirs of their exploits, which is why we are going to immediately destroy this footage. And these exploits need to be conducted in a variety of ways. And finally—" Maddy looked at her daughter with grave seriousness as she sternly said, "This conversation *never* happened and will never happen again . . . um . . . probably. Do you understand?"

Josie looked deeply into her mother's emerald eyes and simply said, "Yes, I understand."

"Man, how *fucked up* is this going to *get*? Now our teenage *daughter* is getting involved in this shit. I mean . . . we knew that this was probably inevitable, but . . . it's *still* pretty fucked up," Erick lamented before failing to hide his excitement any longer. "Oh! But, Josie, all the things that we can now teach you! All the fun family trips we can all take together! All the fun family activities that we can participate in! I really feel as though we've finally come together as a family. Maybe we need a cool name, huh?"

"Oh fuck, yeah!" Maddy cried out as she launched herself onto her beloved husband's lap and kissed him. "Okay, so we already did Trio of Terror. I *still* think that was pretty good, but whatevs. And now, along with Lucy, we're the Unholy Trinity. So, what should we call our little family unit? Hmmmm . . . what would be *cool*? What should it be?" Maddy's face was scrunched up in deep thought as she heard her daughter's innocent voice.

"The Family of Fury."

"Oh fuck, yes!" Maddy cried out. She then said as she playfully messed up her daughter's auburn locks, "*Who's* our little maniacal genius? *You* are!

That's right! *You're* our little maniacal genius!" The trio (not of terror) fell into each other's arms as they laughed hysterically.

They cuddled together on the couch, encased in the deep warmth of their mutual love, until Maddy broke the silence.

"Hey, sweetie?" Maddy stated thoughtfully as she stroked her beloved daughter's lush copper curls. "We're really sorry that it didn't work out with this boy. We both know how painful it is when you get a broken heart."

"Thanks, Mom . . . Dad," Josie replied as she peered at her loving parents' tear-filled eyes.

"You called us mom and dad!" Erick exclaimed before embracing his cherished family once again.

"Yeah . . . I understand now. I'm really tired. I think I'll just go to bed," Josie replied wearily as she stretched and yawned.

"Okay, sweetie," a smiling Maddy softly replied as she wiped a final tear from her eye. "You sleep well tonight. And don't you worry about this boy. As the saying goes, there's always more fish in the sea! Get it? 'Cause she fed those fuckers to *fish*! Get it? Pretty good, huh? Oh, *fuck* you! Don't give me that fuckin' look, mister!"

Why do I get the feeling that parent-daughter bonding time is about to get really messed up? Josie pondered as she crawled underneath her bright-pink covers that were adorned by various cartoon characters. She looked around the room reverentially at all the pictures of herself with her loved ones throughout her short life. There was a smiling Sean holding her up as an infant at the bookstore. Charlie and Rosetta holding a microphone up to her mouth as she sang her first song. Her giggling face as she was dancing with Jacklyn and her aunt Patty. Lucy showing her how to set up her first chemistry set. A group picture with Rosa and her sisters in the Coven, her bright face peeking from under her ill-fitting witch's hat. Jules and Jerry placing a fake tattoo of a flower on her freckled forearm. Pastor Tim and Jeremy in front of their pew with all three smiling and flashing peace signs. Henri and Gregory attempting to look tough as her photobombing eyes peered from behind their brawny shoulders. Vai and the twins teaching her how to play cards. Her aunt Blair smiling proudly as they stood in front of her animal sanctuary. Her big eared novelty hat wearing parents enveloping her in a hug in Paris. Her good friend Rod staring blankly and awkwardly at the camera as she was giving him a kiss on his pasty cheek. And the person who was beginning to become her best friend, Lionnel, behind the bar at LOHAD.

Her lips arched upward in a comforted smile while simultaneously feeling loss and remorse. A single tear dripped down her angelic face. *Yes, this is my family,* she thought to herself. *I don't know what is meant by traditional family, but whatever it is, this* definitely *is not it. But it's* my *family. And I love them all. And may God have mercy on anyone who* ever *tries to hurt any of them again.*

She stretched and yawned once again before turning off her lamp. Stardust was the first to arrive. She nestled under Josie's chin and began purring. Then came Ziggy, who curled up on her chest and let out a comforted mew. Josie was with her pussycats. Josie was with her family. Josie was finally truly home.

CHAPTER 65

SAVE THE LAST DANCE FOR ME

"Isn't it *fabulous*?" a beaming Erick exclaimed to his wife as they stood in the middle of a run-down junk and scrap yard.

"What?" Maddy tersely replied. "*That* hunk of rusted junk with all the *rats* running out of it? What the hell are you going to *do* with it?"

"Oh, it may not look like much *now*," a giddy Erick answered, "but just you wait. It is going to look *bitchin'* by the time Josie's sixteenth birthday rolls around in a year and a half. And she's going to absolutely *love* it!"

"Ummm . . . okay," a skeptical Maddy replied, "if you say so. But I think that thing is beyond repair. Whatevs, do whatcha want. C'mon, we gotta get to the meeting. Oh . . . and who the fuck ever says *bitchin'*?"

Erick began clapping and hopping toward the exit while frequently looking behind him at the foundation of his birthday gift to his beloved daughter.

"Here ye, here ye, here ye!" Maddy bellowed as Erick lightly hit his head on the meeting room table in frustration. "This meeting of Vendetta Degli Oppressi is officially called to order! Here's the deal, gang. CHARLIE units all over the country are mostly in shambles, and the UAM is completely disorganized. Sure, there are still fascist extremist voices out there encouraging the overthrow of democracies, but they are back to the pre-insanity levels of thirty years ago. Most of their previous followers have realized that they had been duped by their bullshit race- baiting and hate-filled propaganda. But there are *still* splinter groups out there who still believe that they can start a race war or at least punish those that they hate, and we have one right here in Brooklyn.

"There's a splinter CHARLIE group of several racist and sexist pricks who have kidnapped at least four prominent women of color in our city. Our informants have told Gregory that they are kidnapping, abusing, and finally murdering prominent women of color, such as business leaders or politicians, to send a message that white males should be dominant over everyone else. Oh, and *these* particular little pricks can't find a partner to . . . use their little pricks with. They're pathetic and radicalized little so- called involuntary-celibates who hate *all* women, regardless of their color or anything else. They think that just because they have a dick women should just bend over for them whenever they want. They don't believe that women are actual human beings. They believe that they are nothing more than their property, and they resent the fact that they actually have to treat women as respected equals to even have a *shot* at getting laid. So, they're taking their pathetic little snowflake frustration out on innocent women. There are at least four who have been abducted. We are going to get them back." Maddy then glared at her crew intensely and said in a deep growl, "And bring those little pricks here too. I want *them*, and I want them *alive*."

The gas canisters of *Toxin A* crashed through the windows of the run-down one-story shack on the outskirts of an industrial park. The four men inside began violently coughing and gagging before falling down unconscious. "Tie them up, boys, and take them to the first van, please!" Josie yelled out to the twins, who emerged from the fog looking even more menacing as their long blonde-white hair framed their all-white gas masks that matched the rest of their customary ensemble.

It was Josie's first mission as lead, and she was being carefully watched by her doting father as Josie commanded her troops to sweep through the five-room shack and find the survivors. The only problem was, there weren't any. "Oh god, Josie," Vai's muffled voice came through her mask, "we're too late. We found all four of them, but . . . you really don't want to see this."

"Out of my way, please," Josie politely ordered. She entered the room and found four beaten and bruised women lying with their swollen purple eyes wide open on filthy, stained mattresses. They were all naked and so bruised that it was nearly impossible to tell what their natural complexion had once been. One woman had barbed wire around her neck. It was obviously the last thing that the city-council woman had felt before mercifully being allowed to exhale her final breath. Josie looked upon the scene in horror and began violently shaking in anger before she heard Henri's voice cry out from another room, "I've found one with a pulse! I've found a survivor! Hurry! Help me get her to the van!"

Erick rushed to Henri's side and lifted the unconscious woman under her arms as Henri firmly grasped her battered legs and placed her on a gurney. The woman's near-lifeless head flopped back, and Erick stared into her swollen face. "Oh, fuck no, goddammit . . . no," Erick muttered as his heart filled with pain-stricken dread while he and Henri began carrying her corpse-like frame to the awaiting van.

"Okay, goddammit," Maddy lamented, "only one survivor. Fuck. I'm going to see if she's being treated all right, and then we're going to have some fun with those four little fuckers who did this."

"Do I get a turn?" Lucy's cold voice emerged from a dark corner of the meeting room.

"Maybe," Maddy replied, "but *not* if you're going to cum all over the floor again! That shit's just *gross*!"

"Well, no promises," Lucy coyly replied while wearing a sly grin.

Erick was trailing a bustling Maddy as she approached the bedroom where the survivor was being tended to by the syndicate's physician, members of the Coven, and the assisting Lionnel. "Maddy, please just wait a moment," Erick pleaded to his wife. "Maddy, *please*, I need to speak with you before you go in—"

Maddy burst through the bedroom door and went to the bedside of the woman. She looked down at her beaten face. She let out a pained wail before falling to her knees and saying, "No . . . please, no. Not you . . . not you . . . Sam."

Erick picked his wife's limp figure from off her knees, wrapped his arm tenderly around her shoulder, and escorted her into the hallway. "I'm so sorry, my love. But she's alive. We'll get her fixed up. And I just want to point out that we have *four* of those fucks in custody but only *three* torture devices. So . . . *one* of them is *expendable*."

He lifted her right hand and placed a set of well-worn and brown- stained brass knuckles upon it. Maddy looked down at her weaponized hand and then up into her beloved husband's caring hazel eyes before saying, "You *always* know exactly what I need. You *are* and shall *always* be my prince. Let's go. I need to work out some . . . aggression."

The three brownshirts could only sit and watch in horror in their piss-stained pants as Maddy thrust the brass knuckles into the face of their companion over and over and over in a blurred fury. Her copper strands were flailing wildly as they were being sprayed with streams of fresh blood. She became focused on the screaming man's right eye that she pummeled until it burst in an explosion of blood and goo all over her black catsuit. His anguished wails continued as she violently hit him repeatedly in his mouth, causing several teeth to become lodged in the gaps of the blood- soaked brass knuckles. Then, she stopped. "Okay, I'm going to take a little breather. You can too. Just sit there and relax while we have some fun with your friends." Maddy went over to her husband, smiled, and whispered, "Thanks, baby. I really needed that. How's Sam?"

"Still being attended to," Erick softly replied. "They'll let us know when they're done."

"Okay, Lucy, pick your . . . um . . . poison," Maddy flatly said while staring at the three remaining brownshirts. "But don't make a fuckin' mess this time!"

"Ohhhh my," Lucy cooed, "it's just so hard to choose . . . but . . . *you're* kinda cute . . . for an ass. Let's put him on the donkey!"

As the twins lifted the panicking bound man and placed him upon the sharpened wooden spikes of the Spanish Donkey, Adam stated, "Oh, how I've wanted to play this game."

"Oh my, yes," came Aaron's reply, "this shall be quite fun. Now, let's attach the weights upon his ankles and see what funny faces and sounds he makes."

The twins sat on unmatched colored midcentury modern chairs on either side of an enthralled Lucy. Their faces wore increasingly wide delighted smiles as the screaming man's weighted body slowly slid down the torture device. It sliced him first through his scrotum. Then up toward his lower intestines. His screams ceased once his body had slid halfway up his torso and his internal organs began clinging to his ribs. The trio continued to watch in fascination until the dead man's body was completely severed in two and his organs randomly laid upon the blood-soaked floors. "Okay, good. Thanks for not making a mess this time, Lucy. Henri, you and Rosa want the next one?" Maddy inquired.

"Hell, yes," Henri replied as he threw the flailing man down upon the rack, and his assistant tied his limbs to the rollers. The man's agonized wails began the moment that Henri began cranking the handle. The wicked man's limbs continued to stretch until a loud pop was heard, and all four of his extremities were completely dislocated. "I think that I'll just let you lie there until you're dead," Henri coldly stated to the agonized man. "No water. No food. Nothing but torturous pain for the next several days until your body finally gives out. And then, motherfucker, I'll see you in hell."

"All right, Henri . . . thank you. Very nice speech," Maddy stated in a congratulatory tone.

"All right sweetie, do you want the last one? I mean, it's called the Iron Virgin, so it seems appropriate for an incel douche like him. And even though I know that *you're* not a virgin, I still thought you might enjoy this one."

"Wait . . . what?" a suddenly panicked Erick exclaimed. "W-what do you mean she's *not* a virgin? When did *this* happen? No, I don't want to know, but who *is* the little fucker? How did this happen? We had the talk! She said that she wouldn't have sex until she was at least forty-five . . . I think. Oh my *god*! Who *did this* to my little girl?"

"Gross, Dad," Josie flatly stated as she strode past her sweating father. "She means that I'm not a virgin at *killing* people. Not *that*. So just calm down."

"Oh . . . killing people," a relieved Erick stated as he wiped the sweat from his brow. "Okay, that's just fine. That's very good. But really, sweetie, whenever you think it's the right time for you to have that . . . um . . . experience, you can always come and talk to me."

The entire room burst into laughter with the exception of the agonized man who was being placed in the iron man-shaped coffin. "I bet you think that it's unfair for you to die before you've had real sex, don't you? I mean, rape doesn't really count now, does it?" Josie inquired of the man who began feverishly nodding.

"Yeah, I think that that is unfair too, so . . . I promise . . . I'll be gentle." Josie's dimples exploded in delight upon her innocent befreckled face as she slowly began closing the lid of the virgin upon the radicalized virgin. He began screaming as the sharp iron spikes in the lid slowly penetrated his face, body, and limbs. His cries became more pronounced as Josie pushed the lid gradually into his flesh. Before giving the lid one last violent shove, Josie yelled out, "Okay! Now let's pop that cherry, heh-heh-heh"

"Okay, sweetie," Erick began in a lecturing tone, "I really do not care for you talking like that. First, the *Deep Throat* reference and now all this talk about popping cherries. It simply is not ladylike, especially for a girl of your age, and I do not approve."

"Oh, shut the fuck up and quit being so overprotective," a dismissive Maddy stated before saying, "C'mon, Rod said the doctor is ready to talk to us now."

———

Sam awoke in a nearly pitch-black room to the sensation of a warm and soft rag being rubbed delicately over her battered arms. "W-where am I?" she asked in a weak voice.

"Somewhere safe," came a woman's caring reply. "Somewhere where no one will be able to harm you ever again."

"M-Maddy?" Sam asked with hesitation as her swollen eyes struggled to adjust to the dim lighting.

"Yeah . . . it's me. And I'm not alone." The lights were brought up slowly to reveal the tearful expressions of Maddy, Jules, and Lucy. "We would hug you, but we'd probably bust your ass up again," Jules dryly stated until she broke down into uncharacteristic tears and yelled, "We're just so happy that you're alive!"

Each woman gently laid one of their hands upon Sam's legs and let out smiles of both sorrow and relief. "I . . . I can't feel your hands . . . my *legs* . . . I can't feel my *legs*!" a panicked Sam cried out.

"I know," a remorseful Maddy began. "Those fuckers messed you up pretty good, Sam. They crushed your spine. I'm so sorry, but you'll never walk again. But . . . hey, listen!" Maddy continued as she lilted her voice while wiping a tear from her green eye. "We have, like, the best fuckin' engineers, and they are building you the best fucking wheelchair in the history of the world! And we have the finest martial arts instructor who can teach you how to kick ass while seated! I know this sucks, but you're alive. You fuckin' *made* it, which is more than I can say about those four fuckers who did this to you. They're all dead . . . well . . . except for one. We were saving him for you . . . y'know . . . if you want."

"Bring him to me," Sam replied in a dark voice. As they were awaiting the doomed man's arrival, Sam looked up at Maddy through her dark purple eyes and said, "I'm sorry about what I said all those years ago. I'm sorry that I wished you dead. I didn't understand. I didn't understand just how messed up and dangerous the world had gotten. And I didn't understand how . . . different Vai and the twins were. Please forgive me."

"There is nothing to forgive. Hell, half of the time, *I* don't understand this fucked-up world. I don't understand if what I'm doing is right or wrong. I don't understand why we have all been called into this. All that I *do* know is that I've had this rage and hatred inside of me since I was a child, and the only thing that frees me of it, at least for a while, is taking one of these mother-fuckin' douchebags off this earth. Well . . . that and looking into the eyes of my prince. *That* usually works too. So, there's nothing to forgive. I'm just happy that you're alive, and I'm happy that we're together again."

The trembling and bound one-eyed man was wheeled into the room. Sam was handed a knife. She felt her hand clench the handle with a strength that she hadn't experienced since her abduction four days ago. She had experienced so much physical and psychological pain at the hands of this evil man and his deplorable companions. She needed vengeance. For herself. For the other women who had suffered and died at his hands. But she was also a soul that was filled with forgiveness. She was *not* Maddy or Lucy. It was not in her to take another person's life, no matter what vile acts they had committed upon her. Her swollen and cracked lips expanded into a pained smile as she dropped the knife.

"It's okay, Sam," Maddy stated caringly. "This shit isn't for everybody. I'll just take him back and take care of it myself. You just rest up now, and we'll all be back in a while."

"No," Sam stated in an emotionless voice, "don't take him away. Don't *ever* take him away. This is what I want you to do. This is what I want *Jules* to do. And I want to watch."

The man screamed out for mercy as Jules, enthusiastic about her first opportunity for a torture session to avenge her friend, sliced through the man's left leg just above the knee, the blowtorch's bright blue-and-white flames cauterizing the wound as it burned through the flesh and bone. The high-pitched wails of despair continued as his right leg was removed. Then, his dominant right arm. His mouth was opened, and Jules pulled his tongue out with a pair of forceps, causing blood to spew out of his anguished mouth and dribble down upon his brown shirt. And finally, Jules removed his pathetic little penis with the slight flick of her hand holding a butcher's knife.

"No wonder he couldn't get laid. He's not exactly packin'," Jules dryly observed as she casually tossed the severed member into the piranha tank to the delight of its inhabitants.

He sat there weeping in agony on two stumps and one hand before being dragged to the side of the bed. Lucy locked the chain around his neck just as Erick entered the room with a tray of wine and cheese.

"Here you are, ladies," Erick dutifully stated as he placed the tray down next to his daughter on a nearby table. "Here is your Wednesday- night treat. I shall leave you now, but . . . what about him? Wednesdays are reserved for ladies."

"No, it can stay," came Sam's chilled reply. "It isn't really a 'he' any longer. In fact, it never *was*. *It* was never a *real* man. *Real* men don't rape. And besides, I *never* want to be without it by my side. It will be a constant reminder to me that true evil exists in this world. No, my dear little Pogo, you and I will *always* have fun together."

As the twins stood outside and listened, Adam whispered, "Oh my, it is so nice to have Aunt Sam back."

"Yes, indeed. I have missed her. And she now enjoys playing games too. Oh, what fun Aunt Sam will have playing games with her little Pogo." "Yes," Adam replied. "It is unfortunate that mother could not rejoin them, however."

"Yes, quite unfortunate indeed. She became not well after father took Alexa away. I hope that she is getting the rest that she needs with those nice men in white coats. It is sad to see our mother suffer so."

———

I just want to go back in time. I just want to live earlier tonight forever and pretend that this never happened. And that is what I' ll do. I' ll just replay it over and over and live there forever until I die, a bewildered Maddy thought to herself as she held her sobbing daughter tightly to the blood-soaked bosom of her yellow-and-white party dress.

Her mind drifted back to the sounds of the preparations for a birthday and anniversary party that was held earlier on that evening of February 14, 2039. Coming from Lucy's bedroom was the song that Sam had requested as her beloved fiancé, Henri, was thoughtfully pulling up her stockings on her paralyzed legs. As she took a seductive drag from her cigarette and listened to Nancy Sinatra's "These Boots Are Made for Walking," she sensually said to Pogo, who was placed next to her on his stumps, wearing blue shorts and a pink shirt that said Mommy's Little Princess, "Gee . . . I bet my *hot legs* are turning you on, aren't they, my little pet? It's really too bad that there is nothing that you can do about it. Well . . . here's something *else* that is hot for you." She then put her cigarette out on his shaven head that was covered in small round burn scars.

Maddy burst into the room in a rage. "What the fuck is *this*?" she screamed.

"Well, Maddy," Sam coldly replied, "I think that you know very well what it is. And I think that you know that you now owe it one dollar."

"No fuckin' way!" Maddy bellowed back. "You don't even fuckin' *live here*!"

"What's all the hububbub?" Erick casually asked as he passed outside in the hallway, and Lucy and Jennifer came racing to see what the commotion was about.

"*This* is the fuckin' hubbub . . . um . . . bub!" Maddy roared. "A fucking *swear jar*! Nope, I love you, Sam, but there's no fucking way that this is going to be in my home!"

"*Actually*, Mom," Josie's cheerful voice appeared as Adrian Belew's "Pretty Pink Rose" blasted from the opened door of her bedroom, "that was *my* idea. You and Dad *really* need to start watching your language. And besides, all the proceeds will go to buying food and supplies for the orphaned animals. It's a win-win for everybody."

A disheveled Jerry and cool-looking Jules emerged from the bathroom down the hall. "Don't worry, Maddy, I've got this," Jules stated before reentering the bathroom. She came back out into the hallway, strode up to Maddy, and put a used condom into the jar. "Problem solved," Jules stated as she adjusted her panties underneath her brilliant-red fringed party dress and walked away from the delighted look upon Maddy's and Erick's faces and the disgusted and dismayed faces of Sam and Josie.

"Why are you still using condoms at your age? You're fifty-one!" Sam yelled out.

"I like the texture!" Jules responded as she began descending the nearby staircase with her dutiful red-faced Jerry directly behind her. "Plus . . . they're ribbed . . . for my pleasure!"

"Okay, now that *that* little tragedy is over, Josie, sweetie, we need to speak to you in our bedroom."

"What? Why?" a red-faced Josie asked in embarrassed confusion. "I swear . . . Lionnel and I are just dating! There's nothing . . . um . . . much going on! I told you that I'm not ready for that!"

Maddy tactfully replied to her daughter, "Why the fuck is everybody in this house so concerned about your little vag? Take a dick, don't take a dick—whatevs. Just be smart about it like your aunt Jules. Now, just get your little ass in here. That's not what we're talking about."

As the Family of Fury walked into the bedroom, Maddy noticed what Erick was wearing for the first time that evening. She looked him up and down, stared into his eyes, and smiled. "You're wearing the suit and slacks from our wedding day!" she excitedly declared as she embraced her adored husband.

"Yes . . . well," Erick proudly replied, "I needed the tailor to . . . um . . . take out a couple of inches . . . like four, I think . . . but yes. I thought that tonight I could handle just a little bit of discomfort to put that smile on your face."

"You *always* put a smile on my face, baby. In the sixteen years that we've been married, I have never *once* been upset with you. Oh sure, you can be a pain in my ass sometimes, but . . . at the end of it . . . you have always made me smile." She then flashed her "silly face" at him, and the loving pair fell upon the bed together, laughing.

"So," Josie impatiently stated, "you guys wanted to talk to me about something?"

"Yes, sweetie," Erick began as he wiped joyful tears from his eyes. "Tonight is not just a celebration of your fifteenth birthday. And it isn't just a celebration of our sixteenth anniversary. Listen, I'm sixty-two years old, and your mother is—"

"Ahem," came Maddy's not-so-subtle cue.

Erick cautiously continued, "Well, let's just say that she is *somewhere* around Jules's age . . . *but doesn't look it—*"

"Yeah, nice save," Maddy acknowledged before allowing him to continue.

"Together, your mother and I have been doing this for a very long time. And whether we want to admit it or not, we aren't immortal and we aren't invincible. I'm wearing down, and your mother is . . . um . . . not . . . but is ready to make a transition into the next phase of our lives together. So, tonight is also our retirement party."

"You see, sweetie," Maddy began as she picked up where her beloved husband left off, "you have made your decision to join this movement. This is not what Aunt Blair wanted. It isn't what your father and I wanted either. We all just wanted you to be safe. So, we think that we have come up with a solution. We are going to transition into full retirement over the next several months. Then, upon your graduation from both high school and college in May, you will take over as president."

"What?" Josie cried out in dismay. "They will never accept me! I'm too young! Too inexperienced!"

"They *will* accept you, sweetie," Maddy responded. "They already know that you are my natural successor. You have earned your stripes on a variety of missions. You're a fucking genius who has sat at the knee of every major player in this syndicate. You know everything about it . . . probably better than *I* do. You are a master tactician. You are a master motivator. Everybody loves you, and you have earned their trust and respect. The only caveat is that they insisted that your father and I stay on as your consiglieres until you turn eighteen. This way, you can still be involved in fighting against the forces of evil in this world without putting yourself in direct harm. You won't need to go on any further missions. These are our wishes, and we ask that you respect them."

"Ummm, okay," Josie tentatively replied before embracing her loving parents in a group hug. The eavesdropping Vai smiled from the kitchen downstairs and thought to herself, *I mean . . . she's fifteen. When is Erick going to get rid of these baby monitors?*

Erick, Henri, Sam, Jules, Jerry, Gregory, Rosa, Lionnel, Rod, Vai, Adam, Aaron, Lucy, and Jennifer had already arrived at the rented nightclub and were seated together at a large round table next to the dance floor. Pogo was chained to a large cinderblock under the table and was frequently being violently kicked by Sam's pointed stilettos whenever the mood struck her. Sam would look at her forty-two-year-old love, smile, and say, "Kick it," at which point Henri would grasp her calf and thrust it upward into the squealing Pogo's scarred face. They would then laugh as Henri would remove her stiletto and show her how much blood had been deposited upon it *this* time.

"Sooo, Lionnel," Erick inquired with a suspicious tone, "so you and Josie have been seeing quite a *bit* of each other, haven't you?"

"Uh, uh, yes, sir," the bashful Lionnel responded meekly as his father and future stepmother knowingly smiled.

"So . . . I think that you are a fine young man. I just couldn't be happier that my daughter is seeing you. But I think that I need to make myself perfectly clear here. There is only *so much* of my daughter that you are going to see right now. Do you understand?"

Before the visibly nervous Lionnel could respond, the DJ announced, "Ladies and gentlemen, especially Erick, it is my great pleasure to introduce to you the arrival of Miss Josie Parker and Mrs. Maddy Sommers!" A white-hot spotlight drenched the pair as they came strutting in. As the sultry chords of Southern Culture on the Skids' version of "Life's A Gas" began playing, Erick burst out into prideful laughter, tears, and applause. He was finally witnessing his loves make their grand entrance together with the accompaniment of their cool theme song. The adorable pair looked nearly identical, with the exception of his daughter's curly locks and a few additional lines upon his wife's face. And their dresses were different. Maddy wore a beautiful little yellow sundress with white patterns. It was the same dress that she had worn on their first date. Josie wore a flowered hippie minidress with white go-go boots. Lionnel gasped as he saw this vision. Erick noticed and jabbed the young man in his ribs with his elbow.

As the song ended, Maddy went rushing up to her husband, gave him a kiss, and bellowed, "It's a fuckin' *party*! Let's fuckin' *dance*!"

The dance floor immediately filled with over one hundred of Murder Incorporated's finest as Maddy's selected playlist of some of her uncle Joe's, aunt Blair's, and especially aunt Patty's favorites boomed through the sound system. Erick would frequently glare at his dancing daughter and Lionnel and yell out, "Hey! That's too fuckin' close! Three feet!"

Josie's delighted face would look over at her overprotective father, roll her eyes, and giggle at him as Maddy would look up at her beloved husband with her emerald-green eyes and say lovingly, "Oh, leave them alone. They're in love . . . just like us."

The couple watched as Henri made his way to the DJ stand. He returned to the dance floor, gently lifted his beloved fiancée from her wheelchair, and began delicately swaying as "Save the Last Dance for Me" by The Drifters enveloped the hall. For Sam, this relationship was not a cold merger of romantic convenience. For Sam, this was truly her first love.

Maddy and Erick chuckled to each other, and they swayed to the music as they stared into one another's eyes. It was just the two of them silently communicating their eternal love to one another. Erick smiled and then winced. A thin trail of blood began dribbling out of his mouth.

"Erick, what the fuck?" Maddy exclaimed before he collapsed upon the dance floor. A thick pool of blood began forming from behind the back of his wedding-day coat. "Oh my god! Oh my god! Oh my god!" was all that could be heard as Maddy dropped to her beloved husband's side and lifted his head. "Hey . . . baby! It's okay! You're going to be okay! Find who fucking did this —now!"

"Okay, okay, okay, okay, just stay with me . . . just please fucking stay with me . . . just look at me . . . just look into my eyes! We need a fucking doctor— now! It's all okay . . . just look at me . . . just stay with me," Maddy pleaded as her husband gazed into her frantic emerald-green eyes. It was just the two of them silently communicating with each other before Erick smiled and meekly said, "Hey . . . wassupbutta—"

"Oh my god! Oh my god! Oh my god! No! No! Don't you *fucking* look at me like that, mister! Don't you *fucking* leave me! You fucking *promised*! You promised to *never* leave me! You have *never* broken a promise to me! You said you would *always* be my prince! *Please* . . . come back!"

CHAPTER 66

BAD REPUTATION

The basement office of the Unholy Trinity was ominously dark, with the exception of a dim backlight in the piranha tank that cast Maddy's silhouette in an eerie glow. "Bring them in," Maddy ordered her daughter in a low, dark voice.

"Mom . . . before I do," Josie began, "we really need to talk about . . . y'know . . . the arrangements for Dad's ceremony."

"There will be no ceremony," Maddy replied coldly. "Your father's body will be cremated, and I shall hold on to his remains through all of eternity. But there will be no ceremony."

"Mom, please, you need this. *I* need this. We need closure. Please be reasonable," Josie pleaded.

"There will *be* no fucking *ceremony!*" Maddy roared back at her beloved daughter as she began violently shaking from pure rage and pain. "There will be no fucking ceremony because your father isn't gone! Oh sure, there were no birds after his passing. I mean . . . where is his bird? There's *always* a bird! A bird to let me know! Where *is* he?"

Josie rushed to her frantic mother's side and wrapped her arms around her as they both broke down again for what seemed to be an eternal stream of tears over the last twenty-four hours since their beloved Erick had been literally stabbed in the back.

Maddy composed herself and once again stated flatly, "There will be no ceremony, sweetie. If we have a ceremony, then I have to say goodbye. And I'm *never* going to say goodbye. I know he's still with us. He's still watching over us. He would never leave me, and I'm never going to leave him. He's out there somewhere, and I'm going to find him. Now, please, sweetie, bring them in."

A fatigued Rosa was the first to enter, still wearing her party gown from the previous evening. She sat nervously in the purple mid-century modern chair in front of the large desk. She had tried all night to make a connection. To try to figure out what had happened. How had she missed this treachery?

"Okay, Rosa," Maddy began calmly, "I know this isn't your fault, but how the fuck did you miss this? How did you not pick up on this evil energy? Please . . . just tell me what happened."

"Um, Maddy," Rosa began with hesitation, "I really don't know. I've been up all night trying to figure it out. There were just so many people there. There was so much energy in that room . . . so much joyous energy that . . . it was just like static. But still . . . I should have picked up on it. If there was murderous male energy in that room, I should have felt it. But . . . I didn't. I really only have two possible explanations. Either this man was able to conceal his negative energy from me, or . . . it was a female assassin."

"Why would gender matter, Rosa?" Josie inquired.

"Well," Rosa began explaining, "as you know, we females have developed the ability to sense threats. Some call it female intuition, and as you know, I'm much more advanced in this ability than others. We can sense negative energy from threats almost like a radar. And for females, *our* primary threat is from heterosexual males. So that is the energy that we're homed in on. We can detect threatening *male* energy, and we can absorb and use positive *female* energy to counter those threats and protect ourselves. That is how we have evolved. We simply don't pick up on threats that might be female. And one more thing. As you know, Maddy, I am unable to pick up on the energy generated by the spirit world. That is not how I have evolved. But some women can. For some women, they can communicate with the spirits who are still here or who may have moved on to the afterlife. I have sensed one such female. She is some-where far away, and I have tried to contact her. I do not know if she received my plea or not. But if she did, she may arrive at some point to help you reach out and find Erick. I'm so sorry, Maddy, that I can't do more than that."

"It's okay, Rosa," Maddy replied softly. "You are incredible, and I thank the universe every day that you are my friend. Just . . . keep working on it, okay? I need to speak to the fucker who did this. And I need to speak to my Erick. Oh, how I have some shit to tell *him*. That's probably why he's hiding from me. He knows I'm gonna give him all *kinds* of shit about leaving me like this—the fuckin' pussy."

Gregory and Rod came bursting through the door with an anxious immediacy. "Sorry to interrupt," a breathless Gregory began, "but we've found him. We've found the assassin. I heard what Rosa was saying before we came in. I'm sorry, honey, but you're mistaken. It wasn't a woman. It was indeed a man."

"Well, *bring* that motherfucker to me then!" Maddy screamed as she was finally able to release some of her rage. "I'm gonna use *all* my torture devices on this douche! He's going to *beg* me to let him die before I get through with him! He's going to be a piece of art that's going to hang on my wall! What are you waiting for? Bring . . . him . . . to . . . me!"

"Well, it really isn't possible," Rod's nasally staccato replied as he stared at the ceiling, unable to make eye contact and not daring to look downward from Maddy's face at this moment. "Yes, we have found him. Someone in his neighborhood tipped us off about a man covered in blood going into his apartment. We know it is him because we found the knife with Erick's blood on it. And he had a picture of Erick on his wall with red crosshairs on it. But . . . it makes no sense. He has no connections to the UAM or any CHARLIE unit. He has no connections to any of our associates. No connections to anyone we have worked for or against in the past. He had been an attendant at a psychiatric institution until just recently. Then, he moved here and was pretty much undetectable. There is no reason for him to have anything against you or Erick or Murder Incorporated. It seems as though he simply murdered Erick . . . for no known reason, then went home, and he . . . hanged himself."

"Well, *that's* fucking anticlimactic," a disappointed Maddy stated as she placed her rage back inside her soul and slumped into her oversized faux leather chair. Then, a chill went up Maddy's spine as she heard Rod utter one final sentence.

"There's one other curious thing. He was hanging there in his living room, and he was clutching a yardstick in one hand and a Bible in the other. I have no explanation for this."

Maddy looked over once again at Rosa with a shocked expression and said, "Rosa . . . you need to find me that fucking medium."

As their colleagues left the room, Maddy and Josie were joined by Jules, Sam, and Lucy. "Hey, guys, what are you all doing here?" Maddy inquired in a weary voice.

"I invited them, Mom," Josie replied. "I thought that you might not want to hold a ceremony, and we all have so much grief and anger in our hearts. That anger has to go somewhere. So . . . how about a ladies' night out? I feel like having a slash dance!"

————

"Why the *fuck* do you just automatically assume that I'm her *mother*? Why can't I be her slightly *older sister* or something?" Maddy screamed at the shaking young man who had approached the table of the nightclub with the intent of obtaining Josie's affection.

"Um . . . I'm . . . um . . . sorry," the disheveled young man stammered before making a hasty retreat back to the safety of his guffawing friends at another table.

"Okay, *that* motherfucker just made the list. Let's find two more," Maddy growled at her sisterhood of Josie, Lucy, Jules, and Sam.

"Mom!" Josie yelled back. "We are *not* going to kill a guy just because he guessed your age. And accurately, *I might add*!"

"Oh, fine. What fucking ever there, jailbait," Maddy barked back. "Just get your little ass out on the dance floor and do your thing. And make sure you tell them your real age and that you're going to a party with us and some of your little school girlfriends. If they're a piece of shit who is trying to get into the pants of innocent teenagers, then they make the list! Got it?"

Seven minutes later, Josie arrived back at the table with three middle- aged businessmen who were sweating in anticipation. "Well, hello there," Lucy stated in a lascivious greeting. "So, do you boys want to come to our dance? We're going to have a *really fun* night. And if you play your cards right, maybe we'll let our little Josie and some of her friends . . . dance . . . as well."

"Uh, yeah, baby!" one of the men excitedly exclaimed. "We're always . . . up . . . for a little fun."

One of the men looked down and noticed Sam's wheelchair. "Uh, no offense, baby, but I'm not sure we'll be able to . . . uh . . . dance with you."

"Oh, trust me, gentlemen," a smiling Sam replied, "what I lack in mobility I make up for in . . . enthusiasm. And I think that you'll be *quite surprised* at what I can do from my chair."

Jules overheard one of the men whisper to another, "Hey, man, a hole's a hole, ain't it? If nothing else, her mouth still works, heh-heh-heh." Jules picked up a fork from off the table and began lifting it until Maddy grasped her hand and slammed it back down while shaking her head.

She whispered into Jules's ear, "Just wait. Take that anger and bottle it up. It's so much more satisfying when you wait. The release is incredible. Trust me. I kinda wrote the book on this shit."

"Okay, boys," Maddy stated cheerfully. "Just sit tight and have a soda or something. We're going to go downstairs and make sure everything's . . . ready." Josie and Maddy were tittering as they began descending the staircase that led to the basement under LOHAD.

"Oh, goddammit!" Maddy cried out. "What are *you* guys doing here? And why are there entrails hanging off the walls?"

"Oh, hello, Aunt Maddy . . . Josie," Adam replied, followed by Aaron's, "Yes, hello. We are making new game parts. Entrails are so delightfully rubbery that we can mold them into any shape that we desire. We do so enjoy games."

Josie looked around at the mess. The tortured wife beater's face was frozen in anguish, and his body had been sliced open. His internal organs were organized neatly on an adjacent table. "Okay, guys. Just put a curtain over this stuff, okay?" Josie requested politely. "And next time you want to use LOHAD for this, just tell me, okay? We have visitors tonight."

"Oh, how fun!" Adam exclaimed.

"Oh my, yes," Aaron responded. "May we play with your guests as well?"

"Nope . . . ladies' night," Maddy coldly replied. "Now, where the fuck is Vai?"

"Oh, she's in the back room," Adam answered, followed by Aaron's, "Yes, she is in the back with another special guest. We think that you might be quite surprised and pleased."

Maddy opened the door to the back room of the basement. Vai had her back to the door and was leaning over another young blonde woman. "Oh, wow, that's really nice, dear. You are so talented," Vai was saying to her guest.

"Uh . . . hey, what's going on?" Maddy asked as she peered over the pair's shoulder to see the entire Manhattan skyline being meticulously painted upon the back of a dismembered human torso.

"Hiya, Aunt Maddy!" the young woman squealed as she jumped up from her chair and embraced her estranged aunt.

"Alexa . . . what the fuck are *you* doing here?" Maddy exclaimed before reciprocating the embrace.

"Well," the blue-eyed, blonde-haired twenty-year-old Alexa replied through her tears of excitement, "after Mom was . . . y'know . . . institutionalized . . . Dad and I went away. Dad was never the same after the twins and Vai left, and Mom went crazy. He started drinking—a lot. I did everything that I could, but he was hell-bent on drinking himself to death. And a few weeks ago, he accomplished that. He passed away, and I came looking for Vai and the twins. I came looking for my family. And I found them. Not only that, but I found all the wonderful games that they have been playing, so . . . they are teaching me what I can do with *my* artistic talent. This particular piece will hang in the living room of the basement. Do you like it?"

"Uh . . . uh . . . uh . . ." was all that Maddy could summon up before Alexa continued. "And so, I've been living down here for the last few days until—"

"Until the time was right to tell you, Aunt Maddy, and more permanent arrangements could be made," Vai interjected. "We did not want anything to disrupt your celebration last night, and then—well . . . we were just waiting for the right time."

"Okay, well, listen, ladies . . . um," Maddy began stating, "you see, we're having one of our slash dances tonight to . . . y'know . . . blow off some steam . . . so . . ."

"What's a slash dance?" Alexa excitedly inquired.

"Well . . . um . . . you see, it's kinda like . . . um—" Maddy attempted to explain before Vai cut her off.

"It's all right, Aunt Maddy. Please just let Alexa and me observe. She has already witnessed some of the Twins' games. I don't believe that this will be much more of a shock."

"Uh . . . yeah . . . okay," Maddy agreed as she opened a drawer and began rustling through it. "But hey, Alexa, do me a favor and put this on, will you? And have the twins go out the back basement exit. We'll be down with our guests in five minutes."

Maddy and Josie began ascending the staircase as the twins were rapidly cleaning up their play area. They entered the main floor of LOHAD, and

Josie said, "Sorry about the wait, fellas. A few of my friends had another party here earlier, and we needed to clean up a little bit."

"Oh, and listen," Maddy interjected as she looked at Jules, Lucy, and Sam, "Ummm, don't freak out or anything, but Alexa's back, and she's downstairs. I'll explain later."

"Alexa!" one of the men exclaimed. "She sounds fun. Who is *she*?" "Oh . . . you're going to really like her. She's one of Josie's childhood friends, and I think that she may be just as fun to play with as Josie is," Maddy replied coyly.

The entire group was laughing as they descended the staircase. There was a black curtain covering the far wall and table. The rest of the area was furnished with red vinyl chairs and sofas with various bright paintings of peace signs, flowers, and smiley faces adorning the walls. The men were too distracted to notice the dull red stains that dripped down the artwork. Vai was sitting in a vinyl chair, sipping a drink in a flirty black dress, and Alexa was sitting on the adjacent vinyl couch. The men's eyes popped out as they saw this blue-eyed, blond-haired beauty sitting there dressed in her school-girl uniform. "Well, *hello, Alexa*!" one of the men shouted out.

"Let's get this party started!"

"Yeah . . . lets," Jules dryly stated as she turned on the disco lights and pushed play on the CD player. The entire group went to the middle of the floor and began suggestively gyrating to "I Feel Love" by Donna Summer.

As their laughing and gleeful faces were rapidly illuminated by the flashing colored lights, Sam pressed a button on the arm of her wheelchair, causing blades to extend from the footrests. She whipped the chair rapidly to her left, and the man nearest her fell to the floor, screaming in agony as his feet had been removed at the ankles. Crimson blood flowed from the shrieking man's stumps as the other four cackling women took knives out of the garments and began slashing at the confused men's faces.

"Slash dance!" Josie yelled out as she sliced through a man's throat with her dagger. She violently thrust the six-inch blade into his soft face repeatedly as he slumped to the slippery yet sticky floor. Lucy looked over at the scene and giggled as she lacerated a third man's face downward from between his eyes to his chin. Maddy grabbed the man's flesh by both sides of the incision and peeled the man's face off his skull as he sank to his knees while screaming in agony. Jules got on top of the stumpy man and gashed his face and torso repeatedly while wearing a maniacal smile. She then took a fork from under her garter and plunged it into the man's left eye, causing blood and goo to squirt upon the bosom of her dark red dress. "Well, *that* should put a fork in it, heh-heh-heh!" Maddy yelled out before the blood-soaked forms of Maddy, Josie, Jules, and Lucy kneeled around Sam's wheelchair in a group embrace as tears and laughter of emotional release began flowing, washing the blood from their shining cheeks.

As Rob Zombie's version of "I'm Your Boogieman" began booming through the speakers, Vai looked at the enthralled face of the young Alexa and said matter-of-factly, "So, dear, that is a slash dance. Do you have any questions?"

"Uh, yeah. Just one," an unblinking Alexa replied as she surveyed the scene of carnage and listened to the final agonized wails of the would-be statutory rapists. "Can I use their torsos for canvas?"

"Of course, you may, dear," came Vai's satisfied reply. "Of course, you may."

CHAPTER 67

PEACE TRAIN

"Okay, sweetie," Maddy began the next morning in a more cheerful tone than what she was feeling, "pack a bag. We're getting out of town for a couple days, okay?"

"Why? Where are we going? I have school!" Josie replied.

"Yeah, like school's a fuckin' problem for you. How many months of assignments ahead are you anyway?" Maddy retorted.

"Well, actually," Josie answered in a slightly embarrassed tone, "I'm pretty much done with my coursework. I just need to hand it in. These classes just go so slow for me. I'm just waiting on finals in May so I can graduate and also get my bachelor's degree."

"Yeah, that's what I figured, smart-ass," Maddy replied as she shook her head and chuckled. "I'll just call the school and tell them you'll be absent for a few days, and you can hand in your next week's coursework. It's not like they won't expect it. I mean, you just lost—I mean . . . well . . . we need to look for your father. They'll understand."

"Mom, please," Josie responded sorrowfully, "please, we need to just admit that Dad is gone. We need to admit that so that we can begin the healing process. Staying in denial doesn't help anything. And I still think that we need a ceremony. Please."

"Nope, *not* gonna fuckin' happen!" Maddy roared back. "*Not* gonna happen because he's *not* gone! Oh sure, he may not be here with us physically, but he's still here. I know it. I can feel it . . . sorta. Maybe he's just lost or something, and that's why there hasn't been a bird to show me a sign. He's probably just got his hopeless ass lost out there in the universe. You know how fucking directionally impaired that man is. I swear, he's so directionally impaired that every time he went to go down on me, he ended up licking my forehead!"

"Mom!" a shocked Josie cried out. "Oh . . . my . . . god . . . *gross*! Don't *say* that to me!"

"Oh, grow the fuck up," Maddy replied dismissively. "You'll get there someday. But . . . heh-heh-heh . . . just know that *now* your father can see *every little thing* that you're up to. You and Lionnel might be able to sneak around behind *my* back, but your father is going to see *everything*. So . . . you just might want to keep that in mind as you engage in your awkward fucking fumbling."

Josie just sat on the edge of the bed with a bright-red face and looked down at the floor as she pondered the possibility of her father being aware of all her actions from this moment on. Her ingenious yet still-adolescent mind resolved at that moment that she would never have sex in her life. It would just be too embarrassing for her and hurtful for her beloved father. "Well, if it's *proven* that Dad is, y'know, watching over me, then I guess that I'll just never have sex in my life."

"Oh, what fuckin' ever!" Maddy exclaimed as she burst into laughter. "And you call yourself a *genius*? Don't worry, sweetie. At some point, your hormones will override the fact that your father can see *every little thing* that you're doing. Every . . . little . . . thing, heh-heh-heh."

"You can be so cruel sometimes, Mom. Now, where are we going?" Josie inquired rapidly to change the topic to something far less personal.

"You'll see. Your father and I were planning on taking you there this weekend anyway, and I don't want to disappoint him. Just pack a few things. We have plenty of stuff there. I just can't *wait* to see the look on your face when your father and I show you this place!"

Josie left the room and went across the hall to her bedroom. A prideful Maddy watched as her beloved daughter exited, and tears began forming in her green eyes. *Jesus, she's just so emotionally strong. So much more so than me. She's the only thing that is helping me to survive this right now. Okay, baby, I'm going to try not to cry when I listen to this song this time. Just please. I know you're out there somewhere. Please . . . just communicate with me, okay? I need to know that you're here.*

She approached the vintage multiple-CD player to once again listen to the song that she had played almost nonstop since her cherished husband's passing. It was the song that he had played as he was getting ready for his mission to infiltrate CHARLIE so many years ago. She had watched him from the doorway as he was sobbing and packing the vials of the antidote to *Toxin X* into his bag. He was playing this song because he knew in his heart that there was a significant chance that he might never see his beloved family again.

Maddy pressed play to listen to REM's "Leaving New York" for one final time. The CD player began whirring as it searched for the chosen track. The music began, and out of the speakers came..."It's A Miracle" by Barry Manilow.

"Josie, Josie, Josie, Josie, Josie!" Maddy excitedly blurted out. Josie came bounding into the room and found her mother clapping and jumping around the room. "What . . . what is it?" she urgently asked.

"How the *fuck* did this CD get in here? Did *you* put it in here?" Maddy asked her daughter with her face beaming with anticipation.

"No . . . no, *I* didn't put it in here. In fact, *this* CD isn't even supposed to be in the house," Josie replied with widened eyes and the pulsing lights of the CD player dancing in her green iris. "Dad took this disc to LOHAD, and he would play a track off it every once in a while and laugh while he was flipping Aunt Patty's mural off."

"I told you!" Maddy squealed in delight. "I fucking *told* you that your father was still with us! Oh, *very* dramatic, mister! Put me through all *sorts* of hell for the last two days! What, didja get yourself *lost* or something? Yeah, probably. Okay, I forgive you. Oh, and you're going to *love* this! I'm taking her to our new place. I haven't told her about it yet, so don't ruin the surprise. And . . . since you're not able to drive, that means that *I'm* going to drive, Mr. Control Freak, and I'm gonna run *every red light* that I can just to piss you off! What do you think about *that*, mister?"

The CD abruptly stopped. There was the sound of a new disc rotating into the play position as Josie and Maddy stared at each other in bewilderment. And then came the uproarious opening laughter of "Don't Get Funny with Me" by The Cramps.

"Oh my fucking god, baby," Maddy expressed as tears began flowing once again. "Okay, this is going to get weird with you communicating with me through songs, but I'll get used to it. I'm just so happy that you're here. I *knew* that you would never leave me. I *knew* that you would never break your promise to me."

"Mom," a rationalizing Josie began as her advanced mind searched for possible explanations. "Listen . . . um . . . there might be another explanation. I mean . . . maybe it's just some weird coincidence or the CD player is broken or something. I mean, it's like forty-five years old."

"Yeah, you think so, *smart-ass*?" Maddy countered. "Okay . . . well . . . let's just see. Hey, baby, did you hear my conversation that I had with our daughter about how you would be able to see everything—and I mean *every-thing*—that she was up to? That you'll *always* be watching her? Did you hear that? What did you think about *that*?"

The music stopped once again. The CD player switched discs, and "Every Breath You Take" by The Police emerged ominously from the speakers.

"Ah, shit, that's so creepy," Josie muttered under her breath as she slowly trudged back to her room to the sound of her mother's hysterical laughter.

———

"We're here!" Maddy shouted out as they pulled their van into the long driveway and approached the main house of the acreage. It was two stories tall plus a basement, of course. Constructed out of large light-gray stones, it seemed to glow in a soft-yellow hue as the sun was setting behind the peace-ful-looking structure.

"C'mon, let me show you around!" Maddy shouted as she pulled Josie from the passenger seat and began dragging her up the eight stone steps to the front door.

She opened the solid oak arched front door and began rapidly explaining, "Isn't this just *beautiful*? Your father and I bought this place to be our retire-ment home. Just a few years ago, this was the home of a UAM oligarch. And now, fittingly, it is ours! All the surrounding neighbors tracked down that evil bastard and hanged him. Just like what happened throughout the country. As people began to realize that they had been lied to and manipulated into believing that pandemic cures were a hoax, elections were a hoax, education was evil, people who weren't white were evil, empowered women were evil, and all that other bullshit, the people banded together. And not just because of *that*.

"They weren't just pissed because they had been lied to and brainwashed into hating other people who were different from themselves. They were also pissed that as the UAM and all their fucking media mouthpieces gained control, they took away their rights. The very people who indoctrinated them into believing that they would protect them actually *took* from them. They took away women's rights first to the point that women would be terrorized into not voting in the UAM counties. Then, the oligarchs took away their land and either forced them to farm their own land for pennies or outright murdered them if they wouldn't cooperate. And they didn't just take their land and their things. They took away their dignity. But once Murder Incorporated and countless other freedom fighters throughout our country and our world beat them back, they *regained* their dignity—in spades.

"They found as many of these motherfuckers as they could. The local fascist leaders. The CHARLIE foot soldiers. The propaganda peddlers and political false prophets in their fancy high-rise apartments, offices, and studios. They found them and dragged them to places like this, and they hanged them publicly. Local authorities just shrugged and turned their back. There were never any witnesses, and every resident had an alibi. Because they had banded together to rid themselves and our world of their cancerous, greedy, narcissistic wannabe overlords. They decided that they weren't going to take their shit anymore, and they exacted *their* brand of justice. They exacted *our* brand of justice. And they did it *together*.

"Just as they have banded together again to share resources to combat the crippling effects of climate change. They share water supplies and irrigation systems. They share their knowledge and ingenuity. They share their tools and equipment. They share their food when someone is going without. They take care of each other's kids. They help each other start local shops and only do business with those local shops, which has led to large corporate stores shutting down. Local shops are thriving because of the pride that their community has in them. Plus, you can't exactly order shit online anymore after what your fucking father, Rod, and Rosa did a few years ago to the wireless systems. That has been a bit of a *fucking inconvenience* for me. But I digress. They share *everything* so that *everyone* can live a peaceful and prosperous life. And they share with *everybody*. There are farmers and shopkeepers and crafts persons and mechanics and builders and laborers and artists here from every walk of life. This county has gone from one of the most oppressive and dangerous counties in the country to one of many of the most peaceful, open, caring, and loving counties. I used to *hate* this county. Now, I wouldn't want to spend my retirement anywhere else. And your father agrees with me . . . *don't* you, mister?"

A single bird flew upon a branch outside of the window and chirped. "Well, are you finally getting the hang of this shit? You coulda done that a little *earlier*, y'know!" Maddy yelled at the bird, which squawked and flew away. Maddy could have sworn that she saw the bird lift a wing and extend a middle feather before its departure.

"Yeah, typical," Maddy muttered before concluding. "And what I'm talking about isn't *socialism* either. GAAAAWD! I fucking *hate it* when those fascist fucks say that shit to frighten and manipulate people! It isn't *socialism* to have respect for another person's point of view. It 'isn't *socialism* to embrace our differences. It isn't *socialism* to care about others who look different than us or worship different than us or love different than us. It isn't *socialism* to support equal rights for *everybody*. It isn't *socialism* to lend a helping hand when someone else is down. To help them rebuild. To watch their kids. To put a smile on their face during hard times. That isn't *socialism* goddammit! It's just fucking *common decency*! It's *humanity*! It's what the *fucking Bible* preaches for fuck sakes! And anyone who says otherwise can just fuck off!"

"Okay," Josie replied in a hushed hesitation. "so . . . are you over your diatribe now? Can we see the house, or do you need to go on for another hour?"

"Naw, I'm good. I feel better now," Maddy cheerfully replied as the pair gazed around the large foyer, with rich wooden walls and a marble floor. They entered the room to the left, which contained a large living area with plush antique furnishings and a grand brick fireplace. Across the hall was a nearly identical room that was to have been Erick's "study," which meant that it would have contained a stereo and wall-to-wall records. To the very back was a large kitchen with modern silver appliances glinting in the setting sun from behind the back picture window.

They rushed up the curved wooden staircase. At the top of the stairs, they abruptly stopped. There were two beefy, hairy tall men silently standing there in camouflage dungarees and T-shirts. Josie immediately reached into her jeans pocket and opened a six-inch knife.

"Oh, fuck," Maddy muttered softly. "I'm sorry, sweetie. Put the knife away. I should have told you about them," Maddy began explaining before one of the men yelled out, "Maddy! We *thought* we heard some commotion downstairs! Welcome home!" He embraced her in a nearly suffocating bear hug.

"And this must be Josie!" the other man squealed out as he embraced her so hard that she dropped the knife. The blade made clinking sounds as it tumbled down the staircase before coming to a rest under a picture of John Lewis. "Oh, my dears," the man stated sorrowfully, "we are *so sorry* about your loss. Erick was such a *fine* man. We absolutely *adored* working with him as he was putting this place together. It is just so tragic. We have been doing *nothing* but crying for the past two days. We are just so sorry."

"Thank you, guys," Maddy stated sincerely as she wiped a single tear from her left eye. "It's okay. Well . . . I mean . . . it's not okay, but we're . . . okay. We're going to be okay. We have come here to find our peace with all this, and we could not be happier to share our home with you. Thank you so much for your sentiments and being here with us."

Josie looked at her mother with a confused expression and said, "Um . . . sharing our home? I'm sorry, but who *are* these guys?"

"Oh! So sorry, sweetie!" Maddy chirped. "Well, this brawny but *slightly vain* gentleman here with all the facial hair that he *continues* to dye black is Paciano."

"Oh, sweetheart," Paciano replied, "are you telling me that *your* lovely copper strands are *still* all natural? Pu-lease! And are you telling me that *my* hair doesn't look *fabulous*? Once again, *pu-lease*!"

"Yeah, yeah, yeah, you look fuckin' great," Maddy sheepishly replied before more assertively stating, "And *yes*, my hair is all *fucking natural*, you ageist fuck!"

The trio burst into laughter. Maddy regained control and said to Josie, "And this also quite brawny and also quite hairy *but naturally gray* gentleman is Stellan. They are a married couple who are going to be our caretakers here in exchange for living here for free. They are wonderful. They are kind. They are intelligent—"

"And we are fucking *fierce*, girlfriend," Paciano interjected.

"Oh, my love," Stellan responded, "must you be so . . . aggressive with your language?"

"Fuck *yeah*, he does!" Maddy yelled out as the four new friends fell into uproarious laughter and embraced.

"Come, come, come, come, come," Stellan eagerly stated. "Come, let's see the rest of the house. There are five bedrooms upstairs. This one is to be used as a guest bedroom. These two are for you two. And these two are *our* little slice of heaven. One is our bedroom, and the other is our sitting room. Now let's go outside, shall we? It's a quite-normal forty-five-degree February evening."

"Ummm, hey," Maddy began inquiring, "why is there a guestroom up *here*? We have a three-bedroom cottage for that."

"Well . . . the guesthouse is a bit occupied at the moment," Paciano replied. "But of course, it is *your* property, and so you may kick them out if you wish. They do tend to be a bit . . . messy, but we have been looking after them."

Stellan then inserted the key into the front door, looked at Josie with a wide smile, and said mischievously, "Come, Josie dear, *you* open the door and turn on the light."

"Awwww . . . goddammit," Maddy stated in a soft, resigned voice as she heard her beloved daughter squeal out, "Kittens . . . and puppies!"

"Yes," Stellan began explaining, "it was the strangest thing. Two nights ago, right after we found out about—well, right after we found out . . . we heard this scratching at the front door. This mother cat and her three kittens and this mother beagle and her two puppies were at the door. They just sat there and looked up at us as though they were expected. We didn't know if you would want them in the main house, so we put them here . . . for the time being."

"Oh! They're *totally* living in the main house!" Josie declared cheerfully. As she was rolling on the floor, bombarded by feline and canine kisses, Josie said to the universe, *Thanks, Dad. You always know what to get me for my birthday. I love you.*

———

"Oh, for fuck sakes!" a still half-asleep Maddy yelled out as she attempted to navigate the blur of playing fur under her feet while attempting to not spill her steaming coffee. "Josie, do something about your animals!" "Sorry, Mom!" Josie responded as she slid down the banister and landed in the foyer. "C'mon, guys! Mika! Get your kittens in order! Mike! Peter! Bill! C'mon! Let's get some breakfast. And that goes for you too, Darcy. Get your pups! C'mon, Joe! C'mon, Bob! Let's eat!"

The mother and daughter spent the day walking around their property in near silence. They surveyed the small apple orchard, pumpkin patch, and area that would be a pink rose garden. They looked around the area that had been developed into an archery range. And they surveyed the apiary. "Bees?" Josie exclaimed excitedly. "We're going to have *bees*? And our own *honey*? Oh, how marvelous! What a beautiful surprise! I can now help the environment by tending to my bees!"

"Uh . . . yeah . . . that's why we did it . . . I guess," Maddy replied. "Actually, this was your father's idea. I had the same reaction as you. I didn't know what he was going for. But he explained it to me and said that you were special and not just because you were his daughter. Everything about you was special, and everything about you connected you to the legends of Saint Valentine. You were born at 2:14 a.m. on February 14. The name Valentine is derived from the word *valens*, which means 'worthy,' 'strong,' and 'powerful,' which you sure as fuck are. It is said that the *real* Saint Valentine's skull is on display in some museum or something and that its crown is adorned with flowers. Your father said that *that* is why he always placed a flower in your hair when you were a baby, and he is always so pleased when you enter a room with a flower in your hair. He has always loved that. He also said that you are one of the most loving souls on this earth and that Valentine's Day is, of course, known best for that. Then, there's the whole you getting into archery thing and the parallels to Cupid and all that shit. But what I *didn't* know was that Saint Valentine was also the patron saint of beekeepers. So, your father had this built . . . for you.

"But . . . one last thing, sweetie. We intend for this place to be a place of peace. This is a place where we can find comfort and love. This is a place that is not to be sullied by the hatred and violence in our everyday lives in the city. This is a place that inspires us to fight for how the world *should* be. This is where our hearts can be at peace and just focus on the love that we have for one another, understand?"

Josie nodded and stood there in silent reverence. Her contemplative silence continued into the evening as everyone was sitting around a blazing fire, cuddling in their pajamas with kittens and puppies. Paciano and Stellan got up from the living room sofa and stretched before Stellan said, "Well, darlings, we're off to bed. Don't forget to put the fire out before coming upstairs."

"Yeah, we won't," Maddy sleepily replied before bellowing, "But hey, keep your shit down! I know how loud you fuckers can be, and we have a minor here!"

Paciano burst into laughter before saying in a singsong voice, "No promises, dearies. You may want to get out your noise-canceling headphones. *I'm* in the mood for a *bumpity* night. Nighty night now, heh-heh-heh."

As the mother and daughter finished the last sip of their hot cocoa and watched the flames recede into the wooden cinders in the fireplace, Josie embraced her mother and said into her ear, "Thank you, Mom. This has been just wonderful. But I need to tell you something. If anyone ever messes with this place, I will tear them apart with my bare hands and paint the walls with their blood. Good night, Mom."

Maddy sat frozen as she watched her cherished daughter exit the room and begin ascending the staircase. As she turned on the radio, she gazed at the fireplace mantel, which she had decorated with a picture of her uncle Joe, aunt Blair, and aunt Patty; the signed SCOTS album from their first date; her DVD copy of *Cinderella*, and her beloved's urn. "There's a Light (Over at the Frankenstein Place)" from *The Rocky Horror Picture Show* came streaming through the tiny speaker. "Yup, you got *that* one right, baby," Maddy stated with reserved satisfaction. "She's both a beacon of hope *and* a fucking monster. And I couldn't be prouder."

Chapter 68

I Have Arrived

"Happy anniversary, baby," Maddy mewed as she extended her five- foot-four (and a fucking half) inch frame for her morning stretch. "I can't believe that it's been a year since . . . well . . . y'know. But let's not focus on that. I can't believe that it's been *eighteen* years since we first met and *seventeen* years since our wedding and *sixteen* years since—oh my god, sorry, baby! I gotta look outside to see if Josie's birthday present has been delivered!"

It was February 14, 2040, and it was indeed Josie's sixteenth birthday. Maddy rushed to the upstairs guestroom in the Brooklyn brownstone and looked out the back window. "Yay! It's here!" she exclaimed as she began jumping on one of the guest beds like a five-year-old at her first slumber party. Although now nearing fifty-two years of age, Maddy still had the exuberance of a child and the looks of a woman at least ten years her junior. "What's all the commotion about?" Josie inquired wearily as she wiped the sleep from her crusty emerald eyes.

"First off, happy birthday, sweetie," Maddy replied, wearing a wide grin. "Now, go jump in the shower because I have a special birthday surprise for you, okay?"

"Aw, c'mon, Mom," Josie whined, "I worked late at LOHAD last night. Plus, it's my birthday, and I wanted to just lounge around today. Please?"

Maddy stroked her chin as she contemplated her response. On the one hand, she had an incredible surprise for her daughter and wanted to spend the day with her. On the other hand, it was indeed Josie's birthday, and she had always been allowed to spend it however she wished, which usually included walking around the neighborhood to attract stray cats and dogs. She did *not* want to begin her sixteenth birthday by fucking this up.

Maddy fucked it up. "Listen here, little missy! *I'm* your mother, so when I tell you to get your *little ass* in the fuckin' shower, then you'll *get* in the fuckin' shower! Then, I'm going to show you a surprise, and we're going to spend the day together, and you're going to have a *great* fucking time! Got it?"

"GAAAAAWWDD! Fine!" Josie screamed as she stormed down the hallway and slammed the bathroom door.

"Well . . . I think that I handled *that* rather well, don't you, baby?" Maddy inquired of her husband's spirit. She thought that it might have been her imagination, but she could have sworn that she heard a lone trombone in the distance going *mwaaa, mwaaa, mwaaa*.

As Josie dragged her feet toward the back door, Maddy exuberantly said, "C'mon, hurry up. Okay, before I open the door and show you your surprise, I need to tell you something about it. This is something that your father has picked out for you and has restored. When he first showed it to me fifteen months ago, it was just a pile of rusted junk. And now . . . and now . . . *drum-roll please* . . . it's this!"

A beaming Maddy flung open the back door of the brownstone. Josie walked onto the back porch, and her jaw dropped. Tears began forming in her green eyes, and she placed her hands over her mouth in disbelief.

Sitting in their back driveway was a completely restored 1976 VW bus. Its bright-yellow paint glistened in the morning sunshine. There were randomly placed seventies-style flowers of multiple colors and sizes painted on the body. The passenger windows had multicolored beaded curtains that could be closed when the bus was not being driven. It was the epitome of utopian hippie freedom. It was the epitome of a symbol of peace. It was the epitome of her father's love for her. For Josie, it was the most perfect gift that anyone could have given her.

"Oh my, oh my, oh my," Josie began blurting out in a torrent of joy. "Oh my god! *Mom*! This is *incredible*! This is the greatest thing in the history of the world! And it's *mine*? I can't believe it. I just can't believe it! You told me that I could have the used crappy 2034 Chevy that we had when I turned sixteen! I just can't believe this! Thank you, Mom! And most of all, thank you, Dad! I love you both so much!"

"Yeah, well, the Chevy thing was just to throw you off. C'mon, let's look inside!" Maddy squealed as she began jumping and clapping. She opened the driver's side door, and Josie climbed in. The polished wood- grain dashboard, console, and steering wheel reflected the bright sunshine that was shining upon it through the crystal-clear windshield. The front bucket seats were a bright-pink vinyl. "This is just amazing," an awestruck Josie said.

"Let's check out the back!" Maddy directed as she pulled her beloved daughter out of the van and slid the side panel door to reveal two bright- pink bench seats sitting upon the black vinyl flooring. "Your father picked vinyl because . . . well . . . it's easier to clean the blood up. And he picked pink because of your love for that color. He wanted to put shag carpeting in but thought better of it because . . . well . . . y'know . . . that would be a *real* bitch to clean up. Oh, and speaking of cleaning up bloody messes, here's the best part!"

Maddy popped a mechanism on the back of the middle seat and tilted it backward to reveal a secret storage compartment. "Your father calls this your toy box. As you see, we have a regular set of bow and arrows, a crossbow with arrows, and a large assortment of knives, swords, throwing stars, and hatchets. Your father said that he was going to tell you that these were for Lionnel in case he gets too fuckin' handsy, heh-heh-heh. Oh, and one last thing, sweetie. Your father searched and searched for a 1976 model because that was the year of our country's bicentennial, and it was a time, although *certainly* far from perfect, when our country had much more civil public discourse and it was at the height of civil rights movements for racial minorities, women, people with disabilities, and the LGBTQ+ community. Oh, and 1976 was *also* the year your father was born, and he thought that this way he could always be with you even after he's gone, which we know *now* isn't *ever* gonna fuckin' happen! Wanna go for a spin?"

Josie climbed behind the steering wheel and grasped the key that had a peace-sign keychain dangling from it. She turned the key and started the ignition. The motor purred like a, well, kitten, of course. Josie and Maddy both squealed in delight and clapped. "Okay, how about some music?" Maddy asked as she pulled open the center console to reveal a set of plastic boxes that were roughly five inches by four inches and less than an inch thick.

"What are *those*?" Josie inquired. "Ummm," Maddy responded, "these are called 8-tracks, and they're like tapes that have music on them. They were really popular in the seventies. That was before cassettes, which were—oh, never mind. Just close your eyes and pick one out. I want to see what your father has to say to you."

Josie covered her eyes and pulled out one of the tapes. Without looking at it, she popped it into the player on the console. Out of the eight speakers came "Sixteen Candles" by The Crests.

"*Jesus*, Dad, you're so corny!" Josie stated as she chuckled and put the bus into reverse.

Josie drove only two blocks toward picking up Lionnel, then Vai, and the twins before Maddy began saying, "Can I drive it now, *hmmmm*? Hey! Can I drive it now? Are you tired of driving yet? Can I drive it? Hey, Josie, can I drive it now, *hmmm*?"

Fifteen minutes later, Maddy pulled up in front of Lionnel's apartment and honked the horn. Henri peered down and said, "Wow, now *that's* a ride! What's goin' on, Maddy?"

"Hey!" Maddy yelled back. "Send Lionnel down. We're scooping the loop or something in Josie's new wheels!"

"Why isn't Josie driving?" Henri asked.

Maddy looked over at her daughter sitting in the passenger seat with her arms folded and a scowl on her face and yelled back, "Oh, she decided it was *my* turn. Now get Lionnel's ass down here!"

As the twins were in the "way back" seat comparing their new miniature chess pieces that were made of human teeth, and Lionnel and Vai were sitting on the middle seat above the toy box, Josie said, "The pet store's down here. It's down here, Mom! *Mom*! Turn *here*!"

"Fuck . . . whatever," Maddy said as she rolled her eyes and screeched the bus around the corner, causing all the passengers to abruptly slide across the pink vinyl seats to their left and crash into the side of the bus. "What's the big fuckin' deal anyway? Why are we going to the pet store?"

"I need to get some supplies for my furry friends at the acreage," Josie replied.

"Oh . . . yeah . . . that makes sense. It's nice of you to buy a present for Paciano and Stellan, heh-heh-heh," Maddy replied jokingly.

"Mom, I *love* you, but sometimes you drive me *crazy*!" Josie exclaimed as she got out of the passenger door and began walking toward the pet store.

"I love you too, sweetie!" Maddy shouted back. "I *know* that I drive you crazy because I'm the one *driving*! Get it? Get the play on words? Hey! How come you're not laughing? That was *gold*! Pure fuckin' go—"

There was a hail of gunfire, and Maddy's petite body was flung five feet backward as she was hit randomly by fourteen bullets. She was gasping for breath as a woman in a purple jacket came rushing to her side and grasped her hand. Josie came running as well and clenched her other hand. A thick pool of crimson blood flowed from under Maddy's lithe frame and crept around the legs of the kneeling women as they heard a woman's voice cackling. As Maddy was attempting to cling to life and looking anxiously into her beloved daughter's frantic green eyes, she listened to the woman's rambling speech while noticing the distinct scent of iron.

"I *told* you, bitch! I fucking *told* you that I'd get you back!" Kristy Anderson was standing fifteen feet away, holding a smoking assault rifle with an expression of absolute glee on her face. "Oh, they all said that I was *crazy*! But they were *wrong*! Could a *crazy* person manipulate an attendant in a psych hospital into helping her escape? Could a *crazy* person frame him for the murder that she herself committed? That's *right*, bitch! *I'm* the one who stabbed your fucking husband in the back! Just like you *both* stabbed *me* in the back! I took him from you, and *now* I'm taking your worthless life!"

And we're going to take the life of your precious daughter too, came a cold nasal voice from Kristy's mouth. *Hello, Madeline, I should thank you for waking me by desecrating my grave. You awoke me, and now I have come for my revenge. You were always such an ungrateful little whore. And now, I am sending you where you belong. All I needed to do was find a human vessel who hated you as much as I did. And I found her. And I entered her body. And I can live here forever and emerge whenever I choose. And now, before you die, I want you to watch as I send your daughter to hell with you.*

"Oh dear," Adam stated flatly, followed by Aaron's, "Yes. Mother is not only crazy, but she has been taken over by a demon as well. And she is a threat to Josie. Come, brother."

The twins approached the body of their mother. Kristy's face looked at them. It was beet red and twisted into a maniacal smile before Maddy's mother momentarily relinquished her control. "Yes, come to your mother, boys. It's time to get Alexa and go home now. We will be a family again. We will be happy. I had to do it. Don't you see? I had to do it to restore our family."

Adam stood directly before his mother as Aaron stepped behind her and placed his hand firmly upon her jaw. The twins simultaneously said, "Thank you for giving birth to us, Mother." There was a loud *CRACK* as Aaron violently twisted Kristy's head. Her lifeless body crumpled to the ground and lay there like soiled laundry in a hamper.

A dark, shadowy cloud of filthy smog emerged from Kristy's warm corpse and looked down upon the carnage that she had created. It began to chuckle before a bright white cloud enveloped it. The two forms were swirling in and around each other in a billowy blur of entanglement. They looked like two curtains being whipped against one another in a violent windstorm as brilliant flashes of dark purple and brilliant light blue flashed in an epic war. The two forms savagely collided one final time and merged into one. There was an impossibly high-pitched tormented shriek, and the battling shrouds dissipated as quickly as they had arrived.

Maddy looked up at her daughter. She was unable to speak, so she said to the universe as she flashed one final smile, *Thank you, Mother. Thank you for sending me to my prince. We will both see you in hell, you fucking bitch.*

Madeline Ruth Sommers exited the world on February 14, 2040. Even in death, her smile was infectious.

Josie wailed in agony as she watched in horror as her mother's brilliant emerald-green eyes faded into a lifeless gray. Josie wailed in agony for yet another tragic loss. Josie wailed in agony because Josie realized that she was now truly all alone.

Chapter 69

———————

Funeral for a Friend / Love Lies Bleeding

"I turned the stereo on and pushed play, but nothing came out, Lionnel," a traumatized Josie stated with disillusionment to her beloved boyfriend as she sat on her parents' bed, staring blankly at the stereo before going to her mother's service.

"They're really gone. I don't know where. I hope it's somewhere where they can be together and be at peace. I hope that they are dancing and laughing together right now. But I feel utterly lost without them. I don't know where they are. I only know that they aren't here with me anymore. I asked Rosa about it. She said that she felt something just as Mom was passing. It was like she felt a connection that she had felt last year after Dad passed. But then it was gone. She's going to keep trying to reach out for someone who might be able to connect with them, but . . . but . . . oh *jesus*, Lionnel, my parents are *dead*!"

Josie broke down in hysterical tears as her dutiful boyfriend wrapped his brawny arm around her shoulders and said softly, "I'm so sorry. I'm so sorry that this happened to you . . . to them. We're all hurting with you today. But I'm here for you, okay? You can yell and scream and throw things at me if it makes you feel better. I'll do *anything* to help you smile again."

Josie looked into the tender face of her beau and simply whispered, "Just kiss me."

Josie hugged every member of the mourning congregation as she entered.

She smiled meekly, took her handkerchief, and wiped tears from Rod's face before giving him a loving peck on his pasty cheek. She hugged Jules and then Jerry who picked her up and squeezed as if he were trying to absorb her pain. She embraced her most recent friends, Paciano and Stellan, whose eyes were nearly swollen shut from crying. She kneeled before Sam and embraced her along with her husband, Henri. She approached Lucy and her girlfriend, Jennifer.

Lucy had rarely shed a tear since the last time that she had been forced into brutal and degrading sex by Maddy's first husband. She swore that she would never allow herself to be that vulnerable again. On this most sorrowful day, Lucy made an exception as decades of anguish and loss came pouring out of her as she clung on to Josie. Gregory gave her a fatherly hug before Rosa, and the entire Coven enveloped her in an embrace of sisterly solidarity. As the sorrowful energy of their souls was entwined, Rosa said softly to Josie, "My sweetie, I'm so sorry. But this may not be over. It is only over if you lose hope. Keep hoping that we can find them, and we shall someday. Today doesn't have to be goodbye. Today can just be a celebration of who they were up until now."

"Thanks, Rosa, but I'm not feeling too hopeful at the moment," Josie replied as she wiped her tears once again and took her seat in the front pew next to Lionnel and in between the twins, Alexa, and Vai.

As Pastor Tim's weary body began approaching the pulpit, a disenchanted Josie looked around. Besides the standing-room-only crowd of mourners, there were armed snipers on the balcony. *Jesus, what a messed-up world. We can't even mourn without feeling threatened anymore. Maybe there is no chance for true peace. And maybe there's just no reason to fight. Maybe we should just bury our heads in the sand and try to find a small piece of happiness as the powerful dominate our lives. What's the point? What's the point of trying to love one another if your loved ones are going to be ripped from you? What's the point in fighting anymore if there is never an end to the battle? What is the point of any of this?*

For the first time since he stood behind a pulpit, Pastor Tim's voice was cracking. "Madeline Ruth S-sommers departed our world on February 14, 2040. She was p-preceded in passing by her beloved uncle Joseph Argento, her b-beloved aunt Patricia Mercy Sommers, her beloved aunt Blair Aubrey Argento, and her cherished prince of a husband. Her s-soulmate and her best friend. And . . . *m-my* friend Erick Parker. She is survived by her adored daughter Josephine Patricia Sommers Parker, her beloved adopted daughter Vai Denhart, and her beloved adopted sons, Adam and Aaron Anderson. And on a personal note, I would like to say—"

Pastor Tim looked down at the podium briefly to collect his thoughts. He wasn't sure that what he was about to say was appropriate, but he was going to say it anyway. He believed that it *needed* to be said, and it *needed* to be heard. This peace-loving man had never been an advocate for violence. But he wasn't an advocate of unconditional surrender to the forces of evil either. "Maddy and Erick are also survived by *everyone* on this earth who appreciates personal freedom. They are survived by *everyone* who is tired of being bullied and harassed and abused and raped and murdered by the cowardly, self-absorbed *infidels* of our world. They are survived by *everybody* who champions righteousness. I know what they did . . . or at least *some* of what they did. And I do not know whether their actions were right or wrong. But I *do* know that they were two of the most loving, caring, and loyal people that I have ever known. I know that the actions that they took came from the very best places in their hearts. I know that their actions prevented many bad men from harming another innocent soul ever again. And I know that their actions serve as an inspiration to *never* take shit from a bully. I pray that their souls are resting easily with our Lord. Because if they are not, then . . . there *is* no fucking God."

As the shocked congregation began to hear the opening notes to Matthew Sweet's "Divine Intervention," Josie thought to herself, *Jesus, Mom! How the hell am I supposed to follow that?*

The song's final note faded into the universe, and Josie rose and began her stride toward the pulpit, flanked by the twins with Vai directly behind her. The moment she took her place behind the podium, a bright ray of sunshine poured through the stained-glass windows, showering her in a kaleidoscopic backlight. The entire congregation let out an audible gasp. *Don't lose it! Don't lose it! Don't lose it!* Josie repeated to herself before she began.

"Well," Josie began with a forced chuckle, "Mom was the one who was good with a joke, so I'm not even going to try. Oh, who am I kidding? We were both just horrible at jokes, and Dad was always quick to point that out to us. Then Mom would say something like, 'Why aren't you laughing, mister? That was pure gold!' And my dad would just roll his eyes at her. And then they would hug and laugh." The congregation nervously tittered before Josie began again as she wiped a tear from her eye. "I am here today to lay both of my parents in everlasting peace. I am here to give their souls back to the universe. I am here to remember their spirits. I am here to say goodbye to them.

"And I am here to say hello to the future. I am here to look forward to a future where we are all able to come together as one. A future where we don't hate one another for our petty differences. A future where we love and embrace one another *because* of those differences. A future where we do not have to live in fear of the bullying bastards who oppress us. Abuse us. Rape us. Murder us.

"That is the world that my parents were trying to build. For me. For you. And they, along with millions of other people throughout the world, took a step toward that. Christ knows they weren't perfect—none of us are. But they tried. They, alongside so many others, fought against the fascist forces of oppression. They fought against the forces of pure evil. And they taught me to do that as well. It's just that—" Josie's voice began to crack. "It's just that .. . I don't know if I have the strength to do this anymore. I've lost *so much* in these wars. We have *all* lost so much in these wars. I just don't know if I can—"

She had to pause for a moment. The pressure of her heartfelt eulogy fell upon her soul like a ten-ton weight helplessly splashing into a dark ocean of despair. The silence of the mourning congregation was deafening as her mind raced. She felt dizzy and heard a slight ringing in her ears. She held her head down so that her lush copper locks covered her tear-filled emerald-green eyes.

This was not supposed to happen. This was a travesty of justice. She had already lost the man who had taught her how to trust and love. Now she had lost the strongest woman in her life. The woman who had nurtured her from birth. The woman who had fostered her own sense of self-worth. Her own sense of being. Her own sense of justice. She had taught her about the power of the feminine spirit and the power of female bonding. And now, without her, she felt utterly powerless.

This was not supposed to happen. They had all been so careful. They had meticulously identified their threats and then took them out one by one. There were no clues. There wasn't supposed to be anyone left. There wasn't supposed to be any further threat to the syndicate or her friends. And most certainly, there wasn't supposed to be any further threat to anyone in her family. She and the younger generation were sure that they had seen to that.

And yet, there she was. Right in front of her. Lying still. Her spiritless corpse painted like an obscene mannequin in the window of a trendy shop in a strip mall. Her beautiful yellow gown covering the fourteen bullet holes that had ripped her life away. It was all over. There was nothing left. She crouched even farther down, trying to become invisible behind the dark mahogany altar. She could not bear this. She had been raised to bear anything. But she could not bear this. Not again.

And then it came. Breaking through the silence was the spirited chirping of a little bird from outside a cracked window. The song penetrated her soul. Buoyed by the hopeful sound, she looked up at the solemn faces of her congregation. This *wasn't* over. This was now *her* responsibility. This is what she had prepared her for. It was now *her* time to ascend.

She gave a comforting and confident smile and then a slight nod to the musical director. He pushed play. As the opening metal riff of AC/DC's "Thunderstruck" boomed throughout the hall, her lithe frame began the confident trek down the church's steps. Her pace quickened, and her stride transformed into a strut as she glided down the middle of the onlooking well-wishers and mourners. When the enormous opening lyric to the song came thundering through the speakers, she tore off her conservative black dress, revealing a skintight green faux leather catsuit. She kicked open the church's doors and screamed to the universe, "Here I am, motherfuckers! Time to fuck some shit up!"

———

"I believe that this is the saddest day that we've ever experienced, Vai," Adam stated, followed by Aaron's, "Yes. Quite sad. Even though we saw this coming many years ago, we were not prepared for just how sad this is. It makes us want to play games, Vai."

Vai looked up at her brothers as Alexa was lying on the floor on her belly and kicking her bare feet while drawing a perfect rendition of Maddy's body lying in her coffin, her corpse clutching the urn of her beloved Erick for eternity. Vai's face was lit only by a single flickering flame from a candle.

"And we shall, my dears. And we shall. Under Josie's leadership, there will be lots of fun games to play. Please send Lucy and Rosa in. We need to begin the preparations for our unearthly battle. We need to prepare to go up against the very essence of evil. We need to prepare to destroy Josie's grandmother."

———

Josie and Lionnel lay together in the warm glow of the raging flames in the fireplace. They kissed one another tenderly before Lionnel's naked frame crawled from under the blanket. He put on his shorts and T-shirt and made his way up the stairs to the music room. *What the fuck is he doing?* Josie thought to herself as she poured herself into her pajamas. He returned and placed a vinyl record on the turntable.

"May I have this dance?" he asked her in a sensitive voice.

"You may *always* have a dance with me," Josie softly replied back as she allowed herself to smile for the first time in days.

They began swaying to Springsteen's "The Ghost of Tom Joad." "I believe you have found our song," Josie purred as her emerald-green eyes gazed into his of dark hazel.

It was just the two of them silently communicating with one another before Lionnel said, "Yes, Josie, I just want to dance with you forever. I want to be with you forever. And I want to fight alongside you . . . forever."

Josie smiled at her love and whispered into his ear, "And you shall. You are my prince, and I am your princess, and no motherfucking douchebag is *ever* going to tear us apart. I promise you that, my love. And I'm my father's daughter. I *never* break a fuckin' promise."

Song Reference List

The author would like to thank the countless musical artists who have enhanced his entire life. In particular, the author would like to give a heartfelt thank you to the following artists for enhancing the experience of both writing and reading this book.

The Cowsills: "The Rain, the Park, and Other Things"
Stephen Bishop: "On and On"
Wayne County & the Electric Chairs: "Toilet Love"
Green Day: "American Idiot"
White Stripes: "Seven Nation Army"
Lou Reed: "There Is No Time"
Joe Jackson: "The Jet Set"
Patsy Cline: "I Fall to Pieces"
Alice Cooper: "Welcome to My Nightmare"
Nine Inch Nails: "Closer"
The Who: "The Kids Are All Right"
The Brady Bunch: "Sunshine Day"
Reel Big Fish: "Trendy"
Fats Domino: "My Girl Josephine"

The Beatles: "Helter Skelter"
Pink Floyd: "Sheep"
The Meteors: "Wreckin' Crew"
The Sonics: "Witch"
Patti Smith: "People Have the Power"
Bob Dylan: "Highway 61 Revisited"
Santana: "Black Magic Woman"
Johnny Cash: "I've Been Everywhere"
The Beatles: "Birthday"
Sparks: "iPhone"
Bruce Springsteen: "Land of Hope and Dreams"
The Cramps: "Let's Get Fucked Up"
The Jesus and Mary Chain: "Darklands"
David Bowie: "Blackstar"
Frankie Goes to Hollywood: "Two Tribes"
Julian Cope: "Beautiful Love"
Todd Snider: "I Believe You"
REM: "I Believe"
Freedy Johnston: "There Goes a Brooklyn Girl"
Blotto: "I Wanna Be a Lifeguard"
Tiny Tim: "Tiptoe through the Tulips"
The Drifters: "Save the Last Dance for Me"
Nancy Sinatra: "These Boots Are Made for Walking"
Adrian Belew with David Bowie: "Pretty Pink Rose"
Southern Culture on the Skids: "Life's a Gas"
Joan Jett: "Bad Reputation"
Donna Summer: "I Feel Love"
Rob Zombie: "I'm Your Boogieman"
Yusuf Islam a.k.a. Cat Stevens: "Peace Train"
REM: "Leaving New York"
Barry Manilow: "It's a Miracle"
The Cramps: "Don't Get Funny with Me"
The Police: "Every Breath You Take"
Susan Sarandon, Barry Bostwick, and Richard O'Brien: "There's a Light (Over at the Frankenstein Place)"
Murder by Death: "I Have Arrived"

The Crests: "Sixteen Candles"
Elton John: "Funeral for a Friend/Love Lies Bleeding"
Matthew Sweet: "Divine Intervention"
AC/DC: "Thunderstruck"
Bruce Springsteen: "The Ghost of Tom Joad"

www.ingramcontent.com/pod-product-compliance
Lightning Source LLC
Chambersburg PA
CBHW061045210726
48294CB00001B/30